By Robert Newcomb

Rise *of the* Blood Royal

RISE *of the* BLOOD ROYAL

Robert Newcomb

VOLUME III OF THE DESTINIES OF BLOOD AND STONE

BALLANTINE BOOKS · DEL REY · NEW YORK

Copyright © 2008 by Robert Newcomb

Published in the United States by Ballantine Books, an imprint of The Random House Publishing Group, a division of Random House, Inc., New York.

BALLANTINE and colophon are registered trademarks of Random House, Inc.

Newcomb, Robert
Rise of the blood royal / Robert Newcomb.
p. cm.—(The destinies of blood and stone ; v. 3)
ISBN 978-0-345-47711-8
1. Title.
PS3614.E58R57   2008
813'.6—dc22   2007028495

Printed in the United States of America on acid-free paper

Map by Russ Charpentier

www.delreybooks.com

2 4 6 8 9 7 5 3 1

First Edition

Text design by Laurie Jewell

CONTENTS

FOREWORD

THIS SAGA'S KNOWN WORLD IS COMPRISED OF FOUR independent nations. To the west lie Rustannica and Shashida. Their great land masses easily dwarf Eutracia and Parthalon, the nations lying to the east. Because of dark magic long since banned by its warring practitioners, the Tolenka mountain range that separates Eutracia and Parthalon from Rustannica and Shashida is insurmountable by those living on either side of its craggy peaks. An azure pass existed briefly that allowed travel through the mountain range, but it was destroyed by Rustannican mystics when they learned that the secret to its use had been granted to the Eutracian prince.

For aeons, a struggle called the War of Attrition has raged between Rustannica and Shashida. Separating these two nations is an area called the Borderlands. Created and controlled by Rustannican mystics, the Borderlands can be morphed at will to create various types of life-threatening terrain, thereby helping to protect Rustannica from invasion by her Shashidan enemies to the south.

The War of Attrition is fought by two opposing groups of craft practitioners. In Rustannica, the ruling body of mystics is called the *Pon Q'tar*. The *Pon Q'tar* members are zealously devoted to the craft's dark side, also known as the Vagaries.

The Shashidan mystics are called the *Chikara Inkai*. They are devoted to magic's more compassionate side, called the Vigors. Although they live under nearly constant attack by the *Pon Q'tar,* the *Inkai* choose to fight a largely defensive war, for fear of destroying the side of the craft practiced by their enemies. Unlike the *Pon Q'tar,* the *Inkai* believe that doing so would collapse both sides of magic and plunge the world into eternal darkness. As in Eutracia and Parthalon, in Rustannica and Shashida it is the presence of "endowed blood" in one's being that allows one to use magic and determines his or her relative power in the craft.

The Emperor of Rustannica, who rules over the *Pon Q'tar,* the Priory of Virtue, and the Imperial Order, possesses the most strongly endowed blood in Rustannican history. The raw power he commands over the craft dwarfs even that of all the *Pon Q'tar* clerics combined.

After centuries of struggle, the less sophisticated nations of Eutracia and Parthalon have seemingly found victory in their fight to overcome the influence of the Vagaries. Dangerous enemies who would have seen the Vigors stamped out forever—some of whom were guided from afar by the *Pon Q'tar*—have been defeated by Prince Tristan of Eutracia and his twin sister, Princess Shailiha. The Eutracian prince rules over the Conclave of the Vigors, a group of fighters and mystics who have been specially chosen for their unique abilities.

Like the Emperor of Rustannica, the Eutracian Prince and Princess possess highly endowed blood. They are the prophesied *Jin'Sai* and *Jin'Saiou,* and it is their mission to unleash their power and bring a just and lasting resolution to the War of Attrition, while ensuring that both sides of the craft continue to coexist peacefully.

But to do this, they must cross the Tolenka Mountains—a seemingly impossible task now that the azure pass is no more. Fulfilling their destinies appears more hopeless than ever. And the Rustannican government, its treasury having been bled nearly white from untold generations of offensive war and costly mass spectacle, is tottering on the brink of a collapse that even the *Pon Q'tar* and its emperor might not be able to stave off.

ROBERT NEWCOMB

I

DEATH AND TERROR

CHAPTER 1

 HE WAS BORN INTO A WORLD FILLED WITH TREACHERY, dark magic, and unresolved war.

His coming had been foretold, and his birth was a joyous event among the few mystics considered worthy to witness it. As his mother gave him life, she and her newborn were surrounded by an azure glow. Soon the glow faded to reveal the crying child for whom the hopeful *Pon Q'tar* clerics had waited so long. They named him Vespasian Augustus I, and it was he who was destined to lead his country to final victory over Shashida, the southern nation that had for so long threatened Rustannica's way of life.

Immediately after the child's birth, his mother and father were taken away. Five veiled wet nurses would take turns suckling him, ensuring that no singular attachment would form in his heart and perhaps mar his later devotion to the clerics who would shape his life. The child was everything; the woman who birthed him and the man who sired him were little more than living suppliers of unique bloodlines. The boy would be raised alone by the mysterious clerics. One day those same mystics would grant him rule over their nation.

The *Pon Q'tar* had explained the boy's sudden appearance and amazing blood quality to the citizens of Rustannica as wondrous gifts of magic that were to be welcomed, rather than omens to be feared. The citizens quickly took Vespasian to their bosom, and as he matured they hungered constantly for news of his upbringing.

He had been born thirty-two Seasons of New Life ago. Today, more of Rustannica's enemies would die.

Small numbers of captured Shashidan soldiers were usually killed outright on the battlefield by the Rustannican Imperial Order. But if the captives were numerous, they were brought in chains to Ellistium, Rustannica's capital city. There, most would be forced into slavery; the remainder would be condemned to fight one another to the death in the "games," a lavish spectacle staged in Ellistium's great coliseum.

Vespasian raised one hand and held it out to Persephone, his empress. Smiling, she placed her palm atop his, and they strode out into the morning sunshine.

As the couple entered the vast coliseum, they were showered with colorful rose petals gleefully tossed down by Persephone's many hand-maidens seated in the stands above. At the sight of their revered rulers, the crowd rose to their feet and roared.

The great coliseum was the largest structure in Ellistium. Its curved stone walls, four tiers high, were covered with colorful mosaic murals depicting a variety of fearsome beasts. On each tier, ivory statues of previous emperors stood in huge carved niches.

The coliseum could accommodate one hundred thousand spectators. As he surveyed the quickly filling stands, Vespasian knew that no seats would go unsold today. These were the first games in nearly three months, and the populace was eager for blood. The mighty Twenty-third Legion had recently been ordered home after a successful campaign, and many Shashidan soldiers had been taken prisoner—sufficient numbers for a full fifteen days of games.

Open arches built into the four tiers allowed light and air into the passageways by which the eager mob entered. Colorful banners fluttered atop the curving walls. Two great red canopies, unfurled from opposite sidewalls, extended nearly to the center of the arena. Their far sides were attached to towering solid turquoise columns that had been sunk into the arena floor. Each column was topped with a gold statue of Vespasian dressed in full military regalia.

The morning sun glinted off the statues and filtered through the red canopies, giving the sand-covered floor the appearance of having already been bloodied and whetting the crowd's appetite for the spectacles that would soon unfold.

The emperor looked from one end of the arena to the other. Massive iron gates stood in the walls at each end, their twin doors guarded by stern Imperial Order centurions. Over each portal was inlaid an elaborate inscription in pure silver. Above the northern doors the inscription read: *The Gates of Life.* The southern one read: *The Gates of Death.*

The emperor's private box was a lavish affair of elegant blue marble furnished with two ivory thrones, along with simpler chairs reserved for privileged advisors and guests. In each of the four corners, banners of purple and gold fluttered from onyx columns, and ivy vines graced the walls. A purple silk canopy lay stretched between the four columns over the box, shielding the emperor and his entourage from the hot sun. In one corner stood the nervous Games Master, the man responsible for the smooth management of the upcoming spectacle.

The emperor's box was flanked by two other elaborate boxes. The one to the left was reserved for the Imperial Order's eighty legion tribunes, though only those few not afield in the seemingly never-ending war against Shashida would attend the games.

The box to the right was reserved for the Priory of Virtue. All twenty seats were carved from solid ivory and lined with red velvet cushions.

The moment the emperor and empress sat down, Shashidan slaves appeared with a multitude of delicacies: wine, sweetmeats, shellfish, grilled breasts of game birds, and boiled eggs; piles of cakes, pastries, and tarts, all sweetened with honey.

As Persephone settled into her chair, the crowd continued to roar and the last of the rose petals fluttered down. She casually employed the craft, causing a golden wine goblet to rise from a tray and float toward her. As she took it in her hand, she turned to regard the man she loved more than life.

Although her marriage to Vespasian had been arranged by the *Pon Q'tar,* Persephone had been smitten at first sight. To her initial dismay, the same had not been true of her intended; but with time, he had come to return her love. The only shadow over their marriage was her failure to produce an heir. Repeated physical examinations of the empress by the *Pon Q'tar* clerics had produced no answers. Even their cleverly concocted fertility potions and specially designed enchantments had not helped her to conceive.

Persephone knew that she had been chosen only because of the unusually high quality of her blood. The *Pon Q'tar* had searched long and hard for a young girl of such highly endowed blood. Persephone had been forcibly taken from her parents at the age of three and, like Vespasian, had been raised and trained by the *Pon Q'tar* clerics. Her instruction in the arts of magic, politics, and war had rivaled Vespasian's in every way—but her specialty was palace intrigue, and some confidants dared to whisper that no one outshone her in that area, not even her husband.

She smiled as she regarded Vespasian beside her. He looked splendid in his dress uniform. Dark blue leather armor adorned with elaborate silver filigree covered a shiny black tunic. He wore dark blue filigreed leather greaves and gauntlets and black sandals. His purple and gold cape was attached to his armor at each shoulder, and a golden dress sword in a filigreed scabbard hung at one hip. In celebration of the games, the traditional crown of laurel leaves fashioned from solid gold sat atop his blond curls.

As she regarded him, Vespasian turned to look at his wife. His dark blue eyes met her light blue ones, and he reached to stroke a strand of her long blond hair. She was wearing a gown of vibrant red silk. Golden snakes wound around her upper arms, and matching earrings hung from her lobes. She looked radiant. Leaning closer, Vespasian gave her a conspiratorial smile.

"I hope that you don't mind attending the games today, my dear," he whispered. "I fear that they have become a way of life."

Persephone smiled in return. "I enjoy the spectacles as much as anyone," she whispered back. "You know that. Besides, my place is with you. The palace is wild with rumors that there is to be some form of entertainment today. I must say that I'm curious."

Vespasian nodded. "Along with the usual lot of criminals and professional combatants, newly captured Shashidan skeens will participate today. They were recently taken by the Twenty-third Legion."

"Did they give up any useful information?" Persephone asked.

Vespasian shook his head. "We heard little that we did not already know."

As he looked back out over the massive crowd, Vespasian couldn't help but be reminded of the immense importance of class structure in Rustannican life. There were four distinct levels, and one's position in society was irrevocably determined at birth by the nature of his or her blood.

The "krithians," those lucky few born with fully endowed blood that complete command over the craft of magic, were protected by special laws and privileges, and considered to be the cream of the Rustannican Empire. Below the krithians were those born with partially endowed blood. They were known as "hematites," or simply "partials." They, too, were able to call on the craft, but their gifts were limited to the craft's organic side, such as herbmastery. The next class of citizens was comprised of those with unendowed blood. Called "phrygians," they were unable to summon the craft in any form. The lowest class was the huge multitudes of slaves, also known as "skeens." By way of continual captures and new births, the slave population had grown so much in recent years that it made up a full third of Rustannica's population.

Regardless of age, gender, or blood type, all skeens were captured Shashidan soldiers, civilians, or their descendants. Those not chosen to supply fodder for the games were sold at auction by the government in Ellistium's great forum on the first of each month. If they had once been magic practitioners, the craft was immediately used to wipe their memories clean of the ability to call upon their gifts, thus ensuring that they would never again present a threat to the empire.

As he surveyed the swelling crowd, Vespasian sat back in his throne, thinking. Most Rustannicans believed that their nation's strength lay in her vast legions and her treasury of gold. But they were wrong. Rustannica's real power lay in the continuing survival of left-leaning endowed blood. That was the true ruling factor here, and nothing would ever change it.

Twelve more people entered the emperor's private box. The seven men and five women greeted Vespasian and Persephone warmly, then took nearby seats. These august mystics made up the revered *Pon Q'tar*. Protected by time enchantments, each was scores of centuries old, and some had even taken part in the ancient revolt against Shashida and the start of the War of Attrition. Their many responsibilities included ongoing craft research, advising the emperor and empress, and overseeing the day-to-day operations of the legions. Each cleric was dressed in a bright white robe, its folds gracefully draping from the left shoulder to the right thigh. A deep burgundy border ran all along the garment's length, signifying its wearer's lofty office.

Shortly after the *Pon Q'tar* arrived, the crowd quieted—a sign that the women of the Priory of Virtue were filing into their box on Vespasian's right. They wore diaphanous white gowns; matching veils fell from simple gold circlets to cover their faces. No other jewelry adorned them, and no badges or symbols of their sisterhood were evident. As they took their seats, the First Mistress of the Priory, also known as the Femiculi, bowed to Vespasian. He bowed in return, and the crowd quickly returned to its raucous ways.

Soon thirty of the imperial tribunes appeared. They were in full dress uniform, complete with gold and red horsehair-combed helmets and blood-red capes. Each man saluted Vespasian by thumping his closed fist against his golden breastplate, then quickly opening his palm and extending his arm straight ahead. They then removed their helmets and took their seats.

By law, each tribune and several of the centurions serving under him had to be krithians trained in the ways of magic as well as warfare. Groups of lesser mystics called Heretics of the Guild also accompanied each legion, to offer additional strength and guidance in the craft.

Once his officers were in place, the First Tribune came to join Vespasian in his box. Lucius Marius had been Vespasian's closest friend since their earliest days when they took their military training together. After Vespasian, Persephone, and the lead *Pon Q'tar* cleric, Lucius was the highest ranking person in Rustannica. With a smile and a respectful nod for Vespasian, Lucius placed his helmet on the floor and bent over Persephone's hand to kiss it.

Persephone liked Lucius. Despite his reputation as a rake and a great lover of wine and gaiety, Lucius was good company and a wise counselor. She returned his smile and handed him a goblet of red wine.

At last, Gracchus Junius, the lead *Pon Q'tar* mystic, quietly rose from his chair and approached the emperor, a worried expression on his aged face. Vespasian placed a hand on the mystic's shoulder.

"What bothers my old tutor?" he asked. "This is to be a happy day!"

Without answering, Gracchus produced a wax tablet diptych from the folds of his robe. The diptych's covers were made of solid gold held together by two jeweled rings.

Vespasian recognized the unique book immediately. It presence meant only one thing: The Oraculum had word for him. If Gracchus was willing to present an Oraculum diptych to his emperor in public, the news had to be of the greatest urgency.

Taking the book into his hands, Vespasian gave Persephone and Lucius a wary look. Persephone pursed her lips; Lucius raised an eyebrow. Vespasian returned his gaze to his cleric.

"It has been some time since she has spoken," he said quietly.

"Yes, Highness," Gracchus said in his gravely voice. "And her newest pronouncements are not reassuring."

Vespasian looked at the book to make sure that Gracchus' personal red wax signet seal was still intact. "Is the news bad?" he asked.

Gracchus paused to look out over the restless crowd. In some areas, squabbles had broken out over the best seats, and the widespread drunkenness and debauchery that usually accompanied the games had begun sooner than usual.

"The news is distressing," he said finally. "Perhaps you should start the games before reading the diptych. The crowd becomes restless."

Vespasian shook his head. "I will read it now. Let the mob wait a little longer."

With a snap of his fingers, he called Gaius, the Games Master, to his side. Once a slave and arena combatant himself, the grizzled old man had long ago lost one eye and several fingers to the games before being given his freedom by one of Vespasian's predecessors. Granting freedom to a slave, criminal, or enemy of the empire who had fought well in the arena was rare, and only the emperor could bestow such an honor. In his twelve years as Rustannica's ruler, Vespasian had never done so.

Now Vespasian looked up into the Games Master's remaining brown eye. "Give them the bread," he ordered. "That should placate them for a while."

"My liege," the man answered with a small bow. He turned and quickly walked to one corner of the box. There stood a series of tall golden staffs that could be easily seen from the arena. Mounted on each staff was a three-sided gilded sign that could be swiveled to signal various commands to ever-watchful centurions prowling the arena floor. Selecting one of the signs, Gaius presented one of its faces to the arena floor.

At once the centurions started walking toward a group of male and female slaves performing acrobatic tricks. Each wore nothing but a simple white loincloth and flowers in their hair. Their oiled bodies glistened in the reddish light filtering through the canopies.

After getting their new orders from the centurions, the slaves disappeared through the Gates of Life. They soon ran back out carrying huge baskets of freshly baked bread. As they tossed the loaves into the stands, the crowd went wild. In honor of the spectators, Vespasian sometimes ordered that thousands of such loaves, each branded with the letter V, be given away. Such royal bread was rarely eaten. Instead it was taken home and displayed proudly as a personal gift from the emperor. There it would remain in some domicile or shopkeeper's window until it molded and fell to dust. The loaves had become so revered that stealing one had recently been made a capital crime. For most Ellistiumites, owning such a loaf of bread was as close as they would ever come to touching royalty. In honor of highly special events, Vespasian sometimes enchanted the loaves, ensuring that they would never spoil. Such was the case today.

With the crowd distracted for the moment, Vespasian opened the diptych and began reading the beeswax pages. The elegant script had been deeply etched with a stylus. As always, Gracchus had personally put the Oraculum's verbal pronouncements in writing, and Vespasian recognized the cleric's unique hand. As he read, his anger rose. He snapped the diptych shut, then handed it to Lucius. As the First Tribune read the pages, his expression mirrored Vespasian's.

Persephone touched her husband on the arm. "What does it say?" she asked.

"The *Jin'Sai* lives," Vespasian whispered. "Despite all our efforts, that son of a thousand fathers escaped Crysenium and returned to Eutracia. Moreover, he now commands the gift of *K'Shari*. He killed Xanthus, the being the *Pon Q'tar* created to lure him to our side of the world. That Vigors bastard seems to have a thousand lives. Perhaps even worse, the Conclave now possesses both the Scrolls of the Ancients and their indexes. I can see no end to the trouble this defeat will cause."

Lucius handed the diptych back to Vespasian, and the emperor angrily tossed it to the floor. "The one blessing in all this is that we were able to kill the traitorous Envoys of Crysenium," he breathed. "But only time will tell how much Tristan was able to learn from them before he fled back to his homeland. Now he is untouchable."

Vespasian turned and glared angrily at Gracchus. "It was the *Pon Q'tar*'s plan to lure the *Jin'Sai* here!" he growled. "In the end, not only did your idea fail, but we were forced to trick Serena into killing herself and her child! In doing so, we lost the last of our Vagaries allies who shared Tristan's blood! The failure is yours!"

"We must accept our misfortune," Gracchus answered. "Our sudden need to summon the Borderlands was regrettable, but no one could have foreseen it. It had to be done because of the Shashidan cohorts that were approaching. I admit that the timing could not have been worse, and had we been permitted to leave the Borderlands dormant, Xanthus would have certainly delivered the *Jin'Sai* into our hands. But what's done is done. Sadly, the azure pass was an amazing opportunity that will likely never come again. We made the best of it that we could. But with the pass gone, just as we cannot threaten Eutracia, those in Eutracia cannot threaten us. And Crysenium and its traitorous Envoys have been destroyed. So it would seem that the *Jin'Sai* lost as much as we. The stalemate persists."

Vespasian thought for a moment. "Directly after the games, I will call for a meeting of the Suffragat," he ordered. "We must discuss this turn of events. I will not tolerate another failure."

"I understand, Highness," Gracchus answered. "And although it grieves me to mention it, there is another urgent matter that we must face. The latest treasury count—"

"I am aware of the treasury count!" Vespasian snapped. Trying to calm himself, he sighed and gave Gracchus a hard look. "The *Pon Q'tar* does little else but whine about it! Do you think I wanted to pay for these games with public funds? But what other choice did we have?"

He angrily rubbed his brow. "I'm sorry, Gracchus," he said. "It seems that I've heard all the bad news I can stomach for now. But you're right about one thing. I doubt that the crowd will be willing to wait much longer. The last thing that we need is another citywide riot on our hands."

As Gracchus nodded and returned to his seat, Vespasian looked at the Games Master and clapped his hands. At once the man walked toward the edge of the box and swiveled another gilded sign. When the crowd saw the centurions again unlock the Gates of Life and hurry through, they stood and shouted, their rising clamor quickly becoming deafening.

Persephone turned to look at Vespasian. Normally at the start of the games her husband showed the same eager excitement as the mob, but now he only looked concerned. She did her best to give him a reassuring smile.

Below, the customary processional sounds rang out. The massive Gates of Life swung open, and dozens of Imperial Order horse-drawn chariots charged into the arena. Driven by accomplished centurions, they began speeding around the arena wall in opposite directions, narrowly missing one another for the amusement of the crowd. Following the chariots, a large band of Imperial Order musicians entered, dressed in their finest uniforms and beating on drums and blowing into trumpets, fifes, and flutes.

Today's killings were special. Seeing the usual lot of common criminals ruthlessly butchered always held great amusement for the Rustannicans of Ellistium. But watching Shashidan fighters taken fresh from the battlefield and forced to fight to the death held a special appeal. By watching the Shashidans die in the arena, the crowd could share in the legions' victories. Vespasian knew that this united his countrymen like nothing else, and so he too welcomed the coming slaughter.

Trying to forget his troubles, Vespasian took up that day's handbill and read it. As usual, the Shashidan prisoners of war possessing low military rank would be killed first. Because of their relative unimportance, they would be creatively tortured and murdered without the right of combat. These first killings served to whet the crowd's appetite for the fighting that would follow later in the day.

As he read further, what the emperor saw on the handbill stunned him. No wonder the crowd was in such a heated frenzy! More than three thousand Shashidan fighters were slated to die during the first act of the games alone. He had never seen such a huge number. Looking angrily out toward the arena, Vespasian shook his head.

"What troubles you?" Lucius asked.

"Look at these tallies," Vespasian answered. "They're far too high! Although I do not object to the way skeens die, I must protest this terrible waste! Most of these slaves should have been branded for sale at auction! Imagine the tax revenue they would have provided to the treasury! Did you know about this?"

Lucius' expression darkened. "I assumed that the *Pon Q'tar* had informed you, as usual, of the number before the handbills were printed."

For the second time that day, anger roiled up inside Vespasian. "Apparently the lead cleric didn't see fit to inform his emperor," he growled. He glanced over at Gracchus, then back to Lucius again.

"I have called for an emergency meeting of the Suffragat to take place directly after the games," he said quietly to his friend. "We have much to discuss. I plan to dress down those willful clerics—especially Gracchus. And I want an audience when I do it, so that my words cannot be misconstrued. For such a supposedly learned mystic, Gracchus sometimes possesses an amazingly short memory. But mark my words—before this day ends he will experience my displeasure." Vespasian sat back in his chair, scowling.

Lucius took a long sip of wine, then smiled. "So be it," he said. "In the meantime, I suggest that you not let the tail wag the dog."

Vespasian nodded. "I couldn't agree more." As he considered his friend's words, a plan started forming in his mind.

Just then more oiled slave boys and girls in loincloths entered the box. Each one carried an elaborate gold tray laden with jewelry, which they presented for the emperor and empress's perusal.

After looking over one tray, Vespasian declined. He glanced over at Lucius. "Spoils from the Twenty-third's recent campaign?" he asked.

Before answering, Lucius watched Persephone select a diamond and sapphire ring. Smiling, she slipped it onto the little finger of her right hand.

"Yes," the First Tribune answered. "They sacked many Shashidan towns before the Borderlands were activated."

"How much raw gold was brought home?"

Lucius shook his head. "Not enough to make an appreciable difference," he answered. Understanding, Vespasian returned his attention to the arena.

As the chariots charged dangerously around the inner walls, the musicians played and the acrobats leaped and whirled. Vespasian quickly ordered the Games Master back to his side and held up the handbill.

"There are far too many slaves marked for execution, you idiot!" He raised his voice to be sure that Gracchus and the other *Pon Q'tar* members heard him. "Have you gone mad, you ignorant son of a street whore? I want the women, children, and one-third of the healthiest men spared for sale at auction on the new moon!" Finished, he lowered the handbill and calmly returned his gaze to the arena without bothering to turn and look at Gracchus.

The Games Master simply stood there, stupefied. Such a huge last-minute change in the program was unprecedented. He turned to look open-mouthed at Gracchus, but the lead cleric seemed strangely unperturbed.

With a shaking hand, the Games Master nervously wiped the sweat from his brow. He had no wish to become a pawn in a dispute between the two most powerful men in Rustannica. But Vespasian had given him a direct order, and he had no choice. Swallowing hard, he looked back at his emperor.

"It will be as you command, Sire," he said.

The Games Master also knew that this immense and unexpected change in the program would have to be handled personally. He would not be able to communicate this new order to the arena centurions by signal. He would have to go down there himself. His greatest fear was how the audience would react when they learned that the first-act killings had been so severely curtailed. Surely the clever emperor had some way to make it up to the crowd, he reasoned.

Just as the Games Master turned to run down to the Gates of Life, Vespasian again surprised him by reaching out and grabbing his wrist.

Calling on the craft, Vespasian augmented the strength in his arm and violently spun the man around to face him. The pain in Gaius' shoulder was excruciating. Vespasian drew the Games Master so close that their faces almost touched. Then he looked over at Lucius.

"Tell me, First Tribune, was this huge group of captured Shashidans first discovered by Blood Stalkers?" he asked.

"They were," Lucius answered.

"And are those stalkers quartered here at the coliseum?" Vespasian asked.

Lucius nodded. "As you know, we must keep them caged when they are not deployed or they would rampage through the streets, killing every Shashidan skeen they could find. The one hundred stalkers assigned to the Twenty-third Legion are locked up below the arena floor. And as your highness also knows, after the huge number of captives was taken, I ordered the entire Twenty-third back to Ellistium. They had been on constant campaign for more than two years and they deserved a visit home."

Vespasian smiled. "Good," he said. "Then we will do something else today that the crowd won't expect. We will publicly honor the stalkers by watching them do what they do best."

When he glared back at the Games Master, Vespasian could see the astonishment in the man's eyes.

"Force one hundred Shashidan skeens into the arena at a time," Vespasian ordered. "Bring no females, for we need them for procreation. Then I want fifty of the Twenty-third's Blood Stalkers turned loose on them. When the first group of skeens is dead you will bring in one hundred more, and so on. See to it that all the skeens are armed. I doubt that we will lose many stalkers, and it will add to the flavor of the first act. Tell the stalkers that they are not to start the bloodletting until they erect their legion standards and form ranks before my box."

The Games Master couldn't believe his ears. Before today, stalkers had never been allowed participation in the games. Although they remained partly human, they were also products of the craft and largely uncontrollable by anyone except an experienced magic practitioner.

"I understand, Sire," Gaius finally answered. "It will be as you order."

Vespasian finally released his grip on the man's wrist. "Good," he said. "See to it at once. And have the crowd informed of the program changes their emperor has made."

Vespasian didn't need to tell the slave twice. As fast as his legs could carry him, Gaius left the emperor's private box and hurried toward the arena floor.

Seated among his fellow clerics, Gracchus smiled as he heard Vespasian give the unexpected orders about the skeens and the Blood Stalkers. *Well done,* he thought. *I couldn't have produced a cleverer countermove myself.*

Benedik Pryam, one of Gracchus' most trusted fellow mystics, sat beside the lead cleric. Casually grasping the shoulder folds of his white and burgundy robe with one hand, he leaned closer. The look on his face was not reassuring.

"Sometimes you push the Blood Royal too hard!" he protested under his breath. "We all agree that he should be continually tested so that he learns how to deal with unexpected pressure—we have done so since the day that he was born. And I agree that such tactics have made him into the strongest and most beloved ruler that the empire has ever seen. But when you defy him in public—and before the entire coliseum audience, no less—you go too far! He *must* have the continued respect of the mob if he is to conquer Shashida for us!"

Smiling, Gracchus turned to look at his friend. Despite his great age, Benedik remained an attractive, vigorous man, because the time enchantments had been granted to him when he had passed only fifty Seasons of New Life. His dark eyes were sharp, and he had a full head of iron-gray hair that he kept cropped close.

"Worried about our young prodigy, are you?" Gracchus asked, as he popped a grape into his mouth. "Don't concern yourself unnecessarily, my old friend. He is everything that we could have asked for and more. If I'm right, this unexpected order of his will do nothing but further embed him into the public's heart. Vespasian knows what Rustannica is. It's the mob, pure and simple. They will soon love him even more for the unprecedented spectacle that he is about to grant them."

"Be careful, Gracchus," Benedik pressed, "lest this monster that we have created get out of hand." But Gracchus only smiled and turned his gaze back to the arena.

As he waited for the news about the change in the program to reach the crowd, Lucius also found himself curious about Vespasian's motives. After taking another sip of wine, the First Tribune turned to look at his emperor.

"What are you playing at?" he whispered. "Blood Stalkers in the arena? That's a first, even for you."

"My guess is that Gracchus planned to take full credit for the huge number of slaves who were to be killed today," Vespasian answered quietly, "even though he is not personally paying for them. I intend not only to spare most of the slaves and sell them, but to upstage that old cleric and steal his thunder at the same time. I'll give the mob something the likes of which they have never seen. We're about to see how Gracchus enjoys having the tables turned."

"And not a day too soon, I might add," Lucius whispered with a smile. "I know that he is your and Persephone's mentor. But he is also your servant, and he sometimes forgets his place. This is not the first time he has openly defied you. He taunts you, but for what reason, I do not know."

Persephone sat back in her chair, waiting for the arrival of the Shashidan prisoners and Blood Stalkers. She knew what Blood Stalkers were, and she was eager to see them in action. Stalkers were captured Shashidan mystics who had been transformed by the craft to serve the Rustannican Empire. The transformation from Shashidan prisoner of war into Blood Stalker changed the captured Shashidans into something less than human. Their sole purpose in life became one of detecting and destroying other Shashidans possessing endowed, right-leaning blood. They also made for excellent legion scouts. It was said that the Coven of Sorceresses used them to great effect in their war against the Vigors wizards that took place several centuries ago on Eutracia. It had been long assumed that Failee—the late Coven's mistress—found the needed forestallment calculations to create Blood Stalkers in the Vagaries Scrolls. Rustannican mystics, however, had possessed the formulas for much longer.

By now more slaves were scurrying around the arena wall, shouting out the changes in the program. Just as Vespasian had expected, the crowd first quieted as they absorbed the news, but almost immediately they became more eager than before. Many started stamping their feet and calling out Vespasian's name in appreciation of their emperor's cleverness.

Just then a shrill bugle call rang out, ordering the chariots, musicians, and slaves to hurry back through the Gates of Life. As the tension in the coliseum mounted, the massive gates closed for a moment. When they opened again, the crowd came to its feet, and its thunderous roar could be heard in the farthest reaches of Ellistium.

The first group of one hundred male skeens was being prodded into the arena by Imperial centurions holding brightly lit torches. If a skeen hesitated he was immediately burned. To the crowd's delight, this happened dozens of times. The smell of burned flesh started drifting its way up into the stands, to the spectators' uproarious approval.

The skeens wore only white loincloths, and their skin was oiled to highlight their bodies for the crowd. Just as Vespasian had ordered, they were armed, some held short swords and shields, others brandished tridents and nets. As they neared the center of the arena they huddled together and stared in wide-eyed terror at the towering stands.

Their jobs done, the centurions retreated through the Gates of Life and locked the iron doors behind them. As the crowd stamped and shouted, the privileged few who were able to command the craft to augment their hearing soon heard the sounds of clanking chains.

An iron trap door in the arena floor slowly opened, revealing stone steps leading into the darkness of the coliseum's subterranean workings. Then, one by one, fifty of the Blood Stalkers attached to the Twenty-third Legion walked up the steps and into the light. Like the skeens, they had never been in the arena before, so they too looked around in bewilderment.

When all the stalkers had surfaced, the trap door closed. Leaning forward on her throne, Persephone regarded the stalkers. She had to admit that they were the most gruesome beings she had ever seen.

At first glance they seemed too large to be men, though they had two legs and two arms like men. Their elongated heads held bloodshot eyes, but there were no noses, only slits in the skin where a man's nostrils would be. On each side of their bald heads lay elongated ears that ended in ragged points of skin. A white fang protruded down from each corner of their mouths. Lathered drool ran from their mouths to their chins and slithered down their hairy chests in long white strings. Their only clothing was fringed leather warriors' skirts, which did little to hide the misshapen male genitals beneath them. Dried excrement clung to the backs of their legs, and each of their elongated fingers and toes ended in a sharp talon. Each stalker wore a collection of dried eyeballs hung around its neck on a leather string—Shashidan war trophies, Persephone assumed.

Each Blood Stalker was armed with a terrible battle-axe the like of which the empress had never seen. The long black helves were randomly patterned with dried blood, and each was crowned with a human skull. From each of the skull's temples a shiny silver axe blade extended outward at right angles. The sunlight filtering through the coliseum's red canopies glinted off the axes' highly polished edges.

Besides their battle-axes, two of the stalkers carried the familiar standards of the Twenty-third Legion. The standards were sumptuous red flags, hung vertically from golden crossbars secured at the tops of long golden staffs. Atop each staff sat a magnificent golden eagle, its wings outstretched in triumph. The flag itself bore the gold-embroidered image of a great bear, the mascot of the mighty Twenty-third. Beneath the bear appeared the number XXIII, also embroidered in gold. At a signal from one of the stalkers, the monsters formed ranks, and the two standard-bearers among them plunged the golden staffs into the sand, allowing the red flags to wave in the breeze for all to see.

Persephone peered closely at the stalkers. She could sense more than ordinary insanity in these creatures, something she could only describe as a crazed need to kill. A shiver of excitement shot through her.

Suddenly the stalker ranks started moving. As if the one hundred armed skeens didn't exist, the stalkers marched around them in lockstep toward their emperor.

Vespasian stood and walked to the front of the viewing box. When he raised his arms, the massive crowd stilled. For the first time today, absolute silence reigned in the arena. He smiled down at the Blood Stalkers. Calling on the craft, Vespasian used his gift to augment his voice.

"Kill them," he ordered.

At his words, the stalkers raised their axes and turned on the skeens. The crowd went wild.

At first the skeens tried to use their superiority in numbers to surround the stalkers and kill them. But it was no good. The drooling monstrosities swung their axes in wide circles, making any approach by their enemies impossible. Realizing that their only viable strategy had failed, the skeens broke ranks. The stalkers chased after them, and the killing started in earnest.

Several skeens died immediately, their blood gushing into the thirsty sand. Only when the survivors finally turned and formed up in numbers against an individual stalker did they have a chance of killing it, and even then their victories were few. Breathless with excitement, Persephone eagerly watched one such struggle unfold.

Waving their tridents and swords wildly, four skeens managed to force an enraged stalker up against a section of arena wall. With a shout, one of the skeens threw his net over the drooling monster. But just as the other three skeens started rushing in for the kill, the stalker unexpectedly laughed.

Reaching up, the stalker gripped the net with his hands and tore it down the middle as if it had been made of parchment. After tossing one half aside, he threw the remaining piece over one of the approaching skeens, trapping him. With one swing of his dark axe the stalker took the skeen's head off at the shoulders and sent it tumbling to the sand. Blood spraying from the gaping neck, the skeen died where he fell.

Screaming wildly, the three remaining skeens tried to rush the stalker all at once. The first to reach the monster raised his sword and shield. But the stalker was much faster. As the bloody axe blade came down it cleft the skeen's shield and plunged into the man's chest. Transfixed, Persephone watched the stalker pull the axe from his victim. With it came the skeen's heart, impaled on the axe blade.

After tearing the smashed shield and bloody heart from his axe, the stalker dispatched the remaining two skeens with equal ferocity. He severed the legs from one and the sword arm from the other. Then, leaving the wounded skeens to bleed to death, the semihuman monster let go a victory scream and lumbered off to find fresh quarry. Persephone took a gulp of wine, her heart beating wildly.

At last the fighting neared its end. All the skeens lay dead save one, and only two stalkers had been rent asunder. Persephone quickly calculated the score. For every stalker that had been killed, nearly fifty skeens had died. She had to admit that she was impressed. Just then she heard the crowd roar with laughter, and she soon saw why.

The last surviving skeen had been surrounded. Rather than kill him outright, the stalkers were taunting him for the amusement of the crowd. But as one stalker moved in a bit too close, the skeen lunged swiftly and plunged his trident into the thing's chest. Impressed by the skeen's courage and skill, the crowd stamped and shouted gleefully.

Knowing that his fate was sealed, the skeen did something entirely unexpected. In a last act of defiance he dropped his net and trident and ran to where a stalker had shoved one of the Twenty-third's standards into the arena sand. Pulling the standard free, he charged the nearest stalker. As the surprised monster tried to parry the blow, the skeen deftly sidestepped and impaled him with the standard's pointed end. Screaming wildly, the stalker fell to the sand and died, taking the red flag and golden staff with him.

The crowd was stunned into silence. For a legion standard to touch the ground was unthinkable, much less that such a travesty might be caused by a worthless slave. The incensed stalkers stood there for a moment trying to absorb what they had seen. Then they collected their wits and charged en masse. Standing his ground, the unarmed skeen screamed out a degrading epithet that he knew would be his last.

Suddenly an azure bolt shot through the air, thundering skyward with pinpoint precision through the gap between the two red canopies. Its explosive sound drowned out even the bloodthirsty mob. Recognizing the signal, the stalkers stopped in their tracks and turned to look toward their emperor's private box. His chest heaving, the condemned skeen also glared upward.

Vespasian was standing at the edge of his viewing box. It was he who had sent the bolt into the air. One azure bolt launched during the games always signaled that the emperor commanded the action to stop. The stalkers had immediately complied, and the crowd quieted. An eerie combination of tension and silence filled the stadium.

Vespasian turned to look at the Games Master. "Send out the branders," he ordered.

"Yes, my liege," the man answered.

Walking to the edge of the box, the Games Master quickly swiveled another of the signs. The centurions manning the Gates of Life opened the gate doors and hurried through. When they reemerged, each man was holding a branding iron. The irons' tips glowed red hot.

The centurions wandered among the vanquished Shashidan slaves lying on the sand. One by one, each victim was branded with the image of the imperial eagle. When the bright red iron touched the slaves' skin, those feigning death were immediately exposed. Seven were found to be still alive, screaming in agony at the unexpected pain. As the crowd cheered, the centurions quickly put them to the sword. When their grisly work was done, the centurions saluted their emperor, then went back through the Gates of Life and closed the iron doors behind them.

Vespasian extended his arms and levitated up and over the wall of his private box, his purple and gold cape fluttering behind him. Every eye in the arena was on him as he landed gracefully before the sole surviving skeen. He turned to look at the dead stalker lying impaled on the Twenty-third's bloodied standard.

Raising one hand, Vespasian pointed at the stalker corpse. At once the monster and the standard rose into the air, the stalker's arms and legs dangling toward the sand, his body dripping yellow, acidic blood where the standard had entered his chest and exited his back. As the blood hit the sand it hissed and smoked.

Vespasian beckoned with his fingers. The standard slowly pulled free from the dead stalker and floated in the air. Then Vespasian pointed downward and the standard plunged itself into the sand to stand upright once more. Vespasian released his hold on the dead stalker, and the monstrous corpse crashed to the ground.

Turning back toward the skeen, Vespasian walked closer. The skeen looked to be about forty Seasons of New Life, with dark hair and a ragged beard grown during his months of imprisonment. Vespasian watched the man's muscles coil as he neared, and he sensed the intense hatred the skeen had for him. Despite the skeen's deadly circumstances, there was a sense of commanding authority in his eyes. This had once been a man of some note, Vespasian guessed. Stopping about two paces away, the emperor folded his arms over his chest.

"What is your name, skeen?" he asked quietly. Vespasian took care to employ the skeen's native dialect, and he used the craft to make sure their words would reach the ears of every spectator.

"I am Tanjiro of the House of the Six Rivers," the man answered.

"What was your rank in the Shashidan army?" Vespasian asked.

"I am the First General of the Twelfth Cohort," Tanjiro answered. "And I do not answer to you."

Vespasian smiled. "Ah, but you are wrong," he answered. "Not only do you answer to me, but you are no longer a general. As a once high-ranking officer, you must also have been a craft practitioner."

"Yes," Tanjiro answered bitterly. "But my gifts are gone, courtesy of your endowed Twenty-third Legion's centurions."

"That's only fair, don't you agree?" Vespasian answered. "After all, your forces do the same thing to our captured officers who are trained in the craft."

Enraged, Tanjiro stepped menacingly toward the emperor. The stalkers lunged to protect Vespasian, but he knew he was in no danger. He stopped his grotesque servants with a wave of one hand.

"We don't murder our captives," Tanjiro growled, "or sell them at auction like cattle! Nor do we work them to death, or use them as sexual playthings! We treat them as respected prisoners of war! Shashida has but one class of people! All people—be they of endowed blood or not—are treated equally!"

His chest still heaving, Tanjiro tried to catch his breath. "That's a concept with which you Rustannican Vagaries worshippers seem to be unfamiliar."

Tanjiro was surprised to see Vespasian's expression soften a bit. Then the emperor stepped closer.

"You Shashidans are as skillful at lying as you are at fighting," he said. "Even so, I find that I like you. Under different circumstances we might have been friends. You have courage. Moreover, you are the first skeen to send one of my standards tumbling to the ground during a coliseum spectacle. You risked everything to dare that last act of defiance. You could scarcely have asked for a larger audience! Had I been in your place, I would have attempted the same thing. But that does not change the fact that we are mortal enemies."

As his words echoed throughout the arena, Vespasian looked out toward the multitudes. Every spectator was on his or her feet, eager to know what would happen next. The emperor decided. He looked back at the slave.

"Get down on your knees," he said.

"No," Tanjiro growled. "Not today, not ever. If you're going to kill me, I demand a warrior's death. Let me remain standing so that I can see it coming."

Vespasian was in no mood to barter with a slave—especially with one hundred thousand citizens, the *Pon Q'tar,* the Priory, and the Tribunes all watching. He extended his hand again. Calling on the craft, he forced Tanjiro to his knees.

"I'm afraid you have no choice in the matter," he said softly.

Reaching to his side, Vespasian drew his dress sword. When it came free of its scabbard, its razor-sharp blade glinted in the reddish light. The crowd held its breath. Persephone leaned forward in her chair.

Vespasian employed the craft to force the slave's head down, exposing the back of the man's neck. He raised his sword, then decisively brought it down.

A collective gasp went through the crowd. Rather than separating Tanjiro's head from his shoulders, Vespasian had buried the sword in the sand before the slave. Tanjiro hadn't flinched. But when he saw the shining blade standing upright only inches from his face, he looked up at Vespasian with unbelieving eyes.

"I free you," Vespasian said. "You fought well, and you were ready to accept death with equal bravery. You are now a Rustannican freeman of the Phrygian class. Arise, Tanjiro. You have but to take possession of my sword to claim your freedom."

The slave was stunned, as was the crowd. Letting the air rush from her lungs, Persephone sat back in her chair. When an emperor gave his sword over to an arena slave, the gesture granted the slave perpetual freedom. From that day forward, the newly minted freeman needed only to show the sword to prove his status.

Lucius smiled to himself, then turned to look at the *Pon Q'tar*. As he expected, they were huddled together, anxiously discussing this unexpected turn of events.

Then the First Tribune remembered what Vespasian had said about wanting to dress down Gracchus. As he took another gulp of wine, he realized that freeing a Shashidan general whom Gracchus had personally marked for death had just done that very thing. And as Vespasian had said, one couldn't have asked for a larger audience!

Well done, my liege, Lucius thought. *This is indeed a day of firsts.*

Vespasian released Tanjiro from his enchanted hold over him. The freeman stood and looked his new emperor squarely in the eyes, then reached down and pulled the sword from the sand. He admired it for several moments. Then, to everyone's astonishment, Tanjiro tossed it away. The mob gasped.

"I reject your offer," Tanjiro said. "Better that I should be killed this day than to live in this monstrous dictatorship and watch my fellow comrades die for your pleasure in the arena. Kill me, Vespasian. Kill me and let's be done with it."

Vespasian respected Tanjiro's answer. As a fellow warrior, he had half expected it. He looked Tanjiro in the eyes.

"Are you sure, Shashidan?" he asked. "I will not ask again."

"Kill me or send me home," Tanjiro answered.

"Very well," Vespasian said. "I have tried to be merciful. Let your death be on your head."

Vespasian opened his palm and held it out toward the sword lying in the sand. At once the weapon obeyed and jumped into his grasp. He stood there for a moment, thinking. After wiping the blade clean he calmly sheathed it.

Tanjiro glared at him. "What are you waiting for?" he demanded. "Get it over with!"

The spectators were again restless for action, and they began shouting and stamping once more. The chant "Kill, kill, kill!" started thundering through the arena.

Vespasian looked around at the decorated arena walls. Choosing an image, he pointed toward a place on the wall just to the right of the Gates of Death. An azure bolt left his fingertips and tore toward it. It struck the stone surface, then flattened out, blanketing the beastly image that Vespasian had selected.

The creature represented on the wall started to come alive. The sight was terrible, mesmerizing. Crying out in agony as it emerged from the dark stones that seemed to give it birth, the thing took form. On recognizing the beast, the crowd roared in approval. The azure glow faded, and the newly born creature launched itself from the wall to pounce, snarling, onto the arena sand.

It looked like a giant wolf, except that it stood on its hind legs. Spotted tan fur covered its body. Its teeth were long and sharp, and its eyes glowed bright red. Its hind feet were padded like a wolf's, but its front legs had five long, taloned fingers. Like the Blood Stalkers, it drooled copiously. Dark armor encased its torso; greaves and gauntlets protected its lower legs and forearms.

Vespasian looked at Tanjiro. "It's called a Rustannican Heart Wolf," he said quietly. "And the heart it wants is yours. You did say that you wanted to see it coming, did you not?"

Vespasian looked over at the hideous creature and then pointed at Tanjiro.

"Kill," he ordered. His menacing whisper reached to the far corners of the arena.

The snarling wolf bounded in gigantic leaps across the arena. Calmly, Vespasian stepped aside. Knowing that there was no escape, Tanjiro stood his ground. Just before the wolf took him, he gave Vespasian a final, defiant look.

The Heart Wolf pounced on Tanjiro, pinning him to the sand and disemboweling him in seconds. Eagerly rooting around in the screaming man's ravaged chest cavity, the wolf latched onto Tanjiro's heart with its jaws and tore it free. With the Shashidan general dead, the monster devoured the heart and then started gorging on the rest of the corpse.

As the giddy crowd chanted his name, Vespasian returned to his private viewing box and reclaimed his seat. Persephone gave him an admiring look; Lucius respectfully tipped his wine goblet toward him.

"Well done, my liege," the First Tribune said. He turned to look at the *Pon Q'tar* clerics. Unlike the overjoyed crowd, they sat in stony silence. Lucius barked a short laugh.

Vespasian called out for the Games Master. The nervous man was at the emperor's side in an instant.

"As usual, your highness no doubt wishes the dead bodies to be dragged away through the Gates of Death?" he asked.

Thinking for a moment, Vespasian sat back on his ivory throne. "No," he answered. "Let us start another new tradition this day. Bring the next one hundred skeens in, but do not arm them. Have centurions bind them to the corpses and body parts littering the sand—including whatever might be left of their beloved general. For the next fifteen days we will watch them starve to death as they are forced to lie there in the heat, bound tightly to their dead, rotting comrades. As that is taking place, send some centurions into the arena to deal with the Heart Wolf. That should provide some interim amusement for the crowd."

"As you wish, Highness," the Games Master answered. "And if I may say so, your idea about binding the living to the dead is an excellent one. It is a fine new tradition, indeed." Without further ado, he hurried away to tend to his orders.

Suddenly pensive, Vespasian watched as the next one hundred skeens were shoved into the arena. The centurions roughly pushed them to the sand and carried out their orders, first binding the skeens hand and foot and then lashing them to their fallen comrades.

Sensing Vespasian's mood, Persephone gave him a worried glance. "What is it, my love?" she asked. "All in all, the day goes well."

Vespasian turned and looked into her eyes. "It is not this day that bothers me," he answered cryptically, "but all the days to follow."

He looked down at the Heart Wolf greedily feeding on what was left of the Shashidan general. Blades drawn, several centurions were cautiously approaching the beast. As Vespasian watched the wolf rip and tear at the mutilated body, admiration showed in his eyes.

"That man died well," he mused. "Part of me wishes that he had accepted my offer of freedom. When my time comes, I hope I can meet death with the same courage that he displayed. They are a tough and determined lot, these Shashidan Vigors worshippers. Often of late, in my nightmares I see us losing this war. Then I awaken, shaking and bathed in a cold sweat."

"I know, my love," Persephone answered quietly. "But we will prevail, I promise you."

The crowd cheered again as one hundred more armed skeens were prodded into the arena to face the vicious Blood Stalkers, and the carnage resumed. For a moment Persephone took her gaze from the games and again looked at her husband's profile.

It will be a long day and an even longer night, she thought. *But most interesting of all will be the meeting that follows the games. It seems that the* Pon Q'tar *have some explaining to do.*

CHAPTER II

AS HE WALKED THROUGH THE PALACE, PRINCE TRISTAN of the House of Galland heard his boot heels echo through the largely deserted corridor. It was well after midnight and sleep had not come. Tiring of tossing and turning, he had finally risen from his bed.

He had quickly donned his familiar black trousers, black leather vest, and knee boots. He then arranged his dreggan, baldric, and quiver of throwing knives over his right shoulder. After running his hands through his salt-and-pepper hair, he left his quarters.

Feeling his stomach growl, he entertained the notion of going to the palace kitchens to get something to eat. As was often the case, earlier tonight the Conclave had taken supper together in one of the palace's elaborate dining rooms. The meal had been tasty enough, provided one liked lamb. But he didn't, and he had eaten little. His twin sister Shail-iha had never cared for it either.

He hoped that eating something would ease his restlessness, but he knew that it wouldn't cure it. Although the Vagaries finally seemed to have been defeated in Eutracia and Parthalon, the events of his recent visits to the other side of the Tolenka Mountains still lay heavily on his mind. In many ways his amazing adventures seemed to be no more than a series of strange, unbelievable dreams. There had been a time when he would have thought anyone who tried to tell him such tales stark raving mad.

But these things hadn't happened to someone else; they had happened to *him*. And as the *Jin'Sai* and leader of the Conclave of Vigors, it was his responsibility to see that the mission entrusted to him by the late Envoys of Crysenium was fulfilled.

As she died in Tristan's arms, the Envoy named Miriam had ordered Tristan and his Conclave to do the unimaginable. She said that they must somehow find a way over the Tolenka Mountains and into Rustannica—the menacing nation that was home to the *Pon Q'tar* Vagaries clerics. Once there, Tristan and his followers were to try to contact the mysterious League of Whispers.

The League was supposedly the secret rebel force of Vigors followers that was trying to unseat the *Pon Q'tar* and bring down the warlike nation that the Vagaries clerics had created. Not unlike the Mistresses of the Coven, the *Pon Q'tar* had aeons earlier started a vicious civil war, attracting to their cause many mystics who also believed that the Vagaries should rule as the sole arm of the craft.

When they had secretly gathered enough followers, the *Pon Q'tar* had declared a huge part of Shashida to be independent, and named the new nation Rustannica. Then they trained their amazing gifts on the long Shashidan-Rustannican border. Using the craft, the *Pon Q'tar* enchanted the border area to create a buffer against a Shashidan invasion. Normally beautiful and serene, the newly formed Borderlands could be morphed at will by the *Pon Q'tar* into various types of desolate, unstable wasteland.

With the secession of Rustannica, the civil disturbance that had spawned her soon grew into a monstrous war between the two nations. It came to be known as the War of Attrition, and it had been going on ever since. Untold millions from each side had perished.

With her dying breaths, Miriam had told Tristan that it was his and Shailiha's shared destiny to secure a lasting peace between Rustannica and Shashida. But Miriam had sternly warned Tristan that in doing so, he and Shailiha must take care to ensure the continued existence of both sides of the craft. For unlike the *Pon Q'tar,* the Shashidan mystics believed that if either side of the craft should perish, so would the other. They also believed that if the world was deprived of all magic, it would plunge into an eternal darkness from which it would never emerge.

Trying to focus on the positive, Tristan took stock of his blessings. So far, he and his Conclave had been victorious, though at a great price. East of the Tolenkas, several savage challenges to the Vigors had been met and defeated. The Sorceresses of the Coven, Tristan's son Nicholas, and Wulfgar—his and Shailiha's half brother—had all tried in their own ways to destroy the Vigors in Eutracia and Parthalon. Most recently, the Conclave had thwarted Serena, Wulfgar's wife, who had vowed to carry on her husband's legacy. Tristan knew that some of those vanquished foes had been counseled and aided by the *Pon Q'tar* clerics.

But the azure pass that had once allowed travel through the Tolenka mountain range was no more. It had been sealed forever by the *Pon Q'tar*, after the clerics learned about the Envoys and how they were helping Tristan to understand and fulfill his destiny. How he wished that those wise mystics were still alive, so that they might somehow help him in his newly realized mission.

Instead, he had seen the results of the butchery inflicted on the well-meaning Envoys by soldiers of Rustannica's Imperial Order. Then he had narrowly escaped the Borderlands with his life, returning to Eutracia just as the pass sealed behind him. With the Envoys gone, no one from the western side of the Tolenkas could help him and the Conclave to cross the peaks into Rustannica, or to contact the mysterious League of Whispers. Clearly, whatever actions he and his allies took must be of their own devising.

As he walked, Tristan allowed his surroundings to distract him from his worrisome thoughts. The massive palace was a wonder, literally sparkling with beauty and cleanliness. Rebuilt and redecorated by Minion and civilian workers after Wulfgar's second failed invasion attempt, the structure had risen to an even greater splendor than before the deaths of Tristan and Shailiha's parents.

Each hallway corner was guarded by two stern warriors of the Minions of Day and Night. They were the savage winged fighters who had originally been conjured by Failee, First Mistress of the Coven, but now swore allegiance to Tristan. The Minions represented the only standing army Eutracia and Parthalon had.

As Tristan approached another corner, the pair of warriors on guard there snapped their heels and came to quick attention. Tristan gave them a cursory nod. The warriors' dark wings were folded behind their backs and their leather body armor shone in the light of the hallway torches. Great curved swords known as dreggans—like the one Tristan carried—hung in scabbards at their hips.

Tristan much admired the Minions and he had relied heavily on them to help him win many bloody victories, both in Eutracia and in Parthalon. But they were not the massively imposing force that they had once been. At the height of their power they had numbered nearly half a million. But losses from so many deadly battles had cut their ranks to fewer than sixty thousand. It weighed on his heart to realize that the warriors might not be much help as he struggled to fulfill his newly crystallized destiny. Even if a way over the Tolenkas could be found, there simply weren't enough Minions remaining to confront the vast Rustannican Imperial Order.

During his time in the Borderlands, from afar he had watched a lone Shashidan force trudging through the snow, only to see it swallowed up by a great chasm that suddenly formed in the earth. To his amazement, the single force had easily numbered one hundred thousand troops. Logic dictated that the Rustannican forces were equally large, if not larger. Moreover, with their dark skin and great wings, Minion warriors would be impossible to disguise, making their use more difficult. It was becoming even more apparent that if Tristan and his followers entered Rustannica, their tactics would have to rely on stealth and cunning rather than brute force.

But the situation wasn't altogether bleak, he reminded himself. Many advantages and much craft knowledge had been garnered during the Conclave's ongoing battles against those who would have the Vagaries triumph.

Most importantly, the Conclave was finally in possession of the fabled Scroll of the Vigors and Scroll of the Vagaries. The Shashidan mystics had granted to Faegan the formula allowing him to use the precious indices to the scrolls. As the Conclave's chief craft researcher, the eccentric wizard could effectively search through the scrolls' vast teachings to pinpoint any forestallment formula the scrolls held. The forestallment could then be imbued into the blood of an endowed person, allowing immediate access to any gift the spell offered. Although part of the Vigors Scroll had been accidentally burned away during Wulfgar's first attempt to invade Eutracia, Tristan believed that its remaining spells would prove a great help in the challenging days to come.

Moreover, the Conclave's newfound ability to change blood signature lean had allowed the rehabilitation of the Consuls of the Redoubt, the lesser wizards who had once fallen prey to Nicholas' dark influence. The consuls' daughters, who had been secretly learning the Vigors at Fledgling House, a castle tucked away to the north at the base of the Tolenkas, had also found their way home to the Redoubt.

Along with the acolytes—the sisterhood of the craft that was the counterpart of the Consuls—the Redoubt bustled with magic students and practitioners of both sexes. Nathan, father of the fledgling Mallory, had been named Lead Consul. And Aeolus, a wizard who had once served with Wigg on the late Directorate of Wizards, had left his martial training school in Tammerland to become a full-fledged member of the Conclave.

Four of the massive Black Ships used during the recent attack on Serena's stronghold in Parthalon had survived and were being repaired in Parthalon. Tyranny, the Conclave's privateer and commander of the ships, would soon bring them home. The small fleet would then be moored at the Cavalon Delta to await Tristan's orders. Tristan was eager to have the ships return, because he guessed that they might somehow prove instrumental in crossing the Tolenkas.

Tristan weighed these things and many more as he continued on toward the palace kitchens. Much had changed, he knew. In some ways, the forces protecting the Vigors east of the Tolenkas had never been stronger. But in other ways, especially given the dwindling numbers of Minion warriors, things had never been more worrying.

Rounding another corner, he saw candlelight framing the edges of the kitchen doors. From behind the doors came tittering laughter. Curious about who else was about at this hour, he pushed open the doors and walked in.

To his mild surprise, Shailiha and the sorceress Jessamay sat at a great butcher's table in the center of the room. Shawna the Short was also there, sweeping the floor and mumbling to herself. As Tristan approached, Shailiha and Jessamay flashed him mischievous grins, and Shailiha beckoned him to come and sit with them.

Removing his weapons and placing them on the table, Tristan took a stool between the two women. He had never liked the formality of the palace dining rooms, and always preferred taking his meals in the kitchen. The notion suddenly crossed his mind that when the Conclave members took their evening meals together, it should be here. Then he realized that Wigg, stickler for royal decorum that he was, would surely protest.

Fires burned quietly in several large brick wall hearths, their orange-red flames welcoming him into the room. Wonderful smells teased his senses. Dozens of shining copper pots and pans hung from racks set low enough for Shawna the Short to reach them easily. A massive wine cellar lay behind an iron and glass door set into one wall. The cellar's thousands of dusty bottles lay in racks, perpetually cooled by one of Wigg's spells.

The table was laid with what looked like a feast: roasted ham, sliced cheese, vegetables, and brown bread were piled on trays. Beside them was a stone container filled to the brim with the spicy ground mustard for which the Eutracian province of Ephyra was famous. Two large pitchers of ale sat on the table, along with some empty pewter plates and tankards. Tristan knew perfectly well that this unexpected meal was Shawna's doing. Gratefully, he built a thick sandwich and filled a tankard. Shailiha gave Shawna a quick glance and slid her stool closer to her brother's.

"It seems that we have been found out," she whispered.

"What do you mean?" Tristan asked.

"Jessamay and I decided to come here and get a snack," she answered. "It seems that she doesn't like lamb any more than you or I. Anyway, we thought that we'd be clever and raid the kitchen without Shawna's knowing."

Tristan laughed. "There's never much chance of that," he answered.

Jessamay smiled ruefully. "No sooner did we get here than Shawna came bustling in to do some late-night cleaning." Raising an eyebrow, she looked over at the busy gnome. "Just watching her exhausts me! I beg the Afterlife—doesn't that little woman ever stop?"

After taking another bite of his sandwich and washing it down with more ale, Tristan shook his head. "Not that I've seen," he replied with a grin.

"Anyway, after we put up with her fussing about how we should have eaten more of her lamb, she finally relented and put this food out for us," Shailiha said. "I suggest that you eat well this time, or we'll never hear the end of it."

Tristan took another swig of ale, then smiled. "You're probably right," he said. "Anyway, I've always thought that simple food was the best. And to that noble end I will be as gluttonous as humanly possible."

As he heard Shailiha and Jessamay laugh, he couldn't help but enjoy the carefree sound. These two women had endured similar—and similarly awful—hardships at the hands of the late Coven of Sorceresses.

Shailiha had been abducted by the Coven because Failee needed her to consummate her mad plan to transform Shailiha into her fifth sorceress. Shailiha had been pregnant at the time. Only after many deadly trials had Tristan and Wigg been able to reach Parthalon and bring Shailiha and her new baby girl home. Frederick, Shailiha's late husband, killed during the Coven's savage attack on Tammerland, had not lived to see his child. Although Shailiha seemed happier these days, Tristan knew that she often felt lonely.

Jessamay, a full-fledged sorceress in her own right, had once been a member of Wigg's famous Black Guard—an elite group of Vigors followers who employed hit-and-run tactics against the Coven during the Sorceresses' War. After being taken prisoner by Failee's forces, she and several others like her had been used by Failee as test subjects for her cruel experiments. More than three hundred years later, Tristan and Wigg found Jessamay cowering alone in the belly of the Recluse, the Coven's onetime stronghold in Parthalon. She didn't look any older than Shailiha and Tristan, since she had been put under the protection of the time enchantments at the age of thirty-five, but she was bent and nearly broken by pain and starvation. After she had recovered, Tristan had offered her a seat on the Conclave. To everyone's approval, Jessamay readily accepted.

As he took another sip of ale, Tristan looked at his sister again. She was as pretty as ever. Long blond hair fell to her shoulders, and her hazel eyes shone with life. Although Shailiha often wore gowns, tonight she had chosen a simple dark blouse, a leather jerkin, green trousers, and soft brown boots. A gold medallion hung around her neck, an exact copy of the one Tristan wore. The medallions, enchanted by the Envoys during Tristan's second and last visit to Crysenium, allowed each to see whatever the other saw. Tristan and Shailiha had used the medallions infrequently, but he believed that they might have great value in the days to come.

Suddenly he wondered about his niece. "Shai, where's Morganna?" he asked, looking around. She tilted her head toward a corner of the room, and then he saw the cot set up there, and Morganna lying asleep, the covers tucked up around her chin. The usually energetic three-year-old looked the picture of peace and contentment.

Just then Shawna quit her incessant sweeping and waddled over to the table, fists on her hips. Knowing full well what was coming, Tristan rolled his eyes at Shailiha.

"So, *Your Highness,*" Shawna began, "it seems that tonight's dinner didn't suit you, either, eh? I'll have you know that my rack of lamb is the best in the kingdom! If you don't believe me you can ask the First Wizard—he'll set you straight! He didn't have to be coaxed into eating three helpings of it!"

She gave a little snort of disapproval as she watched Tristan take another bite of his sandwich. Soon one of her wizened index fingers was waggling before his face.

"I'll have you all know that's not a proper meal you're eating," she added, "even though I laid it out myself!"

Tristan knew that the best way to deal with Shawna was to give back as good as she dished out. Like most gnomes, she didn't respect anyone whom she could intimidate. Before answering, he gave her a knowing look.

What Shawna lacked in stature she more than made up for in tough-minded spirit. Her iron-gray hair was knotted in a severe bun at the back of her head. A stark white apron was tied around her middle over her plain gingham dress. The laces of her no-nonsense shoes were, as always, double-knotted, so that she would never have to stop working for such a silly reason as retying her footwear. Her calloused hands were gnarled but strong. Everything about her bespoke the virtues of hard work and common sense. As her sharp blue eyes met Tristan's, he suspected that she wanted to smile back, but he also knew that she wouldn't allow herself the luxury.

"I just don't like lamb, that's all," he said, deliberately chiding her. "But my sandwich is good." He gave her a quick wink. "I made it myself."

Before Shawna could retort, the kitchen doors blew open and Shannon the Short, Shawna's husband, came charging into the room. His face was almost as red as his beard, and he was out of breath.

As usual, Shannon was wearing a pair of worn blue overalls and a red work shirt, the sleeves rolled up over his beefy forearms. A black watch cap sat at a jaunty angle on his head. One hand held an ale jug, and the other grasped a corncob pipe.

As the pungent smoke curled its way up and out of the pipe and into Shawna's spotless kitchen, Tristan watched her well-known ire rise even farther. She was always upset whenever Shannon came near Morganna with his jug and pipe, however harmless he might be. But this time something in the look on the little man's face told Tristan that trouble was afoot.

"What is it?" the prince demanded.

"It's Master Faegan!" Shannon said, trying to catch his breath. "He told me to fetch you three straightaway! He needs you in the Archives of the Redoubt! All the other Conclave members are already there, saving Tyranny, Traax, and Sister Adrian, who are still in Parthalon!"

Standing, Tristan hurriedly arranged his weapons over his right shoulder.

"What's wrong?" Shailiha demanded, also rising.

"I doubt that even Master Faegan could describe it!" Shannon replied. "He wants everyone to see it with their own eyes! You must come now!"

"For the Afterlife's sake, tell us what's going on!" Tristan shouted as he and the two women hurried for the door. But Shannon had already entered the hallway and was waddling away as fast as he could.

Shailiha was the last one to leave the room. As she reached the doorway, she abruptly stopped to look first at Morganna and then at Shawna.

Shawna smiled back reassuringly. "You know that I will," she said gently. With a quick nod of thanks, the princess hurried after the others.

Running down hallway after hallway, they made their way through the secret passageways leading down into the Redoubt, the labyrinth of hallways and rooms that served as the Conclave's area of craft instruction and research. Even at this late hour the Redoubt was a mass of confusion, with busy consuls and acolytes running this way and that on various arcane errands. Tristan considered stopping one of them to demand what was going on, but then decided not to use up valuable time. Several minutes and a few properly negotiated hallways later, he and the others found themselves standing before the majestic Archive doors.

A crowd of bewildered consuls and acolytes stood before the entryway, obstructing the view. Tristan shouted to everyone to step aside, and they parted to make way for their *Jin'Sai.*

The Archive doors were wide open. No sound came from the room, but a nearly blinding azure glow was pouring through the doors and flooding the hallway. With a worried look, Tristan drew his dreggan and charged in.

CHAPTER III

"O BLESSED FLAME, WE PRAY THAT YOU WILL REMAIN constant in your strength. Fear not that we of the Priory will let your light fail, for as long as our virtue remains unblemished and we are pledged to your everlasting light, your spirit will endure. For wherever your flame lives, so too does the immense power of the Vagaries. In your name and toward that end I deliver this spell of strength."

Her prayer finished, the Femiculi of the Priory of Virtue remained on her knees with bowed head and closed eyes. Now she would perform the second and final part of the all-important ritual. Slowly she opened her eyes and looked up.

As it had done for aeons, a great flame burned in an enormous marble bowl in the Rotunda of the Priory. Like the woman who knelt before it, the flame was pure, serene, and powerful. It burned without heat, smoke, or sound—just a flame so high that it reached halfway to the occulum, the circular hole in the apex of the chamber's domed ceiling.

As the firelight burst through the occulum into the dark night, it reassured Ellistiumites moving about the city that their precious flame still lived. Viewing the heavens above the rotunda each evening was the only way for the citizens to be sure, for admittance to the dome was strictly limited to the emperor, the empress, the *Pon Q'tar,* and the twenty Priory virgins.

The magnificent Priory Rotunda sat atop one of seven hills that surrounded Ellistium. A host of krithian centurions, their weapons always at the ready, continuously prowled the Rotunda's beautifully landscaped grounds.

The Rotunda served three purposes. It housed the eternal flame, provided sanctuary for the women who had dedicated their lives and their chastity to ensure that the flame never died, and housed the ritual known as the auguries. It was believed that the sacred flame empowered the Vagaries. If the flame died, so would the side of the craft worshipped by all Rustannicans. Should the Vagaries die, so too would the nation, for the barbaric Shashidans would surely succeed in crossing the Borderlands and wiping out all that the Rustannicans held dear. The *Pon Q'tar* had commissioned the construction of the Rotunda long ago, soon after Rustannica had seceded from Shashida. Legend had it that another perpetual flame burning in Shashida empowered the Vigors.

It was also said that during the first tenuous days of the empire, the *Pon Q'tar* clerics stole the Vagaries flame just before announcing Rustannica's independence. Those brave clerics had also tried to extinguish the Vigors flame at the same moment, but failed, and thus the civil war began. With the coming of Vespasian and his supremely endowed blood, everyone believed that final victory would soon be within their reach.

Before starting the needed spell, the Femiculi took a moment to look around the Rotunda. She had been a member of the Priory since she was twenty years old. That had been twelve years ago, and even now she remained awed by the structure that was her home.

The massive dome was fifty meters wide at its base and more than thirty meters high. The occulum in the dome's center was ten meters across, and its circumference was ringed with gold. When the flame was at its lowest ebb, stars could be seen sparkling through the occulum. The interior of the dome was made of pure ivory blocks. As the firelight struck the blocks it created shimmering shadows of red, silver, and white.

The huge black altar that supported the bowl and the flame sat in the middle of the floor. A freestanding fluted column of pure gold rose from each of the altar's four corners, and each column was topped by a jewel-studded capital. The floor surrounding the altar was made of highly polished rose and black quartz checkerboard squares.

A second, smaller altar stood between the Femiculi and the bowl. As she looked at it, she shuddered, trying not to think about its grisly purpose.

Now it was time for Julia Idaeus, the reigning Femiculi of the Priory, to commence the spell that would empower the flame through another moon. Slowly she came to her feet and raised her arms. Then she closed her eyes and summoned the craft.

Some said that the wind she summoned had a life of its own, and that it wandered the world as it chose until being called forth on each new moon. Others insisted that each time it came, it drifted to the Rotunda from a secret sanctuary nestled somewhere among the dark peaks of the enchanted Tolenka Mountains. Only the *Pon Q'tar* knew for certain, yet it remained a part of the legend that they refused to share. Nor did it matter, for no one dared to question the clerics' wisdom.

Wherever it came from, the wind always served the same purpose: It fanned the embers at the base of the flame, allowing the flame to burn brightly again for another full moon.

As she called the craft, Julia watched the familiar azure glow fill the Rotunda. She heard the haunting wind arrive and swirl down through the occulum. As it neared her, it parted the folds of her white gown and stirred her hair. Soon the gathering tempest howled so loudly that it hurt her ears and its power nearly took her off her feet. Then the wind turned to fan the flame's embers.

As Julia struggled to control the tempest, her arms shook and her power began to ebb. Soon the embers at the base of the flame glowed brightly again, as if they had been reborn.

The flame strengthened and grew higher. With the last of her powers Julia forced the wind to caress the embers one last time. Then she slumped to the floor. Its job done, the wind whistled hauntingly as it soared back through the occulum and left the Rotunda for parts unknown.

Julia heard footsteps approaching. As she struggled to her knees, several other Priory virgins came to help her up. Agrippina Sertorius, Julia's most trusted Priory Sister, gave her a worried look. Unlike when they appeared in public, inside the Rotunda the women were allowed to go without their veils. Agrippina was five years Julia's junior, with brown eyes and short red ringlets.

"It is done?" Agrippina asked.

Julia looked back at the flame to see that it again roared with life, nearly reaching the occulum. She nodded to her friend. Over the next month the embers surrounding the base of the flame would again dim and the flame would fade, forcing Julia once again to perform the sacred rite of the wind. The ritual had been performed thousands upon thousands of times here in this same place, by Priory Femiculi too numerous to name.

Because the Priory virgins were not protected by time enchantments, Julia would one day become too old to perform the ritual. When that day came, Agrippina Sertorius or another Priory virgin like her would be selected to become the reigning Femiculi. According to custom, Julia would be freed from her duties to live her final days as a highborn Rustannican krithian, with a substantial pension to provide for her living expenses and if she chose, she would be free to marry.

"Let us help you back to your quarters," Agrippina said. "We need our rest—you above all. Vespasian's meeting is to start in less than eight hours. He will want our counsel."

Julia nodded. "I know," she said. As she recalled the day's occurrences, a pensive look crossed her face. "Vespasian seemed different today," she said. "Did you notice? I suspect that he has some important issue that he wishes to discuss." She sighed. "In any event, we will know soon enough."

Agrippina and three other Priory Sisters escorted Julia to the single doorway that led to their quarters. Julia paused to confirm that the flame roared strongly in the center of the beautifully constructed dome.

Satisfied, she left the Rotunda at last.

CHAPTER IV

AS TRISTAN, SHAILIHA, AND JESSAMAY RUSHED TOWARD the Archives entryway, the intense white light coming through the open doors nearly blinded them. Groping about with his free arm, Tristan found one of Shailiha's hands and gripped it.

Just then the wondrous light began to dim. His vision clearing, Tristan saw the crippled wizard Faegan sitting in his wooden chair on wheels, his arms upraised. His face showed intense concentration; sweat had broken out on his brow. His arms shook from the great effort he was expending as he summoned the craft.

Aeolus, Wigg, and Abbey stood by Faegan's chair, their arms also raised.

"What's happening?" Tristan whispered to Jessamay. He let go of Shailiha's hand and quietly sheathed his dreggan.

"I don't know," Jessamay whispered back.

After tense moments, the azure glow vanished at last, and Tristan gazed in amazement at the scene before him.

Books, scrolls, and parchments had been ripped from their shelves and covered the first floor in massive piles. Tristan couldn't begin to imagine how long it might take to set things right.

Tristan beckoned Jessamay and Shailiha to follow him. Trying as best they could not to trample any documents, they slowly walked over to where Wigg, Aeolus, and Abbey stood beside Faegan's chair.

"What happened here?" Tristan asked.

Faegan twisted around and looked sadly into Tristan's face. The ancient wizard wore his familiar black robe. His unruly gray hair lay parted down the middle and reached nearly to his shoulders. Much of his face was covered by a shaggy gray beard, and his lustrous green eyes seemed to bore straight into Tristan's soul. The prince could see that the normally mischievous wizard had been deeply sobered.

"I don't know exactly *what*," Faegan answered. "But I believe I know *why*."

Faegan swiveled his chair around and pointed to the wall on the far side of the room. Everyone turned to look.

Tristan knew that Faegan had brought the Tome—the primary treatise outlining the study of the craft—and the Scroll of the Vigors and the Scroll of the Vagaries here to the Archives for safekeeping. The wizard had used the craft to magically secure them within a five-sided transparent wizard's box high against the marble wall. Only the Conclave mystics had been entrusted with the complex formula that could dismantle the dimly glowing box.

Tristan had approved of Faegan's elegant solution. To the best of Faegan's knowledge, the azure box was impervious to everything except the spell that allowed for its dismantling. But *something* had gotten through. More than the box was illuminated. The Tome and both scrolls were glowing with the same bright white light that had only moments earlier engulfed the chamber. As Tristan gazed at the unprecedented glow, trepidation grew in his heart.

Fascinated, Shailiha stepped nearer. "What is that light?" she breathed.

Wigg shook his head. He was dressed in his customary gray robe. His iron-gray hair was pulled back from his widow's peak into a braid that fell down his back. Despite his advanced age, his tall form remained lean and muscular. His strong hands were gnarled and elegantly expressive, and his craggy face and aquamarine eyes showed deep concern. Sighing, he placed his hands into the opposite sleeves of his robe, then turned to the princess.

"As Faegan said, we don't know," he answered. "Logic dictates that the glow coming from the Tome and the Scrolls has something to do with whatever made such a mess of this room. It took a mighty force to do this. But only the Afterlife knows how or why."

Wigg turned his gaze back toward the glowing box that held the three precious documents. "We can only hope that the box protected them," he added. "Luckily, it seems to be intact. And except for the glow, they appear unharmed. But I suppose that there is only one way to know for sure."

He turned back to look at his old friend. "What say you, Faegan?" he asked. "Do you think it prudent that we dismantle your invention and take a look?"

Faegan, lost in concentration, didn't reply. His eyes were closed and his head was bowed slightly as he pressed his fingertips against his temples.

Tristan understood what Faegan was doing. The wizard was one of the rare few who commanded the gift of Consummate Recollection, allowing him to perfectly recall everything he had ever seen, heard, or read from his birth more than three centuries ago right up to the present. Faegan was almost certainly mentally reviewing the Tome, to learn whether it might shed light on this evening's strange turn of events.

After a time, Faegan raised his head and opened his eyes. His face was pinched with worry.

"The Tome mentions this phenomenon," he said quietly. "Truth be told, until this moment I never gave it much importance. That is because the Tome does not specifically name the three documents that when placed side by side will cause this effect. Now the answer has been revealed. It is only by the greatest chance that we possess all three at the same time. This might be the first moment in history when they have been this close to one another."

"Do you mean to say that your conjured box caused all this?" Jessamay asked.

"No," Faegan answered. "The box is only a means of protection. Still, there is no telling what might happen if it is dismantled. Let me recite the proper Tome passage so that you might better understand."

Closing his eyes again, he leaned back in his chair and spoke:

AND SO IT WILL COME TO PASS THAT IF CERTAIN RELICS ARE PLACED IN CLOSE PROXIMITY TO ONE ANOTHER AND LEFT TO REST, THE RESULTS WILL BE OF VAST IMPORTANCE FOR THOSE TRYING TO UNRAVEL THE SECRETS OF MAGIC. THE AREA SURROUNDING

THEM WILL SLOWLY TAKE ON AN AURA THAT WILL GRADUALLY ENGULF THE DOCUMENTS, CAUSING THEM TO GLOW. PRECEDING THE GLOW A GREAT WHIRLWIND WILL COME, MARKING THE ADVENT OF THE SPELL. AFTER THE PASSING OF THE WIND, THE THREE RELICS WILL GIVE UP MUCH WHEN THEY ARE OPENED.

Faegan sighed and sat back in his chair. He opened his eyes.

"What does it mean?" Abbey asked.

Abbey was nearly as old as Wigg, Faegan, and Aeolus. She too was protected by time enchantments. Like Jessamay, she did not look her age. The herbmistress and partial adept was wearing a simple plaid dress that covered her shapely figure. Her long dark hair was sparsely streaked with gray and her sensual face showed a strong jaw, deep blue eyes, and dark eyebrows. Three hundred years earlier she had been Wigg's secret lover, before the late Directorate of Wizards banished all partials from Tammerland. During the dangerous hunt for the Scroll of the Vigors, Wigg and Abbey had found each other again, and had been together ever since.

"As you all know, the Tome is often difficult to understand," Faegan answered. "I have long believed that the Ones fashioned it to be purposely obscure, so that it would confound friend and foe alike. It seems that we have yet another riddle to unravel."

"What is the code to which the quote refers?" Tristan asked. "Could it be that there is much more to the Tome and the Scrolls than we know?"

Wigg raised an eyebrow. "Have you ever known that *not* to be the case?" he asked. He looked back at Faegan. "You still haven't answered my question," he said. "Do we dismantle your box, or not?"

Faegan turned toward Aeolus. "What say you, Aeolus?" he asked. "We have yet to hear your opinion."

Before answering, Aeolus walked toward the glowing box. He stopped about two meters away and looked at it carefully.

Aeolus was the most recent addition to the Conclave. Once a powerful Directorate Wizard, he had grown tired of war, politics, and the craft and had resigned his membership to pursue a private life teaching martial arts. But by necessity he had become involved in the search for the Scroll of the Vagaries and the struggle against Serena. In the end he had accepted Tristan's and Wigg's offers of a seat on the Conclave.

Three centuries earlier, Aeolus had been granted a time enchantment at the age of eighty Seasons of New Life. Like Wigg, he remained lean and muscular, despite his physical age. His head was shaved and his dark gray beard closely trimmed, and his dark eyes never missed a thing. Out of respect for his late Directorate brothers, he wore a gray robe.

After regarding the box for a time, Aeolus looked at Faegan. "Does your spell incorporate any dangerous components that might harm the documents if it is reversed?"

Faegan shook his head. "No," he answered. "But owing to the need to protect the documents, the spell I conjured is tremendously strong."

Aeolus turned to look at the box again. "My greatest worry is what will happen when the documents are again exposed to the environment of this room," he mused.

"I concur," Faegan said.

"I don't understand," Tristan interjected. "Why would the room harm them? The white light has done its work and it is gone. Aside from the usual oil lamps, the only light comes from the documents themselves."

Faegan gave Tristan a grave look. "That's not true," he said. "The white light is still with us."

Perplexed, Tristan looked around. "I can't see it," he protested.

Wigg shook his head. "Just because you cannot see it doesn't mean that it isn't here," he replied. "We tried, but even our collective gifts could only dim the light to a point that it cannot be seen by those untrained in the craft."

"It's true, Tristan," Jessamay added. "I can still see it."

"So what does all this mean?" Shailiha asked.

"My wizard's box, transparent though it is, might have blocked some of the light from the documents. By conjuring the box, I might have inadvertently hampered the spell. It seems clear to me that the spell was intended to bathe the documents in the light at its brightest. We have no way of knowing what might happen if the Tome and the Scrolls were first partially exposed and then are fully exposed to the light."

As Tristan considered the mystics' concerns, he was again reminded of what a tangled web the craft was. Clearly, the decision whether to continue was a huge one.

Should the documents already be damaged beyond use, the Conclave's struggle to ensure the safety of the Vigors and bring peace to the lands west of the Tolenkas would suffer an unimaginable setback. It was true that Faegan had read the first two volumes of the Tome and could probably recite them verbatim to a consul scribe, but that might take years. And because Faegan had not yet fully read the Scrolls, most of the precious forestallment formulas they held would be lost forever. Perhaps worst of all, the Prophecies—the third and final volume of the Tome that only Tristan was destined to read—would also be destroyed.

He looked back at Wigg. "Although I am the nation's sovereign and the leader of the Conclave, I must leave this matter to those who command the craft," he said. "Only you four have the knowledge needed to decide."

Wigg nodded. "I agree," he answered. He looked at the others. "What say you all?" he asked.

Faegan took a deep breath. "We can't leave the Tome and the Scrolls up there indefinitely," he said. "We need them too badly. We could wait for the spell to subside, but that might never happen. I say we liberate the documents and take our chances. I understand that the risk is huge, but what other choice is there?"

"I agree," Jessamay said.

"As do I," Aeolus replied.

"Very well," Wigg said. "Faegan will dismantle the box. And may the Afterlife grant us luck."

Faegan swiveled his chair to face his invention, then closed his eyes and raised his arms and began his spell of reversal.

For several long moments the box glowed brighter. To Tristan's relief, the three sacred documents inside did not. Slowly, the sides of the box came apart and vanished. Tristan held his breath as Faegan reversed the last fragments of the spell, freeing the three relics from their places high against the wall.

As Faegan opened his eyes and lowered his arms, the Tome and Scrolls suddenly flew toward the center of the room. Tristan looked worriedly at the wizard.

"Was that your doing?" he whispered.

"No," Faegan replied. "What happens now must be the purview of the Ones."

To everyone's amazement, the documents began to spin. Faster and faster they went, until their forms became little more than glowing blurs. Then there was a great explosion, and an intense wind sprang from nowhere.

All the fallen Archives documents went flying into the air. As the precious books and the papers whirled about, three explosions followed in quick succession. Their immense force took the visitors off their feet. Tristan landed hard beside Faegan's overturned chair. He turned his head to see the wizard lying beside him.

Tristan groggily did his best to look through the whirling paper blizzard. He could barely see that the Tome and the Scrolls had stopped spinning. But something else was happening. The three relics were emitting some type of azure dust. The quickly growing cloud grew and grew until it engulfed the room.

As the azure cloud drifted over him, Tristan sensed his consciousness slipping away. He tried to look around; it seemed that everyone except him and Faegan had been overcome.

Tristan managed a last look at Faegan. The old wizard's face showed great delight.

"The legend is true . . ." Tristan heard Faegan faintly whisper, as if the wizard's voice was drifting to him from some faraway place. "Subtle matter exists . . . subtle matter exists . . ."

Unable to stay conscious, the prince finally surrendered.

CHAPTER V

"THAT'S MERE SNIVELRY, GRACCHUS!" VESPASIAN SHOUTED. Raising one hand, he pointed an accusatory finger at the lead cleric. "It was hardly a worthy comment from someone of your station!"

The emperor was clearly angry, as were many others present. Soon the meeting chamber again burst into loud, disorganized rancor.

Lifting his scepter, Vespasian repeatedly banged it on the floor, and the room gradually quieted. From his seat among the other tribunes, Lucius Marius gave his emperor a quick nod of support. Vespasian returned the scepter to the golden holder beside his chair.

The meeting had been going on for nearly an hour. Vespasian had spent some of that time castigating Gracchus not only for what he saw as Gracchus' furtive try to murder an inordinate number of skeens in the arena for his own aggrandizement, but also for what Vespasian saw as a clear affront to his authority. Gracchus had apologized, but Vespasian sensed that Gracchus' contrition was superficial rather than heartfelt, forcing him to doubt whether he had seen the last of his lead cleric's impudence.

It was early morning of the day following the opening of the games. Vespasian knew that this meeting must be brief, for the games were scheduled to resume at midday. As the visitors quieted, Vespasian took a moment to look around the room.

The rulers' meeting chamber was called the Rectoris Aedifficium, or simply "the Aedifficium." Like the Rotunda of the Priory, it occupied the top of one of Ellistium's seven hills. Aside from a few skeens selected to serve them, admittance to the Aedifficium was strictly limited to the emperor and empress, the members of the Priory, the clerics of the *Pon Q'tar,* and the eighty legionary tribunes. Also like the Rotunda, it was guarded by specially chosen centurions. It was here that all laws and important decisions were crafted and voted on.

Compared with many other structures in Ellistium, the Aedifficium was small, taking the form of an amphitheater measuring thirty meters across. Vespasian's chair sat alone in the center of the room facing the curved rows of seats.

The walls, floor, and flat ceiling were made of pure turquoise. Gleaming onyx pilasters stood against the curved walls every six feet, each crowned with a golden eagle, the empire's symbol of authority. Leaded glass skylights let in the morning sun. During nighttime sessions, wall torches enchanted to burn without smoke were set ablaze, granting the Aedifficium an august presence.

The section to Vespasian's left held the seats of the twelve *Pon Q'tar* members. The center section was the province of the twenty Priory women, and the seats on the right were for the eighty legionary tribunes. Custom dictated that the empress always sat in a place of honor beside the First Tribune.

The Aedifficium was seldom in full session because some tribunes were always afield, prosecuting the war. Because the tribunes outnumbered all the other members combined, only the thirty-two highest ranking tribunes could vote, lest the empire's military wing conspire to control every voting session. Taken as whole, the voting body was called the Suffragat.

One legionary tribune was designated the Suffragat scribe, responsible for recording every word. After each meeting, Vespasian and the *Pon Q'tar* heavily censored the scribe's report. Only then was a copy sent to every herald in the city. The heralds would then shout the report's contents from towers standing at each of the forum's four corners, so that interested citizens could hear the Suffragat's latest pronouncements.

A dozen male skeens stood by, waiting to pass important documents among the Suffragat members and to perform other services as needed. As a precaution against the leaking of state secrets, not one Aedifficium skeen could read or write. Additionally, each skeen's tongue had been cut out and his eardrums pierced. Members of the governing body communicated their needs to the skeens by way of hand signals. From the day he entered the service of the Suffragat, every Aediffcium skeen was forced to live out his life in modest quarters on the Aediffcium compound.

As the room finally quieted, from his place on the Aediffcium floor Vespasian again looked his lead cleric in the eyes. Then he glanced toward the tribune scribe, and he smirked. Today's session report would be even more heavily censored than usual, he realized. Because Lucius had already given the war report, Vespasian decided to move on to the next topic. He looked at Julia Idaeus.

"Will the Femiculi please stand?" he asked.

Julia stood from her chair and gracefully smoothed her gown. She was an attractive woman, with a lovely face and long dark ringlets. Julia and her sisters were not allowed to wear their veils in the Aediffcium, largely because the other Suffragat members wanted to be able to gauge the women's expressions as various topics were debated. The Priory was important to the people of Rustannica, and Vespasian knew full well that he needed its support if he was to rule effectively. With her hands respectfully clasped before her, Julia regarded her emperor.

"The full moons are here," Vespasian said. "I trust that the Vagaries flame has been replenished and that should I visit the Rotunda, I would find it in vibrant stead?"

"Yes, Your Highness," Julia answered. "The flame burns strongly again. All is well with the craft."

"Thank you, Femiculi," Vespasian said. "Do you wish to inform the Suffragat of any worthy supplications proposed by the citizens?"

"Not at this time, Highness," she answered.

"Very well," Vespasian said. "You may be seated."

Unlike the commanding way he behaved toward the *Pon Q'tar* and the military, Vespasian always treated the Priory members with utmost courtesy. There were two reasons for this.

First, his respect for the Priory was genuine. The vows of chastity required to join the Priory were taken willingly, and becoming a Priory member was considered a great honor. The vows were an act of faith and central to the women's beings. Should a Sister be caught breaking her vows, the penalty was death. By law, the method of execution was ritual sacrifice, performed on the black altar standing before the Vagaries flame.

In the entire history of the empire, this punishment had never been needed. Even so, the vows of chastity were more than a sacred discipline that the Sisters were obliged to follow. They also symbolized a guiding principle for the populace at large and gave them faith. The citizenry believed that so long as the Priory Sisters remained pure, so would the Vagaries flame that they tended and protected. As went the life of the flame, so did the life of the nation.

The second reason for Vespasian's cultivation of the Priory was more pragmatic. Of the three Suffragat factions, the Priory was the one most attuned to the will of the people. Only Julia Idaeus heard the supplications of the citizens, rather than Vespasian, the *Pon Q'tar*, or the military. The needs expressed by the citizens that Julia deemed worthy of debate were relayed to the Suffragat. If the Suffragat agreed, the request was discussed and a vote was taken. Having the Femiculi's ear was a potent advantage in advancing one's fortunes. People had been known to come from thousands of miles away for a mere chance of being granted an audience with Julia Idaeus. Sometimes the eager pilgrims succeeded, sometimes they did not.

Eager to move on, Vespasian looked at Gracchus. "I will now read the latest treasury report," he ordered.

Gracchus signaled to a skeen who rushed down the aisle and toward his side. After the cleric gave the skeen a large diptych, the servant hurried down to the Aedifficium floor. Reaching Vespasian's chair, he went down on one knee, bowed his head, and reverently handed the gold and beeswax book up to his emperor. After taking it, Vespasian waved the skeen away.

While the council waited, Vespasian read the report. The gold tally had deteriorated to a level that was worse than he had expected. Gracchus was right, he realized. The treasury situation was indeed dire. Would there be enough to finance his new plan? he wondered.

Rustannica's pecuniary troubles had started more than one century ago, during the reign of one of Vespasian's predecessors. It had been his desire to greatly widen the war, hoping to finally bring it to an end. By a narrow vote, the Suffragat had agreed. But in their rush toward final victory, they had grossly underestimated the financial costs to the empire. In a way, Rustannica was a victim of her own military successes against Shashida. The Suffragat was painfully aware that the war was only one part of the problem. The far greater threat was the nation's dwindling gold supply.

As was the case in Shashida, gold was the Rustannican currency. By law, the treasury was supposed to hold a reserve of gold that was at least equal to the value of the gold coins circulating the nation. Unknown by the populace, the law was being wantonly violated by the same Suffragat members who had sworn to uphold it, providing yet another reason to heavily censor the session reports. When an inordinate amount of the treasury reserves were used to intensify the war, the Suffragat's gamble had won out—but not in the way that they had hoped. As the pace and scope of Rustannica's war against Shashida was stepped up, great tracts of Shashidan territory were won. But soon the campaign became a hollow victory, for the spoils taken from those lands were disappointing.

In truth, the Suffragat did not know whether the reputed Shashidan gold hoards had been only rumor, or whether they had existed and had been hurriedly moved to safety ahead of the advancing Rustannican legions. The Suffragat suspected the latter. Worse, they also guessed that the Shashidan military had been forewarned of the new offensive by a spy in their midst, giving the Shashidans time to move their gold. The traitor had never been found.

Because of her greatly accelerated campaign, Rustannica had overextended herself. Soon the cost of maintaining the war was proving too great even for the mighty empire to sustain. But the Suffragat dared not abandon the new lands that she had conquered, for Shashidan cohorts would quickly overrun the area and reclaim the empire's newest source of slaves and added taxation.

Ninety years ago, a change from gold coins to parchment script had been ordered in a try to prop up the treasury, but the experiment was short-lived. The paper script was quickly rejected by the populace and angry mobs literally burned the new money in the streets. Rustannicans liked the sound of coins jingling in their pockets, and only gold's heavy weight and unique texture sustained the people's confidence in the economy's well-being.

For a time, the *Pon Q'tar,* had tried to augment the gold supply by way of the craft. But that project also failed, because even the revered mystics could not conjure gold in sufficient quantities to make an appreciable difference. The empire had tried reducing the amount of gold in the coins, but the public soon caught on and another outcry arose. Worse yet, the Rustannican gold mines were nearing exhaustion and no new deposits had been unearthed for decades. For the first time in the history of Rustannica, her gold supply was nearing a finite amount.

The Suffragat briefly considered stripping all the gold from the public buildings to augment the treasury, but they quickly realized that such a brazen move would only confirm the public's growing suspicions. Moreover, as the population grew, so did the needs of the goldsmiths. Melted and crafted into jewelry, yet more irreplaceable gold was being worn as adornments and buried with the dead that would never find its way back into circulation. For a time the Suffragat actually flirted with the prospect of grave robbing, but the idea was eventually dismissed as too risky and unworkable. While the public worried and wondered, the smell of revolt drifted into the air. Something had to be done to placate the masses while an answer could still be found.

And so, seventy years ago, for better or worse, the great coliseum had been built to distract the mob from Rustannica's constantly rising inflation, ongoing war, and ever-increasing tax rates. But soon the massive costs associated with the grisly theater of death had brought the reverse effect and made matters worse.

Like Rustannica's offensive campaign, the coliseum had been wildly successful on the surface, but it soon created more problems than it solved. The games had become an institution and millions of people now relied on them to make a living. The spectacle employed countless centurions, horse breeders, chariot and wagon builders, animal trainers, slave traders, architects, surgeons, armorers, and untold other types of laborers. Shippers, contractors, and other businessmen also relied heavily on the games.

Not to be outdone, a high percentage of Ellistium's prostitutes counted on the debauchery of the games to supply them with drunken customers who might not otherwise use their services. The men's and women's incomes were heavily taxed by special bands of roving centurions. This unique taxation source had grown more important by the year and would be sorely missed if it stopped flowing.

Indeed, abolishing the games would now mean throwing so many people out of work that the Suffragat feared that it would result in the final collapse of the economy. In short, the games had become more than a diversion. They were the needed drug that numbed the populace to the nation's many problems, allowing the Suffragat to operate as it wished and its dwindling treasury to go largely unnoticed. In an attempt to alleviate the crushing costs of the games, the Suffragat raised the price of attendance, but that did little to help the massive problem.

Soon the coliseum in Ellistium had become so renowned that similar structures dedicated to the same purpose had been erected in other Rustannican cities, further compounding the nation's troubles. And the continual influx of captured skeens and their offspring into the Rustannican society was taking menial jobs away from the hard-pressed phrygian class. Unemployment among the phrygians was nearly rampant. In many ways, the more conquests Rustannica won, the poorer she became.

If the people rioted, Vespasian knew that the Suffragat would surely lose control of the nation. Because of the ever-present war, there were rarely enough legions stationed in the capital to overcome a mass uprising. Vespasian and Lucius secretly suspected that if all the legions were ordered home, even their combined forces would not be able to maintain order for long. And if so many troops were taken away from the front, all would be lost in any event.

Not since the *Pon Q'tar* had stolen the Vagaries flame from Shashida and declared Rustannican Independence had the nation's future been in such peril, and Vespasian knew it. Only a mass infusion of gold would solve the empire's many problems, allow the war to continue in strength, and help ensure the defeat of the Vigors. Ironically, the only way to get more gold was to wage ever-costlier campaigns. And so the dangerous spiral went round and round, threatening to engulf the nation once and for all.

Vespasian lowered the treasury report to the floor, then looked around the chamber. The people sitting before him were the most gifted and dedicated that Rustannica had to offer. Even so, the burden of finding a solution rested largely on his own shoulders. A plan to see his nation through her troubles had been forming in his mind for some time. It was risky, and it could easily mean the end of the empire should it fail. But if it worked, victory might finally be at hand.

As the Suffragat waited, Vespasian rose from his chair and started pacing. The room was silent save for the sound of the emperor's sandals on the polished turquoise floor. Because today's games would start soon, he was attired much the same as yesterday, as were the others.

As was often his habit, Vespasian drew his sword and he placed the flat side of its blade behind his neck and across his shoulders. In one hand he held the hilt, while the sword point balanced delicately against the fingertips of his other hand. Finally he stopped pacing and turned to look at Lucius and Persephone. Then he regarded the entire Suffragat.

"The treasury report is indeed distressing," he said. "We have tried everything we could think of to increase the treasury count, but all our ideas have failed. If we raise taxes again I fear an outright revolt—one that our home legions won't be able to put down. Therefore I have a question for the *Pon Q'tar,* and you clerics must be sure of your answer. The future of our empire might hinge on it." As Vespasian looked directly at Gracchus, the lead cleric calmly returned his emperor's stare.

"All your efforts to destroy the reigning *Jin'Sai* and his Conclave have failed," Vespasian went on. "Although he and his sister remain untrained in the craft and his mystics are supposedly far less gifted than we, they have defeated your plans at every turn. I understand that our direct intervention east of the Tolenkas is impossible, or the *Jin'Sai* and his followers would be long dead. Destroying him and his sister and crushing their Conclave are important issues, but they remain the lesser of our battles. Even so, the Coven of Sorceresses, the *Jin'Sai'*s son Nicolas, and Wulfgar and Serena were all bested by him despite your learned counsel. Make no mistake—I have no fear either of him or of those winged abominations that he inherited from Failee. We could crush their depleted ranks in hours. No, fellow members of the Suffragat—it's his *blood* that I fear, and his willingness to destroy the Vagaries so that his side of the craft might rule. He and the Shashidans share this terrible dream. Rustannica is threatened by their pestilence and stands alone against it. This is what the *Pon Q'tar* has taught me from the moment of my birth, and so this is what I believe."

Sheathing his sword, Vespasian walked closer toward the section holding the *Pon Q'tar.* Only after looking at each male and female member did he again speak.

"And so, my friends, before I announce my plan I must know something," Vespasian said quietly. "Even though the *Jin'Sai* twice navigated the azure pass and spent time with the traitorous Envoys of Crysenium, are you sure—absolutely *sure*—that he and his forces cannot cross the Tolenkas? If the Suffragat ratifies my proposal, I have no wish to suddenly find our legions fighting a war on two fronts."

Gracchus stood and gripped the shoulder folds of his white and burgundy robe. He gave Vespasian a confident look.

"I can speak for the entire *Pon Q'tar* on this matter, Highness," he said. "The *Jin'Sai* cannot cross—of that we are certain! The Oraculum agrees. If we in our majesty have not found a way, then an untrained prince and his ragtag Conclave certainly cannot! Whatever action you have in mind, rest assured that you may proceed without interference from the *Jin'Sai.*"

Taking a deep breath, Vespasian walked back and took his seat. Each time he sat there facing the Suffragat he felt isolated and on display— as if it was his will pitted against theirs. The emperor's chair had been placed there for exactly that reason, he knew. It was but one of the many prices to be paid for holding such immense power.

"May we now inquire about Your Highness's plan?" Gracchus asked. As the Suffragat waited, the Aedifficium grew silent as a tomb.

"Our gold mines are nearly depleted," Vespasian said quietly. "And the Shashidan gold hoards can seemingly be moved quickly, making their capture nearly impossible. But the Shashidan *gold mines* cannot. I want to make a final, all-or-nothing thrust deep into Shashida and take the mines. I intend to lead the campaign personally."

For several long moments no one spoke. Lucius turned to Persephone and he raised an eyebrow. The empress's astonishment was apparent. As she tried to compose herself, she leaned closer.

"Did you . . . know about this?" she whispered. She was so stunned that she could barely get the words out.

Lucius shook his head. "No," he whispered back. "But I have guessed for some time that something weighs heavily on his mind. Now we know what it is."

Persephone's worry became so great that her eyes shone with tears. Knowing that she needed to be strong for her husband, she quickly blinked them away.

"You are his First Tribune," she whispered. "Can we really do this thing, Lucius? Can our legions take the Shashidan mines?"

Lucius narrowed his eyes and rubbed his chin. "That remains to be seen," he answered. "But I know one thing."

"What is that?" Persephone whispered.

"Like Vespasian, I believe that taking the Shashidan gold mines is the only course of action left to us. If we don't, the treasury will soon be bankrupt. Our ability to wage war will come to a complete standstill and the Vigors will prevail."

Persephone clearly understood the immense historical importance of Vespasian's proposal. The Shashidan mines were deep in enemy territory and had long been considered unassailable. For the Rustannican legions to fight their way there would be difficult enough. But to also take the mines and occupy the surrounding lands would require a miracle.

She also knew that Vespasian was not the first emperor to offer such a plan, but in each case the proposal had been voted down because of the staggering cost and hugely long odds. But it wasn't some previous emperor who had again proposed this great adventure. It had been Vespasian Augustus I, whose birth and supremely endowed blood were shrouded in mystery and awe.

Even Persephone had to admit that she did not fully comprehend Vespasian's magical powers. Moreover, Vespasian commanded the overwhelming respect and devotion of his legions like no emperor before him. He had fought with them, drunk with them, laughed and cried with them, and helped to bury their dead. At his word they would follow him to certain death, if need be. This would be a campaign of staggering, unprecedented importance, and its outcome would permit no middle ground. The empire would either survive or fall, and Vespasian's leadership would be the fulcrum on which the scales of history would tip.

Suddenly Persephone's more personal concerns began crowding in. A campaign of this extent could take years, she realized. Her loneliness in Vespasian's absence would be devastating. More important, because she had produced no heir, should Vespasian be killed, Rustannican law dictated that she would rule in his stead until she died or became too feeble to continue. Then the Suffragat would choose a new ruler to fill the power vacuum.

But if Vespasian was killed and his campaign collapsed, what sort of shambles would remain for her to govern? she wondered. Financing this special assault would surely use up most of the remaining treasury funds. If the drive failed and the Rustannican treasury was bankrupted, Ellistium would burst into an uncontrollable riot. Worse, within a matter of months Shashidan hordes would mass outside the city walls. The decimated legions would surely be insufficient to drive them back.

Amid the deafening silence of the Suffragat, Persephone again looked at her beloved husband. He returned a gaze of grim determination mixed with the hint of a secret apology for not having taken her into his confidence sooner. While she nodded her undying support, she found herself wiping away another tear.

The Suffragat strenuously debated the wisdom of Vespasian's proposal for more than two hours. After each group had voiced its opinion, Vespasian again grasped his scepter and banged it on the floor.

"What say you all?" he asked. "May we now vote?"

Gracchus stood. "Before we do, we of the *Pon Q'tar* must ask whether a battle plan has been drawn up for this undertaking," he said. "If it has, we demand to see it."

Vespasian shook his head. "As yet there is no battle plan," he answered firmly. "My reasons for not ordering one are simple. Given its great importance, I wish the plan to be drawn up and approved by the entire Suffragat, rather than only the military. I have but one demand. Once we are in the field, I reserve the right to change any tactics I deem necessary to ensure our success."

"In that case, the *Pon Q'tar* agrees that the proposal should be voted on," Gracchus answered. "But if a suitable battle plan cannot be formulated, the *Pon Q'tar* reserves the right to demand another vote—one that would call for the total abandonment of the campaign. We will of course demand that the First Mistress of the Priory perform the auspiciums to divine our fortune in this endeavor. A favorable answer would go far in convincing the populace of our eventual victory. And there is one other thing upon which we must insist. Should this campaign become a reality, we believe that the Oraculum should be brought along as well. This sets a precedent, we realize, but her visions might be of great use to us."

"The tribunes agree," Lucius said.

"As does the Priory," Julia Idaeus added.

Vespasian nodded. "Very well," he said. "Send the skeens to retrieve the plaques."

With a quick hand signal from Gracchus, each skeen ran to one corner of the Aedifficium. There sat an ivory chest, its sides and top emblazoned with golden eagles. Opening the chest, the skeens removed dozens of gleaming onyx and ivory plaques, each about the size and thickness of a man's hand. One black plaque and one white plaque was delivered to each voting member of the Suffragat. However important or complex a motion might be, voting was a simple process. No secret votes or abstentions were allowed. A white plaque meant yes; a black one meant no.

When the members had been given their plaques, Vespasian looked toward the Suffragat as a whole. "The voting may begin," he said simply.

At once the air filled with plaques as the members cast their votes. As the plaques levitated, Vespasian held his breath.

Not a single black plaque hung in the air. Because there would be no need for a formal count, the members recalled their plaques. As they recognized the full import of what they had done, the Suffragat members went silent again.

Vespasian was astounded. In the entire history of the empire, only two other votes had been unanimous, and those had been "black-plaqued." This had indeed been history in the making.

"The motion is passed," Vespasian announced. "So that all three factions of the Suffragat might be represented, Gracchus, Lucius, and Julia, to you I delegate the responsibility of starting work on the battle plan. Leave no stone unturned."

Pleased beyond measure, Vespasian nodded. "This session is adjourned," he said. "But before we leave for the games, we have one more responsibility."

As Vespasian stood from his chair, Benedik Pryam edged closer toward Gracchus.

"It seems that we finally have our great campaign, after all," he said quietly. "And just as we hoped, it was Vespasian's idea. I pray that the *Pon Q'tar* and this amazing emperor that we have created are equal to the task . . ."

Gracchus smiled. "All in good time, my friend," he answered. "We have taken a greater victory from this day than we could have possibly wished for. I suggest that we go to the arena, drink some wine, and watch more skeens die—for we will soon be on the battlefield."

"Do you mean to say that we are going to accompany him?" Benedik demanded.

Gracchus nodded. "Given that he so cleverly demanded the right to alter the campaign on his sole authority at any time, I'd say that we have little choice," he answered. "But do not fear. I know how to manage our headstrong young ruler. And if I cannot, well, the battlefield can be a very dangerous place—even for emperors. Besides, once his gifts have won the day, his further usefulness will be questionable."

Gracchus watched Vespasian walk across the Aedifficium floor. Against the far wall was mounted a golden war lance. Only the emperor was allowed to handle the lance, and it held great significance for the empire. When the lance was brought before the public, its appearance meant only one thing—that a new and important campaign against Shashida had been ratified by the Suffragat.

Vespasian stopped to regard the sacred lance. He had never held it in his hands. The lance's tip was sharply pointed, and a golden eagle adorned its haft. A gray and white eagle feather dangled from shaft near the tip. Black leather strips were wound around its center, forming a tight gripping surface.

Vespasian reached up and took the lance down from the wall to find that it felt right in his hand. As he marched toward the Aedifficium doors, the entire Suffragat eagerly followed.

Flushed with victory, Vespasian pointed one hand at the massive bronze doors, and they opened quickly. After purposefully striding out onto the massive Aedifficium landing with the Suffragat in tow, he stood among the structure's huge columns and looked down the hill and out across Ellistium's massive forum, the city's great center of trade and commerce. While the Suffragat gathered around him, Persephone and Lucius came to stand by his side.

As was always the case whenever the Suffragat was in session, an eager crowd had gathered on the hill before the Aedifficium steps, waiting to hear news of the meeting. When they saw the war lance in Vespasian's hand, the crowd joyfully erupted, their rising cheers quickly attracting more curious citizens. Soon the entire area was full to overflowing as the mob eagerly waited for their emperor to speak. When Vespasian lifted the war lance above his head, the crowd went wild.

"The Suffragat has granted you a great campaign!" he shouted.

Gracchus smiled at Benedik. "It seems that our creation can do no wrong," the lead cleric whispered. "That man was born to end life."

As Vespasian walked down the hill and toward the coliseum, Persephone took his arm and the Suffragat followed.

In ways that even Vespasian could not have imagined, the die was cast.

CHAPTER VI

HIS NAME WAS ROLF OF THE HOUSE OF BRIGHAM, AND
he had hunted the length and breadth of Eutracia's Hartwick
Wood since his father had given him his first bow. Many said that these
glens and gullies were deeply enchanted by the craft. Rumor also had it
that the woods were the strict provinces of wizards and sorceresses and
that these regions should never be entered, lest an intruder come to
some dark harm. It was also said that an ancient cave lay in the woods,
its opening long sealed by mysterious wizards. Rolf always smirked
whenever he heard those old wives' tales. He had never seen such a cave,
and nothing in these woods had ever harmed him.

Even so, Rolf had more in common with the craft than he realized.
Shortly after he was born, some men in dark blue robes had come to his
parents' home and taken a drop of his blood for examination. They had
then informed his mother and father that he was of fully endowed blood.
At the time, such visits were not unusual, for all newborns were once
tested this way. It was needed for the nation's birth records, the mystics
had said.

Shortly after, an official-looking certificate, complete with a royal
wax seal, had arrived by messenger from Tammerland. Signed by two
Directorate Wizards, it attested to the quality of Rolf's blood. Being

unknowledgeable about the craft, his parents had thought little of the matter and filed the parchment away. Over the years the document somehow escaped to wherever so much of life's flotsam seems to go and hide, never to be seen again. Taken up as they were with the joy of rearing a child, Rolf's parents never told him of the wizards' findings. And because he had never been trained in the craft, his blood showed no signature.

Most of the time, Rolf felt as safe here in these woods as he did on the front porch of his modest farmhouse. He had been ten years old when his father had given him his first bow, and twenty-five more Seasons of New Life had passed since. As he expertly moved across the mossy ground, no sound betrayed him.

Rolf's father was dead, but the birth of his son Dale had helped to fill the void left by his father's sudden passing. And as his father had done with him, Rolf started teaching the boy archery at the age of seven. Now that Dale was ten, it was time for the young man to learn the ways of the forest. During the last three years the boy had become an excellent bowman. But hitting a standing target and killing a living creature were two different things, and that realization was not lost on the nervous young hunter as he trod alongside his father. Although his hands shook, the boy was overjoyed that this day of days had finally come.

It was late afternoon in Eutracia and the sun was starting to hide behind the tops of the trees. The fading sunlight cast ephemeral beacons onto the forest floor, granting the woods the wonderfully surreal appearance that only this time of day could bring. Soon the night creatures would start to prowl and sing and the stars would compete for space in the dark night sky.

One hour ago, the great stag that Rolf and Dale were tracking had unexpectedly turned north. The beast's change in direction had been welcome, otherwise the two tired hunters would have been forced to give up and head for home. They had caught a glimpse of their quarry only once, but that had been enough to convince Rolf that the stag was the largest he had ever seen.

As night neared, Rolf hoped that he and Dale would overtake the deer soon. If so, he would let Dale try to make the kill. If the deer was taken, Rolf would partly dress it, leaving the entrails behind to make the carcass lighter to carry. He would then smear some of the deer's blood onto Dale's face, signifying the boy's first kill. His only real concern was to leave the forest before the Hartwick wolves started their nocturnal prowling, for the scent of stag blood would draw them like flies. As they walked side by side, Rolf turned to look at his son.

When Dale reached manhood he would be tall and lean. His hair was dark blond and his sharp eyes were blue. Like his father, he wore a brown leather jerkin, matching breeches, and a narrow, brimless hat with a jaunty pheasant plume pinned along one side. His arrow quiver was strapped across his back, and he nervously held the ancestral family bow in his sweaty hands. A large hunting knife lay in a sheath secured to his belt, and his knee boots were of soft brown leather. The boy was desperately eager and equally worried about pleasing his father. He too had seen the great size of the stag. If he missed, a chance like this one might never come again.

Stopping for a moment, Rolf knelt down on one knee and looked at the ground. He pointed at the tracks that the stag's hooves had left in the soft moss.

"There," he said quietly. "Do you see how the tracks have become shallower and closer together? That means that the deer has stopped running. The confused track pattern just ahead tells us that he wandered about here for a time. Something must have caught his interest."

Standing, Rolf looked around. After a quick search he found a telling sign. Four low branches of a nearby hinteroot tree had been stripped clean of their berries. An even more meaningful clue was that the same tree trunk was scarred where the stag tried to rub the velvet away from this season's set of new antlers. Rolf called Dale nearer. Narrowing his eyes and rubbing his red beard, Rolf thought for a moment.

"What do these signs tell you?" he asked.

"That our stag was here," Dale whispered back. "He ate the berries and scratched his horns on the tree trunk."

Rolf smiled. "How do we know that our deer did these things?" he asked. "It is not uncommon for deer tracks to overrun each other's. Perhaps we lost him, only to pick up the trail of a different one."

Dale thought for a moment. "No," he answered. "He was here. We have not lost him."

Rolf smiled. "Explain your answer," he said.

Dale pointed to the ravaged tree trunk. "Only a buck could have done that," he said, "because a doe has no horns. And the stag we saw still carried his velvet. Odds are that this was done by him rather than by another."

"Well done," Rolf said. "But this great confusion of tracks makes it difficult to decide in which direction to go. How do we choose?"

Dale shook his head. "I don't know," he answered.

Rolf winked. "It has to do with the missing berries."

"I don't understand."

Rolf smiled again. "He was hungry—he ate four branches full of berries. Deer find them delicious, but the berries always cause them thirst. Unless I'm wrong, he'll soon head for the nearest brook. So we will go east for a time. It's a gamble, but if I'm right it will be worth it."

Changing course, Rolf started leading Dale east. As night encroached, they soon found themselves standing atop a bank and looking down toward a swiftly running brook. Dale knew this stream; he had fished here before. It was a good place for Eutracian black-striped trout.

The steep bank was lined with trees that made for good cover. Without being told, Dale knew that it would provide an excellent place from which to shoot—if only the stag could be found. Guessing that they were nearing their quarry, Rolf silently motioned that they should move on.

Walking stealthily along the ridge of the riverbank, the father and son soon found their stag. As Rolf had guessed, he stood in the middle of the burbling stream, drinking thirstily. Dale quietly slipped a razor-sharp broadhead from his quiver and notched it onto his bowstring.

Rolf put his lips near Dale's ear. "He will lift his head soon, and suddenly," he whispered, so faintly that even Dale could scarcely hear him. "Then he will take a look around. When he does, don't move a muscle! Don't worry—he won't smell us because we're downwind of him. Wait until he lowers his head to drink again. That is when he will be most vulnerable, so draw your bow and shoot. You know where to send the arrow."

Just as Rolf predicted, as though the wary stag were trying to catch some predator off guard, he suddenly lifted his head from the stream. His body was broad and his massive horns held six majestic points on either side. Even to the experienced Rolf, he was a beautiful, wondrous thing. As brook water dripped from the stag's mouth, his dark eyes darted around and his nostrils flared, testing the air. Finally convinced that he was safe, he went back to slaking his thirst.

Rolf knew that the deed now lay totally in Dale's hands, and that all his teaching and care had boiled down to this seminal moment. He watched his son pull the string back to his right cheek, stretching the bow's lacquered sinews nearly to the breaking point. Hoping against hope, Dale let the arrow fly.

His aim was true and the arrow buried itself deeply into the stag's flesh, just behind the right shoulder where the beast's heart lay. But the stag proved stronger than even Rolf had guessed. As the deer twisted in agony, Rolf realized the mighty creature was about to run. If the wounded stag could charge far enough before bleeding out, wolves might claim the carcass first and the situation would turn deadly.

"Shoot again, son!" Rolf exclaimed.

Dale already had another arrow notched and ready. Without hesitation he let it fly.

The second arrow also found its intended mark, slicing into the stag's neck. It severed a major artery, and blood began to gush from the mortal wound. The stag struggled for several steps, but his demise was near. He lumbered heavily from the stream, then fell to the grassy bank.

Rolf let go a deep breath. Dale's two shots had been perfect. There would be other hunts that would further bond him to his son, but this first kill would never come again. Nor could this initial prize have been more wonderful. As he looked at Dale he had tears in his eyes. He placed one hand on Dale's shoulder.

"Well done," he said simply.

"Thank you, Father," the boy said. Despite his modest answer, he couldn't have been happier.

They hurried down to where the stag lay. After warily kicking the animal to be sure that it was dead, Rolf took out his hunting knife and bade Dale to do the same. Soon a pile of steaming entrails lay beside their newly won prize.

Rolf looked again at the mighty deer. For several moments he considered quartering the animal so that Dale could help him carry it from the forest. But because darkness was nearly on them he decided against it. Carrying the deer would be backbreaking work, but if Dale helped hoist the carcass onto Rolf's shoulders, he believed that he could manage. This was no prize to abandon to the buzzards, wolves, and flies.

"Come with me," Rolf said, as he turned toward the stream. "We will wash our hands and knives before we go. I want as little blood scent in the air as possible."

As he bent down and washed his knife, Rolf looked downstream. About ten meters away, the brook emptied into a deep pool before rushing onward. Rolf again looked worriedly up at the sky. *We need to get moving,* he thought.

Just then he felt his knife edge bite into his palm, and a few drops of his blood dripped into the river. He shook his head. The wound was more embarrassing than serious. He had been careless, and he laughed at himself a little. As his blood ran downstream and into the pool, he produced a rag from one pocket and wound it around his hand.

Dale scowled. "Are you all right?" he asked.

Rolf smiled. "Yes," he answered, as he sheathed his knife. "Unlike your foolish father, you must always be careful."

Rolf decided that he would not mind bearing the short, jagged scar that would later form on his palm. Long after Dale had left Rolf and his mother and started a family of his own, the scar would always remind Rolf of this day. *It will be a wonderful story to tell over and over again before the fireplace,* he thought. He put an arm around Dale, and the father and son started back up the riverbank.

As they went, something behind them silently disturbed the surface of the downstream pool. Dark, long, and sharp, two twisted horns surfaced. Next came the crown of a skull that was smooth, hairless, and olive in color. As the horrific thing surfaced, its head and eyes showed next, along with its long, pointed ears. The eyes were wide apart, dully opaque, and held vertical yellow irises. Soon the short nose and wide mouth came into view. As the thing's lips parted, a bright red tongue and rows of sharp yellow teeth were exposed. A pair of snakelike incisors protruded from the upper and lower jaws.

Silently, the hideous thing's body emerged from the depths. Its olive-colored torso was human in form, with muscular arms, a broad chest, and highly accentuated abdominal muscles. Each of its eight fingers and two opposable thumbs ended in a dark talon. But as the rest of the creature broke the surface and the thing hurried toward shore, any similarities between it and a human being quickly ended.

From the thing's waist down, its body was a scaled, snakelike tail. As the tail propelled the creature across the surface of the pool, it whipped to and fro with amazing power. Like the thing's upper torso, the tail was olive in color, but it had dark spots all along its length and gradually tapered to a forked end.

When it reached the shore, the monster silently coiled and reared upright like a cobra, its tail supporting its humanlike torso and supplying the ability to lunge quickly. As it watched the two unsuspecting hunters lift the stag carcass, it curiously twisted its head this way and that. The red forked tongue slithered in and out of its mouth, savoring the evening air.

Suddenly another of them surfaced the pool, followed by another. Soon the dark water was teeming with them, as they too swam toward the shore. As dozens of the things gathered and reared upright, the first one looked at the others. After centuries of waiting, their time for killing had finally come.

Without warning, the first creature lunged straight for Rolf and wound its strong tail tightly around his midsection. Rolf cried out in surprise as he did his best to turn and see what had so suddenly attacked him. His eyes widened in horror. As he tried to reach for his knife, he screamed wildly to Dale to help him.

When Dale saw the terrible thing that had hold of his father, terror seized every fiber of his being, freezing him in place. Finally he had his knife in his hand and he started slashing viciously at the beast seizing Rolf. But the thing saw him coming. Opening its mouth, it let go a nasty hiss. With a quick swipe from one arm, it sent Dale flying across the ground.

The thing's tail suddenly tightened harder around Rolf's body, snapping two of his ribs and squeezing most of the air from his lungs. Terrified, Rolf watched his son fly through the air and land hard. Dale tumbled over and over again, finally landing on his back. As Rolf watched Dale's body come to rest, an awful shock went through him.

During Dale's fall, his hunting knife had plunged into his body. The weapon stood upright in his chest, and blood ran down Dale's already blood-soaked sides and onto the ground. An experienced hunter, Rolf was well acquainted with sudden death. No one needed to tell him that his only son had just been killed. A sudden, savage anger flooded through him, and with his last bit of strength he finally grasped his knife and freed it from its sheath.

While the other curious monsters surrounded them, the one holding Rolf suddenly unwound its tail and dropped him to the ground. Gasping for breath, Rolf stood shakily and slashed at the thing, but it only hissed and then backed away with amazing speed. Before Rolf knew it the monster arched its back and lunged again, this time picking Rolf up with its two muscular arms as if he weighed nothing. Curling its tail beneath itself, and with Rolf still in its arms, the thing levered its upper body several meters high, into another cobralike pose.

Rolf tried to again to stab the thing, but his reach was not great enough. As the monster held Rolf before him, it turned its head this way and that, as if it was examining him for some reason. Then the slimy tongue again appeared to test the night air and retreated into the awful mouth. His strength gone, Rolf could do nothing but wait for death.

The creature reared back, opened its jaws, and bit savagely into the base of Rolf's neck. It tore a large chunk of muscle away, then spat it out. Knowing that Rolf would soon die, the beast let go, sending him tumbling to the ground. Twisting its head this way and that, the thing hissed and looked down at the dying woodsman. To Rolf's added horror, the beasts started wantonly slithering over and under one another in an orgiastic display of victory.

Amid the chaos, in another area of the pool the surface of the water quietly broke again to reveal a different kind of being. This creature was unlike the many others still rising from the depths. Striding from the pool, it walked up the riverbank to stand over the dying Rolf.

The being wore a dark, tattered robe that spilled down over his wrists and feet. So as to hide his face, the hood of his robe was pulled up over his head. He gripped a gleaming silver staff in one hand as he dispassionately watched Rolf suffer.

As his vision slowly dimmed, Rolf watched the strange figure raise his silvery staff. At once a great shaft of azure light streamed from the staff's end and went tearing into the forest. The ground started to shake and Rolf heard explosion upon explosion as the craft mowed down ancient trees and dense brush. Wildfires soon cast their orange-red flames into the dark night sky.

As his azure bolt faded, the robed figure continued to point the staff toward the charred path that he had cleared. Then he looked down at his servants as they hissed and slithered about in their orgiastic frenzy.

"That way, my children," he said quietly. "Our work here is done. Kill no more until you are again ordered to do so." His voice was deep and resonated with the power of the craft.

As the creature that had wounded Rolf slithered toward the path, the others quickly followed. With their great tails snaking back and forth, their speed soon became as great as the swiftest horses. Rolf turned in agony to see still more of the monsters rise from the water and slither up the charred trail.

There had to be hundreds of them by now, he realized. If their rampage continued, the monsters would soon number in the thousands. But his mind could not fathom how or why the terrible things and their mysterious master had so suddenly appeared.

To Rolf's further horror, the hooded figure dispassionately turned and levitated into the air. He then hauntingly glided to a place just above the beasts' onward-flowing column. With his dark robe billowing in the wind and his strange staff gleaming, he flew down the path and shepherded his newborn charges away.

While the forest fires crackled and smoke rose into the air, ever more of the newly born monsters exited the pool to follow their master. As Rolf drifted toward death, he heard a distant Hartwick wolf suddenly call out to announce another night of foraging.

How odd, Rolf thought, as he felt his warm blood spill out onto the ground. *The wolves that once worried me are now the only familiar part of this fiery, monster-strewn madhouse. It seems that the old wives' tales about these woods are true, after all. The craft really does live here . . .*

For the last time, Rolf turned his head to look at his son. If he could summon enough strength, there was one thing left to do. Reaching toward the stag carcass, with a trembling hand he gathered some of the deer's sticky blood onto his fingertips, then gently smeared it onto Dale's cheek. *Goodbye, my son,* he thought. *You did well today.*

As Rolf's eyes closed for the last time, the faraway wolf again let go his plaintive cry.

CHAPTER VII

TRISTAN WAS THE LAST CONCLAVE MEMBER TO AWAKEN. He tried to sit up but his head spun sickeningly, forcing him to lie down again. He soon realized that his weapons had been taken from him and that Shailiha sat by his side. Searching his face, she smiled cautiously.

"So you finally decided to rejoin the world," she said. "Welcome back. We were worried about you."

The princess sat on a chair that had been pulled up beside the sofa on which Tristan lay. He tried to sit up but again his grogginess won out, forcing him back down. As best he could tell, he was still in the Archives of the Redoubt.

"What happened?" he asked thickly.

Shailiha handed him a cup of hot tea. "Drink this first," she ordered. "Abbey laced it with some herbs. It will help bring you around."

Tristan took the cup and gratefully sipped its steaming contents. After giving it back to his sister he finally managed to come up onto his elbows and look around.

As he thought, he was still in the Archives. From somewhere across the room, the other Conclave members were talking in concerned tones. Except for the Tome and the two Scrolls having been released from the wizard's box, the room looked much as it had before everyone passed out. The oil lamps seemed to twinkle even more pleasantly, and mounds of disheveled archives still lay on the floor. Then his vision finally cleared and things came into better focus. A look of wonderment crossed his face.

The entire chamber and all six of its upper levels were sprinkled with a fine azure dust. It lay atop the furniture, coated the displaced archives lying on the floor, and dirtied every oil lamp and chandelier. Then Tristan realized why the lamps twinkled so prettily—their lamplight was filtering through the strange material that dusted them. The dust shimmered with a life of its own, adding a faint azure glow to the room.

When he looked back at Shailiha, he realized that her hair, clothes, and skin were lightly tinged with the stuff. He looked down to see that he was similarly dusted. He collected some of the strange material from his vest and onto his fingers to discover that it felt soft and fine, like highly milled flour. Suddenly he remembered what Faegan had whispered, just before he blacked out.

"Subtle matter," he said, half to himself.

Shailiha frowned. "What did you say?" she asked.

"He said 'subtle matter,' " Wigg's voice announced.

The First Wizard stepped closer. He had brushed most of the azure dust from his person but shimmering bits still clung to him here and there. Kneeling, he placed his face near Tristan's and looked deeply into the prince's eyes.

"Remain still," he announced. "I doubt that you have been harmed. Even so, it seems that you were the most deeply affected. Most of us awakened hours ago."

Tristan was hungry for answers but he did as Wigg asked. Finally satisfied, the wizard stood up. After placing his gnarled hands into the opposite sleeves of his robe, he let go a short smile.

"You'll live," he said drily. "We can only guess that because of the exceptional quality of your blood, you were the most affected. Shailiha has been conscious only a short time as well."

Tristan sat up on the edge of the sofa and looked around. As he did, some of the strange dust fell from his clothing, shimmering beautifully as it drifted to the floor.

"Is everyone all right?" he asked.

Before answering, Wigg reached toward a nearby chair and retrieved Tristan's weapons. The prince nodded his thanks.

"Everyone seems fine," the First Wizard answered. "You have been unconscious for six hours. At first I considered using the craft to try to bring you around. But we are still unsure about what happened here, so we decided to let you come around naturally, like everyone else. It was an interesting experience, wasn't it?"

"Six hours . . . ," Tristan whispered. "It seemed like moments." A look of concern flashed across his face. "What about the Tome and the Scrolls?" he demanded. "Are they safe?"

"Yes," Wigg answered. "Faegan and the others are examining them as we speak. But as we feared, freeing them from the wizard's box seems to have changed them. I think it best that—"

Suddenly Faegan's familiar cackle sounded from the other side of the room. It was full of the same timbre it always held when the eccentric wizard was close to unraveling some puzzle of the craft. Wigg raised an eyebrow, then beckoned the royals to follow him. Tristan stood gingerly and strapped his weapons into place behind his right shoulder. Taking a deep breath, on wobbly legs he accompanied Wigg and Shailiha to the other side of the room.

Jessamay, Faegan, Abbey, and Aeolus were sitting around one of the Archives tables and conferring among themselves. The Tome and the two Scrolls lay before them. As Tristan, Wigg, and Shailiha sat down, the prince regarded the precious relics. At first he couldn't see what Wigg had meant about the Tome and the Scrolls having been changed. Then he looked closer, and he understood.

The massive Tome lay open at about its midway point. Subtle matter lightly coated the Tome's two exposed pages. Its covers of white tooled leather seemed unaffected, but its pages had changed slightly. Until today, the Tome's Old Eutracian script had been written entirely in black ink, but now some of the letters glowed azure. Tristan could discern no reason why only certain of them had been affected.

He then looked at the two Scrolls. The Vigors Scroll lay totally unrolled and stretched the entire length of the table. It too was lightly dusted with subtle matter. Like the Tome, some of its individual markings glowed. But in this case the glowing marks were selected symbols and numbers that helped form the many hundreds of Vigors forestallment formulas. The Vagaries Scroll was unwound. Although it too had been dusted by subtle matter, it seemed unchanged by whatever phenomenon ravaged the Archives.

Tristan was about to speak when Faegan smiled and leaned across the tabletop. The wizard's mischievous gray-green eyes bored straight into his.

"Unless I'm wrong, you were about to demand answers about subtle matter," he said slyly.

Tristan nodded. "What happened here?"

"First things first," Wigg interjected. He raised a bony index finger and pointed it toward the ceiling. "Look there," he said simply.

Tristan and Shailiha raised their faces to see glowing azure lines of script hovering silently in the air high above the tabletop. One line was far longer than the others, and Tristan recognized it as a craft formula. Several more lines hovering nearby formed a short paragraph that was written in Old Eutracian. The four lines wavered to and fro teasingly, as though they were begging to be deciphered. Tristan and Shailiha returned their attention to the mystics.

"You all know that my brother and I can't read Old Eutracian," the princess said. "Where did those lines come from? And perhaps more important, what do they say?"

"Taken as a whole, they seem to be comprised of various letters, symbols, and numbers that have been selected from the Tome and the Vigors Scroll," Jessamay answered. "When the three relics were placed side by side, subtle matter was released from two of them. The amazing things that we all saw just before we blacked out were only the start of the process. The subtle matter seems to have searched the Tome and the Vigors Scrolls for certain letters, symbols, and numbers, then formed them into the paragraph and the formula that you see hovering above us. It appears that the Vagaries Scroll was not a part of that process."

"What does the paragraph say?" Tristan asked.

Faegan looked up at the glowing words.

"*Here lies the coded spell that will unlock so much,*" he read aloud. "*Enacted properly, it will help lead the seekers toward their ultimate goal. After the image appears, travel with care, for many perils await those who would follow the path.*"

"That's not much to go on," Tristan said. "Like the Tome, its message is purposely obscure."

As Tristan thought more about the paragraph, a sudden realization left him nearly speechless. He stared blankly first at Wigg, then at Faegan.

"Do you mean to say that the Tome and the Vigors Scrolls contain some type of a *code?*" he breathed. "And that the Ones used an ancient spell to make it appear from them?"

"That is exactly what we mean," Faegan answered. "We also believe that this is the first time that it has happened."

"And simply placing the three documents side by side caused this phenomenon?" Shailiha asked.

"Correct," Faegan answered. "The idea is quite clever. I believe that the Ones guessed that at some point over the centuries, craft mystics would eventually come to possess all three documents at once. As I quoted just hours ago from the Tome, the catalyst that started it all was placing the three relics side by side and allowing them to remain in close proximity to one another. I unwittingly did that when I conjured my wizard's box. The spell was automatically enacted, causing subtle matter to appear. We must rely on a few assumptions about what happened next, because we were all unconscious. We think that the subtle matter selected the encoded letters, symbols, and numbers from the Tome and the Vigors Scroll to construct the paragraph and the formula that hover above us. The weaker our blood, the less we were affected. But we all blacked out, and that's a pity. The process by which the code formed would have been a fascinating one to watch."

"It seems that the Ones took a terrible risk," Abbey protested.

"What do you mean?" Shailiha asked.

"She means that there was no likely way that the Ones could ensure that the three documents wouldn't fall into the hands of Vagaries practitioners first," Aeolus answered. "Had that happened, the results might have been disastrous."

"Yet the Ones decided to chance it anyway?" Tristan asked skeptically.

"Apparently so," Jessamay answered.

"But why incorporate a secret code into the relics at all?" Tristan asked.

Faegan cackled again. "Ah, why indeed?" he asked in return. "We believe that there is but one answer. Do you remember how the Scroll Master said that you are not the first *Jin'Sai* to seek to fulfill the destiny outlined in the Tome? Moreover, during your time with the Envoys of Crysenium you learned what that destiny truly entails—to bring a lasting peace to Rustannica and Shashida. We believe that this code was meant as a secret way of helping you and your sister to fulfill that task. And if we are right about this being the first time that the code has been released, then you and Shailiha are the first *Jin'Sai* and *Jin'Saiou* to claim this wondrous advantage."

Tristan sat back in his chair, then he looked over at his sister to see that she was equally overwhelmed. *Yet another piece of this ancient puzzle has fallen into place,* he realized. *But what will it reveal?* He looked back into Faegan's eyes.

"It seems that there is only one way to learn what the coded spell holds for us," Tristan mused. "We must enact the formula."

Faegan's expression hardened. "While that is probably true, we must be extremely careful," he warned. "Although it is overwhelmingly tempting, opening the spell could be the worst possible mistake. It might kill us all."

Tristan scowled. "I don't understand," he protested. "Why would the Ones provide us with a harmful spell?"

Just then Tristan noticed that the First Wizard's expression turn decidedly glum, as though some old wound had been reopened.

"What's wrong?" Tristan asked.

As Wigg took a deep breath, then laced his long fingers together atop the table, Abbey moved her chair closer in a silent show of support.

"You're forgetting something," Wigg answered. "For some time we have suspected that Failee possessed the Tome and both Scrolls. What we do not know—and might never know—is whether she possessed them concurrently. If she did—"

"She could have been the first to discover the code!" Shailiha exclaimed. "If that's true, she might have altered it somehow, making it deadly for the next mystics who came across it!"

Jessamay shook her head in disagreement. "I know better than most how brilliant Failee was," she said. "But it seems unlikely that even she could corrupt a spell constructed by the Ones. I still say that the Ones took a terrible risk that the code might first be found by Vagaries practitioners. How could they install the spell and then just trust the documents to the world that way?"

"How could they, indeed?" Aeolus asked. "It might be that the spell holds built-in safeguards, preventing it from forming among enemies. For example, one such protection might be that the spell cannot be enacted in the presence of left-leaning blood. But we cannot be sure. Now you understand the extent of the problem. The question is not *how* to enact the spell, but whether to do so at all."

"You still haven't answered my question," Tristan said to Faegan. "What is subtle matter?"

"We have long suspected the possibility of subtle matter, but until today we had no proof that it existed," Faegan answered. "It is mentioned only in passing in the Tome, making the prospect of its existence all the more tantalizing. This is a great day in our study of the craft—as great, I daresay, as the discovery of forestallments, the two Scrolls of the Ancients, and acquiring the index that allows us to search the Scrolls at will."

Pausing for a moment, Faegan cast his gaze around the table. "You are all familiar with the azure light that accompanies any significant use of the craft," he said. "Simply put, we believe that subtle matter is that same azure light, converted into a tactile form that can then be ordered to perform a mystic's bidding on a molecular scale. The construction of a formula bringing subtle matter into being certainly required power and knowledge of the highest order, and provides yet more proof that it is the work of the Ones."

Tristan shot Faegan a skeptical look. "Or of the *Pon Q'tar*," he added quietly.

"Although we must admit that possibility, the likelihood seems small," Jessamay said. "The Tome and the Vigors Scroll were written by the Ones, and the Vagaries Scroll apparently contributed not one of its letters, symbols, or numbers to the paragraph and the formula hovering above us. There seems little chance that the *Pon Q'tar* or the Heretics had a hand in this."

"But that is not proof positive, is it?" Tristan countered.

Faegan pulled thoughtfully on his beard. "No," he answered quietly. "And there lies the unspoken threat."

"There is still something about all this that makes no sense," Tristan said. "You claim that the Vagaries Scroll lent none of its markings to the secret paragraph and craft formula. Yet it seems that its presence was needed to start the spell working. If that's true, then why would the Ones incorporate the Vagaries Scroll into the spell at all—especially when they did not write that Scroll and they seemingly had no control over its whereabouts?"

"Requiring the Vagaries Scroll's presence is probably another safeguard," Wigg answered. "They wanted to be sure that Vigors practitioners were in possession of all three relics before the code was revealed. That makes sense, because without the Vagaries Scroll, our enemies are far weaker. Moreover, if Vagaries practitioners held the Scroll, they would only be two steps away from discovering the code first."

Tristan nodded his agreement. "The Ones were careful in their plan," he said. "Whatever their message has to tell us, it must be vitally important."

Faegan smiled and gave the prince a knowing wink. "Correct," he said. "It only makes things more tantalizing, eh?"

"But what purpose does subtle matter serve?" Shailiha asked. "I understand that it helped to form the encoded words above us, but surely that is not its only function."

"You're probably right," Aeolus answered. "We will need more time for research, but we believe that subtle matter might allow us applications of the craft that have previously been unavailable."

"What types of applications?" Tristan asked.

"You and your sister have often seen azure bolts used in many facets of the craft," Faegan answered, "such as exploding objects or lifting them into the air. As you know, craft bolts are mostly bright light, highly empowered by magic and ordered to do our bidding. Even so, bolts are limited in their usefulness because they cannot permeate their targets on a molecular level. In addition, they have little or no stealthy quality. We believe that subtle matter can do those things and more, making it far more useful and perhaps more powerful as well."

"I'm not sure that I understand," Shailiha said. "How can subtle matter penetrate where light cannot?"

"Imagine a simple sea sponge," Faegan answered. "If I were to strike it with an azure bolt of very low power, the sponge would singe, but not burst apart. Perhaps of greater importance, the bolt would not truly permeate the sponge. But subtle matter would be a different form of energy, taken to the molecular level. Put another way, think of subtle matter as if it held the same properties as water. Unlike light, even a small amount of subtle matter would presumably insinuate itself throughout the entire sponge, much the same way that the water would do. Then when its energy was released—"

"Unlike the azure bolt, the subtle matter destroys the sponge from the inside out, rather than the outside in," Tristan interjected. "Because its bits are microscopic in size, it can presumably ferret its way into places that other applications of the craft cannot."

Tristan sat back in his chair, thinking. "If you're right, the ramifications of this are immense," he added softly.

"Precisely," Wigg said. "Like forestallments, subtle matter could forever change our use of the craft."

"Even so, we must address the greater question," Tristan said. "Shall we activate the encoded formula, or not?"

As if no one wanted to answer first, each member went quiet for a time. Finally Faegan broke the silence.

"I believe that we should try," he said. "But make no mistake—by doing so we place complete trust in the Ones. There is simply no telling how many Vigors or Vagaries mystics owned the Tome and the two Scrolls before all three finally fell into our hands. We can only hope that the Ones incorporated enough safeguards into the spell to protect us from potential tampering by Vagaries practitioners like Failee. As Tristan said, whatever the formula reveals must be of great importance. Too important, I fear, to ignore." Sitting back in his chair, he cast his gaze toward the prince.

"What say you, *Jin'Sai?*" he asked. "Shall we proceed?"

Tristan knew that he could order the spell enacted, but he wanted the support of the Conclave. Leaning forward, he placed his palms on the tabletop.

"I need everyone's agreement on this," he said, "but I will not demand it." Pausing for a moment, he cast his gaze around the table.

"Do I hear a negative note?" he asked. As the Conclave members glanced at one another, silence reigned. Tristan nodded, then looked back at Faegan.

"It is agreed," he said. "And may the Afterlife protect us all."

Faegan nodded. Closing his eyes and raising his arms high, he started reciting the glowing formula. Shailiha reached under the table and took one of Tristan's hands into hers. He squeezed it and gave her a reassuring smile.

Suddenly the glowing craft formula began to spin. As the formula spun, it coalesced into a tight azure ball, crushing its symbols and numbers into illegibility. Then the ball glowed brighter, hurting everyone's eyes. Tristan raised his free hand to block the light, but it did little good. Suddenly the azure ball exploded, shooting millions of microscopic bits of subtle matter into the air.

This time the subtle matter didn't drift to the floor. Instead, it spread out to form a gleaming rectangle that measured about two meters long by one meter high. Images began forming on the rectangle as it hovered overhead. Moments later Tristan recognized what it was becoming, and it took his breath away. The subtle matter was creating a great map.

Fascinated, the Conclave members watched the Ones' spell unfold. Soon they could read the words and images forming on the map.

Rustannica, the letters read on the upper half.

Shashida, they soon formed on the lower half.

The Borderlands, the subtle matter etched into the vast area in between.

I beg the Afterlife! Tristan thought. *That is a map of the lands west of the Tolenka Mountains!*

Transfixed, the Conclave members watched as the subtle matter went on to illustrate various landmarks and geographical terrain, such as rivers, cities, mountains, valleys, and lakes. Just when Tristan thought that the spell had finished its handiwork, some of the subtle matter drifted toward the eastern side of the map. It collected onto an area southwest of Tammerland, in the northwestern part of Hartwick Wood.

The subtle matter swirled about that spot to create another geographical representation. The resulting landmark was small, dark, and oblong. Unlike the other landmarks, it glowed with a light sage color, causing it to stand out from everything else. Something about its shape tugged at Tristan's memories.

Soon a series of smaller numbers took form on the map just below it. At first Tristan thought that they might be another craft formula, but from his time spent aboard the Black Ships he soon recognized the numbers for what they were. *They're a series of maritime coordinates, pinpointing an exact spot,* he realized. Then the subtle matter vanished, leaving its spellbinding creation hovering in the air.

Even without the coordinates, Tristan instinctively knew what the small area represented. It was the entrance to the Caves of the Paragon— the place where Wigg had first discovered the Paragon and the Tome more than three centuries ago, and where Tristan's only son Nicholas had poisoned him while attempting to build the Gates of Dawn. Within those labyrinthine nether regions also lay the red waters of the Caves and the mysterious Azure Sea—the wondrous ocean that Nicholas had unwittingly set free during his enlargement of the caves, and about which the Conclave still knew so little.

Tristan's had long suspected that the Caves of the Paragon might hold the answers to his many questions, and now every fiber of his being suddenly told him that he must brave those mysterious caverns again, no matter the cost. As he felt Shailiha's hand tighten around his, he knew that she also grasped the Caves' renewed importance.

Suddenly more subtle matter collected and swirled about the room.

After a time the matter gradually spread out. For several mesmerizing moments it formed a sentence in Old Eutracian that hovered over the meeting table, teasing everyone with its meaning. Then the sentence vanished, never to return.

Tristan gave Faegan an anxious look. The old wizard seemed so stunned that he couldn't speak. Tristan quickly glanced at Wigg, Jessamay, and Aeolus to see that they were similarly amazed. He quickly glanced at Faegan again.

"What did the message say?" Tristan demanded.

Faegan could only summon a dumb, vacant stare. Desperately wanting answers, Tristan stood from his chair and took Faegan by the shoulders. He gave the wizard a gentle shake.

Finally Faegan snapped out of it. Before looking into Tristan's eyes, he blinked hard and shook his head with astonishment.

"To reach Shashida," Faegan quoted, "you must first cross the Azure Sea."

CHAPTER VIII ·

THE BOY HAD SEEN ONLY TEN SEASONS OF NEW LIFE and he was terrified of what might happen next. He never knew what awful things they might force him to do or to witness. "Schooling," the beings called it.

As he waited to be summoned he felt his warm urine run slowly down the inside of his left leg. Although the room was not cold, he shivered. *"What does not kill you makes you stronger,"* one of his strange masters had once said. But the boy didn't want to become stronger—he just wanted to die, so that he would never have to come here again.

The dank stone room in which he waited was small and bereft of light. His simple wooden stool was the only furniture. He always regained consciousness in this terrible place before they came for him. Then he would rise from the stone floor and sit on the stool to wait, with no memory of where he had been before now, or where he always went afterward.

Oddly, he could remember nothing of his life outside these walls. *Perhaps I have no other life,* he thought. As far as he could remember he had no name, no identity, and no other reason for living save for his "schooling." But when he was here, he could always recall his past sessions in this place.

Sometimes he waited for hours in this nightmarish sensory deprivation; sometimes it lasted only moments. In the end, the same being always came to collect him. There was no way to know how long he had been here this time. Hours, he guessed.

He heard the door open and a narrow shaft of light stabbed its way into the room. The boy raised one hand, partly to protect his eyes from the light and partly because he so dreaded seeing the one who always came to fetch him.

The door open fully and a figure entered. He was dressed in a dark hooded cloak. As the boy's eyes adjusted to the light, he was reminded of his master's hideous nature.

The being had no face.

The confines of his cloak hood held nothing but blackness. There was no head—just a terrible empty void that somehow spoke orders to him. The voice was always the same. It was clearly male and it commanded respect. The figure crooked an index finger.

"Come," he demanded. "It is time."

His legs shaking, the boy rose from the stool. As he walked toward the dark figure, the faceless man placed one arm around the boy's shoulder and escorted him from the room. The door closed heavily behind them.

As always, the hallway was narrow and brightly lit, and the white walls, floor, and ceiling gave the passageway a cold, sterile feel. White doors lined the walls, and each door had a golden handle. The identical handles stretched as far as the eye could see.

The boy shivered again. *Which door will my faceless master take me through this time?* he wondered. *Will I be able to bear what lies on the other side? Or will I fail and disappoint him?*

The mysterious figure finally stopped before one of the glistening white doors. As the empty hood turned toward him, the boy cowered.

"Today's lesson is one of the most important that you will ever learn," the man said. "This time you will not be asked to participate, only to watch. You will watch carefully, and do so over and over again, if needed, until you grasp the concept. Do you understand?"

His voice lost to his overwhelming fear, the boy nodded.

"Good," the faceless man said. "Follow me."

The gold handle levered downward and the door opened. During each previous lesson, a different room had been used, and today was no exception. The boy obediently followed his master inside.

The wood-paneled chamber was about eight meters square. Sawdust covered the sunken floor. Thirteen seats overlooking the floor sat in elevated rows along one side of the room. Two wooden doors lay on opposite sides of the short square wall surrounding the sunken floor. Eleven more hooded figures in dark robes, their faces also missing, sat in the chairs. Two empty seats sat in the front row. The air was cool and smelled pleasantly of the fresh-hewn sawdust.

The man led the boy to the empty seats and they sat down. Fearing what might come next, the boy wrapped his arms about himself, then hunched over in his chair. The empty cloak hood again turned his way.

"No," the master said sternly. "Sit up like a man."

The boy did as he was told. Born more of fear than the coolness of the room, goosebumps started breaking out on his skin.

"You are about to watch something," the faceless man said. "When it is over we will ask you to explain its meaning. You will frame your answer in a single sentence. You will not turn your face away or close your eyes, nor will you be allowed to leave this place until you have correctly explained the point of the lesson. Each of us will be watching you. Do you understand?"

His voice still frozen with fear, the boy again nodded. Whatever was about to happen, all he wanted was for it to end.

"Good," the man said. "We shall start."

The two opposing doors in the sunken wall slowly slid to one side. Only darkness showed beyond. From behind one of the doorways came a soft growl. As he waited and watched, the terrified boy again felt the warm liquid run down one leg. This time its presence unnerved him as it reminded him this was not a dream, but real.

Fearsome black dogs suddenly charged through the opposing doorways and lunged across the sawdust-strewn floor toward each other. On reaching the limits of their chains, they were abruptly halted in their tracks. With their deadly muzzles only inches apart, drool ran from their mouths as the dogs snapped and barked viciously, and sawdust flew as their claws dug at the floor. As they snapped and lunged, the boy did his best to screw up his courage and look at them.

The hounds were huge, with sleek coats and muscular bodies. They seemed to be identical in every respect. Cropped ears stood tall on either side of their heads. Their tails had been closely bobbed, and their slanted eyes were a haunting yellow color. White teeth and fangs continually flashed as the savage animals struggled to break free from their bonds and tear into each other. The faceless master placed one hand on the boy's shoulder.

"The two dogs are identical in every respect, save for one," the mysterious master said. "It will be your task to identify the difference between them. They have been intentionally starved and are nearly insane with hunger. Each knows that his survival hinges on killing the other and eating him. It is this way throughout all nature, even for us supposedly enlightened humans. Do you understand?"

The boy finally found his voice. "Yes," he whispered.

"Good," the master replied.

No sooner had the faceless master stopped talking than the chains disappeared, freeing the savage dogs. Terrified, the boy watched the two starving animals tear into each other.

At first neither dog could claim the advantage. The one on the right appeared quicker, but the other one seemed stronger. As the dogs tangled, the boy soon lost track of which one was which.

With a vicious growl, one of them bit savagely into the other's shoulder. Just as he did so, the other dog tore into his opponent's neck. Blood gushed from the fresh wounds to wildly paint the sawdust-strewn floor. The boy desperately wanted to close his eyes, but his fear of his master's wrath far outweighed his revulsion, so he watched.

Because neither dog would release his grip on the other, the struggle would hinge on which one lasted longer. Soon the dog whose neck had been bitten started to wobble from blood loss. Sensing a victory, his enemy dug his teeth in harder, causing the wound to deepen. A renewed torrent of blood gushed to the floor.

Soon the weaker dog's front legs collapsed, followed by his hindquarters. Without waiting for his victim to die, the victor removed his teeth from the neck wound. Amid the other's dog's desperate cries, he started eating his victim alive.

After a time the victorious dog suddenly stopped feeding and lifted his head. The beast's muzzle was dripping blood, and bits of flesh lay trapped between his teeth. His yellow eyes bored straight into the boy's. Then the two dogs suddenly disappeared and the sawdust was refreshed, leaving no trace of the carnage.

The faceless master leaned nearer. "What did you learn?" he asked.

Glad that the spectacle was finished, the boy did his best to think. He would do anything not to have to watch another such battle.

"One dog lived and one died," the boy offered quietly.

"True," one of the cloaked figures said from behind him. This time the speaker was female. Her voice was understanding, almost compassionate. "But that is not the answer we seek. Try again."

"The dog that won was bigger," the boy answered, not knowing what else to say.

"Like a poor marksman, you keep missing the target," the man beside him said. "You must do better, or be forced to watch again. The next time will be worse."

The boy desperately wanted it all to end. His will broken, he felt salty tears run down his cheeks. "I don't know!" he cried out. "Please don't force me to watch another contest!"

"Men do not cry," the female voice said. "They lead. Answer the question correctly and you may go."

The boy wiped his eyes and thought hard about what he had just seen. At last it came to him: "The winner attacked a weaker spot . . . and he stayed stronger," he finally said.

Had it been possible, the boy would have seen his faceless master smile. "Well done," the mystery man said. "Now apply that answer to nature's entirety, rather than just the two animals you watched struggling to kill each other."

As the boy thought, long moments passed. "Only the strong survive," he said, praying that he had finally been right.

"Yes," the master answered. "You have grasped it. It is a lesson that you must always remember." But this time the master's words sounded strangely hollow, as though they were coming from far away.

"Only the strong survive," he repeated, his voice echoing strangely through the room. "Only the strong survive . . . only the strong survive . . . only the strong . . ."

His face and naked body covered with sweat, Vespasian Augustus bolted upright in his bed. Instinctively grabbing the jeweled dagger lying on his nightstand, he launched from the bed and charged toward the far corner of the room. As his naked skin touched the balcony draperies he cried out, as if the harmless cloth were trying to entangle him and kill him. Although still asleep, his eyes were wide open. In a manic haze he slashed at the draperies like a madman.

Persephone leapt from the bed to stare at her enraged husband. His recent dreams had been terrifying, but nothing like this had happened to him before. An accomplished sorceress, she correctly guessed that he needed to be awakened before he hurt her or himself. But given the great strength of Vespasian's blood, she hesitated.

Screaming again, Vespasian caught Persephone's shadowy form out of the corner of one eye. Believing that she was the threat he so feared, he raised his dagger and charged at her. Realizing that she had no choice, Persephone sent a weak azure bolt directly toward the emperor.

Her bolt struck Vespasian squarely in the chest, lifting him off his feet and sending him crashing to the floor some three meters away. Hoping against hope, she immediately ran to him.

Vespasian's chest was singed, but he looked otherwise unharmed. The sudden pain had broken his terrifying reverie and fully awakened him. With a groan, he dropped the dagger to the floor. Desperate with worry, Persephone kneeled and took her husband in her arms.

For several moments she lovingly cradled her stricken husband. Then the silence was shattered as royal bodyguards started pounding on the bedroom door. Persephone cleverly used her nightgown train to cover Vespasian's chest burns.

"Be still, my love," she whispered. "I will protect your secret."

She looked up to see that the magnificent oak door was starting to give way and soon it would surrender altogether. It would do no good to try and call the legionnaires off, for the disturbing noises coming from the bedroom had been too great to explain away.

In a hail of shattered wood and sprung crossbraces, the door finally gave way. Their swords drawn, two legionnaires charged into the room.

"Is everything all right, my lady?" one of them shouted as he looked around warily. After Persephone told him that Vespasian was unharmed, he turned to see the ripped draperies. Then his eyes went to the dagger lying on the floor.

"Was there an intruder?" he asked.

"No," Persephone insisted. "Your emperor suffered a bad dream— nothing more. I am quite able to tend to him."

The legionnaire looked closely at Vespasian's drained face, then back at Persephone. "The emperor looks ill," he protested. "Does your grace wish me to summon a physician?"

Persephone shook her head. "No," she answered. "Leave us now. First thing in the morning, arrange to have the shattered door repaired. If I change my mind about the physician, I will call for you."

"As you wish," the legionnaire answered. With that, the bodyguards saluted her and reluctantly exited the room.

As Persephone looked down into Vespasian's sweaty face, she watched him go unconscious. Closing her eyes, she placed her palm to his brow. His mind had gone deep, but he was unharmed. Then she looked around the ravaged room.

This was far more than a bad dream, she realized. *The craft has been at work here. But why,* she wondered, *and on whose orders?*

Deciding to speak to no one about this until Vespasian regained consciousness, she stood. Raising one arm and calling the craft, she gently levitated her husband's body back onto the bed. She would lie with him until morning. If by then he didn't awaken, she would use the craft to gently rouse him.

She knew that the only surefire way to protect Vespasian's secret would be to have the two guards killed. It was a pity, for she knew them well and they had only been doing their duty. Even so, she couldn't allow the slightest hint of this episode to surface—especially so close to the start of Vespasian's massive new campaign.

As she lay beside him, she silently gave thanks to the all-powerful Vagaries flame that Vespasian had not unconsciously used his powers. Had that happened, he might have killed them both and destroyed the entire royal residence. Once she knew that Vespasian was well, as a token of her gratitude and devotion she would order the Priory maidens to slaughter a white bull in the Rotunda. Still worried about her husband, she held him closer.

She would remain that way until dawn.

CHAPTER IX

AS TYRANNY OF THE HOUSE OF WELBORNE STOOD AT THE bow of the *Tammerland,* the sun's rays started warming her back. Her fleet of four Black Ships was heading west and fighting a fierce headwind. Every hand had been awake all night.

With the Eutracian coast nearing, Tyranny could smell land. As usual, she planned to moor the Conclave fleet in the Cavalon Delta bay, where the ships could reprovision and take shelter against the unpredictable Sea of Whispers. It would be good to be home.

Despite how she loved being at sea, she would find an indulgent bath and one of Shawna's wonderfully prepared meals very welcome. Although Tyranny preferred living aboard her flagship, Tristan had granted her personal quarters in the palace. When not at sea she often availed herself of the royal luxury. Even so, not one Conclave member would dare to call her a landlubber.

The fleet of Black Ships had been at sea for the past week. Of the six original vessels, two had been sunk while trying to attack Serena's island stronghold. The late Vagaries Queen had somehow conjured a massive tidal wave that surged west, smashing the *Florian* and the *Malvina* into matchsticks.

The *Tammerland,* the *Ephyra,* the *Cavalon,* and the *Illendium* had survived, but each suffered damage. Only the *Tammerland* had remained seaworthy enough to sail home straightaway; the other three needed to stay in Parthalon for repairs. Tyranny and Adrian had sailed the *Tammerland* home ahead of the others. After the Minion shipwrights declared the work on the other three vessels finished, the remaining acolytes had piloted the ships home. While she awaited the arrival of her fleet, Tyranny had prowled the palace like a caged tigress. When they finally arrived, she took immediate action.

Although the Minion shipwrights were immensely skilled, they knew that their workmanship must pass Tyranny's muster. After giving the vessels a sharp visual inspection, she had insisted on a full week of sea trials. Traax and four Minion phalanxes had accompanied her.

Adrian empowered the *Tammerland,* while the acolytes Astrid, Phoebe, and Marissa piloted the other Black Ships. Tyranny pushed the women hard and ordered the Minions to perform rigorous combat drills in the sky and on deck. During the trials the Minions' seafaring fighting skills had sharpened and the sisters' abilities to fly the great vessels improved markedly. With the trials all but over, Tyranny felt confident that she could give her *Jin'Sai* a report that soundly testified to the fleet's readiness. The report would also recommend that the same four Minion phalanxes be assigned to the fleet on a continual basis, and that Adrian, Phoebe, Marissa, and Claire become the Black Ships' permanent pilots.

Tyranny looked northward. Their dark shapes glinting in the rising sun, the three sister ships were also flying high over the waves. Sailing through the sky was an exhilarating feeling and one that the Conclave privateer wasn't entirely accustomed to. She had spent most of her life bounding atop the waves, not flying over them. She smiled. Her life had been nothing if not eventful.

After a hard run of nonstop flight yesterday, she had ordered the four acolytes to empower the ships all through the night as well. That had set a precedent. She hadn't issued the harsh order because she felt hurried to return home; rather, she needed to know whether the sisters could endure the effort. Like the other Conclave members, Tyranny hoped that the threats to the Vigors east of the Tolenkas had finally been quashed. Even so, Tristan had taken her aside and told her that he wanted the acolytes and the Minions pushed to the limit during these trials. Like Tristan, she suspected that the fleet would be instrumental in somehow crossing the Tolenkas and finding Shashida.

Tyranny reached into her leather jacket and retrieved her new cigarillo case. It was solid gold and inscribed with the letters *TW.* She removed a cigarillo and a match, then returned the case to its resting place. She was proud to be a member of the prince's Conclave, and her adventures had made her the richest woman in all Eutracia. But she had come to realize that her seat on the Conclave meant far more to her than her wealth ever could.

For the first time in her life she felt like a valued part of something greater than herself, and so she had marked the occasion by buying the gold case. The privateer had been careful to avoid letting her newfound wealth turn her head; the case was one of the few purchases she had allowed herself. To this day her vast hoard of kisa—the gold coin of the realm—lay behind locked doors in the depths of the Redoubt.

As she turned her gaze westward she stabbed the cigarillo between her lips. Any time now, the Eutracian coastline would materialize and she would order the acolytes to put the ships down onto the sea. Reaching down, Tyranny prepared to strike the match against one of her knee boots.

"I can help you with that," a familiar voice called out. Turning, Tyranny saw Sister Adrian approaching. The acolyte was carrying two cups of hot tea.

As she neared, Adrian called on the craft. At once the tip of Tyranny's cigarillo glowed bright red. After inhaling a deep lungful of smoke, the privateer smiled.

"That's a neat trick," she said, raising her face to blow the smoke skyward. "If I had endowed blood, I would ask you to teach it to me. It would save much time, not to mention the wear and tear on my boots!"

Adrian laughed and handed Tyranny a teacup. "But I wouldn't do it!" Adrian answered. "It would only make poisoning yourself with those things all the easier!"

Tyranny snorted out a short laugh. After taking a welcome sip of tea she tossed the unused match overboard.

During the past week, Tyranny and Adrian had become fast friends. Their relationship had matured far beyond the fact that each woman served on the Conclave. Despite being opposite personalities, they shared a common goal, and during the sea trials each had impressed the other with her unique abilities.

Adrian was as modest and thoughtful as Tyranny was brash and outspoken. Tyranny's defenses were her wits and her weapons, while all Adrian needed to defend herself was the craft. Moreover, the two women bore not the slightest physical resemblance to one another. They were an odd couple, but one that commanded respect from friend and foe alike.

Clearly the prettier of the two, Tyranny was tall with an attractive figure. Her short, dark, urchinlike hair moved with every turn of her head. Her wide, dark blue eyes rested above high cheekbones. She wore tight striped pants, a short leather jacket with a high collar, and worn knee boots. A gold hoop earring dangled from each earlobe. A sword hung at her left hip, and a sheathed dagger lay tied to her right thigh. A brass spyglass hung across her chest from a leather strap around her neck. Even her pungent cigarillos seemed to suit her rakish nature.

In contrast, the First Sister was short and plump. Her dark red acolyte's robe, tied around the middle with the traditional black knotted cord, did little to change that impression. She had a pleasant but unremarkable face, soft brown eyes, and loads of curly sandy hair. What she lacked in stature she more than compensated for with dignity, bravery, and an ever-growing command of the craft. As the First Sister of the acolytes and a respected member of the Conclave, she was quickly becoming a force to reckon with.

Tyranny took another sip of tea. "You and the other acolytes have done well," she said. "I didn't know whether you could empower the ships all night, but you did. I also see that you four have acquired the ability to fly the ships while walking about and doing other things as well. Before now I had seen only Wigg, Faegan, and Jessamay do that."

"Thank you," Adrian answered. "The craft is much like anything else. The more one practices, the better one becomes." Reaching into her robe, she produced three small parchments and offered them to the privateer. "You should know that I just heard from the other sisters by way of Minion messengers. They are exhausted, but they should be able to empower the ships the rest of the way to the coast."

Tyranny decided that there was no need for her to read the messages. Instead, she nodded her understanding and took another pull on her cigarillo. She turned to look aft, down the *Tammerland*'s seemingly endless topside. Although Tyranny had been commanding these great vessels for more than a year, they still held her in awe.

Each ship was an inky black color and built largely of magically enhanced hardwoods held together with cast iron fittings. They had been constructed by the late Directorate of Wizards more than three centuries ago, during the height of the Sorceresses' War. The vessels were largely impervious to battle damage and could survive tremendous storms.

With ten full masts each and spars as thick around as several tree trunks combined, every ship was easily quadruple the size of a standard man-of-war.

Each vessel held eight full lower decks, allowing for the simultaneous transport of thousands of Minion warriors and enough food, water, supplies, and weapons to fight a protracted sea campaign. A massive hinged door took up the stern of each ship. The doors could be opened and lowered to a safe distance above the waves much the same way a drawbridge could be lowered from within the walls of a castle. Even the sails were black, and each was adorned in its center with a bright red image of the Paragon. Hundreds of male and female warriors swarmed over her topside, masts, and spars, and among her eight lower decks.

Despite their massive size, the ships' greatest advantage was their amazing speed. They could sail atop the waves like normal vessels, and when they did their progress was astounding. But when taken aloft and empowered by a trained mystic, the sea drag on their hulls was eliminated and their airspeed was even greater, easily rivaling that of the swiftest Minion fliers. At one time crossing the Sea of Whispers had taken at least thirty days. Now the voyage could be done in less than six. The ships could soar with equal efficiency over land.

On Tristan's orders, four massive wooden cradles were being built on the palace grounds so that the ships could rest in them and be easily maintained, supplied, and taken aloft at a moment's notice. When Tyranny had word that the cradles were finished, she would order the vessels overland to their new resting places. She smiled wryly as she imagined the incongruous sight. *Like fish out of water,* she thought, and sighed. With the ships stationed full time in their cradles, she would probably give in for good and stay in her luxurious palace quarters permanently.

Just then the two women heard the warning bell ring out three times from the *Tammerland*'s forwardmost crow's nest. Because of the vessels' great size, when a warrior shouted out from so high above, his or her voice was often lost to the elements. Recognizing the problem, Tyranny had worked out a series of bell signals. Three loud clangs meant that land had been sighted off the bow.

The Minion scouts I ordered aloft two hours ago have finally sighted land, she realized, *and they have returned to inform the warriors manning the crows' nests.* Grasping her spyglass, she pulled open its brass cylinders and looked to the west.

As was often the case at dawn, the Cavalon Delta bay was heavily shrouded in fog. Tyranny lowered the spyglass, thinking. She had two choices. She could order the ships to fly in circles as she waited for the rising sun to burn away the fog. They could then approach the coast with confidence and moor the fleet. But she also knew that the acolytes needed rest, and she was eager to get the ships down as soon as possible.

The second choice was to set the ships atop the waves straightaway, then take soundings as they cautiously approached the coast through the fog. When the depth was right they would lower the anchors and let the ships swivel into the wind, digging their anchor blades firmly into the seabed.

As Tyranny considered her options, Traax walked up. He was accompanied by Scars, Tyranny's giant first mate, who had been with her long before she became a member of the Conclave. The two had heard the warning bells.

Tyranny lowered her glass and looked at Scars. "Your opinion?" she asked.

Scars rubbed his chin, thinking. To those who did not know him well, his fearsome appearance overshadowed his sharp, seafaring mind. At nearly seven feet tall he seemed more like some freak of nature than a human being. His head was shaven and he wore only ripped trousers with no belt. His feet were continually bare. When asked why, his only response was that bare soles gave him a better feeling for the movements of the great ship. A ragged scar—the result of wrestling sharks during his youth—ran down his forehead, near one eye and down the length of his left cheek. Yet more such scars graced his arms and chest.

"I say we descend and take soundings," he answered, in his unexpectedly erudite way. "The sisters are near exhaustion. Should they lose control, the result might be unpleasant. Besides, my sailor's bones tell me that the fog bank does not extend all the way to the waves."

"I agree," Tyranny said. She turned to look at Traax.

The Minion second in command was an even more fearsome presence than Scars. Tall and muscular, he was also clean shaven—something of a rarity among male warriors. Long dark hair fell down behind his back and was secured with a bit of worn leather string. With his dark wings folded behind his back, his leather body armor in place, and his dreggan and returning wheel hung at opposite hips, everything about him suggested sudden death. To know Traax was to also know of his legendary devotion to his *Jin'Sai.*

Everyone was eager to return to Tammerland, but Traax's wish to make his way home ran especially high. Just three months ago he had become a husband. His new wife, the warrior-healer Duvessa, eagerly awaited him at the palace. These sea trials had been the first time he had left her side since the wedding, and he missed her keenly.

The couple had been wed by the *Jin'Sai* personally. During the ceremony, Shailiha's daughter, Morganna, had been the bearer of the two jeweled pins that symbolized the betrothed warriors' love for each other. Traax was a member of the Conclave, and Duvessa commanded all the female warrior-healers, an elite cadre of fighting women who were expert healers as well. As Tyranny looked into Traax's eyes she understood how badly he wanted to get home. But there was still work to do.

"Traax, when we reach the sea, have your warriors take soundings," she ordered. "I want the depth called out in one-fathom intervals. Have all the sails furled and tied off."

Traax nodded. Tyranny knew the waters of the Cavalon Delta like the back of her hand. By the changing depths alone, she would be able to gauge the fleet's nearness to the coast and keep the ships from running aground.

"Send three warriors aloft and have them deliver a message to the other acolyte pilots," she continued. "Tell them that we are going to descend through the fog and land on the waves. When they see us start down, they are to follow. They must stay close enough to continually see us." She shot a sly smile at Adrian, then looked back at Traax.

"This maneuver will need some tricky flying to prevent the ships from colliding," she added, "but I think that the acolytes can handle it. Tell them to consider it their final test. When we drop anchor, they are to do the same."

"As you wish, Captain," Traax answered. He turned on his boot heels and hurried off.

Tyranny turned back to Adrian. "You may start your descent," she ordered. "Take us down slow and level."

"Aye," the First Sister replied. "Slow and level as she goes."

Adrian altered her hold over the craft and the *Tammerland* started a slow vertical descent. The First Sister kept the ship perfectly level, so that the entire length of her keel would touch the water at once and keep the ship from heeling over.

Tyranny looked at the sky. The sun had finally risen in earnest, and it would soon start burning away the fog. Until now the *Tammerland* had been flying in the clear, but she would soon enter the fog bank below.

Like Scars, Tyranny guessed that the fog did not reach all the way to the sea and that they would soon break clear. Even if they were wrong, at this slow rate of descent the *Tammerland*'s landing might be blind, but it would be gentle. The privateer glanced again to starboard to confirm that the other three ships were following the *Tammerland*'s lead.

Soon the great ship entered the dense fog. As the fog crept higher it engulfed the hull, then the topside, and finally the masts, furled sails, and spars. The fog soon grew so thick that Tyranny lost sight of the other three ships, causing her concern. *Perhaps I place too much confidence in the acolytes' abilities,* she worried. Then she heard Minion voices hauntingly calling out in the gloom. For the benefit of the four acolytes, they were announcing the distances between the vessels. That must have been Traax's idea, she thought, and it was a good one.

As the *Tammerland* descended, Tyranny, Adrian, and Scars grabbed hold of some nearby rigging to steady themselves. More tense seconds ticked by. Without warning, the great vessel hit the waves. She listed hard to port for a moment before settling down. Soon they heard the other three Black Ships splash down, and it was over.

As the *Tammerland* started to drift, Tyranny turned to Scars. "Drop anchor!" she shouted. Scars immediately ran to carry out her order.

Soon the two women heard the anchor chain rattling across the foredeck, and the anchor splashed into the sea. The *Tammerland* swiveled hard to port before settling down again. Then she tugged hard on her chain, digging the anchor blade deep into the sea floor.

Exhausted, Adrian closed her eyes and let go a deep breath. She had no doubt that her sister acolytes were equally spent.

"Well done," Tyranny said. "You have earned a well-deserved rest."

Just then Traax and Scars reappeared. "The other three ships are successfully moored," he said, "and they are far enough apart so that they will not strike each other as they turn in the wind. Shall we take our first sounding, raise the *Tammerland*'s anchor, and head for shore?"

Before answering, Tyranny turned and gazed westward. She smiled.

"That won't be needed," she answered.

The others turned to look. The fog was slowly parting. As it did, shafts of golden sunlight streamed down here and there from the sky above, spotlighting the ships and the waves. It was a welcome sight.

Tyranny saw that the coastline was starting to appear. Raising her spy-glass again, she turned its lenses to the west.

The fleet was moored about a hundred meters from shore. She could see the lush foliage of the delta and one of the three major tributaries that poured the Sippora River's fresh water into the sea. Several fishing villages clung to the delta coast, one of which lay dead ahead. Birming-ham, she realized.

Then she saw something odd on the rocky beach, and she froze. Hur-rying forward, Tyranny leaned hard against the gunwale and again raised her spyglass. At first she refused to believe her eyes. But as she looked further, the terrible reality sank in. She slowly lowered the glass.

"I beg the Afterlife," she whispered, her face contorting in cold rage.

Of her three officers, Scars knew Tyranny best. Even so, he had rarely seen such a look overtake his captain's face. "What's wrong?" he asked anxiously.

Tyranny quickly beckoned them all forward. Reaching out, she took Traax by his shoulders and pulled his face to within inches of hers.

"Save for a skeleton crew left aboard each Black Ship, I want every warrior armed and aloft this instant!" she ordered. "Have them circle above until I order differently! I want my litter made ready, and bring the other three acolytes here immediately! We're all flying ashore!" Traax clicked his heels and was gone in an instant.

Scars gave Tyranny another questioning look. The privateer's only re-sponse was to remove the spyglass strap from around her neck and thrust the scope into Scar's beefy hands. The first mate raised the glass and turned it toward the coast. After a time, he swallowed hard.

"Tyranny . . ." Adrian breathed. "What's going on?"

The hard-nosed privateer reached for her gold case. After stabbing another cigarillo between her lips and lighting it, she finally answered the acolyte.

"I suggest that you employ the craft and look for yourself," she growled.

Adrian hurried to the gunwale. As he looked toward the coast, Scars stood stock-still beside her like some great marble statue. Calling on the craft, Adrian augmented her eyesight and looked westward.

Like Scars and Tyranny, the acolyte had already experienced much during her relatively short life. But what she saw this day froze the blood in her veins.

CHAPTER X

WITH EVERY STEP GRACCHUS TOOK, HIS CONCERN mounted. The Oraculum had reached out to touch his mind less than one hour ago, and he feared that her latest vision might be disturbing. The war plan to take the Shashidan gold mines was nearly ready to submit to the Suffragat, and he had worked, schemed, and killed for far too long to let his dream die now. With one hand gripping the opposite shoulder of his white and burgundy robe, he hurried on.

The subterranean hallway he trod was dank and mildewed. Wall torches, enchanted to burn forever and without smoke, showed the way and lent the twisting passageway a haunted feel. Specially chosen centurions sworn to secrecy on penalty of death stood guard at every turn. As the lead *Pon Q'tar* cleric hurried by, they snapped to swift attention.

The secret hallway that Gracchus navigated lay far below Ellistium. Aside from the guards, only the *Pon Q'tar* and the Suffragat knew of its existence. Aeons ago, after selecting the site for the new capital city, the *Pon Q'tar* had secretly built this subterranean labyrinth. It had come into being while the magnificent capital had risen so many meters above it.

Gracchus soon came to a large square room built from cut stones. Before him lay a granite landing that overlooked a wide subterranean lake. More torches burned in iron wall brackets. The lake was dark, dirty, and deathly still. Three more centurions stood guard there. As they came to attention, Gracchus hurried to the edge of the landing.

"Bring me the boat," he ordered.

At once a centurion saluted, then walked to the far end of the room. Reaching down, he untied the line that secured a common wooden rowboat to the landing. He towed the boat to a place before the lead cleric.

Gracchus walked down a short series of steps cut into the landing and climbed into the boat. The centurion tossed the line into the boat, setting it free. Gracchus took up a wooden staff from the bottom of the boat and started to pole his way across the dank lake.

As he went, here and there the putrid water rippled ominously. *Good,* he thought. The deadly creatures that he and his fellow *Pon Q'tar* members had conjured so long ago to protect what lay on the other side still lived. So far, their savagery had not been needed. Still, he was glad to know that they were there, constantly searching the water for intruders.

The boat trip would not take long. He knew the way well, for he had come here thousands of times before. Soon he saw his destination. As he reached the opposite side he tied off the boat and walked up another series of short steps.

Like the preceding chamber, this one was square in shape and built from rough-hewn stone blocks. More wall brackets held burning torches. As Gracchus mounted from the landing, a startled rat squeaked and scurried off into the gloom.

Finally alone, Gracchus walked to the far wall. A casual observer would have seen nothing unusual about its many rough-hewn stones. After choosing one unremarkable block from among thousands, Gracchus summoned the craft.

At once the stone glowed bright azure. Gracchus then caused a small incision to form in his right wrist. As he liberated one drop of his endowed blood, it hovered before him and twisted itself into his unique blood signature. He calmly watched the incision close and the resulting scar disappear. He then sent the blood signature flat against the glowing stone.

The enchanted stone quickly recognized the cleric's blood. Soon a bright azure line formed down the center of the wall and the two halves parted, allowing Gracchus access to the chamber beyond. He hurriedly entered, and the walls scratched closed behind him. The subsequent chamber was as pristine as the preceding one was dank.

As Gracchus walked into the room he was comforted to see that nothing had changed. *And why would it?* he asked himself. *I have been the only visitor to this place for thousands of years. The being I imprison here will never reclaim her freedom, despite the immense power she once commanded.*

The chamber was large and well lit. Its four walls and ceiling were built from finely hewn alabaster blocks. The floor was solid onyx, polished to a magnificent sheen. Solid gold wall brackets held engraved oil globes, their flames combining to cast a soft glow over the room, and the air was warm and odorless. But the chamber's beauty meant little, he knew. The real reason for this secret place stood across the room.

The entire far wall glowed with a soft azure hue. Its depths seemed limitless. Curved shards of swirling white light continually wheeled and streaked amid the azure aura that imprisoned them. The strange masterpiece of the craft emitted a soft roar and a crackling sound, much like a blazing fire.

As he regarded the mesmerizing sight, Gracchus was reminded of how long it had taken him and his fellow *Pon Q'tar* clerics to create it. Fifty years, to be exact—ten years of ceaseless toil to refine the formulas, then forty more to construct this chamber, the two landings, the lake, and the secret tunnel that led here from aboveground. The skeens who had been forced to do the construction were long dead and had taken this place's secrets with them to the Afterlife.

The lead cleric raised his hands and called the craft. At once the glimmering wall started to slide closer. As it neared, a transparent roof and equally glassy sidewalls formed, ensuring that the azure light remained imprisoned. The amazing construct slowed, then stopped about three meters from where he stood.

The result was a glistening cube that measured eight meters square, the entire space within it filled with azure light and darting white shards. Despite how many times Gracchus visited here, he always found the cube a wondrous thing to behold.

The lead cleric stepped closer. "Show yourself," he ordered.

From the foggy depths a woman emerged. Her eyes and wrinkled skin were so old that they were nearly dust. Her long, brittle hair was the purest white and flew about wildly. Her dark eyes darted about the room, then stared straight at him, boring their way into his own. The tattered gray gown she wore had once been pure white. Like her hair, its tattered ends swirled in the azure mist. Wrinkled arms and hands lay quietly by her side while her bare feet dangled just below the hem of her tattered gown. As she hung weightless in the cube, she said nothing.

"You touched my mind," Gracchus said calmly. "What have you seen on the other side?"

"The Orb of the Vigor has shown me much, lead cleric," she said. Her ancient voice was tremulous, hollow. "Two more important manifestations of the craft have occurred east of the Tolenkas. You are fortunate—I had barely enough energy remaining to witness each. You will be pleased to learn of one. The other will doubtless cause you great distress."

Gracchus eagerly stepped forward. "Tell me," he ordered.

A short smile crossed the Oraculum's lips. Gracchus guessed that she would deliver the distressing news first, because she would enjoy it. He and the woman had been enemies for aeons. Even so, in a perverse way they needed each other.

"The Conclave has discovered subtle matter," she said. "Although the *Jin'Sai's* mystics cannot yet employ it, it seems only a matter of time until they learn. It might become a potent weapon for them."

Gracchus was stunned. "How did this happen?" he breathed. "Their knowledge of the craft is not sophisticated enough to have done this on their own!"

"It was revealed to them through a secret spell incorporated by the Shashidans into the Tome and the Scroll of the Vigors aeons ago," the Oraculum answered, her gown and hair floating about her as she hovered in the azure light. "Even I did not know of its existence. When Faegan placed the three relics side by side for safekeeping, the subtle matter was released."

"Subtle matter is never released without need," Gracchus mused. "What purpose did it serve?"

Reveling in his discomfort, the Oraculum smiled again. "You're right," she said. "The ancient spell that was enacted did far more." She went silent again, purposely allowing the tension to build.

"Tell me, you half-dead bitch!" Gracchus raged. "Or I will kill you here and now!"

"No, Gracchus," she answered. "We both know you won't do that. You might torture me. But you can't afford to kill me—especially not now, when there is so much left for you to learn."

Seething with rage, Gracchus shook his fist at her. "Tell me!" he screamed, "or I *will* torture you! And I'll enjoy it!"

"Very well," she said. "The subtle matter has told the *Jin'Sai* that he must traverse the Azure Sea to reach Shashida. As yet, he and his Conclave do not know how that is to be accomplished. But the *Jin'Sai*'s wizards are clever. If they learn enough about subtle matter, they might devise a way to cross the sea. The Tolenka Mountains on which you have so long relied to keep the *Jin'Sai* and the *Jin'Saiou* trapped on the other side of the world might no longer be the obstacle that they once were."

"But how can that be?" Gracchus breathed. "Its expanse is too vast and its dangers too great! Even our strongest spells cannot overcome its many obstacles!"

"I can only guess that the subtle matter will somehow lead the way," the Oraculum explained. "If the *Jin'Sai* finds it, I do not know what might follow. Nor does the *Jin'Sai* know. But there is more to it. The subtle matter also supplied the Conclave with a detailed map of the territories west of the mountains. My guess is that the map is aeons old and might well be flawed, given the shifting changes in the boundaries that you say have taken place over time. Even so, it should be of great help to them should they somehow cross the sea."

For several moments all Gracchus could do was to stare blankly down at the onyx floor, his mind a whirl of misgivings. He could not have imagined worse news. He finally collected himself and looked the Oraculum in the eyes.

"And because all my Vagaries allies in the east have been defeated, there is no way for me to stop the *Jin'Sai* from trying," he whispered, half to himself.

At first the Oraculum did not answer as she floated silently before him, imprisoned in the mist. "That is not entirely true," she finally replied.

Her heart broke as she said the momentous words. Even so, she had no choice but to tell him. Gracchus could easily torture the information from her, and he had often done so by magically altering the environment of her bizarre prison. Many centuries ago when she was younger and stronger, she had tried lying to him about what she saw on the other side of the world. But he had always found out and the torture started. Now she was too feeble to survive it. To stay alive, her only course of action was to tell the truth—no matter how much it grieved her to do so.

"You're referring to your second sighting, aren't you?" Gracchus demanded. "Tell me of it!"

The Oraculum sadly closed her eyes. "You *do* possess a new Vagaries ally on the other side," she said. "If the legend is true he has the ability to commune with you, for Failee's last attempt to find the needed forestallment formula was successful. To order him to do your bidding, you need only to reach out and touch his mind."

Sensing a glimmer of hope, Gracchus took another step closer. "Who is he?" he demanded.

"The Viper Lord has risen," she answered, "as have his many servants. The legend seems true, after all. Failee's genius for reaching out from the dead to influence the here and now continues to know no bounds."

Gracchus' heart leaped in his chest. "How did the Viper Lord come into the world?" he asked. "Did it happen as we always suspected?"

The Oraculum nodded. "A few drops of left-leaning endowed blood were inadvertently released into a spring in Hartwick Wood, thereby enacting the spell," she explained. "As we know, during the Sorceresses' War, Failee had hoped to end the war there. But the Directorate did not take the bait and chose to fight elsewhere. Even so, what little blood was spilled was enough. Since your rebellion against Shashida, whenever an important use of the craft occurred on the other side, I have witnessed it. Like you, I command the gift of Consummate Recollection, and I can easily recall the day that Failee enchanted the waters."

Gracchus's mind started racing. He had long known that the Viper Lord might rise, and he welcomed the coming of Failee's long-lost creation. But the discovery of subtle matter by the Conclave and the idea that Tristan might try to cross the Azure Sea posed new threats of dire proportions—especially now, when he and the *Pon Q'tar* were so close to realizing their dreams.

But if the Viper Lord could intervene and keep the *Jin'Sai* from crossing the sea, perhaps the campaign to take the Shashidan gold mines and the rest of his secret plan could still be salvaged. In any event, he would inform Vespasian only of the Viper Lord and not of the Conclave's discovery of subtle matter, for if Vespasian learned of the latter, he might choose to postpone the new campaign. Gracchus looked back at the Oraculum as she hovered in her beautiful prison.

"Where is the Viper Lord now?" he asked.

"I can only tell you that I saw him and his servants flee Hartwick Wood," she answered. "They travel northeast, presumably searching for more populated venues. Without direction from a higher Vagaries power, the Viper Lord is doubtless searching for his former mistress, and committing his preordained mayhem as he goes. When he does not find her, he will assume her to be dead. In her name he will continue to blindly seek revenge against all of Eutracia. With each victory his servants are systematically removing certain organs from endowed corpses. As you know, revenge was one of the First Mistress's greatest motives. If she could not win, she ensured that those who had bested her would continue to suffer her wrath. Unlike the failed Swamp Shrews of Parthalon, the Viper Lord might finally succeed in carrying out her vengeance." The Oraculum paused for a moment as the azure mist swirled about her.

"When the *Jin'Sai* learns of the Viper Lord, he will face a difficult choice," she continued. "Will he lead his Minions against this new threat, or will he take up the larger challenge and try to cross the sea? If the *Jin'Sai* succeeds in reaching Shashida, the Orbs cannot follow him. I will no longer be able to monitor the *Jin'Sai,* or any other Vigors mystics he might bring with him. If he reaches this side of the world, the only way to find him is by seeking out his all-powerful blood. Given Shashida's immense size, doing so seems highly unlikely—even for you and your fabled *Pon Q'tar.*"

Gracchus turned away from the Oraculum and he started angrily pacing the room. He needed time to think and he didn't want to endure the Oraculum's self-satisfied gaze. His thoughts soon turned to the recent past.

Although Failee never possessed the convoluted forestallment that allowed her direct communion with the Heretics or with the *Pon Q'tar,* by way of the Oraculum the Vagaries masters had monitored the First Mistress's valiant struggles with great hope. But now it seemed that she had perfected one aspect of the formula, allowing Gracchus to touch the Viper Lord's mind. That was at least one stroke of luck that he would soon make use of. Even without the *Pon Q'tar*'s help, Failee had nearly defeated the wizards and destroyed the Vigors east of the Tolenkas. *She was indeed brilliant,* Gracchus thought. *Given enough time and training, she might even have risen to join the ranks of the* Pon Q'tar.

Had Failee won the Sorceresses' War, the Vagaries east of the Tolenkas would have finally been victorious. But it was not to be, for the Directorate prevailed. Despite Failee's well-planned attack on Eutracia three hundred years later and her brilliant plan to kidnap Shailiha and turn her into her fifth sorceress, Tristan had killed her and the entire Coven. Worse, for the first time a reigning *Jin'Sai* was threatening *this* side of the world, and had at his disposal knowledge and weapons more potent than any *Jin'Sai* before him. *That bastard seems to have nine lives,* Gracchus fumed.

The lead cleric knew that this news was a potential disaster in the making. But the unexpected coming of the Viper Lord might help counter that. The Oraculum was right—Tristan would soon face a difficult choice. Gracchus found himself hoping that the *Jin'Sai* would live up to his impetuous reputation and battle the Viper Lord first. That might temporarily keep him from finding a way to cross the Azure Sea and interfering with the *Pon Q'tar*'s scheme. Even better, the Viper Lord might well kill him.

Another thought crossed Gracchus' mind. He stared at the Oraculum.

"Can you reproduce the map that the Ones supplied to the Conclave?" he asked.

The Oraculum nodded. "But what good will that do you?" she asked. "It won't stop the *Jin'Sai* from crossing the Azure Sea."

Fueled by the bad news and his growing frustration, Gracchus' anger toward the Oraculum finally burst open. "Just do it, bitch!" he shouted. "I have my reasons!"

"Very well," the Oraculum said. As she continued to hang weightless in the glowing cube, she raised her arms and closed her eyes.

An exact replica of the map given to the Conclave began to form beside her. As it materialized, it hung weightless in the azure mist. Gracchus soon saw that the sage-colored diagram was indeed a detailed representation of the lands west of the Tolenkas. Parts of western Eutracia were also shown. As the Oraculum had guessed, certain areas of the map were out of date. The Oraculum was right about something else, too, he realized. If the Conclave somehow crossed the Azure Sea, even this flawed portrayal would prove invaluable to them.

He then looked for the Caves. A series of coordinates lay just below the oval mark. After committing the entire map to memory, Gracchus nodded, and the Oraculum caused the map to vanish.

"Do you believe that the *Jin'Sai* will try to cross the sea?" he asked.

"I do not know," she answered. "I see only what the orb sees—and only when an important act of the craft occurs. I cannot predict the future for you, Gracchus. I can only tell you what has already happened on the other side of the world. That is how it has been since the day you imprisoned me in this glowing cage."

The Oraculum smiled again. "Will you inform the Blood Royal of these recent developments?" she asked.

"That's none of your affair!" the lead cleric exploded. "I am done with you for now! When you have something else of importance to tell me, you are to reach out and touch my mind immediately!"

Gracchus raised his arms and called the craft, causing the glowing azure cube to retreat. As it went, its transparent roof and sides melded into the rear wall. Soon all that remained of the cube was its glowing face lying flush against the far alabaster wall. The Oraculum gradually retreated into the mist, then faded from view altogether.

Gracchus anxiously rubbed his brow, thinking. Not since Rustannica broke away from Shashida had so much been at stake. The next few months would forever determine the future of the world. There was much for him to do and too little time in which to do it.

Gracchus called the craft and commanded the great doors behind him to part. As they scratched their way open he walked swiftly from the chamber. When the doors closed, the torches in the chamber went out, leaving only the strange azure glow and the whirling white shards to pierce the gloom.

Faced once more with her overpowering loneliness, deep within the azure cloud the Oraculum sadly hung her head. As the heart-rending guilt washed over her for having told the monstrous *Pon Q'tar* cleric so much, she wept.

CHAPTER XI

TYRANNY, SWORD IN HAND, CAST HER GAZE ALONG THE rocky shore. The morning sun had finally risen in earnest. As the remaining fog burned away, the scene before her only worsened. Taking a deep breath, she lowered the tip of her sword.

What a strange thing death is, she thought. *How full of life a person can be one moment, then gone the next, leaving the body behind to become an empty, decaying vessel. Do we really possess souls?* she wondered. *If so, where do they go? It seems that even the wizards cannot answer such questions.* She sighed and shook her head. If the mystics did know, they weren't telling.

She looked at Sister Adrian to see that the acolyte was crying and her face was covered by her hands. But Tyranny had no such tears, for the rage she felt easily overcame her grief. She had seen much during her struggles against the Vagaries, but nothing equaled the sheer brutality of this.

Hundreds upon hundreds of Eutracian citizens had been systematically murdered, their corpses lining the shore for as far as the eye could see.

The victims were impaled on long staffs, freshly cut from a nearby beechwood grove. Even women and children had been brutally killed. The bodies were naked, bloody, unmoving. Human entrails lay scattered far along the shore, telling Tyranny that the carnage had taken place over a wide area. There was so much blood that she could scarcely tell that the rocks beneath her feet were black.

She saw no discarded weapons or clothing, suggesting that these poor souls had been stripped first, then brought here to be killed, and that most had died without a fight. Fearing that they had come from Birmingham, she had ordered two Minion phalanxes to immediately fly there and investigate. As Tyranny and her group stood staring, not one of them spoke, the only sounds coming from the restless waves as they lapped at the shore. As the fog lifted for good, the extent of the disaster was fully revealed.

Row after row of impaled corpses lined the shore as far as the eye could see, the stakes holding the victims' bodies upright. Their sharpened tips had been viciously shoved into the victims' groins, then threaded up through their abdomens and forced out near their collarbones. The lower end of each stake had been plunged into the rocky shore. Each corpse's hands had been raised over the head, then clasped together and pierced through.

Shorter branches had been lashed to the stakes just below the victims' feet and hands, keeping the corpses from sliding down the poles. Every corpse's abdomen had been systematically disemboweled from the throat to the genitals. In some cases their internal organs dangled from the gaping wounds. Some stretched so far as to reach the ground.

Tyranny came to stand before an impaled young woman. She had been lovely, with blond hair and a strong jawline. A look of terror was frozen on her face. Tyranny sheathed her sword and reached up to gently close the woman's eyes. As she did, Traax, Scars, Adrian, and the other three acolytes approached.

Tyranny turned toward Traax. "Have our scouts reported back?" she demanded.

Traax shook his head. "Given that you ordered every building to be searched, it will take some time. My warriors will not report until either they find who did this or their search is otherwise finished."

"And the other two phalanxes that I ordered to ring this area?" she asked. "What of them?"

"They continue to search," Traax answered, "but they have found nothing. Unless the killers remained behind in Birmingham, they are probably long gone."

Tyranny turned to look out to sea. As though they were eager to take sail again, her four Black Ships tugged at their anchors. Several dozen fishing boats lay moored between the shore and the fleet, and two long wooden piers jutted from the shoreline into the restless waves. The nearby fishing village of Birmingham had been instrumental in supplying the Black Ships with goods and provisions whenever they moored in this wide delta bay. But as she saw dark smoke rising in the west, Tyranny feared that Birmingham was no more.

The privateer looked skyward. Her instincts told her that the day would become sunny and hot. Swarms of black vultures already wheeled overhead, and the greedy birds would soon swoop down to collect their next meal. Unless something was done, there would be much for the birds to gorge on.

Tyranny looked at Adrian. "Was the craft at work here?" she asked.

Adrian came to stand before the woman whose eyes Tyranny had just closed. The acolyte spent some time looking at the gaping abdomen. She pursed her lips thoughtfully.

"At first I wasn't sure," she answered, "but on closer examination, I believe that it was." Adrian pointed to the wound and beckoned everyone nearer.

Tyranny soon saw what the acolyte was talking about. The privateer was no mystic, but she had seen enough azure bolts used to recognize the telltale marks that they left behind. The edges of the wounds were precise and singed black. Tyranny pointed at them.

"These wounds were caused by the craft, weren't they?" she asked.

Adrian nodded. "Yes," she said. "Do you see how smooth the cuts are? I know of no traditional weapon that can produce such perfect incisions and singe marks at the same time."

Traax shook his head. "With all due respect, First Sister, you're wrong," he countered. "There is such a weapon, and I know the warrior who wields it."

Tyranny nodded. "You're right," she said. "The warrior is Tristan, and the weapon is his dreggan. During the fight to take the Recluse, when he called on his gift of *K'Shari* his dreggan glowed. It sliced though his enemies as if they were made of paper and caused these same burns. But does that mean that there is another *K'Shari* master roaming Eutracia with the same skills?"

Adrian again turned her attention to the corpse. She bent down and looked at the internal organs lying at the victim's feet. Lifting the hem of her robe, she trod through the blood and regarded the next impaled victim in the same way. This time her inspection became more focused, as if she was searching for something specific. She quickly moved on to look at two more corpses. Thinking, she walked back to stand beside Tyranny. There was a puzzled look on her face.

"What is it?" Tyranny asked.

Adrian scowled. "Aside from the obvious, two of the four victims that I just examined have another thing in common," she mused.

"What are you talking about?" Scars asked.

As though she couldn't believe what she was about to say, Adrian shook her head.

"They are missing their livers," she said. "Like the exterior wounds, the cuts that allowed their removal are equally precise and darkly singed."

Tyranny shot Adrian a skeptical look. "Show me," she ordered.

Adrian pointed to the dead woman's gaping wound. Some organs were missing and dangled toward the ground. "Look there," she said. "Do you see those interior cuts? They allowed the removal of the liver."

"How do you know that only the liver is missing?" Tyranny asked.

Adrian gave Tyranny a rueful look. "All her other organs are accounted for," she said quietly. "They lie at your feet. It is the same with the others. Only their livers are gone."

Tyranny scowled and ran one hand through her hair. "What in the world . . ." she breathed. "You are that conversant with human anatomy?" she asked.

Adrian nodded. "All acolytes are. It's part of our training. The craft has to do with blood; blood has to do with the organs; and the organs— well, you see."

Tyranny shook her head again. She was starting to understand these horrors less and less. It was an unsettling feeling.

"But why would some attacker want their *livers*?" she asked incredulously. "Does that also have to do with the craft?"

"Probably," Adrian answered. "On the anatomical level, magic has much to do with the liver. A person's entire blood supply—be it endowed or unendowed—flows through it. We might be dealing with something never seen before. Either way, only our more senior mystics might answer that. I strongly suggest that we take several of these corpses to Tammerland. Faegan will certainly want to do necropsies. And there is one other thing that you need to know."

"What is that?" Tyranny asked.

"Although each victim was impaled and rendered, the livers were taken only from those victims who possessed endowed blood. Clearly, there is much more going on with these horrors than first meets the eye."

Wanting to look at another corpse, Tyranny beckoned Adrian to walk with her. The privateer stopped before the second victim that Adrian had examined. When she looked at the corpse's face she saw that the dead man had been injured in ways that the woman had not. At first Tyranny thought that she might become ill.

Parts of the man's eyes were missing. The entire front of each eyeball was gone, leaving only the rear walls intact. A trail of dried vitreous material ran down each cheek. The edges of the eye sockets were not singed like the man's abdominal wounds. Rather, they looked pitted, ragged. As Tyranny looked closer she saw that the man's face was similarly injured by what looked like fresh pox marks. His liver remained intact, telling Tyranny that if Adrian was right in her assumptions, this fellow had been of unendowed blood. She looked curiously at Adrian.

"What destroyed his eyes?" she asked. "And what caused these red marks on his face?"

Adrian shook her head. "I don't know," she answered. "It looks as though acid or some other caustic material was sprayed onto his face. That might also be what destroyed his eyes. But one thing is certain."

"What is that?" the privateer asked.

"If these poor souls were alive during their mistreatment, they suffered horribly," Adrian answered. "I'm talking about *terrible* pain, Tyranny—the kind that drives even the strongest mystics mad. What happened here is an outrage of massive proportions. I fear that a new Vagaries scourge has somehow been loosed on Eutracia. If we don't stop it soon, more such atrocities seem sure to follow. But why bring these people here and then impale them? If they hail from Birmingham, herding them to this shore took great effort. They could easily have been tortured and killed in town."

Tyranny cast her gaze back out across the sea. "I know why," she said. "It was meant to be a warning. They knew that the fleet would arrive soon, and they wanted this travesty to be the first thing that we saw. It worked."

Adrian was about to reply when she heard the flurry of Minion wings. As two warriors landed nearby, everyone hurried over to greet them. One of the warriors was male and rather young; his senior officer was an older female. They quickly approached Tyranny and clicked their boot heels together.

"We have finished the shoreline body count that you asked for, Captain," the female warrior said. "The impaled victims number two thousand six hundred and thirty-three. There are no survivors."

Tyranny's heart fell. If these people came from Birmingham, it likely meant that the entire population of the town had been wiped out.

"Is there word from Birmingham?" Traax asked.

The female officer pointed toward the western sky. Everyone turned to see a cluster of dark specks approaching.

"A patrol returns from the village as we speak," she answered.

As the figures in the sky grew larger, Tyranny soon realized that six of the twelve warriors were carrying a litter. She couldn't tell what the litter contained, but she was eager to find out. As the patrol descended toward the shore, everyone ran over to meet them.

The newly constructed litter was about three meters square and made of freshly cut tree branches lashed together with rope. It was more like a cage than a litter, Tyranny realized. As she ran nearer, she finally saw what it contained. She and her group came to a quick stop.

The Minion warriors had captured a snarling, hissing beast. Tyranny had never seen anything like it. She approached cautiously, stopping about three meters away.

The half-man, half-serpent was a grotesque creature. The hairless skull was olive in color. A pair of twisted, sharp horns rose from either side of the skull. Long pointed ears lay on either side. The eyes were wide apart, with dully opaque whites and vertical yellow irises. Its mouth soon opened, sending a bright red forked tongue slithering forth to test the air. Before the mouth closed again, Tyranny saw sharp yellow teeth and a pair of deadly incisors flash in the morning sun.

Its upper body appeared to be human, and its muscular arms looked strong. From the waist down its body was a scaly, snakelike tail. Like the thing's torso, the tail was olive in color, but it had dark spots all along its length and gradually tapered to a forked end. When it saw Tyranny approach, it coiled up and viciously hissed.

Without warning the creature suddenly shot forward and grasped one of the litter's wooden braces. Hissing madly again, it used all its strength to try to rip the cage apart. The sturdy cage rocked wildly, but it held. The defeated beast then slithered toward the back of its beech wood prison and coiled up protectively. As its dark eyes bored into Tyranny's, a quick shudder went through her.

Her mouth agape, she looked at the senior officer, who had also been one of the litter bearers. His name was Davin, and Tyranny had come to respect him during the past week's sea trials. Although Davin was a graybeard, few warriors could outdrink or outfight him.

Tyranny pointed at the monster in the litter. "What in the name of the Afterlife *is* that thing?" she breathed.

Davin unsheathed his dreggan. Before answering, he shoved his dreggan blade into the cage and poked at the creature. It hissed again, exposing its deadly teeth.

"We don't know," Davin answered, "but most folks wouldn't want to meet it alone on a dark night! When we found it, it was lying in one of Birmingham's streets, unconscious. One of the citizens must have stunned it. When we tried to capture it, the thing came awake. It injured one warrior, then spat at another, blinding him. It hasn't spat again since its capture, so we think that a certain amount of time must pass before it can do that again." Davin pointed to the rows of impaled corpses. "We believe that this thing and many more like it are responsible for these atrocities."

"Can it speak?" Tyranny asked.

Davin shook his head. "Not that we have seen," he answered. "But we all know that means nothing."

Adrian took a step closer. "A warrior was blinded, you say?" she asked.

Davin quickly raised one hand, warning the sister to stay back. "That's close enough," he said. "The venom it spits seems to be acid. It burns the skin and harms the eyes. We have several healers caring for the warrior that this bastard blinded. They are hoping that the blindness is temporary, but they can't be sure."

Adrian looked at Tyranny. "That would explain the strange facial wounds that we saw," she said. "My guess is that many more of these victims have them as well."

Davin turned to look at Tyranny. "If it please the captain, the blinded warrior should be seen by one of the Conclave Wizards. I request that he be flown to Tammerland immediately."

Tyranny nodded. "See to it at once," she ordered. "But before you go—what of Birmingham?"

A dark look crossed the warrior's face. "Birmingham no longer exists," he answered. "Every building was set afire. By the time we got there, most were already consumed. We saw no citizens—dead or otherwise. It seems that they were all herded here and then killed. The phalanxes are doing what they can to control the last of the flames."

As she sheathed her sword, Tyranny looked angrily at the ground, then back at the rows of grisly corpses. She had learned all that she could from this butchery, and it was time to go home and inform the Conclave. Her task would not be a pleasant one. She cast a hard gaze toward Adrian.

"I head for Tammerland," she said. "Traax will come with me. You, the other acolytes, Scars, and the four phalanxes will remain here until you receive word that the ships' new cradles have been finished. While I am gone, you are in command. If more of those beasts appear, get the Black Ships and the phalanxes into the air immediately. The monsters don't seem to have the power of flight, so being airborne will give you a great advantage. But I don't think those creatures will return."

"And why would that be?" Traax asked.

Tyranny sadly cast her gaze toward the rows of corpses once more. "Because if Adrian's suspicions are true," she answered softly, "these monsters got what they came for."

The privateer turned to look at Davin. "Build another litter," she ordered. "I am taking six of these corpses back to Tammerland for further inspection. After I have gone, I want the remaining bodies burned. The Conclave failed to protect these people. Immolating their remains seems the least that we can do."

Davin clicked his boot heels together and went to carry out his new orders.

"The bodies that you take back should be preserved by the craft," Adrian offered. "Faegan would insist on it."

Tyranny nodded. "You're right," she answered. "Please enchant on six of them. Make sure that at least one of them is without a liver. But leave the impaling staffs in place. I want Faegan and the other mystics to see exactly how these people died." Adrian nodded her agreement, then walked off to start her grisly task.

As she waited, Tyranny looked out across the Sea of Whispers. The freshening wind smelled clean, making her wish that she could go straight back out to sea. Instead, as she stood in the drying blood among the glistening entrails, her heart became heavy once more.

Reaching for her gold case, she produced a cigarillo, then struck a match against one knee boot. As she lit the cigarillo, the first lungful of smoke calmed her. Even so, from the moment she had first seen the grisly impalements, the same question kept haunting her.

Why?

CHAPTER XII

"AS YOU CAN SEE, CONQUERING THE LANDS WHERE THE six rivers join will be of prime importance," Lucius Marius announced. He pointed to the large azure battle map floating in the air. "But *keeping* these lands while the gold is being extracted is even more vital. It is widely rumored that the Shashidan mines are inexhaustible." Pausing for a moment, he smiled and turned to look at the Suffragat.

"If we are lucky," he added slyly, "we will learn whether the legend is true."

As Vespasian sat in his throne before the entire Suffragat, he cast a quick glance at Persephone. The empress was seated in her usual place, and she looked splendid in a beautiful blue gown. Blood-red ruby earrings adorned her earlobes, and a matching necklace lay around her neck.

Persephone gave her husband a welcome look of support. Vespasian's recent night terror had shaken him, she knew. Even so, he had skillfully controlled every nuance of the session.

After Vespasian had finally awakened from his terrors, he and Persephone had talked for hours. He described his dream to her in great detail. As she listened, Persephone grew more worried about him. When she asked him who the unknown boy had been, he could not answer. In the twisting maze that had been his dream, Vespasian was certain of only one thing—this latest reverie had been far more real than any of those before it.

At Persephone's suggestion, Vespasian had reluctantly trumped up some charges against the imperial guards who had rushed into their rooms that night. He accused them of being members of the League of Whispers, saying that they had broken down the door and tried to assassinate him and Persephone. He had considered killing them on the spot, Vespasian added, but he wanted the public to witness the traitors' executions.

His orders were carried out the following dawn. The bewildered guards had gone to the gallows loudly protesting their innocence. It had been all that the guilt-ridden emperor could do to keep from commuting their sentences at the last moment. He knew these men, and they had served him well. But the stakes were too high, so the executions went forward. With the guards dead, his secret was safe.

During his youth, Vespasian's dreams had always been florid and often frightening, sometimes so much so that he had once confided to Gracchus about them. But none of those earlier episodes had been as alarmingly violent as this most recent one. The lead cleric had told his young student that his dreams were caused by the highly unusual strength of his endowed blood. As Vespasian grew older, the dreams would slow, then stop altogether, Gracchus had said. And until last night, they had.

Even so, something about this latest terror told Vespasian that no one other than Persephone should know of it. Not even his best friend Lucius would be told. It was vitally important that he continue to display the leadership and strength that had always characterized his reign—especially when Rustannica would soon launch her greatest campaign.

The Suffragat had been in session for the last three hours. The *Pon Q'tar,* the Priory of Virtue, and the Imperial Order centurions had come to learn about and vote on the war plan to take the Shashidan gold mines. Because the session was highly secret, no skeens were present.

The war strategy was everything that Vespasian had hoped for. Taking the mines would produce greater stability at home and ensure the empire's continued ability to wage war. Conversely, it would drastically curtail Shashida's defensive capabilities and limit her power to supply the domestic needs of her people. The tables would be turned. And if the mines could be held indefinitely, an eventual Rustannican victory in the War of Attrition would be nearly assured.

The intricate plan that Gracchus, Julia, Persephone, Vespasian, and Lucius had finally agreed on had not come easily. Intense bickering had persisted for days while Vespasian steadfastly settled one dispute after another. It came as no surprise that most of the disagreements arose between Gracchus and Lucius. The military and the *Pon Q'tar* had struggled for dominance since the empire's earliest days, and little about that rivalry had changed.

The attack on the Shashidan mines would be Vespasian's fourth campaign as emperor. His earlier crusades had been aggressive but far from decisive. During those struggles he had learned that the military and the mystical wings of the Rustannican war machine badly needed each other, whether they wanted to admit it or not. Without the legions, even the vaunted *Pon Q'tar* was of limited usefulness, because they were relatively few in number. Conversely, the military desperately needed advanced forms of magic to help win its battles.

Vespasian knew that once the campaign started, the military and the *Pon Q'tar* would likely snap at each other like the vicious dogs in his recent night terror. Once again, this would be especially true of Gracchus and Lucius. Because he was First Tribune, Lucius was also a trained mystic of notable power. Lucius mistrusted most mystics who were not military personnel, and he saw Gracchus as a particularly grasping and manipulative cleric. Gracchus thought Lucius to be a hedonistic upstart who owed his quick rise to a close friendship with the emperor. Vespasian knew that each of his headstrong servants was at least partly right. But during times of war there were no two allies that he would rather have by his side.

As he thought about the campaign, Vespasian felt the pressure to succeed crowding in on him again. It would be his responsibility to keep the peace among his forces while making war on the enemy. That was why he had demanded the right to unilaterally change any aspect of the battle plan once his forces were afield. In the end, the burden of victory would be his alone. As the days progressed it weighed ever more heavily across his shoulders.

He again regarded the azure battle map. Lucius was still speaking—overstating, as expected, the military's importance to the plan. Never to be upstaged, Gracchus would surely ask for equal time to emphasize the critical role of the *Pon Q'tar*. Beneath the map hovered hundreds of script-laden columns that detailed the attack and listed the vast hordes of legionnaires and the huge amounts of war materiel that would soon be needed. The requirements were staggering.

Save for a few legions left behind to keep order in Ellistium, all the empire's land forces would attack Shashida in a huge thrusting movement and take the mines. While the legions advanced, great barges would cruise down the six majestic rivers that stabbed deep across the Borderlands and into Shashidan territory. The legions would ruthlessly take one Shashidan riverside town after another and secure the surrounding territories. According to Vespasian's intelligence, the precious mines lay farther south, where all six waterways joined to form one torrential force of nature called the Alarik River. It would be there that Vespasian's legions would stop, at least for a time.

Once all six rivers were secured, the gold would eventually be sailed to Ellistium on legion cargo vessels. But before he could allow that, Vespasian needed every Shashidan town along the twelve riverbanks to be firmly under Rustannican control. This would ensure that the mines stayed in Rustannican hands while the cargo vessels spirited the gold to Ellistium.

Special groups of legionnaires trained in mining and engineering would bear the responsibility of taking the purloined gold from the ground. Shashidan miners who survived the attack would become Rustannican slaves and be forced to help supply their enemies with their own gold. Those who refused would be killed. It was a brazen, complicated plan that would need precise timing. If it worked, Shashida would be weakened and Rustannica strengthened beyond all precedent. But if it failed, all of Rustannica might go crashing down to final defeat. With her treasury nearly empty, she would never again be able to mount such a massive campaign.

Vespasian returned his attention to Lucius' presentation. The vote had already been taken and the battle plan overwhelmingly approved. Therefore, Gracchus' previous suggestion to take another vote to quash the entire concept proved unneeded. Then Lucius had asked Vespasian for some extra floor time to make several additional points on the military's behalf. As Lucius' self-aggrandizing talk progressed, Vespasian smiled. He knew that he badly needed Gracchus. But Lucius was his closest friend and had always been a greater confidant than his mentor in the craft. *They're such an odd but effective pair of allies,* he found himself thinking.

Vespasian then regarded the *Pon Q'tar* as a whole. As they listened to Lucius' specious talk, many of the imperious clerics were wriggling uncomfortably like a mess of trapped eels. Vespasian soon found himself wondering whether any of them had done one day's worth of manual labor in their entire lives. *One never finds dirt under a* Pon Q'tar *cleric's fingernails,* he thought.

Lucius soon finished his talk. After bowing to his emperor, he took his customary seat beside the empress. Wishing to regain control of the proceedings, Vespasian lifted his gold scepter from its nearby holder and banged it against the floor.

Before Vespasian could speak, Gracchus stood. Vespasian noticed that the cleric held a gold diptych in his hands. The emperor's eyes narrowed. The Oraculum, he realized.

"With all due respect to the emperor, I wish to approach," Gracchus said.

Vespasian beckoned the lead cleric forward. Gracchus neared and handed the gold diptych to Vespasian. As Vespasian broke the red seal and read the beeswax pages, a wide smile spread across his face. Puzzled, the Suffragat waited in silence.

"Can this be true after all these years?" Vespasian asked of Gracchus. "As you know, I too am familiar with the legend."

Gracchus nodded. "The Oraculum dares not lie," he answered. "She knows that her life is in my hands."

Vespasian was overjoyed. The *Jin'Sai* would be suddenly preoccupied just as the Rustannican siege of Shashida went forth. It was a huge stroke of luck. He smiled at Gracchus.

"I suggest that you explain the Oraculum's latest vision to everyone," he said. "It is news worthy of this fine session."

Gripping the shoulder folds of his robe, Gracchus turned to face the Suffragat.

"The Oraculum brings excellent news," he announced. "Our prayers to find a way to continue our fight with the *Jin'Sai* on his side of the world have been answered. It seems that we again owe much to the failed First Mistress of the Coven. After more than three centuries, the Eutracian Viper Lord has risen. He and his servants have already started their rampage. In due course, all resistance in Eutracia might well be eliminated. If the Viper Lord is victorious one can only guess that he will then sail to Parthalon to wreak his mistress's special brand of vengeance there as well. We might see the death of *all* right-leaning blood east of the Tolenkas. This is indeed a glorious day."

Pausing for a moment, Gracchus looked straight at Lucius Marius, then smiled. "For those military personnel who might be unschooled in the legend, I will provide a brief explanation."

The Suffragat listened as Gracchus explained at some length the coming of the Viper Lord. Happy expressions surfaced all around. Even Lucius momentarily forgave Gracchus' thinly veiled insult and went so far as to stand and start the raucous applause. As the ovation gradually subsided, Gracchus returned to his seat.

Vespasian stood and looked toward Julia Idaeus. Despite the affirmative vote on the war plan, one more hurdle remained before the emperor could pronounce the campaign official.

"Are you prepared to perform the auspicium?" he asked.

The Priory Femiculi stood. "I am," she said. "The sacred birds await us."

Vespasian nodded. "Very well," he said. "Let us all adjourn to the courtyard."

By custom, Persephone was the first to leave her seat and approach the emperor. As the remaining Suffragat members followed her, Vespasian led the group across the floor.

Raising one arm, Vespasian pointed toward one of the many onyx wall pilasters, and it soon glowed with the familiar azure color of the craft. Then the pilaster vanished to show a secret tunnel in the Aedifficium wall. The courtyard beyond was called the Rustica, and it was known only to the Suffragat. Built at the same time as the Aedifficium, it had been constructed in secrecy and at great expense. The sacred ritual of the auspiciums was the Rustica's sole reason for being.

Taking Persephone by the hand, Vespasian led her into the arched tunnel and out through the far end. When they emerged into the Rustica, dappled sunlight and the pleasant warbling of songbirds greeted them.

The Rustica held marble seats arranged against one of its four walls. Another, far less grandiose throne for Vespasian sat on the floor before them. While the members found their places, Vespasian beckoned Persephone to take her seat. As he settled into his throne, the emperor looked around. Vespasian loved the Rustica, for he always sensed a measure of intimacy here that he found lacking in the Aedifficium.

The closed courtyard was square, measuring twenty meters on each side. As a tribute to the azure glow of the craft, the walls and floor were built of turquoise blocks, polished to a high sheen. There was no roof. Over time, lilac and crinkleberry vines had become so overgrown that the walls could scarcely be seen. The combined scents of the hardy vines wafted pleasantly on the afternoon air. The sky was bright blue and without a hint of cloud.

Vespasian turned to look toward the wall opposite the Suffragat. As Julia had promised, ten white birds sat atop a golden rail. The birds' feet were tethered to the rail. The auspicium would produce a foretelling of either good or bad fortune and was always performed before a major event such as the trying of an important new craft formula, the implementation of a new law, or the advent of a major military campaign.

During the empire's earliest days, the *Pon Q'tar* had insisted on performing the ritual themselves. Later, they graciously bequeathed that honor to the reigning Femiculi. It had remained that way ever since. Because her heart was known to be pure, the Femiculi could be relied on to perform the ritual honestly and without prejudice.

How the sacred birds could divine either good or bad fortune was a secret of the craft that only the clerics knew. Even Rustannica's emperors were never informed. Vespasian did not object to this, because in the entire history of the empire, the birds had never been wrong. By mutual agreement of the Suffragat, an auspicium decreed whether a proposed event should go forward.

If the birds foretold bad fortune, the impending event was quickly canceled. If the decree was good, the event was carried out with confidence. During the early days of the empire, a few quarrelsome military tribunes had refused to believe an auspicium warning of bad fortune. The secret campaign they launched proved disastrous, and Shashidan forces had slaughtered them to the last man. Since then, not one member dared doubt the validity of the ritual.

Vespasian knew that the fate of the campaign to take the Shashidan gold mines rested on what happened here. If the auspicium went badly, his magnificent plans would be canceled. Even he would be unable to change that. If the decree was for good fortune, the campaign would be launched. Once in the field, Vespasian would order yet more auspiciums to help him lead his forces to victory.

Each of the sacred songbirds was pure white, like the gowns and veils of the Priory maidens. The maidens tended the birds carefully, always ready for the day when the *Pon Q'tar* would notify them that another auspicium was needed. Like the *Pon Q'tar* clerics, the birds had been granted time enchantments, and they were thousands of years old. These same ten birds had been used in every auspicium ever conducted.

As Julia waited for Vespasian to summon her, her heart pounded. This would be the most important auspicium of her life—perhaps the most important in all of Rustannican history. As Vespasian turned her way, she felt the weight of his gaze.

"You may begin," he said simply.

Julia rose from her seat and walked toward the far wall. Save for the soft cooing of the birds, the Rustica was bathed in silence. After stopping before the birds, Julia pointed in their direction. At once the tethers binding the birds' feet to the golden rail vanished. Even so, the birds knew better than to fly away until their mistress willed it. Julia raised her arms and closed her eyes.

After the Femiculi recited the sacred chant, the birds would be free. They would wing their way home to the Rotunda and enter the building through the oculus. If they turned north first, the decree was favorable. If they turned south before flying for home, the decree dictated ill fortune. Julia took a deep breath and bowed her head.

"O sacred flame of the Vagaries, grant us the wisdom to receive this auspicium, and to be guided by its decree," she said. "Allow your divine magic to drive the sacred birds skyward to show your servants which path is best. We ask for your guidance in the upcoming campaign. In your name we offer our thanks and our continued servitude."

With that, Julia opened her eyes and raised her arms higher. Among a quick flurry of white wings, the birds took to the sky.

For several tense moments the birds circled overhead, giving no inkling of their decree. Then suddenly, as though of a single mind, they wheeled around to soar in one direction before finally turning toward the Rotunda. Vespasian held his breath as the birds chose their path.

They flew due north. With every person's gaze trained on the birds, no one saw that Gracchus had narrowed his eyes slightly.

The Suffragat erupted into cheering. Letting go a deep sigh of relief, Vespasian looked at Persephone. She gave him a reassuring smile. Then tears started forming in her eyes as she hoped that when they said goodbye to one another it would not be for the last time.

For Vespasian the moment was bittersweet. As he watched Persephone's eyes well up he made a silent pact with himself that he would treat each remaining moment with her as though it were their last. He then looked at Lucius. Already eager to be in the field, the beaming First Tribune gave his emperor a rapacious wink.

And so it was that the campaign to take the Shashidan gold fields had been officially ratified and could be put into motion. It would take time to assemble the needed troops and materiel. Even so, nothing could stop the attack now.

Persephone came to join her husband and he escorted her from the Rustica. By custom, each time an auspicium decree was favorable, a great banquet was served in the royal palace to celebrate the joyous event. Tonight would be no exception, and Vespasian was looking forward to it.

As the Suffragat left the courtyard, two *Pon Q'tar* clerics remained behind. Gracchus looked up at the sky and he smiled. Aegaea Mithridates, one of Gracchus' most trusted *Pon Q'tar* confidants, came to stand beside him. She had a pleasant face and flowing gray hair. As if she could again see the sacred birds winging home, she too looked to the sky.

Only hours ago Gracchus had informed the *Pon Q'tar* of the Oraculum's complete vision. Unlike Vespasian, Persephone, the Priory, and the Tribunes, nothing that the lead cleric had told the *Pon Q'tar* during today's Aedifficium session had come as a surprise. As had been so often the case over the centuries, once again their playacting had been flawless.

"And so you have succeeded once more, Gracchus," Aegaea said.

"Don't I always?" he asked in return.

Taking her gaze from the sky, Aegaea looked the lead cleric in the eyes. "Tell me," she asked, "had you not intervened, which way do you believe that the birds would have flown?"

Gracchus looked at her. "We'll never know," he answered. "Nor does it matter. All that matters now is that we have our war."

"And what is to keep the *Jin'Sai* from crossing the Azure Sea?" she asked.

Gracchus smiled. "I will address that issue shortly, my dear," he answered. "Do not fret. Tonight our only concern is to enjoy our emperor's renowned hospitality."

As Gracchus escorted Aegaea from the courtyard, the late afternoon sun slipped down behind the Rustica's western wall.

II

TERROR AND MAGIC

CHAPTER XIII

Although revenge will taste sweet, it is not so much for myself that I do this thing as for my lost beloved.

— KHRISTOS

WIPING THE SWEAT FROM HIS BROW, TRISTAN TOOK A break from his labors and reached down to grasp a nearby stone jug. He raised the vessel to his lips and drank greedily of the cool water before pouring some onto his head. Smiling, he ran the fingers of one hand back through his salt-and-pepper hair, then tossed the jug to Ox.

Ox caught the jug between his huge palms and drained its remaining contents in a single draught. After letting go a wet belch, he wiped his mouth with the back of one hand and dropped the jug to the ground.

"Not good as akulee, but Ox thank *Jin'Sai*," the huge warrior said. "The day be hot, but work almost done. Then ships can come." Tristan responded with a smile.

It was midafternoon on the third day following Tyranny's return to Tammerland. The sky was hot and bright. As he stood amid the great hustle and bustle, Tristan shook his head, thinking. So much had happened in such a short time that he hardly knew what to make of it all. He wasn't alone in his confusion, for every Conclave member felt the same.

His mystics had been secluded in the Redoubt for the last two days, trying to unravel the strange mysteries that had recently appeared. So far they had sent no word about their findings. To dispel his nervous energy, Tristan had come to help the Minion workers and engineers with the massive project that he had assigned to them several months ago. He was glad that the job was nearly done.

The *Jin'Sai* took another deep breath. Raising his sledge high, he brought it down squarely against an iron spike that would help seat another of the great laminated timbers into place. Hundreds of Minion workers were also pounding away in various areas on the same project. After driving six more spikes home, Tristan again stopped to catch his breath.

The huge construction area was a beehive of activity, with hundreds of male and female Minion warriors working tirelessly toward one goal. Tristan had selected a spacious field just outside the palace walls as the permanent resting place for the Black Ship fleet. Of all the Conclave mystics, only Jessamay was here to apply the craft when needed. Tristan wanted the fleet returned home as soon as possible, for his heart told him that he would soon need them.

He had seen the horrific creature and the impaled corpses that Tyranny brought back, and their surprising existence caused him great concern. He realized that many such wicked beasts would have been needed to commit the thousands of grisly atrocities that Tyranny found at Birmingham. Despite Tristan's earlier hopes that the Vagaries had been vanquished east of the Tolenkas, another strange threat from the craft's dark side had somehow risen. Every fiber of his being told him that the danger needed to be dealt with quickly.

Moreover, the Conclave's confirmation of subtle matter and learning that Shashida could be reached by crossing the Azure Sea had been astounding. But Tristan had absolutely no idea how to accomplish such a daunting task. Ships would be needed to cross that strange sea, and in the depths of the caves there were no raw materials from which to build them. Nor did Tristan dare order his warriors to try to cross the sea by air, for he knew nothing about the distance involved.

Tristan shook his head again. Only three days ago he had been dead certain that he should leave for the Caves straightaway. But with the grisly impalements and the coming of the man-serpents, his next course of action became unclear. As was often the case, his mystics' advice would figure prominently in his decision.

Even so, he had ordered that Minion phalanxes start flying over Eutracia to search out the deadly monsters. He knew that it would be akin to finding a thimble in a sneezeweed stack, as Abbey was so fond of saying, but he had to try. Because the Conclave still knew so little about the beasts, even if they were found, he had ordered that the warriors were to take no action unless citizens were again being threatened. It chafed at the *Jin'Sai* to give his troops such cautious instructions. Not leading them himself chafed even more. But other matters commanded his duty now.

Placing one palm above his eyes to shield them from the blazing sun, he again looked out over the huge construction site. Three of the massive cradles were finished and the fourth was nearly so. Because so many warriors had been freed after building the first three, the final cradle was swiftly nearing its completion.

The cradles' frameworks were shaped exactly like the Black Ships' hulls, only larger, so that the vessels could fit into them. Great laminated timbers that formed the cradles' spines lay on huge stone foundations so that the cradles wouldn't shift in the soft earth. The cradles pointed east, ensuring that when the ships lay in them, their bows would face into the prevailing wind coming off the Sea of Whispers. Each massive spine measured just over one hundred meters long and curved skyward for fifty meters at each end. Huge timber braces curved away from the spines at regular intervals and also rose upward for fifty meters. Buttresses made of more stout wood stood angled against the braces, their opposite ends shoved deeply into the earth for support.

Wigg had searched high and low for the original Black Ship plans, and he had finally found them buried among the countless other documents that had been scattered about in the Archives of the Redoubt. With the plans at their disposal, Jessamay and the Minion engineers could ensure a perfect fit when the four Black Ships finally came home to roost. The aft ends of the cradles were left open so that the huge stern doors of the ships could be easily lowered for the loading and unloading of supplies, weapons, and troops.

Tristan would be greatly relieved to have the vessels stationed so near to the palace rather than moored at the Cavalon Delta. With the ships constantly supplied and their Minion crews and acolyte pilots always at the ready, the ships could be ordered airborne at a moment's notice. Tristan had read Tyranny's sea trials report and he had accepted her suggestion about permanently assigning the four Minion phalanxes to Black Ship duty. He had also told the acolytes Astrid, Phoebe, and Claire that they were to be the ships' permanent pilots. But Tristan believed that

Sister Adrian was too valuable to be assigned to the flagship *Tammerland* on a permanent basis. When Adrian returned with the fleet he would order her to select and train another acolyte in her place.

Tristan laid down his sledge and turned to look at Ox. "I've had enough of pounding these spikes for a while," he said. "Shall we go and see how Jessamay is doing?"

The giant warrior smiled. If ordered by Tristan, he would gladly swing his heavy sledge until his heart gave out. He gave his *Jin'Sai* a wide grin.

"Ox glad to quit," he said. Reaching down, he retrieved Tristan's weapons from the ground and handed them to him. As Tristan strapped his sword and throwing knives into place, Ox looked around the construction site.

"Minions do well here," he said. "Me hope *Jin'Sai* be proud."

Tristan smiled and laid one hand atop the warrior's shoulder. Ox had saved his life more than once, and there were few souls in the world that he trusted more.

"Since entering my service that fateful day in Parthalon, the Minions have always given me pride," he answered, "and sometimes you above all."

As though Tristan had just given Ox the keys to the kingdom, the warrior puffed his chest out with pride. Without further ado the pair started over to where Jessamay was working.

Cutting the thousands of trees needed to build the ships' cradles had been a daunting enough task. But carefully heating and bending the massive, freshly laminated braces so that they would exactly conform to the Black Ships' hulls was another matter entirely. Tristan knew that given enough time, the Minion warriors could probably have done the job. But he wanted ships home soon, so he had decided to speed the process via the craft. Intrigued by the challenge, Jessamay had eagerly volunteered. For the last three months she had done little else but toil on the massive cradles.

The Vigors sorceress stood about thirty meters away, occasionally waving her arms and shouting out orders to the warrior engineers assigned to help her. With her long blond hair tied behind her back and dressed as she was in leather trousers, scuffed knee boots, and a simple white linen peasant's blouse, she looked more like a Eutracian commoner than a valued member of the Conclave. Tristan smiled as he approached. Jessamay was many things, but commonplace wasn't one of them.

The warrioress Duvessa was standing by Jessamay's side and barking out orders with equal verve. As Minion Premier Healer and the leader of the cadres of female combat warriors, she commanded great respect. Traax's wife was an attractive Minion with green eyes. As it was today, her black hair was often tied into twisted braids. A pair of crossed feathers was embroidered into the breastplate of her leather armor. The white feather showed her rank as Premier Healer, and the red one signified her command of the female warriors who participated in combat.

A crude worktable stood before the two women, its top strewn with parchments and diagrams. A stout canvas lay stretched atop wooden poles, shielding the women and the ancient documents from the sun. As Tristan and Ox gratefully took advantage of the shade, the women looked up.

"How is it coming?" Tristan asked.

"We're nearly done," Jessamay answered. "There's just one more brace to shape and install." She raised her arm and pointed toward the construction site.

Tristan looked out from the shade to see several dozen horses being led their way by Minion warriors. Taken from the palace stables, the thirty-six steeds were harnessed in pairs to a huge, flat cart that had been built solely for moving the massive uprights. Despite the powerful horses, the cart and its odd-looking load neared with agonizing slowness. Realizing that this last brace measured a good fifty meters long and another ten meters around, Tristan couldn't begin to imagine how much the thing weighed.

As the sweating horses finally pulled the cart to a stop, Jessamay scooped up one of the parchments from the table and went to inspect this last brace. Tristan, Ox, and Duvessa followed.

Like its brothers, the brace was a wondrous example of Minion craftsmanship. The warriors had selected Eutracian oak because of its great strength and high resistance to inclement weather. The massive brace was actually a series of smaller and thinner oak slats that had been carefully cut to size, then glued together. Just now the brace was as straight as an arrow, but that would soon change.

Jessamay spent much time looking at the brace, then consulting her diagram, then looking back at the brace again. She then produced a long measuring string from her trousers and used it to confirm her findings. Finally satisfied, she nodded and returned the string to her pocket.

"It'll do," she said simply.

Tristan smiled as he anticipated the next part of the process. He had seen Jessamay do this several times before, and each time it had amazed him. Because of the great length and thickness of the laminated braces, even Jessamay could only bend them a little at a time. This brace would be no exception.

The Vigors sorceress ordered the Minions to unharness the horses and lead them away; then she asked that Ox, Tristan, and Duvessa come and stand behind her. As the three spectators moved into place, Jessamay raised her arms.

At once the far end of the massive brace started to glow. As the azure hue intensified, Jessamay concentrated harder. Soon the near end of the beam began to curve, and hissing steam rose from it to disappear high into the air. When the sorceress was satisfied, she dropped her arms and the azure hue vanished. Taking up her parchment and her string again, she went to check on the first stage of what would be a long and arduous process.

For the next two hours she fussed, measured, and employed the craft to repeatedly force the length of the beam into the proper shape. The curve had to be just right, lest the last cradle become misaligned and cause its Black Ship to sit crookedly. Worse yet, if one beam was misshapen, the others might not be able to withstand the added strain, causing the entire cradle to collapse.

Once the beam cooled, she would order the Minions to ferry it to the last cradle. The warriors would then use great cranes and pulleys to lift it into place and immediately buttress it with side shores. They would then pound spikes into it to join it to the spine, just as Tristan and Ox had been doing. Finally the hundreds of needed crossbraces would be added to strengthen the cradle and to hold the entire framework together.

Glad to be done with her work, Jessamay walked tiredly back to the makeshift shelter. Taking a bottle of claret and several wooden cups from a nearby picnic basket, she placed them on the worktable. By the time the others joined her, all four cups were filled.

Raising her cup, Jessamay watched the others follow suit. She then looked out at the four massive cradles sitting side by side on their stone foundations. Lined up that way, they took up a huge area. Once the

Black Ships lay in them, the sight would be even more impressive. Proud to have been a part of this effort, she returned her attention to the others.

"To the Black Ships!" she toasted. "May they take us far and always bring us home again!"

Everyone smiled at that. After draining his cup, Tristan refilled it. But just as he was about to take another drink, he noticed an odd tingling in his blood. He looked up to see that everyone was staring strangely at him. He soon realized that they weren't looking at his face, but at the gold medallion lying around his neck. He looked down to see that the medallion was glowing.

Tristan was delighted. This was the first time that Shailiha had called on her matching medallion to communicate with him. Placing his cup on the worktable, he grasped his medallion and turned it over.

As he expected, the medallion's opposite side showed an image of his sister. She was seated in her chair at the great mahogany table in the Conclave meeting chamber, deep in the bowels of the Redoubt. Tristan could see Traax seated on one side of her; the empty chair on the princess's other side belonged to Jessamay. Caprice the field flier sat perched at the top of Shai's chair and was gently opening and closing her great wings. Given the limited confines of the medallion, Tristan could not tell whether anyone else was in the room.

As he looked closer, he saw that his sister's face bore a worried expression. She held up a parchment, and he saw that its words were written in her handwriting. As Tristan read them, a sudden chill went down his spine.

Come quickly, the parchment said. *The wizards need us.*

CHAPTER XIV

 IN THE END, THE CITIZENS OF TANGLEWOOD NEVER stood a chance.

As the once beautiful city burned in the night, the vicious man-serpents raged wildly through the streets. Tanglewood held many more inhabitants than had Birmingham. But that was of no consequence, for even now more snakelike beings continued to rise from the stream in Hartwick Wood to swell the monsters' ranks. As though there were no end to their numbers, they flowed through Tanglewood like a dark, undulating river. Standing in the town square, their leader watched as his servants went about his bidding. He would kill every human he encountered during his quest to find and serve Failee.

From all around him came the screams and sobs of the innocent, as one by one they were impaled like those killed along the Birmingham shore. Because there were so many more victims here, the process would take far longer. But that didn't matter, for he had all the time in the world.

The grisly impalements were ingenious, ensuring the immobilization of his captives while leaving his servants free to rummage about in the victims' innards. Some succumbed straightaway after being impaled; others lingered in agony before dying. The crude impalement poles and their bleeding human adornments already filled the great

square, and their numbers had started overtaking the connecting av-
enues and byways. In many cases the impalements wound far up the
cobblestoned streets and out of sight, into the inky blackness of the
night.

The master turned to look at the writhing victim impaled directly
before him. The man had once been hardy and vigorous. He appeared to
be somewhere near fifty Seasons of New Life and he had thick, graying
hair. Although he had been one of the first to be impaled, he still lived.
Despite how tenaciously he clung to life, his death would soon be at
hand.

Like all the Birmingham victims, he had been stripped of his clothing. A sharpened pole had been viciously shoved into his groin, then
threaded up through his abdomen to emerge near his collarbone. His
hands were raised above him and impaled through his palms; pieces of
wood had been fixed to the pole below his hands and feet to prevent him
from sliding down the bloodied staff. Blood dripped slowly from his
groin and onto the dirty cobblestones. Like all blood, it looked black in
the dark of night.

How curious, the serpent master thought. *Sometimes the men die so
quickly, while the physically weaker women, children, and the elderly often
linger for hours.* It no doubt had to do with whatever bits were punc-
tured, he reasoned. Clearly, the impaling process was not a precise one.
Nor did it need to be.

Hearing another building cave in, he turned to look. Every structure
in the city was ablaze. Carrying torches, the grotesque man-serpents had
furtively slithered into the dwellings and set them afire, or simply tossed
their blazing torches atop the thatched roofs and left them to do their
work. Many screaming victims fled the infernos with their clothing and
hair afire, and they were allowed to burn to death before being impaled.
Some buildings had already tumbled into ruin, while others still spewed
orange-red flames from their destroyed doorways and smashed windows.

The crackling of the fires sometimes drowned out the wailing of the
victims, and thick, choking smoke curled into the air, blotting out the
stars. Many people tried to run, but they were invariably snatched up
by the man-serpents' strong arms or winding tails. Children toddled
about aimlessly, wailing and crying out for parents who would never
again hold them. Some people emerged to find friends and loved ones
already impaled. Many collapsed in grief, sobbing as they hugged their
beloveds' bloody feet before they too were taken up.

The serpent master smiled. Despite ordering the fires to be set, he cared nothing about destroying the city. Rather, the fires were an easy way to force the humans from their dwellings so that they could be caught and spiked. He enjoyed seeing their hovels burn, even though he too had once been human.

He watched as his grotesque servants dragged ever more struggling citizens toward the square. Stacks of freshly hewn impalement poles lay nearby on the blood-slicked cobblestones. There the captives were stripped naked and impaled and their clothing tossed into the raging fires. If they resisted, their livers were harvested quickly by the monsters' slashing talons and biting teeth, and their dead bodies were impaled anyway.

To better view the grisly scene, the master reached up and lowered the hood of his robe. As he did, the raging fires highlighted his grotesque face. He was called Khristos, and his tale was a twisted one.

Like the heads of the man-serpents that he commanded, his cranium was also hairless, with long, pointed ears. Although his face could not be called entirely human, it was less snakelike than those of his followers. He bore no sharp, twisted horns, and his skin, nose, and lips were human. But his eyes, his tongue, and his teeth told a far different tale.

His large eyes were human in contour, but they held almond-shaped pupils that lay embedded vertically in bright yellow irises. Like those of his followers, his teeth were long, sharp, and yellow, and he possessed the same two pairs of incisors. Also like his servants, his long tongue was bright red and forked, and continually tested the cool night air. The rest of his muscular body was human.

His simple black robe was tattered, and in one hand he held a gleaming silver staff. As he had hundreds of years before, he again commanded the craft with a power and a mastery that easily rivaled any wizard in Eutracian history. And of perhaps even greater significance, there was a secret about Khristos that only a few surviving mystics knew.

Three centuries ago—long before his transformation into the being that commanded the terrible man-serpents—Khristos had been Failee's secret lover.

Khristos returned his gaze to the impaled man. Somehow the fellow still lived. But whether the man was alive or dead was of no importance, for he would not survive what Khristos was about to do to him. Khristos raised his staff and pointed it at the bleeding man. At once the entire instrument shone, and the death-dealing began in earnest.

An azure beam, so narrow that it could hardly be seen, leapt from the staff and struck the man squarely in the chest. As his skin burned and smoked, he struggled against his impaling pole and cried out in agony. But he soon realized that it was no use, for the more he struggled, the greater the searing pain became.

Khristos used his glowing beam to carve an incision down the man's body from his throat to his groin. Then he ordered the beam to crack apart the victim's sternum and separate his rib cage, exposing the man's working organs. As the sickly-sweet smell of burning flesh rose into the air, it took only a few more moments for Khristos to find and free the man's liver. By this time the man had died, his chin slumping forward onto his chest. Like wriggling serpents suddenly liberated from a snake charmer's basket, the man's glistening intestines slipped free from his gaping body cavity and dangled toward the ground.

His job done, Khristos recalled the azure beam, and his staff reclaimed its gleaming silver color. Using his free hand, he calmly pointed toward the prize he sought and ordered it to float into his grasp. Smiling as blood ran down his hand, Khristos admired the liver in the moonlight. It was a fine specimen, but many more like it would be needed. He turned and handed it to one of the man-serpents standing by his side. Hissing with satisfaction, the monster greedily accepted the bloody prize and devoured it on the spot.

Turning, Khristos walked to the next victim. This one was an elderly woman who was already dead, but neither of those distinctions mattered. Amid the constant screaming and begging of those still being impaled, he once more raised his silver staff. The azure glow again began building within the shining instrument of death.

Just as he was about to incise her body, Khristos heard an unknown voice call out from everywhere, nowhere. Its sudden and unexpected presence startled him.

"*Khristos . . .*" it said. Then it was gone.

Turning this way and that, he saw no one except the many terrified victims and his servants who were still hard at work committing the grisly atrocities. With no answer at hand, he again raised his staff. Just as he did, the strange, otherworldly voice visited his mind again.

"*Khristos,*" the voice repeated. "*Stop your work and hear me.*"

At first he was overjoyed, hoping that the voice might be that of Failee. But no, he realized sadly, for it had been male. Suddenly gripped by an overpowering yet unexplained need to supplicate himself, he went down on his knees. He placed his staff on the ground beside him and bowed his head. Amid all the gore and mayhem, he waited.

Despite his great prowess in the craft, Khristos did not know what to do. Three centuries ago Failee believed that she might one day have the power to reach out and touch his mind. Now, three centuries later, he somehow understood that he needn't speak to answer the voice's mysterious owner.

"I am here," Khristos thought. *"Who are you? What do you wish of me?"*

"First, know this," the voice said. *"Your beloved mistress is dead."*

Like a raging river, an intense, overpowering sorrow flowed through Khristos' being. He wanted to weep and wail, but he steadfastly held his posture of supplication. He dared not move, for a being that could reach out and touch his mind this way must surely be more powerful than he. Summoning up his courage, he decided to ask the question that burned so hotly in his heart.

"How did Failee die?" he asked. *"Was she killed in the Sorceresses' War?"*

"No," the voice answered. *"Nor did the Coven win that war. The Directorate of Wizards prevailed."*

"Which of them killed her?" he demanded. *"Was it Wigg? Does he live still? Tell me and I will force that Vigors worshipper to rue the day that he was born."*

"It was not Wigg."

"Who, then?"

"Failee was killed by the reigning Jin'Sai. *He murdered her less than three years ago. The* Jin'Saiou *also walks the earth."*

As Khristos' sorrow turned to rage, his anger became so great that he could barely respond. His body trembled; he cried aloud; he beat his fists upon the bloody cobblestones. Finally he relented and he returned his attention to the mysterious voice.

"Who are you who knows so much and commands such wonders of the craft?" he asked.

"My name is Gracchus," the voice answered. *"Listen carefully and I will tell you many things. Much has happened since Failee committed you to the river. With the First Mistress gone you must abandon your search for her. In her stead, you must now serve me."*

"Why should I do so?" Khristos asked. *"With my beloved dead, I am a free entity."*

"True," Gracchus answered. *"But your new, overriding concern is to kill*

the Jin'Sai *and his followers, is it not? Like you, I serve the Vagaries. Unlike you, I command powers that you could only dream of. But even with all your newly born servants you cannot touch the* Jin'Sai, *for he hides behind the palace walls with his Conclave and his grotesque winged army. If you join forces with me, together we can destroy him. Should you succeed, I will grant to you a reward beyond your wildest dreams."*

"*What reward?*" Khristos asked.

"*You will have complete rule over Eutracia and Parthalon,*" Gracchus answered. "*Destroy the Conclave and all this will become yours.*"

"*But how am I to destroy the* Jin'Sai," Khristos asked, "*given how well protected he is?*"

"*He will soon depart the safety of the palace,*" Gracchus answered. "*But only I know his destination. So tell me—do we have an arrangement?*"

Khristos raised his head for a moment and looked out over the atrocity-laden square with nearly unseeing eyes. The events of the last few moments had been stunning, life-altering. He and his servants had been released from the river for but a few hours, yet already had come another great crossroads to navigate. Is following this unseen mystic what Failee would want him to do? he wondered. Could the sacred trust she instilled into him still be honored if he accepted this strange voice from the beyond as his new master? After thinking for a time, he again lowered his head.

"*I will serve you,*" Khristos finally answered. "*Tell me more.*"

Amid the fires, the chaos, and the sudden death, for the next full hour Khristos listened intently to Gracchus' every word. Gracchus told him of the worlds on the other side of the Tolenka Mountains and of the great campaign that Rustannica was mounting against Shashida. He also enlightened Khristos about the outcome of the Sorceresses' War, of Failee's banishment to Parthalon, of her failed plan to abduct the *Jin'Saiou* and to turn her into her into her fifth sorceress, and how the *Jin'Sai* had defeated Nicholas, Wulfgar, and Serena. When the *Pon Q'tar* cleric finished, Khristos was unwaveringly committed to his new master.

"*I understand, my lord,*" Khristos answered. "*What are your orders?*"

"*Leave this place,*" Gracchus answered. "*Take your army of Blood Vipers and head south to the Caves of the Paragon. There you will await the* Jin'Sai *and his forces. They will surely enter the Caves. That is when you will strike.*"

"*Very well,*" Khristos replied. "*We will do as you say. When will you reach out to touch my mind again?*"

"*When the* Jin'Sai *draws near,*" Gracchus answered. "*Until then, travel only by night, for the* Jin'Sai's *winged ones are undoubtedly hunting for you. Enter the safety of the Caves unseen and await my word.*"

Understanding his new task, Khristos bowed deeper. "*It will be as you say,*" he replied. With that, he felt Gracchus' presence leave his mind.

Standing, the newly indentured Viper Lord turned to look at the ravaged city that had once been Tanglewood. Nearly all the buildings lay in ruins as dawn crept over the horizon. Victims sobbed and wailed as they were being impaled. Children still cried; the fires still burned. But he would leave all this work unfinished, for he had been given a far more important and worthy task. If he was successful, he could still avenge Failee's murder and forever secure his place in history.

For several moments he thought of the magnificent Failee—of her great beauty, of her majesty, of her immense prowess in the craft. Then his mind turned toward the *Jin'Sai* and his intense hatred began to rebuild. Failee had told him that the Tome predicted the coming of the *Jin'Sai* and the *Jin'Saiou* and that they must be dealt with to protect the Vagaries. But in those days even the First Mistress did not know when they might appear. None of that mattered now, he realized. The sun would rise soon, and it was time to be on the move.

Summoning his many Blood Vipers, Khristos issued his new orders.

CHAPTER XV

AS TRISTAN TOOK HIS SEAT AT THE ROUND MAHOGANY table in the Conclave meeting room, he was eager to hear what his mystics had to say, yet he was also fearful that their pronouncements might cause him even greater worry. For the last three days nearly all he could think about was the conundrum of how to cross the Azure Sea and reach Shashida, as well as finding and crushing the mysterious man-serpents that had so ruthlessly tortured and killed every man, woman, and child who had once lived in the coastal village of Birmingham. There had been no word from the Minion search parties that hunted the monsters, and that only heightened his restlessness. Each of these new challenges was of immense importance, and the dark consequences of their simultaneous arrival were not lost on him.

As Shailiha and the mystics waited in silence, the remaining Conclave members took their seats. Sister Adrian would be the only member not in attendance, for she was still piloting the Black Ships home. Once the nine members were situated, Tristan looked around the table. The people gathered here formed an impressive group, and he could think of no better allies to have by his side during the dark and challenging days that lay ahead.

To his immediate left sat Tyranny. Tristan was surprised to see her smoking one of her cigarillos—a Conclave meeting first. The bluish haze already starting to fog the chamber was garnering the privateer more than a few disparaging looks. But the set of her jaw told everyone that she would not appreciate being asked to forgo her habit. Failing to save the Birmingham impalement victims still deeply angered her, and whenever she was agitated, a lit cigarillo could be found clamped between her lips. In truth, Tristan had never minded her habit. But he smiled wryly as he wondered how long it would take Wigg to make a fuss about it.

To Tyranny's left sat the First Wizard. His craggy face looked worried and drawn, perhaps due in part to lack of sleep, Tristan guessed. There was also a hint of sadness there, as if he had been reminded of some deep personal pain. Secured to its familiar gold chain, the Paragon hung around the wizard's neck. The herbmistress Abbey sat on Wigg's other side. A pot of steaming tea, nine cups, and a platter piled with sugared scones sat before her.

Tristan knew how much Abbey loved Wigg and that despite the wizard's protests, Wigg secretly enjoyed the way she looked after him. The *Jin'Sai* respected her deeply. As he watched her pour a cup of hot tea for Wigg, he found himself hoping that she had laced it with one her esoteric stimulants. It had already been a long day, and like Wigg, he too could do with a bit of propping up.

Next to Abbey sat Faegan, comfortably situated in his chair on wheels. Like Wigg he looked desperately tired. In his hands he held Nicodemus, his centuries-old dark blue cat, and his precious violin lay on the table before him. Nicodemus purred pleasantly as Faegan absentmindedly scratched the cat's throat.

The next seat was vacant, for it belonged to Sister Adrian. Then there was Traax. Like Tyranny, Traax seemed agitated. He too had been devastated when they had not been able to intercept the grotesque manserpents. As Tristan looked at him, the warrior clenched his jaw and shifted in his seat, eager for the meeting to start. Traax respectfully nodded back at Tristan, his dark eyes reflecting a mixture of devout loyalty and his deep need to hunt the monsters that prowled Eutracia.

Shailiha sat on Traax's left. Clothed in a simple blue dress, she wore a string of freshwater Eutracian pearls, and two more hung from her earlobes. She regarded her brother affectionately. As was often the case during Conclave meetings, Caprice perched quietly atop the princess's chair, gently folding and unfolding her butterfly wings to keep her balance. Tristan pointed at his medallion, then gave his sister a knowing smile. Shailiha nodded and smiled in return.

Next to Shailiha sat Jessamay. Like the other mystics, the Vigors sorceress seemed tired. But Tristan knew that her fatigue came from her long hours of helping the Minions construct the new Black Ship cradles, rather than from conferring with her fellows in the craft.

On Tristan's immediate right sat Aeolus. The bald-headed mystic and *K'Shari* master sat peacefully, waiting for the meeting to start. He did not seem as tired as the other mystics. His years of martial training accounted for that, Tristan guessed.

Seeing Aeolus reminded Tristan of something, and he instinctively looked down at one of his upper arms, then the other. Like Wigg and Aeolus, Tristan bore the dual tattoos of Aeolus' martial schooling. And like Aeolus, Tristan commanded the gift of *K'Shari,* allowing him to gain total calm during battle—a priceless advantage to any warrior. Tristan had gained the gift of forestallment, immediately granting his endowed blood expertise in hundreds of martial techniques, many of which he had yet to realize. Although Aeolus had been working with him to bring them to the fore, they believed that Tristan had only scratched the surface of what he might ultimately attain. To the best of Tristan's knowledge, he and Aeolus were the only two people in the world who claimed the gift.

Tristan again regarded his tattoos. One was that of a serpent, indicating hand-to-hand combat mastery. The other was a sword, attesting to expertise with various weapons. He was proud of those two marks, and he knew that they would be with him until the day he died.

In the center of the table lay the Tome of the Paragon and the two Scrolls of the Ancients. The Scrolls were wound tight and secured at their centers with golden bands. Each relic still showed slight traces of azure subtle matter, reminding the prince of the other reason this meeting had been called. The rest of the room was littered with various scrolls and texts that had probably been taken from the still-disheveled Archives of the Redoubt and used in the mystics' research.

Curiously, Failee's centuries-old red leather tooled grimoire sat atop the table as well. It had been some time since Tristan had seen it, and he had to admit that he had nearly forgotten about it. Taken from the depths of the Recluse, the book was said to contain many of Failee's most secret spells, her private correspondence, and her personal memoirs. Tristan had no idea how much of the book Wigg had read, and out of respect for the wizard's feelings he had never asked. Even so, the grimoire's presence here today would surely serve some important purpose.

Feeling a pinch in his back, Tristan realized that he was still wearing his weapons. Unbuckling his baldric and knife quiver, he placed them over the back of his chair. The fire in the hearth across the room burned and snapped pleasantly, its comforting flames and pleasant odor belying the wizards' possibly dark pronouncements. Tyranny let go yet another lungful of smoke into the air; Jessamay poured herself a cup of Abbey's strong, dark tea.

Tristan looked first at Wigg, then at Faegan. "What have you learned?" he asked simply.

After scrubbing his face with his hands, Wigg tiredly leaned forward and placed his forearms on the table. He took another sip of Abbey's tea, then looked Tristan straight in the eyes.

"There is so much to tell that we scarcely know where to start," he said.

"Better too much than too little," Tristan answered. "I suggest that you start at the beginning, old friend."

Wigg nodded and sat back. "The terrible creatures that tortured and killed the people of Birmingham are called Blood Vipers," he began. "Like the Swamp Shrews that once tormented Parthalon, they serve but one purpose—exacting revenge. The formula for their conjuring was perfected by Failee late in the Sorceresses' War, when the defeat of the Coven was near. There are probably tens of thousands of Blood Vipers loose in Eutracia by this time. But unlike the leaderless Swamp Shrews, these creatures are commanded by a shrewd and cunning master. He is called the Viper Lord, and he will stop at nothing to wreak vengeance in Failee's name. He commands the craft in the name of the Vagaries."

"With all due respect, how can you know this?" Shailiha asked skeptically. "Surely you did not unearth all this information simply by examining the creature and the six corpses that Tyranny brought home."

"No," Wigg answered. "While Faegan was performing a necropsy on the blood viper, Aeolus, Abbey, and I searched the Tome and the Scrolls for information that might help us understand more. I soon wondered whether Failee's grimoire might shed some light on the mystery. I was right. Despite how well I thought I knew Failee, what I found there shocked me. When these secrets were coupled with Faegan's necropsy report, we had many of our answers. We then concentrated our efforts on researching the subtle matter and how we might cross the Azure Sea. Some of what we are about to tell you will seem incredible, but you must hear us out."

Intrigued, Tristan leaned forward. "Go on," he said.

"Failee's formula to conjure the Blood Vipers was found in her grimoire," Faegan answered. He paused to give Nicodemus another welcome scratch. "Even now we are just starting to understand how brilliant she was. Like the Swamp Shrews that she conjured to take revenge on innocent Parthalonians, she created the Blood Vipers to take revenge on Eutracians should she lose the Sorceresses' War. It was a part of her failed scorched-earth policy. But in several ways this plan was even more diabolical."

"How so?" Shailiha asked.

Faegan gave the princess a short smile. "The first difference should be obvious enough," he answered. "Unlike the leaderless shrews that appeared soon after her death, here in Eutracia the Blood Vipers came alive only after lying dormant for more than three centuries—long after the war had ended. One day not long ago they arose, and with them came their lord. They quickly started exacting vengeance in Failee's name, starting with the poor souls in Birmingham. Unless they are stopped, they might well kill every person in Eutracia."

Tristan rubbed his chin, thinking. "If the vipers and their lord were conjured by forestallment, there are two possibilities," he said. "Either some act triggered their coming, or they were brought alive after a certain amount of time had passed. Which was it?"

For the first time in several days, Wigg smiled. "Well done," he said to Tristan. "It was an event-activated forestallment. At first we couldn't be sure, but then I found something else in the grimoire that helped us deduce the answer." Another look of sadness overcame the wizard. "That, plus a few personal recollections from the distant past that I'd rather forget," he added softly.

Wigg reached across the table and took the red grimoire into his hands. As he did a pained expression came over his face, as if he wished that his explanation could be handled some other way. Tristan saw that a slim golden bookmark had been inserted between two of the grimoire's many gilt-edged pages. Wigg opened the book to the marked place, then ran a bony index finger down the two facing, wrinkled pages. After a time he found what he had been searching for, and he returned his attention to the group.

"Here is the forestallment formula that she devised to conjure and later summon the serpents," he said. "They were first conceived as embryonic beings, and she protected them with time enchantments so that they would not die as the years passed. These notes state that the embryos would be placed in a deep stream in Hartwick Wood. There they would lie in wait. The Viper Lord was also placed there, but in his already fully realized form. He too was protected by time enchantments." Closing the book, Wigg looked around the table.

"When some predetermined event finally occurred, the spell automatically took effect," he added. "The Blood Vipers appeared and their master rose with them. The grimoire also states that the Viper Lord was once a fully realized Vagaries wizard who served Failee in the war. In her notes she reveals no qualms about morphing him against his will into some kind of cross between a human being and a serpent. He might look much like the many creatures he commands. This was supposedly done so that the Viper Lord and his servants would feel like kindred spirits, bonding them to each other. She would then condemn him to the river along with her embryonic vipers. The notes go on to say that the mission of the Blood Vipers and the Viper Lord would be to search out all right-leaning endowed blood and destroy it. The plan's entire motive was vengeance, pure and simple."

Shailiha pursed her lips. "Much like the Blood Stalkers," she murmured.

"What was that?" Tristan asked.

Shailiha looked into her brother's eyes. "The Viper Lord is much like the Blood Stalkers that the Coven used during the Sorceresses' War," she answered. "The stalkers were morphed wizards, turned to Failee's purposes. They became partly human and partly . . . something else. They could also detect endowed blood, and like the Viper Lord they were used to hunt down and kill the Coven's enemies." She turned to look at Faegan. "I'm right, am I not?" she asked.

Faegan nodded. "But these new threats are even more dangerous," he added. "We believe that the Blood Vipers already far outnumber the late Blood Stalker ranks. Worse, they are commanded by a wizard—one who probably still commands the craft."

"Does the grimoire reveal this wizard's identity?" Tristan asked.

Aeolus turned toward Tristan. "Despite the many myths that have grown up over time about the Sorceresses' War, Failee had many wizards in her service," he answered. "The Viper Lord might be any one of them."

"Why do the Blood Vipers—or perhaps their lord—remove the livers from their victims?" Traax asked. "That makes no sense."

Tristan watched as Faegan reached into a pocket of his robe to produce a small rectangle of glass. The prince soon realized that there were in fact two pieces, with something red sandwiched between them. Faegan placed it on the table.

"I took this from between the teeth of the Blood Viper that Tyranny brought home," Faegan said.

"What is it?" Tyranny asked, taking another lungful of smoke and blowing it toward the ceiling.

Wigg scowled and waived a hand in her direction. "*Must* you practice that foul habit here?" he demanded.

Undaunted, Tyranny scowled right back at him. Clearly neither was in a mood to take orders from the other.

"No," she answered, "but I like it." Taking another pull on the cigarillo, this time she blatantly exhaled the smoke through her nose.

Wigg shook his head. "I'm too tired to argue about it," he said. "Pollute yourself with that stuff if you must. But at least allow an old wizard to breathe some clean air while you do it."

Wigg raised one arm and the gathering fog quickly disappeared. Tristan correctly guessed that each time Tyranny exhaled more smoke the same thing would happen. It seemed that the two intractable Conclave members had found a compromise. Tristan glanced over at Shailiha and winked. The princess smiled back. As Faegan let go a muted cackle, Tyranny sighed and shook her head.

Wigg cleared his throat. "That red bit taken from the Blood Viper's mouth came from a human liver," he continued. "It was no doubt part of one that was incised from one of the many Birmingham victims." He paused for a moment as he looked around the table. "Not only is the Viper Lord impaling his victims, his servants and perhaps even he himself are eating the excised livers."

For several long moments the room was silent. Shailiha could scarcely believe her ears, and she fought back the urge to become ill. After taking a quick sip of tea, she looked aghast at Tristan to see that her brother was equally stunned. She gazed back at Wigg with wide eyes.

"But *why?*" she breathed.

"I can answer that," Jessamay said. "During the Sorceresses' War many Vagaries practitioners believed that devouring the fresh liver of an endowed person immediately granted the eater greater power in the craft. This was never practiced among Vigors mystics, but it was common among our enemies. The Old Eutracian phrase for this selective form of cannibalism is known as *cannabae carnetorus,* or simply *carnetorus.*

Although the theory was never proved beyond a doubt, there is some lingering evidence indicating that it worked."

His mouth still agape, Tristan sat back in his chair. "I beg the Afterlife," he said. "But why eat only the liver?"

"Because the liver performs a unique function in the human body," Faegan answered. "All one's blood—be that blood endowed or unendowed—is filtered through it. The theory postulates that as this happens, certain aspects of endowed blood's power are continually left behind and trapped there. The lost power is later regenerated as it courses through the bloodstream and is again exposed to the Paragon—or so goes the theory. Vagaries practitioners believed that if the liver was eaten raw, these filtered bits of errant power could be taken as one's own. It logically follows that the higher the quality of the victim's blood, the greater the purloined power will supposedly be."

Pausing for a moment, Faegan thoughtfully pulled on his beard. "In truth, the idea is not as far-fetched as it sounds," he added quietly. "The entire notion of using the endowed blood of others for various reasons has teased both sides of the craft for centuries."

Tristan shook his head. "It's monstrous," he said softly.

"Yes," Aeolus replied. "Like so many Vagaries practices."

"Is it likely that the Viper Lord is also doing this?" Tyranny asked.

"Perhaps," Wigg answered. "But there is an even larger question that must be answered."

"And that is?" Jessamay asked.

"Whether the Viper Lord knows that Failee is dead," Wigg answered. "If he has somehow been informed, then what becomes of his mission? And if not, will he continue to ravage Eutracia in an effort to continue her revenge? My guess is that he will, because that is what Failee would have wanted. Only a Vagaries mystic of far greater power might induce him to stop. And as far as we know, no such persons remain on this side of the world."

Tristan reached out to pour a cup of tea. As he sipped it he could sense its stimulating effects take hold almost immediately. He nodded his appreciation to Abbey; the herbmistress nodded back.

Tristan put down his teacup. "Two things still need clarification," he said. "First, is there a spell of reversal in Failee's grimoire that might help us deal magically with these monsters and their lord? And second, do you have any idea what act initiated the forestallment allowing them to rise from the river?"

"The grimoire contains no reversal spell," Faegan answered sadly.

"And what act triggered the forestallment?" Abbey asked.

Wigg again reached out to take up the grimoire. *It is such a small book when compared to the Tome,* Tristan thought. *But its secrets can loom equally large.* He watched Wigg open the book to another page beyond where the golden bookmark lay. Wigg placed the opened book onto the table, then beckoned everyone to view its pages.

Tristan leaned forward and saw that the pages were written in green ink. He had seen the book only briefly when he, Wigg, and his late wife, Celeste, had first found it deep in the bowels of the Recluse, the Coven's onetime stronghold in Parthalon. Seeing it again reminded him of Failee's elegant handwriting. These pages held only handwritten text, seeming to suggest that Wigg had opened the book to the section that held the First Mistress's private memoirs.

Tristan again looked at the First Wizard's face and saw that the sadness had returned. Despite Failee's madness and her devotion to the Vagaries, Wigg had once loved her with all his heart. How much pain had it caused him, Tristan wondered, to have read these pages and to relive even so few moments from those terrible, heart-wrenching days?

Gathering himself up, Wigg pointed to a paragraph on the left-hand page. He cleared his throat.

"I will place the viper embryos and their morphed lord into a river flowing through Hartwick Wood," he quoted from the grimoire. *"And toward that river I will try and draw the bulk of the Directorate's forces. That is where I and my sisters will make our final stand. Should we lose and the river run red with Vagaries blood, I will know that I have failed. Then and only then will the Blood Vipers and the Viper Lord arise to take vengeance in my stead."*

"What does it mean?" Traax asked.

"Hartwick Wood was where Failee wanted to start her final push toward victory," Aeolus answered. "She needed the dense cover that the woods provide, and now we know that this other part of her plan was why she chose that place as well. But the Directorate didn't take the bait. We chose to meet her out in the open on the fields of Farplain. It would prove to be the largest battle of the war, and we won the day. Even so, it was not the final conflict."

"From what we have learned, it seems that endowed, left-leaning blood must somehow have entered the river that Failee mentions in her grimoire," Faegan said. "With no formula of reversal to neutralize it, the spell keeping the embryos and the Viper Lord alive survived to this day. We suspect that the amount of blood entering the river needn't have been large. In fact, the forestallment might have been activated by only a few random drops. We do not know whose blood it was or how it came to be in the river. In truth, we might never know. The blood might even have entered the water by accident rather than with malicious intent. We suspect that if Failee had been able to have her battle there, if she saw that it was going badly she would have released some of her own blood into the stream. Even if she had died, she would thus still have had her vengeance. After all these years the problem has become ours to deal with."

Thinking about Faegan's explanation, Tristan sat back in his chair. Failee's plan had been brilliant. It had finally been put into action, perhaps by one or more persons of endowed blood who had no idea of the ramifications of what he or she had done. Despite the many loose ends regarding all of this, one thing was certain. The rampaging monsters and their wizard lord had to be killed. And it must be done soon, before more Eutracians died and before the Viper Lord's depraved cannibalism perhaps increased his powers to such a degree that even the Conclave and the Minions could not overcome him.

Deciding to change the subject, Tristan momentarily shelved his concerns about the Blood Vipers. He gave Faegan a commanding look.

"What about the subtle matter?" he asked. "Do you have word about that as well?"

For the first time since the meeting started, Faegan smiled. Tristan knew that smile—it always appeared whenever the crippled wizard possessed a secret that others were eager to learn. Before answering, Faegan lifted Nicodemus from his lap and gently placed the cat on the floor, where he began affectionately winding his body and tail around Wigg's legs. The First Wizard scowled.

"What we have learned about subtle matter will surely amaze you— perhaps even more than did our news about the Blood Vipers," Faegan said, wiggling his eyebrows up and down for emphasis. "Prepare yourselves," he warned, "for the tale that you are about to hear astonished even us old wizards."

As Faegan talked, Tristan leaned forward, hungering for every word. In the end, the crippled wizard would be right.

CHAPTER XVI

MY WINGS ARE SO HEAVY, SIGRID THOUGHT. *HOW I WOULD love to give the order to land so that my warriors could rest and warm themselves beside a roaring fire. I have led this patrol for the last sixteen hours straight, and still we have not found the man-serpents. But we are Night Witches—we never surrender, we never give up. So I will lead my warriors onward until dawn. When the sun comes up, perhaps then we will have better luck finding the monsters that plague Eutracia.*

Banking to the west, Sigrid knew that she needn't confirm whether all her fellow Night Witches still followed her. They were among the best fliers that the Minion ranks had to offer, and each warrior's resolve and talents equaled her own.

Forming these special reconnaissance groups had been Commander Duvessa's idea, and the *Jin'Sai* had heartily approved. Three such groups existed, and the moment one group landed, another took flight. Each consisted of thirty female Minion warriors who had volunteered from Duvessa's elite fighting cadres. Specially trained in long-distance reconnaissance, the women had been chosen for their stamina, fighting skills, and sharp eyesight.

Since learning of the existence of Rustannica and Shashida, Tristan had used the Night Witches to check on Eutracia's far-flung borders should the *Pon Q'tar* mystics somehow find a way to cross the Tolenkas and attack Eutracia. News of the Night Witches' exploits traveled fast, and the patrol groups were quickly becoming legendary. Even the few remaining Minion males who stubbornly grumbled about fighting alongside females had been heard whispering that if something needed to be found, send a Night Witch to find it, for she would not come home empty-handed.

Sigrid was cold and nearly exhausted. She knew that the warriors following her would be equally spent. Closing her eyes for a moment, she did her best to stretch her tired back muscles as she pulled her strong wings through the air, then used her stiff fingers to clear the gathering frost from her face and eyelashes.

It is so cold at this altitude, she thought, shivering slightly. *But the higher we fly the farther we can see. If the man-serpents are ransacking another town, they might have set it ablaze as they did Birmingham. So it is the fires that we seek rather than the creatures themselves. At this altitude and in the dark of night, finding the man-serpents on the ground would be nearly impossible.*

She let go a quick smirk. *Even for Night Witches,* she realized.

At twenty-five Seasons of New Life, Sigrid was young to command one of the newly formed reconnaissance groups. That was partly because she was highly qualified and partly because of the high attrition rate suffered by the Minions in their service to the *Jin'Sai.* Although the warriors had fought well, their battles against Nicholas, Wulfgar, and Serena had taken a great toll. It would take many generations of peace to replace their numbers. And like many warriors, Sigrid believed that true peace would not prevail for a long time, if ever.

Duvessa formed the three groups because of her conviction that if Eutracia's borders and coastline could be better watched, future battle losses might be averted. She had never agreed with the Conclave that all the Vagaries threats east of the Tolenkas had likely been quashed. She had been saddened to learn of the man-serpents, even though their sudden appearance had proved her right.

Because the duty would be hazardous, Duvessa insisted that only unattached females from her fighting cadres be allowed to volunteer for the new units. After selecting and training the ninety women herself, she had conducted a short ceremony during which she awarded each new scout a pair of silver threaded wings to be sewn onto her body armor at the right shoulder. The women wore them with pride, and the approving glances that soon came from unattached male warriors had been a welcome side effect. Being a member of the Night Witches quickly became a great honor.

Sigrid smirked again as she remembered how the name "Night Witches" had come into being. They did not patrol only at night, but the name had stuck anyway. It was Traax who had unwittingly granted them the title. Sigrid and her group had just returned from a long night patrol to descend near the massive Minion camp lying just outside the palace walls. As it was tonight, the sky had been dark and cloudless and the patrol had been a long one.

Landing tiredly on the dewy grass, Sigrid and her group had looked around to see Duvessa and Traax standing nearby, waiting to perform a surprise dawn inspection on the unsuspecting camp. Traax had walked over to speak with Sigrid. Eager to hear how Sigrid would comport herself, Duvessa accompanied him. Despite their great fatigue, Sigrid and her warriors came to swift attention.

Traax walked up and down their lines, looking them over with a steely gaze. He finally stopped before Sigrid and stared into her dark eyes. As she had been trained to do when approached by a superior officer, Sigrid squared her shoulders and focused her attention on a spot somewhere just above Traax's left shoulder. As the Minion second in command admired the silvery wings embroidered into her leather body armor, Sigrid remained emotionless.

"Impressive," he said simply. He turned to look at his wife. "So this is what you've been doing with your spare time, eh?" he asked. He looked back at Sigrid. "How long was your patrol?"

Sigrid promptly clicked her heels together. "Twenty consecutive hours, my lord," she answered. "Nineteen of which were flown at an altitude of three thousand meters over the slopes of the Tolenka Mountains."

"Why do you fly so high?" he asked.

Sigrid was no fool. Traax was a member of the Conclave—he would already know the answer. Just the same, she was duty-bound to reply.

"Since learning of the nations west of the Tolenkas, the *Jin'Sai* wants us to be on guard against a Rustannican invasion force that might somehow cross over the mountains," Sigrid answered. "We patrol the coastline as well, searching for seaborne threats. Should we discover an incursion, flying high will grant us a broad view of the enemy force, allowing us to better gauge its size."

Taking another step forward, Traax raised an eyebrow. "Are you sure that you're not embellishing, subcommander?" he asked. "There is little breathable air at that height. So little, in fact, that I can think of few *male* warriors who can fly for so long at such altitudes. And we all know that our male warriors are stronger, wouldn't you agree?"

Sigrid immediately bristled at that remark, but aside from a slight narrowing of her eyes she didn't flinch. But she did break with protocol and look at Traax directly, putting him on notice. "It's the truth, my lord," she answered sternly. "If you would like to consult with any of my fliers to confirm our height and speed—"

Traax waved one hand. "That will not be necessary, subcommander," he answered. Then he grinned widely, telling her that he had only been teasing. *It seems that the Minion second in command is in a good mood this morning,* a relieved Sigrid thought. *Perhaps he hopes to catch some lazy warriors still sleeping in their cots after reveille has sounded . . .*

"I believe you," Traax added, placing a comforting hand on her shoulder. "Duvessa has told me all about your exploits. Well done. You and your sisters do a great service to the *Jin'Sai.*"

Traax turned to smile at his wife. "They are indeed as proud as you say," he offered. "And just as arrogant, I might add! Given the way that they can fly, perhaps they are all Night Witches!" He turned back to look at Sigrid. "You and your group get some rest," he ordered. "You've earned it."

Sigrid abruptly clicked her heels again. "Thank you, sir," she answered.

Just then everyone heard the camp bugler sound reveille. Turning away, Traax and Duvessa eagerly hurried through the encroaching sunrise to begin their surprise inspection. *They will be ruthless with anyone they find still asleep,* Sigrid thought. *Good. They need to be.*

Traax hadn't realized it, but every warrior in Sigrid's group had heard the name he had called them. And like all good names, this one stuck. By now many more females had offered to join the Night Witches and new patrol groups were being formed. But no matter how many Minion women joined, Sigrid would always be proud that she had been among the first. During the early days, Duvessa led this group; then she had promoted Sigrid to the rank of subcommander.

Banking south this night, Sigrid changed course again. This new line would take her patrol directly across the southern fields of Farplain, skirt the western boundaries of Shadowood, and return them to Tammerland. *It will be good to be home,* Sigrid thought. *I will grant each of my witches an extra ration of akulee for flying so well.* Her customary smirk emerged again. *I doubt that anyone will refuse,* she thought. *Not only can my witches fly and fight as well as most Minion males, they can outdrink some of them, too.*

Picking up the pace, she continued leading her group on this line for another quarter hour. Still she saw nothing unusual. *A quiet patrol,* she thought. Just then she saw an orange-red light twinkle against the dark ground some leagues ahead.

Narrowing her eyes, she pressed on harder, wondering whether she was seeing things. Sometimes at great altitudes Minion warriors imagined things that weren't there. Such false visions were usually depictions of things that they desperately wished to see, such as shimmering oases when the warriors were near death from thirst. When airborne, the warriors called such teasing phantoms "sky mirages," and they were known to be caused by prolonged exposure to the thin air found at high altitude.

Duvessa had taught the Night Witches well about sky mirages, for she too had experienced them. This would not be Sigrid's first encounter with the seductive apparitions. Because they were seen while airborne, sky mirages were more deadly than land mirages. They could cause the death of an unsuspecting warrior as surely as any weapon made of steel, and nearly as fast.

There was but one way to deal with these phantoms. Duvessa had taught them. You must dive as though your life depends on it. If not, you will suffer lightheadedness, followed by unconsciousness. The fall to earth will be a quick one, with little hope of recovery before the end comes.

Wasting no time, Sigrid snapped shut her wings and dived straight down. Every Minion knew that the quickest way to bleed off altitude was to perform a free fall. As she watched the dark earth come barreling toward her, each of her fellow Night Witches followed suit.

The cold wind was blinding at this speed, causing her eyes to water mercilessly. This made seeing the ground even more difficult, creating a special danger all its own. *"Watch carefully!"* she heard Duvessa's voice call out to her again. *"Pull up before you get too close! Only then will you know whether the image that you questioned was real or imaginary!"*

As the wind whipped by her and the air warmed, Sigrid's labored breathing eased. She strained to see the ground. Suddenly a treeline materialized out of the darkness, the tops of its branches approaching far too quickly.

She snapped open her wings and pulled up hard, as she had done so many times while training under Duvessa's watchful gaze. Missing the tops of the trees by only a few meters, she leveled off, then finally looked behind her. Seeing all twenty-nine of her Night Witches perform the same heart-stopping maneuver was always an impressive sight. Reaching up with one hand, she wiped the melted frost from her face and eyes, then swerved to change course again and she gained a bit more altitude. *Now we shall see,* she thought.

Several minutes later the mystery was partly answered when Sigrid smelled dark smoke, pungent and sickly sweet. Having already seen far too many Minion funeral pyres during her young life, she quickly recognized the telltale odor.

Suddenly another stand of very tall trees loomed up ahead, their black branches nearly indistinguishable from the dark blue sky. Pulling up hard, she narrowly missed them as they brushed against her body armor. Just then she again saw the orange-red glow, telling her that this had been no sky mirage after all.

Tanglewood was on fire.

Swooping lower, Sigrid waved one arm, signaling that she wanted her second in command to fly up alongside. Valda came quickly. She was a strong and especially brave Night Witch, and Sigrid trusted her with her life. Her hair was a lighter color than most. Like that of the other Night Witches, it had been tightly braided and tucked beneath her body armor so that it wouldn't harass her during flight.

"What are your orders?" Valda shouted.

Reaching to one hip, Sigrid unsheathed her dreggan. Even with the night wind whipping by, she could hear the blade briefly ring out as it cleared its scabbard. To a Minion warrior, that sound was always a comforting, exciting thing to hear. Immediately after, she heard another welcome sound as twenty-nine more dreggans simultaneously cleared their scabbards, their ring unmistakable. With the light of the three Eutracian moons highlighting her face, Sigrid turned to look at her number two warrior. The smile Valda saw was predatory.

"Take half the witches and start a search!" Sigrid shouted. "You curve to the east! I'll curve to the west! Take no direct action unless you are attacked! May the Afterlife be with you!"

Raising her free hand, Sigrid waved her fist first in one direction and then another, signaling that the force should divide into predetermined halves. Each Night Witch knew with which half she belonged, and the well-practiced maneuver was over almost as quickly as it started.

Sigrid looked over to see that Valda and her fourteen witches were gone. Then she quickly turned to look behind her. Those witches still following her were close behind, their dreggan blades shining in the moonlight. Her face grim, Sigrid led them directly over the heart of the city.

Most of the buildings had collapsed from fire. Black smoke and the sickening odor of burning flesh rose into the air, limiting the witches' ability to see and turning their stomachs. Soot soon darkened their faces, their body armor, and their weapons. Sigrid reached up to wipe it from her face, only to wonder a few seconds later whether the soot had once been part of a living human being. Hysterical men, women, and children ran everywhere at once, some of them bloodied and naked. The insane screams of the tortured and the dying seemed to fly alongside her through the smoky air.

It's like Birmingham all over again! she realized. *The man-serpents must be here—but where?*

Changing course, she led her witches toward the town square. Suddenly the grisly impalements came into view along with the thousands of horrific man-serpents and the human victims on whom they were doing their terrible work.

Sigrid clenched her jaw and tightened her grip on the dreggan. What was happening here easily rivaled the atrocities that the Minions had been ordered to commit against the helpless citizens of Parthalon when they served the iron will of the Coven. As in those terrible days, the brutality she saw this night was heinous, and total in its depravity. Then she saw a lone figure in a dark robe, standing in the center of the square. Swooping lower yet, she took her witches down for a better look.

The bloody square was something straight out of some madman's nightmare. Thousands of citizens had been impaled; in many cases their organs dangled from their ravaged bodies. Most looked dead, while others still writhed in agony, waiting for the reaper to come and gather up their souls. Swooping closer, Sigrid took a good look at the figure in the dark robe.

What she saw stunned her. The being's face wasn't quite human, nor could it be called fully reptilian. The tattered black robe that he wore spilled down over his wrists and boot tops. In one hand he held a silver staff.

He was surrounded by thousands of obedient man-serpents. The creatures listened intently as their master shouted out orders that Sigrid couldn't hear. It seemed that his servants were abandoning their grisly work. Coiled up on their tails and rearing into the air, ever more of them gathered around to hear their master's words.

That was when Sigrid realized that she had flown too low and had attracted the attention of several man-serpents. Hissing loudly, they pointed to the sky. Soon thousands of them were staring up and hissing viciously at the careening Night Witches. As Sigrid swooped by, she saw their master snap his head around and glare at her with his yellow reptilian eyes. To her surprise, he smiled.

Well aware that attacking would be suicide, Sigrid did her best to dig her wings into the night air and gain some altitude. Her fourteen Night Witches followed her, but not one of them knew that the Viper Lord commanded the craft. Realizing that he was seeing the *Jin'Sai*'s winged servants for the first time, Khristos eagerly raised his staff.

The azure bolt that soared skyward was unlike any that Sigrid and her brave Night Witches had ever seen. It pierced the dark night as a narrow beam and hurtled straight toward the center of their group. Then the bolt suddenly flattened out and exploded with an eardrum-shattering bang.

Eight of Sigrid's witches died immediately, their bodies, heads, and wings ripped apart by the bolt. Two more were burned beyond the ability to stay airborne, and they crashed to the bloody cobblestone square. The savage man-serpents set on them at once, tearing off their leather armor and ripping their bodies apart even before they could lift their heads. To the delight of their fellows, the creatures lifted the warriors' body parts high and paraded them about the square. Others writhed among themselves in orgiastic triumph.

Sigrid and the three remaining witches were burned but remained airborne. She immediately screamed out an order to head south, but even as the words left her mouth she realized that it was too late. Just as they started to turn, another azure bolt from Khristos' staff came tearing through the air.

The second bolt proved equally deadly. When it exploded, it killed Sigrid's three remaining witches immediately. This time Sigrid became showered with blood and bits of destroyed organs and bone. She survived only because her fellow witches had been behind her and their bodies had absorbed most of the blast.

Although she lived, Sigrid was shocked to the point that she could barely fly. Dazed and weakened, she too started tumbling down. Desperately trying to think, she groggily realized that she needed to break her fall. As she tried to straighten out her wings and regain control, the best that she could do was to head toward one of the few thatch-roofed buildings that wasn't ablaze. As she tumbled through the air she knew that the end was near.

Then from somewhere she heard Duvessa's stern voice counsel her again. *"You're a Night Witch!"* the voice said. *"Never give up—never surrender! Think! Do whatever you must to stay alive!"*

Summoning her strength, Sigrid snapped her wings closed to protect them. She then took her dreggan tightly into both hands and did her best to raise it over her head. Just before she crashed into the roof, she brought the razor-sharp blade down with everything she had left.

She felt the blade slice into the bundled straw and cut straight through a slender roof joist, clearing a path for her to fall through. Suddenly her dreggan struck against something hard and metallic, the blow resonating so strongly that the sword was knocked from her hand.

Amid a hail of dust and loose straw she tumbled end over end into the building. At the same time a great ringing sound suddenly tormented her ears as if she were standing in some great steeple and someone was madly ringing its bell. As she crashed into the room, two more resounding explosions came from overhead, combining with the mysterious clanging to create a deafening cacophony.

Tearing through the roof, she tumbled the rest of the way down to crash hard upon a wooden worktable. Like a dry twig being snapped in two, she heard as much as felt her left forearm break. Then the table collapsed under her weight and she smashed hard onto the stone floor. Her eyes closed and her head lolled over to one side. Some time passed; she would never know how much.

As she lay there, a dense fog seemed to surround her. Her body felt weightless, her mind without care. *Is this what it means to be dead?* she wondered. Her thoughts seemed forlorn and far away, like the plaintive cry of a lonely wolf. *Were those noises I heard the sacred death bells that our graybeards talk about when a valiant warrior dies in battle and goes to the Afterlife?*

Groaning, Sigrid opened her eyes. Lying on her back, she looked up to see the lifesaving cut she had made in the thatched roof. A dark patch of sky lay beyond, silently embracing its network of twinkling stars. Then the pain in her broken left arm reached out to bite her. She groaned again and used her good arm to cradle her bad one.

It seems I'm not dead after all, she realized. *But where am I?* Then her mind cleared and she remembered what had happened. Her blood ran cold as the deadly nature of her predicament set in.

Sitting up was a huge struggle; standing was an even greater one. She hobbled to lean against a wooden beam and took stock of herself. She hurt everywhere. Night Witch blood, bone, and flesh still clung to her skin and body armor. Her returning wheel remained fastened to her hip, but her dreggan was missing. Miraculously, only her left arm seemed to be broken. She could still fly, but fighting would prove difficult. Then she remembered the terrible man-serpents and their powerful master. She snapped her head around, all her senses on alert.

Why haven't they come for me? she wondered. *Perhaps the blinding light of the second explosion shielded my crash through the roof. If not, the terrible things will be on me in moments. But what caused all those awful clanging noises? Didn't the man-serpents hear them, or did the last two explosions mask them?*

Sigrid looked around to see her sword lying in the pool of moonlight filtering down through the hole in the roof. She hobbled toward it and picked it up. *At least I will die with a dreggan in my hand,* she thought. Then she looked around the room, and the reason for all the clanging noises became evident.

She had crashed straight through the thatched roof of a bellmaker's shop. Cast iron bells of all descriptions hung from the ceiling and from wooden crossbraces and lay scattered across numerous work tables. A hearth full of dwindling coals lay on one side of the room. A massive bellows stood beside it as if waiting for the bell master to return and use it to set the hearth glowing brightly again. More tables held variously sized bell knockers, casts, and odd bits of hardware. An old sign that had seen better days hung crookedly on one wall, reading "House of Ryburn and Sons, Bellsmiths."

Then Sigrid remembered her dreggan striking something hard after it sliced through the roof joist. *One of the bells,* she realized. A quick look at her sword showed that its blade was undamaged. *Bless our Minion swordsmiths,* she thought.

Suddenly she heard a sharp scream pierce the night. It seemed to come from the square. She turned in that direction to see a smashed-out window frame in the far wall, moonlight streaming through it onto the dirty floor. Cradling her left arm, she quietly crept toward the opening and peered outside. She soon discovered what was occupying the man-serpents' attention.

Eight of the brave Night Witches from Valda's group were being systematically impaled. Like Sigrid's group, the rest must have been killed while airborne. *That explains the last two explosions I heard,* she realized. In anguish, Sigrid watched the grisly process unfold. Tears formed in her eyes as her fellow Night Witches began dying one by one.

Tyra was the first to suffer. She was already stripped naked and standing before the serpent master. He seemed to regard her with particular interest—perhaps because he had never seen a Minion before, Sigrid supposed. Finally he seemed satisfied. He snapped his fingers and his servants began the grisly process.

As four of the awful creatures impaled Tyra she screamed insanely and fought back as best she could, but it was no use. Soon the hideous task was finished, and the lower end of the sharpened stake was pounded into the ground among the bloody cobblestones. Then the dark master walked toward Valda, the next Night Witch waiting in line. As he neared, she shouted out a Minion epithet, then spat in his face. Unperturbed, the serpent master nodded, and the process started anew.

Nearly insane with desperation, Sigrid grasped her dreggan handle so tightly that her knuckles went white. She tried to ignore Valda's screams, but it was no use. How she wanted to go charging into the square and somehow get close enough to the mysterious serpent master to cut him down! But she knew that would be suicide. Her chest heaving, she turned her back toward the wall and slid down it, squatting on her haunches. Placing the cool dreggan blade flat against her forehead, she closed her eyes.

Think! she ordered herself. *You're a Night Witch Commander! What will you do?*

Suddenly Duvessa's training returned. "*Always remember these words, Night Witches,*" she had warned them. "*Your first responsibility is to survey and report, regardless of the circumstances. Bring your precious information home at all costs. Worry not for your own life. Because you are a Minion, it ended the instant you were born.*"

Sigrid realized that she had to find a way to escape and get home. But that would mean leaving her sisters to their awful fates. *Can I really do it,* she wondered, *only to forever know that I abandoned them?*

She opened her eyes and looked around again. Perhaps there was another way out of the bell shop. If she could find it she might be able to take to the dark sky unnoticed. After several nerve-racking moments she saw a wooden door in the back wall. She looked again around the abandoned shop. What few exits she found were not promising.

There were few ways out. Using the front door or the smashed window frame was out of the question because each faced the square, and every other window was too small to crawl through. The gaping hole in the roof was a possibility, but she would need two uninjured arms to climb up and reach it. The only alternative was the far door, but she had no idea what horrors might lie beyond it.

Deciding that she had no other choice, she quietly crept for the far door. About halfway there she heard a strange tinkling that sounded like breaking glass. Holding her dreggan high, she swiveled around to look. Her blood ran cold.

One of the horrible man-serpents was slithering through the smashed window frame that she had just abandoned. Because the thing was about the size of a man, it barely fit through. As it came, bits of broken glass still lodged in the woodwork scratched at its body, became dislodged, and fell to the floor. Fully intent on squirming its way into the room, the monster hadn't seen Sigrid. Holding her dreggan high with her good arm, the Night Witch quietly retreated, melting into the shadows.

Using its strong arms, the monster finally forced its way into the room. It quietly dropped free of the window frame and started slithering across the floor. After traveling a few feet, it stopped. Coiling its spotted tail, the thing reared into the air, much like a Eutracian cobra just before it strikes. Its yellow eyes darted around the room. After letting go a soft hiss, the beast opened its mouth and its red, forked tongue slithered forth to test the dank air.

Sigrid held stock-still, waiting for her chance. *Can the thing smell me with its tongue?* she wondered. Despite the coolness of the night, sweat started beading on her forehead and her hands became slippery. As the awful thing hissed again and tested the air, Sigrid did her best to steel her resolve.

She considered running for the nearby door, but then she realized that it might be locked. She could probably smash the lock open with her dreggan, but she didn't know how fast the man-serpent was, and losing those precious seconds could kill her. And so she waited. *Come to me, you vile bastard,* she prayed. *Come to me and we will do this thing.*

Hissing loudly, the man-serpent started savagely ransacking the room. It seemed oblivious to the great ruckus it was making. Using its muscular arms it crazily scattered bells, threw hardware, and upended furniture as it scoured the place, searching for more Night Witches. Sigrid cringed as she begged that the clamor wouldn't attract more of the awful things into the shop.

She looked down at the returning wheel attached to her left hip. She was an expert at throwing the wheel—some said that she ranked among the best. In these close quarters, missing was almost unthinkable. If she launched the wheel at the beast from the darkness of her hiding place, the thing would never know what hit it. Given all the noise the beast was making, even if the wheel sliced straight through it and struck one of the interior walls, the crash would surely mix with the ongoing clamor. But if she was going to do it, it must happen before the awful thing stopped rummaging about. She desperately needed to escape, and time was fleeting.

Silently sheathing her sword, she reached down to her left hip and freed the shiny, saw-toothed wheel from its carrying place. Raising it high, she drew it back over her left shoulder, coiled the muscles in her throwing arm, and waited. The beast was still rifling through the shop, angrily scattering things and turning over furniture with abandon. *Just a little closer,* she silently pleaded.

As though it had read her thoughts, the man-serpent suddenly stopped to listen. When it heard nothing, it used its long tail to propel it nearer the center of the room, scattering more objects as it went. Sigrid tried to calm her heartbeat, but suddenly her broken left arm shouted at her again, making her wince. Steadying herself once more, she watched the awful thing come nearer.

That's right, she begged silently as the thing slithered closer yet. The red tongue appeared again to quickly taste the air, then disappeared back into the grotesque mouth.

Come to me, Sigrid thought. *Come closer and taste my sharp surprise.*

Still the monster neared. The time had come.

Throwing the wheel with everything she had, Sigrid held her breath and watched it go spinning across the room.

The monster's reflexes were amazing. As the throwing wheel flashed through the beam of moonlight shining down through the hole in the roof, the beast moved with unheard-of speed and dropped straight to the floor. Sigrid watched in horror as her wheel flew harmlessly above the beast only to bury itself in the far wall.

Knowing that she had no other choice, the night witch drew her dreggan and quietly stepped from the shadows. Hearing Sigrid's blade ring out, the monster snapped its head around and let go a vicious hiss. It quickly coiled upright again, its yellow eyes flashing greedily as they finally sighted their prey. Without hesitation it reared back, then launched straight for her.

As the creature sped near, Sigrid swung her dreggan in a flat arc, hoping to separate the monster's head from its body with one swing. But again the man-serpent was too fast.

The beast deftly sideslipped the blow, and the dreggan severed nothing but air. Before Sigrid could summon another swing, the monster dropped flat to the floor again, this time raising its powerful tail. The tail cracked through the air like a bullwhip, its far end wrapping tightly around the hilt of Sigrid's dreggan. The beast quickly snapped its tail again, ripping the sword from Sigrid's grip and sending it flying across the room.

The precious dreggan skidded across the floor and disappeared into the shadows, putting the man-serpent squarely between Sigrid and her fallen weapon. The Night Witch nearly panicked as she realized that her sword might as well be ten leagues away for all the good it did her now.

As the beast hissed and glared at her, Sigrid quickly reached down to unsheathe her Minion dagger, but it wasn't there. She had no time to mourn the loss, for the terrible creature suddenly launched itself at her again. Sure that she was about to die, Sigrid charged forward to meet it.

As the two enemies clashed in the center of the room, the monster swiftly took each of Sigrid's wrists into his hands. The pain in her broken left arm lashed out and Sigrid screamed, exposing her injury. Seizing on its unexpected advantage, the monster let go of her right wrist while tightening his grip on her left one. Screaming again, Sigrid had no choice but to drop to her knees.

Helpless, she watched the awful thing move its face near hers. The terrible mouth opened again. Sigrid tried to turn away as the monster sent its tongue sliding over first one of her cheeks and then the other, exploring them, tasting them. Finally the awful tongue retreated into the waiting mouth.

Knowing that Sigrid was beaten, the thing finally let go. Pointing to the front door of the shop, it hissed again. There could be no question about what it wanted, Sigrid realized. She was to leave the shop as his prisoner. Like Valda and the other Night Witches, she would soon be impaled at the viper master's pleasure.

There was only one more weapon available to her. It was one that all Minions were born with, one that they carried forever after, and one that Sigrid knew how to use with deadly expertise. It was her last hope, but she was too close to the beast to use it. Everything depended on her gaining some distance from the monster, and the timing had to be perfect.

She nodded submissively, suggesting her surrender. The monster smiled and pointed toward the door, silently ordering her to go first. Clearly he had no intention of turning his back on her. Putting on her best look of defeat, Sigrid shuffled past the beast, then quickly put some precious distance between them. The man-serpent hadn't counted on her marching to her death so quickly, and that was just what Sigrid had hoped.

When she was about two meters away she abruptly stopped, then turned to the right, placing her at right angles with her captor. Summoning every bit of strength remaining, she snapped open her right wing.

The man-serpent never saw it coming. As Sigrid's wing flew open, its hard-boned leading edge caught the monster directly across the throat. At first the thing just stood there, gasping and retching. Sigrid immediately retracted her wing and repeated the blow. This time it struck the beast in the forehead. As the light went out of its eyes, its neck made a cracking sound. The thing's head fell rearward to dangle at an unnatural angle. Then the man-serpent collapsed like a house of cards, dead before it hit the floor.

Cradling her left arm, Sigrid hurried for the rear door. Hoping against hope, she grasped the rusty door handle and gave it a turn. Blessedly, it opened.

The alleyway beyond was dark, dirty, and deserted. Wasting no time, Sigrid ran a few quick steps, then did her best to launch into the air. Her left arm didn't matter—nothing did, save for getting away. As she struggled to gain altitude she heard another of her Night Witches scream out.

As she curved her way south toward Tammerland, this time her watery eyes were not caused by the passing wind.

CHAPTER XVII

AFTER TAKING A SIP OF ABBEY'S ROBUST TEA, TYRANNY stabbed another cigarillo between her lips and lit it with a match. The Conclave meeting had been going on for some time and she doubted that it would conclude soon. As she casually blew the smoke out her nose, she turned her skeptical gaze toward Faegan.

"We're listening," she said drily. "By all means, amaze us with your acumen."

Tristan smiled. He knew that Tyranny's sarcasm was in jest. But like Tristan, she accepted nothing on faith, and she was quite comfortable with challenging the Conclave mystics and their theories.

Faegan let go a little laugh. "Very well," he answered quietly. "I will try to do that very thing."

Pushing away from the table, he wheeled across the room to a mahogany cabinet. He opened one of the cabinet doors and produced a cylindrical object. Cradling it in his lap, he returned to his place, then gently set the strange item on the table for everyone to see.

Tristan leaned forward to look. The glass jar was about a foot high and six inches in diameter. Its top was sealed with red wax, and it was nearly filled to the brim with subtle matter. The flickering firelight seemed to bring the microscopic bits to life. *Such a wondrous and beauti-*

ful thing, he thought. *I suspect that my venerable mystics have yet to unravel all its secrets.*

Faegan pointed at the jar. "As best we know, this is all the subtle matter that exists on our side of the world," he said. "There is no known way to produce more. But we have learned a little about how to use it."

"This is the same material that formed the maps of Rustannica and Shashida, and the formulas and the written words that hovered below them," Shailiha mused. "How did it get into the jar?"

"After the rest of you left the room, Wigg and I stayed behind talking," Faegan answered. "To our surprise, something else started happening. For the last three days we have done little but try to unravel its secrets. We have made some meager progress, but there are many more riddles about subtle matter that are far from solved. But one use for the amazing substance has come to light."

"And what is that?" Traax asked.

Wigg leaned forward over the tabletop. "A way to help us cross the Azure Sea," he answered.

The room went silent. It seemed that no one wanted to ask the obvious question for fear that doing so might make the answer disappear. Finally Tristan placed one hand atop Wigg's.

"Tell us," he said softly.

Wigg pointed at the glass jar, causing it to slide toward him. He picked it up and regarded it with great reverence. Then he looked over at the *Jin'Sai.*

"Before now, we believed that only three things could truly employ the power of the craft," he said. "Can you name them?"

"Certainly," Tristan answered. He looked at the jewel dangling against Wigg's chest. "One is the Paragon."

"And the others?" the First Wizard asked.

"Endowed blood and the red waters of the Caves," Tristan answered.

Wigg gently placed the jar back atop the table. "Correct," he said. "Our recent discovery of subtle matter makes four such things. These are indeed days of great importance in our understanding of the craft. But subtle matter holds rare properties that even the Paragon, endowed blood, and cave water do not."

"What do you mean?" Shailiha asked.

"As you already know, the Paragon and endowed blood are tools by which the power of the Vigors and the Vagaries are made available for certain human beings to use," Jessamay said. "This power comes from the two opposing orbs. But even the Paragon and endowed blood are mere conduits. Simply put, subtle matter is a unique form of pure magic that has been captured rather than simply empowered. Normally we do not see the magic itself, only its results. But this is magic that can be literally held in one's hand. The treatise confirmed our suspicion that it is the light of an azure bolt, changed into a different physical form. It is no oversimplification to say that if there is such a thing as enchanted dust, this is it."

Tristan again stared at the mysterious powder. *How incongruous,* he thought. *So powerful a substance, trapped inside such a fragile vessel.* He looked back at Wigg. "Is it alive like endowed blood?" he asked.

Faegan shook his head. "No," he answered. Then he thoughtfully tugged on his beard, thinking. "Or perhaps I should say that it is not 'alive' by any definition of the word that we understand," he added. "We now command one of its uses, but most of the others still escape us."

"How did it become trapped in the jar?" Shailiha asked. "Was that the strange happening that you referred to?"

Wigg nodded. "Faegan and I watched in horror as the subtle matter unexpectedly scattered, breaking apart the map, the associated formulas, and the treatise. The subtle matter then coalesced into a cloud and began careening around the room. At first we couldn't imagine why. Was it about to form another message, perhaps? The longer it flew about, the more it seemed to be searching for something. When it found what it wanted, we got our answer."

"And what was that?" Tristan asked.

"It needed a resting place," Wigg answered. "When it neared this ordinary glass jar sitting atop one of the Archives shelves, the jar magically emptied. It previously held several scrolls of small importance. As the scrolls drifted to the floor, the subtle matter immediately flew inside. The red wax seal formed immediately after." Wigg raised an eyebrow. "It was an interesting process to behold," he added. Wigg's talent for understatement was far from lost on him, the prince smiled.

"What then?" Traax asked. "How did you come by all this newfound knowledge?"

"Part of the information hovering below the map was a craft treatise written by the Ones," Faegan answered. "My guess is that it only scratches the surface of this particular discipline. Only a few uses for subtle matter were shown. No doubt the Ones wished that the entire discipline not be given away for fear that the Tome and the two Scrolls—the relics from which all this new information was so recently gleaned—had simultaneously fallen into the wrong hands. The information is sparse, and because the Tome and the two Scrolls were its originating source, it is aeons old. Because so much time has passed since the writing of the Tome and the two Scrolls, there is simply no telling how much farther the Ones have advanced the craft. Despite what we consider to be the treatise's supreme complexity, for the Ones it might be little more than some schoolchild's lesson. It was written in a complicated dialect of Old Eutracian that we have yet to completely decipher. But we have learned enough to know that it was a short discourse in several uses of subtle matter."

"And because the subtle matter swirled its way into that jar, whatever hasn't already been learned is lost forever," Traax lamented.

Aeolus let go a soft cackle. "You're forgetting something, my winged friend," he said. "True, the message that the subtle matter briefly formed has been disassembled and transferred to that jar. But Faegan read it first! And in its entirety, I might add! Remember, he commands the gift of Consummate Recollection. The message is gone, but it will never be forgotten. Because of its highly important nature, Faegan recorded the entire treatise on parchment. He has done the same with the formulas and with the map of the territories west of the Tolenkas. Each document rests safe under lock and key in the Archives. Along with the Tome and the two Scrolls of the Ancients, I daresay that they rank among the Redoubt's greatest treasures."

Impressed, Traax glanced at Faegan. The crippled wizard's only response was to smile and bounce his bushy eyebrows up and down.

"I'm confused," Abbey said. "How can subtle matter help us to cross the Azure Sea?"

Cackling again, Faegan jabbed a bony index finger into the air. "How indeed?" he asked. "Allow me to perform a brief demonstration."

Looking around the room, Faegan spied an unlit oil lamp resting on a nearby bookshelf. With a wave of his hand the lamp lifted into the air and came to land atop the meeting table. Then he commanded the jar full of subtle matter to slide toward him.

Faegan pointed his index finger at the wax seal. It soon disappeared, leaving the jar open at the top. Beckoning with the same finger, he caused some of the microscopic bits to leave the jar and float into the air. The individual particles were so tiny and few that had they not twinkled, the Conclave members would not have seen them. Faegan moved his finger again, causing the tiny particles to hover directly over the oil lamp. He placed his hands flat on the tabletop.

"Observe," he said quietly. The wizard closed his eyes and called on one of the spells found in the treatise.

Tristan watched as the twinkling bits of dust descended toward the oil lamp. At first nothing happened. Then the twinkling stopped and the entire lamp started to glow. Tense seconds passed. Tristan's mouth soon fell open with astonishment.

The oil lamp was shrinking.

Smaller and smaller it became until it was no larger than a thimble. As the lamp stopped glowing, a hush fell over the room.

His mouth still agape, Tristan looked first at Faegan, then at Shailiha. Faegan only smiled. The stunned look on Shailiha's face mirrored her brother's.

Tristan finally found his voice. "I beg the Afterlife . . ." he breathed.

"Oh, this has little to do with the Afterlife," Faegan exclaimed, laughing.

Lacing his fingers together, Wigg leaned nearer. "Faegan is right," he said softly. "The act of the craft that you just saw was true miniaturization. We mystics have long thought it possible, but until now it was quite beyond our knowledge."

"Is the oil lamp the same in every respect save for its size?" Tyranny asked. She was still so amazed that she could barely speak.

"Yes," Aeolus answered, "except for its weight. That property is now also reduced to a level commensurate with the lamp's new size."

As though still unable to believe, Shailiha leaned forward to touch the shrunken lamp. As she did, Faegan gave Tristan a knowing wink. Just as Shailiha's fingertip touched the lamp, Faegan used the craft to set the lamp's tiny wick alight. Jumping back, Shailiha let go a little shriek. As the other Conclave members laughed, Shailiha's face reddened briefly.

Faegan reached out to pat her hand. "I'm sorry, Princess," he said, "but I just couldn't resist. As Aeolus said, save for its reduced weight and size, the lamp is the same in every respect." He gave her a quick wink. "It can even produce light."

Tristan's thoughts soon returned to Abbey's earlier question. He looked over at the First Wizard. "This is all very interesting, but how does it help us to cross the Azure Sea?" he asked.

Faegan gave him a little smile. "Can't you guess?" he asked.

Tristan shook his head. He clearly remembered the Azure Sea. It was a vast, beautiful, and most likely very dangerous place. *I can imagine only one way to cross it,* he thought. *But we can't do that because . . .* Suddenly understanding, he looked at Faegan as if the wizard had just gone mad.

"You must be joking," he whispered.

"Oh?" Wigg countered. "And why is that?"

"You can't do it, that's all!" Tristan protested. "It would never work!"

"And just why not?" Aeolus countered. "After all, you saw what happened to the lamp."

"But to shrink them to such a small size—could it really be done?" Tristan asked.

"Perhaps," Jessamay said. "But the process wouldn't be without its problems, nor would the ensuing journey."

"What are you talking about?" Tyranny demanded.

Shaking his head, Tristan gave the Conclave privateer a look that said he was still stunned. "They mean to shrink the Black Ships to a size that can be carried into the Caves of the Paragon," he said, hardly believing his own words. "We would then transport them to the shore of the Azure Sea—presuming that we can find it again. The vessels would be placed onto the water and set adrift. From there I can only guess that more subtle matter would be used to restore them to their original size."

He turned to glare at Wigg. "Could such a thing really work?"

"Perhaps," Wigg answered. "Unless we try, we might never reach Shashida. Remember, the Tolenkas cannot be crossed—even by the Ones and the *Pon Q'tar.* Sailing north or south on the Sea of Whispers will only bring us up against dangerous ice packs. We know—it was tried many times during the Sorceresses' War while attempting to outflank the Coven's forces. We could fly the ships over the ice, but for how long? That too has been tried without success. Worse yet, going in either of those directions might take us farther away from Shashida rather than toward it. Of even greater importance is the message formed by the subtle matter. 'To reach Shashida you must first cross the Azure Sea.' It seems that we might have found a way after all."

Wigg again raised an eyebrow. "Unless you know more about this than the Ones, and you can imagine a better way to do the same thing," he added drily.

Tristan let go a deep breath and sat back in his chair. He still couldn't believe that he and his fellow Conclave members were sitting around a table and talking about such a bizarre thing. As the notion settled in, he looked back at Wigg.

"How would we proceed?" he asked.

"First let me show you something else," Faegan said. The wizard closed his eyes. A few more subtle matter bits freed themselves from the jar to land atop the lamp. Soon the shrunken lamp glowed again. Then it started to grow. On reaching its original size, it stopped. The lamp was again itself in every respect. Even its restored wick was still alight.

Faegan sat back in his chair. "We had to know whether the process could be reversed. As you have just seen, that is the case. But major hurdles remain."

"What hurdles?" Shailiha asked.

"Many, I'm afraid," Aeolus answered. "First, our supply of subtle matter is finite and we have no way to produce more. We do not yet know whether there is enough to do the job. We cannot use more than one-fourth of it to shrink the four ships."

"Why?" Tristan asked.

"Because an equal amount will be needed to return the ships to their original size atop the Azure Sea," Aeolus answered. "If we find Shashida and return, more will be needed to shrink them again to take them from the Caves and yet more to return them to their normal size—unless we decide to moor them on the Azure Sea and leave them there. Without enough subtle matter, the ships will never return home. Before we make our first attempt we must calculate how much subtle matter is needed to perform each transformation. We simply can't afford to waste any."

"There are other concerns as well," Jessamay said. "The ships must be free of all crew members before the process starts, because we cannot know what effect the subtle matter might have on living things. Conversely, the ships must be fully loaded and as totally prepared as possible for a voyage of undetermined length. We cannot know how far our journey might take us or what we will face on the way. We will be literally sailing into the unknown. Moreover, we are assuming that the ships' cargoes will shrink inside them. If not, the cargoes will be crushed or the ships' hulls damaged. It is obvious that we must understand all these things before we dare to take the ships into the Caves."

"But damage to the ships or their outright loss might not be as catastrophic as it first sounds," Faegan said. "As you know, Wigg finally found the ships' long-lost plans. If need be, another fleet might be built. It might take years, but it could be done. Because the cost and manpower needed would be enormous, if the four Black Ships that currently serve us can be safeguarded, we must make every attempt to do so. We will therefore try to supply and transform one ship first, rather than all at once."

"And despite these obstacles you believe that the basic theory is sound?" Tristan asked.

"Yes," Wigg answered. "What works for an object like that lamp should work for any object, regardless of its size or weight. It seems that the only limiting factor will be our finite supply of subtle matter."

"How will you compute the amount needed?" Tristan asked. "It seems impossible."

"It won't be as difficult as you think," Aeolus answered. "From the original plans we already know how much a Black Ship weighs unloaded. The tricky part will be estimating the cargoes." He turned to look at Traax.

"That's where you and your warriors come in," he said. "You will fill one of the ships to the rafters with supplies and arms. As you do, weigh and list each item that is taken aboard and compile a total sum. We will then add that number to the empty weight of the ship to arrive at a total."

"And then?" Tristan asked.

"The treatise states how much subtle matter is needed to miniaturize one pound of given material," Faegan answered. "From there we will formulate our calculations. We need enough subtle matter to perform sixteen such transformations, or four times per vessel. If we have enough, after Jessamay brings the fleet home and the ships are resting comfortably in their new cradles, we will empty the ships of their crews, load them, and try our first transformation. If it works, identical cargoes will be loaded onto the other ships and we will then miniaturize them as well."

Tyranny gave Faegan another skeptical look. She never liked having "her" ships tampered with, to say nothing of this new madness that the mystics were proposing. Overwhelmed by what she was hearing, she tousled her urchinlike hair.

"To what degree will you shrink the ships?" she demanded. Then she scowled and shook her head—she still couldn't believe that she was asking such a thing.

"That is of critical concern," Faegan answered. "The smaller the object is to become, the more subtle matter is needed. To put it simply, we will shrink the ships at least to a size that fits through the opening to the Caves. As each ship shrinks, so too should its cradle. Each ship and cradle will be packed into a crate for safekeeping and carried to the Azure Sea by Minion warriors. They should be able to handle the loads, because as each ship shrinks, its weight becomes commensurate with its decreased size. If the warriors cannot easily carry them, we can help them with the craft."

Tristan reached for his cup and poured some more tea. After a time he shook his head, thinking.

Can such a thing work? he wondered. *If such learned mystics as Faegan, Wigg, Aeolus, and Jessamay believe so, then it must be possible. After all, the oil lamp shrank before my eyes. But a simple oil lamp and a massive Black Ship are very different things.* After taking another sip of tea he placed the cup back atop its saucer. *I'll believe it when I see it,* he thought.

"Assuming for the moment that we are able to miniaturize the ships, some crucial decisions must be made," Wigg said. Reaching out, he took Abbey by the hand. The look on the First Wizard's face had again become somber.

"Only certain Conclave members should make the voyage," he added, "because some must remain behind to deal with the Viper Lord and his servants. Deciding who goes will not be easy. For some it will mean staying behind to wonder whether their loved ones will ever return. For others it will mean sailing off into the unknown, perhaps to their deaths. Who goes and who stays will be of prime importance, not only to reach Shashida but to protect Eutracia as well. The goals are equally important. In any event, one thing is certain."

"What is that?" Shailiha asked.

"Regardless of what the other Conclave members do, Tristan must lead the voyage. And you must remain here, Princess," Wigg answered.

"Why?" Tristan asked.

Faegan leaned forward. Like Wigg, his expression had turned gravely serious.

"There are several reasons," he said. "First, we know nothing about the Azure Sea or about what dangers it might hold. There is a great chance that whoever goes on this voyage will not survive it. If you and your sister die, the world will lose both the Chosen Ones. We cannot allow that to happen."

"Moreover, you are the *Jin'Sai,*" Wigg added. "The Tome clearly states that it will be you who must first try to fulfill your and Shailiha's mutual destinies. The Envoys of Crysenium stated that it should be you who first returns to the other side of the world, not your sister. We believe that the late Envoys' wishes should be respected. Regardless of who else goes, you should lead the voyage and Shailiha should remain here."

As usual, Wigg's logic was irrefutable. Hoping that his sister hadn't been hurt by the news, Tristan looked over and took one of her hands into his. "I'm sorry," he said, "but Wigg is right. Will it disappoint you to stay behind?"

Before Shailiha could answer, Faegan spoke up. "Do not worry, Princess," he said. "Your mission will have equal importance with your brother's. You must command the Conclave in its war against the Viper Lord. We mystics fear that the struggle will be far larger and deadlier than you might suppose. Failee's ancient servant will not be easily defeated. Unless we win, Eutracia could perish, leaving Tristan and his group no one to come home to."

Understanding, Shailiha gave her brother's hand a squeeze. "It seems that we each have our work cut out for us," she said. "Just promise me one thing."

"Anything," Tristan answered.

The princess put on her best look of mock ferocity. "Just come home in one piece," she ordered. "I've gotten rather used to having you around."

Tristan smiled at her. Just as he was about to respond, an urgent pounding came on the meeting room door. "Enter!" Tristan shouted.

The door blew open to show Ox standing there. His chest was heaving and his face showed deep concern. Crossing the threshold, he hurried into the room.

Tristan stood from his chair. "What is it?" he demanded.

"Pardon, but one Night Witch patrol find man-snakes and their leader," the warrior said. "Sigrid only one to survive. She hurt but Duvessa say she will be all right. All other Night Witches impaled. Sigrid say Tanglewood nearly all destroyed by fire and most people there dead." As the massive warrior did his best to tell the tragic tale, Tristan could see the hatred building in his eyes.

"Ox want to kill all man-snakes," he said, his voice lowering to nearly a whisper. "Will *Jin'Sai* come and lead us?"

Tristan looked around the meeting table, then into his sister's eyes. *I will start this fight,* he thought. *But if I sail for Shashida, Shailiha must finish it.* As if she were reading her brother's mind, the princess nodded. He grimly nodded back.

The war against Failee's Viper Lord is beginning, Tristan realized. *May the Afterlife protect us.*

CHAPTER XVIII

IT IS HOT AGAIN TODAY, VESPASIAN THOUGHT, AS HE STARED out over the massive, bloodthirsty crowd. It was barely midday and already the huge red canopies had been stretched over the arena, shielding the spectators from the sun. After taking a sip of wine, the emperor again looked down at the carnage.

So many skeens, centurions, and wild animals had already been killed that one couldn't tell whether the sandy coliseum floor was bathed in blood or simply tinted by the sunlight filtering down through the red canopies. Scattered limbs, bodies, and organs lay partly submerged in the sand like bizarre islands in a sea of blood. Shattered chariots and smashed carriages lay about as though they had been tossed there by giants. Dead and dying horses, wild beasts, and weapons of all types could be seen by the hundreds.

And yet the first act has not concluded, Vespasian thought. The games had been going on for four hours, but even now the first group of hard-fighting skeens continued to resist.

The emperor turned to look at Persephone. Sensing his gaze, she returned his glance and smiled. She looked splendid in a yellow silk gown and delicate gold jewelry. Vespasian reached out to grasp her hand. Despite the ongoing spectacle, for a moment her easy smile made it seem as if the insane world inside the coliseum didn't exist.

She is so beautiful, he thought. *And I love her beyond words. Surely she is the best part of me.* After taking another sip of wine, Vespasian returned his attention to the games.

This was the seventh day of what would soon become nearly a fortnight of death and mayhem taking place on the coliseum floor. Thousands of skeens and centurions and a host of wild animals had already perished for the amusement of the crowd. Every day seemed to bring with it some higher form of savage cruelty. Surprisingly, the unprecedented games had produced another effect besides delighting the mob. Because he had personally ordered these games, Vespasian's already great popularity had risen even higher. Moreover, his newly proclaimed campaign against Shashida and his announcement of the successful auspicium had also added to his charisma.

Graffiti had sprung up throughout Ellistium providing adoring testament to the emperor's bravery, his vision, his amazing ability to use the craft. Heralds had taken to writing their own scripts that proclaimed Vespasian's magnificence, and they were brazenly reading them aloud from their citywide towers. Young men—each one suddenly eager to become a part of their emperor's new campaign—were joining the legions in record numbers. For the first time in decades the mood sweeping over Ellistium was wildly joyful. From the most august krithian all the way down to the lowliest phrygian tradesman, each believed that his august emperor could do no wrong.

Vespasian looked around his viewing box. As usual, the *Pon Q'tar* clerics were in attendance, as were the maidens of the Priory of Virtue. But Lucius and the other Tribunes were absent, readying their mighty legions for the new campaign. Those forces of the Imperial Order that were afield had been sent new directives telling them to withdraw from their current struggles and to turn north toward home. Vespasian realized that an order of that magnitude would surely alert the Shashidan Ones that something was brewing, but that couldn't be helped.

When the forces stationed in the capital were ready, they would move south to join their brothers. There they would regroup and head toward Shashidan territory. While the barges sailed south on the six rivers, the legions would curve around from the west and east, devouring Shashidan towns and armies while approaching the mines in a gigantic pincer movement. One week from now the capital troops would be ready to depart Ellistium. Once they joined their fellows, the combined invasion force would dwarf any in Rustannican history.

Hearing the crowd roar again, Vespasian looked back down at the grisly spectacle. The combatants were reenacting the Rustannican victory at Messalina, a city that had been lost to the Shashidans three centuries ago and then retaken in one of the bloodiest and most protracted battles ever fought in the War of Attrition. Reenacting Rustannican victories was something that the mob especially relished. Although no details about the new campaign would be made public, its impending start was reason enough for the crowd to revel even more joyfully than usual in today's retelling of a Rustannican military triumph.

Vespasian watched as the Gates of Life swung open. Another ten chariots bearing three tribunes each raced into the arena to go charging toward the Shashidan skeens still alive on the sandy floor. Each chariot held a driver, an archer, and a lance thrower, every man an expert in his field.

Of the one thousand skeens that had been shoved into the arena at the start of the day, only thirty remained standing. Most of them were bloodied and broken, and Vespasian doubted that they would survive this fresh onslaught by the tribune charioteers. Even so, he reminded himself that he could be proved wrong. The surviving skeens were clever and battle-hardened, and like all Vigors worshippers they would fight to the death. The crowd knew this and reveled in it. Chanting and stamping, they watched breathlessly as the ten chariots thundered in.

Unlike other spectacles, battle reenactments were staged affairs that more or less accurately portrayed famous Rustannican military victories. With help from the craft, the entire coliseum floor could be flooded, allowing mock warships to actually fight and sail atop the waves. Reenacted sea battles were especially popular, and sometimes the small ocean entrapped within the arena walls was filled with sharks and other man-eating creatures, adding a brief but grisly flavor of unpredictability.

Although their outcomes were a certainty, these reenacted battles were not entirely without a twisted brand of fairness. The Games Master was always careful to set equal numbers of centurions and skeens against each other. No craft use was allowed by the centurions, because all Shashidan skeens had been stripped of their power to use magic. The skeens were well armed and given various forms of terrain that they could use as cover. Beasts were often conjured from the mosaics adorning the arena walls to threaten and kill centurions and skeens alike, adding another unpredictable facet to the spectacle. The skeens were even granted food and water so that their strength would not falter and anger the crowd.

Because the battle to retake Messalina had been fought in rugged terrain, a miniature mountain had been constructed of wood, painted gray, and placed in the center of the arena floor. Measuring nearly fifty meters across and nearly as high, during the previous night it had been brought piece by piece into the arena, where it was painstakingly rebuilt. Complete with rocks and foliage, from a distance the small mountain looked amazingly genuine. Wild man-eating animals that had been starved nearly to death roamed the entire area, threatening skeens and centurions alike.

Despite such concessions made in the name of authenticity, the result was always a Rustannican victory, lest the usually drunken crowd stage a riot. And so ever more centurions—usually volunteers who were paid handsomely for the privilege of showing off their various skills before an adoring public—were continually sent in until the last of the skeens and the wild beasts were annihilated. If the skeens were proficient, killing them might take an entire day. Despite their contrived outcomes, the finales always resulted in jubilant crowds. Whenever a land or a sea battle was reenacted, the best seats often went for double the normal price, and the bet takers, wine merchants, and prostitutes were even busier than usual.

Vespasian watched one chariot speed straight toward a group of skeens who had not been quick enough to take refuge on the mountain. The specially crafted chariot was a beautiful thing—too beautiful, Vespasian thought, to serve such an ugly purpose.

The chariot was painted dark blue and adorned with gold filigree. Two magnificent black stallions sped it across the sand. The axle shafts running through each wheel hub had been extended, reaching a good two meters sideways from either side of the cart. The wildly spinning axles were also adorned with gold, and along their sides lay sharpened steel blades that spun madly with the revolutions of the chariot's wheels. As the driver whipped the team the archer drew back his bow and the lance thrower hoisted his shining spear over one shoulder, preparing to strike.

But the clever skeens acted quickly. Banding together, they placed their shields side by side and over their bodies, creating a dome that would provide them cover. Knowing that he had little time to lose, the chariot archer loosed his arrow. It pierced a skeen shield but did not reach its owner.

Still the driver charged his chariot onward, directly toward the fragile house of shields. It seemed that he was intent on driving his team straight into it regardless of the outcome. Then the lance thrower tried, but his weapon skidded harmlessly across one of the angled shields and fell to the sand.

The three charioteers immediately drew their swords. As the chariot charged ever nearer, the turtle of shields defiantly stood its ground. Just then Vespasian realized that the defiant skeens surely had a plan. *They must act soon,* he guessed, *or they will be mowed down.*

Sensing that a great collision might occur, Vespasian quickly stood and cheered his centurions onward. Seeing their beloved emperor rise to his feet caused the crowd to shout even louder as they too anticipated the crash.

Just as the chariot was about to mow them down, the skeens abandoned the turtle tactic and formed two straight lines on either side. Unable to change direction quickly enough, the chariot charged straight through the gap. But three of the skeens hadn't been quick enough. Although they tried to jump aside, the axle spikes found them, slicing each of them through at the waist. Spurting blood, the grotesque halves tumbled to the thirsty sand.

As the horses tore between the skeen lines, the surviving slaves plunged their swords deep into the stallions' chests and struck out at their front legs. Screaming wildly, the two horses went down, the stumps of their severed front legs burying into the sand. As the crowd roared, the horses flipped forward onto their backs. Still harnessed to the team, the chariot also launched into the air, turning upside down and crashing ahead of the tortured horses. The three charioteers went flying onto the sand some distance away.

The tables had been turned, and the centurions were now at the mercy of the skeens. Because the other nine chariots and their riders were busy elsewhere, Vespasian realized that this trio was done for. Before they could rise to their feet, the jubilant skeens were on them, hacking them to pieces. Starving animals then rushed in to pounce on two of the busy skeens and to devour the scattered corpse halves.

Vespasian took a deep breath. *So much blood and violence,* he thought as he again sipped his wine. *But that part of our nature must remain if we are to defeat the Shashidans. We must stay hard, brutal, and unyielding, for the price of our freedom is constant vigilance.* Looking down, he used an index finger to thoughtfully trace the rim of his wine goblet.

Perhaps if the Vigors are defeated we can someday forgo all violence, he mused. *That is my secret dream. But I fear that brutality might be forever ingrained in our blood signatures. After aeons of cultivating violence, it will not be easily dismissed, even if I can secure a lasting victory.*

He turned to look at Persephone again. Flushed with excitement, she watched eagerly as the fighting raged on. More centurions were being let into the arena to take the place of their fallen comrades, while the exhausted skeens could do nothing but watch and wonder how much longer it would take them to die. As Vespasian's attention focused ever more on Persephone, he was reminded of the great request he had made of her the day before . . .

"WHAT BOTHERS YOU SO, MY LOVE?" PERSEPHONE ASKED.

Dipping her sponge into the warm water again, she soothingly used it to rub Vespasian's naked back. Closing his eyes, the emperor luxuriated in his wife's loving gesture.

There were only two places in the world where Vespasian felt that he commanded total privacy, and they were both in the royal residence. The first was in his and Persephone's vast and luxurious bedchambers. The other was here in their private bath.

Like attending the games, bathing—both public and private—had become something of an addiction in Ellistium. Most people used the public baths, but some of the wealthiest citizens possessed private baths. The public baths were often linked to other facilities such as massage rooms, meeting places, exercise areas, eateries, and shops. Sometimes the water was heated by the craft, but most often it was warmed in underground boilers connected to wood-burning furnaces and was then piped into the bathing pools. As would be expected, the royal bath was a sumptuous affair. Unless Vespasian and Persephone deigned to invite guests, this place was for their use alone.

The room was large and beautifully appointed. Measuring thirty meters square, its walls and ceiling were made of the finest turquoise and onyx. The floor was a subtly patterned mosaic of white marble squares. A large rectangular skylight in the center of the ceiling allowed sunlight to flood in. A dozen fluted columns stretched from the floor to the ceiling to support the four sides of the massive skylight. The rest of the ceiling was comprised of a series of indented squares, each one bordered by ornate gold moldings and painted with a different scene from Rustannican antiquity. Shaped like the dark blue mosaic pool lying directly beneath it, the skylight let in not just sunlight but also rainwater, reducing the need to continually add more water.

The bath walls were covered with colorful frescoes, separated every few meters by decorated pilasters reaching from floor to ceiling. Scented water burbled from a golden spout in the center of each wall to fall into another stone pool. Luxuriously upholstered sofas and chairs and ornately framed mirrors had been placed about the room, and a host of handmaidens stood by to serve every need of the Blood Royal and his wife. Two of the handmaidens provided lyre and flute music, and caged birds added a soft chorus as sunlight streamed down through the atrium to shimmer in the pool water. Vespasian's personal masseur, a stout skeen who had served the emperor for two decades, stood ready to employ his strong hands and exotic oils.

As Persephone gently rubbed his back, Vespasian flexed his naked body. He loved the royal bath, but his mind remained troubled. His recent night terror had shaken him and he feared that another might come. But even more worrisome was the thought that he might somehow be struck down by one of these terrifying visions during the day for everyone to see. He knew that he could not afford such an occurrence— especially with the advent of his new campaign.

He turned to look at Persephone. *Only she understands me,* he thought. *Not even Lucius knows me so well. Nor does he know about my secret weakness. How I need this woman . . .*

Reaching up, he removed the elegant diamond clasp that collected her long blond hair. Tossing it across the floor, he shook her tresses free, letting them slip into the warm water, and pulled her naked body to his. Persephone smiled knowingly as she playfully laid her wet forearms on his shoulders and looked into his eyes.

Smiling, she touched the tip of one index finger to the end of her husband's nose. "You still haven't told me what troubles you," she said. "Arousing me won't stop me from asking, you know."

Vespasian nodded. "Come," he said. "Let's talk."

Looking across the chamber, he snapped his fingers at the handmaidens and the masseur. At once they gathered up their things and left the room, bowing as they went.

Vespasian led Persephone through the shoulder-deep water toward the pool steps. As they walked up he reached out to a nearby table and took up a heavy white robe, which he draped around her wet body. Smiling, she squeezed the water from her hair.

Vespasian donned a matching robe, then led her to one of several lounging sofas and bade her lie down. After filling two wine goblets resting on a nearby table, he handed one to her. As he sat down beside her, the look in his eyes became searching.

She reached out to touch his face. "It's your night terrors, isn't it?" she asked. "That's what you need to talk about. I understand, my love. They would frighten anyone. But the two guards have been killed. Only I know your secret, and it will never leave my lips."

Looking down at his goblet, Vespasian shook his head. "It's more than that," he said. He took a deep breath. "There is something that I must ask you to do for me. It will be dangerous, but I hope that you will consent."

"I would do anything for you, you know that," she answered softly.

Vespasian put down his goblet. "I want you to accompany me on the new campaign," he said simply. "We leave in one week."

Persephone was overjoyed. Her eyes widened and she took a quick breath.

"You know that I will!" she said.

Tears started welling up in her eyes. She had desperately feared watching him go to war, just as she had done all the times before. But this time was different. This was to be an all or nothing campaign, and the greater dangers involved had been driving her nearly mad with worry. As Vespasian brushed away her tears, a short laugh of relief escaped her. *At least if he dies I will die with him,* she thought.

"But why this time?" she asked. "I have never accompanied you before."

As Vespasian sipped his wine his eyes took on a thoughtful, faraway look.

"There are several reasons," he answered. "First and foremost, I have not been convinced by the *Pon Q'tar* that the *Jin'Sai* won't somehow find his way into our side of the world. He is amazingly resourceful, as are his mystics. If that happens you will be far safer afield with me and the legions than here in Ellistium, protected only by the Home Guard."

"What leads you to worry that he can cross over?" Persephone asked. "If it is impossible for us to do so, then surely the *Jin'Sai* and his mystics cannot. After all, their powers in the craft pale when compared to ours."

"That's true," Vespasian answered. "But Tristan has surprised us before. And remember, we still cannot know the full extent of what he might have learned from the traitorous Crysenium Envoys. But there is something more . . . something tugging at my heart since experiencing my first night terror. It is almost as if he and I are connected somehow, despite the mountain range that separates us. I can almost see him trying to reach us." Shaking his head, he gave Persephone a reassuring smile.

"But do not worry, my love," he said. "If he should come we will deal with him and his flying monstrosities."

"And your other reasons?" she asked.

"I no longer trust Gracchus as I once did," Vespasian answered. "I haven't done so for some time. I do not brand him a traitor, but I sense that he has some personal mission that does not entirely match mine. Like my suspicions about the *Jin'Sai,* these are feelings that I cannot justify. But my instincts are strong enough to tell me that should I be killed on this campaign, Gracchus might not continue it in the way that I have planned—and our victory is vital. Four days ago, his scheme to sacrifice so many skeens in the arena without my consent only added weight to my convictions. While it's true that Lucius might protest a change in the battle plan that Gracchus engineered, even the First Tribune is outranked by the lead *Pon Q'tar* cleric. But you outrank them both. With you in attendance, my wishes would be carried out. To override you, Gracchus would first have to kill you while deep among Lucius and the combined legions. Lucius would immediately become suspicious. Even the *Pon Q'tar*'s powers in the craft could not overcome their combined strength, and Gracchus knows it. He would have no choice but to honor your commands."

"I understand," Persephone said. "But there is more to all this, isn't there? I suspect that your need to have me near also has something to do with your recent night terror."

A grim look came over Vespasian's face. "Yes, my love," he answered. "I must admit that it does. You are the only person that I dare trust with my secret. I have considered confiding in Lucius, but even he needs to remain convinced that his emperor is totally fit and able to conduct this campaign. And I am fit, aside from these strange and terrifying episodes. But there remains something else about them that worries me even more."

Reaching out, she lifted his chin and turned his eyes toward hers. "And what is that?" she asked.

"That someday one of these awful visions will overtake me while I am awake, for everyone to see," he answered. "I have no proof that such a thing will occur. Again, it's only a feeling. But should it happen I will need you by my side. You might be able to spirit me away before anyone realizes that I am in such terrible distress. Should I suffer such a daytime attack in public, Gracchus might well have me declared mad. According to Rustannican law, that is his right, but only if he has reliable witnesses of my supposed incompetence. A day terror would provide him with more evidence than he would ever need. With you by my side, should I fall ill, you can make the needed excuses. Such explanations will be far more commanding coming from the empress than from the First Tribune."

As she listened to Vespasian's words, Persephone realized that her husband was right. She would gladly accompany him to the ends of the earth if it meant helping him win this new campaign—to say nothing of keeping him in power.

"How will you explain this to the *Pon Q'tar?*" she asked.

Vespasian gave her a wry smile. "You need to stop thinking in those terms," he said. "If something happens to me, you will become the new ruler of Rustannica. You must quickly put your personal grief aside, no matter how overwhelming it might be, and immediately take charge. Gracchus and the others will start appraising your performance from the first moment. Stop worrying about how *you* will explain things to *them.* Rather, it is *their* task to worry about whatever orders *you* might give. To answer your question, I am the emperor. I will simply command that you come, and I will do so without giving my reasons. To be forced into explaining myself would be seen as a sign of weakness. That is something that we cannot afford—especially now."

"And what of Rustannica?" Persephone asked. "If the campaign fails and we die, who will oversee our beloved country?"

"After I announce that you are joining the campaign, I will ask Lucius to recommend a tribune who commands his full trust," Vespasian answered. "He will remain here and oversee the nation. It is the most that we can do." Vespasian sighed and took another sip of wine.

"But if the campaign fails, given the state of the treasury there will surely be a citywide riot," he added. "It might not be immediate, but it would surely come eventually. As the news of the defeat and the treasury collapse spread, anarchy will devour the nation. With most of our forces destroyed, we will be wide open for attack. The Borderlands will become useless, and the Shashidans will be able to walk into our country unimpeded. The Vagaries will be destroyed and the Vigors will rule forever."

Persephone gave him a somber look, then lowered her face. "If I had been able to give you an heir, some of our troubles would be solved for us," she said softly. "The child would be young, but at least someone of our bloodline would rule after we were gone. I'm so sorry, Vespasian. I wanted a child more than anything in the world. But it was not to be . . ."

Vespasian put his hands on her cheeks and looked into the eyes that he so loved. "We haven't failed," he said with a smile. "We simply have yet to succeed. We are far from the day when there will be no more reason to try." As he looked at her, his gaze suddenly became hungrier.

"I suggest that we waste no more time talking," he said. "Actions speak far louder than mere words."

Standing, he removed his robe. As he did, Persephone looked up to see his muscular body still wet and glistening with bathwater. She parted her robe, readying herself for him.

As Vespasian took her, the empress trembled and cried out as never before . . .

AS ANOTHER TERRIBLE SCREAM REACHED HIS EARS, VES-pasian's thoughts returned to the present. A Rustannican Heart Wolf freshly conjured from the arena walls was rooting about in the innards of a fallen skeen. For a moment the dreadful creature paused its feasting to look around the huge crowd. Fresh blood dripped from teeth and muzzle. As expected, the mob cheered and stamped, begging for more.

Vespasian took a quick count to find that only five skeens remained standing. For the sake of moving on toward the next act, the last skeens would be dispatched quickly. Then would come a brief intermission while the fabricated mountain was dismantled and taken away. Another act of today's games would soon follow, then more after that until nightfall. When Vespasian reached over to take Persephone's hand, she turned and gave him a short smile.

This morning the emperor had publicly issued his order regarding Persephone's attendance on the impending campaign. As a precaution he had also handwritten the proclamation, then commanded that the heralds shout it from every tower in the city even before the news was made available to the Tribunes and the *Pon Q'tar.*

Vespasian had little doubt that the public would receive the news favorably. They loved their empress, and he rightly guessed that seeing her go to war alongside her beloved husband would only endear her to them more. He was quickly proved right when Persephone's name was soon being joyfully shouted aloud both in the city streets and amid the mayhem that was the coliseum. But it had not been only for Persephone's benefit that Vespasian had done this. Rather, if the public widely approved, the *Pon Q'tar* would be harder pressed to accept his terms.

So far Vespasian's gambit was working. He had heard rumors of some minor grumbling among the *Pon Q'tar* and of surprise among some of the Tribunes. Even so, no formal protest had been lodged. Vespasian knew that the longer the public rejoicing in this matter reigned, the better his council would come to accept his edict.

Even so, despite the overwhelming agreement among the populace, Vespasian remained somewhat worried that the *Pon Q'tar* had accepted his new order so gracefully. The surprising lack of discourse usually accompanying so unexpected an order had unnerved him, forcing him to again question the clerics' motives.

Turning around, he looked at Gracchus. The lead cleric was on his feet, waving his fists in the air as he cheered the deaths of the remaining Shashidan skeens. When at last he found Vespasian's gaze upon him, he bowed and smiled broadly. It was a wry smile, forcing Vespasian to guess at what might lie behind it. Nodding in return, Vespasian again faced the arena, wondering.

As the last of the skeens died, hundreds more centurions rushed through the Gates of Life to start disassembling the fabricated mountain and removing the debris. It would take some time, Vespasian realized, for much of the mountain was littered with blood and the bodies and body parts of skeens, centurions, and wild animals. Vespasian took another sip of wine and sat back in his ivory throne. He would never forget that moment, for in the space of an instant his life suddenly changed.

First the dizziness took him. It did not come all at once, but gradually, like the onset of too much wine. Then the sweating started. As he tried to put down his goblet, he spilled a bit of wine. Soon his hand was trembling, and he knew.

Desperately hoping that he could hide his condition from everyone but Persephone, he immediately leaned over as best he could and touched her hand. When she turned to look at him, she knew.

"Can you walk on your own?" she urgently whispered.

The best response that Vespasian could muster was to nod. Standing, he and Persephone started making for the rear entryway that led to their private hallway. The empress knew that if she and Vespasian could reach their private litter waiting just outside the coliseum walls, she could draw the litter blinds and tend to him.

As they left the viewing box, everyone else stood and bowed. Luckily, most of them quickly returned their attention to the arena floor. After quietly telling a few of the clerics that she and Vespasian would return after the intermission, Persephone wasted no time following her husband out.

Entering the relative safety of the hallway, she turned to look back. No one was following. Breathing a short sigh of relief, she considered taking one of Vespasian's arms to support him, then thought better of it. If their charade was to go undetected, the emperor must be seen entering his litter under his own power.

As they finally exited the coliseum, Vespasian was on his last legs. Summoning the craft, he used it as best he could to help himself. His head still held high, he entered the ornate blue and gold litter bearing his insignia. Persephone followed, then drew the curtains and called to the litter bearers and the accompanying squad of centurion bodyguards to proceed quickly back to the royal residence.

Vespasian lost consciousness in Persephone's arms, leaving her to wonder again what was happening to her husband's mind and why. They were safe for the moment, she realized, but when would Vespasian return to her, and what would he be like when he did? Despite her many questions, one thing was certain.

Vespasian's day terrors had begun.

CHAPTER XIX

THOSE NEW CRADLES HAD BETTER HOLD UP, ADRIAN THOUGHT. Standing on the bow deck of the *Tammerland,* she looked westward to where the strange structures lay beside the royal palace. *I hope the other Conclave mystics know what they're doing,* she worried. *If the cradles collapse, we'll suffer troubles that I can't begin to imagine.*

Turning to starboard, she watched the other three Black Ships dutifully soar through the sky alongside hers. Sometimes they drifted so near that she could identify the acolytes who piloted them. Satisfied, she again cast her gaze westward. Soon the new cradles came into view.

The cradle spars rose hauntingly up from the earth like the bare rib cages of some monstrous half-buried beasts. They were stunning things to see. *Will they support the great weight of the ships?* she wondered. *And who among us would have guessed that the Minions could build such wondrous things?* The warriors surely had some help from the craft, she guessed. It would have taken more than a smattering of magic to build them so quickly.

As the wind ruffled her hair and robe, Adrian grabbed hold of some nearby rigging to better steady herself. She felt drained, just as she knew her three acolyte pilots also did. Even so, the trip from the Cavalon Delta to Tammerland had been short and uneventful.

When Tyranny had finally sent word by Minion messenger that the cradles were ready, Adrian and the other sisters had been pleased. But when the messenger went on to inform them about the lost Night Witch group, their happiness vanished. The flight home became a somber rather than a happy affair.

Nearly an entire Night Witch patrol has been lost to those horrible creatures, Adrian thought as the wind swirled about her. *Twenty-nine brave and talented female warriors—many stripped naked and impaled. I can imagine no more humiliating death for Minion females.*

Two of the Night Witches had been mates of warriors serving aboard the Black Ships, and it had been all that Adrian could do to keep the grieving husbands from leaving then and there to seek vengeance. But in the end their Minion sense of duty prevailed and they stayed aboard. Adrian felt sure that Tristan would have ordered warrior parties to bring home the dead, and that thought had helped to calm the raging widowers.

Every fiber in my being tells me that we are in for another terrible fight, she thought as the massive cradles loomed nearer. *May the Afterlife see us through it.* Little did she know how much the other Conclave mystics had recently learned, or what added wonders she would soon witness.

Just then she saw a Minion litter approaching from the west. As it neared she could make out Tyranny and Tristan sitting in it. She watched Tristan shout out an order as he pointed toward the *Tammerland.* Soon the litter landed safely on the flagship's bow deck, not far from where Adrian stood. Tristan and Tyranny departed the litter and came to stand by her side. After exchanging greetings, for the next few moments the three allies simply watched Tammerland draw nearer. Finally Tristan turned to look at Adrian.

"Was your trip uneventful?" he asked.

Before answering, Adrian noticed that the *Jin'Sai* seemed unusually anxious. *And with good reason,* she thought. Tyranny also seemed particularly vexed. Adrian watched the Conclave privateer place a cigarillo between her lips and light it. She smiled.

"So you still haven't given up those things," she chided Tyranny. "Given that the four cradles are about to be tested, I can understand why."

Exhaling the smoke through her nose, Tyranny waved the match out and tossed it over the side. As if she didn't know how to answer, she let go a disparaging snort and tousled her hair. "You don't know the half of it," she growled softly.

Tristan gave Adrian a stern look. "Your *trip*, First Sister?" he demanded.

Adrian pursed her lips. "I'm sorry, *Jin'Sai*," she said. "The voyage went well. There is nothing untoward to report save for my sorrow over the loss of the Night Witches. How is Sigrid?"

"She was injured but she will survive," Tristan answered. As he let go a sigh, his expression softened. "I apologize for being short with you," he answered. "What you have yet to learn is that seating the ships in their cradles will seem like child's play compared to what the wizards want to do next. I understand their plan but I still can't believe it. The Conclave and the entire Minion camp eagerly await us. This will be a far more eventful day than you first realized."

"What do you mean?" Adrian asked.

As Tristan explained the Conclave's plan to shrink the ships, Adrian's breath caught in her lungs and her eyes grew as large as hen's eggs. Finally she found her voice.

"They actually believe that such a thing can work?" she breathed.

Tristan nodded. "They claim that the theory is sound. But Tyranny and I have our doubts. It seems that she and I remain the two great skeptics."

Adrian shook her head in disbelief. "You can add my name to that list," she said. "What are your orders?"

Tristan looked out at the looming cradles. It was nearly midday and the shadows created by the great wooden ribs stretched long across the grassy field. He pointed toward them.

"As the fleet approaches the cradles, you will slow the ships to a crawl," he said. "Then you and the other sisters will cause the ships to hover over the empty ground lying east of the four cradles. Wigg and Faegan will take a litter aloft while the others watch and wait on the ground. They will then lower the ships one at a time. Jessamay and Aeolus will stand ready to help with the craft should anything go awry. Do you understand?"

"Yes," Adrian nodded.

"Very well," Tristan answered. "Then this is where we leave you. Good luck."

After Tyranny tossed her cigarillo overboard, she managed to give Adrian a wry smile. "If you wreck my ships I'll have your hide," she said quietly. Knowing that Tyranny was only half joking, Adrian swallowed hard and nodded back.

After saying goodbye, Tristan and Tyranny walked back to their litter. Soon they were aloft and heading back to the landing site.

Taking a deep breath, Adrian worriedly scrubbed her face with her hands, then called for a messenger. The female Minion was by her side in an instant. She clicked her boot heels together.

"I live to serve," she said.

After repeating Tristan's orders word for word, Adrian gave the warrior a stern look.

"Relay my orders to the other three acolyte pilots," she said. "Leave nothing out. Should the acolytes have questions, bring their inquiries to me straightaway. Be sure to follow my orders to the letter lest you be responsible for the crashing of all four Black Ships." Adrian turned her gaze westward once more. "I doubt that the Conclave would look kindly on such a disaster," she added sternly.

For a moment the warrior's face blanched, but she quickly recovered. "All will be as you say," she replied.

"Then stop wasting time staring at me," Adrian said. "Get going."

The warrior again clicked her boot heels together, took a few quick steps, and launched into the air. After watching her land on the deck of the *Ephyra,* the First Sister looked west again. She hadn't meant to be so stern with the messenger, but like Tristan and Tyranny, she was nervous. Soon her earlier thoughts about Wigg and Faegan echoed in her mind, this time with even greater concern.

I hope those sly old wizards know what they're doing.

"ARE YOU SURE THIS IS GOING TO WORK?" WIGG ASKED Faegan.

To say that the First Wizard was worried would have been the grossest of understatements. Like Abbey and Faegan, he was exhausted by the long hours and the mental stress of the last few days. After boarding the litter, Abbey affectionately touched Wigg on one arm, and Faegan situated his wheeled chair to his liking. As six stout Minion warriors took the litter aloft, Faegan cradled the precious jar of subtle matter in his hands. His usually impish demeanor gone for the moment, he gave Wigg a somber look.

"Will the cradles hold?" Faegan asked. "I don't know. But they are the least of today's worries, for they can be fixed if need be. The truly disconcerting part will come when we try to shrink the ships."

Pursing his lips, Faegan looked at the subtle matter trapped in the simple glass jar. "Such amazing material," he mused. "I suspect that we have only scratched the surface of its powers. But without more help from the Ones we will never grasp its true potential."

"I know," Wigg answered, "and I find that thought even more worrying."

Suddenly an old wizard's adage sprung from Wigg's memories. His father first spoke it to him centuries ago, long before Wigg met Failee and she started the destructive rampage that would become the Sorceresses' War.

"*Worry is much like the payment of a debt before it comes due,*" his father said, "*neither of which will do one any good.*" For the first time today the First Wizard let go a short smile.

As Wigg looked out over the grassy fields he was again awed by the mountain of wooden crates lying nearby. The crates were chock-full of supplies, foodstuffs, potable water, and arms. Each one had been precisely weighed by the Minions and the tally given to the Conclave mystics. The job had been a massive one. Even so, given the thousands of warriors taking part, the task had been finished in less than two days.

Then the mystics had painstakingly calculated the amount of subtle matter needed to do the job. The results were discouraging, for there wasn't enough of the amazing material to perform all sixteen transformations. Only a bit more than half of what was needed lay imprisoned in the glass jar. If the expedition to Shashida was to go forward, the plan had to be changed.

And so a compromise was agreed to. Tristan suggested that they try to miniaturize only the *Tammerland* and the *Ephyra,* leaving the *Cavalon* and the *Illendium* in their original states. This would provide Shailiha with two ships to use as she hunted down the Viper Lord and his servants. It also meant that only two ships could try to find their way across the Azure Sea to Shashida, but that couldn't be helped. Aside from the fact that Tristan would lead the expedition, it had yet to be determined who among the other Conclave members would accompany him.

The wizards' plan for the ships was simple on its surface, but it would be amazingly complex in its execution. If the cradles successfully held the monstrous vessels, the warriors would then load the *Tammerland.* The cradles had supposedly been engineered with enough strength to support the great ships even after the vessels had been loaded to their bursting points. But the mystics could not be entirely sure about that, nor could they know whether the cargoes would successfully shrink along with the ships. As the first vessel descended, Aeolus and Jessamay would be standing by to use the craft should it be needed. Once the *Tammerland* was loaded, the next part of the great experiment could start.

Wigg looked east to see the Black Ship fleet approaching. They were wondrous things to see as their bright red images of the Paragon painted onto their huge black sails shone brightly in the sun. Wigg was proud of the acolyte pilots; they had learned to fly the Black Ships well. *That's a good thing,* he realized as he watched the ships fly ever nearer. *We might soon need the acolytes' services as never before.*

As the ships reached the landing area, Wigg watched their Minion crews take to the air to furl the hundreds of red and black sails. The ships then hovered in the air alongside the massive cradles, their hulls casting huge, looming shadows across the grass. Faegan shouted out an order to the Minion litter bearers. Soon the litter was also hovering just a few meters away from the *Tammerland*'s gunwales.

"Ahoy!" Faegan shouted at Adrian. "Is all well?"

The First Sister left her place in the bow to come and stand at the gunwale. "Yes!" she shouted back. "You may start!"

Faegan turned toward Wigg. "It's time," he said. After Abbey gave Wigg a supportive squeeze on his arm, the First Wizard went to stand beside Faegan. "I'm ready," he said simply.

"Slowly release your hold over the ship!" Faegan shouted out to Adrian. "As you do, we will take control!"

"Very well!" Adrian shouted back. Grateful that her part of the process was done, the First Sister gradually retracted her power, and the two wizards took up the task.

For a few moments the *Tammerland* rocked gently as the transfer of power was completed. Because Wigg and Faegan were both doing the job, the strain on each man was not unduly great.

Faegan looked over at Wigg. "Just as we discussed, First Wizard," he said. "We'll take her down nice and easy."

As the remaining Conclave members and thousands of Minion warriors looked up in awe, the amazing process began to unfold. After Faegan carefully handed the jar to Abbey, the two wizards raised their arms.

Little by little, Wigg and Faegan caused the *Tammerland* to float sideways to a place directly above her new cradle. Then the wizards rotated her bow due east, perfectly aligning her keel with the cradle's spine.

Soon the great ship began drifting downward. While Wigg verbally dismissed the warriors carrying the litter, he partitioned his power to take personal control over it so that its descent might more perfectly match that of the Black Ship. Seeing that the process had started, the thousands of warriors aboard the *Tammerland* crammed up against the gunwales to watch.

Her hull creaking softly, the *Tammerland* descended past the tops of the cradle ribs. Seeing that an adjustment needed to be made, Wigg and Faegan changed the ship's lean slightly toward starboard. As she continued to descend, the *Tammerland*'s keel neared the spine of the cradle. Wigg took a deep breath. *Now we shall see,* he thought.

With a great creaking of her timbers the *Tammerland* settled into her new cradle. At once the cradle leaned frighteningly toward starboard. Wigg and Faegan immediately brought the ship a few meters back up, alleviating the stress.

Jessamay, Aeolus, and several thousand warriors ran over toward the cradle's starboard side. As the mystics helped with the craft, the warriors quickly pounded more buttress timbers into the ground and shoved them up against the cradle's starboard ribs, returning it to the vertical. When the cradle had been righted, Wigg and Faegan allowed the *Tammerland* to descend once more. Soon the ship's keel was again nearing the curved spine.

With a great groan the *Tammerland* again settled into her cradle. For a few moments the cradle ribs and spine creaked loudly in protest as they bore the massive weight for the first time, and the earth beneath them shuddered. Then all was still.

They did it! Tristan realized as he stared up at the wondrous sight. The huge Black Ship and her cradle were motionless, awe-inspiring. Soon the *Tammerland*'s massive stern door lowered and Adrian made her way to the ground, followed by the several thousand warriors who also served aboard.

Letting go a deep breath, Faegan looked at Wigg and Abbey and smiled. "It seems that we've done it, old friends!" he said. "Let's go down and take a look!"

Wigg landed the litter near where the Conclave members were waiting. As they touched down, the thousands of warriors who had worked so tirelessly on the great project erupted into raucous cheering, their sudden outburst so deafening that no one could hear himself think. As the ruckus went on, the three mystics triumphantly exited their litter and were quickly engulfed by the throng. Soon the joyful warriors saw the *Jin'Sai* and the other Conclave members approaching, and they dutifully formed a pathway through their midst.

Running ahead of her brother, Shailiha grabbed Wigg up in a great bear hug and kissed him on the cheek. As Wigg's face reddened, Faegan and Abbey chuckled at the First Wizard's expense.

"Well done!" the princess shouted. Soon Tristan and the other Conclave members joined them.

"I couldn't have said it better myself," Tristan said. "Well done indeed." He looked up to see the *Ephyra,* the *Illendium,* and the *Cavalon* still hovering in the sky.

"But this is no time to rest on your laurels," he added with a smile. "There's still work to be done."

Tristan turned to look at Traax. "Have your warriors start loading the *Tammerland*," he ordered. "Given how many are available to do the job, it shouldn't take long."

Traax clicked his boot heels together and hurried off to carry out his orders.

Faegan turned to look at Wigg. "Shall we go for another ride?" he asked.

Wigg pursed his lips and placed his hands into the opposing sleeves of his gray robe. "And once we have cradled all three ships?" he asked. "Do you still intend to try to shrink the *Tammerland?*"

"But of course, my dear fellow!" Faegan exclaimed. The crippled wizard's mischievous smile reappeared. "Only he who attempts the ridiculous can ever achieve the impossible! Follow me!"

Without further ado Faegan levitated his chair high over the crowd to soar back to the litter. Wigg took the jar from Abbey, then wended his way through the crowd to join him. Soon they were again soaring through the sky to approach the *Ephyra.*

Two hours later all four ships lay safely nestled in their new cradles. Each time, the process went more smoothly. Tyranny and Scars came to stand beside Tristan and Shailiha. Now that the *Tammerland* had been loaded, the time for the more complex experiment had come. The Conclave privateer looked more worried than ever. Touching Tristan on one arm, she bade him walk with her.

"What is it?" he asked, as they left the crowd to stride across the grass.

For a time Tyranny said nothing as she walked beside her *Jin'Sai.*

Then she stopped and searched his face with a deeply worried expression. As though she didn't know how to start, she sighed deeply.

"I know that I don't *own* those ships," she said. "And I will never be able to repay you for all your kindnesses. But . . ."

Pausing for a moment, she looked back at the massive vessels that she so loved. For her, seeing the ships cradled on dry land seemed unnatural, almost a travesty. But her seafaring nature found what the wizards planned to do next even more blasphemous. She turned back to look into Tristan's eyes.

"Those ships are my life," she said quietly. Then one of her wry smiles appeared, only to vanish as quickly as it came. "I suppose that my well-known sense of pride would never allow me to say that to anyone but you. *Must* we try this thing?"

Tristan nodded. "Although I hold the same misgivings as you, my mind is made up," he said. "I know that it's risky. Whenever I get these feelings, I put my trust in Wigg, Faegan, Aeolus, and Jessamay. It's all that we can do. What will be will be. Besides, if the worst happens and the *Tammerland* is destroyed, we will still have the other three ships." He gave her a crafty smile. "I'll even make a deal with you," he added.

"What sort of deal?" she asked skeptically.

"If the *Tammerland* is wrecked, I will order that another be built," he said. "You can have a hand in outlining her specifications."

"Agreed!" Tyranny answered.

Just then they heard the crowd roar, and they turned to look. An azure glow was settling over the mastheads and the crow's nests of the *Tammerland.* Wigg and Faegan's litter hovered above the great ship like a tiny fly badgering some great beast. Then the haunting glow moved lower, engulfing the entire ship. As Tristan watched, the breath caught in his lungs. *It has begun!* he thought.

Their hearts in their throats, the *Jin'Sai* and the privateer ran back toward the spectacle as fast as their legs could carry them.

CHAPTER XX

AS KHRISTOS LOOKED AROUND HE REALIZED THAT EVEN his lost love Failee could not have created such an exquisite place. Silver staff in hand, he turned and ordered his thousands of hungry servants to wait behind.

Walking on, he crossed the ornate portal that granted him access to the magnificent chamber waiting beyond. As he entered, he found the room to be every bit as stunning as Gracchus had told him. Several hours ago, Khristos and his servants had not only entered the Caves of the Paragon, but with Gracchus' help had found their way into its lower regions. These were sacred places that were once known only to a privileged few. Excepting the newly arrived Viper Lord, all the other mystics who knew of this place had taken their knowledge to their graves.

After killing the Night Witches in Tanglewood, Khristos had used the remaining darkness to herd his creatures south toward Hartwick Wood. Because he assumed that more of the *Jin'Sai*'s flying patrols were searching for him, traveling across open ground during daylight was unacceptable. But if he could enter the forest before sunup, his forces could hide amid its dense cover as they continued toward the caves. Pushing his servants hard, he and his vipers reached the forest's edge just as dawn arrived.

Gracchus had unexpectedly reached out to touch Khristos' mind once more, soon after the last of the female Minions had died. The *Pon Q'tar* cleric told him much—including how to safely navigate the labyrinthine caves. Most of what Gracchus told him sounded too fabulous for words. Even so, Gracchus' guidance had brought Khristos to this place of places. As his servants hissed and writhed behind him, Khristos walked deeper into the room.

Like the many chambers and passageways that led him here, this magnificent underground room had been hewn from living rock. Measuring several hundred meters in both directions, the room's walls and floor had been clad with light green marble shot through with streaks of black. It shone beneath the light of hundreds of enchanted sconces and chandeliers lining the seemingly endless walls; each light source had been enchanted by its maker to burn forever and without smoke. Despite the great size of the room, the air was stifling and the temperature was warm, even hot.

But even more amazing were the contents of the room. On the floor, stretching as far as Khristos could see, lay countless rows of huge, broken eggshells, their thin white sides translucent in the light. Just as Gracchus had predicted, what remained of the eggs' contents still glowed brightly with the color of the craft.

It's true, Khristos realized. *Nicholas' spell still lives.* Taking several more steps, he looked closer at the shells.

Each of the broken, slimy eggs dripped a thin azure fluid down the outside of its shell. The fluid seemed fresh—perhaps as fresh as when Nicholas had first conjured these treasures of the craft three years ago. The stinking fluid from the many eggs had pooled on the floor, adding to the fetid odor pervading the room.

Singling out one shell for examination, Khristos levitated his body so as not to step into the stinking fluid. As he glided closer, he became even more impressed by Nicholas' gifts.

Standing about five feet high and four feet wide, the shell had been pecked open at its top, showing how the creature that had grown inside it finally emerged to join the world. Conjured by the thousands, Nicholas' hatchlings had been instrumental in his attempt to open the Gates of Dawn and unleash the forces of the Vagaries west of the Tolenka Mountains on Eutracia. But it was not to be, for Tristan and his Minions had battled Nicholas' winged servants high in the sky over Farplain and then issued the final blow later, near the entrance to Shadowood. Khristos hadn't the immense knowledge required to create such wonders, nor did he need it. His only concern was that these masterpieces of the craft still existed, and that they could be used to further his purposes.

Nicholas had been Tristan's bastard son, Gracchus had said. A product of one of the Coven sorceresses' rape of the *Jin'Sai,* Nicholas had been one of the most perfect beings ever seen on this side of the world. Because of the quality of Nicholas' magnificent blood, the spell used to conjure these eggs might survive for all time. So too would remain this wondrous chamber and the secrets that it contained. Secrets, Khristos began to realize, that would spell the final downfall of the *Jin'Sai,* his twin sister, and the pompous Conclave.

Khristos levitated a bit higher so that he could peer down into the broken shell's depths. He smiled, for what he saw relieved his worried heart.

The bottom of the egg still held some glowing azure fluid. That was welcome, but it was only part of what he needed. The real prize lay amid the fluid still trapped in the egg's curved bottom. It was the red umbilical cord that had nourished the hatchling while it gestated in this egg, only to become detached and abandoned when the creature broke free to join its brothers.

Khristos did not know how the nurturing process had worked. Perhaps the azure fluid had been the creatures' food and it had once nearly filled the eggs. The cords might have been the devices that supplied the fluid to the growing embryos. *But that doesn't matter now,* he realized. *What counts is that they are still here and they remain usable.*

He looked down the seemingly endless rows of broken eggs and he smiled. *Gracchus was right,* he thought. *There are more than enough here to serve my needs.* He turned and looked at the thousands of Blood Vipers who waited behind in a room nearly the size of the one he had just entered.

"Come, my children!" he shouted. "Come and feast on the wonders of the Vagaries that have been left behind! Take your strength for the struggle that is to follow!"

As though they were possessed of one mind, the famished creatures slithered into the massive room to gorge themselves. As they entered, Khristos hovered higher so as to not hamper their feeding frenzy.

The famished beasts ripped into the eggs with abandon. The fluid ran down their faces and arms as they chewed savagely on the cords, and Khristos smiled as he realized that his great concern had been overcome. Before making his pact with Gracchus, Khristos' only purpose had been to exact Failee's revenge. But to his dismay he soon realized that his lost love's goal would be nearly impossible to achieve.

Because he had been released from the river, he immediately knew that the sorceresses had lost the war, making his duty clear. But as Khristos ransacked Eutracian towns, it became evident that finding and killing enough persons of endowed blood to sustain his throngs of followers would be nearly impossible. So that their strength would continually grow, Failee had engineered the Blood Vipers to feed only on the livers of the endowed. After they had fed on enough endowed victims, even the *Jin'Sai*'s Conclave would be unable to stop them.

But Khristos soon realized that Failee's plan was hopelessly flawed. Because not enough endowed persons could be found, Khristos's vipers had begun to starve before his eyes. Then he made his highly unexpected pact with Gracchus and everything changed. Now there was a new foe to vanquish in Failee's name. Khristos would do everything in his power to destroy Tristan and to see that the Vagaries ruled unopposed everywhere east of the Tolenkas, just as Failee had hoped. It gladdened his heart to know that the First Mistress's great vision might yet be fulfilled.

Now there is plenty for my servants to eat, bringing the final victory even closer, he realized. *Gracchus is indeed wise.* As he watched the creatures gorge, Khristos' consciousness drifted back in time to the previous night, when Gracchus had reached out from across the Tolenkas to again touch his mind.

Sensing Gracchus' ken, Khristos kneeled reverently in the bloody cobblestone square. Seeing their master supplicate himself, all the Blood Vipers stopped what they were doing and bowed.

"*Khristos,*" the Viper Lord heard Gracchus say.

"*I am here,*" he answered. "*Command me.*"

"*Go to the caves,*" Gracchus said. "*From your experiences in the Sorceresses' War you know where they can be found. What you do not know is that while you lingered in the river, the late son of the reigning* Jin'Sai *enlarged the caves, then set them to a particular purpose—one that failed but can still serve us. Because of the great power of his blood, Nicholas' spell lives there still. Let your vipers feed on what nourished his growing hatchlings, for it will provide the same increased powers as that which you took from the bodies of the endowed. The* Jin'Sai *will come soon, and you must be ready for him. He must be stopped from crossing the Azure Sea at all costs. Let your vipers feed and grow stronger, for soon the greatest struggle of your life will begin.*"

"*I will obey,*" Khristos answered.

As his mind returned to the present, Khristos let go a smile. His vipers could gorge themselves to their hearts' content and only increase their strength. As he watched his servants feed, he found himself eagerly waiting the impending fight.

Come to me, you filthy Vigors worshipper, he thought. *Let us finish what was started so long ago.*

CHAPTER XXI

THE YOUNG BOY SAT ON THE FLOOR AND SHIVERED. THE usual wooden stool was not here this time. He briskly rubbed his arms, trying to warm himself as the chilliness seeped through the damp floor and crept into his bones. He did not realize that the goose bumps forming on his skin came more from his rising fear than from the cold.

As usual, he had awakened prone upon the floor. And like the times before, he could not remember who he was or where he would go after his next lesson with the robed ones. Despite his fear he decided that he didn't care. He only wanted these sessions to end so that he might never have to come here again. Had the barren room offered up a way to kill himself, he would have done so gladly rather than face another unknown horror.

Perhaps they know that, he thought. *That is why they took the stool away, thinking that I might use one of its legs to stab it into my heart and end this madness.*

After a time the door creaked open to show the boy's faceless master. As the door parted, a shaft of bright light cut through the darkness, hurting his eyes. His vision slowly adjusted, and another shiver went down his spine. Finally he looked up into the empty confines of the dark cloak hood.

If only my master would show his face, he thought. *If his countenance was kind, I might not be so afraid.*

The master extended one hand, then crooked a finger, beckoning the boy to stand.

"Come," he said simply. Like the times before, his voice sounded hollow but commanding.

The boy stood on shaking legs and walked to the door. The hallway beyond looked the way he remembered, with its two rows of opposing white doors. The stark corridor held no scent, no sound, and no life except him and the tall cloaked figure standing by his side. Placing one hand atop the boy's shoulder, the faceless master started guiding him down the seemingly endless hallway.

Soon they stopped before a door. The master pointed at the gold door handle and it levered downward. As the boy followed the master into the room, he was surprised and saddened by what he saw.

Like the hallway, the chamber was stark white and without furniture. A man stood naked in the center of the room, his hands and feet chained to four iron rings embedded in the floor. He looked to be about forty Seasons of New Life. He was filthy and emaciated, and his body bore many battle scars. His eyes seethed with hatred as he struggled against his chains.

Looking closer, the boy saw a square beeswax plaque hanging around the man's neck from a leather string. The plaque served but one purpose, the boy knew. This man was a recently captured Shashidan who would soon be sold into slavery in Ellistium's great forum. When the final bid was accepted and the gavel came down, the auctioneer would record the price and the buyer's name into the plaque with a stylus. Then the slave's new owner would lead him in chains to one of the many cashiers' tables to arrange payment.

Suddenly another thought went through the boy's mind. As the realization hit home he felt even colder and more alone.

How can I know such things, he wondered, *when I can remember nothing else? I understand about Shashida, the slave market, and Ellistium, but I cannot even speak my own name.*

Before he could find his answers his master spoke again, breaking the boy's concentration. He had been on the verge of something, he realized. Even so, he wisely decided to say nothing of his newfound revelations. The master pointed at the man chained to the floor.

"He is a worthless convict," the master said. "Worse, he was once an enemy soldier and a magic practitioner of the worst kind. He cannot speak to you, because after he committed his crime, his tongue was cut out in punishment."

Pausing for a moment, the master pointed at the beeswax plaque hanging from the man's neck. "He has been marked for sale at auction," the master said, "but with no tongue he won't bring much." Then the empty hood hauntingly turned toward the boy's face.

"He killed his slave handler while on the way to the forum, dealing the poor man a gruesome death," he added. "It is up to you to determine his fate. There is only one correct decision, and choosing wisely will be today's lesson. It is one of the most important that you will ever learn."

The empty hood turned toward the chained slave once more. "His future rests in your hands," the master said. "Over the course of your life you will be forced to make many such choices, and each must be the right one. There can be no mistakes and no second-guessing, for such errors will be taken as a sign of weakness by those who would destroy you."

Before continuing the master placed his hands into opposite robe sleeves. "The usual penalty for murder is death," he added sternly. "But one day you will have the power to commute such sentences and show mercy, should you wish to. So what is it to be? Will you spare him and send him back to the auction block? Or will you order his demise?"

Before the boy could answer, the master waved an upturned palm. At once a gleaming sword appeared in his hand. He held it out.

"Take it," he said. "Make your choice, but first know this: If you wish the slave to die, it must be by your own hand. Moreover, should you choose to free him, unpleasant consequences could arise."

With trembling hands the boy took the sword. Despite its heaviness it felt like it belonged in his grasp. The feeling surprised him.

"What consequences?" the boy asked.

"I will not say," the master answered. "In life one must suffer the unknown results of his decisions, whatever they might be. That is how it will be today. Choose."

As the boy looked at the slave his whole body started to tremble. *Why should the decision be mine?* his mind cried out. *Who am I to have the power of life and death over others?*

The boy lowered his sword. "I will not choose," he answered. "Nor can you force me to do so."

He raised his face to again look into the empty, frightening hood.

"The choices you offer are worse than nothing. You say that I must either condemn this helpless man to slavery for the remainder of his life or kill him here and now . . . I do not know which fate is worse."

The master stepped nearer, his imposing presence stabbing even greater trepidation into the young boy's heart.

"You *will* choose," he ordered. "And you will do so this instant. Indecision can be as deadly as the blade in your hand. Choose—or you will remain in this place, learning one harsh lesson after the next until you are an old man and your bones turn to dust. What is it to be—mercy or death?"

The boy looked back at the seething slave. "If I must choose, I choose mercy," he said. "Free him and return him to the auction block."

"Very well," the master answered. "Be prepared to deal with the consequences of your decision."

Before the boy could answer, an azure cloud gathered around the faceless master. Two seconds later the cloud vanished, taking the master with it.

Stunned, the boy quickly turned to look at the slave. As he did, several smaller azure clouds formed around the slave's hands and feet. Soon the Shashidan's manacles vanished, leaving him free.

To the boy's astonishment the slave let go a wicked smile and charged straight for him, tendons knotting and teeth flashing.

This can't be happening! the boy thought. *I just saved him from certain death! Surely he knows that!*

But the time for wondering had passed. There was only one course of action, the boy realized. He would have to defend his life.

As the slave neared him the boy felt a sudden, unbidden tingling course through his veins. As though it were second nature he quickly turned on the balls of his feet, then raised his sword high and brought it around with everything he had, taking the slave's head off at the shoulders with one cut. As the blade passed through the slave's neck, for the briefest of moments the boy thought that he saw it glow azure. Then the severed head and the body to which it had once belonged crashed to the white floor, spurting blood as they went. The headless body convulsed and bled for several moments before finally going still. The killing had taken less than six seconds.

His chest heaving, the boy again lifted the sword and regarded it with wonder as the slave's still warm blood ran down it and onto his hands. He watched as the strange azure glow slowly left the blade.

Has all this been a dream? he wondered.

Dropping the sword, he lifted his hands before his face and stared at them with horror as if they belonged to someone else—a cattle butcher, perhaps, who cut into flesh as a way of life and was accustomed to having his hands bathed in blood.

Yes, he thought. He stared back down at the dead slave, marveling over how simple a thing it had been to kill another human being. *I am much like that cattle butcher. But I have now become a butcher of men . . .*

Just then another azure cloud appeared. Seconds later, the faceless master stepped from its midst. With a wave of one hand he caused the cloud, the corpse, and the severed head to vanish. As he turned toward the boy he again placed his hands into opposite sleeve robes.

At first the boy couldn't find his voice. Finally the words came in a whisper.

"How?" he breathed. Had the boy been able to see his master's face, he would have found the approving expression that he had hoped for earlier.

"You possess a rare gift," the master said. "It is called *K'Shari.* I granted it to your blood as you lay asleep on the stone floor. As you grow to manhood you will learn much more about it—how to harness it, embrace it, and make it your own. But for now that is all you need to know about it."

For the first time since coming to this bizarre place, enough anger roiled up inside the boy to finally overcome his fear. He took a threatening step closer to the frustrating mystic.

"You left me alone with that freed slave!" he shouted. "You knew that he would try to kill me, didn't you? Yet you vanished, you coward, only to reappear after it was over! Why bother to teach me these strange lessons if you value my life so little?"

"You are wrong," the master answered. "Your life is more highly valued than you could possibly imagine. Despite your youth, because of *K'Shari* you were never in danger. I vanished because I wanted you to know that you must not rely on others to save your life. But that is not what we must discuss."

"What, then?" the boy demanded.

"Your wrong choice," the master answered.

"Why was my choice wrong?" the boy protested. He had become so angry that his voice shook.

Good, the master thought. *He is starting to assert himself.*

"You chose to be merciful toward someone whom you knew to be a dangerous enemy," the master answered, "and toward someone who had already killed one of your own kind. Your only reward for that generosity was to be forced into defending your life. That is all that Shashidans know—how to hate, take, and destroy. Never forget that. You must always strike first, and strike to kill."

The boy calmed a bit. Turning, he looked at the blood on the floor. "Surely there must be some good in everyone, no matter what they believe or where they come from," he offered.

"No," the master answered. "Now, then—tell me what you learned here today."

Perhaps the master is right after all, the boy thought, as he felt his dread of the faceless mystic continue to wane. *It was kill or be killed. And I'm the one still standing.* This time the boy's answer came quickly.

"Mercy is a weakness," he said.

"True," the master replied, "but that answer is not definite enough—especially coming from someone so gifted as you."

Stepping closer, he placed a hand on the boy's shoulder. This time the young man stood his ground and did not shrink from the mystic's touch.

"Purify that thought, then take it one step further," the master ordered. "The words are in your heart—you have but to say them."

The boy thought for a moment. As his new response formed, he found that he longer mourned the slave who tried to take his life.

"Mercy has no purpose whatsoever," he said softly.

"Not quite," the master answered. "Sometimes a display of mercy can enhance one's image, among other things. Even so, it always comes at a price—one that might be too steep to merit payment. Should you choose to be merciful, always do so to further your own goals rather than for mercy's sake alone. Mercy without a secret purpose is worse than weakness—it will soon rot away your power over others. You will then become the one needing mercy rather than the one who grants it."

The master snapped his fingers and the azure cloud reappeared. Placing one arm around the boy's shoulders, he escorted him toward its foggy embrace.

"You still have much to learn, my young charge," the master said. "But you have taken a great step forward. You have not only grasped today's lesson, you have also lost your fear of me. We will be together for a long time, you and I, and these small victories of yours will serve us well in the days to come."

As they stepped into the azure cloud it gathered closely around them and they were gone.

AS THE ROYAL LITTER JOSTLED ITS WAY THROUGH THE streets of Ellistium, Persephone looked down at her husband's face. Holding him close, she removed the crown of golden laurel leaves from his head and lovingly smoothed his curly blond hair.

Vespasian's face looked pale and drawn, and he sweated so profusely that his dress uniform was starting to soak through. Suddenly he let go a quiet moan, causing the empress's concern to rise even further.

Not knowing what else to do, she decided to allow the litter to continue on its way home. Somehow she must find a believable excuse to explain why she and the emperor did not return to the games. Worried beyond reason, she rocked Vespasian to and fro in her lap much as she might have cradled the child that she never had.

What can be causing these terrors? she wondered frantically. *And how can we possibly hide another one?*

Then she struck on an idea. After making sure that the litter's curtains were fully drawn, she called the craft and pointed a finger at Vespasian's wrist.

A small incision opened in his skin, allowing one drop of his blood to rise into the air. Persephone used the craft to close the wound, then looked at the evolving blood signature. Soon the familiar design formed fully. As always, angular lines made up one half, while flowing lines comprised the other half. Also as usual, hundreds of forestallment branches led away from the signature. Like the blood signature of every endowed person, Vespasian's was an amalgam of those inherited from his father and his mother.

Vespasian had never known his parents, and for that Persephone had always been sorry. The *Pon Q'tar* said that they had died in a tragic accident while Vespasian was still an infant. They went on to explain that when they first became alerted to the nature of his magnificently endowed blood, for the sake of the nation they had raised him, trained him in the ways of the craft, and decided that he should one day become emperor. After Gracchus convinced the reigning Suffragat that Vespasian might well be the one to lead Rustannica to her final victory over Shashida, the governing body had eagerly voted to one day crown him emperor.

We have much to thank Gracchus for, Persephone realized, *even though Vespasian is coming to distrust him.*

As Vespasian lay in her arms, Persephone continued to examine his hovering blood signature and its many branches. When she saw that it looked normal in every respect, she didn't know whether to feel anxious or relieved. *His blood holds no answers for us,* she thought sadly. With a wave of her hand she caused the blood signature to vanish.

Just then Vespasian groaned again, and his shallow breathing deepened. Soon he regained consciousness. Unlike when he awakened from his previous terror, this time he seemed calmer. As he looked up into Persephone's eyes she gave him a reassuring smile.

"We are in my litter . . ." he ventured weakly.

Persephone kissed him on the forehead. "Yes, my love," she answered. "We travel home now."

"And the games?" he asked. "Did we manage to leave without my attack being detected by the others?"

"Yes," she answered softly. "But we must make some excuse to explain why we did not return."

Vespasian shook his head. "No," he said. "I am the emperor and my new campaign has already been heralded among the populace. The *Pon Q'tar,* the Tribunes, and the Priory all need me more than ever. They will simply have to accept our absence."

Vespasian reached up to gently touch her cheek. "Do you want to hear about my dream?" he asked.

"Of course, my love," she answered. "Together we will discover what these dreams mean and how to put an end to them."

"Do you remember the Shashidan general I tried to free that day not long ago in the coliseum?" he asked. "To spite Gracchus, I decided to grant the general mercy."

"Of course I remember," she answered.

"My dream has much to do with that day, I fear," he said. "But I'm not sure why."

As the emperor told her of his recent terror, tears gathered in Persephone's eyes and rolled down her cheeks.

CHAPTER XXII

TRISTAN SAT ON THE BALCONY OF HIS PRIVATE QUARTERS and took another sip of wine. The day had been tiring and the drink was producing its welcome effect. He would purposely imbibe a bit too much this night, he decided, and with good reason. Tomorrow might prove the most momentous day of his life, and he was determined to enjoy this evening.

At the least, the morrow would see his departure from Tammerland— perhaps forever. At the most, his expedition might reach Shashida. *What will happen if we do?* he wondered, thoughtfully rolling the wineglass between his palms. His emotions about the impending journey remained in conflict, for the prospect of reaching Shashida both thrilled and unnerved him.

He turned to look at the table by his side that was laden with his favorite foods. Roasted quail, loin of beef with ground horseradish, fresh vegetables, black bread, and Shawna's famous redberry cake all sat waiting to be consumed, their wonderfully pungent aromas drifting into the air. He smiled as he remembered how it had all come to be here.

The ever-industrious Shawna had cooked up a great feast, then insisted in her own inimitable way that the Conclave members hold a farewell dinner before parting ways in the morning. But to her dismay,

Tristan put his foot down and ruled against it. He knew that Wigg and Abbey would want to spend this last night quietly, just as he wanted to dine alone with his sister. He might never see Shai again, and he needed to bid her farewell in private.

Putting down the wineglass, he rose from his chair and wandered into his private bedchamber. The room was large and magnificently appointed, and as usual his weapons had been casually tossed atop the great four-poster bed. A marble fireplace stood in one wall, its logs burning brightly.

He sighed as he looked at the lonely urn that held his late wife's ashes. It rested atop the mantel beside her farewell letter. For a time he had considered taking them with him, then he realized that their rightful place was here, where he and Celeste had spent so many loving hours. As he sadly realized that he might be leaving them behind forever, he closed his eyes. *What would she think of this mad scheme?* he wondered.

For the thousandth time he recalled his late wife's beauty, her intelligence, her sensitivity. Celeste had been the love of his life, but now she was gone. She would say that that he must go, he decided, even if it meant never seeing each other again. After all, that was the risk that Wigg and Abbey were taking. Were Celeste alive today, could she and Tristan do less?

Placing his thoughts aside, he walked deeper into the bedchamber and toward a large oak table that stood near the far wall. As he looked at what sat upon it, he again found himself filled with awe.

Late in the afternoon, Wigg and Faegan had attempted the miniaturization of the *Tammerland* and the *Ephyra*. To Tristan's amazement, the experiment had been a complete success, right down to the thousands of crates and sundry items that the Minions had loaded aboard the ships beforehand. It had been a mesmerizing process to watch, and were the two ships not sitting on the table before him, Tristan would have never believed such a thing possible.

Each Black Ship now measured just over one meter long from bowsprit to stern and about the same distance from the keel to the top of the mainmast. Had he not known differently, he would have thought these ships nothing more than amazingly accurate models. Their sails were furled and they nestled in their new cradles, which had also been miniaturized. When the process was finished, Tristan ordered the ships brought to his quarters for safekeeping. Tomorrow morning they would be crated, and the free space in the crates would be enchanted by Faegan to cushion the vessels during what would surely be a hazardous journey through the labyrinthine caves.

Bending down, Tristan looked more closely. Each ship still twinkled with the subtle matter that had accomplished their miraculous transformations. Wigg and Faegan thought that they might stay that way permanently, and Tristan suspected that the twinkling substance might help camouflage the vessels when sailing on the Azure Sea. *Is this something that the Ones planned for?* he wondered. *Unless we reach Shashida, we might never know.*

Walking back to the balcony, he again took up his wineglass. The sun was starting to slip down behind the western horizon. As he watched it disappear, his mind drifted back to the Conclave meeting that he had called immediately after the miniaturization of the ships.

Because of the many important issues to be settled, the meeting had become a spirited, often raucous affair. More than once Tristan had been forced to intervene to keep the discussion civil. The stressful tenor of the meeting had not been because of any personal rancor among the members, he knew. Rather, it was that they would soon be splitting into two groups, and those in each group might never see the others again. Because everyone was eager to see Shashida, trying to decide who would go with Tristan had been a particularly difficult issue to resolve.

In the end it was agreed that Wigg, Tyranny, Scars, Astrid, Phoebe, and Jessamay would accompany Tristan on the expedition. Faegan, Traax, Aeolus, Abbey, and Adrian would stay behind to follow Shailiha into battle against the Viper Lord. Also, the *Tammerland* and the *Ephyra* would carry the same two Minion phalanxes that had trained with Tyranny and Adrian during the recent sea trials. By common agreement it was decided that the Tome, the Scrolls of the Ancients, and the Paragon would stay behind under Faegan's care.

Tristan refused to allow personal relationships to play a part in these decisions, demanding that his group members be selected only for their unique abilities. Wigg was chosen rather than Faegan largely because of Faegan's limited mobility. Faegan had been deeply disappointed but agreed that of the two of them, Wigg should be the one to go.

Tyranny was selected because of all the Conclave members she had the most seagoing experience, and that could prove vital. As usual, Scars would serve as her first mate. Because Jessamay commanded the unique ability to determine an endowed's blood signature lean by looking into his or her eyes, she too was chosen. The acolytes Astrid and Phoebe would relieve Wigg and Jessamay in the piloting of the Black Ships. Marissa and another acolyte would remain behind to pilot the *Cavalon* and the *Illendium* under Shailiha's command.

But the most distressing problem—and the one that would have no resolution until Tristan's group entered the Caves of the Paragon—was how to find the subterranean Azure Sea.

Tristan was the only Conclave member who had seen it, and sometimes even he wondered whether it had been real or some mad dream. Wigg had been with him at the time, but unconscious. It was on the sandy shores of that strange sea that Tristan and Wigg were scooped up and flown away by Nicholas' hatchlings, only to be released by Nicholas after suffering cruelly at his hands. By that time Tristan had also lost consciousness, ensuring that neither he nor Wigg knew how far the hatchlings had carried them or how long it had taken. Even if they could find the sea again and restore the ships to their original size, they would be literally sailing into the unknown.

Will Shashida really lie on the other side? he wondered. *And if so, how long might it take to reach it?*

Just then a soft knock came on the double doors. Tristan walked over and opened them to see his sister standing there. Morganna stood by her side and Caprice floated lightly overhead.

Tristan smiled and beckoned them into the room. Shailiha looked radiant in a yellow gown, matching satin slippers, and a golden chain. The medallion lying against her bosom twinkled in the candlelight. Three-year-old Morganna looked adorable in a red dress fringed with white lace.

As Shailiha escorted Morganna into the room and Caprice obediently followed, the princess put on a brave smile. Tonight would be difficult for her and Tristan. They had seen the death of their parents, and each had lost a spouse whom they loved more than life. So far, the journey toward fulfilling their common destinies had been terribly costly. Without saying so, each understood that despite how much they had already endured, their struggle was far from over. And tomorrow they would part, perhaps forever.

"I thought you'd never come," Tristan said as cheerfully as he could.

Shailiha's eyes widened as she watched her ever-curious daughter walk toward the Black Ships. "Don't touch!" she cautioned.

Morganna stopped and turned, her bright eyes still curious but respectful. "I won't, Mamma," she said. She quickly turned back again to look with that innocent, wide-eyed gaze that it seems only children can muster.

Tristan was soon reminded of how much Morganna was starting to resemble her late grandmother. The queen had been a remarkable woman, and she was many years ahead of her time. It had been she who had convinced the late Directorate of Wizards to break with more than three hundred years of tradition and again allow the teaching of the craft to females. This teaching had taken place at a secret castle called Fledgling House nestled at the base of the Tolenka Mountains. Some of those girls, and a group of specially selected sons of the Redoubt Consuls, now took their training in a similar school in the Redoubt.

Morganna will soon attend that school, Tristan thought. Then his smile faded as he remembered that he might never see that day. He looked back at his sister.

"Would you like some wine?" he asked.

Shailiha nodded vigorously. "After hearing the Conclave members bicker for two hours, I could use some!" she answered. She turned to look at her daughter. "Come, Morganna!" she said.

Shailiha escorted her daughter to the balcony and boosted Morganna into one of the chairs. As might be expected, Morganna's eyes went straight for the cake icing. Before Shailiha realized it, the child had poked three of her fingers into it and shoved them straight into her waiting mouth. Her satisfied smile said it all.

Tristan laughed as he poured another glass of wine. "She takes after her mother," he chided. "It seems that she's developing your taste for sweets."

Shailiha wiped Morganna's mouth, then quickly moved the cake a safe distance from her daughter's energetic fingers. "So you noticed, did you?" she asked. After fixing a proper plate and cutting the food for the child, the princess took her first sip of wine.

For a time Tristan and Shailiha ate Shawna's delicious food in relative silence, with few sounds to accompany them aside from the night creatures and Caprice's delicate wings fluttering overhead. They dawdled over their food, realizing that the meal provided a welcome reprieve from the conversation that would follow. But after finishing two slices of cake and several cups of tea, they both knew that the time had come.

Shailiha looked over to see that Morganna had fallen asleep in her chair. The princess carried her into Tristan's bedroom and laid her on the bed. After moving Tristan's weapons to a nearby sofa, she again joined her brother on the balcony. As he looked into her eyes he could see tears welling.

Leaning closer, Shailiha took his hands into hers. "Please be careful," she said quietly. "I know that you must do this thing. More than once you have gone away only to return. But tomorrow might be very different. No one knows where the Azure Sea will take you or what you might have to face to get there. And we have only recently seen the coded message left by the Ones that tells us you are doing the right thing. That spell was likely written aeons ago—Wigg said so himself. What if it is no longer true? What if the *Pon Q'tar* is out there waiting for you instead? What if—"

Tristan gently placed his fingers against her lips. "There can be no more 'what ifs,' " he said. "I'm going and that's that. Of course I'll do my best to return. But if I do not, you must be prepared to rule Eutracia. Value the advice of the remaining Conclave members, but make each decision your own. They're not always right, you know." Smiling again, he wiped away one of her tears.

"Besides," he added, "as you said, they certainly like to bicker!"

"Yes," Shailiha added, "especially Wigg and Faegan."

Tristan reached out to take her medallion into his hand. "Don't forget this," he said reassuringly. "You can see me whenever you want. But remember—do not overuse the spell, and be sure that the medallion remains in your possession at all times. When Miriam charmed our medallions, she warned me of these things. Always keep them in mind."

Tristan let the medallion fall back onto Shailiha's chest. "Have the Viper Lord and his followers been sighted?" he asked.

Shailiha shook her head. "Even the Night Witch patrols cannot find them. It's as if they dropped off the face of the earth. How can a force that large simply vanish?"

Tristan shook his head. "They might be using the craft to help them hide," he offered. "But it would seem that even a wizard as powerful as the Viper Lord would eventually tire and reveal his position. I admit that it's puzzling. When you find them, let Faegan help form your plan. But when it comes to the very real and dirty business of fighting, take your advice from Traax. You can rely on his judgment completely. In many ways I wish he was coming with me. But because only two phalanxes sail with my group, he will better serve us here."

Deciding that the time had come to say goodbye, Tristan smiled at his sister as best he could. "If I don't come back—"

"Don't say that," she insisted. "I just know that—"

Just then another knock came on the double doors. Wondering who it might be, Tristan rose from his chair.

"Enter," he called out softly, trying not to wake Morganna.

The doors parted to reveal Aeolus standing there. Tristan beckoned him inside. After Aeolus paid his respects to the princess, Tristan bade him sit down. The mystic's expression was serious.

"Forgive the intrusion, *Jin'Sai,* but I wanted to speak with you privately before you leave tomorrow," he said.

"Is something wrong?" Tristan asked.

Aeolus gave Tristan a weary smile. "Do you mean aside from Eutracia being overrun by beings of the Vagaries and you and half the Conclave sailing off into the unknown tomorrow?" he asked. "Truth be told, before you leave I want to talk to you about your gift of *K'Shari.*"

Suddenly the wizard's expression darkened a bit. "If this is a private moment, I will gladly return later," he added quietly.

Tristan smiled. "Whatever you would say to me you can say in Shai's presence as well," he answered. "There are no secrets between us."

"Good," Aeolus answered. He poured a glass of wine and took a discerning sip, then looked into Tristan's eyes.

"I wish we had been able to train together longer," he said. "Even so, I have come to understand that you are the real master and I the student. Always remember that your *K'Shari* will be stronger than mine because your blood is much more powerful. During your travels, should you need to call on your gift, you must be careful. Do not become overconfident, and take nothing for granted."

Tristan's eyes narrowed. "What do you mean?"

Before answering, Aeolus set his glass on the table. "The beings you might meet on the other side are presumably far more advanced than we—especially in the science of the craft," he said. "Moreover, the forestallment formula that granted you *K'Shari* was found in one of the Scrolls. That means that they had the gift long before we did. If you must fight, always remember that your opponent might command *K'Shari* too—and to a higher degree and with greater experience than you possess. Furthermore, your gift is called forth automatically, while mine is not, and only your sword glows with the color of the craft. Despite many hours of searching for an answer, Wigg, Jessamay, and I still cannot explain it. You must trust in your gift, for that is all you can do. Do not fight the feeling when it comes over you, and let your actions flow through your body naturally. Only then might you defeat an enemy on the other side with equal talents."

Tristan appreciated Aeolus' advice. During the battle to retake the Recluse, fighting techniques both armed and unarmed had come to him unexpectedly and effortlessly, allowing him to do wondrous things. And his sword had indeed glowed with the color of the craft.

Later in Crysenium he had fought and defeated Xanthus, his first opponent who also commanded the gift of *K'Shari.* The battle had raged like some desperate war between two titans. Whenever Tristan's dreggan or Xanthus' axe missed its target and struck something else, they had utterly destroyed it. Tristan had never felt such power, and he had to admit that a part of him was eager to experience it again. But until now he had not considered the dangers that Aeolus was describing. Like Wigg and Faegan, sometimes Aeolus could make him feel very small.

"You're right," he said quietly. "I hadn't looked at it that way. Thank you."

"My pleasure," Aeolus answered. "And now I will take my leave."

As the mystic stood, Tristan stood with him. "Please watch over my sister while I'm away," the prince said. "I'm relying on you two to destroy the Viper Lord and his servants."

Aeolus gave Tristan reassuring wink. "I wouldn't miss it for the world," he answered. After saying good night to Shailiha he let himself out, the doors closing quietly behind him.

Tristan continued to gaze at the closed doors for several moments, thinking.

"He's a good man," he finally said. "Despite what our mystics might say about the quality of your blood and mine, we'll never fully appreciate everything they've gone through for the sake of the Vigors. Sometimes I have to force myself to remember that each of them is more than three centuries old."

Shailiha looked back at Morganna to see that her daughter was still fast asleep. When she looked back at her brother, her expression was sad but resigned.

"It's late and we should go," she said. "Just promise me that you'll return."

Tristan stood, as did his sister. He gave her a short smile.

"Such a promise would be unfair," he answered. "But I will do my best. In your absence make sure that Shawna looks after Morganna. You could never find a better nanny, despite how ornery she can be!"

Shailiha's laugh sounded brittle and forced—as if she wanted to let go but couldn't find it within her to do so. Grabbing the lapels of Tristan's worn leather vest, she tugged on them and gave him a ferocious look.

"Just come back," she ordered. "Don't force me to come to Shashida and find you!"

The princess went to take Morganna into her arms, the child grumbling softly before settling back down into a deep sleep. On reaching the doors Shailiha gave her brother a final, lingering look, then she was gone. Sighing deeply, Tristan sat down again and sipped his wine.

Goodbye, my sister, he thought. *May we each find what we're searching for.*

As it happened, he would not sleep that night, but sat on the balcony until dawn, lost in his thoughts.

III

MAGIC AND GOLD

CHAPTER XXIII

Given that the Jin'Sai *cannot be easily killed, taking the life*
of the Jin'Saiou *will do equally well.*

—GRACCHUS JUNIUS

"I HAVE BEEN BID FIVE HUNDRED SESTERCES FOR THIS prime example of Shashidan pulchritude!" the slave auctioneer shouted. "Who will give me six? Come now—just look at her! Won't some fine krithian give me six?"

When no one in the crowd responded, the auctioneer put on his best look of astonishment. It was a well-practiced deception, and one that had served him well over the years. The slave's current owner had told him that six hundred was the least he would accept. The price was relatively high but not unreasonable for such attractive, untouched goods.

Trying to entice new bidders, the vulgar auctioneer smelled approvingly of the naked woman's long dark hair, then pointed lasciviously to her ample breasts. As expected, the crowd drew nearer. Like hundreds of other slaves waiting to mount the block, she wore an unmarked beeswax plaque around her neck.

"Only twenty years old and still a virgin!" the auctioneer shouted. "And she has been bathed in scented oils! That alone is worth one hundred sesterces! Just think of the many skeen children this one will bear! Why, she'll easily pay for herself ten times over! Come, now—who will give me six?"

"Six, then, you robber!" a red-robed krithian man shouted from the back of the crowd. "But I'll not give you one sesterce more! And she'd best be as fertile as you say!"

The auctioneer smiled broadly. He had finally reached the minimum bid, and he could soon move on to hawk his remaining merchandise. He gave the young woman another leering look.

"Fear not!" he shouted back. "In my vast experience, the worst Shashidan slave girl I ever had was wonderful!" This time the crowd roared with laughter.

As Julia Idaeus passed by she looked up at the humiliated young woman standing on the block, then stared across the great forum. The huge plaza was busier than usual, partly because it was auction day. But it was more than that, she realized.

The announcement of Vespasian's impending campaign had restored the public's confidence. With that had come a renewed loosening of their purse strings and a slight surge in tax revenue. It was not enough to greatly help the treasury, but it was sufficient to convince the Suffragat that the final day of games should serve as a special celebration of Vespasian's impending departure, to build yet more public confidence in final victory. After some discussion, the emperor had given his blessing.

Seating in the coliseum would be free, first come, first served. For once, krithians and hematites would intermingle at the games gladly, with no rancor over who could afford the best view. Much free food and wine would be given away, and an unusually high number of slaves and animals were to be sacrificed. This would be the greatest single spectacle ever held in the coliseum, and the excitement was already at a fever pitch. The celebration would occur in two more days, and hundreds of people were already standing and sleeping in long lines outside the coliseum, hoping to be among the first to claim a good seat.

As Julia regarded the trembling slave girl, she was glad for the white veil covering her face, for it kept the mob from noticing her sadness. Deciding not to linger, she held her leather valise closer and continued on her way down the broad forum. As she passed through the crowd, many of those not intent on watching the auction bowed reverently to her.

Because of its massive size and great beauty, many Ellistiumites considered the forum to be their greatest achievement. At one end stood the Aedifficium, and far away at the opposite end could be found the emperor's residence. The forum lay in the heart of the city, deep in the oblong valley created by the seven surrounding hills. Traveling across Ellistium was a long and complicated affair unless one traversed this bustling place and thereby added to the usual congestion.

Made of pure white marble, the massive rectangular plaza was surrounded by many public buildings, some of which towered several stories into the air. Among these were baths, a great library, and offices for such professionals as barristers, moneylenders, and land vendors. Other areas were devoted to cattle, vegetable, and fish markets. A gleaming colonnaded portico lay at the forum's center, complete with covered walkways, eateries, and more shops of every description. From one end to the other, the forum measured more than half a league. Despite how often Julia ventured here, each time she revisited this place her sense of majesty was renewed. As she continued on toward her destination, today proved no exception.

Ellistiumites from all four classes bustled to and fro, giving her the impression that even the poorest of phrygians couldn't wait to dispose of their hard-earned sesterces. As usual, everyone from highborn krithians traveling by personal litter to the lowest skeens being led to the auction block were present.

Some ladies carried parasols while they strolled about, and robed men eagerly gathered to discuss the events of the day. A marble tower stood at each corner of the forum, from which heralds shouted the latest news that few besides Julia knew to be heavily censored by the Suffragat. Food vendors cajoled with promises that his or her delicacies were the freshest and the cheapest. Proud horse traders displayed their animals before prospective buyers, magicians surprised and delighted the crowds, and ever-watchful centurions maintained order. The atmosphere was festive and carnival-like, and skeens were bought and sold here no differently than those same horses or the fine gold jewelry that adorned highborn krithian women.

Suddenly a breeze came up, threatening to lift Julia's veil. Grasping it quickly, she clutched her leather valise tighter and hurried on. Soon she reached the famous landmark known as the Columns of the Emperors. It lay at the far end of the forum, just before the elegant entryway into the royal residence. The two opposing rows of giant columns were made of solid black onyx and rose to a height of one hundred feet. Each gleaming monolith was capped with a solid gold capital; atop each capital stood a marble likeness of a past emperor.

Walking among the massive columns always gave Julia a profound sense of history and sometimes made her feel insignificant, despite her important role as the reigning Femiculi. On reaching the final column she looked up to see Vespasian's likeness shining in the midday sun. Purposely avoiding the guarded entryway to the palace, she turned right and walked on.

Soon she arrived at her destination. The Hall of Antiquity held a special place in the hearts of all true Rustannicans, from the most highborn krithian to the lowliest phrygian street beggar. Skeens were denied entry, even when accompanied by their owners. Pausing for a moment, Julia took in the impressive structure.

The building stood four stories high, each level boasting an ornate recessed archway every forty feet. Within each archway stood a marble likeness of an important figure from Rustannican history. People known for their contributions to the military, the arts, and the Vagaries were represented, along with members of previous royal families. More statues lined the flat rooftop.

One hundred stone steps led the visitor first to a broad landing, then up a narrower stairway to the huge columned entrance. Manicured cypress trees and thousands of colorful flowers adorned the grounds on either side. The battle frieze carved into the triangular pediment represented the famous Rustannican victory at Aegates, a onetime Shashidan city lying far to the south. Julia started the trek upward, eventually finding herself atop the last landing and among the massive fluted columns.

After taking a moment to catch her breath, she walked over to the huge sundial standing on the terrace. She was surprised to see how late it had become; she must not dally. As she smoothly turned to enter the building, armed centurions guarding the massive oak doors bowed to the Femiculi.

As she entered the great foyer, imposing works of art and artifacts of Rustannican history came into view. Despite their great number, they were only a smattering of what lay deeper within. Striding across the foyer, she stopped for a moment and looked around.

The Hall of Antiquity was both an art museum and a monument dedicated to the glories of the empire's war machine. Many of its hundreds of exhibition rooms were filled with Rustannican paintings, sculptures, and tapestries, some of them aeons old. Other rooms devoted to the history of the Rustannican military exhibited ancient battle charts, war machines and weapons, tributes to past leaders, uniforms, and spoils from Shashida. Coming here to learn about Rustannican culture and the empire's war machine was a required part of every krithian, hematite, and phrygian schoolchild's education. As the children were escorted through the place by their teachers, the war displays sowed the seeds of a military career—a sentiment that the *Pon Q'tar* did nothing to discourage.

From the grand foyer ran seven hallways, each named for one of Ellistium's seven hills and leading to a different series of exhibition rooms. Sheathed in gleaming white alabaster and blue marble, the foyer atrium reached all the way to the roof, where skylights let the afternoon sun stream in. In the event of rain, shutters could be pulled across the skylights to protect the priceless exhibits.

The hall was busy today with a high number of visitors and several gaggles of noisy schoolchildren being escorted by their ever-watchful teachers, their eager voices and quick footfalls echoing loudly against the marble floor and walls. Without exception, everyone who crossed Julia's path stopped to bow and pay heartfelt respects. To keep from being further delayed, she politely circumvented another approaching group of visitors and made for one of the gleaming hallways, then quickly climbed another flight of stairs.

Reaching the second floor, she turned and walked up the first hallway on her right and into one of the many exhibition rooms. She took her usual seat on a marble bench across from a wall covered with paintings. There were few people about just now, and that suited her purpose. Opening her leather valise, she withdrew her sketchpad and her colored chalks, then placed the valise on the floor.

The room she chose was devoted to a group of Rustannican painters known as the Ravennans. Ravenna was a small town in the south of Rustannica known for its magnificent sunlight and colorful foliage, especially during the Season of Harvest. The Ravennan painters had been a tightly knit group, never numbering more than twelve. Painting some two centuries ago, they displayed an uncanny ability to capture dappled sunlight while showing wholesome themes of hard work and loyalty to the Rustannican Empire. These patriotic qualities had quickly brought their work into favor with the ever-watchful *Pon Q'tar.* Like so many other aspects of Rustannican culture, all artwork was subject to the approval of the clerics before it could be sold privately or displayed in public. Conversely, all captured Shashidan artwork was immediately deemed degenerate and summarily destroyed by whatever legions came across it.

Despite Rustannica's brutal nature, the Ravennans depicted their warlike nation as compassionate. Each brushstroke added layer on layer to the great hoax that was Rustannica. Only Julia and the *Pon Q'tar* knew the truth about the craft, but the *Pon Q'tar* had yet to learn that Julia was aware of it. It was that same dreaded secret that gave her the courage to come here once each month. Just the same, she lived with the constant fear of being found out, tortured, and killed.

As she looked at the paintings, Julia saw the same sanitized agenda over and over again, and she hated the Ravennans for it. These works mirrored the great lie, leading her to understand why the *Pon Q'tar* valued them so much. Like a painter who reused a canvas to cover a failed effort, Julia was painfully aware of the ugly truth that lay beneath the *Pon Q'tar's* treachery and deceit.

As she started to sketch the painting before her, her sense of revulsion grew. Her well-known pastime of sketching was nothing more than an excuse to leave the Priory and come here. She had chosen this place for her excursions precisely because she hated it so, and she frequented the Ravennan room because of all the chambers here, she hated this display the most. The military exhibitions were gruesome, but at least their depictions were honest. But here in the Ravennan room, surrounded with charming lies made of paint and canvas, Julia was best reminded of her intense hatred of all things Rustannican and the importance of her mission. For Julia Idaeus was far more than the reigning Femiculi.

She was a Shashidan spy and a member of the League of Whispers, embedded into the highest reaches of the Rustannican government.

As she sketched, people wandered by but left her alone. She was known here, and most visitors respected her privacy. That was another reason why the Hall of Antiquities was the perfect choice for her assignations. Because this was a public place, even the deeply suspicious *Pon Q'tar* would never suspect that something so damaging to their cause might happen within these walls. Her hatred for this place and all it represented was the perfect fuel for her passionate devotion to the Vigors cause.

Closing her eyes for a moment, she called the craft.

"I am here," she said silently.

"*We hear you,*" the many voices answered in her mind. Their harmonious timbre was reassuring. "*Are you well?*" they asked.

"*Yes,*" she answered. "*There is much to tell you.*"

"*And there is much for us to tell you, child. Is your secret still safe?*"

"*Yes.*"

"*Then you may continue.*"

For the next quarter hour Julia silently communed with her Vigors masters over vast distances incomprehensible to the average mind. She told them everything, including Vespasian's impending campaign to take the Shashidan mines and its reasons. When she finished she sat and waited, all the while being sure to glance from time to time at the hated Ravennan landscape and to continue sketching a copy of it.

For a time her masters did not answer, causing a flood of fear to pour through her. *Have I been detected?* she wondered. *Are centurions on the way to arrest me?* Then she realized that it must have been the stunning nature of her message that had given her masters pause. When they finally replied, she was greatly relieved.

"*Are you sure of these things?*" the voices asked. "*Defending the mines against such a major attack will be a huge undertaking, and you must be absolutely certain.*"

"*Without question,*" she answered. "*Vespasian even allowed me to help form the battle plan.*"

Again the masters paused for what seemed an unnerving period. "*Tell us of the plan,*" the voices finally ordered.

After outlining the campaign, Julia again fell silent, waiting for a response.

"*So Vespasian has requested that you go on this quest to perform the auspiciums,*" they said. "*That will prove useful.*"

"*Indeed,*" Julia answered.

"*Does Gracchus continue to subvert the auspiciums to help perpetuate the great hoax?*" the many voices asked.

"*I believe that he does,*" the Femiculi answered. "*He is still unaware that I know. I have also been informed that Persephone will accompany Vespasian on the campaign.*"

"*That is interesting and perhaps useful as well,*" the voices said.

"*There is more,*" Julia continued, fearful that she was pushing the limits of her subterfuge. Since she had sat down, no Rustannican had tried to speak to her. But it would only be a matter of time until some fawning citizen wanting to be seen in the company of the Femiculi came over to address her.

"Vespasian is acting strange," she told them. *"He left the games for no reason two days ago. I believe that he could be ill, but I do not know what is wrong with him."*

"That is also of great interest," the voices replied. *"But time grows short, so we will discuss it more during our next communion. While on the campaign it is imperative that you find a safe place in which to commune with us. Thank you for all that you have told us and for your constant bravery as you continue to serve us from the belly of the beast. Before we leave you, there is something important that you must know. If it happens, the results will be earth-shattering."*

"What is it?" she asked.

"The Jin'Sai *and some of his Conclave are about to try to cross the Azure Sea,"* the Ones answered. *"They have seen subtle matter for the first time, and they also discovered the message that we left hidden in the Tome and the Scrolls so long ago. Tristan is the first* Jin'Sai *to do so. If he reaches Shashida alive, our world will change forever."*

Julia began to tremble, her shaking hands suddenly drawing unruly lines. It was all she could do to keep from erupting in joy. Finally allowing her tired fingers to rest, she took a deep breath and calmed herself.

"It is time for us to sever our link lest our communion be discovered," the Ones said. *"Stay safe, Julia Idaeus, and remain brave in the face of the many changes that will soon come."*

Even before she could say goodbye, Julia felt the bond between her mind and theirs dissolving, then it was gone. She felt tired but elated. Gathering up her valise, she put away her drawing things and turned to leave the Ravennan chamber. As she walked across the hated room, several Ellistium toadies bowed and scraped to her and attempted to engage her in small talk. But she did not mind, nor did she need to hurry, for hope was finally at hand.

As the Femiculi finally left the Hall of Antiquity to navigate her way back through the busy forum, from behind the protection of her veil she smiled.

CHAPTER XXIV

"IS THERE ANY SIGN OF THE CONCLAVE?" KHRISTOS asked. He gave his lead Blood Viper a stern look. "I must be notified the moment the *Jin'Sai*'s party is detected."

The creature hissed and shook his head. "No, my lord," he answered. "Rest assured that when they arrive, we will be ready to strike. As you have ordered, some of us wait in hiding near the cave entrance. When they approach, we will enter the Caves ahead of them and inform you."

"Very well," Khristos answered. "Be sure to report to me the moment they are seen. But do not engage them or otherwise alert them to your presence. Let them enter the Caves peacefully. Only then will we take our revenge."

"Understood, my lord," the Blood Viper answered. The creature bowed respectfully, then slithered away with several others of his kind to go about its duties.

As he watched his servants go, Khristos smiled. Before committing the viper embryos to the peaceful river in Hartwick Wood, Failee had enchanted a handful of them with the power of speech. These specially gifted ten would one day serve as Khristos' captains, she had told him. Because of the Blood Vipers' extremely violent and nearly uncontrollable natures, Failee feared that allowing all of them to converse with one another might lead to discord, perhaps even rebellion.

Some of these specially gifted ones served as Khristos' eyes and ears above ground, while the others helped to convey his orders to the multitudes. Those that could talk did so in a hesitant, guttural fashion, reflecting the violent nature of their dark personalities. Despite the vipers' rather inhuman way of speaking, Khristos smiled as he remembered the late First Mistress's brilliance. The Blood Vipers were among her precursors to the Minions of Day and Night, Gracchus had said.

How ironic, he thought. *The first of Failee's many attempts to develop the Minions are about to battle the final products. The results should prove interesting.*

On entering the caves, Khristos unerringly followed Gracchus' directions and led his servants to the chamber where they could feast on Nicholas' glowing eggs. With each egg that they consumed he watched them grow stronger and more willing to kill and die, if need be, in the late First Mistress's name.

Then Gracchus had again communed with Khristos, ordering him to travel deeper yet into the Caves. Again following the lead cleric's directions, the Viper Lord led his monsters to the shores of the Azure Sea. From there, supply lines had been established so that more eggs could be delivered to the waiting vipers to feed on and build their strength.

Before communing with Gracchus, Khristos considered ambushing the *Jin'Sai* above ground near the entrance to the Caves. But Gracchus had commanded Khristos to let Tristan enter unharmed, bringing his Black Ships and all of his warriors with him. The process would be time-consuming but worth the wait, the *Pon Q'tar* cleric said.

Only after making sure that the enemy had traveled too far into the bowels of the earth to order an effective retreat would Khristos finally spring his trap and slaughter them all. His superior numbers would savagely overwhelm the Vigors worshippers and the winged beasts they commanded. Then he would enjoy watching Tristan's precious Black Ships burn.

When the *Jin'Sai* and all of his followers were dead, Khristos would take the fight aboveground again and redirect his rage against the *Jin'Saiou* and those remaining Conclave members and Minion warriors who followed her. With Tristan, his Minions, and half of the Conclave killed, Khristos' victory in this last struggle would be far more assured.

He would then go on to ransack Tammerland, destroy the royal palace, and tear the Redoubt of the Directorate apart from stem to stern. Moreover, he would burn the Tome and the Vigors Scroll to ashes, ensuring that no endowed person could use them against him. Then his next mission could begin as he and his vipers went on to murder every endowed man, woman, and child of right-leaning blood he could find. Vigors blood in Eutracia would exist no more.

After completing his scorched-earth campaign, he would then take his servants to Parthalon in the *Jin'Saiou*'s two Black Ships. He did not know how to sail them through the air, but that did not distress him. He could easily round up any number of Eutracian sailors living along the coastline, just as he had done with the citizens of Birmingham and Tanglewood. He would use the craft to bend the sailors to his will and force them to take him across the ocean in the traditional way. Once he reached Parthalon, the entire country would fall prey to him and his Blood Vipers. He would then stand astride both nations like a colossus and enjoy the just rewards of dictatorship that Gracchus had promised to him.

Hearing the sounds of the ocean, Khristos turned. While he and his grisly servants eagerly awaited news of the *Jin'Sai*'s arrival, Khristos took in the amazing sight.

The cavern in which he stood was huge—so mammoth, in fact that he could not see its limits. A great subterranean ocean lay before him, its blue waves stretching away from the rocky shore. Hundred of meters above him, a ceiling of rock lay where the sky would normally have been. The millions of radiance stones ensconced within it lit this place brightly with a sage-green hue, stretching as far as his eyes could see. Even the ocean itself, wide and foam-crested, seemed endless.

The smell of the cool breeze blowing in off the waves reminded him of the coast of Eutracia. The froth-tipped waves were the exact hue produced by the craft. They rushed toward him over and over again, crashing noisily upon the sandy shore some fifty meters from his feet. Behind him lay a long, jagged stone wall, reaching from the sand to the top of the cavern. Hundreds of cave openings pierced the wall, their dark holes often lying many meters above the sand. With Gracchus' help, Khristos knew that each one stretched for leagues into the living rock. Within those caves his thousands of servants lay coiled and ready to strike at a moment's notice.

This is where the Jin'Sai *will finally meet his death,* Khristos thought as he watched the waves constantly assault the sandy beach. *Before that can happen, he and his mystics must again find this place, but even that has been skillfully arranged.*

Leaving the beach, he trod the sand back to where one of the dark cave entrances stood. From just within its depths he would be able to clearly see the *Jin'Sai* and his forces arrive, for there would be but one entrance available to them—the one that Gracchus and Khristos wanted them to use. Only then would he order the attack.

As he waited among his eager servants, his mind slowly drifted back to the violent era known as the Sorceresses' War. Failee was losing her struggle for dominance over the craft, but much more blood would be spilled and far more combatants killed before she would finally be defeated. The three Mistresses of the Coven and their forces had gathered deep in Hartwick Wood, hoping to entice the Vigors forces into a trap and annihilate them. It had also been the time of Khristos' great love for Failee and of her secret plan to commend him and the viper embryos to the peaceful-looking river . . .

"WHAT TROUBLES YOU, MY LOVE?" KHRISTOS ASKED. Turning over, he looked deeply into Failee's eyes. *Sorceress's eyes,* he thought as he became lost in their luster for the thousandth time. Her hazel orbs sometimes seemed to glow, and they were but one of the mysterious qualities that drew him to her. She had coupled with him even more frantically this night, like a desperate woman who feared she was lying with her mate for the last time. For him it had been glorious, overpowering, mesmerizing. But as he waited for a response and got none, he worried.

When he had first approached her and offered his services as an accomplished Vagaries wizard, the First Mistress had reacted with aloofness. It seemed that she regarded him as little more than yet another among the many hundreds of wizards who wished to follow her cause and to see the Directorate destroyed. Later, as his wartime exploits and notoriety blossomed, she took an increasing interest in him. A mutual attraction soon developed, finally enticing them to share a bed.

But as his love for her grew, other than their frenzied physical couplings he could sense no emotional need in her for him. All that he ever saw within those wondrous eyes was her obsession to win this terrible struggle that she had started. Like her prosecution of the war, she approached her frantic lovemaking as if it too were some battle that must be won. She controlled every aspect of her terrible war with methodical savagery, and her carnal need for Khristos was no different.

The magnificent First Mistress, he thought as he searched her beautiful face. He continued trying to guess her thoughts even though he knew it was impossible. *She is also the estranged wife of Wigg, Lead Wizard of the Directorate. What a strange path this war has woven for us. Only the Afterlife knows how it will all end. If I ever see Wigg again, how might such a bizarre scene play out?*

Saying nothing, Failee rose from the luxurious bed and walked naked to the other side of her war tent. As she went, he watched her graceful curves glint in the candlelight. Long dark hair streaked with silver hung far down her back, swishing gently to and fro and brushing her perfect skin.

There was no other sorceress on earth like her and there would never be again, his heart told him. Whatever she asked of him he would do. Not simply because Failee was his lover, but also because he had never known so strong and infallible a leader as she. Her talents in the craft were legendary, her ruthlessness on the battlefield uncompromising.

Sitting down at her dressing table, the naked First Mistress looked into the mirror, then took up a tortoiseshell brush and began pulling it through her lustrous hair. When she went silent like this, there was no use trying to prod her, Khristos knew. Like everything else in her life, conversing was strictly on her terms.

As he waited, Khristos sat up in bed and he looked around. Despite how many times he had visited the First Mistress's war tent, it never ceased to amaze him. Had he not known better, he might have thought himself to be in the private bedchamber of some queen's castle rather than amid a huge military camp deep in Hartwick Wood. As usual, wherever the Mistresses of the Coven ventured, every conceivable luxury had been provided for.

The tent was very large, its four long sides and pointed ceiling sturdily supported by gleaming golden poles rather than the customary wooden posts. The dense canvas was dyed dark green to match the forest that surrounded it. Ornately carved furniture and patterned rugs adorned the area, while dozens of candles and oil lamps gave off soft, reassuring light. One table held war charts, texts, and scrolls relating to the craft. Scented oils wafted on the evening air while outside the tent, the familiar sounds of soldiers at arms, neighing horses, and other camp activity sounded into the night.

Two handmaiden mystics armed with swords and daggers stood motionless near the tent entrance, ready to execute any order given them by their First Mistress. As so many times before, tonight they silently watched as Failee and Khristos performed their grasping brand of lovemaking. At first Khristos had found their cool gazes unnerving, but because of his carnal need for Failee, he soon adjusted. For a time he had wondered whether the women were there to protect their mistress should Khristos ever threaten her. Then he had laughed aloud when he realized that Failee would need no help to kill him should she wish him dead. It was widely rumored throughout Failee's massive war machine that she could kill with a single thought, as could Succiu, Vona, and Zabarra, the other three lesser but equally devoted Mistresses of the Coven.

As Khristos looked into Failee's mirror, his face reflected back to him alongside hers. The image was serene, like some idyllic portrait of a contented husband and wife lovingly set upon a fireplace mantel. But this image was false, for she bore no love for him. Nor was there any contentment in her, for her war had yet to be won.

Taking a deep breath, Khristos continued to gaze at his reflection. At forty Seasons of New Life he was already an accomplished wizard with few equals. Curly black hair adorned his head, and he was handsome and strong. He had taken many lovers over the course of his life, but none had compared to Failee. As her eyes finally met his, he looked at her with concern.

"You haven't answered me," he said softly. "What troubles you so?"

Faille put down her hairbrush as she continued to stare into his eyes from the depths of the mirror. Her answer would surprise him.

"Do you love me?" she asked simply, her usually commanding voice perhaps granting him a bit more compassion than usual.

Sensing that something had changed in her, Khristos sat up in the great bed. "You know that I do," he answered, "even though you cannot return my love."

"Then why do you stay with me?" she asked.

"Perhaps it is in the hope that your feelings will one day change," he answered honestly. "Call me a fool if you will. But the heart wants what the heart wants."

Failee rose from her dressing table and walked back to the bed. Sitting down beside him, she looked at him in that way only she could. No one in the world had ever made him feel so brave yet so timid, so important yet so small.

"If you really love me you will listen to what I have to say," she said quietly. "What I tell you now is for your ears alone. Even Vona, Zabarra, and Succiu have not been informed." Leaning closer, her hazel eyes bored their way even deeper into his. "Be sure that you wish to hear this, Khristos," she added. "If I learn that you have betrayed my trust, I will kill you without reservation."

Khristos took a sharp breath. She had always been stern with him and he had never objected to her dominance—on or off the battlefield. Even so, until now she had never threatened his life. After some careful consideration he finally decided.

"What is it?" he asked.

As though some sudden shame had poured over her, Failee turned her face away. *Now it will come,* he thought.

"We are losing this war," she said softly.

Her words struck Khristos like a thunderbolt, the simple statement earthshaking. Had it come from anyone else he would not have believed it. Even when uttered by the First Mistress it was a difficult concept to fathom.

No one in their mighty army had the confidence of Failee. Not even the other three Coven mistresses were so sure of victory, and Khristos knew them well. Moreover, her forces had just scored a significant victory over part of the Vigors army near the plain called Heart Square, south of the capital. Soon after, her war scouts reported that the wizards had fled the battle to seek refuge in Tammerland.

Sensing that her great chance had finally come, Failee chased after them and laid siege to the capital. As her forces hammered at the outskirts of the city, Tammerland became a fortress and her people began to riot and starve. Rumors soon spread that many were demanding the wizards' surrender. Anything, they said, was better than watching their children starve before their eyes. With the wizards cornered and losing control, it seemed that Eutracia would finally belong to the Coven.

But then something unsuspected happened. It was learned by her scouts that the wizards' "retreat" to Tammerland had been a ruse. They and the bulk of their forces had circumvented Hartwick Wood to the west, then traveled northeast toward Tanglewood to regroup. Failee immediately understood that her army must meet the wizards' forces soon, while they were still reeling from their defeat at Heart Square. Because the Vigors mystics were not in Tammerland, the city had no more strategic significance than did any other, and so she abandoned her siege.

Because she dared not risk an all-out assault in which her forces could be seen advancing for miles, she devised a plan to draw the Directorate's army into the forests of Hartwick Wood. The dense forests lay not far from where the wizard army was camped, making the temptation even greater.

Khristos had never known how Failee planned to encircle and destroy the wizards' forces once they entered the forest, but he did know that these woods were rife with magic—magic that perhaps only Failee and the other Coven members understood and could use. This was perhaps why the wily wizards had not taken the bait, or perhaps they simply did not wish to abandon a position from which they could see enemy forces advancing from leagues away. But for whatever reason, they did not come. And so Failee's chance to trap and annihilate the Vigors worshippers, first in Tammerland and then in Hartwick Wood, never materialized. Even so, Khristos had never dreamed that those missed opportunities might somehow signal that the war was lost.

"What makes you say this?" he asked, still unable to believe. "Although the wizards refused to follow us into Hartwick Wood, we stunned them at Heart Square and inflicted many casualties on their ranks. They're reeling, Failee, surely you see that! I say that now is the time to move our forces to Tanglewood and strike them with everything we have!"

She turned to look at him angrily. "Don't you think I know that?" she growled. "A fool could see it! Under normal circumstances victory could still be ours. All I would need to do is to reach out and take it! But these are far from normal times, Khristos! My spies tell me that something has happened that will irrevocably alter the outcome of this war. I fear that this news will forever change the science of the craft. Unless I am wrong, victory has become impossible. But I will continue this fight nonetheless. It is what I was born to do, despite the massive advantage the wizards have obtained."

"What advantage?" Khristos asked. "What could possibly have happened that might cause us to lose this struggle?"

To his surprise, Failee balled her hands into fists, and her body started shaking. She lowered her head, and her hair fell to cover her face. Even during her darkest moments he had never seen her so overcome. It wasn't some new fear that consumed her, he realized. She was far too brave for that. Rather, he sensed that it was some strange combination of immense dread and frustration that had so quickly engulfed her. He tried to put his arm around her, but she roughly shoved him away. Closing her eyes, she angrily swept her long hair back with one hand.

"The wizards have found a great book," she said softly. "And with it was a blood-red stone, bathed in vibrant red water. It is rumored that these two seemingly innocuous items will forever change our knowledge of the craft. The book and the stone will make the wizards powerful, Khristos—more powerful than we can ever become unless we also gain the knowledge and power that these artifacts are said to provide. Even so, we have no choice but to fight on. But if the book and the stone are as important as my spies say, the wizards might already possess advantages over us that we can never surmount. It is said that the book is called the Tome, and the stone is called the Paragon. They were left behind by our long-lost ancestors for us to use and learn from. But the wizards found them first, and I can see no way to take the Tome and the Paragon from them. Had we discovered the book and the stone first, our war might already be won."

"Where were these artifacts found?" Khristos asked gently.

To his great surprise, Failee suddenly threw her head back and laughed. It was a strange, desperate cackle, lacking the slightest trace of humor. When she stopped, he noticed that she was no longer shaking and her domineering nature had returned. Rising from the bed, she began pacing the tent like a caged lioness.

"That's the truly maddening part!" she exclaimed. "My spies tell me that the artifacts were found in a deep cave not more than three leagues from where we are now camped! Three leagues! That's all that stood between us and total victory! Supposedly the cave entrance was covered with rocks and vegetation, making it difficult to see. I cannot be sure when the caves were found." Just then her face took on a familiar expression of disgust. "But I do know *who* first discovered them and secretly removed the sacred artifacts."

From the look on Failee's face, Khristos immediately knew the answer. "Wigg," he breathed.

"Yes," Failee answered quietly. "The wizard Wigg—my traitorous husband, and the Vagaries' greatest enemy."

"What are your plans?" Khristos asked.

"I will continue this war as best I can," she answered. "Despite this setback we have come too far to turn tail now. But to finish my plan I will need your help. Will you help me, Khristos?"

"Of course," he answered. "What do you wish me to do?"

"Get dressed," she said. "We are about to travel through the woods to a special place. Once we have arrived I will explain how you can aid the cause like no other wizard at my command."

Failee and Khristos dressed quickly under the ever-watchful gaze of the two women guarding the tent door. When they were ready, she led him from the tent and toward a wagon to which a pair of horses were harnessed. A dark canvas covered the wagon bed.

As they walked through the massive camp, the three magenta moons shone their light down through the trees, giving the bustling place a surreal appearance. Because Failee had ordered that no fires be lit this night, the camp stretched darkly for leagues into the dense forest. Hundreds of wizards, sorceresses, and Blood Stalkers walked to and fro, going about their business. Thousands of mindless but otherwise healthy male citizens who had been captured and magically turned to Failee's purpose as battle fodder could be seen everywhere, and screaming shot into the night as Failee's wizards transformed captured Vigors mystics into yet more drooling Blood Stalkers. The morale of her many mystics remained high, and they were clearly eager for another chance to meet the Vigors wizards and end this war.

Khristos smiled wryly as he wondered how the mood of Failee's many followers might change if they heard the strange news about the two recently found artifacts. Knowing better than to speak of it, he climbed aboard the wagon and sat beside Failee.

Khristos watched as Succiu, Second Mistress of the Coven, approached. Dressed all in black leather, she gave Failee and Khristos a curious look. The bullwhip hanging at her left hip and her black knee boots glinted in the light of the three red moons, as did her silken straight black hair. As Succiu neared the wagon, her exotic almond-shaped eyes searched Failee's face. Of the other three sorceresses, Succiu was the most rebellious, never missing a chance to question the First Mistress's authority. Reaching out, she brazenly grasped the horse's bridle and looked into Failee's eyes.

"Where are you two going at this hour of the night?" she asked. One corner of her lovely mouth came up. "Surely it's far too late for a picnic," she added. Knowing better than to interfere, Khristos remained silent.

Failee gave the Second Mistress a hard look. Khristos knew that Failee respected Succiu's talents in the craft, for among all four sorceresses they were second only to her own. But Succiu could be difficult and her personal predilections bizarre. He knew that this was the time for Failee to control her protégée rather than obey her request and honestly answer Succiu's pointed question.

"You have no need to know," Failee answered. "But perhaps I will tell you after we have returned. Now unhand the horse."

Succiu smiled. "As you wish, First Mistress," she answered. "But when you return, I and my fellow sisters will want answers."

Reaching down, Succiu uncoiled the whip lying at her hip and expertly snapped it out across the dewy grass. Then she raised it high and brought it down sideways, directly across the haunches of both horses.

As Failee's anger built, she quickly employed the craft to control the rearing horses and settle them down. Deciding to deal with the Second Mistress's insult later, she charged the wagon from the clearing.

Failee and Khristos rode the rumbling wagon for two hours without speaking. After Succiu's brazen actions, he knew better than to try to strike up a conversation. Besides, he had been told that everything he needed to know would be explained to him when they reached their destination. So he sat quietly beside Failee, trying to imagine what part he might play in her great scheme. Finally they approached a babbling brook and Failee pulled the horses to a stop. She climbed down from the wagon, and Khristos followed suit.

Khristos found the place unremarkable. The brook emptied into a deep pool about ten meters away, and one of its banks was a high hill covered with dense foliage. As the innocuous stream burbled along, the trees lining the bank swayed in the wind and the moonlight gently caressed the water, grass, and foliage.

Khristos turned back toward Failee to see that a strange expression had come over her face. He was about to speak when she quickly raised her arms.

The twin azure bolts that streamed from Failee's hands were among the brightest he had ever seen, and they gave him no time to react. As they hit him, he was caught up in a wizard's warp and lifted high into the air. The gleaming light that surrounded him held him tightly in its powerful embrace, allowing him only the ability to move his head and blink his eyes. He tried to cry out, but words wouldn't come. He tried to call the craft and break her spell, but her gifts were too powerful. As he hung imprisoned in the glistening azure light, he saw that Failee's face had become menacing.

"I have a mission for you, Khristos," she said, as she continued to empower the strange spell. Lowering her hands, she stepped closer and examined him approvingly, much as she might regard some fine object of art.

"It is of the utmost importance to me and it will require much sacrifice on your part," she said. "Because of that, I have taken away your power to resist me. You see, you have no choice in the matter. But once you hear me out you will better understand my motives. You might even agree with them.

"As I confided to you in my tent, I might soon lose this war," she continued. "I have no real way of taking the newly found artifacts from the wizards, save for defeating them outright. And if they are already on the path to becoming more powerful, that seems unlikely. If my sisters and I are defeated, I want the wizards and all other persons of right-leaning blood to suffer mightily for daring to oppose the Vagaries. That is why I have brought you here, Khristos. Should the war be lost, you and thousands of creatures who shall become your servants will wreak my revenge."

Returning to the wagon, Failee again raised her arms. The canvas flew away to reveal numerous earthen vessels. She used the craft to lift them gently into the air and deposit them one by one on the riverbank. A shudder went through Khristos as he tried to imagine what they might hold. Turning, the First Mistress again faced him as he hovered helplessly in the night.

"We shared some tender moments, you and I," she said. "But now they are finished. You must be wondering why I chose you for this, rather than some other wizard or sorceress. The answer is simple. You have come to love me, Khristos, and too much, I'm afraid. That makes you the logical choice. From the moment I first learned of the Tome and the Paragon, you became no more to me than a means to an end."

Fearing for his life, Khristos again tried to scream. But as before, his voice was gone. All he could do was stare in horror at the determined First Mistress as she stood there in the moonlight. Then she detailed her plan for him.

If it became clear that the war was irrevocably lost, she would return to this brook and commit suicide, releasing her blood into the water, Failee said. That would activate the final part of the spell and release Khristos so that he could start his grisly mission. Khristos would rise from the water a new being. His existence would have but one goal, as would the lives of the evolving creatures that would serve him. As he listened he silently begged her to stop, to change her mind, to abandon this madness. But she did not. When she finished her tirade she turned and walked back to stand near the many earthenware jugs.

Failee levitated the first of the vessels into the air and caused it to float to a place directly over the deep pool. Suddenly the plug flew out and landed on the dewy bank. Then the jug tilted toward one side, emptying its haunting contents into the water.

The bright azure fluid coming from the jug was slimy and slick-looking. Holding thousands of Blood Viper embryos, it caused the pool to churn and glow. One by one Failee did the same with the remaining jugs. After returning each jug to the wagon bed and again covering them with the canvas, she turned to look at Khristos. For the briefest of moments he thought he saw hint of sadness cross her face. Lowering her hands, she walked down the riverbank to where he hung in her carefully crafted warp.

"Goodbye, Khristos," she said quietly. "We shall never meet again."

At once Khristos floated out over the pool. Again he desperately tried to break the sorceress's spell, but it was no use. As he entered the cold brook water there was nothing he could do but succumb to Failee's trickery. Little by little the water rose until it covered his chin, his nose, his vision. His last view of the world was of Failee's cold, beautiful eyes staring at him.

As Khristos submerged, the brook again churned and glowed with the color of the craft. Then the water settled down, showing no trace of what had happened. After staring at the brook for a time, Failee turned and mounted the wagon. Clucking to the horses, she started back to her war camp.

In the end, Failee's war would take her far afield, never giving her the chance to return to this brook or to send an emissary of left-leaning blood to do her bidding. Little did she know that her spell would intern Khristos and the vipers for centuries, only to be activated by a common hunter whose endowed blood meant nothing to her. Nor could she have known that when Khristos and his servants were finally liberated, Gracchus and the *Pon Q'tar* would intervene and set the Viper Lord on a parallel but different course.

As the centuries passed and the spell held its sway, the newly minted Viper Lord came to understand Failee's need for revenge, and his heart softened against her treachery. He still loved her, he realized, and he always would—despite how she had used him.

So much for what my life might have been, Khristos mused as his mind returned to the moment at hand. There had been no report of the *Jin'Sai,* but he knew that it would soon come. *And so I again wait in darkness with my many servants,* he mused. *But this time my prey is far more important. Come to me,* Jin'Sai, he thought as the azure waves pounded against the shore.

Come to me and meet your fate.

CHAPTER XXV

"THE NATION WILL BE DIFFICULT TO CONTROL IF I AM not victorious," Vespasian said sternly. Taking a deep breath, he looked Tribune Flavius Maximus squarely in the face.

"You must understand that," the emperor added. "In the end there may be little glory in this task that I offer you. Should we fail to secure the Shashidan mines, the depleted state of the treasury might well give rise to a revolt. Only two legions will remain here in Ellistium with which to enforce martial law. Moreover, all the *Pon Q'tar* and Heretic ranks go with me, for I will need them in the field. That leaves only you and a handful of other tribunes who can employ the craft. I do not envy you this job."

Turning away, Vespasian resolutely folded his arms across the breastplate of his dark blue dress armor and looked around the room. He would be leaving the palace soon, perhaps never to return. He would miss it.

Vespasian stood in his private office. Broad and spacious, the room was magnificently decorated. Massive oak doors lay in the far wall, closed for the moment and guarded by two centurions on the other side to ensure privacy. The floor was made of highly polished onyx and alabaster checkerboard squares, and in its center was inlaid the letter *V* in solid gold. The walls were tall, with fluted pilasters between the many colorful frescoes. A wide skylight let in air and sunlight. Vespasian's elaborately carved desk stood nearby, its top littered with parchments, beeswax plaques, styli, and abaci.

Vespasian turned and walked out onto his balcony, thinking. His legions and armada were ready and the momentous day had finally arrived. The forum lay before him, its beautiful columns and majestic buildings glistening in the midday sun.

Looking down at the impatiently waiting throng, it seemed to him that every single Ellistiumite had come to this spot to cheer the war procession's departure from the city. The sun was high and the day hot, and the eager spectators had already waited for hours. Turning back to look at Flavius Maximus, Vespasian realized that the citizens would have to wait longer still, for he refused to leave the tribune in control of the capital until matters were clearly understood.

"What say you?" he asked sternly. "Are you up to the task? Will you and your two legions fight to the death if need be to maintain control in my absence? If not, simply tell me and I will appoint another in your stead. I will attach no shame to your decision should you decline. But I must know that whomever I leave in charge can be relied on."

Putting down his wineglass, Flavius rose from his seat at the meeting table he shared with Persephone and Lucius Marius. Without hesitation he walked to his emperor. Thumping his clenched right fist against his chest, then opening his palm and thrusting it forward, he gave Vespasian his best military salute. Vespasian eyed him warily, wondering whether the show of loyalty was a bit too hearty.

"You have my devotion unto death," Flavius answered. "Surely you know that. We have fought in many battles together, and I wish I were going with you yet again. But we each know that a soldier cannot choose where he fights. I have every confidence that you will succeed in taking the Shashidan mines and return home in triumph. Seeing our forces parade back through the forum with countless wagons full of Shashidan gold will indeed be a day to tell our children's children about."

Thinking about how his course had come to be set, Vespasian thoughtfully walked farther out onto the balcony, this time allowing the adoring crowds to see him. At once thunderous cheers arose and thousands of flower petals filled the air like so many snowflakes suddenly in a blizzard. Despite having secured the public's badly needed confidence, Vespasian remained worried, ever calculating.

My subjects desperately want this campaign, Vespasian thought as he waved back at them. *And why wouldn't they, after the Suffragat took such pains to persuade them of its righteousness. But what do civilians know of war? Just one day on the battlefield would change many minds, but there can be no going back now.* As he watched the crowd, his thoughts drifted back to the difficult Suffragat meeting that he had overseen yesterday.

The ordeal of choosing a tribune to rule in Vespasian's absence had been politically charged and time consuming. The *Pon Q'tar* had wanted a man named Magnus Attilus to oversee Ellistium in Vespasian's absence, and in many ways Attilus would have been a good choice. Attilus was mature and wise, a brilliant field commander and a powerful craft practitioner. He might have served well, and he had been on Vespasian's list of choices.

But in the end Attilus was the *Pon Q'tar*'s man through and through, and because of Vespasian's growing concerns about Gracchus' motives, the emperor had finally rejected him. As expected, the *Pon Q'tar* immediately voiced an outraged protest. The Suffragat had then bickered for hours like maids at the market until Vespasian became disgusted and finally used his power of official decree to proclaim Flavius as the new Imperator Tempitatus, or temporary ruler. Flavius was well aware of how he had come to be chosen, the emperor's defiant act further cementing his well-known allegiance to Vespasian even more.

Hoping that he had chosen wisely, Vespasian took another deep breath, then turned to again look at the man who would serve in his stead. If there was ever a stalwart tribune, it was Flavius.

Short, stocky, and sturdy as a marble column, Flavius wore a neatly trimmed red beard. Dark blue eyes and a flat, crooked nose that had been crushed twice in battle highlighted his imposing face. His hair was red, close-cropped, and thinning slightly at the temples. As he stood before Vespasian he looked splendid in his dress uniform, complete with golden breastplate and matching gauntlets, greaves, and blood-red cape.

Flavius was a devoted family man with a loving wife named Atia and three sons of fully endowed blood, each of whom was a centurion in the famed Twenty-fifth Legion. Vespasian knew that watching their sons go would be hard for Flavius and Atia, but their loyalty to the empire was unswerving.

He looks every bit the commanding emperor, Vespasian thought as he studied Flavius. *That is good, for his lot here will not be an easy one.*

Vespasian glanced over Flavius' shoulder to give the First Tribune a questioning look. Lucius took another sip of wine, thinking. After placing the wine goblet back atop the table he nodded, signaling his agreement. Vespasian looked back into Flavius' eyes.

"Very well, then," he said simply. "It is done."

Walking to his desk, Vespasian took up a rolled-up parchment and a gold ring, then walked back to stand before Flavius. He handed the parchment to the new Imperator Tempitatus. Flavius accepted it gratefully.

"This official decree holds my and Gracchus' signatures," Vespasian said. "It is also marked with my seal, further proving that I have appointed you to your new station. In the absence of the Suffragat it additionally empowers you to declare martial law and to do away with the right to trial should you see fit. If a revolt arises, immediately set an example by executing several of the suspected rabble-rousers. Their guilt or innocence is unimportant—nothing deters anarchy like very sudden and very public killings. Make their deaths slow and gruesome before giving their bodies to the usual lot of corpse collectors and bone grinders."

Vespasian then handed the gold signet ring to Flavius. It was a gorgeous piece of jewelry, produced overnight on the emperor's order. The letter *F* was deeply inscribed into the face of the ring. Vespasian watched as Flavius reverently placed it onto the third finger of his right hand.

"Guard that ring with your life, just as I guard mine," Vespasian said. "It is the only way that I will know that your messages are genuine. Most of your communiqués will be by mental communion with Gracchus. But if you wish to tell me something in secret, send a parchment containing your seal by messenger bird. It will take longer, but I will have no doubt of its veracity."

Flavius gave Vespasian another crisp salute. "All will be as you order," he said. Then he stepped nearer and placed one hand atop Vespasian's shoulder. "And I thank you for this honor," he said softly.

Vespasian gave a short laugh. "Don't thank me yet, old friend," he said wryly. "The time for that will be if I come home laden with Shashidan gold."

"You mean *when*!" Lucius laughingly shouted.

Vespasian looked over to see that the First Tribune had risen to his feet. Taking another slug of wine, he smiled broadly, then sauntered past Vespasian and Flavius and out onto the balcony. The impatient crowd promptly roared again, this time so loudly that it nearly hurt everyone's ears. Smiling, Lucius turned back to look at Vespasian.

"Now that the formalities are over, it's high time we got going!" he said with a wink. "Those poor civilians waiting down there are starting to wilt."

Vespasian nodded at Lucius, then looked at Persephone and reached out to her.

"My love," he said simply.

Persephone rose from the table to take her husband's hand. As she did so, Vespasian stretched his other hand out toward Flavius. The Imperator Tempitatus responded by slapping his palm against the inside of Vespasian's forearm and grasping it firmly, signaling the common greeting between devoted legionnaires.

Vespasian smiled. "Walk out with us," he said to Flavius. "I want the people to see you standing by my side in your new role. It will help to cement the transition."

Vespasian raised one hand and called the craft. As the massive doors parted and Persephone, Lucius, and Flavius passed through, Vespasian paused for a moment to take a last look around the room in which he had agonized over so many difficult decisions. For better or worse, from this day forward all of his choices would be made in the field. Finally he turned and followed the others out.

In the end it would take hours for Vespasian's lead chariot, Persephone's personal litter, the litters of the *Pon Q'tar* members and Julia Idaeus, and the two valiant legions that would return to serve under Flavius' command to navigate the broad forum and wend their way among the thousands of adoring citizens. Trumpeters and drummers heralded Vespasian's departure while untold multitudes of colorful handkerchiefs waved and thousands more flower petals rained down from windows and balconies. In two days the procession would link up with the remaining twenty-eight legions awaiting them at the fountainhead of the Six Rivers, near the boundary of the Borderlands. From there the *Pon Q'tar*'s azure portals would transport them the thousands of leagues to where the fighting would start in earnest. It would be a campaign like no other, and regardless of its success or failure, it would forever change the fate of Rustannica.

As Vespasian guided his two white stallions through the forum and toward the city limits, even now he worried about the great venture that he had birthed. Little did he understand the ever-rising danger of what he had set in motion, for there were forces awaiting him the likes of which no Rustannican emperor had ever seen.

Deciding to meet his destiny head-on, Vespasian grimly slapped his reins across the stallions' haunches.

CHAPTER XXVI

FROM HIS VANTAGE POINT ON THE CAVE FLOOR TRISTAN looked up to watch ever more Minion warriors walk down the stone steps and enter the Caves of the Paragon. The torches they carried cast macabre shadows across the cave walls, reminding him of how eerie this beautiful place could be.

Wigg, Scars, Tyranny, Astrid, Phoebe, and Jessamay stood nearby, each of them stunned into silence by this wondrous place. Tristan had come here several times before and he knew what this first chamber looked like. But some members of his party had never visited here, and amazement registered on their faces. Despite Tristan's familiarity with the Caves, their magnificence again took his breath away.

The journey to the Caves had been uneventful, but Tristan and his group remained unaware of how to find the Azure Sea. As a precaution, each warrior carried a supply of food and potable water strapped across his or her back, in case the search became protracted. But Tristan still hoped that they might somehow find the sea without great difficulty, allowing them to soon be on their way to Shashida. Looking around again, he recalled what he knew of this sacred place.

The Caves had supposedly been carved out of living rock aeons ago by the Ones Who Came Before, but no one on the eastern side of the Tolenkas knew for sure. The Conclave believed that a previous *Jin'Sai* and *Jin'Saiou* had used the caves as a hiding place for the Tome and the Paragon after their unsuccessful bid to secure their destinies, and one could only assume that they were long dead.

More than three hundred years ago, Wigg had found the Caves quite by accident. The Paragon had been suspended amid the rushing red waterfall, the vibrant waters supporting the life of the stone while it awaited its new masters. Those new masters were to become the Directorate of Wizards, the Vigors mystics aligned against Failee, her Coven, and the forces of the Vagaries in the struggle known as the Sorceresses' War. Had the two precious artifacts come into the possession of Failee rather than the Directorate, the world east of the Tolenkas might have become a far darker place.

As Tristan watched, Wigg raised one hand and called the craft to bring flame to the many torches lining the cavern walls. With the added light came a better view of this amazing first room.

Tristan and the others were standing on the floor of a huge, irregular underground cavern that was at least several hundred meters long in each direction as well as high. Stalactites of every color and description hung from the ceiling, some so long they almost reached the floor. Many of their older brothers had found the floor some time ago, creating here and there the impression of marvelously beautiful stone columns.

As yet more Minions cautiously entered the cave, the roar of the nearby waterfall continued to assault Tristan's ears, and he turned to look. The waterfall was nearly the same height as the stone steps—about forty feet—and at least as wide. Springing from a tunnel in the opposite wall of the cavern, the water traveled about twenty feet across a smooth stone slab before finally falling gracefully over a precipice into a large stone pool at the bottom. At the far end of the pool, the water ran out through a low tunnel in the rock, ensuring that the basin would never overflow. Looking at the other walls, Tristan noticed a great variety of plants and flowers growing on them that he had seen nowhere else, and the floor was also covered with thick green foliage. Every plant was huge, its colors amazingly vibrant.

Against one stone wall stood a large, square-cut tunnel entrance, and Tristan knew by experience that entering it was the only way to penetrate deeper into the Caves. It was obviously man-made and at least ten feet high and fifteen feet across. A smooth rectangular panel carved into the stone wall above it contained an inscription in Old Eutracian. As

Tristan thought about what lay beyond it, he recalled the many added passageways and confusing intersections that his late son Nicholas had excavated while preparing to construct the Gates of Dawn.

But there was more about the Azure Sea that confounded Tristan and Wigg besides the seemingly impossible task of finding it again. Ragnar, the traitorous consul who had served Nicholas, had told them that the sea was a byproduct of Nicholas' excavation of the Caves to house his hatchlings as they matured. Ragnar had gone on to say that another underground river ran through that area, not unlike the falling red waters of the first chamber that had for so long supported the life of the unattended Paragon. During the excavation, the unusual spring was laid bare, he claimed, flooding the entire area around it and creating the strange sea. But rather than being red, these waters were azure—the color generated during a significant manifestation of the craft.

Even so, with the discovery of the subtle matter message claiming that the way to Shashida lay across the Azure Sea, Ragnar's explanation suddenly made no sense. The message was supposedly aeons old, yet Nicholas' excavation of the Caves had occurred fewer than three years before.

So who was telling the truth? the Conclave wondered. Had the consul lied knowingly? Had the madness caused by his partial transformation into a Blood Stalker caused him to believe the lies he told? Or was he simply playing some twisted prank on Tristan and Wigg while he had abused them? The Conclave mystics had discussed the matter for hours and arrived at no satisfactory conclusion. In the end they agreed that the only true answer lay with the Ones in Shashida. And to get there the Conclave must first cross the Azure Sea.

No matter what the truth might be, our path is clear, Tristan thought. *We must enter that forbidding tunnel. But from the first confusing intersection to the last, we will be walking into uncharted territory.*

Just then Tristan realized something else. Every other time that he had come here, the red waters of the caves had exerted a strange effect on him, causing his heart to beat rapidly, his breathing to become labored, and a feeling of faintness to overpower him. More than once these symptoms had nearly killed him. Wigg and Faegan had long assumed that the high quality of Tristan's blood caused the cave water to affect him adversely whenever he neared it. He had in fact been dreading his entrance into this first chamber for just those reasons.

But today he felt no such life-threatening symptoms. Smiling, he again turned to look at the waterfall. Not being affected by the water was a wonderfully liberating feeling.

Just then Wigg approached. Raising one eyebrow at Tristan, the wizard placed his hands into the opposite sleeves of his robe.

"You seem to remain well this time," he mused.

"Yes," Tristan answered. "It's amazing. Why do you think that is?"

Wigg scowled with thought. "I can only guess that this unexpected development has to do with your unique blood," he answered.

"In what way?" Tristan asked.

Wigg shook his head. "Unknown," he answered. "It might be because your blood was once azure, but a better explanation eludes me. Yet another question for the Ones, it would seem."

Tristan turned to look at the Minion warriors still descending the stairs. Two full phalanxes had accompanied him here—one phalanx for each Black Ship—for a total of four thousand. He then looked around the massive stone room and back at the First Wizard.

"We need to make a decision," Tristan said. "The tunnel entrance is only about fifteen feet across, yet every warrior must follow us in. Even so, this first chamber seems large enough to accommodate everyone at once. Should we wait until all the warriors have assembled, or shall we enter the tunnel while they are still descending the stairs?"

Wigg turned to look at the tunnel entrance, thinking. Then he looked at the seemingly endless parade of warriors still entering the Caves. It would take many hours for them all to assemble, he realized. And even then only a certain number could enter the tunnel at once. He turned to look at Tristan.

"The Conclave members should go now," he said, "followed by the first group of warriors. We'll leave Ox in charge here to oversee the flow of remaining warriors into the tunnel and then bring up the rear. In any case, it's important that—"

"Wigg!" Jessamay shouted from somewhere behind them. "Come here—I need you!"

The Conclave members turned to see Jessamay standing before the tunnel entrance. There was a strange, searching look on her face. When her eyes met Wigg's she hurriedly waved him over. As the Conclave members neared her, she hushed them into silence.

"Do you hear that?" she asked Wigg.

Wigg called the craft to augment his hearing. Soon the look on his face told Tristan that whatever sound Jessamay was talking about, the First Wizard now also heard. Unable to detect any noise but the rushing waterfall, the others simply stood there, baffled.

"I do," Wigg answered. "How odd . . ."

Taking a step backward, he looked into the depths of the tunnel. "It's coming from in there," he said. "But this sound is something new. I have never heard it before."

"What are you talking about?" Tyranny demanded. "I can't hear anything except our voices and the waterfalls."

"Nor is it likely that you would," Wigg answered the privateer. "Only a craft practitioner could detect this."

"What does it sound like?" Tristan asked.

Wigg looked at Jessamay. "Help me," he said simply. Guessing Wigg's intentions, Jessamay nodded.

The two mystics turned to face the vibrant waterfalls. After looking at one another, they raised their hands and again called the craft. To Tristan's amazement, the waterfalls stopped producing any sound, even though the water still tumbled down into the stone pool as vigorously as before.

Tristan was about to speak again when he too heard the new sound. At first he couldn't identify it. But he finally recognized it for what it was. It was the sound of wave after wave crashing against some distant shore.

Is this the Azure Sea we hear? he asked himself. *But how could that be? The sea supposedly lies far away from this first chamber. And even if it is the Azure Sea, why do I hear it this time but never before?*

Tristan looked at Wigg with unbelieving eyes. "How . . ." he breathed.

Wigg shook his head. "I don't know," he answered. His expression was worried. "But two things are certain. First, this sound is being carried here by the craft. Given how far away the sea probably lies from this chamber, that must be the case. And second, the sound is meant to draw us in and to help us find the sea."

"But who would do this?" Tristan asked. "Few craft practitioners know about this place. Fewer still would have the ability to enact such a spell."

Wigg turned to again look at the tunnel. The ocean noises continued unabated. *Come to us,* the distant waves seemed to whisper. *Come to us, for your destinies lie this way.*

After thinking for a time, the First Wizard looked at the Conclave members.

"There is but one likely answer," he said. "The Ones did this. I believe that they left this spell behind to be activated when the subtle matter message was released in the Redoubt. While it's true that the message did not mention this phenomenon, I believe that the coincidence is too great to be anything else. In any event, we have no choice but to enter the tunnel. Take heart—following the sound should make our quest an easier one."

Tristan glanced over at Tyranny to see her shoot him a decidedly skeptical look. Tristan shared her suspicions, but he also understood that they had no choice but to follow the sound wherever it led them.

"All right," he said. "We'll go."

Tristan turned to look at the growing number of eager Minions milling behind him. "Ox!" he called out. "Come here!"

A few moments later the stalwart warrior appeared by Tristan's side. He came to attention and clicked his boot heels together. "I live to serve," he said.

Tristan gave him a commanding look. "Have the two crates brought forward," he ordered. "Make sure that they are handled carefully!" Ox quickly disappeared into the crowd to do his duty.

Soon the huge Minion's bellowing voice could be heard again as he led the way back, roughly parting the warrior crowd as he came. Behind him walked two pairs of hand-picked male warriors, each pair bearing a wooden crate hung between two poles. On Tristan's order they gently set the crates down near his feet. Tristan gazed at the crates, part of him still unable to believe what they contained.

Each crate held one miniaturized Black Ship that rested securely in its cradle. The empty space surrounding each ship had been enchanted to hold the vessels in place and to buffer them against jostling or—Afterlife forbid—dropping. One of the crates also held the jar containing some of the remaining subtle matter, the rest left behind in the Redoubt for safekeeping.

Each dark wooden crate stood about three feet high by two feet wide and was divided in half down its center. The bottom seams were connected by brass hinges, and the halves were held together by leather straps with brass buckles. Stout poles ran beneath the straps so that each pair of warriors could carry a crate by placing the poles atop their shoulders, the crates suspended between them as they walked along. Each crate glowed hauntingly with the hue of the craft.

Tristan looked at the four warriors who would carry the precious crates. Each was a battle-scarred graybeard carefully selected for his strength and loyalty. Although Arron, Taredd, Rhun, and Rafal were older than many, Traax had heartily recommended each of them, and Ox and Duvessa had agreed. Tristan gave each warrior a hard look.

"These crates and their contents are your responsibility," he warned them. "You will guard them with your lives. They are the keys to getting across the Azure Sea and back alive. Not only do the ships and the subtle matter rest in your hands, but so too does the fate of everyone taking part in this expedition. Do you understand?"

At once all four warriors came to attention. "Yes!" their leader answered sternly. "We will make sure that the *Jin'Sai* will not regret the trust he has placed in us."

Tristan nodded. "See that you do," he answered.

Tristan looked back at the tunnel entrance with suspicion. There was very little about this imminent journey that he liked, but they must undertake it if they were to reach Shashida. Ragnar had poisoned Tristan and blinded Wigg in those murky depths while Nicholas prepared to raise the three Gates of Dawn. In the end Nicholas had failed, but the savage horrors inflicted on Tristan in these caves still lingered in his heart and gave him pause.

Worse yet was the inescapable fact that so many warriors would be moving through many passageways at the same time, creating a logistical nightmare. If Tristan's group was attacked, there would be little fighting room, and those warriors following behind him would be nearly powerless to help. But there was nothing to be done about it.

Tristan was about to give the order to enter the tunnel when he looked up at the inscription, probably placed there by the Ones. The elegant Old Eutracian script meant nothing to him. He turned toward Wigg and pointed at the words.

"You never told me what that means," he said.

Wigg smiled. Without needing to read it, he solemnly recited the ancient inscription:

"*Quicumque ambulare semtae accipere veritas,*" the wizard answered. "Whoever walks these paths shall learn the truth."

"That doesn't mean much," Tyranny protested.

Wigg shook his head. "On the contrary," he answered. "The search for the truth is why we're all here, is it not?"

Saying nothing more, the wizard raised one arm and called the craft to illuminate the millions of radiance stones embedded in the tunnel ceiling. At once the passageway glowed with a pale sage-green light. Tristan looked far into the tunnel but could see no end to its depths.

After nodding to Wigg, Tristan stepped inside, and the other Conclave members followed. As Ox waited behind to direct the flow of warriors into the tunnel, Taredd, Rhun, Arron, and Rafal lifted the poles bearing the crates atop their shoulders and also entered. Watching them go, Ox clenched his jaw.

Go safe, Jin'Sai, he thought, as Tristan's back finally became lost in the crowd. *This time Ox will be too far behind to protect you.*

CHAPTER XXVII

 IN TWO MORE HOURS THE SUN WOULD RISE, MAKING IT more difficult for the lead cleric to hide his face.

As Gracchus skulked through the dark war camp, his need to be anonymous was irritating. It made him want to rebel, to stand erect, to announce his august presence to these lowly legionnaires. But to succeed in his plan, the *Pon Q'tar* lead cleric would have to swallow his pride for the moment and do what he must. And so he hurried on, bent over like some nameless, crippled beggar trying to avoid wandering centurions as he navigated the camp.

The war procession had halted for the night among broad, rolling fields well south of Ellistium. Behind Gracchus the luxurious tents of the emperor, the Tribunes, and the *Pon Q'tar* retreated into the distance, the oil lamps inside each tent casting their soft glow through the canvas and into the night. Between him and his destination were thousands of legionnaires ringing the camp's center, not to mention the caged animals and the thousands of carts, chariots, and wagons that always accompanied great Rustannican campaigns.

Hurrying on, Gracchus put as much distance between himself and the Blood Royal's compound as he could. For a moment he regretted the decision to leave the secret structure so far from the center of the camp, only to realize again that he had little choice if he was to visit it without others knowing. He had explained the decision to Vespasian by insisting that the structure would be safer by making it invisible and not circling it with centurion guards, just as it had been when it secretly left Ellistium with the war procession. Vespasian had at first been skeptical of the idea but he finally agreed, largely because his forces had not yet entered enemy territory.

Gracchus had wisely replaced his white and burgundy *Pon Q'tar* robe with the drab brown one he now wore, but it added to his grating sense of ignominy. Pulling the hood higher, he continued to cloak his endowed blood as he hurried across the dewy grass, circumventing yet another group of tired legionnaires as they sat drinking beside a roaring campfire.

There were tens of thousands of empire soldiers in these two accompanying legions alone, and each one knew Gracchus by sight. Worse, there would be many more of them to avoid once Vespasian's group joined up with the forces waiting at the head of the Six Rivers. Their added numbers would make his visits to the secret building far more difficult, but the die was cast and there could be no going back.

Above all, Vespasian, Persephone, and Lucius must not learn of his secret assignations. Should legionnaires challenge him, Gracchus would silently kill them with the craft, then magically dispose of the bodies. Although desertion among the legions was rare, it was not unheard of, But even Gracchus hoped that that would not be needed—not because he would shrink from murder to achieve his ends, but because it would further complicate his already devious plan. Should the Oraculum give him unwelcome news, he surely didn't want Vespasian aware of his visits beforehand.

Finally exiting the camp without incident, he scrambled down a small gully, then traveled up a dry river bed for about fifty meters. The great oak tree standing on the riverbank served as his landmark. He stopped and looked around.

The night was still, the three red moons casting their magenta glow over everything with their customary beauty. The night creatures that had stopped singing when he neared gradually took up their songs again as he stood motionless, his endowed senses searching for a sign of human life. When his surroundings finally returned to normal, Gracchus decided that he was at last alone. He raised his arms and called the craft.

Soon a temple appeared in the center of the riverbed, its structure gleaming serenely in the moonlight. Small and low, it was made of white alabaster with a peaked roof and seven steps leading to its columned portico. Heavy marble doors locked from the outside stood high and broad in the facing wall. Although the temple had but one purpose, it was vital to Gracchus' plans. Despite being a huge encumbrance, the entire Suffragat had agreed that it should come on the campaign. But Gracchus had his own reasons for insisting that the temple be brought along, for there were secrets that only the *Pon Q'tar* must know if the Vagaries were to rule this side of the world as well as the other.

The lead cleric hurried up the stone steps, then called the craft. At once the massive doors swung wide. He walked into the temple, and the doors silently closed behind him. Had anyone been watching, he would have seen the temple start to shimmer, then disappear from sight, leaving only the night creatures to attest that it ever existed.

Lowering his hood, Gracchus walked midway across the highly polished floor. Looking at the far wall he was relieved to see that the *Pon Q'tar*'s wondrous construct had survived the journey intact. The inside of the temple was simple and bare, with only a handful of enchanted wall torches providing light. The air was warm and odorless.

As he had hoped, the far wall glowed with a soft azure hue. Its depths seemed limitless. Curved shards of white light wheeled and streaked through the azure aura. The strange masterwork of the craft emitted a soft roaring, crackling sound like that of a blazing fire. Raising his hand, Gracchus again summoned the craft. At once the shimmering wall slid closer, causing the familiar glowing cube to take form. The cube came to a stop a few meters from his boots.

"Come to me," he ordered.

As the Oraculum emerged, a strange look showed on her face, and her dark eyes searched the unfamiliar room. Her tattered gray gown flowing about her in the mist, she said nothing as she hung weightless in her endowed prison.

"Do you know where you are, Matsuko?" Gracchus asked almost politely.

"I know that this room is not the one in which I have been imprisoned for so many centuries," she answered. "I could sense that this structure was moving and that until only moments ago it was surrounded by the workings of the craft—a spell of invisibility, perhaps. But I do not know where we have come or why."

"We are on a great campaign against Shashida," Gracchus answered.

"You are now housed in temple built of solid alabaster and especially enchanted to keep you imprisoned. I caused a spell of forgetfulness to pass over you while you and your cube were moved from belowground. We call this place the Oraculum Tempitatum. But you need be told no more than that."

"A great campaign," Matsuko mused. At first the news stunned her, but soon a slight smile crossed her lips. "This is the first time that you have taken me from my underground prison. Your reasons for bringing me with you must be important, considering that you could simply have left me in Ellistium and touched my mind to hear my pronouncements. Why am I here, Gracchus?"

The cleric's jaw hardened. Bringing the Oraculum along on the campaign was a great hardship, but a necessary one. With Vespasian's blessing, this temple had been hastily constructed by the *Pon Q'tar* to move the Oraculum without fear of her escaping imprisonment.

Moving her glowing cube from one locale to another without encasing it within another strongly walled object was unthinkable—she remained far too powerful for Gracchus to trust such pedestrian measures of confinement as mere chains or barred cages. Only solid, enchanted stone might keep her trapped should she somehow slip the bonds of her azure cube. That was why she had been imprisoned beneath the ground so long ago and why she and her glowing cube were being transported in this gleaming temple, its alabaster sides enchanted by the craft to strengthen them and to cloak the presence of her highly endowed blood.

Causing the temple to become invisible and to float through the air among the advancing legions had been a huge drain on several of the cleric's gifts. The strain in the coming days would be no less severe. But it was needed because the legions would soon be linking up, then entering Shashidan territory, the Oraculum's onetime home world. Moreover, the Oraculum was unknown to anyone other than the Suffragat, and so she had to be spirited from the capital in secret. If her pronouncements could be secretly used to their advantage in the war, the clerics' and emperor's victories would seem all the more inspired.

Despite her advanced age, Gracchus suspected that the Oraculum's powers were still great. The Vigors worshippers would not only kill to get her back, but they would consider her return to their midst a huge moral victory. Her escape would be a no less stunning defeat for those who ruled the Rustannican Empire, so no chance could be taken that she might somehow vanish. Gracchus needed her visions if he was to wisely manage the ongoing struggle being carried out by the Viper Lord. But there was another, far more personal reason why he had insisted during the Suffragat voting session that the Oraculum accompany the legions on this mighty campaign. It was one that only he understood and could put into practice. He needed to look into her face as she offered up her pronouncements.

Gracchus had never dared to rely on the convenience of distantly touching her mind to learn what she had to say. Instead, he had for aeons visited her personally. He needed to look into her eyes, to see her face, to hear the quality of her voice to determine the veracity of her words. Indeed, by now his ability to judge her persona had become so keen that he immediately knew when she was lying, and because of it she had not dared do so for centuries. Even so, should he abandon visiting her in person and rely only on touching her mind, he had no doubt that her lying would recommence. Like the desperate campaign against Shashida, the struggle being carried out by the Viper Lord was of the utmost importance. The intelligence gleaned from the Oraculum must be genuine. And for that, only being in her presence would do.

Gracchus refused to answer. She knew why she was here, he realized. Besides, her inquiry was meant only to taunt him, and he would not honor her with a response.

"Tell me what you have seen," he said.

Again the ghostly, knowing smile crossed the Oraculum's lips. As it did, a tingle went down Gracchus' spine.

This is why I come to see her, he thought. *It is small gestures like this that tell me if her words are genuine. Her smile says that she has bad news and that she will enjoy telling it to me. That alone is enough to ensure that her information is genuine.*

When Matsuko did not speak as soon as the anxious cleric wanted, he took a quick step forward, glaring into her weathered face.

"Tell me, you wizened crone!" he demanded. "What have you seen?"

Again her curious smile surfaced. "I have seen many things," she answered, "not one of which you will like."

Gracchus' heart fell. "Go on," he said cautiously.

"The *Jin'Sai*'s mystics have miniaturized two of their Black Ships," she answered. "He and two Minion phalanxes enter the caves in search of the Azure Sea. They bring the ships with them. I needn't tell you why. The other two ships remain full size and were left behind for the

Jin'Saiou's use in hunting down the Viper Lord. They rest in newly constructed cradles that sit alongside the royal palace in Tammerland."

Gracchus took an involuntary step backward, stunned. "How . . ." he breathed.

"They used some of the subtle matter to accomplish their ends," the Oraculum answered. Then she went still again as she floated hauntingly in her majestic cube. Gracchus found her defiant silence infuriating.

Enraged by her teasing answer, he shook his fists at her. "Of course they used the subtle matter, you Vigors bitch!" he shouted. "But how did they come by the specialized knowledge to employ it?"

"From the Shashidans," she answered. "They left behind both a message that Shashida lay across the Azure Sea, and a formula showing the *Jin'Sai's* mystics how to transform the ships. Their plan was perfect. And now the most powerful of all the *Jin'Sai*s ever to walk the earth has finally uncovered it. As we speak, he and his mystics search the Caves. If they are not intercepted and destroyed—"

"I know full well what will happen if they are not destroyed!" Gracchus screamed. He had become so uncharacteristically incensed that his whole body was shaking. Calling the craft, he arduously settled his nerves, then gave the Oraculum a seething look.

"You have made a grave error, Gracchus," Matsuko said. "Why did you order Khristos and his servants to wait inside the Caves rather than attack the *Jin'Sai* aboveground? Tristan has but two phalanxes with him. By allowing this you have granted him a great advantage, it would seem. Every step he takes brings him that much closer to Shashida."

The Oraculum smiled again. "Things are unraveling on you, Gracchus," she said. "It would seem that the lead *Pon Q'tar* cleric is not as invulnerable now as during the heady days of yesteryear."

Gracchus paced the floor, fuming. He would not tell her why he had allowed the *Jin'Sai* to enter the caves, even though there had been no other choice. He could not let her know that Khristos' servants were starving for lack of endowed bodies on which to feed and that the only way to sustain them in such multitudes and simultaneously augment their powers was to send them into the caves to devour Nicholas' glowing eggs. But as he considered the situation further, he again took heart.

Khristos still had the element of surprise. Moreover, the *Jin'Sai's* forces would be heavily outnumbered. Despite the Oraculum's grim pronouncements, Gracchus' plan still had the edge. He could of course commune with Khristos and call off the attack, but that would allow the *Jin'Sai* to reach the sea unimpeded.

No, he realized. It would be better to let things stay on course even if Tristan did bring two ships with him. But the Conclave would have to be stopped at all costs, for Gracchus could not fathom the troubles that would ensue if the *Jin'Sai* crossed the Azure Sea. Even now he could imagine Khristos employing the spell that he had ordered him to use, causing the sounds of the sea to reach the first chamber of the caves and draw the *Jin'Sai* near.

"Tell me, Gracchus," the Oraculum said, interrupting his thoughts. "Does the Blood Royal know how badly things have gone awry on the other side of the world? If he does, I can only imagine how angry he must be with you. And if not, there must be some facet about all this that you hide from him. Either way, the future does not bode well. You are playing a very dangerous game."

The sudden combination of the Oraculum's bad news and her growing insolence caused Gracchus' anger to finally reach the boiling point. Deciding to teach her a long-awaited lesson in humility, he raised his arms and called the craft.

At once the Oraculum began writhing in exquisite pain—the same pain that Gracchus had used when she had first tried lying to him so long ago. She had not felt such agony for aeons, and it came as a total shock. But this time she was not being punished for lying, because her words had been true. Instead, Gracchus wanted only to reestablish his personal brand of terror.

As Gracchus continued to torture her she felt hot, searing pains burn along her nerve endings like blazing fires running amok through a tinder-dry forest. She screamed as Gracchus' wicked gifts continued to pass through the cube—the cube that had been enchanted in such a way that his spells could reach her, but inside of which only her ability to see what the Orb of the Vigor saw was of use to her. She had tried for aeons to secretly unravel Gracchus' manipulative spell that enforced this one-sided effect, but to no end. And so she hung helpless in the azure mist, her body jangling like a marionette manipulated by a cruel master.

Gracchus finally stopped the spell, and the Oraculum crashed to the floor. He hadn't killed her—that would be unthinkable, even for him. He needed her alive, at least until his secret plans involving Vespasian, the campaign, and the Viper Lord had come to fruition. But when that day arrived, he would relish watching her die.

As she lay sobbing on the cold stone floor he called the craft and ordered the glistening azure cube to again retreat into the far wall. Pulling up the hood of his well-worn robe, he ordered the doors to open and briskly exited the Oraculum Tempitatum. There were new things to be done, including communing with Khristos as soon as possible.

When the doors closed, Matsuko slowly raised her head. She felt broken, used, abandoned. Tears filled her eyes, their coming as much a result of having to tell Gracchus the truth as of the intense pain he had inflicted on her. The physical pain would go away, she realized, but the psychological torment of continually having to help Gracchus defeat her Shashidan countrymen would remain, just as it had done for countless centuries.

Suddenly she could again sense Gracchus' unique application of the craft, suggesting that this strange new prison in which he was now housed had once more become invisible. Her fellow Shashidans might soon be looking right at it and not know that it existed or that she was imprisoned inside. That thought pierced her being more painfully than any torture the lead cleric might inflict on her.

How clever, Gracchus, she thought as what strength she still possessed slowly returned. But the lead cleric had said too much, she realized. Unless she missed her guess, she and this strange new temple would soon be in Shashidan territory. For what reason, she still did not know. But one thing was certain.

If there was a way to escape this new prison, she would find it and take her sweet, long-overdue revenge.

CHAPTER XXVIII

"HEAR ME, KHRISTOS," GRACCHUS ORDERED. *"YOU MUST COMmune with me, even if the battle has started! What I have to tell you is of the utmost importance!"*

Waiting among some of his many servants in one of the dark tunnels facing the Azure Sea, Khristos immediately sensed the cleric calling out to his mind. His lead vipers had returned, saying that the *Jin'Sai* was nearing the cave entrance. It would only be a matter of time now.

Cloaking his blood while also forcing the ocean sounds through one of the many tunnels was severely taxing his gifts, but he would prevail. As Khristos patiently waited he hungered for Failee's killer to come nearer so that he might personally avenge her. Since learning that it had been Tristan who murdered his love, his need to face the *Jin'Sai* had become overpowering. Clutching his silver staff in one hand, he fell to his knees and closed his eyes.

"I am here, Gracchus," he answered silently. *"The battle has yet to be joined."*

"Good," the lead cleric answered. *"The* Jin'Sai *brings with him prizes that must be destroyed at all costs. Two of his Black Ships have been shrunk by a craft device called subtle matter. He means to use the ships to cross the Azure Sea. I understand how badly you want to see the* Jin'Sai *die, for I share the same dream. But destroying the ships and the subtle matter is of equal importance. Destroy them, Khristos, and do not fail!"*

For a moment the Viper Lord was dumbfounded that the ships could be so radically transformed. Even Failee would have not dreamed it possible.

"*We will not fail,*" he said. "*Consider the ships destroyed and the* Jin'Sai *as good as dead.*"

As he sensed Gracchus' ken slipping away, Khristos opened his eyes and came to his feet. Knowing that time was short, he started urgently whispering new orders to his lead vipers, then concentrated again on sending the ocean sounds through the length of a nearby tunnel—the one the *Jin'Sai* and his traitorous Vigors worshippers would soon exit. Then the Viper Lord smiled.

The game was afoot.

THREE HOURS LATER, TRISTAN STOOD JUST INSIDE THE entrance to a rough-hewn tunnel that looked out onto a sandy beach. The Azure Sea, white-capped and restless, lay beyond. On Tristan's orders, no one had ventured outside the tunnel. Unlike the times before, this trip had been uneventful, something for which the prince and the First Wizard were grateful.

Sword in hand, Tristan could see and hear the waves strike the sandy shoreline about fifty meters away. Because of the ongoing ocean sounds, reaching the sea had been a far simpler matter than first assumed when the Conclave discussed this journey in the Redoubt. But that was not to say that the trip hadn't been a confusing one.

Many intersections loomed along the way, most of which were unfamiliar even to Tristan and Wigg. The haunting ocean sounds whirling through the connecting chambers were confusing, forcing Wigg and Jessamay to use the craft to decide down which of the various tunnels they should travel. The last time Tristan and Wigg had come here they had been forced to descend a narrow circular stairway that hemmed them in on both sides. Tristan feared no man or the blade he carried, but tight spaces bothered him greatly. He badly wanted to leave this claustrophobic tunnel and set sail over the Azure Sea, for his destiny lay there and he would not be denied.

Wigg could sense Tristan's restlessness to get moving, but the wizard remained apprehensive. Something tugged at his senses—something to do with the craft. The feeling had become stronger as he neared the tunnel exit. *Perhaps it is the Ones' spell,* he guessed as he pondered the matter.

Wigg looked behind him to see the other Conclave members standing there. Farther down the tunnel, endless hordes of Minion warriors stood bunched together as far as the eye could see. Many more Minions still followed the trek's strange path, their extended lines perhaps reaching as far back as the waterfall chamber.

Wigg could imagine Ox still trying to control the eager warriors with little at his command save his booming voice. Perhaps more than any of them, Ox would want to be here, standing beside his *Jin'Sai.* As Wigg looked down the tunnel, the millions of radiance stones in the ceiling added ghostly highlights to the warriors' stern faces.

Tristan had been right about one thing, Wigg realized. Trying to move so many warriors through these tunnels was creating a monstrous logjam. They badly needed to exit onto the sandy beach, where everyone could get some breathing room. Still, something gnawed at the old wizard's well-known sense of danger.

Standing just behind the Conclave, Taredd, Rhun, Arron, and Rafal had discharged their duties well and carried the two Black Ships without incident. At Wigg's order the dark wooden crates had been set down on the tunnel floor. One crate still held the last of the precious subtle matter.

Tristan's impatience was starting to overcome him, and he knew that Scars, Tyranny, Astrid, Phoebe, and Jessamay were also eager to walk out onto the beach. He gave Wigg a questioning look.

"Why are we waiting?" he asked. "We have arrived without difficulty. We must proceed!"

Wigg pursed his lips as he again looked out the tunnel exit. "There's something strange out there," he said, half to himself, "something more than the Azure Sea. There is a craft presence here that is eerily familiar yet also foreign."

"Can you tell what it is?" Tristan asked.

Wigg shook his head. "Only that the craft is at work," he answered.

The First Wizard glanced over Tristan's shoulder, and he beckoned Jessamay to come forward. The sorceress squeezed through the crowd to stand with Tristan and Wigg. The First Wizard gave her a searching look.

"Do you sense anything unusual?" he asked.

Jessamay closed her eyes. When she opened them, a look of confusion crossed her face.

"I do," she answered, "but it's faint. How long have you sensed it?"

"For the last quarter hour," Wigg replied.

Jessamay smiled. "Your gifts were always stronger than mine," she said. "Had you not asked me to search it out I might have missed it altogether."

"Can you identify it?" Wigg asked.

Jessamay narrowed her eyes while testing her gifts. "Sometimes the sensation feels like partly cloaked blood. But it changes from one moment to the next—it ebbs and flows much like the sea lying before us."

Wigg nodded. "Exactly," he said. "Would you care to hazard a guess about what it might be? I want us in agreement before we depart this tunnel."

Jessamay thought for a moment. "I believe it is the spell that the Ones left behind to force the ocean sounds through these many passageways," she finally answered. "It must be that because of the way it ebbs and flows. Otherwise I cannot say."

Wigg again turned to look out the tunnel and toward the tempting sea. Its sounds still called to him, but now he was so close that it was impossible to say whether it was the sea that he heard, or the spell left behind by the Ones.

Jessamay must be right, he decided. *Her analysis makes sense. Still . . .*

Wigg turned to look at Rhun. "Bring me the crate containing the subtle matter," he ordered. Rhun immediately came forward with one crate and placed it at the wizard's feet.

"What are you doing?" Tristan asked.

"If Jessamay and I are wrong, I want the subtle matter with me," Wigg answered. "The two ships can be replaced if need be. The subtle matter cannot."

Wigg called the craft and pointed a bony finger at the crate. Soon the crate started to glow and the leather belts surrounding it unbuckled themselves and slumped downward. Wigg used the craft to slowly open the crate's sides and lower them gently to the floor.

The *Ephyra* sat in her miniaturized cradle, still twinkling with subtle matter. By way of the craft, a glass vial containing the subtle matter had been attached to the ship's cradle. The jar was about half full of the strange, twinkling material. Wigg reached down and freed it from its resting place.

Before his group had departed the palace, Tristan had watched as Wigg and Faegan transferred the subtle matter into the flat vial. They had then attached a stout leather cord to the vial's top. The First Wizard now placed the cord around his neck, allowing the vial to fall to his chest, hidden beneath his gray robe. A faint outline of the vial could be seen, but it would hardly be noticed unless one knew what to look for.

Then Tristan saw something unexpected. A smaller glass vial containing still more subtle matter had been attached to the inside of the crate. Before he could ask Wigg about it, the wizard employed the craft to close and secure the crate with its leather straps.

Tristan scowled. "I saw a second vial," he said. He turned and pointed at the other crate that stood among the warriors. "Does that crate have one inside it too?"

"It does," Wigg answered. "Faegan and I fitted each crate with one before we left the palace."

"Why do that?" Tyranny asked.

Wigg gave the privateer a wink. "Call them insurance," he said simply. He then turned to face the *Jin'Sai.* "It's time to go," he announced.

Tristan nodded and looked down the passageway. "Draw your swords!" he shouted.

At once the sound of several thousand Minion dreggans resounded through the tunnel, the combined ring of their blades unmistakable. Each armed Conclave member also drew his or her weapon.

"I want a group of warriors to surround the crate bearers and the Conclave members as soon as they exit the tunnel!" Tristan shouted. "Move toward the shoreline as quickly as you can! As the phalanxes grow in size I will issue further orders! Let's go!"

Eager to be free of the oppressing tunnel, Tristan pushed past Wigg and led the way toward the exit.

UNKNOWN TO THE CONCLAVE, KHRISTOS HAD HEARD every word.

The Viper Lord had first sensed the *Jin'Sai's* supremely gifted blood nearly an hour ago, telling him that Tristan was nearing the shore. Forty minutes later, he and many of his vipers had quietly left their hiding places to flatten their bodies against the rock wall on either side of the tunnel. Its exit lay about one meter above the sandy beach and was the one from which the Vigors forces would soon spill forth to meet their deaths. Even now, more vipers slithered from other tunnels to take up places along the length of the rocky wall. When the Minions exited their tunnel they would be blindsided and slaughtered, their many comrades bunched up behind them ensuring that retreat would be impossible.

As Khristos stood eagerly waiting beside the tunnel exit, he called on the craft to linger over the great quality of the *Jin'Sai's* endowed blood and listen to every spoken word. The sea waves crashed against the shore, and the beach lay pristine and unbloodied. *But not for much longer,* he thought.

For a moment he was tempted to simply stand before the tunnel entrance and loose bolt after bolt into it, killing as many Vigors worshippers as he could. Because of the enclosed space, he would surely destroy many of them. But he could not know whether Tristan, the two Black Ships, or the subtle matter were positioned farther down the length of the tunnel. If so, they all might escape. And so he waited patiently, determined to kill his enemies one by one as they exited the tunnel into which he had so cleverly lured them. Gripping his silver staff tighter, he held it steady alongside the rock wall, eagerly awaiting his prey. His enemies wouldn't know what hit them.

Then he heard Tristan give his order to take the beach.

HAD TRISTAN'S GIFT OF *K'SHARI* NOT SUDDENLY WARNED him of the impending danger, he would surely have died.

No sooner did he start to cross the plane of the tunnel exit than his blood started tingling wildly, signaling the rising of his unique gift. This time he followed Aeolus' advice and he did not question it.

Leaping from the tunnel, he curled his body into a tight ball, presenting a smaller target. As he hit the sand he heard a deafening explosion. With his blood telling him that it was kill or be killed, he somersaulted twice across the beach, then came up swinging.

The bolt that Khristos sent raging from his staff had been meant to tear Tristan in half. Instead it missed him by mere inches, singeing his hair and skin. Unfazed, the bolt narrowly missed Khristos' vipers that lay in wait on the tunnel's other side, then went crashing into the curved rock wall surrounding the beach to send tons of rock shards crashing down.

Swinging his dreggan at the first viper he saw, Tristan sent the tip of the blade slicing across the monster's throat. The thing's head partly separated from its body and the viper crashed to the sand, its tail snaking about wildly before the beast died. But there was no time for Tristan to revel in his victory, for not only was Khristos again raising his silver staff, but several more vipers were charging him at once.

Turning on his heels, he let his *K'Shari* take over again and quickly positioned himself so that the onrushing vipers were directly between him and the unknown being who so powerfully commanded the craft. Suddenly a shocking realization went through him.

No wonder our Night Witch patrols could not find the vipers! They were here waiting for us! But how . . . why . . .

Suddenly Khristos' silver staff loosed another bolt. Employing his gift again, Tristan quickly fell to the sand. The bolt soared over the beach to crash into the vipers before him, then shot across the sea to finally fall into the waves, sending plumes of seawater and steam rocketing skyward. The three monsters facing Tristan exploded in a cacophony of blood, bone, and skin.

Tristan quickly came to his feet to find that he was covered with bloody offal, the grisly sight nearly causing him to vomit. Determined to stay alive, he hacked down one viper after another. But given the huge number of servants at Khristos' command, he knew that his death would not be long in coming.

Cursing his luck as he crouched by the rock wall, Khristos saw Minion warriors leaping from the tunnel to land on the sandy beach at an alarming rate. He then saw the other Conclave members exit the tunnel, surrounded by even more ranks of warriors. In moments the beach became a riotous madhouse of death-dealing.

At first the valiant Minions were killed with deadly precision by Khristos' bolts and the vipers' flashing talons and sharp teeth the moment they left the tunnel. But then some of the charging Minion ranks began fighting back. As their numbers grew, so did their chances of survival. Soon a huge battle raged from which neither side could expect any retreat or quarter, as countless more warriors and vipers swarmed from the many tunnels to join their fellows.

In the midst of the mêlée, Khristos quickly looked around to try to find Tristan and the Black Ships. But the *Jin'Sai* had become lost to him among the struggling multitudes, and the Black Ships were nowhere to be seen. Suddenly the Viper Lord's eyes caught something floating high above the Azure Sea. When he raised his face skyward he was stunned by what he saw.

"Wigg . . ." he breathed.

The hated Vigors wizard looked older than Khristos remembered, but there could be no forgetting Wigg's craggy face or his highly arched widow's peak. Wigg hovered high in the air some distance out over the ocean. A female craft practitioner hovered beside him—another Conclave member, Khristos guessed. The two cowards were looking down on the battle, refusing to engage. But then Khristos saw something else, and he immediately understood. A flood of emotions ran through him as he realized that Wigg might already have bested him.

Wigg held a wooden crate in his arms, as did the woman hovering by his side. Before Khristos could act, the First Wizard and Jessamay called the craft and set the crates free onto the air. As the crates flew farther out over the waves, Khristos realized what they contained, and he immediately raised his silver staff to destroy them.

But Wigg and Jessamay had seen the Viper Lord. Just as Khristos pointed his staff at the first of the hovering crates, Wigg and Jessamay raised their arms. The twin bolts that they sent streaking down at Khristos were met head-on by one the Viper Lord sent upward. The three azure beams collided in a great explosion over the Azure Sea, about half the distance to the hovering crates.

The explosion's sound and fury were so massive and the resultant blacklash so great that Khristos was knocked off his feet and sent crashing against the rock wall, rendering him unconscious. Wigg and Jessamay were also affected when the echoing shock wave reached them and were thrown dozens of meters higher into the air as though they had suddenly being caught up in a hurricane.

Hovering weakly, his body and robe singed, Wigg desperately tried to regain his senses while the terrible battle raged on the distant shore. Jessamay was in still worse straits, but she remained airborne—at least for now. Knowing that Khristos would soon recover and attack again, Wigg summoned all the energy he had left, and he pointed at the nearest hovering crate.

Soon the crate turned azure and its leather belts slipped free of their brass buckles. But this time only one side of the crate lowered, while the other remained upright to reveal the *Ephyra*. Again pointing his hand at the case, Wigg focused his energy on the small vial of subtle matter that had been fixed to the top of the crate's upright side. He watched breathlessly as the vial stopper wriggled free, allowing the subtle matter to sprinkle with agonizing slowness down over the *Ephyra*.

The First Wizard then put the reverse forestallment into effect that would restore the Black Ship to her original size.

But before Wigg could turn his attention to the other case, he heard Jessamay moan. He turned to see her suddenly go unconscious and start tumbling through the air toward the sea. Wigg quickly sent a wizard's warp toward her, catching her in midair. He saw her back arch violently, but there had been no other choice. She might have suffered a broken spine, but hopefully her life would be saved.

With Jessamay safe for the moment, Wigg turned his attention to the other crate and quickly duplicated the process he used on the first one. As the vicious battle seesawed back and forth on the bloody beach, he watched the two crates with wide eyes, desperately hoping that his and Faegan's plan would work.

With a groaning heave the *Ephyra* began expanding in midair. Soon she outgrew her crate, splitting it apart and sending it crashing to the sea. The *Tammerland* followed suit and also started growing, splintering its wooden crate into matchsticks. As the crate bits fell away, Wigg watched the craft do its amazing work.

Each ship agonizingly lengthened and grew taller, her spars, hull, sails, and masts groaning in exquisite pain like tortured souls being stretched on dungeon racks. On and on the spell went, continuing to enlarge the vessels until they regained their original size. Their huge bulk soon overshadowed the beach, the effect so mesmerizing that some of the desperate fighters paused for a moment to gawk up in abject wonder.

Although the ships had been enlarged, Jessamay dangled precariously some one hundred meters below Wigg, and the First Wizard's plan was unraveling fast. Jessamay was to have empowered the *Ephyra* and kept her aloft while Wigg did the same with the *Tammerland*. But Wigg was still dazed, and the strain of simultaneously holding Jessamay and enacting the One's spell had weakened him far too much for him to empower both ships.

He stole a few precious moments to look down at the battle. Even now, neither side had gained the upper hand. Explosive azure bolts streaked here and there among the fighting, but from so high up he couldn't tell who was casting them. Nor could he learn whether Tristan or any of the other Conclave members had been killed. Knowing that there was little he could do to change the outcome, he concentrated what remained of his energy on saving Jessamay and the two Black Ships.

Just then the Ones' spell ended, leaving Wigg's rapidly dwindling gifts the only way to keep the ships airborne. To his horror, the massive vessels began plummeting toward the sea, listing crazily as they fell. With a monumental effort he empowered the *Tammerland* on her way down, holding her steady in the air while she righted herself. With his other hand he lifted the warp holding Jessamay, then moved her toward the *Tammerland* and let her fall onto the ship's bow deck. But he had been too late to save the *Ephyra*. As he watched her plummet toward the Azure Sea, he felt his heart rend in two.

I beg the Afterlife, he thought. *What have I done?*

Finally regaining consciousness, Khristos gathered himself up from the sandy beach to see that many of his vipers had surrounded him and were staving off the vicious Minions who wanted him dead. He quickly levitated into the air above the fray, then pointed his silver staff at the cluster of warriors ringing the vipers.

Khristos' azure bolt launched straight into the warriors' midst, sending blood, armor, and body parts flying. Landing in a blood-soaked clearing a few meters away, Khristos looked up just in time to see one massive Black Ship hovering in the sky and the other plummeting crazily toward the sea.

With a mighty crash the *Ephyra* hit the waves, sending a plume of water high into the air. She bounced, then crashed violently down again into the ocean. As the seawater fell around her, Khristos strained his eyes, hoping that the ship had been smashed into kindling. When the scene cleared, he raised his fists and shook them at the sky.

The *Ephyra* had survived.

He watched transfixed as the Black Ship heeled over and nearly capsized. To his chagrin, she finally righted, her rigging swinging violently to and fro as she settled down. Many of her spars were broken and one of her masts lay across the main deck, but she looked otherwise intact.

Casting safety to the winds, Khristos cursed and ran toward the shoreline. Again raising his silver staff, he pointed it at the stricken ship's bow. If he couldn't destroy both ships, he would at least try to send one of the black bastards to the bottom.

But just as he raised his staff, a figure lunged across his path, blocking his view. Khristos snarled and was about to sidestep the fighter when he saw the pair of dark blue eyes boring into his and sensed the stranger's supreme blood quality.

The *Jin'Sai.*

As the battle whirled around them, for a moment the two enemies glared at one another. Then Khristos screamed and pointed his staff at Tristan's chest.

With the imminent threat washing over his senses, Tristan's blood tingled with yet greater strength and his sword blade suddenly glowed with a bright azure hue. This had happened only once before, during the climactic battle to take the Recluse. But there was no time to think. With Aeolus' warnings again ringing in his ears, Tristan widened his stance and stood his ground.

This second bolt Khristos sent at Tristan was again a narrow one, designed to cut the *Jin'Sai* in half. Tristan raised his sword with blinding speed. As the searing bolt struck his dreggan blade, its power was immediately reflected back toward Khristos. Had the wizard's reflexes not been so fast, it would surely have killed him.

Khristos wheeled but the bolt struck his right shoulder, causing him to drop his staff. Tristan lunged forward and kicked the craft weapon far across the sand. Weakened with shock and falling to his knees, Khristos again tried sending a bolt Tristan's way, this time from his fingertips. But the bolt fizzled halfway to its target and crashed into the beach, sending charred sand high into the air. As the sandy cloud cleared, Tristan raised his dreggan high and charged in for the kill.

But again the wizard was too fast. Summoning his last bit of power, Khristos levitated from the sand and soared away to seek protection among his many vipers. As he left the ground, Tristan swung his blade at him, but it fell short.

Enraged, Tristan tossed his sword into his left hand, then reached behind his right shoulder to grip a throwing knife and let it fly. The silver dirk cartwheeled over and over, its double-sided blade a whirling blur.

Seeing the knife coming, Khristos twisted in midair, causing the blade to miss his heart. But he hadn't been fast enough to avoid it altogether, and the dirk buried itself in the same shoulder that had been struck by his returning bolt. Screaming in agony, he pulled the knife from his shoulder, then crossed the sand and landed amid another group of battling vipers. Hissing and drooling, the hideous things quickly surrounded their beloved master and defended him with their lives.

Khristos could no longer be seen, but Tristan knew where to find him. The *Jin'Sai* was about to charge across the bloody sand and tear into the group of vipers when he felt a strong hand grip the back of his left shoulder. Knowing that he was being attacked by another viper, he had no choice but to forget Khristos and whirl around.

Reaching across his chest with his right hand and raising his bloody sword high with his left, he grasped the enemy's wrist and swiveled left. As he came around he found himself staring into a familiar face.

There stood Ox, bloodied and exhausted. Ox immediately shouted out an order, and he and Tristan were quickly surrounded by more Minion warriors to keep yet another throng of advancing Blood Vipers from reaching them. The massive Ox gave Tristan a desperate look.

"Wigg say you must come now!" he shouted above the fighting. "Black Ships safe but we losing fight! Wigg say hurry! Must cross blue sea!"

That wasn't what Tristan wanted to hear. Instead of sailing away, he wanted to kill the unknown Vagaries wizard if it was the last thing he ever did. Then Ox grabbed Tristan by the shoulders and roughly spun him around to face the rocky wall on the other side of the beach.

"Look, *Jin'Sai*!" Ox screamed. What Tristan saw sent icewater pouring through his veins.

The sand between him and the rock wall was covered with the dead and the dying, blood, and body parts from both sides. The casualties seemed to be roughly equally divided between Minions and vipers, but in the continuing mêlée Tristan couldn't be sure. Then he looked to the rock wall, and he knew.

Thousands more vipers still poured from hundreds of tunnels, threatening to engulf the Minions once and for all. But no more fresh warriors were jumping to the beach to confront them. The tunnel floor from which the warriors had exited dripped blood down the rock wall, and vipers were slithering inside it to look for wounded stragglers. Some of the Minions still struggling on the beach had taken to the air to hack their dreggans downward on the vipers. Even so, it was clear that the odds were turning against them. Tristan knew that without an order to retreat, his forces would fight and die to the last. He swung around to look into Ox's pleading eyes.

"Wigg say we must go now!" Ox shouted. "There be too many vipers! He say if we stay, all warriors die!"

"Where are the other Conclave members?" Tristan shouted. "Are any dead?"

"Ox not know!" the warrior shouted back. "But we must go!"

"Have all our warriors exited the tunnel?" the prince shouted. "I refuse to leave anyone behind!"

"Only warriors in tunnel be dead ones!" Ox answered. "I be last one out! *Please, Jin'Sai!* We must go *now!*"

Finally surrendering to the desperate situation, Tristan angrily put aside his desire to continue the fight.

"Blow the retreat!" he shouted.

With a relieved look on his face, Ox quickly reached for his bugle. He sounded the retreat call twice, then scooped Tristan up in his beefy arms and took to the air. On hearing the bugle and seeing their *Jin'Sai* leave the beach, the surviving warriors also took flight, many of them carrying wounded comrades in their arms. As the warriors soared away, the thousands of vipers slithered toward the shoreline, waving their arms and hissing loudly in celebration of their bloody victory.

Tristan looked out to sea to find the *Tammerland* and the *Ephyra* sitting atop the waves about one hundred yards from shore, each twinkling brightly with subtle matter. One of the *Ephyra's* masts and some of her spars had come down, but Tristan was sailor enough to know that she could be repaired. And then to Tristan's amazement this subterranean world began to change.

It didn't start slowly, or with prior warning. Instead, its coming was sudden and earsplitting. Because Tristan was being carried in Ox's strong arms, he could do nothing but watch in horrified wonder.

The Azure Sea started to churn, and great steaming geysers exploded from its depths to launch hundreds of yards into the air. Tristan couldn't believe what he saw next, but the irrefutable proof lay directly before him, bewildering his senses. The Azure Sea was literally boiling.

Suddenly worried for his fleet, he snapped his head around to see another geyser erupt just off the *Ephyra's* port bow, sending the great ship dangerously rocking atop the waves. Nearly capsizing, she listed hard before righting.

Then Tristan heard terrible screaming, and he saw some Minion crewmen being tossed from the *Ephyra's* pitching deck toward the boiling sea. The quickest snapped open their wings and took flight just before reaching the superheated water. But some could not and they hit the boiling waves, the sea immediately overcoming them, and they perished on the spot. Tristan watched in horror as their scalded bodies and limp wings bobbed atop the boiling sea, some of them bumping against the *Ephyra*'s hull.

As yet more geysers and superheated steam exploded into the air, Tristan soon doubted that he and Ox would reach the *Tammerland* alive. As the sea birthed one geyser after the next, the rising steam had become so thick that Tristan could barely see his hands before his face, to say nothing of the Black Ships. Tristan suspected that Ox was straying off course, but turning around to fly back to the beach and its thousands of swarming vipers was unthinkable. And so they pressed on, the air becoming hotter and deadlier by the moment.

As he wondered how many loyal warriors had survived the beach only to be boiled alive in the sky and on the sea, Tristan's stomach turned over. Soon the smell of cooked flesh reached his nostrils to confirm his fears. Then he heard more horrible screaming and saw hundreds of Minion corpses, their dark silhouettes barley visible in the fog, tumbling downward and splashing into the sea.

"Higher, Ox!" Tristan screamed, desperately hoping that the heat would dissipate with more altitude. "You must take us higher!"

Straining with everything he had, Ox angled upward and his strong wings started to climb. Tristan's skin burned and there was so much hot water running into his eyes that he could hardly see. He knew that unless Ox soon climbed out of the steamy fog, the end would be near for them, too.

Just then Ox broke through the rising water vapor to find clear air. Desperately wiping the water from his face and eyes, Tristan ordered Ox to fly in a circle and search for the ships.

Soon the terrible geysers stopped, and the water vapor began to dissipate. The prince looked down to see the azure waves littered with bobbing Minion corpses, sometimes grouping like tiny dark islands adrift on a sea of death. Then through a break in the parting clouds Tristan saw the *Tammerland.* He pointed to the ship and Ox immediately understood. Diving through the rent in the superheated fog, they plummeted toward the flagship.

As they neared the *Tammerland,* Tristan was relieved to see most of the heated fog diffusing and some of the Conclave members gathered on the bow deck. The ship was covered with hot seawater, its main deck still steaming in the gradually lessening heat. Ox set Tristan down atop the slick deck and the *Jin'Sai* immediately ran over to where Wigg stood at the starboard gunwale.

"What's our situation?" Tristan demanded.

When the First Wizard turned around he looked hunched and frail. He stared at Tristan without seeing him, his aquamarine eyes glassy and unfocused. Tears streamed down his cheeks.

"I should have known," he said faintly. "Jessamay and I knew that it felt like cloaked blood . . . so many warriors dead, Jessamay hurt, and it's all my fault . . . how could I have been so blind . . . then the geysers came . . . so many more died . . . the water is full of bodies . . ."

Tristan grabbed the wizard by the shoulders and shook him roughly.

"Wigg!" he shouted. "Take hold of yourself! I must know our situation!"

With Tristan's commanding voice ringing in his ears, the First Wizard seemed to partly regain his focus. His skin, hair, and robe were steaming and soaked through, telling Tristan that the wizard had nearly been killed. He collected himself, then he wiped the tears from his face.

"We have lost many warriors," he said, "not just to the vipers but also to the terrible geysers. But the geysers have stopped, and it seems that the man-serpents will not swim into the superheated sea. Aside from Jessamay, the other Conclave members were not badly hurt."

Tristan let go of Wigg and he took a quick look around.

Jessamay lay unconscious atop a Minion stretcher, being tended to by anxious warrior-healers. She was scalded and soaked, and her injuries appeared severe. Parts of her body could be seen here and there through ragged burn holes in her drenched doublet, boots, and breeches.

Tyranny stood nearby with an open wine bottle in one hand and a smoldering cigarillo dangling between her lips. She too was soaked, her dark hair matted. Her sword, its hilt stained with viper blood, lay sheathed on her hip. She said nothing as she looked into Tristan's eyes, then lifted the bottle to take another long slug. Her left hand was bleeding, but she ignored it; viper blood covered much of her clothing. Scars stood behind her, his torso and trousers also smeared with viper blood and offal.

Tristan turned back to face Wigg. As he did so, he saw thousands of warriors winging their way back to the Black Ships. Many were so tired and injured that they were crash-landing onto the decks.

"What caused the geysers?" the *Jin'Sai* shouted.

The First Wizard drunkenly shook his head. "I don't know," he answered. "I've never seen their like. Perhaps the release of the subtle matter caused them . . ."

"Where are Phoebe and Astrid?" Tristan demanded.

"They're here aboard the *Tammerland,* awaiting further orders," Wigg answered weakly. "They are exhausted but unhurt. We cannot fly the ships out of here, Tristan. We are too exhausted, and Jessamay is unconscious." Then Wigg finally managed a short smile. "But the wind is good," he added.

Heartened that all the Conclave members had survived, Tristan returned Wigg's smile, then affectionately placed one hand atop the wizard's shoulder.

"You did the right thing by sending Ox to me," he said. "Had we not retreated when we did, we might have lost everyone."

Tristan turned to look across the waves. The sea had calmed and the fog was gone, but the water still steamed. Thousands of Blood Vipers still congregated at the shoreline, hissing and writhing about each other in an orgy of victory. The sight incensed Tristan, enticing him to return to the bloody beach and kill them all. He turned to again look at Wigg.

"Those monsters are under the control of a hideous-looking Vagaries wizard," he said. "He seems to have been morphed by the craft for some reason. I had two chances to kill him but I failed."

Wigg nodded. "Khristos," he said.

"You know him?" Tristan asked.

Wigg nodded. "He is a dark part of my past—the past that I foolishly thought I had forever left behind. But even now Failee's deeds continue to rear their ugly heads." Tired and shaking, Wigg looked at Tristan with worried eyes.

"Khristos is a powerful Vagaries wizard," he said, his eyes going glassy again. "He must be dealt with decisively . . . it seems that the craft has changed his appearance, but I recognized him just the same . . . Shailiha must be told about . . ."

Just then Wigg's aquamarine eyes rolled back and he fainted away. Tristan caught him and handed him over to Ox. The huge warrior lifted Wigg into both arms as though he weighed nothing.

No sooner had Ox taken up Wigg than another unsettling sound tore through the cavern. Tristan wheeled around, looking and listening. This time the noise was different. Not only was the sea roiling again, but the entire subterranean cavern was shaking violently, and the rumbling sound grew louder by the second.

On and on the terrible rumbling came, causing the swelling waves to crash against the ships' gunwales and once again put them in danger of capsizing. Tristan lost his footing on the slick deck, and only by grabbing some rigging did he keep from tumbling overboard into the deadly sea.

Tristan looked across the deck. "Tyranny!" he shouted.

The privateer and her first mate were already struggling to reach him, but the going was hard. Without warning another terrifying manifestation of the craft appeared.

On either side of the ships, two giant dark walls started rising from the depths. They nearly scraped the ships' sides as they came roaring upward. Tristan, Tyranny, and Ox could only stand and watch, bewitched by what they saw.

The craggy rock walls rose straight up past the ships, thundering so loudly that Tristan thought his eardrums might burst. Their flat tops stretching for endless leagues, higher and higher they rose until they neared the ceiling, thousands of yards above. On reaching the ceiling, their flat tops ground agonizingly against the radiance stones. Tons of rock debris came crashing down into the sea, narrowly missing the ships and sending plumes of water high into the air. Then everything went deathly still.

Tyranny and Scars carefully made their way across the slick deck to stand beside Tristan. At first not one of them could speak, stunned as they were by the amazing sight.

The two Black Ships lay trapped in a narrow channel of aquamarine water that stretched away into infinity. The black rock walls loomed up from the channel on either side like dark giants waiting to crush the vessels between them. Sharp and forbidding, they seemed to stretch away forever on either side of the slim waterway.

As the channel water calmed and slapped gently against the ship's sides, Tristan collected his senses and looked around. Ahead could be seen only the limitless expanse of the tunnel-like channel. Behind them lay the viper-infested beach. The ceiling radiance stones lying trapped between the opposing rock walls provided bright, constant light.

As the last of the rubble broke free and tumbled into the channel, the rock walls settled and the wind calmed. Then, as if some great pair of protective hands had just reached down from the Afterlife to grasp them, the two ships stopped drifting atop the water and hauntingly held their positions, well clear of the deadly walls. The sensation was eerie, unnatural.

Tyranny turned to stare at Tristan, dumbfounded. "What just happened here?" she breathed.

Tristan shook his head. "I am as much at a loss as you," he answered softly, still awed by what he saw. Trying to focus his thoughts on the ships, he finally turned and looked at Tyranny.

"But whatever else has just occurred, the mystics are too exhausted to pilot the ships," he said. "If we are to leave here, we must sail atop the waves. Are the ships seaworthy?"

Her hands shaking, Tyranny removed the cigarillo from between her lips and ground it beneath the sole of her boot. She tousled her wet hair, thinking.

"The *Tammerland* is," she answered. "The *Ephyra* can probably also sail, but her fallen mainmast, spars, and sails must eventually be repaired. She'll be slower without them, but our Minion shipwrights can repair them as we go. Either way, this discussion is meaningless, because there is no wind. Nor can I understand why the ships don't drift. The craft must have done all this . . ." she added softly, her voice trailing away.

Taking another slug of wine, she turned to look back at the shoreline and its thousands of jubilant vipers. "Even so, we must somehow get away from here as quickly as possible," she said. "I saw that disfigured bastard at work and I don't want to suffer any more of his tricks. We must find a way to move these ships."

Tristan nodded and looked at Ox. "I want a Minion casualty report as soon as possible," he ordered. "Have Wigg and Jessamay taken below to their quarters and see that they're looked after by warrior-healers. I also want a report on their condition as soon as I can get it. And have Astrid and Phoebe also tend to Wigg and Jessamay—their healing gifts will be useful. If they are not too tired, send the Night Witches out on staggered patrols down the length of this channel. I want to know what lies ahead of us."

Ox snapped his boot heels together smartly. "I live to serve," he said. He turned and hurried away, the First Wizard's arms and legs dangling toward the steaming deck as Ox bore him belowdecks.

Tristan turned back to look at Scars. "You will serve as the *Ephyra*'s captain until our mystics can empower the ships through the sky. Make arrangements for a warrior to fly you there right away."

He then turned to look again at the bloody shoreline. "We must somehow find a way to leave here," he said. "Something tells me that we haven't seen the last of that Vagaries bastard."

As Tyranny walked up beside him she sighed and tousled her hair again, causing Tristan to raise an eyebrow. He knew that look—it always brought bad news. "If there's something else on your mind, you'd best tell me right now," he said sternly.

"I'm sorry to report that our instruments don't work here," Tyranny said. "They just spin crazily, as though they are being affected by the craft. Even the enchanted one that Shailiha and I used to find our way to the Citadel won't function properly."

After everything else that had happened, Tristan wasn't surprised. "What about the sextant?" he asked.

Tyranny shook her head. "We should have realized back in Tammerland that our instruments might be useless on the Azure Sea. There is no sky here, Tristan—only radiance stones, and they show no discernible pattern. Even Faegan's enchanted sextant needs changing points of reference to confirm our position. Even if we escape this channel we can navigate only by line of sight. I don't like it any better than you, but there it is."

"Then line of sight it is," he answered.

Tristan turned to look down the strange channel. The air was motionless, ensuring that the ships would be going nowhere. Moreover, the twin walls that hemmed them in rose straight up and seemed impossible to land on.

Just then a strong offshore wind freshened, and with it the waves became restless. Whatever force had been holding the ships in place suddenly set them free, allowing them to drift across the waves. Recognizing the coming danger, Tristan quickly turned to look at Tyranny and Scars.

"Get the sails up so that we can maneuver, or we'll crash into the walls!" he shouted. "Take the only course available to us—straight down the channel while the wind remains astern! If it changes direction it might blow us back to the beach!" Wanting to use Tyranny's spyglass, Tristan quickly relieved her of it before sending her on her way.

Tyranny immediately ran to carry out the orders while a warrior picked Scars up and flew him over to the other ship. As the Minions hurried to unfurl the *Tammerland*'s sails, Tristan held his breath as he watched her drift ever closer to one of the deadly rock walls. Then her sails caught the breeze and she heeled over at the last moment, missing the rock wall by only yards. With Scars finally taking control of the *Ephyra*'s wheel and her sails starting to appear, she too narrowly avoided the other wall, then heeled over and began following.

Only once the great vessels were finally sailing down the mysterious channel and away from the bloody beach did Tristan's frayed nerves begin to settle down. Finally alone with his thoughts, he started the long walk toward the *Tammerland's* stern. As he passed by wounded and exhausted warriors they attempted to stand and pay their respects, but many simply could not. Giving them reassuring smiles, he walked on.

On reaching the stern deck he stood against the curved gunwale and looked toward the bloody shore. Thousands of vipers still milled there in joyful celebration.

They think they've scored a victory, Tristan thought. *And in some ways perhaps they have. Many warriors died, but in the end we gave as good as we got, and the subtle matter and the Black Ships were spared. For those things we can be truly thankful. But what caused this strange channel, and where will it lead us?*

Then he saw a dark speck on the beach. Raising the scope to one eye, he twisted its cylinders, bringing the faraway scene into focus.

Khristos stood on the shore watching the Black Ships make their escape. The right shoulder of the wizard's robe was bloodied and partly burned away. The *Jin'Sai* smiled at that.

Tristan already knew why Khristos had led his vipers into the caves. The *Pon Q'tar* had ordered him to do so in an attempt to kill him and the Conclave and to destroy the subtle matter and the Black Ships.

He grimaced as he realized that this probably also meant that the *Pon Q'tar* was watching Shailiha, causing his worry for her to grow. Her task of destroying Khristos and his servants would not be an easy one, and he must use his medallion as soon as possible to inform her of the danger. But many unanswered questions remained about Khristos and the Blood Vipers—questions that only Tristan's mystics might answer. As soon as Wigg was strong enough, Tristan would press him for details.

Tristan raised the glass once more to the retreating shoreline. Khristos still stood there, silver staff in hand, angrily watching his prizes slip away. Despite the day's horrific events, the *Jin'Sai* remained optimistic. All his Conclave members were alive and his ships were finally on their way, despite the strange arrival of the rock walls and the narrow channel they created. As he watched Khristos' dark form recede from view, he decisively closed the scope cylinders.

Your Pon Q'tar masters will not be happy to hear of your failure to destroy my expedition, Khristos, he thought. *But don't worry.*

The Afterlife willing, we'll be back.

CHAPTER XXIX

 "WE CAN AFFORD NO MORE FAILURES, GRACCHUS!" BENEDIK Pryam shouted.

The incensed cleric could scarcely control his emotions. He and the others could see no end to the troubles this latest defeat might cause. Rising from his seat, he started anxiously pacing the room.

"You told us that the *Jin'Sai* would be stopped in the Caves!" he went on, venting his fury. "Now you bring us word that Tristan, part of his Conclave, and two Minion phalanxes sail the Azure Sea in his Black Ships! Moreover, the sea walls have risen! Surely we needn't remind you of this campaign's importance—the same campaign that you said would bring an end to all our troubles! Who knows what might happen should the *Jin'Sai* reach Shashida! Tristan and his twin sister must be destroyed once and for all!"

Pausing for a moment, Benedik stopped pacing and glared angrily into Gracchus' eyes.

"The state of our treasury is such that this campaign must succeed!" he added, his tone deadly serious. "We waited for aeons for the Blood Royal to be born, just as the current mystics living on the world's other side waited for their reigning *Jin'Sai*. I also needn't remind you that despite their lesser prowess in the craft, Tristan's mystics are not so different from us. Vespasian is perfect for our needs, and his like might never be seen again. But the same can be said for Shashida and the *Jin'Sai*! Admittedly, the depleted state of the treasury and the Blood Royal's coming of age are unfortunate coincidences. Even so, our course has been set. Our primary concern was once the taking of the Shashidan mines, not the killing of the reigning *Jin'Sai*. But with every step that brings Tristan closer to Shashida, we are no longer certain which struggle is more important!"

Gracchus fumed as he watched Benedik pace and rant. How could they possibly doubt him? he asked himself. He was the most learned and powerful of them all. Had it not been he who launched the successful revolt against Shashida, ensuring that the cause of the Vagaries would survive? Had he not succeeded those many centuries ago, the hated Shashidan Vigors worshippers would still rule all the land west of the Tolenkas. Their pompous self-righteousness would to this very day stifle the craft's admittedly more chaotic but infinitely more appealing opposite side, refusing to allow it to flower. The revolution he brought forth had been unprecedented, earth-shattering. Rustannica owed its very existence to him, and no one here could deny that. Characteristic of his vaunted ego, he considered the failure to stop Tristan a temporary setback rather than an outright defeat. But of even greater import was Gracchus' other plan—the one that involved destroying Shailiha. And this time he would not fail.

The camouflaged tent in which the *Pon Q'tar* convened sat far away from the main body of Vespasian's war camp. Like the Oraculum Tempitatum, it too was shrouded in invisibility. This was not a full meeting of the Suffragat, nor was it meant to be. Only the twelve clerics were present, and by meeting in secret this way they were breaking one of Rustannica's highest laws.

Called the Vetare Secretum, the Law Prohibiting Secrecy, it forbade the *Pon Q'tar,* the Tribunes, or the Priory to meet in secret for the purpose of conspiring. The penalty for violating the law was death. Proposed more than ten centuries ago by an emperor named Polydorus, the law was quickly passed.

Like Vespasian, Polydorus had become suspicious of the *Pon Q'tar.* Also like Vespasian, Polydorus had been greatly admired by the military, birthing like-minded concerns of eroding influence among the paranoid clerics. Like many ad hoc laws formed by struggling governments, the Vetare Secretum was ratified more out of personal need to retain power than from an altruistic desire to help the nation.

Truth be known, the scheming *Pon Q'tar* had violated the law from the start, despite the harsh punishment they would suffer should they be discovered. Given Vespasian's powerful command of the craft and his close ties to the Legionary Tribunes, violating the Vetare Secretum under his rule was far riskier than during the reigns of previous, weaker emperors.

Because they were the most experienced craft practitioners in all the land, the *Pon Q'tar* were immensely powerful, to be sure. But even they realized that should they be caught violating Vetare Secretum, with a snap of his fingers Vespasian could command the military to execute them all, and do so lawfully. If the *Pon Q'tar* chose to fight, the ensuing battle would be monumental. But in the end the military wing would triumph because of their overwhelming numbers. And so the future of the imperial monarchy always tilted on a strange fulcrum that was the reigning emperor, weighted on one side by the *Pon Q'tar* mystics' secret schemes and on the other by the military's overwhelming might.

The war tent in which the *Pon Q'tar* met this night was uncharacteristically small and conspicuously missing the elaborate trappings usually accompanying the clerics' lofty stations. They sat on simple wooden stools, and a single oil lamp hung from the rafters. The tent's canvas sides and top were dyed black to match the night that surrounded them, should for some reason the craft cloak be broken.

Each member had traded his or her white and burgundy robe for a drab one, in case they should be found conspiring in the night and need to escape quickly. But that likelihood was not great, for not only was the tent shrouded by the craft, but the clerics' words were enchanted to travel no farther than the canvas sides and roof that entrapped them. Even so, far greater risk prevailed in this canvas house afield than in Ellistium. There such traitorous meetings could be held in hundreds of secret places, safely contained by far sturdier walls and far from prying eyes, roving centurions, and eavesdropping ears.

Gracchus had communed with Khristos only hours ago. When he reached out to touch the Viper Lord's mind he had desperately hoped that the *Jin'Sai* was dead, his ships burned, and his Conclave and Minions killed to the last. But then Khristos told him the bitter truth.

The news had been far worse than Gracchus had anticipated, but even so he would tell the *Pon Q'tar* the unvarnished facts. Despite how easily he might betray and manipulate Vespasian, Persephone, the Tribunes, and the Priory, he was always honest with his fellow clerics.

Seated before them in much the same way that Vespasian presided over the Suffragat in the Rectoris Aedifficium, Gracchus suddenly felt naked and alone as he endured their harsh stares.

Even so, he refused to be intimidated. Rising from his seat, he grasped the shoulder folds of his robe in one hand and looked Benedik squarely in the eyes.

"You overstate the threat, my friend," Gracchus answered. "While the best strategy was to stop the *Jin'Sai* in the Caves, he and his forces remain a long way from Shashida. Just as we have the Borderlands, the Ones have their Azure Sea. Moreover, they cannot be sure whether their long awaited *Jin'Sai* is truly sailing those waters, because their seer is no more adept at viewing what happens in the caves than is our Oraculum. Simply put, the dangers of the Azure Sea will conspire against the *Jin'Sai* just as if we were crossing rather than he. He has but one course available to him. He will not survive the journey—of that we can be sure."

Another cleric rose from her seat to address Gracchus. Lowering the hood of her robe, she showed herself to be Cynthia Flavanius, one of the *Pon Q'tar*'s most powerful craft practitioners. As he looked at her, Gracchus felt a pang go through his heart, just as he always did when he found himself in her presence.

More than any other cleric, Cynthia Flavanius had supported Gracchus during the dark, early days when Rustannica split from Shashida. Her counsel had been invaluable, her allegiance to the Vagaries unshakable. She had fought beside him, given him hope, and later shared his bed.

As the centuries passed, Rustannica developed into a powerful nation and the capital city of Ellistium became secure from attack. The *Pon Q'tar* was formed, and Gracchus and Cynthia became members. Not long after, they were married. Their only child, a son named Ajax, soon followed.

Because of the high quality of his fully endowed blood and the prominent positions of his parents in the Rustannican hierarchy, Ajax seemed destined for great things. Some said that he would become emperor one day, despite the many misgivings voiced by the other factions of the Suffragat that the direct descendants of serving members should never rule the nation. Unlike now, during those early days there had been no law prohibiting nepotism.

But in his inimitable way Gracchus had anticipated those obstacles and soon plotted to overcome them. When he came of age, Ajax would take military training and become a legionnaire, Gracchus decided, and later a Tribune. If Ajax could garner enough support among his fellow Tribunes, the anticipated vote in the Suffragat to declare him emperor would be far more assured.

But like any mother faced with the prospect of watching her son march off to pursue a military career, Cynthia had her misgivings. She first asked, then pleaded, then finally demanded that Gracchus alter the course he had set for their only child. But Gracchus would not be dissuaded, nor would their young son, whose head soon became filled with tales of Rustannican military glory and honor. When Ajax entered his training, then attained the rank of Tribune some years later, Gracchus could not have been prouder. But Cynthia's worried heart trembled even more for her only child.

Knowing what was expected of him, Ajax understood that being an ordinary Tribune would not be enough to achieve his father's plan. To one day become emperor, Ajax must also become a national hero. And so time after time he volunteered for the most hazardous duty, for only that would secure his needed fame. With that duty came many successes and the growing loyalty and admiration of his fellow Tribunes, some of whom were older than he and serving on the Suffragat. His path seemed certain, and with his father's guidance the once looming obstacles in his way were easily devoured.

Then one day came the shattering news. As Gracchus read the scroll, his hands trembled and his heart broke.

During a campaign to take some Shashidan high ground, Ajax had been killed. There hadn't been enough of his body left to send home, adding to Cynthia's and Gracchus' inability to properly mourn. The shocking news sent Cynthia first into hysterics, then into grief, and finally into rage at Gracchus for so cruelly manipulating their only child. Even Gracchus finally saw his mistake, but by then it was too late. He extended an olive branch by offering to adopt a child, but Cynthia had become too bitter, and her heart had fallen into too many pieces to be repaired. With her love for Gracchus irreparably shattered, she petitioned for divorce.

Save for service in the legions, from the beginning of the Rustannican Empire women enjoyed the same rights as men in all things. The right to petition for divorce was no different, and there was no social stigma attached to it. Moreover, when a divorce was granted, the woman could demand the return of her dowry, helping to ensure that she would have financial independence and not become a burden to the state.

This was especially true of the krithian class, in which dowries could reach fantastic sums, making divorce very expensive for the husband. Paying back a woman's dowry was seen as a matter of honor. Any husband who refused or could not do so was socially ostracized, and his further advancement in Rustannican society remained unlikely until proper restitution was made. Even then the stigma remained, and few such recalcitrants saw their fortunes improve. Cynthia's dowry had been huge, and its subsequent return from Gracchus' coffers helped make her one of the richest women in Rustannica. With such wealth added to her great command of the craft and her membership in the *Pon Q'tar,* she was a force to reckon with.

Gracchus watched as Cynthia lowered the hood of her robe. To this day she took his breath away, and he again felt his heart ache not only for the loss of his son, but for the loss of her love. That had been many centuries ago, and neither of them had remarried.

Granted the time enchantments at the young age of forty-three, she looked as lovely now as she did then. Her eyes were blue and wide-set; graceful eyebrows arched over them, lending them an exotic look. A mass of dense blond curls reached to her shoulders. Her graceful jawline was firm and strong, her lips full and inviting. Her form was seductive, its alluring shape only partly hidden by the ill-fitting robe.

Because of her many obvious attributes, it was said that over the centuries hosts of suitors had asked for her hand, but not one was chosen. It was also rumored that she had taken many lovers in an attempt to dull her grief, but not even Gracchus knew for sure.

As he looked again into her lovely face he wondered what she might say. Would it be a further condemnation of his failed plan? he wondered. Or would it be some other way to hurt him again for his mistakes of so long ago?

"You are forgetting something, Gracchus," she said. "You are right when you say that because the *Jin'Sai* sails the Azure Sea, we can no longer take direct action against him. But there is something more to this puzzle that you have avoided. I was wondering whether you might address it, but since you haven't, I feel the need to do so in your stead."

Gracchus steeled himself against her next words, for he now knew what she would say.

"What of his blood?" she asked. "We have been told that his blood will open many locked doors and remove many obstacles in his path, simply because of its majestic quality. As you know, this information was gleaned long ago from more than one highly placed Shashidan mystic whom we captured in battle and later tortured. The information was obtained many separate times over several centuries. Its veracity is irrefutable."

Pausing for a moment, Cynthia gazed deeply into Gracchus' eyes. As she did, he found the loss of her love far more defeating than anything else she might say.

"So tell us, Gracchus," she said. "Might the *Jin'Sai*'s blood not guide him safely across the Azure Sea? Despite your reassurances, is there still not cause for great concern?"

"Perhaps," he answered. "But you know as well as I that the information gleaned from those Shashidan mystics has never been tested. We have no way of knowing whether it is true. And after all, every one of our ships and crews that tried to cross that sea was never heard from again."

A short smile crossed Cynthia's lips. "In any event, because of your recent failures it seems we will soon have our answer," she said. "And if the answer is the wrong one, all our plans for Vespasian might come to naught. You must judge the import of all that for yourself. I have already formed my opinions, and I find them distressing. Of perhaps even greater concern is that you promised Vespasian that the reigning *Jin'Sai* couldn't possibly leave his side of the world. Should that prove untrue, I for one would not wish to endure our emperor's wrath. Your twisted creation might yet turn on you."

Still on his feet, Benedik turned to again glare at Gracchus. "Cynthia is right," he said. "What say you about all this?"

"I say that it doesn't matter," Gracchus announced, still refusing to be humbled. "We cannot know what will become of the *Jin'Sai*. Thus it becomes pointless to worry about it. What will be will be. I will deal with Vespasian should the need arise. For now I suggest we discuss something about which we *can* take immediate action."

"And what is that?" Aegaea Mithridates asked.

"The destruction of the *Jin'Saiou*," Gracchus answered. "Never forget that she carries equal importance. She must be dealt with while we still possess the means to do so. I know that the hour is late, but you must hear my plan."

"Very well," Benedik answered.

As the single lamp burned and the night wore on, Gracchus outlined his scheme to destroy Shailiha. In the end, even Cynthia Flavanius was impressed.

CHAPTER XXX

TRISTAN LEANED AGAINST THE *TAMMERLAND*'S STERN gunwale watching the two Black Ships bound across the azure waves. Tyranny captained the *Tammerland* while Scars skippered the *Ephyra.* The wind was brisk and they were making good time. Then Tristan wondered about that.

Trying to gauge the ships' progress in this strange place was frustrating, for the only way to do so was to watch the monolithic rock walls slip by on either side. One couldn't estimate the rate of travel by looking up at the millions of glowing radiance stones embedded into the massive channel ceiling, for as Tyranny said, they showed no discernible pattern. Sailing this way was dangerous, the craggy walls waiting to tear the ships apart should they drift from their courses and strike them. To travel more safely, the *Ephyra* followed the *Tammerland* rather than sail beside her. With the dark walls looming on either side, Tristan couldn't escape the gnawing feeling that they might be sailing straight into another trap.

He still had no answer as to why the dark walls had suddenly risen. They had not appeared the first time he visited the Azure Sea, nor had they been present during the first part of the battle against Khristos and the vipers. Only after Ox was ferrying Tristan toward the ships had the walls thundered up from the depths to meet the glowing cavern ceiling.

But they surely existed now, and their overpowering presence disturbed him, for he could do little but watch the dark stone walls move silently by, their surfaces forbidding and treacherous.

The channel down which the *Tammerland* and *Ephyra* sailed was uncomfortably narrow. Tristan guessed it to be about one-eighth of a league wide. The riverlike channel trapped between the walls often snaked back and forth, making it impossible to see what lay beyond. Night Witch patrols had flown nearly to the point of no return, only to report that nothing laid ahead save for more of the same. Trying to navigate such treacherous waters was something that no one aboard had ever experienced.

Nerves were starting to fray, especially those of Tyranny and Scars. Their sure hands were constantly needed on the ships' wheels, and Tristan knew that the privateer and her first mate grew more tired by the minute. Tristan guessed that when his mystics could sail the ships through the air they would be less subject to the whims of the wind and the water and the going would be safer. But he did not know when that might be, so until then they could only press on atop the waves.

Four hours had passed since they set sail. Or at least that was what the ships' hourglasses said. But Tristan wondered whether even time could be confidently measured here. Not long ago he and Tyranny had guessed that the sage-colored light emitted from the radiance stones might never dim. If so, there would be no night, and that phenomenon would bring problems all its own. Sleep patterns would be disrupted, forcing the Minions to rest belowdecks in rotating shifts. Moreover, the great ships could not stop and weigh anchor, for although soundings had been taken, the channel bottom was never found.

Still, some encouraging signs remained. A water sample taken from the channel revealed that it was fresh, rather than salty, granting them an unlimited supply of drinking water. Even so, he ordered that the azure channel water not be used for any purpose until his mystics had assessed it.

Foodstuffs remained the other advantage, at least for now. Feeding everyone represented no immediate problem, for the ships' lower decks held enough provisions to last for several months. Still, from what Tristan saw of this eerie place, there would be no chance to live off the land, and when the food was gone, his expedition would starve. No creatures or vegetation clung to the rocky walls or populated the azure water, nor had a single bird or insect been seen. Only the warm, odorless wind, the forbidding rocky walls, and the mysterious radiance stones existed here. Save for the usual noise made by busy Minion crew members, the only other sound was the crashing of the waves as they split against the ship's bows. The environment was eerie, soulless, unsettling.

Closing his eyes for a moment, Tristan wearily ran his hands through his salt-and-pepper hair. He was desperately tired, but the continually shining light made sleep elusive. His fatigue ran deeper than just in his mind and his muscles, he knew. For some time now it had been seeping its way deep into his soul.

He didn't want to admit it, but the feeling could not be denied. The last few years of struggle had taken their toll, forcing him to wonder how much longer he could keep trying to fulfill the task that the late Envoys of Crysenium had explained to him during his first wondrous trip to the world's other side. For a long time his mystics assumed that his destiny meant combining the Vigors and the Vagaries for the benefit of all mankind. But to his great surprise, the Envoys had said otherwise.

Instead, Tristan was to finally bring an end to the War of Attrition, the ongoing battle raging between Rustannica and Shashida. He would then unite the two nations and become their lone ruler, ensuring that they never again went to war. But the Envoys were savagely murdered by Rustannica's Imperial Order before Tristan could learn how this great task might be accomplished. And so he struggled on to reach Shashida and to find the many answers still eluding him.

But it was more than just the uncertainty of it all, he knew. Since the return of the Coven of Sorceresses four years ago he had known little besides death, war, and personal loss. He was sick of killing and of seeing others killed, regardless of which side of the craft they served.

Nearly his entire family and the beloved Directorate of Wizards had died either by his hand or because of his personal destiny. That was to say nothing of the thousands of Minion warriors who had willingly perished while serving him, and the many enemies of the Vigors he had personally killed. The numbers were too great to count, and as the tally grew, so did his sense of guilt for leading so many souls ever deeper into his personal war.

But what else could he do? he wondered as he watched the rocky walls silently slide past. He was the *Jin'Sai*. Like it or not, he had been born for this mission. His greatest hope was that if he could stop the War of Attrition, the lives he might save could somehow justify the deaths of all the others—a balancing of the Afterlife's ledgers, if you will. But how many more would perish before he might somehow end that terrible war?

And when they died, how would that alter his imaginary balance sheet of death? Whom else might he lose in this struggle? Wigg, Shailiha, Faegan, Tyranny? Would he possess the strength, the spirit, the will to—

"Pardon, *Jin'Sai*," a familiar voice suddenly broke in. Tristan turned to see Ox standing there.

"Wigg and Jessamay conscious again," he said. "They ask for meeting, and say all Conclave members must come. They also want Scars and acolytes there."

Tristan nodded, then thought for a moment. The only way that Tyranny and Scars could attend would be to stop the vessels somehow, for he trusted no one else to sail them the traditional way through these treacherous straits, and allowing them to drift was unthinkable. Because the soundings had found no channel bottom, the ships could not be anchored.

"Return to Wigg and ask if he and Jessamay have regained enough strength to empower the ships and hold them still in the channel," he told Ox. "If so, tell them that we will come. Send a messenger to the *Ephyra* to inform Scars. When the ships stop, have that messenger bring Scars here. We will then furl both ship's sails."

"Yes, *Jin'Sai*," Ox said.

As Ox went to confer with Wigg, Tristan walked up the *Tammerland*'s main deck to stand behind Tyranny at the ship's wheel. For a time he admiringly watched her thread the ship through the strait as if through a swerving needle's eye. She did more than simply react to the changing wind and waves, he realized. She anticipated them, her marvelous seafaring skills a natural part of her being.

Walking nearer, he gently touched her on one shoulder. Despite her demanding task she turned and smiled warily at him before returning her sharp gaze to the ship's bow.

"You might fancy yourself a pilot," she said slyly. "But if you've come to relieve me, you can forget it! You'd have us up on those rocks in minutes!"

Tristan let go a short laugh. "I don't doubt it!" he answered. "Anyway, I'm not going to relieve you—Wigg is. You and Scars could do with a rest."

Tyranny nodded gratefully. Moments later the *Tammerland* stopped

dead in the water and held still in the center of the channel. No longer
seeing the craggy walls slide dangerously by was a welcome relief.

After tying off the ship's wheel, Tyranny ordered the Minions to furl
the *Tammerland*'s many sails, lightening Wigg's burden. Tristan looked
astern to see that the *Ephyra* had also stopped and that her warriors were
scrambling up her masts. A female Minion could be seen flying back to
the flagship with Scars in her arms.

Tristan gestured toward the ship's bow. "After you," he said. Tyranny
nodded. After stretching her tired back muscles she led the way forward
toward one of the many open deck hatches.

The air surrounding the *Tammerland* was warm and humid, making
the crowded atmosphere belowdecks even more uncomfortable. As he
followed Tyranny down two gangways and along the length of deck
three, he took in all the sights and sounds common to a busy warship.

Stacked crates of food, water barrels, and arms lockers lay all about,
making traversing the decks difficult. Minion warriors were everywhere,
busily going about their duties. As Tristan and Tyranny walked by, they
snapped to attention, then pressed their bodies up against the walls to
allow their superiors easier passage. Oil lamps enchanted to burn forever and without smoke lined the walls, giving the hallways an eerie
appearance.

Coming to the end of one hallway, Tyranny opened a door and
walked through. Following her, Tristan soon found himself in the *Tammerland*'s huge galley.

The place was a beehive of activity. There were so many warriors aboard
that they were forced to eat in round-the-clock shifts, and so the galley
never shut down. Warriors constantly chopped, stirred, cooked, and
baked to provide enough food for their hungry brothers in arms. Tristan
had long enjoyed Minion fare, and the enticing smells soon got his stomach growling, reminding him of how long it had been since he last ate.

At the far end of the galley Tyranny opened another door and they
walked down another hallway. More busy warriors saluted and made
way for them. Finally Tyranny stopped before a mahogany door on the
hallway's starboard side and double-knocked.

"Enter!" Wigg's voice called out. Tyranny opened the door and she
and Tristan walked into the First Wizard's private quarters.

Like the all the quarters assigned to Conclave members, Wigg's private rooms were spacious and attractive. Patterned rugs lay atop the
hardwood floor and tall leaded glass windows swiveled wide to catch

the sea breeze along the starboard wall. A great four-poster bed stood in one corner and a desk in the other, its top littered with parchments, texts, scrolls, and other tools of the craft.

Although all the windows were open, Wigg's rooms seemed little cooler than the passageways Tyranny and Tristan had just navigated. On the salon's port side was another door leading to the wizard's private washroom. Tristan also noticed that the flat glass vial containing the remainder of the subtle matter had been securely mounted onto the wall behind Wigg's desk against the whims of the waves and the shifting breezes. A large gilded oil lamp hung from the center of the ceiling but remained unlit because of the bright light pouring through the many open windows.

Wigg sat gingerly in a chair on one side of the room while Jessamay lay on a sofa with her legs propped up. Between them sat a low table, its marble top covered with plates of cheese, fresh fruit, dark bread, and flagons of red wine. A rolled-up scroll lay there as well. Tristan noticed that Wigg had replaced his seared robe with a fresh one, and in order not to aggravate her burns, Jessamay had donned an oversized doublet and equally blousy breeches.

Wigg managed a smile as he beckoned Tristan and Tyranny into the room. Tristan walked to Jessamay's side, and as Tyranny followed she pulled up a chair for her and one for the prince. After sitting down, Tristan gave Jessamay a concerned look.

"Are you all right?" he asked.

The Vigors sorceress nodded. "I am, but I'd be dead if Wigg hadn't caught me in his warp. At first I thought that I had broken my back, but luckily I didn't. Even so, every muscle throbs. I can't recall anything after that until waking up in my quarters, but Wigg has kindly told me the tale. He has also granted me a spell to control my pain, and another of accelerated healing to help with my burns."

The blond sorceress winced as she gingerly rearranged her burned legs, then gave Tristan a meaningful look. "We were lucky, you know," she added quietly. "Khristos is a very powerful wizard, and his Blood Vipers are equally vicious. I know that we lost many warriors, but Wigg says that we likely killed an equal number of the enemy."

"So, like Wigg, you know who Khristos is?" Tristan asked.

Jessamay nodded, but the look on her face said that Wigg should be the one to explain.

Tristan nodded, then folded his arms across his chest and looked into Wigg's aquamarine eyes.

"And you, old friend?" he asked. "How are you faring?"

Wigg's face was scalded, and painful-looking blisters showed on his hands and forearms. Even so, he seemed more energetic than did Jessamay.

"I'll be all right," he answered. "The important thing is that the subtle matter and the Black Ships were saved. I'm sure that you will want to know about our losses—I have the report right here."

As Wigg reached for the scroll lying on the tabletop, he winced, then decided that it wasn't worth the effort. Just as Tristan tried to help, the First Wizard called the craft and levitated the scroll into the air, eluding Tristan's grasp.

Wigg raised an eyebrow in the *Jin'Sai*'s direction. "I might be burned, but I'm not helpless, you know," he muttered. The scroll then unrolled in midair and Wigg started reading it aloud.

"Eight hundred thirty-seven male and female warriors were killed outright on the beach," Wigg said solemnly. "One thousand two hundred thirty were wounded, of whom about seven hundred are expected to recover and fight another day. Another one hundred or so remain unaccounted for. Ox informs me that those warriors who do not heal sufficiently or who lost limbs will be restricted to duties that no longer include combat. So a full one-third of our fighting force has been neutralized, even after the wounded return to duty."

The news was even worse than Tristan feared. Taking a deep breath, he slumped in his chair and laid back his weary head. Hearing Wigg read those numbers sadly reminded him of his imagined death ledgers. *Yet more marks for the debit page,* he thought. Putting his thoughts aside, he turned to Tyranny.

"What is the status of our ships?" he asked.

Just as the privateer was about to answer, another knock sounded on the cabin door. "Enter!" Tristan called out.

The door swung open to reveal Scars, Astrid, and Phoebe. As Tristan beckoned them into the room, Tyranny set out three more chairs.

Scars looked exhausted, a rarity for him. As usual he wore only his torn trousers. Astrid and Phoebe also looked tired and drawn, and their red acolyte robes needed some serious scrubbing.

"Are you all right?" Tristan asked them at once.

Scars nodded. "I am well," he said.

"As are we," Astrid answered for the two sisters. "We are all lucky to be alive."

Tristan nodded appreciatively as he looked at the two acolytes. Astrid was short and plump, with a profusion of brunette ringlets. Phoebe was just the opposite—tall, with a willowy figure and straight blond hair. Each sister had been handpicked by Adrian to empower the Black Ships, and they had become very good at it. No one need tell Tristan how valuable these women would be in the days ahead. Like Wigg's and Jessamay's fingertips, the sisters' were darkly charred from loosing bolt after bolt against Khristos' forces. Tristan turned back to look at Tyranny.

"Your report?" he asked.

After pouring a cup of wine, the privateer sat back tiredly and crossed one long leg over the other. "The *Tammerland* is seaworthy," she answered, "which is a bloody miracle, given all that she's been through. I can't speak for our sister ship, because I've been too busy keeping the *Tammerland* off the rocks to go and take a look at her."

Tyranny took a long slug of wine, then looked over at her gigantic first mate. "What say you, Scars?" she asked. "Are you taking good care of my other boat?"

Tristan smiled. This wasn't the first time he had heard her say that, nor was it likely to be the last. From the beginning, Tyranny considered all four Black Ships to be *her* vessels. It was a sentiment he didn't try to discourage.

"Aside from her downed mast and spars she is fine, Captain," Scars answered. "Some of her sails were torn, but they're being mended. As I'm sure you know, keeping her straight in this damnable channel is a struggle. She's slow and more than a little sluggish on the wheel because of her reduced sail surface, but the mast and spars should be repaired soon. It's a good thing that we brought along spare timber. It takes up much space belowdecks, but it's worth it. Because of Sister Astrid and Sister Phoebe's help, my Minion shipwrights say that we'll have everything set right in twelve more hours."

"Good," Tristan said. "We need to travel as fast as we can. We have much food and water aboard, but it's not limitless."

Tristan looked back at Wigg. "When can you and Jessamay empower the ships?" he asked.

"We have discussed it and we believe that we can start tomorrow,"

Wigg answered. "It will be difficult for Jessamay to stand, so some sort of seat must be provided for her while she pilots the *Ephyra*. When we tire, Astrid and Phoebe will take over. We will then establish regular shifts."

"Good," Tristan said. "Once we are airborne we should make better time. But it is nearly impossible to gauge the rate of travel in this place. The Night Witches report that nothing lies ahead except more of the same. I will keep sending them out, because this channel must have an end somewhere. We can only hope that we reach it before we run out of supplies."

Wigg nodded. "I know," he answered. "But starvation was always a risk, wasn't it?"

"And the azure water beneath us?" Tristan asked. "Have you analyzed it?"

"Such pursuits lie more within Faegan's purview than mine," Wigg answered, "but Jessamay and I did what we could. The water seems to possess an energy all its own. Truth be told, I've never seen anything like it. For now it should be used for no purpose whatsoever. We'll keep trying to learn more, but you must continue your wise prohibition. You should also know that there's something about the azure water that particularly disturbs us. It was a notion that we failed to consider before we left home."

Tristan's expression darkened. "What is it?" he asked.

"We fear that the azure water might be adversely affecting the ship's hulls," Wigg said. "When the Directorate built these vessels they enchanted them to withstand many things, but this azure water was not one of them. Because the Black Ships were originally designed to sail the Sea of Whispers, there was no need for such considerations."

"But if we stay airborne most of the time, that shouldn't matter," Tyranny said.

"Not necessarily," Jessamay replied.

"Why?" Tristan asked. "What Tyranny said seems logical enough."

"True, but you two didn't help build these ships," Wigg answered. "If you had, you would know that part of what keeps a ship's hull waterproof is the swelling that its timbers incur when it is first set atop the waves. The dry wood absorbs the water, locking the timbers tightly together. This effect is normal, and the shipbuilding process wouldn't be complete without it."

"That's true," Tyranny replied. "But the Black Ships are hundreds of years old. After spending so much time atop the Sea of Whispers, their hull timbers are the best seasoned I have ever seen. I'm sure that they have drawn in all the moisture that they ever will. If you're worrying about them absorbing much azure water, I doubt that could happen."

"You're forgetting something, Captain," Scars said quietly. "Wigg is right—we failed to consider it before we left Tammerland."

At first a perplexed expression crossed Tyranny's face. Then she suddenly grasped Scar's meaning and her visage went ashen.

"I still don't understand," Tristan protested. "What is the threat?"

"We shrank the ships," Wigg answered, "and the power that the subtle matter generated to perform that task was immense, unlocking high degrees of heat. Also, the ships sat landlocked in their cradles for days while Minion warriors loaded them with supplies. There can be no question that the hulls dried to some degree. How much so, we might never know. But if the dried hull timbers are absorbing azure water, the ships could be deteriorating as we speak. I'm sorry, Tristan, but no one expected this. Even Faegan would be surprised."

Sighing, Tristan sat back in his chair. "When will we know?" he asked.

"As soon as the ships can be flown," Wigg answered. "When the hulls are lifted from the sea we will send Minion shipwrights soaring down to examine them. Until then, there is only one sure way to tell."

"And what is that?" Tristan asked.

"If either ship starts to take on water and list," Tyranny said softly. "But by then the end will already be in sight. And as we already know, the channel seems bottomless."

Like Tristan, Tyranny could hardly believe what she was hearing. Second only to her service on the Conclave, these ships had become her life. To lose one on the high seas during battle where the decisions and responsibilities were hers she could understand, even accept. But losing them to some unexpected and insidious aspect of the craft seemed cowardly and honorless. Worse, this was a foe that she didn't know how to combat. She looked back at Wigg with angry eyes.

"Is there nothing we can do?" she asked.

Wigg pursed his lips, thinking. "We must get the ships airborne as soon as possible, then do everything in our power to keep them free of the azure water. But the best solution for all of our problems is to reach Shashida quickly."

Tristan suddenly had a thought. "Please find some parchment, some ink, and a quill," he asked Phoebe.

Wigg raised an eyebrow. "What are you doing?" he asked.

"You'll see," Tristan answered.

"Very well," Wigg answered. "Phoebe, you'll find what you need at my desk."

Phoebe went to Wigg's desk and sat down. Soon she had collected what Tristan asked for.

"I'm ready," she told him.

Tristan nodded. "I want you to take notes of this meeting," he said. "Be concise, but also be sure to include all the important points. Start with the battle against Khristos and then go on to our new worry about the ships."

"As you say," Phoebe answered.

She dipped the quill into one of the ink bottles. Using the craft to speed her task, she started writing about the recent battle and the fresh concern about the ship's hulls, the point of her quill noisily scratching across the page.

Jessamay shot Tristan a puzzled look. "Why do we need notes?" she asked.

"You'll understand soon enough," he answered. "Right now there are things I need to learn." He looked at Wigg again.

"I know how much it pains you to talk about Failee," Tristan said. "But when I asked you about Khristos earlier, you also mentioned her. Why was that?"

Before answering, Wigg caused his wine cup to levitate, then grasped it and took a long swallow. The drink seemed to help prepare him for what he needed to say. Slowly rolling the cup between his palms, he looked Tristan in the eyes.

"Khristos is an ancient Vagaries wizard," he said. "He is quite powerful. The call of his left-leaning blood enticed him to Failee's cause. He soon became one of her best wizard-generals. But in the end he was much more."

"What was that?" Tristan asked.

Wigg sighed deeply. "Failee's lover," he answered softly.

"I'm sorry," Tristan said. "I didn't know. But the Sorceresses' War ended more than three centuries ago. Where has he been all that time? Why did he choose now to surface?"

After sipping some more wine, Wigg shook his head. "I have no idea," he answered. "When the war ended and Failee's forces surrendered, Khristos was not among the captured. The Directorate assumed he was killed. Seeing him on that bloody beach was one of the greatest shocks of my life."

"Did Blood Vipers serve Failee during the war?" Astrid asked.

"No," Wigg answered. "Like all of you, I had never seen one until Tyranny brought the captured one to the palace."

"Khristos doesn't look entirely human," Tyranny offered. "He resembles the Blood Vipers at his command. It's ghastly. Was he always that way?"

Wigg shook his head. "When I knew him, he was as human as we. Something happened to him in the meantime—something that I cannot explain. Clearly, his changed appearance has to do with the Vagaries. Perhaps Faegan and Aeolus can answer that."

"They also knew him?" Tristan asked.

"Yes," Wigg answered. The First Wizard paused to take another sip of wine.

"Khristos was a well-known wizard in his day," he added. "But what strange course his life took after the war is a great puzzle. Even so, two things seem certain. After failing to stop us, he will soon go after Shailiha."

"And what is the other?" Phoebe asked.

"Khristos took his army into the Caves to try and stop us from reaching Shashida," Wigg said. "And I think I know who ordered him to do it."

"So do I," Tristan said. "It was the *Pon Q'tar.* They have found a way to commune with him. It's the only answer that fits. For some time now it seems that they have been watching us. How can this be?"

Wigg rubbed his chin, thinking. "I don't know," he answered. "It's all a great mystery."

"Why did the rock walls suddenly rise?" Tristan asked.

"It might have to do with the sudden nearness of your blood," Wigg answered. "Jessamay and I have discussed it, but we can attain no greater insight about it than that."

Phoebe suddenly looked up from her parchment. "There might be another reason," she offered from across the room.

Everyone turned to look her way. "What could that be?" Tristan asked.

As Phoebe put down her quill a thoughtful look came over her face. "The Ones tempted us to come here by way of their subtle matter message," she said, "telling us that we must cross the Azure Sea. If that's true, then the rock walls might exist for our benefit."

Tyranny shook her head. "With all due respect, Sister, that can't be true. Those walls are just waiting out there to destroy these ships. They're far more of a threat than a help, I assure you."

Phoebe shook her head. "Not necessarily," she said. "Don't you see? At first, the Azure Sea looked endless in every direction. Then the walls rose to create this channel."

Wigg smiled. "Well done," he said. "Well done indeed."

"What is she talking about?" Scars asked.

"It's all so clear now," Wigg said. "Who knows in what direction we might have sailed had we had our choice? Like Tyranny says, the compasses and sextants don't work here. We might have sailed in circles while using up all of our supplies. The coming of the channel ensured that only one course was available to us. We were forced to take it, like it or not!"

"To Shashida?" Tristan asked.

"Still unknown," Wigg said. "Unless you want to go back, we must keep going through the channel."

Tristan sat back in his chair. What Phoebe said made sense. But for now the time for talking was over and another task needed his attention. He looked back at Phoebe.

"Are you finished with the notes?" he asked. "Make sure that you include mention of the Minion losses."

"Just a moment," she answered, her hand still moving like lightning. "There," she said a few moments later.

"Good," Tristan answered.

He walked to stand beside the desk. Reaching out, he took up a blank sheet of parchment, then asked for Phoebe's quill. After unrolling the parchment on the desk he loaded the quill with more ink. The acolyte watched with curiosity as Tristan scrawled two short words onto the paper:

FIND FAEGAN

Taking up Phoebe's notes, Tristan walked to the other side of the room, then placed the parchments atop the meeting table.

"What in blazes are you doing?" Tyranny asked.

"Patience," he answered.

Tristan took his gold medallion into his hands, then called forth one of his two forestallments. In his mind's eye he pictured two medallions side by side. Soon they merged into one. Tristan opened his eyes to see the medallion hanging around his neck start glowing with the color of the craft. He then turned it over.

At first he saw only the shiny golden obverse. Then an image slowly started swimming to its surface to show Shailiha's face smiling back at him. The scene's outline was blurry, but it seemed that she was in the Archives of the Redoubt.

Reaching out, he took up the parchment asking her to go and fetch Faegan and he held it before the disk. But that wasn't needed, for soon the crippled wizard's face appeared alongside Shailiha's. Wasting no time, Tristan dropped the first parchment, then took up the one with Phoebe's notes and held it before the disk, knowing that if Faegan read them they would immediately be committed to his gift of Consummate Recollection and never be forgotten.

As the moments passed, Wigg's quarters became deathly still, and the once happy expressions on Faegan's and Shailiha's faces slowly darkened.

CHAPTER XXXI

THOUSANDS OF LEAGUES SOUTH OF ELLISTIUM AND JUST across the *Pon Q'tar*–controlled Borderlands lay a gently rolling plain. Stretching for many leagues, its grasses waved gracefully beneath the midday sun. The only sounds came from the passing wind and the black and yellow striped honeybees buzzing about in search of their daily nectar.

A lone oak tree stood broad and tall in the midst of the plain. Its gnarled trunk had struggled skyward thousands of years ago from a single acorn carried there by some meandering bird. The tree's thick branches and deep green leaves cast an irregular shadow over the grass, the ever-moving umbra slowly tracing a path around the trunk as the sun chased it from east to west. Dark mountain ranges loomed to the east of the field, their tops capped with ice and snow that melted each year to replenish the fountainheads of the Six Rivers.

Under normal circumstances the idyllic scene might have granted a place where lovers might couple unseen amid the waves of tall grass. But this day the tree and the rolling grassland surrounding it would serve a far darker purpose than providing some secret trysting place. Instead, it would soon become the staging area of Vespasian's campaign against Shashida.

Had those imaginary lovers truly been there they would have seen a strange pinprick of azure light form in the air near the tree trunk. Soon the mysterious star broadened into a whirling spiral, its outer edges gaining speed and size to form a circle many meters across. The azure spiral grew darker, then parted down the center to unleash the first of many horrors that would eventually mass in the quiet field.

While one rider led the way, ninety-nine more followed him out of the azure spiral. The one hundred mounted Blood Stalker scouts attached to the mighty Twenty-third Legion rode quickly across the grass to become the vanguard of Vespasian's invasion force.

As their horses pawed and snorted, the riders formed one line. Each was eager to start the hunt, but first they would search the immediate area for right-leaning endowed blood. Only then would the main body of Vespasian's forces start arriving by way of hundreds more vortices, each far larger than that which had just formed. The stalkers knew that their sweep of this place had to be thorough, for Vespasian's forces must arrive unseen.

Unlike those that once served Failee, some Rustannican Blood Stalkers retained their intelligence and their powers of speech. But less than one in one thousand of them were high-functioning, because among their many other deformities, the vast majority always suffered irreparable brain damage and cleft palates during their forced conversions from captured Shashidan mystics to Blood Stalkers. Only those Shashidans mystics of great intelligence and inordinately highly endowed blood kept their ken and their vocal gifts fully intact. From the earliest days the *Pon Q'tar* clerics had recognized the usefulness of such superior stalkers and used them for a higher purpose than that of their drooling, less sentient brothers.

Because the lesser stalkers could be rebellious, only the intelligent ones were allowed to command patrols without the aegis of an Imperial Order Tribune. Known in Old Eutracian as "carnefiis," or "tormentors," a famous carnifex commanded this first reconnoitering. Some of the regular stalkers here with him today—also known as "vulgarium," or common—had proudly taken part in the recent coliseum massacres during which Vespasian offered phrygian status to one of the Shashidan captives. It would be the task of the carnefiis to take charge of the individual groups formed when the stalkers split up to start their far-ranging search.

Because of their rarity, carnefiis were valuable assets to the legions. On surviving the painful transformation with their intellects and vocal skills intact, all memories of their previous Shashidan lives were cleansed from their minds by *Pon Q'tar* clerics. The forestallment allowing them to sense right-leaning blood was granted while all their other gifts save for the ability to launch azure bolts were wiped away. They were then given Rustannican names and indoctrinated body and soul into the empire's war machine. Like the vulgarium, their devotion to the Vagaries was unshakable.

The carnifex commanding this mission was named Aegedes, and although he no longer remembered it, several centuries ago he had been an important Shashidan mystic. Like all carnefiis he had been granted the time enchantments that protected him from sickness and old age. If carnefiis served the empire well they were sometimes rewarded with gold, lands, and captured Shashidan women. Aegedes was many centuries old, his exploits and skills legendary among the legions. He enjoyed killing Shashidans and he was especially good at it.

Although his grotesque bodily appearance was the same as other stalkers', Aegedes' uniform resembled that of a tribune. He wore a gold breastplate and leather greaves and gauntlets. A golden helmet topped with a red horsehair comb sat on his head. Like all stalkers he wore a fringed warrior's skirt and thick battle sandals laced up the calves. Around his neck hung a collection of desiccated eyeballs, grisly trophies he had taken over the centuries from Shashidan victims.

At his left hip hung the legionary sword, or gladius, and in one hand he held a traditional stalker's axe, its bottom end resting in one stirrup, its shiny opposing blades topped with the skull taken from his first victim, a gold imperial eagle with outstretched wings bolted to its forehead. The eagle signified Aegedes' rank of Carnifex Magnus, allowing him to command not only all common stalkers, but all other carnefiis as well. Aegedes was the only Carnifex Magnus in all Rustannica. It was a singular title that he bore proudly.

Sitting atop his war mount, Aegedes said nothing as he too employed the craft to search out Shashidan endowed blood. His gift revealed nothing. Spurring his horse, he rode down the long line of waiting stalkers, looking sternly at each vulgaris and carnifex in turn. Each stalker shook his head, indicating that he too sensed no right-leaning blood.

Satisfied for the moment, Aegedes ordered his most trusted carnifex from the line. The stalker obeyed instantly and spurred his mount forward.

The carnifex's *Pon Q'tar*–given name was Paganus, and he had served with Aegedes in many campaigns to capture and kill Vigors worshippers. Unlike Aegedes he wore no gold breastplate or helmet. Two shiny black leather belts crisscrossed his chest and attached to his warrior's skirt at opposite hips. A shiny gold disk engraved with the imperial eagle lay where the belts crossed, showing Paganus' rank as a carnifex. He too wore battle sandals and a warrior's skirt and carried the traditional axe. Like all carnefiis, he wore a gladius at his hip. Pulling his horse to a skidding stop, Paganus looked into his master's eyes.

"Yes, my lord?" he asked.

"Send them out," Aegedes ordered simply. The Carnifex Magnus possessed a strong voice and its tone was always decisive, commanding deep respect from his underlings.

"Three leagues in every direction should suffice," he added. "I want this done quickly, Paganus. My group and I will wait here and protect the portal. When all nine patrols have reported and I am sure that this area is clear, I will return to the war camp and inform the First Tribune. Be quick, for he eagerly awaits our word. Remember, we are not here to take slaves, only lives. Follow these directives to the letter and there'll be no need to subject you to an Imperial Order court-martial." Turning to look back at the line of waiting stalkers, Aegedes clenched his jaw. "Should any of the patrols fail in their duties, I will kill you personally."

From atop his impatient horse Paganus immediately gave his master a crisp legionary salute.

"All will be done as you say," he answered. Spurring his horse, he returned to the long line of eager stalkers and started barking out orders.

Aegedes watched as his stalkers broke into groups of ten, with one carnifex leading each group save for his own. As he rode his horse back toward his waiting group, the other nine patrols charged off in different directions, their horses' shoes flinging grass and dirt as they went. While riding away for three leagues, each group would use their specialized gifts to search for endowed blood. If none was found, Aegedes could be certain that an invasion staging area measuring six leagues in diameter was free of Shashidan mystics.

Under normal circumstances, Aegedes' standing orders were specific. When Shashidans were found, they were to be taken alive if possible, then sent home to meet their fates atop the slave block in Ellistium's great forum. If Shashidan mystics were met, they were to be killed or taken as prisoners of war. But capturing mystics was a risky business, often resulting in many stalker deaths.

The orders for this all-important mission were different. This time the First Tribune had warned Aegedes that the taking of slaves was strictly prohibited. Feeding them and trying to return them to Ellistium would only create hardships. This time, no matter whom the stalkers met, they were to be summarily killed. This campaign was about taking the Shashidan gold mines, not human beings. If the mines could be won, their immense wealth would dwarf the rewards of slave-taking thousands of times over. Lucius had also said that should Aegedes need to kill any unruly stalkers as an object lesson to help maintain discipline, no questions would be asked.

Aegedes looked at his nine remaining vulgarium. Drooling and eager, they sat restlessly atop their horses, hoping that the Carnifex Magnus might change his mind and let them attend the killing spree.

"Dismount," Aegedes ordered. "Keep trying to sense endowed blood. Until the others return, we wait here."

As his stalkers left their saddles, Aegedes heard some of them utter rudimentary sounds that resembled grumbling. They communicated only in throaty tones, nonsensical syllables, and sweeping gestures. Some Rustannican mystics had learned the strange vulgarium way of speaking, as had each carnifex and legionary tribune.

After the lumbering stalkers climbed down from their horses, Aegedes noticed one of them starting to collect branches that had fallen from the massive oak tree. Clearly, the lumbering fool was about to light a fire.

Swinging one leg over his saddle pommel, Aegedes dropped to the grass. As he slipped up behind the stalker, the Carnifex Magnus silently unsheathed his sword.

Raising the blade high he brought it around swiftly, its broad side slapping hard against the vulgaris' bare back. Although the blow was not meant to kill, the stinging pain and the red mark would last for days, branding the stalker with the ultimate humiliation of unworthiness.

Screaming in agony, the stalker swiveled around, intent on murdering whoever had struck him. When he found himself face to face with the Carnifex Magnus he lowered his bloodstained axe and let go a deep growling sound.

Sheathing his sword, Aegedes looked each stalker in the face.

"No fires!" he ordered. "You know our orders—this is a clandestine patrol! The next one who disobeys me dies!"

The stalker Aegedes struck pointed obstinately at the small woodpile he had collected, then gave the Carnifex Magnus a nasty glare. It was clear that he had not given up on a fire, foolish as it might be.

"Hach-a-garrr!" he shouted.

"No!" Aegedes shouted back, determined to keep control. He didn't want to kill the glowering vulgaris, but if need be he would remove his head from his body without hesitation. This was the most important campaign of Aegedes' life and he would allow no drooling underling to rob him of his glory.

To stress his resolve, Aegedes reached across his body to touch the hilt of his gladius. Growling in protest, the petulant vulgaris finally lumbered off to join his brothers as they continued to search out endowed blood. Deciding to take a look around, Aegedes walked down the gently sloping field.

His group had barely entered Shashidan territory, but their incursion constituted an act of war just the same. He couldn't be sure about how long it would take his patrols to return, but the longer they were gone, the likelier it was that they had met Shashidans who needed killing. Although he treated his carnefiis and vulgarium harshly, he was proud of them. No stalker ranks had taken as many heads or captives as had his, and he meant to keep it that way. Part of him wanted no Shashidans to be found, for that would better ensure the stealthy nature of Vespasian's advance. But he also wanted his stalkers to take many heads this day, giving him the ability to submit another glowing report to Lucius. As he thought about it, Aegedes smiled. He could live with either outcome, he decided.

Turning east, he looked toward the Vertex Mostim, the immense mountain range bordering Rustannica and Shashida on their eastern sides. Tall and snow-capped, the granite peaks were beautiful but forbidding. It was said by the *Pon Q'tar* that the civilizations on the Vertex's eastern side were uncultured, their craft use primitive, and that their people called these same mountains the Tolenkas. But that didn't matter, he realized. After the empire's legions took the Shashidan mines and went on to conquer the entire nation, there would be all the time in the world to find a way to cross the Vertex and crush whoever lived on the other side. By then nothing could stand in the empire's way. The world would finally be theirs, and they would have paid for it dearly in Rustannican blood.

As he scanned the Vertex, Aegedes could barely see the six majestic waterfalls bursting from the sides of the peaks. Each one had loosed its fresh, cold water for aeons, and each was responsible for forming and sustaining one of the six rivers that clawed deep into Shashida like jagged fingers. The empire's barges would soon ply those rivers, taking city after city to protect the transport of stolen gold on its way back to the waiting portals. Curving around on either side, Vespasian's mighty legions would sweep each armada's flanks clear of any land-based resistance, then take the mines. It would be an amazing fight, and one in which Aegedes would be immensely proud to play his small but important part.

Aside from Shashida's reputedly massive gold mines, Rustannicans greatly envied her other, perhaps even more valuable natural resouce— namely, her abundant supply of clean water and the six wide rivers that so briskly carried it due south into her heartland. In Rustannica, the Vertex peaks also supplied water, but not in such copious amounts or of such wonderful purity. Rather than forming rivers, in Rustannica the base of the Vertex had become swampland—most of it unrecoverable, even for their mystics. And so the precious Rustannican water springing from the Vertex had to be manually collected and channeled down a clever series of *Pon Q'tar*-designed aqueducts that carried it to Rustannican cities. The aqueducts worked well, and the Shashidans had never invaded far enough into Rustannican territory to endanger them. Although two full legions continually guarded the aqueducts, their lengths were so vast that areas of vulnerability always existed.

Looking back to the south, Aegedes thought for a moment about the Borderlands, the massive tract of Rustannican territory that separated the two warring nations along their entire east-west border. The countryside it encompassed was beautiful and lush—unless the *Pon Q'tar* activated the powerful spells that turned it into a living nightmare from which there was no return. Differing spells could be chosen to morph the inviting terrain into a fiery desert or a frozen wasteland, neither of which could sustain life. Because of that, the Borderlands had always remained uninhabited. Meant to protect Rustannica from invasion by Shashida, the Borderlands killed anyone trapped in their midst. That was not to say that the Borderlands were summoned every time the

Shashidans tried crossing it, for the power needed to do so was severely draining to the *Pon Q'tar* clerics and was therefore used only in the direst of emergencies. But effective as it was, the unique environmental weapon had other drawbacks.

When the Borderlands were summoned, everyone there—be they Rustannican or Shashidan—soon died from exposure to the harsh elements. The Borderlands took no notice of one's allegiances, killing indiscriminately. Aegedes also knew that the *Pon Q'tar* was not above summoning the Borderlands even if legionnaires were patrolling there, provided that a greater number of Shashidan soldiers could be killed at the same time. The Carnifex Magnus snorted at that notion. *War of Attrition, indeed,* he thought.

Moreover, when the Borderlands were summoned, all other uses of the craft were negated there—including magic portals like the one his stalkers had just used to come thousands of leagues across its great expanse. Coming on patrol in Shashida this way was always risky, for if the Borderlands were summoned during a mission, there would be no way home again until the *Pon Q'tar* deemed the threat past and the spell was dismantled. Aegedes had once heard that the magic summoned to bring the Borderlands to life was so awesome that it overpowered all other craft uses, rendering them too feeble to be called forth. In truth he didn't know, nor did he care. But one tale he had heard about the Borderlands did awe him. During the entire known history of the Borderlands, only two beings had entered its deadly midst and survived. One of them was said to be called the *Jin'Sai,* a man of wondrous blood that lived on the world's other side.

Looking back toward the south, Aegedes' thoughts returned to how his marauding stalkers were faring. Deciding to rest a bit, he walked back up the grassy knoll to await the return of his patrols.

THE NEXT SHASHIDAN TO DIE AT PAGANUS' HAND WAS A girl child, aged no more than seven years. No endowed blood had been detected in the small village lying four leagues due south. Even so, the Carnifex Magnus had been explicit. Kill every Shashidan you find, he had said, whether of endowed blood or not.

Spurring his war horse, Paganus charged through the flowery field and soon caught up to the screaming, fleeing child. As he deftly swung his gladius, the blond girl's neck sliced open like paper and her head fell from her shoulders to go tumbling to the ground. Her body followed, its arms and legs flailing about madly in all directions. Wheeling his horse, Paganus lowered his bloodstained axe and looked down the hill toward another gruesome scene.

The entire village was ablaze. It had been small, holding only a few wooden buildings and a smattering of Vigors-loving souls unworthy of life. It had also been quite pedestrian, showing little of the usual Shashidan propensity toward garishness that he so hated. He much preferred the stark and martial aspects of Rustannican architecture, with its marble columns, broad forums, and statues of heroic emperors.

This village held the usual cross section of Shashidan scum—men, women, children, and the elderly. Azure bolts loosed from Paganus' fingertips had set every building ablaze, and the structures were now little more than smoldering shells. He didn't know the name of the place, nor did he need to. All that mattered was that everyone in this forlorn village died. As his warhorse danced beneath him, Paganus could smell the sickly-sweet odor of burning flesh, telling him that the job was nearly done. Dismounting and gathering up the dead girl's head and body, he slung them across his saddle, then mounted again and galloped back toward the village.

Riding into the town square, he pulled his horse to a skidding stop. It seemed that his vulgarium had done their jobs well. According to their orders, they were dragging the corpses into the square and heaping them into a pile. Others were busily using their axes to chop the bodies into pieces to make their immolation more efficient.

Walking his horse forward, Paganus unceremoniously shoved the girl's severed head and lifeless body from his saddle onto the growing pile. As it landed, one of the drooling, axe-wielding stalkers stopped chopping and stared up at him.

"Rach-tu-lag?" he asked.

"Of course that one too, you cretinous hulk!" he shouted. "Why do you think we came all this way?"

Paganus was about to jump down from his horse and give the nearly mindless vulgaris a good tongue-lashing when he heard a woman scream. Swiveling in his saddle, he turned to look.

One of the stalkers had found a survivor. She was young and pretty, and she seemed to be unharmed. She was insane with fear, and much of her dress was covered in someone else's blood. The stalker dragged her by her hair from a smoldering building and tossed her to the ground.

Standing astride her, he started to remove his fringed warrior's skirt, making his intentions all too plain. As he dropped down atop her, the other vulgarium started cheering and shouting.

Whipping his horse, Paganus drew his gladius and charged straight toward the aroused vulgaris. As he neared, he took the stalker's head off with one swing of his sword, and the headless corpse collapsed atop the young Shashidan woman. Screaming insanely, she managed to shove the stalker off herself, then sprang to her feet. Wheeling his horse, Paganus charged back toward her. In moments her severed head and lifeless body lay alongside those of the rebellious stalker, their yellow and red blood commingling to feed the thirsty dirt.

Paganus turned and glared harshly at his other eight vulgarium. Pointing his sword at them, he shouted, "You know your orders! There is no time for this! Now do your duties and finish cutting up those corpses! We still have two more leagues to cover!"

Amid much growling, the eight vulgarium finished their grisly task, with the heads and other body parts of the dead stalker and the young woman finally added to the pile. Swarms of hungry flies had already started feasting on the easy prey of gaping wounds and open, unseeing eyes.

After looking around the smoldering village one last time, Paganus ordered his vulgarium to mount their horses and form a line. Walking his horse closer, he raised one hand and pointed it at the pile of corpses. At once the pile burst into flame, adding yet more stink to the air.

Ordering his stalkers onward in the search for right-leaning endowed blood, Paganus led the charge from the destroyed village, and the stalkers again headed south.

TEN HOURS LATER, AEGEDES RESTED AGAINST THE TRUNK OF the lone oak tree. Reaching into the pack that he had taken from his horse, he grasped some more dried jerky and his water flask. Because he wanted his stalkers to move fast, such meager rations were all that he had allowed each one to bring along. The jerky was tough and the water warm, but they would do for now.

Aegedes looked up at the sky. Night had fallen and the cloudless heavens held too many stars to count. The three red moons beamed down peacefully, belying the mayhem that would soon accompany Vespasian's mighty war machine. With his nine vulgarium gathered quietly around him, Aegedes waited.

Soon the first of his patrols returned. They had killed some Shashidans traveling the roads, but otherwise their area of responsibility had been clear of endowed blood. As more patrols returned, their stories were much the same. The souls they had killed were few, the resistance meager, and there had been no stalker injuries.

Finally Paganus and his group rode up the grassy slope. Pulling his horse to a stop, the carnifex dismounted and bowed to his master. From his resting place against the base of the tree Aegedes took another sip of water and regarded his carnifex calmly. The fact that one stalker was missing was not lost on him.

Aegedes listened intently to Paganus' report, including the killing of the unruly vulgaris. The Carnifex Magnus stood up before replying.

"It seems that our job is done," he said, "and that the area in question has been cleared." Walking to his warhorse, he swung up into the saddle.

"I go to report to the First Tribune," he said, his horse dancing eagerly beneath him. "While I am away, do not leave this place. Keep trying to sense endowed blood, and above all protect this lone portal with your lives. If endowed blood is detected, search it out immediately and kill its owners. This is the most important campaign in the history of the empire and we cannot afford mistakes. You will likely see hundreds more portals forming within the hour. At that time, the tribunes will issue us new orders. You have done well, but our bloody work has just begun."

Paganus gave Aegedes a crisp salute. "As you say, my lord," he answered.

Wasting no time, Aegedes galloped his horse directly into the center of the azure portal, then he was gone.

Looking around the meager campsite, Paganus breathed a sigh of relief. For the time being their mission was over. Aegedes seemed pleased and he was off to give his report. Soon many more portals would form, then the Rustannican war machine would start pouring through them and this quiet place would become a madhouse of activity.

Deciding to take what rest he could, Paganus sat down in Aegedes' place and leaned his tired back against the lone tree.

CHAPTER XXXII

"I AGREE," FAEGAN SAID. THE WIZARD'S TONE WAS UN-characteristically dour, his mood pensive.

"The outlook is not promising," he added, "and it seems that whatever could have gone wrong *did* go wrong. Who knew that Khristos and his Blood Vipers would be waiting on the shore of the Azure Sea, or that those rock walls might suddenly arise?"

He gave Shailiha a reassuring smile and reached out to touch her hand. "But take heart," he added softly. "Tristan and his group are a sturdy and resourceful lot. If anyone can reach Shashida, it is they."

Sighing, the crippled wizard lifted Nicodemus from his lap. But the still-sleeping cat was not ready to be dislodged from the warmth of his master's care, and his claws remained hooked in the fabric of Faegan's worn black robe.

With a smile the wizard called the craft to gently release the cat's claws and he set Nicodemus down on the floor. Not to be denied, the cat stretched lazily and wended his way among the meeting attendees' legs, rubbing his arched back against them.

The topics being discussed in the Archives of the Redoubt were worrisome. Faegan, Traax, Shailiha, Abbey, Aeolus, and Sigrid sat at a meeting table, each person's face long with concern for their beloved friends who were sailing into the unknown. Three days had passed since Tristan's message had reached Shailiha by way of their matching medallions, and the princess was becoming anxious. Compounding her worries was that little could be done until Khristos and his vipers surfaced. Faegan and Aeolus had explained Khristos' history to everyone, and Shailiha had been surprised to hear of him.

Several times since receiving Tristan's message, the princess had been tempted to contact her brother before finally deciding against it. When the Envoys of Crysenium had enchanted Tristan and Shailiha's medallions, they had warned the *Jin'Sai* that the gift could be easily overused, risking its loss altogether. And so Shailiha resolved to call on her medallion only if there was something of importance to convey to Tristan. So far, nothing had arisen. After getting Tristan's message, Aeolus and Traax had led a group of Minion warriors deep into the Caves in a try to hunt Khristos down, but they returned empty-handed. Nor had Aeolus divined a hint of endowed blood.

Even so, the Vagaries wizard and his servants could still be hiding there, for the Caves were immense and the areas that Nicholas had excavated remained largely unexplored. Night Witch patrols searched the length and breadth of Eutracia, but they could find no sign of the Vagaries wizard or of his macabre forces. With no one to fight, Shailiha and her Conclave members felt stymied and frustrated. And so they anxiously waited for word from the Night Witches, for only then could a proper attack be planned.

But how does one fight a ghostlike enemy that can seemingly vanish at will? Shailiha wondered. *And even if we find him and his vipers, will we prevail?*

"Let's review what we know," Aeolus offered, rousing the princess from her thoughts. As she looked across the table, she found his calm manner comforting.

"First, Wigg and Jessamay are injured, but they will heal," he said. He gave everyone around the table a little smile. "If I know those two, they'll be back on their feet annoying everyone in no time."

Shailiha looked over at Abbey to see the herbmistress smile for the first time in two days. She was terribly worried for Wigg, as they all were. But because she was Wigg's lover, the First Wizard's injuries struck a far more sensitive chord in her than in the others. After having been apart from Wigg for more than three centuries, she had no wish to lose him all over again. She had been desolate when it was decided that she would not accompany him on the journey, but she knew it was for the best. As she glanced back at Shailiha she tried to give the princess a hopeful look.

"The rock walls that rose from the sea floor are dangerous to navigate, but if Phoebe is right, the Ones might be funneling the Black Ships toward Shashida," Aeolus went on to say. "If that is true and they can keep the ships clear of the walls, the path to Shashida is ensured."

"Unless all this is a Vagaries trap, engineered by the *Pon Q'tar*," Traax countered. "And even if Phoebe's theory is right, problems remain. Their fighting force has been cut by a full one-third. That's a staggering loss, and Tristan knows it. I can only imagine how savage the fighting on that beach must have been. Then there is this added business about the azure water perhaps damaging the ships' hulls. I am fully aware that's only a possibility, but should they lose those ships—"

"We can't change those things," Faegan interrupted. "So no matter how difficult it might be, we must not worry about them."

Shailiha sighed and sat back in her chair. Faegan was right—worrying would do no good. Tristan had chosen his path, and nothing could prevent him from following it. It was what he was born to do, and everyone knew it.

She turned to look at Sigrid. The female warrior's broken right arm was in a sling from tumbling through the bell shop roof in Tanglewood, but it was healing. Shailiha knew simply by looking at the devoted Night Witch that the pain Sigrid felt at not being able to lead her patrols far outweighed the suffering from her injured arm.

"There is still no sign of Khristos and his vipers?" Shailiha asked.

As Sigrid adjusted her sling, she winced. "No," she said sadly. "It's as though the earth swallowed them up. How does one move such a huge force without being seen from the air? It's nonsensical—unless they're still in the Caves. I fully understand that Khristos intended to kill Tristan's group to keep them from reaching Shashida. And as Tristan's message said, with Failee dead it is likely that Khristos has come under the control of the *Pon Q'tar*. But Tristan escaped, so why would Khristos linger in the Caves? At any given time several Night Witch patrols search Eutracia from above. My witches are exhausted, but finding the enemy has become a matter of honor. They'll keep looking until they fall from the sky."

"What are Khristos' plans, indeed?" Faegan asked. He pulled thoughtfully on his beard for several moments. "There can be but one answer. Having failed to kill Tristan and his group, he will come after the *Jin'Saiou*."

"How can you be so sure?" Shailiha asked.

"With Tristan free from Khristos' reach, you present the most important target," Aeolus answered. "If the *Pon Q'tar* cannot destroy your brother, they will settle for killing you. Khristos might be the last of the Vagaries worshippers on our side of the world whose gifts are powerful enough to commune with them and to do their bidding. They will surely use him to their greatest advantage."

Shailiha's expression hardened. "Then let him and his vipers come," she said softly. "I welcome it! To reach me, he must first enter Tammerland. All the Minions have been put on alert, and the warriors patrolling the city streets have been doubled. If he and his forces enter the city, they will be seen. So I say let the fighting start! Anything is better than this infernal waiting!"

Just then an urgent pounding came on the Archives doors. "Enter!" Shailiha called.

The doors opened to show a Minion warrior standing there. Shailiha recognized Lars, the officer in charge of palace security. He was deeply out of breath. Running to the princess's chair, he quickly went down on bended knee.

Realizing that something was wrong, Traax immediately stood. "Speak!" he shouted. "What is happening?"

"Tammerland is overrun by the Blood Vipers!" Lars cried. "The night is dark, but even so, we should have seen them coming! No one knows how they got into the city unseen, and their numbers are overpowering our street patrols! The citizens are at their mercy!"

"Are they marching on the palace?" Faegan demanded.

Lars vehemently shook his head. "That's the strange part," he said. "They seem to have no interest in the palace. The beasts are flowing down the streets like rushing rivers, burning buildings and killing people at random. The few warriors who survived the initial onslaught are fighting back, but they cannot last long!"

Snatching up his dreggan and baldric, Traax hurried to strap them on. "Has the Minion camp outside the palace walls been mobilized?" he demanded.

Lars turned toward Shailiha. "They have, Your Highness!" he answered. "They circle in the sky above the palace! Litters await you in the courtyard!"

Suddenly energized, Shailiha leapt to her feet. This was the moment she had been waiting for! At last the vipers had exposed themselves! Even so, she decided to withhold her orders until she and the Conclave could get into the air and take better stock of the situation.

As though of one mind, Lars, Sigrid, and the Conclave members charged from the room.

CHAPTER XXXIII

THIRTY-SIX HOURS EARLIER, KHRISTOS HAD STOOD ALONE just outside the entrance to the Caves of the Paragon. It was early evening, and he felt assured that he could linger there in safety. Shailiha and her Conclave would likely not yet know about his recent battle with Tristan and the Minions, and would therefore not think to search the labyrinthine caves. He had sadly informed Gracchus of his failure to kill the *Jin'Sai,* and of the strange rock walls that had surfaced from the Azure Sea. Even so, he had destroyed many Minion warriors, and for that he was glad. Following the orders Gracchus had given him during their earlier communion, he had come to this spot alone, leaving his vipers behind in the caves.

"Take no further action until you again sense my ken," Gracchus had told him. *"Worry not that you failed to kill the* Jin'Sai. *Exit the caves and await my word. At that time I will give you new orders that will spell the end of his twin, the* Jin'Saiou. *In many ways she is an even greater prize, and killing her will be equally delicious, I assure you. When Tristan hears of her death, the pain he will suffer will be even greater than had you killed him with your silver staff on that bloody beach."*

And so Khristos left his servants behind in the caves to come and tarry in the magenta moonlight.

As he stood waiting, the wind came up, ruffling the hem of his robe. The moonlight glinted off his staff, and the night creatures that had stopped singing when he first arrived slowly adjusted to his presence and took up their odd-sounding choruses again. The grass was heavy with dew, its countless stalks looking like row on row of tiny, glistening sword blades. This place was peaceful and beautiful, but he had little appreciation for it, because in his heart he only hungered to redeem himself and for his fight to start anew.

As he waited for Gracchus' word he dropped the hood of his cloak, his hairless cranium shining in the moonlight. He then thought about Failee and smiled, wondering how she would have interpreted his new mission.

Although he was not taking her revenge in the manner that she had planned, this way was better, he decided. The Directorate of Wizards on whom she had originally wished to wreak vengeance were all dead, save for Wigg, Faegan, and Aeolus. And so he now did his best to kill those directly responsible for foiling Failee's plans for Shailiha and for causing her untimely death. *It is fitting,* he reasoned.

Even now he missed the First Mistress, despite the wicked way she had tricked and used him. In truth his devotion to the Vagaries would allow him no other sentiment. Bearing a left-leaning blood signature of such great quality meant undying loyalty to the cause and unswerving devotion to those Vagaries mystics whose gifts outshone one's own. So it had been with Failee, and so it now was with Gracchus.

What Khristos could not know was that before Gracchus deigned to again commune with him, the *Pon Q'tar* cleric would first meet in secret with his fellows in the small invisible war tent—the same tent that stood far away from the main body of Vespasian's camp as the emperor awaited word from the Carnifex Magnus that the invasion could safely start. Because Gracchus had given the other *Pon Q'tar* members the bad news about Tristan's escape and outlined his further plans for the *Jin'Saiou,* Gracchus was free to communicate his new orders to Khristos.

Just then the Viper Lord felt Gracchus' mind reaching out to touch his. Going to his knees in the dewy grass, he bowed his head.

"I am here," his thoughts said.

"Good," Gracchus answered. *"Pay close attention to my orders. You will soon use one of Failee's spells with which you are intimately familiar. Following my instructions to the letter will take you far toward your final victory, and soon Eutracia and Parthalon will be yours to rule. Listen now and I will tell you all . . ."*

As Gracchus outlined his plan, Khristos was surprised and impressed. The *Jin'Saiou* and her Conclave would never see the attack coming. Tammerland would be just the first step, but also the most important one. As he turned back to reenter the Caves, he smiled as he wondered what it would soon be like to sit on Tristan's throne . . .

NINE HOURS LATER, KHRISTOS AND HIS SERPENTS HAD EX-ited the Caves, and they stood along the southern bank of the Sippora River as it rushed eastward along the northern edges of Hartwick Wood toward the coast. Dawn would arrive soon, but for now the sky was still dark, its stealthy embrace hiding him and his servants from prying eyes. His Blood Vipers waited eagerly, their immense numbers stretching along the riverbank for nearly two full leagues. At his signal they would all leave this place and start their secret trek toward Tammerland. Then Khristos' private war could start again.

To Khristos' amazement, Failee's three-hundred-year-old spell—the same one she had used to condemn Khristos to the water and give the viper embryos the chance to survive and to grow—still endured in them, Gracchus said. Moreover, when Khristos and his vipers again entered the water, like the time before, the spell would sustain them and they would no longer need to seek food. He had not known this, and he fully realized the many advantages that this new knowledge would bring. Failee's spell that had once entrapped him and his vipers could now be used at will to further his ends.

How I wish that she could be here to see this night! he thought. *What my love tried so hard to achieve is nearly in my grasp! When my task is done, the Vagaries will rule everywhere east of the Tolenka Mountains.*

Having given his lead vipers their orders in the Caves, they had informed all of the others. As his Blood Vipers waited on the riverbank they eagerly writhed and hissed, wanting to be on their way. The time was now, Khristos realized. Raising his staff, he pointed it toward the river.

At once the thousands of Blood Vipers dived into the rushing Sippora and submerged. Failee's unique spell that gave them life and allowed them to survive the depths would sustain them all the way to Tammerland, and the current would carry them along.

As he watched his servants vanish into the depths, he knew that they would not surface again until they were well into the heart of Tammerland, for the Sippora ran straight through the city's center. Only then would they surface to climb the banks and enter the city. Their great numbers coupled with the huge advantage of surprise would quickly overcome the meager Minion patrols wandering the streets, and the killing could start. Even so, this part of Gracchus' plan was only a diversion to help serve the more important stage that would follow.

In the heart of Tammerland the Sippora split into two branches before joining again and continuing toward the sea. The southernmost branch ran close by the royal palace. As the main body of Blood Vipers continued on, Khristos and the others would split off and keep traveling along the riverbed bordering the palace grounds.

After the main body exited the water to engage the Minion street patrols, the alarms would go out, bringing the palace grounds to life and summoning the Minions into the heart of the city to deal with the sudden threat. With the palace and its grounds nearly unguarded, Khristos and his viper group would exit the river and start their work. The savage killing of any Minion skeleton force left behind to guard the palace would serve as a welcome bonus.

With all his vipers waiting in the river, Khristos dived into the water and began leading his forces on the trek toward Tammerland.

FORTY-EIGHT HOURS LATER, KHRISTOS AND HIS FORCES had reached the heart of Tammerland undetected. Because of Failee's spell, despite the murkiness of the river water he and his vipers could see one another plainly. Using hand signals, Khristos ordered some of his servants to stride up the sloping riverbanks and to enter the unsuspecting city. It was evening in Tammerland, and many citizens would still be walking the streets.

Good, Khristos thought. *The more mayhem that is caused, the better things will go for us.*

As half of his servants crawled up the underwater banks on opposite sides of the river, the Viper Lord ordered his remaining force to wait behind. They would travel on to where the river branched. By the time he reached the area bordering the palace grounds, he knew that his vipers exiting the river in the city would have caused so much death and destruction that the palace would be nearly abandoned, as would the prizes that he sought. Motioning his forces forward, they traveled on.

Dripping water as they came, the thousands of hissing Blood Vipers entered the city, and with them came the first screams.

CHAPTER XXXIV

SITTING AT HIS DESK IN HIS PRIVATE QUARTERS ABOARD the *Tammerland,* Wigg heard the ship's bell, telling him that it was midafternoon. Putting down his quill, he stopped to listen. Wafting through the open starboard windows from three decks above, the bell's chimes were reassuring yet frustrating. Tristan had been right when he said that time had no meaning in this underground labyrinth of azure water, rock walls, and bright radiance stones. Despite all that he had experienced during his more than three centuries of life, Wigg was forced to admit that the absolute lack of nighttime was something truly extraordinary.

After placing the quill into its holder and closing the leather-bound volume before him, Wigg put the book to one side. Since the final defeat of the Coven he had been writing almost daily in his private journal, recording all the amazing things that he had witnessed. Part of him wished that he had been doing so since he was a boy, because the idea of being able to revisit any previous day of his choosing held a certain attraction for him. But as with so many of life's projects, the needed resolve had come late. Because his life had been so hectic in recent years, his journal often went unmarked. But it was a worthwhile project, he reasoned, even if parts of it were written days or weeks later. He smiled wryly as he thought about Faegan and the crippled wizard's gift of Consummate Recollection. He had no need for such a mundane tool as a daily journal.

As Wigg rose from his desk, his burns unexpectedly snapped at him again. Wincing, he nearly cried out. He took a deep breath and called the craft, forcing the pain back into its lair. Only then did he walk gingerly to the room's starboard side and recline on the upholstered bench lying beneath the row of open windows. Reaching out to the table before him, he poured a glass of wine, then turned to gaze outside.

The *Tammerland* and the *Ephyra* were making good time, or so he supposed. But because the monolithic rock walls surrendered few clues about how fast the Black Ships traveled, gauging the ships' speed seemed as pointless an endeavor as trying to measure the passing time. Like the others aboard, Wigg found that sleeping in perpetual light was nearly impossible. Three days had passed since the channel walls had arisen and Tristan's little fleet had escaped Khristos and the Blood Vipers. Because of the constant light and the mind-numbing sameness of the scenery, those three days had seemed like three weeks.

Tristan kept ordering Night Witch patrols out ahead of the ships, a decision with which Wigg heartily agreed. But with the return of each patrol the report was always the same: Nothing lies before us except this endless channel. Even so, everyone kept hoping that the devoted witches would sight something that might give the conclave an inkling about where they were headed and what they were facing. Gingerly placing his legs atop the bench, Wigg sighed and took another sip of the excellent wine.

Just now Astrid was piloting the *Ephyra.* Jessamay was topside, piloting the *Tammerland* from the comfort of an upholstered chair near the ship's bow. Wigg smiled again as he supposed that the ever watchful Tyranny was surely standing by Jessamay's side, second-guessing every course adjustment the sorceresses made.

Although her burns were worse then Wigg's, Jessamay insisted on fulfilling her share of the piloting duties. So far there had been no mishaps, but the rocky walls always loomed near, and not one of the four mystic pilots could afford to let his or her guard down when empowering the vessels. It was exhausting work, and Wigg knew in his heart that it would be a miracle if the ships didn't eventually strike the walls, or—Afterlife forbid—collide with one another.

As soon as the ships left the waves, Minion shipwrights had performed airborne inspections of the ships' hulls. Everyone was relieved when the warriors reported that they saw nothing suspicious. The ever-skeptical Wigg had insisted that one of them carry him in her arms and let him see for himself, but even the First Wizard could find no apparent damage.

Still, Wigg remained concerned. He knew that these first inspections might mean little, for if azure water had seeped into the ships' timbers, it could be doing damage sight unseen. Because there was no way to be certain, all he could do was wait and continue to order regular inspections. Of perhaps even greater concern was the supposedly great distance to Shashida—if indeed that was where they were headed. But other worries also gnawed at the old wizard—concerns that had less to do with the perpetual light, the monotonous view, or the state of the ships' hulls.

Like Tristan, Wigg was bone-tired and sick of seeing so much death and destruction. The three centuries since the end of the Sorceresses' War had given him a long time to reflect. Then the Coven had unexpectedly returned, and with them yet another period of violence, political uncertainty, and upheaval in the craft that had persisted almost without pause right up to the present day. Although he tried his best not to show it, the defeat of the Coven and the powerful Vagaries servants who followed them had taken their toll on him. There had been little time in which to simply laugh, live, and love—the truly important things that make life worth living. Moreover, he adored Abbey and missed her keenly, every passing day forcing him to wonder whether he would ever see her again.

But even these concerns paled when compared with the singular worry that had troubled him from the moment the subtle matter had been so unexpectedly released in the Redoubt and tempted him and his friends into this strange quest. More than anything, he worried about what they might find in Shashida and what effect it would have on Tristan.

Wigg was not Tristan and Shailiha's father. Even so, since their births he had carefully watched the *Jin'Sai* and *Jin'Saiou* grow to adulthood. He had done all that he could to shape their values and beliefs according to the principles of the Vigors, and had he been their real father he could not be prouder. He had witnessed their nearly simultaneous births while using the craft to help their mother, Morganna, deal with her pain, and he had comforted Nicholas I as he watched his wife suffer. As had been foretold in the Tome, an azure glow surrounded the blessed event, assuring all that the Chosen Ones had finally come. And since the deaths of the king, the queen, and the other members of the Directorate of Wizards on that tragic day of Tristan's aborted coronation, Wigg knew that he alone could best serve as the Chosen Ones' mentor. As his responsibility grew, so did his worry for them.

This is what vexes me so, he realized—*the loss of so many loved ones and friends to the horrors of the Vagaries. The loss of the Chosen Ones would be felt by us all, to be sure, but such a catastrophe would tear my heart in two.*

In truth he had always worried more for Tristan than for Shailiha, and there were ample reasons why. Tristan was the impulsive one, the headstrong one, the one who always challenged every answer with yet another question. Shailiha was more thoughtful and better able to harness her emotions. She was every bit as capable a leader as her brother had come to be—perhaps even more so, given her greater proclivity to think before acting. But because Tristan was prophesied to be the first of them to try and bring peace to the warring nations of Rustannica and Shashida, Wigg's worry for him was the greatest.

Every soul aboard these two ships was risking his or her life to find Shashida, and not knowing the nature of its culture was also deeply unsettling. If the Ones truly were the world's greatest masters of the Vigors, it should follow that they would be compassionate and understanding. But what if they were not, and their only interest in Tristan was some arcane use of his blood to win their terrible war for them? Wigg wondered. Could this be what the Tome referred to when it said that Tristan's blood would serve some higher purpose than had ever been seen before? After so many aeons of war, had the Ones become like the *Pon Q'tar,* and were they now willing to win at any price—including Tristan's death? Or in the end would they—

Suddenly an urgent pounding was heard on the doors. Pushing aside his thoughts, Wigg placed his wine glass on the table.

"Enter!" he called out.

The doors parted and Scars stood there. Without invitation the first mate hurried into the room and approached Wigg, a concerned look on his face.

Wigg sat up quickly. "What is it?" he asked. "Has something happened?"

"One of the Night Witch patrols found something ahead in the channel," Scars answered. "Tristan wants you to come right away."

Wigg came to his feet, his eagerness temporarily brushing aside his pain. "Is it Shashida?" he asked breathlessly.

"I wasn't told," Scars answered. "Come—we must hurry!"

Just then Wigg felt the *Tammerland* stop in midair, telling him that Jessamay was causing the ship to hover. Wasting no time, Wigg and Scars headed for the cabin door.

When they reached the bow topside they found Tristan, Tyranny, and Jessamay there, huddled around a lone Night Witch commander and simultaneously bombarding her with questions. Many warriors had also rushed forward to hear what she had to say. Wigg approached and elbowed his way through the crowd.

"A ship, you say?" he heard Tristan ask. "What kind of ship? Where is she?"

The Night Witch Tristan was questioning looked rather young, and she seemed intimidated by her anxious superiors. She looked at her *Jin'Sai* with an expression of subservience.

"Yes, a ship," she answered. "She looks very old and her timbers are black. I daresay she's easily the size of ours."

Seeing Wigg, Tristan asked, "Could she be another Black Ship? Did Black Ships exist before those that you and the other wizards built to serve in the Sorceresses' War?"

Wigg scowled. "It's possible, I suppose, although I never considered it. The plans and accompanying enchantments for the Black Ships were found in the Caves of the Paragon, so someone might have used them before we did and then returned them to their hiding place. We always assumed that the documents were left behind by the Ones, but we could never be sure."

Wigg gave the Night Witch a commanding look. "What is the condition of this ship?" he asked. "Is anyone aboard her?"

The Night Witch shook her head. "We saw no one," she answered. "Nor did we board her, for fear that craft use might be afoot. Her hull is nearly gone, and she lies beached on a huge rock shelf along one channel wall. She rests on what remains of her port side. Much of her is smashed beyond salvage."

Wigg nodded. "You were right not to board her," he said. "Can you tell us anything else?"

"Only that if you wish to view her, you should do so from a hovering litter," she answered. "The channel narrows up ahead and it looks barely large enough for our ships to pass through. From here on, the channel zigzags. Trying to keep the ships away from the rock walls while also inspecting the wreck from the ships' decks would be difficult."

"How far away is she?" Wigg asked.

The young Night Witch thought for a moment. "Distance is difficult to gauge here, but I would guess that the site is about two leagues off our bow. Fresh warriors should be able to keep a litter hovering for a sufficient time as you search the wreck and then bring you home without difficulty."

"Thank you," Tristan said. "You have done well. Go and rest."

After clicking her boot heels together, the tired young warrior gave Tristan a short bow, then went off to go belowdecks and find a place to sleep.

Tristan gave Wigg a wry smile. "What say you?" he asked. "Do you feel up to a little adventure?"

Perhaps it was only his earlier thoughts come back to haunt him, but Wigg sensed peril up ahead. The discovery of a vessel resembling a Black Ship gone aground in this newly birthed channel seemed impossible. Of even greater concern was whatever terrible force had tossed her onto the rocks, and that the channel narrowed markedly. Even so, he knew that this find must be seen.

"Very well," he answered Tristan. "But we must be careful."

Tristan looked over at Scars. "Wigg, Tyranny, and I will go," he ordered. "Have a litter made ready at once. Two hundred armed warriors will accompany us. Tell them to stay alert, because we cannot know what awaits us. You and Jessamay will stay here to mind the *Tammerland.* And send a messenger to the *Ephyra,* informing Astrid and Phoebe what's going on."

As Scars rushed off, Tyranny gave Tristan a grateful look. "Thank you for taking me along," she said. "Truth be told, if you hadn't asked me, I'd be pitching a fit right now."

Tristan let go a short laugh. "I know," he answered. "But don't chalk it up to kindness. I will need a maritime expert out there, and that's you."

He turned to see a litter being untied from the deck and a host of warriors rushing to man it. "Let's go," he said to Wigg and Tyranny. "If nothing else, this should prove interesting."

Wigg raised an eyebrow in Tyranny's direction and the privateer smiled back, acknowledging Tristan's gift for understatement. They climbed into the litter, and the Minion bearers took it aloft.

No sooner had the litter become airborne than its passengers heard a great tumult from the *Tammerland*'s crowded decks. As hundreds of Minion warriors cried out in wonderment, Tristan, Wigg, and Tyranny turned to look.

The subtle matter secured in Wigg's quarters had somehow freed itself from its glass vial and come soaring through one of the open windows on the *Tammerland*'s starboard side. The amazing substance twinkled brightly in the light of the radiance stones as it flew in a long stream to find its freedom in the air above the water. Everyone stood gaping as it collected near the departing litter for a moment, then streamed away over the water and down the length of the channel.

Knowing how important the magical substance was to their safe return home, Tristan shouted out orders to the litter bearers to follow it and keep it in their sight. Like Wigg, he was terrified that they might lose possession of the subtle matter forever.

What is it doing? Tristan asked himself as he felt the litter lurch forward and pick up speed. *And what in the name of the Afterlife caused it to so suddenly free itself?* Suspecting correctly that the ride was about to become a wild one, Tristan gripped one side of the litter for dear life, then shouted to Wigg and Tyranny to do the same.

As they tore down the length of the channel in pursuit of the subtle matter, the oncoming wind ripped at their hair and clothing and caused their eyes to water. Tristan had never seen Minion warriors fly so strenuously, and he knew that they couldn't keep this pace up for long. But the priceless subtle matter was pulling away from them, despite how hard the straining Minions pulled the litter through the sky. Knowing that they would soon lose track of it, Tristan made a decision.

"Despite your injuries, can you empower this litter and fly it faster?" he shouted at Wigg. "We're falling behind!"

"Yes!" Wigg shouted back, trying to be heard above the rushing wind. "But if I do, the litter bearers must release us and then follow as best they can! That means we will arrive at the shipwreck unguarded, and there is no guarantee that I can keep pace with the subtle matter! I won't be able to keep this speed up for long, but it seems that I must try if we are to have any chance of staying with it!"

"Then do it!" Tristan shouted back.

He immediately worked his way to one side of the litter, then the other, as he barked out identical orders to the bearers. On his hand signal, the Minions simultaneously let go of the litter, then started trying to keep pace alongside.

To Tristan's horror, the litter plunged straight down toward the azure waves. Just as it was about to hit, Wigg's use of the craft blessedly took hold and the litter lurched upward again and gained more speed. But as he strained to look ahead, Tristan could see that their maneuver had cost them precious time and that the subtle matter had gained even more ground in its chase toward the unknown.

Suddenly a sharp right turn loomed up ahead. The subtle matter veered effortlessly to negotiate it, then disappeared around the bend between the two rock walls. Hanging on as best they could, Tristan and Tyranny nearly fell from the careening litter as Wigg banked it hard to the right, trying to make the dangerous turn. Zooming through the narrow bend, the litter righted quickly and tore on in pursuit of the fleeing subtle matter.

Tristan strained his vision to try to make out the subtle matter, but the oncoming wind made seeing difficult. Holding onto the litter for dear life, he inched his way closer to Wigg.

The strain showed clearly on the wizard's face, forcing Tristan to wonder how much longer Wigg could keep them aloft. No one knew what effect the azure water might have on humans should they crash into the channel, and the prospect terrified him. Inching closer, he placed his mouth near Wigg's ear.

"Can you see the subtle matter?" he shouted.

"Yes!" Wigg shouted back, the wind whipping violently at his hair and robe. "But it still gains ground! When we reach the wreck we must decide!"

"I know—we must either carry on after the subtle matter or stop and view the wrecked ship!" Tristan answered. "But the ship is going nowhere! We must keep after the subtle matter at all costs!"

"Perhaps!" Wigg answered, every fiber of his being trying to summon yet more power into the speeding the litter. "But I'm nearly exhausted! If we crash into the azure water, no one knows what will become of us!"

As another sharp bend approached, Tristan considered Wigg's warning. The subtle matter was important, he decided, but it wasn't worth their lives.

"Then put the litter down alongside the wreck, if you must!" he shouted.

Still trying to keep the subtle matter in view, Wigg nodded, then threw the litter around another sharp bend, nearly driving the litter into the rock wall on the left-hand side. Then came another quick series of sharp turns. During the third turn, the right leading corner of the litter struck the rock wall, smashing part of the litter to bits. Most of the litter's right side suddenly gave way and tumbled into the azure water with a great splash. As Wigg desperately negotiated the next few blind turns while also trying to keep up speed, the damaged litter rocked sickeningly, threatening to throw everyone from its meager safety and into the sea.

As the litter rounded the next bend, the sidewalls started to narrow dangerously, adding another threat to the pursuers' plight. Then they were suddenly around the bend and chasing down another length of straight channel. As the litter carried them along above the waves, Wigg, Tristan and Tyranny finally saw the shipwreck in the distance. Looking farther, they saw something else—something disheartening and totally unexpected.

They were fast approaching a dead end.

Like the channel walls, the rocky edifice at the channel's end rose straight up out of the sea. Its craggy surfaces reached all the way to the radiance stones lining the channel ceiling, and it stretched from one side to the other, leaving no option but to stop the litter in midair. As Wigg slowed the litter, Tristan scanned the wall. He could find no cracks or caves in it, telling him that their journey to Shashida had reached an abrupt and unsuccessful end. Tristan and Tyranny looked around for the subtle matter that had led them here, but it had vanished.

Using his last bit of energy, Wigg gently set the litter down atop the huge rock ledge in the right-hand channel wall. The litter was dwarfed by the ledge and the great wrecked ship that lay on it. As the three passengers left the wrecked litter, the two hundred armed Minions finally reached this strange place. At a hand signal from Tristan they drew their dreggans and landed warily atop the rocky shelf.

Tristan gave Wigg a sad look. "It seems that this is where our dream ends," he said. "I had such hopes . . ."

"You're right," Tyranny said. "We can do nothing but go back. If Khristos still waits for us on the far shore, we will have to fight our way out of the Caves."

"So it would seem." Wigg replied. "But for now let us finish what we came here to do." As Wigg turned to look at the great wrecked ship, so did Tristan, Tyranny, and the hundreds of warriors.

Despite her ravaged condition, the vessel remained magnificent. Easily the size of the *Tammerland,* she rested on her port side, just as the young Night Witch had reported. Her hull seemed cannibalized, as though her hull ribs and timbers had been chewed on by some great unknown beast. In some places, parts of her ribs still arched away from her gunwales like wizened fingers. Broken masts and sail spars lay everywhere atop the rocky ledge, and battered and torn sailcloth draped her topside like dingy burial shrouds.

Like those of the *Tammerland* and the *Ephyra,* her timbers were dark as night. Seeing such a once magnificent vessel looking as if it had been fed upon by some ravenous creature was an eerie feeling. As the wind blew through her wooden bones it whistled hauntingly, as if trying to warn the audacious visitors to flee before they too came under the spell of whatever had done this terrible deed.

Tristan walked to the wreck and reached up to touch one of the few remaining hull ribs. Ashen flakes loosened from it to drift away on the channel breeze. Hoping to find more clues to the ship's history, he led Wigg and Tyranny on a long walk down her side and toward her stern. An elaborately carved plaque affixed to her stern read *Intrepidus.*

"Is that Old Eutracian?" he asked Wigg.

The wizard nodded. "In our modern tongue, she would be known as the *Intrepid.*"

"She is easily as large as the *Tammerland,* and she shows similar lines," Tristan said. "I think that she was built from the same plans that you and the Directorate members used so long ago to build your fleet against the Coven. Could she have been one of yours?"

Wigg shook his head. "No," he answered. "We had no Black Ship by this name—although her name could have been changed, I suppose. But I agree that she is much like the *Tammerland* and the *Ephyra.*"

"You're right." Tyranny agreed. "But who built her? And how did she come to be wrecked on this ledge?"

Wigg pursed his lips. "There are two possibilities," he answered. "Either some great force threw the ship here, or her crew purposely beached her."

"Why would they beach her?" Tristan asked. "They could simply have reversed course."

"Perhaps they didn't have the chance," Tyranny offered. "If they were being chased by something, they mightn't have had that luxury. One doesn't exactly turn these great ships quickly. Besides, the dead end meant that they couldn't go on."

"Well said," Wigg replied. "But there might be another answer as well."

"Such as . . . ?" Tyranny asked.

Raising one arm, Wigg called the craft to send a narrow azure beam against one of the few remaining hull ribs. He held the beam in place for a time, then moved it back and forth with a sawing motion. Soon an end of the rib fell to the rocky ledge.

The three visitors and a host of curious Minions walked nearer. Nodding, the First Wizard pointed at the smooth end of the rib. To everyone else's surprise, its freshly exposed interior glowed brightly with the distinctive hue of the craft.

"So the spells used to strengthen the *Intrepidus* remain in place," Tristan said. "That's surprising after all this time, but it doesn't explain your other reason why she might have been deliberately beached."

Wigg lifted an eyebrow. "Doesn't it?" he asked. "I suggest you think again."

Tyranny grasped the frightening possibility before Tristan. "It's because of the azure water in the channel!" she exclaimed. "What we feared might happen to our ships happened to this one! The water seeped into the *Intrepidus'* hull and destroyed it little by little! That's why it looks like it's been eaten away!"

Wigg nodded. "It would explain a great many things," he said. "And if this is truly what happened to the *Intrepidus,* the future doesn't bode well for the *Tammerland* and the *Ephyra.*"

"But we can fly our ships back," Tristan argued. "With any luck, we won't have to put down in the water again."

"True," Wigg answered. "But for all we know, the *Intrepidus* was in the water for no longer than were our ships—perhaps less. If this is what happened, I suspect that the damage is insidious, eating the wood from the inside out. And if that's true, then by the time the damage is seen it might already be too late."

"That could be what happened," Tristan agreed. "But it still doesn't explain how she came to be beached this way."

"As Tyranny said, if they were being chased and they encountered this dead end they might have had no choice but to set her down on this rocky shelf," Wigg replied. "In any event they would have done every-thing in their power not to set her back down on the water. But when they landed her on the ledge, her rotting hull gave way and she rolled over on her port side, marooning her here forever. If her crew was being chased, they might all have been killed. If not, they probably starved to death."

"A precious Black Ship and her gallant crew, all lost," Tristan mused. "What a terrible waste."

Wigg placed his hands into opposite robe sleeves, then cast his dis-cerning gaze up the side of the great vessel that lay there like some monstrous beached whale.

"Don't be so quick to mourn either this ship or her crew," Wigg replied quietly.

"What do you mean?" Tristan asked.

"Although the *Intrepidus* was likely built and skippered by mystics, who's to say that they were Vigors practitioners?" the First Wizard asked.

"Do you have reason to believe that this ship was manned by Va-garies worshippers?" Tyranny asked.

"Unknown," Wigg answered. "But the possibility seems equally likely."

"All of which raises other questions," Tyranny said. "What freed the subtle matter? Or did it somehow free itself? Why did it lead us here, and where is it now?"

Tristan took a quick look around but could see no trace of the beau-tiful material that had a mind all its own. "It's gone," he said. "We can presumably fly our ships back through the channel and reach the sandy shore, but what then? Without our subtle matter or a way to produce more, the *Tammerland* and the *Ephyra* must be left behind. With no way to build cradles for them, they will be forced to sit atop the waves and later suffer the same fate as the *Intrepidus*."

"And if the *Intrepidus* perished because of the water, we dare not sal-vage anything from her, because it might only make matters worse," Tyranny said.

Wigg shook his head. "I disagree," he countered.

"Why?" Tristan asked.

"Probably the only damaged parts of her were those that touched the water," Wigg answered. "As one looks at the ship from the waterline up, she seems sound."

Before Tyranny could protest, the wizard quickly raised a hand, stopping her.

"But do not assume for a moment that we might dare to start dismantling her and taking her lumber back to our ships," he added. "I'm fully aware that such drastic measures would require much forethought."

Tristan was about to reply when a Minion officer came forward to salute him. "Pardon, *Jin'Sai,*" he said, "but there is something you need to see."

"What is it?" Tristan asked.

"Human remains," the warrior answered solemnly. "And some that don't look as human as the others. We also found unfamiliar weapons and other war materiel."

"Show us," Tristan ordered.

As the officer led the way back across the rocky ledge and toward the the *Intrepidus,* Tristan soon realized that the Minions must have flown up along her damaged hull and entered through one of the many smashed windows to gain entrance to the ship's interior. He resolved to do the same.

"I want three of you to fly us up the side and help us enter through the windows," he said. "Then you can lead us toward what you've found."

The warrior saluted and beckoned two others near. They soon had Wigg, Tyranny, and Tristan in their arms and were soaring up the black sides of the great ship.

Tristan found that viewing the ship from this perspective was an eerie sensation. He also guessed that trying to navigate their way through the stricken ship would be even more disorienting, for they would have to walk along the inside of the port hull as they searched her. Finally reaching the first row of windows, the warriors helped the three explorers inside. They let Wigg, Tristan, and Tyranny go and watched them slide down the interior wall until they reached the deck below.

Tristan was the first to go. Narrowly missing some overturned crates along the way, he skidded down the wall feet first and landed with a thud against the joint where the wall met the deck. He came to his feet to find that he was standing directly in the floor joint, and staying upright was difficult. He then saw Tyranny and Wigg come skidding into the room in the same fashion. Finally the Minion search party followed. As Tyranny and Wigg collected themselves and the warriors formed ranks, Tristan looked around. Because of the brightly lit radiance stones shining down from the cavern ceiling, the interior of the ship had ample light.

The room they had entered was huge, and its odd angle gave one the sensation of being drunk. Because the *Intrepidus* lay on her port side at about a forty-five-degree pitch, everything was cockeyed. Tristan realized that one could attempt to scale the sloping walls to reach the windows, but after reaching only so far, he or she would invariably slide back down again to land in the joint where the ship's sides met the deck. Nearly all the objects in the room had tumbled toward the joint to create a long line of debris that was piled high in many places.

It seemed that they had entered the ship's armory. Tristan easily recognized the uses for the war weapons he saw scattered about, but their designs were unfamiliar to him. Covered in dust and dumped along the length of the floor joint lay examples of the most beautiful and exotic craftsmanship he had ever seen. Some of the longer weapons like lances and spears still lay in their holding racks lining the ship's sides.

Then he saw some of the skeletons that the Minion officer had spoken of. They lay about in strange poses as if they had been tossed there by the fates, their joints often broken and lying at unnatural angles. To a man they wore magnificent gold breastplates and matching greaves and gauntlets. Iron spears, metal shields, and odd-looking gold helmets with cheek guards could be seen lying about. Strangely, the dust-laden images on the shields appeared to be eagles with outstretched wings. The skeletons' leather battle sandals and warriors' skirts had long ago fallen to dust, leaving little behind but faint imprints to tell Tristan what they had once been.

As everyone started exploring, Tristan walked a few paces forward while trying to keep his balance. The task was not an easy one. Spying a sheathed sword still in the grasp of a skeletal hand, he reached down to pick it up. As he did, the hand bones fell apart and the leather tooled scabbard turned to dust, leaving behind only the metal weapon it had once protected. Wiping the dust from the sword, Tristan held it to the light of the windows and regarded it with an expert eye.

The sword was beautiful and marvelously crafted. It was shorter than his dreggan, leading Tristan to believe that it was made more for stabbing than for swinging. It seemed to be forged of soft iron that had been strengthened with coal powder, a swordsmith's technique that was also common in Eutracia. But this was no Eutracian sword.

The two-sided blade still remained exceptionally sharp and had a V-shaped tip. Rather than a blood groove running down the blade's length, as on a dreggan, each edge of the blade sloped gently upward to form a ridge running down the center, which would cause blood and offal to slough off during battle. The rectangular hilt resting just above the silvery blade was made of solid onyx. The handle was a cylinder of solid ivory with carved finger grooves that perfectly fit Tristan's grip. At the end of the handle was a round ball of shiny onyx that prevented the sword from slipping from the bearer's grip.

Lifting the sword higher, Tristan spun it several times through the air. It produced a distinctive hum not unlike that of his dreggan, and because of its shorter length it whirled faster. The sword was impressive, perfectly balanced and no doubt very costly to produce. To whom this sword had once belonged he could not know, but one thing was certain. From the looks of their weapons and armor these dead soldiers had once been a force reckon to with, perhaps easily rivaling the expertise and savagery of his Minions.

As he lowered the sword, Tristan noticed an inscription on the blade. It read:

CARNIFEX MARCUS

LEGIONUS XXIII

The inscription had no meaning for him. Looking across the tilted room, he saw Wigg examining one of the many dusty skeletons.

"Wigg!" Tristan called out. "Please come here!"

Wigg looked up and carefully wended his way over to where Tristan stood. As the wizard neared, Tristan held the sword up.

"What do you make of this?" he asked.

Wigg shrugged. "They're everywhere," he answered. "They're finely crafted, but that one doesn't look different from the others." It seemed clear that Wigg found the skeleton he had been examining far more interesting than the sword and that he wanted to return to it. "Is this the only reason you called me over?" he asked.

"This one has writing on the blade," Tristan answered. "Can you tell me what it says?"

His interest piqued, the First Wizard took the sword into his hands and held it up to the light.

"Carnifex Marcus, Legionus Twenty-three," he muttered thoughtfully. After thinking for a few moments he handed the sword back to Tristan.

"The root of the word *carnifex* likely signifies 'murderer' or 'scoundrel,'" he said. "And the word *legionus* clearly means 'legion,' or some other variant of a word describing a sizable military force. 'Marcus' would be a man's name. These markings doubtless identify the sword's owner—one Marcus, the great murderer of the Twenty-third Legion, or words to that effect. I suspect that if we took the time to inspect all of these dusty old swords, we'd find that each one bears a similar inscription. Where did you find it?"

Tristan pointed to the skeleton from which he had taken the sword. Wigg walked to it, then beckoned Tristan to come nearer. Noticing what was going on, Tyranny wended her way through the debris to join them.

Tristan and Tyranny grimaced as Wigg calmly bent down, grasped the skeleton's head, and gave it a sudden, twisting yank. After the neck vertebrae snapped, Wigg lifted the skull high and blew the dust from it.

"I beg the Afterlife," Tyranny muttered. "Why on earth did you do that?"

"It's just as I thought," Wigg said, his curiosity forcing Tyranny's question aside. Holding the skull out, he turned it to face them. As the empty eye sockets glared at them from the distant past, they looked eerie, menacing.

"Does either of you see anything unusual about this skull?" Wigg asked.

Tristan was intrigued, and he walked nearer. There *was* something unusual about it, he realized. The skull was highly elongated. He looked back into Wigg's eyes.

"It's oddly shaped," he answered. "It doesn't look entirely human."

Just then the Minion officer neared. "This is what I was referring to earlier, *Jin'Sai,*" he said. "There are many human skeletons here, and some look like this one. This armory is but one room. I can scarcely imagine what we might find if we were to search the entire ship."

"Why does the skull look like that?" Tyranny asked. "What was wrong with him?"

Wigg smiled. "There was nothing wrong with him," he answered, "for a Blood Stalker."

"That's a Blood Stalker skull?" Tyranny asked.

"Yes," Wigg answered. "Believe me—I saw enough of them during the Sorceresses' War to know."

"What were Blood Stalkers doing aboard this ship?" Tristan asked.

"Serving their superior masters, I presume," Wigg answered. "In any event, we can now be sure of at least two things. First, this stalker was named Marcus, and he held the title of Carnifex. And second, the *Intrepidus* was commanded by Vagaries worshippers, for only they employed Blood Stalkers." After setting the skull down, Wigg took another look around.

"If this ship could talk, her tales would surely be fascinating," he added softly.

Just then Tristan heard several of the Minion warriors cry out, and he turned to look. The subtle matter had returned and was flying into the armory through one of the many smashed windows lining the tilted port hull. After all of it entered the room, the amazing substance gathered itself up for a moment and hovered above the dusty weapons, armor, and skeletons. Then without warning it divided into three distinct streams, and they headed straight for Wigg, Tristan, and Tyranny.

Tristan panicked as he felt the azure matter wrap around his waist and hold him fast in its iron grip. In moments Wigg and Tyranny were similarly caught up. Before Tristan could cry out, the subtle matter stream lifted him high into the air. Wigg and Tyranny soon followed him, and the three of them could only look aghast at one another.

"Don't fight it!" Wigg shouted as he watched the others struggle. "We have no choice but to obey! If the subtle matter wanted to kill us, we would have been dead long ago!"

Tristan started to shout out something, but before he could, the subtle matter whisked him up toward one of the smashed-out windows. Wigg and Tyranny watched in horror as the azure powder dragged Tristan out through the window. Before he knew it, Wigg was taken out the same way, followed by Tyranny.

Dazed and frightened, the wizard and the privateer soon found themselves hovering in the air by Tristan's side, directly over the narrow channel. Tristan could hear his warriors shouting from inside the ship, and the many others still on the rocky ledge started desperately running as they tried to come to the aid of their *Jin'Sai*. Some took to the air in an attempt to free Tristan from the subtle matter's grasp, but Wigg sternly ordered them back.

For several moments the three captives hung in space and looked at one another in terror, wondering what might happen next. But before Wigg could shout out another warning, he got his answer.

The three subtle matter streams spun their captives around to face the dead end. To their amazement, the edifice started to rumble and thunder, just as had the rocky walls near the sandy shore when they first rose to meet the cavern ceiling. The captives watched breathlessly as a thin azure line formed down the center of the end wall. Then the wall began to part, its divided surfaces magically receding into the side walls and sending tons of loose stone crashing down into the channel. The terrifying space in between looked pitch-black and infinite.

Suddenly an awful wind arose, its force so strong that Tristan thought it might throw the *Intrepidus* free of the rocky shelf and into the channel. The waves rose to many times a man's height and swayed violently to and fro, imprisoned between the unforgiving walls. Just when Tristan thought he could take no more, a vortex suddenly appeared within the depths revealed by the parting rock walls. It reminded him of Faegan's portal, but this could not be Faegan's work, for it was far larger than any portal that Faegan could summon, and its color was much more dazzling.

Soon the howling wind and the whirling vortex had become so overpowering that the three prisoners blacked out. As the wind tore at them, they hung unconscious in the subtle matter's grasp, and awaited their unknown fates.

Tristan was the first to be called. Without warning the subtle matter holding him flew directly into the depths of the whirling vortex. His arms and legs flailing in the air, Wigg soon followed. Tyranny went next. When the three were gone, the vortex disappeared and the rock walls rumbled shut, leaving no trace of what had just happened. The terrible wind died, allowing the channel waves to again find their equilibrium.

As the stunned Minions looked on, a deathly stillness crept over the channel, the rocky ledge, and the mysterious ghost ship that lay upon it.

TRISTAN AWAKENED GROGGY AND DISORIENTED. HE WAS lying prone, and he had no idea how much time had passed since he had been pulled into the vortex. His vision was fuzzy and his head swam sickeningly.

Raising himself up on his elbows, he saw several figures standing before him, but their images were too hazy to distinguish. He tried to look around to find Wigg and Tyranny, but his blurred eyesight failed. He shook his head, trying to clear his vision.

Fearing that he had entered Rustannica, he sat up groggily and reached behind his right shoulder to grasp his dreggan. To his horror, he found that his sword and his throwing knives were gone. He also realized that his clothing had been changed. He now wore a dark blue silk robe wrapped oddly around his body. His knee boots were gone; in their place, thick socks and wooden thong sandals clad his feet.

"You will not need your clumsy physical weapons here in the People's Palace, *Jin'Sai*," he heard a female voice say. "Please calm yourself. We mean no disrespect, but our magic is far more powerful than that of your Conclave mystics. You feel drugged because you are unfamiliar with our vortex. We deeply apologize for any discomfort you might have suffered, but it was the only way. The feeling will pass, and your vision will clear momentarily."

As he tried to see through the haze, Tristan thought he saw one of the figures raise a hand and point it at him. At once his eyesight began to improve.

First the cloudiness disappeared, then his double vision cleared to reveal a scene of startling beauty. The room in which he lay was magnificent in its exotic splendor, and the woman who had just used the craft to aid his eyesight was remarkably beautiful. Her long dark hair was piled atop her head in a strikingly unusual way, and a silken robe wound around her body revealed a tantalizing hint of the graceful figure that lay beneath it. Several more women dressed the same way stood beside her, their hands folded gracefully before them.

"Who are you?" he demanded. "What have you done with my friends?"

"They are well," the woman replied. "Because of the strength of your blood, you are the first to awaken."

"Where am I?" he asked.

The woman bowed deeply from the waist. As she did so, the others followed suit.

"You are safe," she answered as she remained bowed in his presence. "You are the first *Jin'Sai* to reach our side of the world, and your arrival has long been anticipated."

Rising and looking into Tristan's dark eyes, she smiled. "Welcome, *Jin'Sai*," she said. "Welcome to Shashida."

IV

GOLD AND DEATH

CHAPTER XXXV

Sadly, more often than not the difficult thing to do is also the right thing.

—MASHIRO OF THE HOUSE OF CRANES

AS TAMMERLAND BURNED AND THE CRIES OF HER TER-
rified citizens rose into the night, Khristos' lead viper looked
around and smiled.

Just as the Viper Lord had planned, the surprised Minion patrols wandering the city had been no match for the thousands of Blood Vipers that
came slithering up from the depths of the Sippora. Caught off guard, the
winged warriors had fought well, but the vipers' superior numbers soon
ruled the night. The lead viper knew that the alarm had gone out to alert
the royal palace and that the hordes of Minions camped there would soon
arrive. He welcomed their coming, for the Viper Lord's plan depended
on that very thing. As the heart of the city burned, the viper in charge of
the carnage slithered about, taking stock of the scene.

Hundreds of citizens and Minion warriors lay dead in the streets, their
blood pooling in the gutters and their bodies lying wherever they had
fallen victim to the vipers' talons, fangs, and venom. Scores of buildings
had been set afire by marauding Blood Vipers carrying torches. Winding
their bodies and tails around Tammerland's many lampposts, the seething
man-serpents slithered up them to smash the glass globes and eagerly
light their torches. The torches were then tossed through the windows of
shops and homes and the vipers gleefully watched them burn. Anyone
caught rushing from a burning building was summarily killed, and the

many thatched roofs in the city provided opportune targets as the torches tossed on top of them set them ablaze straightaway. Many citizens with endowed blood were being ruthlessly gorged on while still alive, their screams ringing out into the night as the vipers—once again hungry now that they had been freed from the water—searched for fresh endowed livers on which to feed.

Despite the great destruction and bloodshed, it was not the Viper Lord's plan to occupy the city or to kill all its inhabitants. Seeing how many weak-minded mortals could be murdered meant nothing to him, nor did the growing numbers of burning buildings. Killing Minions was advantageous, but just as the main body of warriors arrived to relieve the city, most of the Blood Vipers would slither their way back down the riverbanks to reenter the Sippora and escape unseen. This would be no cowardly retreat, but a clever tactical maneuver.

To add believability to their charade, some vipers would be ordered to stay behind and fight to the death. Their ranks would be enough to trick the Minions into believing that they needed to remain in the city and fight on, but not so great that Khristos would miss them during the next part of his plan. Viper sentries waited on many rooftops, constantly searching the southern sky. At the first sign of Minion relief troops they would wave their torches, signaling that the retreat into the Sippora should start.

As the carnage wore on, the lead viper also looked skyward. The Minions would arrive soon, he realized. Turning back to survey the battle, he smiled once more. Hopefully enough time would remain to kill the few surviving Minions and devour many livers of the endowed.

After ordering another viper to watch for their sentries' signals, he hungrily slithered across the dewy square and used his talons to rip into a young man's corpse.

BY THE TIME SHAILIHA AND HER FORCES ARRIVED, TAMMER-land's center was nearly destroyed, and fires were spreading outward in every direction.

From her place in the litter she gazed out aghast over a sea of flames. Dead humans and Minions lay everywhere. Vipers voraciously fed on human victims as others madly set fire to yet more buildings. Heartened by their success, the grotesque monsters writhed about each other in a sickening orgy of victory. As her litter neared the scene, the princess pulled her sword from its scabbard, gripping it so hard that her knuckles turned white.

Faegan, Abbey, and Aeolus rode with her. Flying alongside, Traax commanded the bulk of the Minions, while Duvessa led her specialized cadres of female warrior-healers. At Traax's suggestion, only a skeleton force had been left behind to guard the palace and the Redoubt. As they neared the battle, the rising smoke choked their lungs, and terrible screaming could be heard as its chilling tenor rose into the night.

Our people are dying down there, Shailiha thought. *My failure to find and kill Khristos and his forces has brought this tragedy on us. But now the fight is finally joined. Khristos' rampage must end here and now, on this night of nights.*

Shailiha signaled her troops into the fray. Their dreggans flashing, thousands of Minions swooped down to tear into the soothing vipers, while Faegan and Aeolus loosed azure bolts at the monsters with everything they had. The battle was joined.

KHRISTOS WAS THE FIRST TO STEALTHILY BREAK THE SURface of the river. His timing was perfect and his resolve unshakable. Smiling as he looked across the water, he realized that Gracchus' plan was proceeding perfectly.

While thousands of his vipers waited unseen in the murky depths, Khristos surveyed the area. Just as Gracchus had told him, the palace lay near the river bend. Between the river and the palace lay a great field, its dewy expanse providing the huge area needed to contain the great Minion war camp. Untold lines of shadowy war tents seemed to stretch forever into the distance, their openings flapping gently in the nighttime breeze. Just as Khristos had hoped, it seemed that every available warrior save for a few sentries had been called out to quell the mayhem raging in the heart of the city. Quietly turning around in the water, he confirmed the orange-red glow in the sky.

Looking back, he saw the royal palace standing west of the campsite, its many lit torches shining down onto its barbicaned parapets. The moat surrounding the castle looked deep and tranquil, and the drawbridge had been raised and locked into place between its twin gate towers. To an untrained observer the magnificent structure would surely appear unassailable, but on this night that perception would be wrong. Even so, the largely unprotected palace and the many treasures it housed were not Khristos' first goals. Looking to the south, the Viper Lord smiled again as he spied the first of Gracchus' targets.

The two magnificent Black Ships that Tristan had left behind sparkled in the moonlight as they rested in their massive wooden cradles. Khristos' heart leapt as he realized that only a handful of Minion sentries guarded them. Without the great ships, the *Jin'Saiou*'s ability to hunt him down would be greatly curtailed, and she could no longer sail across the Sea of Whispers. These ships would therefore be Khristos' targets.

Following Gracchus' orders, he would set fire to one and steal the other, filling it with his vipers and then using it to his further purposes. Having fought and sailed alongside Failee during the Sorceresses' War, he could empower Black Ships as well as any mystic alive. But even he could fly only one ship at a time, so the other must be made useless to the *Jin'Saiou* here and now. These things must be done quickly, before Shailiha and her Vigors mystics realized that the battle in the square was a diversion and hurried back to the palace. The time was right, the setting was all Khristos could have hoped for, and Gracchus' plan was ready to be executed.

Submerging again, Khristos waved his thousands of vipers forward. They would quietly climb the riverbanks, then slither silently on their bellies through the tall grass to flank both sides of the Minion camp and rush in to dispatch the remaining sentries. Soon after, the warriors guarding the ships some distance away would follow their brothers into the Afterlife. If both attacks succeeded quickly and quietly, those in the castle would perceive no threat until one Black Ship was in the air and the other was in flames.

As the magenta moonlight gently licked the waves of the Sippora, Khristos and his vipers started to surface, their huge numbers slithering up the dark riverbank like a menacing tide.

SWINGING HER SWORD IN A PERFECT ARC, SHAILIHA SLICED its blade through the throat of another attacking viper. The thing stood frozen in time for a moment before falling to the cobblestones, dead where it lay.

Daring to lower her sword for a few precious moments, the princess found that her arms were leaden and that her lungs clawed to capture each new breath. Her mind wanted to keep fighting, but more and more her body refused to obey. She and her forces were exhausted, and to her dismay, seemingly endless hordes of vipers still poured around street corners and down dark alleyways to come and challenge them. The princess's face and body were peppered with blood and offal, and she knew that her muscles would soon give out. Even so, like her comrades, she had no choice but to fight on. Faegan and Aeolus were somewhere on the far side of the square, still loosing azure bolts, their fingertips long since blackened and singed. The acolyte and consular cadres who had followed in separate litters were doing the same all across the macabre urban battlefield.

Shailiha took a quick look around to see that the Minion corpses seemed at least equal in number to those of the vipers that had been blown apart by azure bolts or cut down by Minion swords or returning wheels. As more Minions landed in the streets, terrified citizens ran madly in every direction as they tried to escape the raging vipers.

Shailiha desperately hungered for a battle report, but Traax had not yet brought one to her, forcing her to wonder if her valiant commander was dead. She knew that to effectively lead this fight, she must understand what was going on around her. But in all this madness, finding Traax seemed impossible. Shailiha had lost track of Abbey long ago, and she had yet to see Khristos. Not finding the Viper Lord worried her, but aimlessly searching through the raging battle would surely get her killed. Knowing that she must learn how her troops were faring, she realized that there was only one way to do it. She would take to the air again and view the battle from above.

Just as she was about to summon some warriors to her side, Shailiha saw another viper coming. She instinctively backed up and lifted her sword high with both hands, readying herself for its attack. Then the deadly viper unexpectedly stopped short and glared directly into her eyes. With its talons outstretched and its strong tail coiled up beneath its humanlike upper body, the thing ominously levered high into the air, then looked down on her and let go a menacing hiss.

Standing her ground, Shailiha knew what the monster would likely do next, for she had seen it happen dozens of times this terrible night. Rearing back, the viper would suddenly launch at her, its talons and incisors flashing as it came. Holding her ground, the *Jin'Saiou* summoned her courage and defiantly glared back.

But rather than charging, the Blood Viper opened its mouth wider, hissing again and exposing its forked tongue. Only too late did Shailiha sense the danger and swivel to one side. As the viper spat its venom, the shock of seeing the acidic poison fly through the air was so great that the danger seemed to come at her in slow motion. Even so, she could not move fast enough.

The green substance flew through the air and hit the left side of her face. Smoke immediately rose from her burning skin, and the pain ripping through her eye was unimaginable. Screaming wildly, she covered her stricken face with one hand while trying to hold onto her precious sword with the other. But the pain was too much and she fell to the bloody square, her sword slipping from her grasp to rattle down onto the bloody cobblestones. Sensing his chance, the viper moved in for the kill.

Slithering forward, the thing reared up alongside Shailiha's prostrate body to hiss viciously and look down on its greatest victory. The liver of the *Jin'Saiou* would grant it inordinate power.

Bending closer, the thing curiously tilted its awful head back and forth as it luxuriated in the sight of its terrible handiwork. Despite the many dangers surrounding the viper, it knew that this woman of supremely endowed blood was the conquest of a lifetime, and he was determined to savor her. First he would kill her slowly by strangulation; only then would he rip her open and take her liver. Smiling, the thing spread wide its talons and reached down for Shailiha's exposed neck.

He never saw the silver blur that killed him. Coming directly from behind, the Minion's returning wheel sliced straight through the thing's neck, severing its head from its body without stopping. Soaring on nearly unfettered, the wheel careened through the air in a perfect circle back toward its master.

Reaching up, Traax expertly caught the bloody wheel in the leaded glove covering his left hand, then quickly returned it to its resting place at one hip. Running with all his might, he abandoned any thought of his own safety and tore across the chaotic square to kneel beside the stricken princess. When he turned her over and looked at her face, the air rushed from his lungs.

Shailiha was near death, the left side of her face ravaged by the viper's venom. Smoldering and hissing, the terrible venom was still doing its awful work and burning deep craters in her skin. Traax hurriedly removed a kerchief from beneath his armor, but when he tried to wipe away the venom, the cloth also started to hiss and steam, forcing him to stop.

Reaching down, he touched the side of her neck. He found a heartbeat, but its rhythm was weak and slow. Just then the *Jin'Saiou* started to regain consciousness, and her burned eyelids fluttered open. Screaming and writhing in exquisite pain, her one good eye beseechingly looked up at Traax. As she did, the Minion commander tried his best to hide his shock.

Shailiha's left eye had been nearly destroyed.

The eyeball was pitted and glassy, and vitreous fluid ran from it, crazily tracing down her severely pockmarked cheek. Traax could easily tell that the eye was blinded, and he sadly guessed that it would never again see the light of day. As her good eye moved frantically about, her damaged one did not copy its movements, telling Traax that the muscles of the affected eye had also been damaged by the viper's venom.

Screaming again, Shailiha madly reached out to grasp Traax's shoulders. There was only one thing to do, he realized. Quickly overpowering her with his strong arms, he wrestled her back down atop the bloody cobblestones.

"Forgive me . . ." he said quietly.

Reaching out, he used two fingers of one hand to find the carotid artery on the right side of her neck, and he pressed hard. Eight seconds later the princess was again unconscious. Picking her up in his arms, Traax unfolded his strong wings and took to the air.

"IS SHE DEAD?" AEOLUS ASKED.

Faegan did his best to wipe the tears from his face, but even more came to take their places. "Yes," he answered simply, his voice little more than a tremulous whisper. Taking his eyes from the shrouded body lying before him, he sadly looked around.

After much hard fighting, the battle had finally been won. The last of the Blood Vipers had been corralled, and incensed Minions were eagerly beheading them on Faegan's orders. Khristos had not been among the dead, nor had anyone reported seeing him. That realization continued to deeply worry Faegan despite his overwhelming grief.

He and Aeolus had loosed azure bolts at the enemy until they had nearly collapsed with exhaustion, killing hundreds of vipers in the process. The acolytes and consuls who had also rushed here from the Redoubt had killed many more. Four loyal acolytes and seven worthy consuls lay dead, not to mention the still uncounted Minions who had also perished. Each surviving mystic had suffered venom burns and talon wounds, some of them serious.

Much of the stricken neighborhood remained aflame, but the Minions were battling the fires. Faegan watched as throngs of citizens wandered aimlessly through the bloody streets in search of loved ones. The sounds of crying children, neighing horses, wildly barking dogs, and groaning citizens and Minions still filled the air. Duvessa and her warrior-healers were doing everything they could to stem the suffering, but they too were exhausted and could only do so much. The gutters ran red with blood, bodies and body parts littered the shiny cobblestones, and hungry flies were already gathering atop the corpses. As the news of the singularly important death spread, all the surviving mystics and hundreds of spent Minion warriors had congregated to mourn the shrouded corpse lying in the street.

Faegan wearily moved his chair closer. *Her courageous death will long be remembered,* he realized, and her life's story would resonate in everyone's consciousness for longer still. *How can we possibly tell Tristan and Wigg about our failure to protect her?* he wondered. *Will either of them ever trust us again?* Still unable to believe, with a trembling hand he reached down and pulled back the makeshift shroud.

Abbey had died quickly, they told him. She was last seen fighting three vipers at once, and she had succumbed to their attacks before Minion warriors could reach her. She bled out quickly from the viper talons that had slashed at her throat, then she had fallen to the ground, where her innards were ravaged by the terrible beasts. Finally some frantically struggling warriors reached her and ensured that the vipers responsible for her death had suffered horribly before being killed.

Faegan looked down at her face with bleary eyes. The herbmistress and partial adept had been instrumental in defeating Wulfgar and Serena, and in ensuring that the Vigors had not perished from the earth. Many of the people gathered here owed their lives to her several times over. She had been a handsome woman, with long dark hair lightly streaked with gray, a strong jaw, and a shapely figure. The only partial adept on the Conclave, her specialized use of the craft would be sorely missed. Faegan had enhanced her time enchantments so that her body would not immediately fall to dust, even though she had been more than three centuries old. Raising his head, Faegan looked out across the carnage-ridden neighborhood.

Wigg will be inconsolable, he thought. *Because I am his oldest friend, the grim burden of telling him should fall to me. But how does one do such a thing?*

Just then Faegan saw a Minion warrior approaching in the night sky. As the warrior neared, the wizard saw that he carried someone, the victim's arms and legs dangling lifelessly earthward. On finally recognizing the warrior and his charge, Faegan's blood ran cold.

Traax landed before the crowd and quickly handed the princess over to Aeolus.

"You must help her!" he shouted urgently.

As Aeolus and Faegan stared in horror at Shailiha, the blood drained from their faces. "What happened to her?" Faegan demanded.

"She was struck by viper venom!" Traax answered. "It continues to burn her even now! But I fear that her eye took the worst of it!"

"Hand her to me!" Faegan shouted.

As Aeolus quickly laid the princess in Faegan's lap, Faegan looked at the burns and pockmarks on her face. Calling the craft straightaway, he induced a spell over the venom to try to stop it from doing further damage. He also called another spell to help control her pain and to keep her unconscious. Then he carefully lifted the damaged lid of her left eye. He closed his own eyes and bowed his head in sorrow.

"How bad is it?" Aeolus demanded.

"Very bad, I fear," Faegan answered. "We might be able to help her, but to do so we must hurry back to the palace. There is no time to lose!"

Seeing Abbey's corpse for the first time, Traax took a sharp breath. "Is she—?"

"Yes," Faegan answered. "We can no longer help her. Shailiha is now our greatest worry. Summon a litter at once! Half of our forces will remain here and continue to quell the fires and help the wounded as best they can. The rest of our warriors will accompany us home. Duvessa and her group will remain here as well. Go and give the orders! We must leave now!"

As Traax hurried off, Faegan reached down and removed the gold medallion from Shailiha's person and placed it around his neck. After doing so, he sadly rocked the princess in his arms, just as he might cradle a child who had been taken mortally ill.

"Why did you take her medallion?" Aeolus asked quietly.

"I did it for both Tristan's and Shailiha's sakes," Faegan answered. "There is no telling when Tristan might again use his medallion to contact his sister. Do you want his next glimpse of her to be like this?"

"I understand," Aeolus answered. "But doesn't Shailiha need to be wearing the medallion for it to work?"

Faegan shook his head. "No," he answered. "The needed spell is contained in the two medallions, not in their wearers' blood. That is why the Ones cautioned Tristan so strongly about not letting the medallions fall into the wrong hands."

"And you know how to call the spell?" Aeolus asked.

Before answering, Faegan cradled the stricken princess closer. "Yes," he answered simply. "We can only hope that Tristan does not contact us before we have had some time to try and help her."

Just then a litter arrived, its six stout warriors landing it quickly before the hushed crowd. With Shailiha still lying in his lap, Faegan levitated his chair up and over the litter's sides. Aeolus joined him, and before they knew it they were soaring through the air toward the royal palace.

As the litter gained speed, Faegan looked down at the stricken princess's face, then back toward the fires that were finally starting to come under control. Keeping pace alongside, Traax and half the exhausted Minion survivors accompanied the two wizards and their fallen leader. As they hurried on, Faegan sadly closed his eyes.

You have won this day, Khristos, he thought. *We killed many of your vipers, but Abbey is dead and the* Jin'Saiou *will likely never be the same again. If it is the last thing I ever do, I will hunt you down and kill you, I swear it. But where were you this night, you bastard product of the Vagaries? If attacking Tammerland was so important, why weren't you there, leading your vipers?*

All at once the terrifying realization hit him, and Faegan took a sharp breath. Looking over at Traax, he barked out new orders as fast as he could.

THE MINION SENTRIES DIED QUIETLY. AFTER SLITHERING on their bellies up the banks of the Sippora, Khristos' vipers had quietly flanked the camp. They then closed the circle to surprise and kill the unsuspecting sentries by first blinding them with their venom and then slitting their throats. Some of the warriors had seen them coming and fought back, but the several hundred Minions were no match for the thousands of Blood Vipers that commanded the element of surprise. Confident that the palace had not been alerted, Khristos again motioned for his vipers to slither their way through the dewy grass toward his next targets.

Watching from the safety of the camp, the Viper Lord wished he was going with them. But he would hold back where he could not be seen from the palace's parapets. Nor could he use his silver staff to help his servants kill the Minions guarding the Black Ships, for that would certainly cause uproar among those warriors guarding the palace. While he stood alone among the Minion dead, his servants expertly went about his bidding.

Fifty warriors patrolled the area surrounding the two Black Ships, and they died as quickly and as quietly as had their more numerous brothers who had guarded the war camp. When one of his lead vipers slithered back to whisper news of their success, the Viper Lord rushed to where the others waited for him. As he looked up at the great ships, he knew that he must hurry in his mission, for once it started, those Minions left behind to guard the palace would surely see what was happening and attack him.

The *Cavalon* and the *Illendium* rested peacefully in their massive wooden cradles, their hulls and masts twinkling beautifully in the night. Deciding to steal the *Illendium*, Khristos ordered his vipers to stealthily board her in the darkness. Silently slithering their way up the cradle spars, the thousands of monsters took possession of the great ship.

Once they had all boarded, Khristos would remain on the ground as he empowered the ship into the air. Only after he had taken the *Illendium* a safe distance away from the palace grounds would he set fire to its mate, then fly through the air and land on the *Illendium*'s topside to spirit her away. Those vipers that had secretly left the battle in Tammerland to slink back into the Sippora had been ordered to travel submerged downriver. Only after they were well away from Tammerland would they again surface to meet and board the pirated *Illendium*. Satisfied that his vipers would soon be aboard his new flagship, Khristos turned his attention to the *Cavalon*.

She was equally beautiful, and in a strange way he almost regretted having to destroy her. Knowing that he must hurry, he looked back at the *Illendium* to see one of his lead vipers signal that all his servants had boarded, and he smiled when he saw their huge numbers crowding the gunwales and slithering quickly up the masts. With no time to lose, he raised his arms and called the craft.

At once the *Illendium*'s black and red dark sails tumbled free of their spars. Expertly manipulating the craft, Khristos then summoned the first of the powerful forces that would lift the great ship and send her skyward. Her hull groaning and her masts straining against the pull of the sails, she slowly left her cradle to rise into the night air. Moving his hands, he expertly guided her to a safe distance from the *Cavalon,* then set her hovering. With the *Illendium* airborne, he again gathered up his power to finish off the *Cavalon.*

Raising his silver staff, Khristos pointed it at the great ship. Because of the many enchantments used by her builders to protect her, setting her afire would not be a simple feat, but once she started burning, her ages-old timbers would become a raging inferno. Summoning all his remaining power while also causing the *Illendium* to hover, he loosed the first azure bolt from the tip of his staff.

AS FAEGAN AND AEOLUS NEARED THE PALACE AND SAW THE first of Khristos' bolts strike the *Cavalon,* their worst fears were confirmed. *How could we have been so blind?* Faegan asked himself. Cursing the heavens, he pounded his fists against the sides of the litter.

Worse, Shailiha still lay unconscious in his lap, her fragile soul barely clinging to her wounded body. If she didn't receive treatment soon, the venom coursing through her bloodstream would surely kill her. Even so, Faegan didn't dare hurry her into the Redoubt for fear that the palace had also been overrun.

Then they saw the *Illendium* hovering in the air, and even from this distance they could see that it was filled with Blood Vipers. With one Black Ship taken and the other destroyed, the Conclave's ability to defeat Khristos would be drastically weakened—perhaps to the point that the Viper Lord could savage all of Eutracia at will. The death and destruction that he could cause with even one Black Ship at his command, while the Conclave had none with which to counter him, would be unstoppable.

As Khristos' next bolt struck the hull of the *Cavalon,* Faegan started to doubt his assumptions about what the Viper Lord was trying to accomplish. Trying to destroy a Black Ship with azure bolts could be done, but it would take a long time—more time than Khristos had available. And then Faegan understood fully. Khristos was trying to set the *Cav-*

alon ablaze. Shouting out to the Minions, he beseeched them to fly faster and take him within range of the Viper Lord.

Seeing the Minion forces cross before the three magenta moons, Khristos cursed, then loosed another bolt against the mighty ship. The first two had been largely ineffective, but the third highly concentrated beam sent against the same spot finally sent wood shards flying from the *Cavalon*'s starboard side, and smoke started drifting into the air from the jagged wound that had formed. Khristos had little time before the enemy would be on him, and he knew that he must work fast if he and his vipers were to escape in the *Illendium.* He quickly backed away from the ship to gain a different perspective.

Khristos pointed his staff directly at the *Cavalon*'s mainmast. At once her furled sails were set free and went tumbling down. Knowing that the sails were far more vulnerable to fire than were the ship's timbers, he loosed a narrow bolt from his staff to thunder straight toward the exposed mainsail. At once it burst into flames, then started setting fire to the others around it.

Laughing into the night, Khristos caused all the other sails to come rolling down and quickly set fire to them as well. Returning his attention to the smoldering hole in the *Cavalon*'s starboard hull, he quickly loosed bolt after bolt against it, finally setting it ablaze. But just as he was about to join the *Illendium* and fly her away, the litter bearing Faegan and Aeolus appeared in the night sky. Soaring toward the *Illendium,* the Conclave wizards seemed determined to stop her from escaping before attacking Khristos or trying to save the burning *Cavalon.*

Knowing that he could not defeat both wizards at once, Khristos cursed aloud. He realized that if he was to escape with the *Illendium,* his best course would be to board her quickly and spirit her away. While the *Cavalon* burned, Khristos quickly made for the riverbank.

As they neared the *Illendium,* Faegan and Aeolus understood the unfolding disaster all too well. The *Cavalon* was burning, and their badly outnumbered and exhausted Minions couldn't retake the *Illendium* without suffering unacceptable losses. Cursing his decision to leave half the warriors behind in the center of Tammerland, Faegan looked at Aeolus

"If we deal with the *Illendium* first, do you believe that we can then save the *Cavalon* from destruction?" he shouted.

As the fires raged aboard the *Cavalon,* Aeolus anxiously tried to decide. He desperately wanted to save the burning ship, but the threat from the viper-laden *Illendium* was great. If the *Illendium* turned to attack the palace, the vipers aboard might well take it. Of equal worry, the ghostlike Viper Lord might escape them yet again. While Traax and the throngs of exhausted warriors hovered alongside the wizards' litter, they desperately hoped for an order that would send them to attack the vile creatures that had commandeered the *Illendium*.

"Perhaps!" he shouted back at Faegan. "With Shailiha incapacitated, you are in command! What are your orders?"

Faegan decided that there was but one course of action. It was drastic, and once he set the needed spell into motion there could be no going back. Clearly the vipers must be dealt with first, and in a way that would cost the fewest Minion lives. The Conclave could continue battling Khristos without the Black Ships, but not without enough warriors. His mind made up, he looked at Aeolus.

"I'm going to call the spell!" he shouted. "There seems no other choice!"

Aeolus gave Faegan a grim look, then nodded. Harsh as the crippled wizard's decision was, Aeolus could also see no other way.

"Very well!" he shouted back. "But you must allow me and the warriors to start trying to save the *Cavalon*! If the fires advance farther we will surely lose her!"

"I understand!" Faegan shouted back.

Looking over at Traax, Faegan barked out a series of sharp orders. Unable to believe what he just heard, Traax gave Faegan a searching look.

"You want us to *retreat?*" he demanded. "But the enemy hovers directly before us. They're *taunting* us to attack! I beg you to let us finish this here and now!"

"No—you will follow my orders!" Faegan angrily shouted back. "There are not enough of you to win, and Khristos knows it! Take Aeolus into your arms and then order all your forces to obey him! You must do your best to save the *Cavalon*! Leave only my litter bearers behind! You are to also order a patrol into the palace to see if it is safe! If so, the princess must be immediately taken to the Redoubt!"

Although he could not fathom Faegan's logic, Traax had no option but to obey. "I live to serve!" he shouted. Scooping Aeolus up in his arms, the Minion commander shouted a series of orders to his troops, and they all flew toward the stricken *Cavalon* as fast as their wings could take them.

Left hovering in the night air with only Shailiha and his litter bearers, Faegan looked across the night sky toward the *Illendium.* Soon after the discovery of the subtle matter and the decision that two of the Black Ships would try to sail across the Azure Sea and find Shashida, Tristan had insisted that his Conclave mystics combine their knowledge to devise a unique spell—one he hoped he would never be forced to use. Even so, he ordered that it be infused into every Black Ship and readied for immediate use should their path lead them to Rustannica and the *Pon Q'tar* rather than to Shashida and the Ones. It was that same spell that Faegan would now be forced to call forth. It remained untested, for summoning it successfully would have produced the direst of consequences. As he hardened his heart, Faegan raised his arms.

Summoning all his power, he recalled the elegant series of calculations. Straining and shaking, he finally loosed the spell that had been laid deep into the age-old timbers of the *Illendium.*

The resulting explosion seemed to tear apart the heavens. Bursting from the inside out, every rib, beam, mast, spar, and other bit of wood that was the *Illendium* ruptured mightily in a massive azure detonation of the craft. As the shock wave and debris reached Faegan's litter, for several awful moments the wizard was sure that the warriors bearing it would lose their grip. Yet despite the awful concussion, the warriors held fast.

When the great ship exploded, so too did every Blood Viper aboard her. Soon blood and bits of flesh rained down, and Faegan, Shailiha, their litter, and the warriors bearing it were covered with the awful stuff. Leaving behind no surviving part of the *Illendium* larger than a matchstick, the cacophony finally subsided as tons of debris fell to the ground. As the smoke cleared and the Minion bearers regained control of the litter, only the nighttime sky remained where the mighty *Illendium* had hovered moments before.

Lowering his hands, Faegan sadly looked around. The enchantment for the *Illendium*'s self-destruction had worked well. Although he had killed every Blood Viper aboard her, he felt little sense of accomplishment. Shouting out a new set of orders, he told his bearers to take him and Shailiha to the palace as quickly as he could.

From his place by the river's edge, Khristos watched the unexpected explosion with mixed emotions. He had lost many vipers this night, and he had failed to take the *Illendium* for his own. But the Conclave he so hated had lost much more. Many of their warriors had been slaughtered; one Black Ship was destroyed, and fires still raged aboard the other. Had he also known that the wounded *Jin'Saiou* lay near death, he would have judged the night a near total success. Smiling, he walked down the riverbank and entered the Sippora to join the rest of his forces waiting downstream.

Moments later he was gone.

Chapter XXXVI

As Tristan followed the four women down the elaborate hallway, his mind reeled with unanswered questions and tempting possibilities. Having lived his entire life in the royal palace, he was well acquainted with opulence. But that had been in Eutracia, and this was a different world. The farther he walked, the more he realized that nothing in his experience could have prepared him for Shashida.

The room in which he awakened was amazingly luxurious, and he guessed that it was only a brief taste of the splendor he would find elsewhere. The floor was made of solid onyx and the walls were built from an unfamiliar blue stone that sparkled with a life of its own. The bed had been fitted with sumptuous silk sheets, and a diaphanous canopy was stretched from its four marble posts. Fluted pilasters adorned the walls and an elaborate fountain graced the center of the room, its tumbling water creating a wonderfully soothing sound. Dappled sunshine streamed in through skylights in the gilded ceiling overhead.

After Tristan rose from the bed, the four women graciously asked that he follow them. On leaving the room, they began walking down a long hallway. The women had not told him what purpose this wondrous building served or where they were headed, only that he was being taken to their masters. As he walked, he was glad to realize that the dizzying effects of the vortex were gone and his eyesight had returned to normal. Eager to finally come face to face with the supreme masters of the Vigors, he dutifully followed the mysterious women onward.

Each of the women sent to fetch him was young and beautiful, with long black hair that hung down to her shoulders like strands of pure silk. Colorful long-sleeved embroidered robes wrapped their bodies and reached all the way to their ankles. Open-toed wooden thong sandals graced their feet, and their faces had been lightly brushed with a pale powder. Tristan found their appearance immensely attractive, and he admired their polite but commanding behavior.

The hallway down which they trod was opulent. The walls were white and the elaborately patterned carpet dark red, its luxurious fibers so thick that it seemed he was walking on soft grass. Golden candelabra graced the walls every few meters, and an enticing aroma of fresh-cut mint hung in the air. Tristan hoped to see more Shashidans along the way, but aside from himself and the four women, the hallway was deserted.

After a long walk they reached an intersection where eight hallways joined. On one side stood a pair of tall black lacquered doors, their intricately carved panels adorned with representations in gold of exotic birds and animals the likes of which Tristan had never seen. On reaching the doors, the four women turned and bowed.

The one who had addressed Tristan earlier stepped forward to look at him. Her large, dark brown eyes seemed full of mystery.

"They await you," she said simply. "On behalf of all Shashidans, we welcome the *Jin'Sai* into our midst. We have anticipated your coming for aeons."

With a wave of one hand she called the craft, and the lacquered doors swung open. As they did, she stepped back among the other women, and they again bowed.

Still unsure of how to behave in the women's presence, the *Jin'Sai* bowed in return. "Thank you," he said quietly.

Eager to learn what lay beyond, he walked into the room, and the doors closed behind him. The moment he stepped into the magnificent chamber he knew that he was about to learn the answers to his many questions.

The room was large, about twenty meters square. In its center stood a magnificent round table fashioned from exotic wormwood. Twelve men and women sat there. Several more chairs stood empty.

Like the room where Tristan had awakened, this room had a high gilded ceiling pierced with skylights through which dappled sunshine streamed. The walls were of flecked alabaster, and the floor was made of highly polished interlocking hardwood strips. The entire far side of the room was an open colonnade, revealing a courtyard that held winding garden paths, exotic plants, meandering streams, and burbling fountains. Exotic paintings hung on the walls, along with ornate tapestries. Gold vases and other priceless decorative items also adorned the room, and crystalline wind chimes hanging in the garden trees sent a soothing melody into the chamber. It seemed apparent that this room served as a meeting place.

As if they were of one mind, the twelve strangers stood and bowed deeply to him. Tristan counted six men and six women. Each was dressed in an elaborate robe much like his own, with two exotic-looking swords held against their waists by silk sashes. The swords were unlike those he had seen on the wrecked ship, reaffirming that the armor and weapons he saw there had been Rustannican. Most of the people looked very old, with gray hair and deeply lined faces, but two of them looked his age.

Still unsure of the proper etiquette, Tristan bowed in return. As eleven of the people sat down, one of the older men remained standing. Their leader, Tristan guessed.

The man's hair was stark white and pulled back from his forehead to form a short queue secured with a gold ornament. A large white mustache graced his upper lip, its ends drooping downward past his chin. The deep lines carved in his weathered face spoke of a fully experienced life. His body appeared muscular and lean, and his blue eyes gleamed with wisdom.

He was dressed differently from the others, his more elaborate clothing further suggesting his status as their leader. His magnificent silk robe was deep red with bright yellow cranes embroidered into its fabric. Over the robe he wore a sleeveless long black silk tunic, its wide, pointed shoulders extending past his body on either side. Like Tristan he wore dark socks with open-toed wooden thong sandals.

The two swords secured at his left hip were beautiful creations. The upper sword was short, and the lower one longer than its brother by about one-half its length. Each gently curved wooden scabbard was lacquered in black and adorned with intricately painted red butterflies resting on delicate tree branches. The swords' oblong hilts were made of onyx, and their ivory handles were slim and intricately wound with black cord. In the spaces among the crisscrossed cords lay small, finely crafted gold ornaments that Tristan guessed would allow for a better grip and tell the sword's owner when his hands were properly situated for fighting. As the man looked at Tristan, he smiled warmly.

"Welcome, *Jin'Sai*," he said reverently, his voice strong and firm as an old oak tree. "My name is Mashiro of the House of the Yellow Cranes. So that you can understand us, while in your presence we will speak only your native Eutracian dialect. Like your fellow countrymen we have chosen to recognize ourselves by mentioning our family house, even though those living in Rustannica have long since abandoned that custom. In the name of our people, we twelve humble Vigors mystics welcome you to Shashida. Collectively, you know us as the Ones Who Came Before. You have endured much to reach us, and you and your two friends are the first from your side of the world to do so. We are immensely grateful for the suffering that you have endured to help ensure the survival of the Vigors."

Tristan was about to reply when the doors behind him swung open. Turning to look, he saw Wigg and Tyranny enter the room. Each of them was dressed as he was. When they stepped into the room, their faces quickly mirrored the same awe and wonder that Tristan's had shown when he first entered.

Relieved, he hurried toward them. "Are you all right?" he asked urgently.

The First Wizard and Tyranny nodded. "Yes," Wigg answered for both of them, "but it took time to overcome the effects of the portal. I have never experienced such an overpowering use of the craft. When we awoke we were dressed in these clothes. Then some women escorted us here. It also seems that my pain is gone and my burns are fully healed."

After looking around the room, Wigg's eyes settled on the twelve people at the great table. "Are we in Shashida?" he asked reverently. "Are you the Ones Who Came Before?"

Mashiro bowed. "You may call us that," he answered, "although we prefer another name for our humble group. You have our apologies, my friends. We understand that you are unaccustomed to our higher uses of the craft, but once you reached the channel's dead end, our portal was the only safe way to help you complete your journey. It is much like the portal your wizard called Faegan uses, but ours is infinitely more powerful. We also took the liberty of treating the First Wizard's injuries."

"You know who we are?" Wigg breathed. "How can that be?"

Mashiro smiled again. "In truth, we know all about you," he answered, "and we are intimately familiar with the many trials you have suffered. There is much to discuss, and at long last your questions will be answered. Please come and sit at our modest table."

The three visitors did as they were asked, with Tyranny sitting on one side of Tristan and Wigg on the other. Tristan looked over at Tyranny to see that for the first time since he had known her, she seemed truly dumbstruck.

As Mashiro took his seat, Tristan wanted to pose question after question, but he realized there was no hurry. He had finally reached Shashida, and his heart told him that everything he so hungered to know would come to light soon enough. Forcing back his need to speak, he looked around the table.

Regardless of age or gender, the twelve ultimate masters and mistresses of the Vigors were immensely imposing. Mystics like Wigg, Faegan, Aeolus, and Jessamay all projected a sense of calm power. The Ones were also august, Tristan realized, but far more so. Ten of them looked immensely old, like Mashiro, but one woman and one man looked more like Tristan's age. As Tristan focused his attention on the younger-looking woman sitting across from him, he took a sharp breath.

She was a truly arresting creature. Parted on one side, her hair was long, straight, and black, lying atop her shoulders in undulating waves. Her face was sensual, with even features and a strong jawline. Sleek eyebrows rested above dark brown irises that lay partly hidden beneath their upper lids, and her lips were full and finely drawn. Rather than cheapening her natural beauty, her faint blue eyeshadow and deep red lipstick accentuated her loveliness. The light blue robe that crisscrossed the swell of her breasts was embroidered with graceful images of multi-colored flower blossoms.

"Forgive me, *Jin'Sai*," Mashiro offered. "I must introduce you and your friends to the other members of the *Chikara Inkai*. Because we usually speak an advanced dialect of Old Eutracian, our names will no doubt sound odd to you."

"This group is called the *Chikara . . . Inkai?*" Tristan asked.

Mashiro nodded. "In your dialect it means Vigors Council. Just as you have your Conclave and the Rustannican Empire has its *Pon Q'tar*, we have our *Chikara Inkai*, or simply the *Inkai*. One or more members of the council can also be referred to as *Inkai*. The people you see here are the world's greatest Vigors mystics, duly elected by the Shashidan populace to oversee the nation and to conduct the War of Attrition. Shashida is divided into ten provinces that we govern. Each of the people here represents one such area, and the designs you see on their robes portray something for which their prefectures are particularly well known."

As Mashiro introduced each *Inkai* member, the names did seem strange to the three visitors. When the time came to name the beautiful woman sitting directly across from Tristan, Mashiro called her Hoshi of the House of Lotus Blossoms, and he said that she was the supreme commander of the Shashidan armies. The young man seated beside her was introduced as the first admiral of the Shashidan armada.

At first Tristan was surprised that younger people held such important posts. Then he reminded himself that in the maze that was the craft, one's perceived age was meaningless. When Hoshi was introduced to the *Jin'Sai,* she bowed slightly, but she did not speak.

As if suddenly embarrassed, Mashiro's expression darkened. "Forgive me, *Jin'Sai,*" he said. "You and your fellow Conclave members must be hungry and thirsty. Would you like to dine as we talk?"

Not wanting to delay the conversation, Tristan shook his head. "We can eat later," he answered. "But we could do with some wine, if it please you."

Smiling, Mashiro nodded. "We have something better," he said.

Mashiro clapped his hands and three servants appeared through a side door. Two men and one woman entered, each dressed in a silk robe and bearing a silver tray laden with silver pitchers and handleless cups. As they served everyone, Tristan noticed that the liquid they poured was steaming. Tristan picked up his cup and smelled its contents to find its aroma deeply pungent and unlike anything that he had smelled before. After everyone was served, the servants left the room as swiftly and quietly as they had come.

Tristan looked over at Mashiro. "Might I ask what this is?" he inquired.

Mashiro smiled. "It is called *umake,*" he said. "It is a distilled spirit that is laced with seasonings and best served hot. One must be careful of its potency, especially at first. Our blood is accustomed to umake, but yours is not."

Tristan, Wigg, and Tyranny each gingerly took a sip of the heady liquid. Closing his eyes, Wigg swallowed hard. Despite her love of spirits, Tyranny coughed outright, producing smiles from some of the *Inkai.*

But Tristan, accustomed as he was to drinking harsh Minion akulee, found the brew to his liking.

Putting down his cup, Mashiro looked at the three visitors. To Tristan's surprise, the *Inkai* leader's expression had grown serious.

"Before we tell you of our world, we must inform you of recent developments in Eutracia," he said. "What you are about to hear will disturb you, but that cannot be helped."

Immediately concerned for those he left behind, Tristan stiffened. "How can you know what happens on our side of the world?" he asked. "Are you in communion with one of my mystics?"

Mashiro sadly shook his head. "No, *Jin'Sai*," he answered. "At this moment none of your mystics possesses the needed forestallment. Like the *Pon Q'tar*, we have an Oracle in our service. What the Orb of the Vigors sees, she also sees. It has been this way since the earliest days of the War of Attrition."

Intensely interested, Wigg leaned forward. "What is an Oracle?" he asked.

Mashiro smiled. "I appreciate your curiosity, but there will be ample time to discuss matters of the craft," he said. "First you need to hear us out. I am sorry to tell you that one of your Conclave members has been wounded and another has been killed. You have our deepest condolences."

Tristan felt his stomach lurch. *Shailiha,* he feared. After quickly turning to look at Wigg and Tyranny, he cast a worried gaze back toward Mashiro.

"Who are they?" he breathed.

"The *Jin'Saiou* has been gravely injured, but she lives," Mashiro answered. "The Viper Lord attacked your capital city of Tammerland. She was struck in the face by viper venom and blinded in one eye. Of greater worry is that the venom still runs through her bloodstream. Your wizards Faegan and Aeolus are tending to her as we speak, but her fate remains uncertain."

Heartbroken, Tristan buried his face in his hands and fought back his tears. After several quiet moments passed he took another much-needed swallow of umake, then looked back at Mashiro.

"Who was killed?" he asked, his voice little more than a raspy whisper.

Mashiro sadly turned his gaze toward Wigg. "Abbey of the House of Lindstrom died while fighting off the Blood Vipers," he said quietly. "We are deeply sorry, First Wizard. Each *Inkai* member knows how much you loved her."

For several moments Wigg's eyes widened and his jaw worked up and down, but no words came. As his eyes welled with tears, he suddenly cried out and reached for Tristan, burying his face in the *Jin'Sai's* shoulder. Tristan held the ancient wizard as Wigg's tears came freely and his body shuddered with the terrible news. Stunned by what he had just heard, Tristan turned to look at Mashiro.

"What of my sister?" he asked. "Will she live?"

"That is unknown," a female voice said from across the table. "It is only because of her extraordinary blood quality that she still clings to life. But hope remains, however dim."

Tristan looked across the table at the woman who had just spoken. He remembered Mashiro introducing her as Midori of the House of Snowy Mountains. Her white hair was long and her green eyes kind, and her dark brown robe was embroidered with snowy mountain peaks resembling the Tolenkas. Like Mashiro, expressive lines creased her ancient-looking face.

Trying to collect himself, Wigg looked blankly around with tear-filled eyes. He still trembled, but now the cause was pure rage.

"Did Abbey suffer?" he asked.

"I will not lie to you, First Wizard, because that is not our way," Midori answered sadly. "Yes, she suffered before dying. Even so, you can be assured that the vipers that killed her suffered far more before your Minion warriors ended their lives. But I regret that there is more to tell you. We possess these facts because I am the Oracle to whom Mashiro referred earlier."

"What is an Oracle?" Tristan asked again.

"Aeons ago and long before the War of Attrition started, twin baby girls of right-leaning blood were born here in Shashida," Mashiro answered. "Like your wizard Faegan, they were born already possessing a very rare gift of the craft. In Faegan's case, it is his gift of Consummate Recollection. Here on this side of the world, the twin girls were born as seers, or Oracles. What the Orb of the Vigors overlooks, the Oracles also see. But their visions do not occur constantly. They happen only when an important use of it is made, for it seems that the orbs are drawn to such occurrences."

"Fascinating," Wigg said. "Where is Midori's sister?"

"Her name is Matsuko," Midori answered sadly. "During the civil war engineered by the *Pon Q'tar*, Gracchus spirited her away. She has been his prisoner ever since. We have no doubt that he forces her to use her gift in the name of the Vagaries, just as I use mine in the name of the Vigors. It is my deepest wish to someday see her freed."

"So this is how you know so much about our side of the world," Wigg mused. "For many centuries, Midori has informed you." Thinking, Wigg sat back in his chair.

"This explains much," he added quietly.

"Yes, but as I said, there is more to tell you," Midori replied.

"What is it?" Tyranny asked.

"Not only were many of your minions killed, but the *Illendium* has been destroyed and the *Cavalon* burns," another *Inkai* member answered.

This time the voice was male. Tristan, Wigg, and Tyranny looked over to see the man who had been introduced as the head of the Shashidan armada. His name was Renjiro of the House of Daggers.

Renjiro was a handsome man of about Tristan's age. As was seemingly the custom among Shashidan men, his dark hair was pulled back from his forehead to form a short queue held in place with a gold ornament. But unlike the other men at the table, Renjiro had shaved the top of his head, leaving hair only on the sides. The effect was chilling and rather fearsome.

His robe was made of black silk embroidered with beautiful silver daggers. Renjiro radiated a particularly powerful sense of self-discipline, and as he again sipped his umake, his movements were smooth and economical, leading the *Jin'Sai* to wonder whether Renjiro possessed the gift of *K'Shari*. But whether Renjiro commanded *K'Shari* or not, Tristan recognized an accomplished warrior when he saw one, and he had no doubts about Renjiro's abilities. Aghast at the loss of two of his Black Ships, Tristan turned to look at Mashiro with unbelieving eyes.

"What happened?" he demanded.

"The Viper Lord's attack on Tammerland was a diversion," Mashiro answered. "Sadly, your Conclave members were taken in by it. Tammerland was never Khristos' real objective—the ships were. He tried to steal the *Illendium* and then set fire to the *Cavalon*. Rather than see it fall into Khristos' hands, Faegan destroyed the *Illendium* with the subtle matter that your mystics imbedded into its timbers. He also sent many

Blood Vipers to their deaths in the process, but Khristos escaped. Even now your forces try to quell the fires ravaging the *Cavalon.*"

"Where were Shailiha wounded and Abbey killed?" Wigg asked, his overpowering rage barely allowing him to speak.

"In the Tammerland battle," Mashiro answered. "They acquitted themselves well, of that you can be sure."

Tristan suddenly remembered the gold medallion hanging around his neck. Desperately wanting to see his sister, he grasped it and turned it over. But before he could call the needed spell, Mashiro raised a hand.

"It is best that you hear us out before you see the *Jin'Saiou,*" he said. "In any event, Faegan now wears the medallion, and you would see only what he wishes."

Although he was disappointed, Tristan followed Mashiro's advice and let the medallion fall back to his chest. "Why has Faegan taken Shailiha's medallion?" he asked.

"He wishes to spare you needless heartache, *Jin'Sai,*" another *Inkai* member answered. "He also wants to help Shailiha recover before you see her. Her feelings must also be considered."

Tristan looked across the table at the man who just answered him. He had been introduced as Kaemon of the House of the Rising Moons. He was ancient and bald, his hairless cranium shining in the sunlight streaming down through the skylights. Three crescent-shaped magenta moons adorned the left shoulder of his gray robe.

Tristan shuddered as he thought about his once beautiful sister and what she might look like now. "Is it that bad?" he asked quietly.

"Yes," Kaemon answered, "I regret to say that it is."

"I know that the distance between Shashida and Eutracia is vast, but can you help her?" Tristan asked Mashiro.

Reaching out, the ancient mystic patted Tristan on one hand. "You're right," he answered, "the distance is indeed vast. Despite that, we have already taken action to help your sister."

"How . . . ?" Wigg breathed in wonderment.

"While the *Jin'Sai* was unconscious we used Tristan's medallion to contact Faegan," Mashiro answered. Despite the serious subject matter, the *Inkai* leader let go a quick smile.

"As you might imagine, the wizard was amazed to see us," he added. "We showed him some enchantment formulas that should help Shailiha's system fend off the viper venom. He and the one called Aeolus are no doubt employing them at this moment. We can only hope that they are not too far beyond your wizard's abilities. They will find them puzzling at the least, but we daren't risk simplifying the enchantments too much, lest they become baffling and of no use at all. Because we were not privy to the workings of Failee's original spell that created the Blood Vipers, we cannot ensure that our formulas will succeed. We also informed your Conclave that you reached us safely."

"And what of our two Black Ships and everyone still aboard them?" Tyranny asked. "Are they safe?"

"Yes," Hoshi answered, speaking in Tristan's presence for the first time. Her voice had an alluring, smoky quality that he found attractive.

"The ships and your people need to finish the journey here," she added. "Because your forces would probably not obey us, one or more of you will have to return to the waiting ships to inform your crews. From there all your forces and your two ships can be brought here the same way that you were."

For the first time, Hoshi gave Tristan a smile. "My *katsugai mosota* are eager to learn whether your Minions of Day and Night are everything that our Oracle says they are," she added.

"Katsugai . . . mosota?" Tristan asked.

"You have forgotten yourself, Hoshi," Mashiro gently admonished. "We must remember to speak only the eastern dialect while among our guests."

Hoshi bowed. "My apologies, *Jin'Sai,*'" she said. "*Katsugai mosota* is the Shashidan phrase for 'loyal warriors.' They would rather commit suicide than face the shame of defeat or dishonor."

"I understand," Tristan answered. "My Minions have sworn an oath that is much the same." Interested in learning more, he decided to press a bit.

"I have not seen your fighters in action," he said, "but I'm sure that they are excellent. Even so, I find it hard to believe that they could easily overcome the Minions' great tactical advantage."

Hoshi gave him a wry smile, showing that she appreciated his little boast. Undaunted, she leaned across the table.

"You refer to the Minions' powers of flight," she answered.

"I do," Tristan answered.

"A great advantage, to be sure," she replied. "But can your warriors shoot a winging sparrow from the sky with a bow and arrow at two hundred meters and never miss? Can they perform the same feat with a thrown dagger, or accomplish both while riding a galloping horse? Are their hand-to-hand combat skills so good that they can easily kill an enemy with one blow while blindfolded?"

For several moments Tristan was awestruck by Hoshi's boasts, but then he understood. Nodding, he politely acknowledged what might be the Shashidan armies' superior tactical advantage.

"Do all your katsugai command the gift of *K'Shari*?" he asked.

Realizing how quickly the *Jin'Sai* had uncovered the answer, Hoshi smiled again. "Only those with endowed blood," she answered. "They are our army's most elite warriors."

Leaning forward, Wigg laced his long fingers together. He was desolate over the loss of Abbey, but he also meant to master his emotions in this august company. His mind awash with questions, he looked at Mashiro.

"Tell me," he asked, his voice still brittle. "Do the Rustannicans also speak the Shashidan dialect?"

"By and large, no," Mashiro answered. "Our dialect has evolved far more than theirs during the aeons since Rustannica split away and became a rogue nation. And because so much time has passed, our cultures have evolved in strikingly different ways. However, most Rustannicans who hold positions of power are fluent in the Shashidan dialect."

"I suspected as much," Wigg replied. "The wrecked ship we found held Rustannican skeletons and weapons. I was able to partly decipher some writing on one of the swords. It seems that they once used Blood Stalkers in their campaigns. Do they use them to this day?"

"Yes," Renjiro answered, "and with greater effectiveness than did the Coven of Sorceresses."

Tristan was immensely eager to learn all he could about Shashida and Rustannica, but he knew that the shocking news from home must take precedent. Looking around the table, he fixed his gaze on Mashiro.

"We know who Khristos is," he said. "But what we cannot understand is why he finally surfaced again after all this time. What does he hope to gain?"

"At first his mission was solely to fulfill Failee's mad need for revenge," Renjiro answered. "She condemned him and her embryonic vipers to a river in Hartwick Wood to wait in silence until she called them forth. One droplet of left-leaning endowed blood entering the river was all that her spell needed to release her former lover and his fully evolved servants. Like Failee's vicious Parthalonian Swamp Shrews, her vipers were to be a means of retribution against the Vigors wizards should she lose the war. But because the First Mistress is dead and Khristos now serves the *Pon Q'tar,* he hopes not only to destroy your Conclave and Minions, but to one day rule your side of the world. Unless he is stopped soon, that might well happen."

"What do you mean when you say that Failee condemned Khristos and the viper embryos to a river?" Tyranny asked. "Surely some body of water cannot be where they waited for three centuries, only to emerge now and wreak their havoc."

"Ah, but it was," Kaemon answered. "With the permission of my fellow *Inkai,* allow me to tell you the tale. You will find it a fascinating one. Failee was nothing if not brilliant."

For the next hour Kaemon explained Failee's search for vengeance and conquest, including the recent battle in Tammerland and Khristos' attempt to steal one Black Ship and to destroy the other. When Kaemon finished, it was plain to see that Wigg, Tristan, and Tyranny were deeply troubled by the story. But it also explained many of the mysteries surrounding Khristos—not the least of which was his ability to hide from the Night Witches, only to suddenly emerge elsewhere to cause further mayhem.

Determined to stop Khristos at any price, Tristan leaned over the table and looked at Mashiro. "Can the *Inkai* help my mystics in Eutracia defeat the Viper Lord?" he asked. "With so many Minions dead, Shailiha injured, and the Black Ships useless, their ability to stop him has been drastically curtailed. And although Faegan is an accomplished herbmaster, Abbey's unique craft abilities will be sorely missed. If there is a way to help, we must do so."

"Although victory over Khristos cannot be certain, yes, we can help," Hoshi said.

"How did Khristos know that we were going to cross the Azure Sea?" asked Wigg. "He and his forces ambushed us there and we barely escaped with our lives."

"We can only surmise that the *Pon Q'tar* ordered him to attack you in that place," Mashiro answered. "Most likely it was Gracchus who gave the order."

"Gracchus?" Tristan asked.

Mashiro nodded. "As the lead *Pon Q'tar* cleric, he is my Vagaries counterpart in Rustannica."

"What about the Azure Sea itself?" Tristan asked. "Wigg and I were told by the half–Blood Stalker Ragnar that the sea was unexpectedly re-

leased when my son Nicholas further excavated the Caves. He was trying to capture the energy from the Paragon as part of his plan to raise
the Gates of Dawn, and he nearly succeeded. Was Ragnar telling the
truth?"

"No," another *Inkai* answered.

Tristan looked to the right to recognize the woman who had been introduced as Tamika of the House of Green Forests. A row of green pine
trees was embroidered on her white silk robe. Her long white hair had
been wound atop her head with care, and black lacquered wooden sticks
held it in place.

"So Ragnar lied after all," Tristan mused. "If that's the case, was the
Azure Sea always there?"

"No," Mashiro answered. "Just as the Rustannicans have their Borderlands, we have our Azure Sea."

"I don't understand," Tyranny said. "Do you mean to say that you *created* it?"

"Yes," the *Inkai* leader said. "The explanation is a long one, and it is
probably best told later. For now, suffice it to say that when we inhabited
all the lands that are now known as Eutracia, Parthalon, Rustannica,
and Shashida, just after the sudden rising of what you call the Tolenka
Mountains, we became landlocked here in the west. Then Rustannica
split away to become a martial rogue nation. The *Pon Q'tar* conjured
the Borderlands as a defense between our two warring states. Once the
mountains rose, the Caves became the only way for someone east of the
mountains to reach Shashida. And just as the *Pon Q'tar* felt the need to
isolate Rustannica from Shashidan incursion, we needed a way to prevent those of left-leaning blood from using the Caves to invade Shashida
from the east. You saw the rock walls rise from the Azure Sea because
the water detected the sudden presence of so much high-quality right-
leaning endowed blood. Part of the spell that we devised to conjure the
sea also included the channel. If the azure water detects sufficient power
of right-leaning blood, the walls rise and guide its owners to the rocky
dead end where our portal can sense their presence and come to their
aid. If the water detects left-leaning blood, rather than forming a channel to the dead end the walls also rise, but in that case they form a long,
winding maze from which there is no escape. As the enemy is forced to
endlessly sail the maze they eventually die from dehydration and starvation. Although the concept seems simple, its application was not, I as-

sure you. The water did not detect Khristos' left-leaning blood because unlike your group, he alone possessed it."

"Amazing," Wigg breathed. "But tell me—did Nicholas ever try to cross the Azure Sea?"

"We do not know," Midori answered, "but it is unlikely. The quality of his blood would probably have called forth the maze, and even he would have died while trying to navigate it. He likely knew better than to try because he was in communication with the Rustannicans. In truth, Nicholas knew much that he never told you."

"But his hatchlings carried Wigg and me across the Azure Sea and delivered us to another area in the Caves," Tristan protested. "That is where Ragnar blinded Wigg and poisoned my blood. Why didn't the rocky walls rise while we were waiting by the shore? And how did Nicholas get across the sea without the maze being summoned?"

"We might never know, but the walls probably did not rise because they did not detect sufficient quantities of endowed blood," Mashiro answered. "Much of yours and Wigg's blood had been drained to weaken you and make you more manageable. Had that not been the case, the walls would have surely risen. As for Nicholas, we might never know the whole truth. But the Caves are vast. He and Ragnar mightn't have needed to directly cross the sea to reach where they awaited you and Wigg. Instead, they might have simply found a way to go around it."

"And the wrecked Rustannican warship that we saw beached on the rocky wall?" Tyranny asked. "How did that get through the maze?"

"That was the first and last Rustannican vessel ever to do so," Kaemon answered. "It was part of a Vagaries strike force from the east that managed to get that far because at the time our spell was incomplete. Far more Rustannican warships rest at the bottom of the channel maze, I assure you. Like you, they used subtle matter to shrink their war vessels, allowing them to be transported through the caves for use on the Azure Sea. It is interesting how minds of the endowed often think alike, regardless of whether their owners' blood favors the Vigors or the Vagaries! Before our development of the formulas allowing for the maze, many great naval battles took place on that Azure Sea."

His mind awhirl, the *Jin'Sai* sat back in his chair. He knew that there remained a staggering amount to learn about this side of the world and the people in it, and the mere thought of it all seemed overwhelming.

Deciding that the time had come to put other questions aside, he resolved to ask about the great personal mystery that had eluded him for so long. The first time he had used the vanished azure pass to travel through the Tolenkas and reach this side of the world, he had learned that it was his and his sister's destiny to somehow stop the War of Attrition so that the practitioners of the Vigors and the Vagaries might live together in peace, in one unified nation under the guidance of one ruler. That ruler, he had been told, was to be him.

But in his heart he knew that there must be far more to this ultimate riddle. How could he—an untrained person from a faraway land—ever hope to accomplish what these supremely august mystics could not? Although he had defeated many enemies in the name of the Vigors, and he was the only *Jin'Sai* to have reached this side of the world, the nature of what these people required from him seemed impossible in the extreme. Summoning up his courage, he looked Mashiro in the eye.

"It's time that I was finally told about my true destiny," he said. "My entire life has been leading up to this moment. How is it that I might ever hope to accomplish all that you need from me?"

As if to tell Tristan that he understood the *Jin'Sai*'s frustration, Mashiro gave him a compassionate look.

"As you already know," Mashiro began solemnly, "the War of Attrition must be brought to an end. We understand that you find it impossible to believe, but only the *Jin'Sai* can do it, for the *Pon Q'tar* has no wish for peace. Even so, it is our wish that the two countries be unified under the rule of your supremely gifted blood. But what you have yet to learn are the other deeds that must be accomplished as well if your destiny is to be fulfilled. The world must be reunited as it was before the outbreak of this terrible and costly war and the sudden rising of the Tolenka Mountains that separated it."

"What deeds are these?" Tristan asked.

For several moments Mashiro looked down at his hands. When he finally lifted his face he looked first at Wigg, then Tyranny and Tristan. When his gaze met the *Jin'Sai*'s it was stern, resolute.

"What I am about to say will no doubt shock you," he said quietly. "Nonetheless, it needs to be heard."

When Tristan did not respond, Mashiro drew a deep breath. As Tristan waited for Mashiro to answer, the silence became deafening.

"With your help," the *Inkai* leader said at last, "we mean to destroy the Tome and the Scrolls of the Ancients and dismantle the craft as we know it."

CHAPTER XXXVII

WHILE DESPERATE FIGHTING RAGED IN THE DISTANCE, Vespasian stood in his war tent. Looking down at the table before him, he tensely consulted the freshly updated war map that Lucius Marius had supplied to him only moments ago. Alongside the map lay several beeswax diptychs that had been rushed from the front by hand-picked centurion messengers. The map displayed the Imperial Order's progress in taking the next Shashidan riverside town, while the diptychs held detailed information about enemy soldiers and civilians killed, casualties suffered among the Rustannican forces, and tallies of supplies, food, and arms both used and still flowing to the front from the safety of Rustannica.

Vespasian was pleased with the progress of his war. So far his casualties had been surprisingly light and great areas of Shashidan land had fallen to his legions, causing many of his tribunes to believe that a great victory lay at hand. Even so, the same concerns that worried Vespasian when he first conceived this campaign had started to surface again, and the Shashidan gold mines still lay many leagues away.

Like previous Rustannican thrusts through the Borderlands and into Shashida, the distances to objectives of real importance were vast and immensely difficult for so great an army to traverse—even with the help of the azure portals. Should the Shashidans somehow negate the use of his portals, his entire invasion force would become stranded in enemy territory. Worse, it would take many years of marching to reach the Borderlands, then cross them and return home. And because the Borderlands could not be summoned without killing his own troops as they crossed them, Shashidan forces could harass them every step of the way, killing them off little by little.

Therefore it was imperative that Vespasian's overland escape route be fiercely protected. This meant that the lands already taken had to remain in Rustannican hands for the duration of the campaign, forcing valuable troops and materiel to remain behind in strategic places along the way. The sands in the hourglass of war were falling quickly, he knew. If the Shashidan mines were to be seized and held long enough to send at least some of their prized contents home, Vespasian's advance must not only take the entire area surrounding the Six Rivers and the lands between them and the mines, but also hold them for as long as possible.

Lifting his gaze from the map, Vespasian looked out the tent entrance and toward the horizon. The sun was starting to rise, bringing with it the promise of good weather. *It will be a fine day for killing Shashidans,* he decided.

Gracchus Junius, Lucius Marius, Empress Persephone, and Julia Idaeus stood by his side waiting to hear his daily orders. After the Twenty-third Legion's Blood Stalkers had secured the staging area near the headlands of the Vertex Mostim, Imperial Order legions and armed barges had arrived by way of hundreds of azure portals. They then advanced south and subdued the first few Shashidan towns along the banks of the Six Rivers. Soon they had reached the strategic place where the Six Rivers joined to form one huge, rushing current known in the Shashidan dialect as the Togogawa, or Abundant River. From there the Togogawa led to the gold mines.

Surprisingly, few Shashidan troops had been met, and the meager enemy forces trying to resist Vespasian's monstrous invasion had been swiftly overcome. While the *Pon Q'tar* and most of the tribunes saw that as a good omen, Vespasian and Lucius Marius found it unnerving. Surely the *Inkai* knew by now that Vespasian's advance was no brief incursion to be taken lightly. *So why hasn't the full weight of their armies rushed north to meet us?* Vespasian wondered. As he looked back down at his war map, that worrisome question and others like it gnawed greedily at his self-confidence.

The Shashidan riverside city to which his forces currently lay siege was much larger than those already in his hands. This was yet another hindrance to his war plan, for as his forces advanced to the south, the cities became far larger and therefore more problematic to conquer. Because so few Shashidan troops had been met, the first few riverside cities had been taken easily. But this next city was protected by far more Shashidan troops than the others had been, and taking it was chewing up more time than Vespasian had planned on.

Such delays might significantly lengthen his timetable and supply the Shashidan forces with precious time to reinforce their troops that protected the gold mines. That was a turn of events that Vespasian could not afford, for his plan depended on reaching and surrounding the mines with lightning speed. At the same time all the captured lands north of his current position must remain firmly in his hands should his forces need to retreat without benefit of the enchanted portals. Of added concern was that given the specific direction of Vespasian's advance downriver and its markedly narrow east-west line of attack, the emperor's goal would soon become clear.

If he was to take the mines, he must reach them soon, before the entire Shashidan army arrived to stand in his way. Yet another worrisome possibility was that the enemy might postpone an outright confrontation and instead flank his narrow thrust on its eastern and western sides. This would allow them to at first avoid his forces, then turn and march directly toward each another. If they could link up, they would split his forces in two and sound their death knell.

Moreover, with every step south, his supply lines became farther stretched. Food, soldiers, and materiel from Ellistium still poured through the portals, but given the ever-increasing distance from home, the supply situation might soon grow dangerously tenuous. Time was of the essence in this campaign, as Vespasian had known from the moment he first proposed it to the Suffragat that fateful day in the Rectoris Aedifficium.

Raising his gaze from the map, Vespasian turned to look at Lucius. "The battle for the next town still rages?" he asked.

"Yes, Blood Royal," Lucius answered.

Vespasian shook his head. "We are moving too slowly," he mused. "There are few prizes worth taking this far north, but to secure our route home, it must be done. And that, my friend, is the confounding part of this war! We must capture and hold thousands of leagues of useless grasslands before reaching objectives of substance. The best plan would have been to use the portals to take our forces straight to the gold mines. But should the Shashidans somehow render them useless, without having first secured an overland escape route home we would become hopelessly surrounded in a matter of days."

"That is true," Lucius answered. "But we had no choice. If we don't hold those lands and the Shashidans negate our portals—"

"I know, I know," Vespasian interrupted. "I have had enough of running this war from charts and reports. I will visit the battle firsthand." He turned to look at Persephone, Gracchus, and Julia. "Wait here," he said. "I will return shortly. Lucius, come with me."

After grabbing up their helmets, Vespasian and Lucius left the war tent to become part of the riotous scene outside. In the entire history of Rustannica there had been no greater invasion force than this, and even now Vespasian remained awed by its sheer size and ferocity.

The empire's colorful command tents stood atop a rise overlooking a gently sloping valley. Through the rich green valley snaked the mighty Alarik River, or the Togogawa, as the enemy called it. In some places the huge waterway measured over two hundred meters across, making it a formidable force of nature. In the distance could be seen the burning Shashidan riverside town to which the empire's troops laid siege.

The town would eventually be taken, Vespasian knew. Then his forces could recommence their advance downriver and seize the remaining towns standing in their way. Soon his invasion would cross these broad, useless flatlands and reach a mountainous area through which the raging Alarik flowed. According to Vespasian's intelligence reports, it was there that the Shashidan mines would be found, their massive deposits having been slowly laid bare as the Alarik spent countless centuries carving its way through the mountains.

Hurrying to his chariot, Vespasian quickly jumped aboard, and Lucius followed suit to stand beside him. Taking the reins from his horse handler, Vespasian snapped the whip, and his two white stallions charged down the hill with the gleaming white and gold chariot in tow.

The awe-inspiring scene was like some bizarre warrior's dream. While trumpets blared and drums rolled, hundreds of thousands of armed legionnaires, bowmen, archers, and lancers marched side by side in lockstep down the hill toward the enemy city in uncountable rows measuring half a league wide. Dark Rustannican barges laden with yet more men and war materiel sailed down the mighty Alarik to take part in the siege. Giant war machines engineered by the *Pon Q'tar* sat in countless rows, their vast numbers quiet for now but threatening to pour forth death and destruction at any moment. Monstrous war beasts conjured for this campaign lumbered down the hill and cried out to one another under the watchful eyes of legionary animal handlers, their huge numbers causing the earth to tremble beneath their feet.

North of the command tents lay countless square leagues of conquered grasslands, their endless swells covered with the much-needed support mechanisms that sustained Vespasian's monstrous advance. Thousands of provision wagons and camp tents provided refuge and work areas for the legions' armorers, fletchers, cooks, surgeons, paymasters, prostitutes, and more, their vast numbers stretching northward as far as the eye could see. Mammoth supply lines snaked across the landscape to provide the goods, armaments, and manpower needed to sustain the gargantuan invasion force.

Whipping his horses again, Vespasian continued down the slope toward the stricken Shashidan town. He soon saw the flames that were ravaging the city and smelled the telltale odor of burning flesh. As his legions parted to clear a path for their emperor's chariot, the soldiers cheered and saluted. Taking the reins in one hand, Vespasian saluted them in return.

Soon he and Lucius came upon yet more of the legions' handiwork. Wanting to take a closer look, Vespasian pulled hard on the reins and slowed his stallions to a walk, steering them rightward onto a dirt road running alongside the Alarik River that led directly into the burning town. Like the slope he and Lucius had just descended, the dusty road was choked with eager legionnaires on their way to finish the job of destroying the city and killing what remained of the town's inhabitants and soldiers. As their chariot slowed, Vespasian and Lucius looked first to one side of the road, then the other, taking in the results of the emperor's imaginative orders.

No slaves would be taken in this war, Vespasian had decreed. This far from home, prisoners were nothing more than liabilities to feed and care for, and no extra personnel or supplies were to be made available for such useless compassion. But that did not mean that certain Shashidans could not be put to good use.

To instill terror among the populace, Vespasian had ordered that his tribunes take several thousand Shashidan civilians and soldiers alive. Their protracted deaths would serve as a warning to those who would dare defy the empire. Looking along the opposing roadsides, Vespasian reviewed those unfortunate Shashidans who had been chosen to serve as his object lessons.

Thousands of long, sturdy timbers had been pounded into the ground along either side of the road down which the legions thronged. Near the top of each timber, a shorter one had been placed at right angles to the first and then inserted into a carved notch. Wooden plugs pounded through the shorter timber into the longer one held the arrangement in place.

Naked Shashidan men—military and civilian alike—hung upside down from the sturdy crossbraces. Their ankles had been tied to the ends of the crossbraces, and their bodies and arms hung downward to face each other from opposite roadsides. With their legs widely splayed and their blood rushing to their heads, their deaths from exposure to the elements would be slow and agonizing. To prevent escape, legion officers segregated those with endowed blood, then wiped their memories clean of the craft.

Many of these victims were already dead, but as Vespasian and Lucius kept going they soon neared those who had been recently hung and remained alive. They would die soon, Vespasian knew, for his legionnaires were strictly obeying the other part of his orders.

As the legionnaires walked by, from time to time they reached up with their spears or gladii to poke at the dangling victims. Each of the countless jabs was to be short, clean, and expertly done. The goal was not to kill the victims straightaway but to see how long they could survive such exquisite pain. The stronger the subject was, the longer it took him. So as to prolong the spectacle, Vespasian ordered that only healthy men be subjected to this traditional brand of Rustannican butchery. The process was called *mortem obirein incisurae,* or "death by a thousand cuts."

To Vespasian's amusement, one victim had the courage to shout an epithet as the emperor drove by. Pulling his horses to a stop, Vespasian looked at him. The Blood Royal knew that he was a Shashidan soldier because his unique battle armor had been stripped from him and lay scattered by the roadside, and because of his unique hairstyle. Hundreds of bleeding wounds pierced the man's torso, face, extremities, and genitals. If the cuts were done right, the victims died from slow exsanguination. But even the expert legionaries sometimes cut too long or too deep. If they did so, the victims' internal organs became exposed and eventually slipped from the body cavity to fall earthward before their faces, making them the suspended prisoners' last sight before dying.

So that the man might know his identity, Vespasian removed his helmet. Vespasian found that staring into the man's upside-down bloody face was a disorienting experience. Like all tribunes, *Pon Q'tar* members, and Heretics, Vespasian spoke perfect Shashidan. Shaking his head with disgust, he turned to look at Lucius.

"Such subhumans these Shashidans are," he said. "Do you see how they persist in shaving their heads? And what bizarre armor they wear!"

Vespasian again looked into the man's eyes. "What is your name?" he asked in the man's native dialect.

The prisoner seemed to be somewhere near thirty Seasons of New Life, and despite his wretched condition he possessed a modicum of vitality. Hatred filled his eyes as he stared back at Vespasian. Like all *katsugai mosota*, the top of his head was shaved. The gold ornament that usually held his queue in place had been stolen by some greedy legionary, allowing his long black hair to dangle earthward. Rather than being a war crime, stealing the traditional gold ornament was considered an extra payment for doing the dirty job of stripping filthy Shashidan barbarians and hanging them from the makeshift crosses. Some of the more industrious legionnaires owned hundreds of the gold trinkets, which they proudly displayed on their body armor or sent home to their wives, lovers, or mistresses.

When the man did not answer, Vespasian moved his chariot nearer.

"I demand to know your name!" he shouted.

"I am Akeno of the House of Bamboo," the man answered. Much to the emperor's and Lucius' surprise, the man smiled, his bloody lips bizarrely curving earthward rather than upward. The effect was strangely chilling.

"I have recently come from the south," Akeno said. "I prayed that I might live long enough to see you ride by, you illegitimate Vagaries bastard. I am an acquaintance of the *Inkai,* and I have a warning for you."

Incensed by the Shashidan's insult, Lucius immediately drew his gladius, but Vespasian grabbed his arm. Clenching his jaw, Lucius grudgingly sheathed his sword.

"What is your message?" Vespasian demanded.

Once more the bloody inverted smile appeared. "The *Jin'Sai* is coming to Shashida," the captive answered. "He might already be among us.

Rustannica's days are numbered, Vespasian. If you value your life and the lives of your troops you will stop this mad invasion and go home. You will need every one of your vaunted legionnaires when the *Jin'Sai* comes for you and the barren whore that is your empress."

Although the news was highly valuable and Vespasian would later curse himself for not interrogating the prisoner further, this time even he could not contain his rage. Summoning but a tiny fraction of his power, Vespasian raised one arm and sent an azure bolt tearing toward the dangling katsugai.

The bolt blew the man to pieces, sending blood and offal high into the air. The resulting noise was so great that even the disciplined legionnaires marching by stopped to look. For several moments Vespasian's stallions reared violently, nearly sending the chariot tumbling sideways to the ground.

As the scene quieted, Vespasian glared angrily at the smoking, damaged cross. Save for wet bloodstains and glistening bits of flesh and bone that still clung to the wood, the man had been vaporized. Nor was there much left of the sturdy crossbrace from which he once hung. Vespasian and Lucius watched as what remained of the torture device fell apart and tumbled to the ground.

Realizing his mistake, Vespasian took a deep breath, then scrubbed his face with his hands. The Shashidan's warning had shaken him, and he was stunned by what he had just heard. *Perhaps it was only the Shashidan's way of tormenting me before dying,* he thought.

He turned to look at Lucius. "That was foolish of me," he said angrily. "I should have ordered him interrogated before killing him."

Lucius shrugged his shoulders. "Perhaps," he offered. "But before we started this campaign the *Pon Q'tar* assured us that the *Jin'Sai* cannot reach this side of the world. We must ignore the dead barbarian's babbling for the tripe that it was. Let us continue onward to the battleground."

Vespasian nodded and took up his reins. "You're right," he answered. "We have larger concerns than the mad ramblings of one dying katsugai who wished to insult me." Taking up his whip, he prepared to get his stallions moving again.

But just as Vespasian raised his arm he again felt the dreaded, all too familiar sensation overcome him. Within moments his heart was racing wildly and cold sweat poured from his skin. His muscles trembled uncontrollably, forcing him to drop the reins and whip.

Persephone, he thought desperately as he sensed his consciousness fading. *Only she understands . . . I must return to her before Lucius knows . . . and my troops . . . above all else, they must not see their emperor fall . . .*

Sinking to his knees, Vespasian realized that it was already too late. He weakly reached up to grab at Lucius' armor as the stunned First Tribune looked down at his lifelong friend in horror.

"My emperor!" he gasped. "What overcomes you so?"

"Take me back to Persephone!" Vespasian whispered. "Only she knows what to do! Hide me in the chariot and be sure that no one else sees me like this—my fate is in your hands—above all, do not let the *Pon Q'tar* see me this way . . ."

Finally losing consciousness, Vespasian collapsed to the chariot floor.

Nonplussed, Lucius looked around. Hordes of legionnaires still obediently passed by the chariot on their way toward the battle scene. Some had surely noticed what happened, Lucius realized. He also instinctively knew that whatever was wrong with his emperor, above all else, Vespasian must be hurried away from here.

With Vespasian's desperate pleas still ringing in his ears, the First Tribune reached down and gently slid Vespasian's limp body forward near the chariot's riser where it would not be seen. Then he quickly took up the reins and slapped them hard across the stallions' haunches.

Wheeling the chariot around, he charged back up the hill.

CHAPTER XXXVIII

IN THE END IT WOULD TAKE THE PRINCESS OF EUTRACIA twelve hours to regain consciousness. As her mind slowly sharpened, the last thing she could recall was looking up in terror as the Blood Viper's talons slashed down toward her throat. Moments later, a lesser degree of the terrible pain that had ripped through her entire system, and especially her left eye, returned. As her acuteness continued to strengthen, she took stock of her surroundings.

It was nighttime in Eutracia, and she lay in her private quarters. The royal palace and the surrounding grounds were peaceful, with only the usual sounds of the night creatures wafting through the air to keep her company. She was dressed in one of her nightgowns, and as she came around, the pain that still racked her body, face, and left eye slowly rose. *But I am alive,* she thought gratefully, *although I may have no right to be.*

She soon realized that her vision was deeply compromised; everything looked darkly shadowed and her depth perception was markedly skewed. The effect was chilling. Because only one candelabrum on the far side of the room was in use, her chambers looked unusually dark. *Perhaps that is why I cannot see as I should,* she thought. Then she sensed an unfamiliar pressure against her left eye.

Moving as best her sore muscles and joints would allow, she leaned over toward one bedstand and grasped the hand mirror that always lay there. With a trembling hand she started to lift it before her face.

But just as she did, an unseen power forced the mirror down and away. As though her arm suddenly belonged to someone else, she felt an unearthly force press it down onto the bed. The sensation was not painful, and she soon realized that there was no point in trying to fight it, for it was born of the craft. Clearly she was not alone.

"I am sorry, Princess," came a familiar voice from the shadows along the far side of the room. "I thought it necessary that we talk before you see your reflection. I apologize for not removing the hand mirror from your bedstand earlier. I should have guessed that it would be the first thing you'd reach for after you awakened."

Although Shailiha desperately wanted to see her reflection, she knew that there was no use in arguing. The voice had been Faegan's, and he would use the craft to enforce his wishes. Because of how much he cared for her, his decisions would surely be in her best interests. But unlike many times before, on this night she was not easily comforted by his presence. Clearly he was preventing her from seeing her face, causing her to wonder just how bad her injuries were. Like a spectator unable to take part in some drama she was watching, she saw the mirror slide from her grip and float across the room to disappear into the shadows. After taking a deep breath, she lay back on her silken pillows.

Moments later Faegan wheeled his chair from the shadows to come and sit by her bedside. He looked tired and drawn, and her hand mirror lay in his lap. Although he tried to smile, even with her hampered vision Shailiha could see that his cheerful expression was forced.

"How long have you been here?" she asked.

"Twelve hours," he answered, "the same as you. I have been with you every moment since Traax brought you to me. It was he who saved you from the viper."

"How bad are my injuries?" she demanded. "You must tell me the truth if I am to lead Eutracia. Like each of us, I am only as good as my limitations."

In the flickering candlelight Faegan smiled again, and this time she thought that his expression seemed more genuine. "You're starting to reason like a sorceress," he said. "I'm going to have to be more careful around you." In a silent attempt to avoid her question, he grasped her down comforter and pulled it up a bit higher.

"You still haven't answered me," Shailiha insisted as she tried to sit up. But the strain of moving suddenly increased her pain and she was forced to again lie back. Sighing, she closed her eyes for a moment. As she did so, she felt the lashes of her left eye brush against something, and she knew.

She turned toward Faegan and looked into his face as best she could. "I'm wearing an eye patch, aren't I?" she asked.

Faegan nodded.

"Is my left eye blind?" the princess asked quietly.

"Only you can answer that," Faegan said. "In one more hour I will remove the patch and we will know."

"Why must we wait?" she asked.

"The Shashidan *Inkai* said that the enchantment would do its best work in thirteen hours," he answered. "The craft formula that they supplied to help heal you was the most elegant and convoluted that I have ever seen. It took Aeolus and me two hours to grasp it, and even now we're not sure whether we applied it correctly."

"The Shashidan *Inkai?*" Shailiha asked. "What are you talking about?"

Faegan smiled and placed his hand atop hers. "There is much to tell you," he said. "And like most news, only part of it is good."

"Is Morganna all right?" Shailiha demanded.

"She's fine," Faegan answered. "Shawna looks after her."

"Did we defeat Khristos?" the princess asked.

Faegan shook his head. "The Viper Lord and many of his servants escaped us again. I wish that I could tell you that we gave as good as we got, but I can't. The *Illendium* has been vaporized, and although the *Cavalon* is repairable, she was severely damaged by fire. Khristos' goal wasn't to take Tammerland or to see how many people he could kill. The attack on the capital was only a ruse designed to draw the Conclave and our forces away from the palace so that he could steal one Black Ship and destroy the other. I'm sorry to say that he nearly succeeded."

Shailiha looked away in shame. "It's my fault," she said softly. "I ordered us straight into it."

"No," Faegan said. "We're all to blame. Even Traax agreed that we needed to rush every available warrior into the heart of Tammerland. But there is other news, Your Highness, and it grieves me deeply to be its bearer."

"Is it about Tristan?" she asked urgently.

"No," Faegan answered. "He, Wigg, and Tyranny have finally reached

Shashida and they are safe. The others remain aboard the Black Ships. But during the fighting in Tammerland we lost a valuable Conclave member."

Shailiha closed her eyes. "Who . . . ?" she asked.

"Abbey is dead," Faegan answered. "I am sorry."

Heartbroken, Shailiha sank lower in her bed. She had loved Abbey, as they all had. Then she thought about Wigg and how badly her death would hurt him.

"Does Wigg know?" she asked.

"I can't say," Faegan answered. "As we speak, he, Tristan, and Tyranny are conferring with Mashiro and the other *Inkai* members for the first time."

"Mashiro . . . ?" Shailiha asked. "That's a strange-sounding name."

"Indeed," Faegan answered. "The Shashidan dialect contains far more idiosyncrasies than we had imagined. In any event, Tristan, Wigg, and Tyranny were rendered unconscious when the Shashidans took them into their portal to help finish their journey. While Tristan was unconscious they used his medallion to contact us. They told us much about themselves, including how they knew that you had been injured. But they cut the session short so that they could give us an enchantment to apply to your blood. They promised that after their meeting with Tristan they would contact us again."

Despite all the bad news, a mischievous smile crossed Faegan's face. "We've done it, Shailiha!" he said. Slapping his hand against one knee he let go a self-satisfied cackle. "At long last we've reached Shashida!"

Shailiha wanted to demand that Faegan tell her everything that he had learned about Shashida, but her sense of duty returned to insist that the situation in Eutracia take precedence. Putting her curiosity aside for the moment, she asked, "Has Khristos been sighted since the last attack?"

"No," Faegan answered. "Even so, there's good news regarding him."

"What do you mean?" she asked.

Faegan gave the princess a conspiratorial wink. "The *Inkai* know much about him," Faegan answered. "They explained how he appears and disappears at will and why he is trying to destroy the Conclave. Because he is a Vagaries wizard, he feels compelled to destroy the Vigors but the full answer goes far deeper than that. And as has so often been the case, the explanation has to do with Failee."

For the next half hour Faegan told the princess about how Khristos and the embryonic vipers had been condemned into the river by Failee, how and why they had finally arisen after all this time, and that the *Inkai* suspected that Khristos was now in the service of the *Pon Q'tar*. The *Jin'Saiou* listened intently, hanging on the wizard's every word. When he finished, she tiredly nodded her head.

"That explains much," she said. "But because they can hide in Eutracia's many rivers and use them to travel about unseen, finding and killing them will be very difficult. It's no wonder that our Night Witches couldn't find them. They can seek refuge anywhere a river runs."

"There's more to the tale," Faegan said, "but the *Inkai* did not relate it to us. They wanted to be sure that you were looked after first. In any event, they said that they might be able to help us destroy Khristos and his vipers—not by direct intervention, but in some oblique way. I can only hope that they will tell us how when we next view each other."

Just then Faegan and Shailiha saw an azure hue build on the room's far side. The glow soon revealed a large hourglass sitting atop a table. As Shailiha looked at it, she saw that a few remaining sand grains were tumbling from the top globe into the bottom one. When the last grain fell, the azure hue disappeared.

"The thirteen hours are up," Faegan said. "It's time to check your vision. Close both eyes. Do not open them until I tell you."

Shailiha's heart hammered in her chest. With her eyes shut she saw only darkness. *Is this all that my left eye will ever see again?* she wondered. Knowing that she must resign herself to whatever Faegan wanted, she took a deep breath, then nodded her assent.

Faegan moved his chair closer and gently removed the dark patch and its strap from her face and head. As the patch was lifted away, the temptation to open her eyes gripped the princess, but she did as she had been told and kept them shut.

For several moments she felt Faegan's fingertips gently explore her left cheek and eyelid. Waiting in silence this way was torturous, and she desperately wanted to open her eyes and learn the truth. Then she remembered that this was Faegan she was dealing with and that only what he wished to happen would come to pass. As the maddening seconds went by she could only wait and wonder. Finally his probing fingers left her skin.

"You may now open your eyes, Princess," Faegan said. "Tell me what you see. Allow your vision to adjust, and be in no hurry to answer."

Hoping against hope, Shailiha opened her eyes. Several moments later her heart fell. To her horror, her overall vision was worse than when she had worn the eye patch. The scene coming through her left eye was milky, as if a white fog covered it. The vision in her right eye was fine, but with her left eye so badly occluded, she found herself in the dreadful position of nearly asking Faegan to put back the eye patch. Although while wearing the patch her depth perception was flawed, at least the milky fog wasn't visible. Tears welled up, but she grimly blinked them back.

Sensing the worst, Faegan looked at his hands. Soon the telltale shininess in his eyes rivaled hers.

"Tell me," he said softly.

"My left eye is blind," she answered.

"Is it totally blind," he asked gently, "or only occluded? The *Inkai* said that occlusions might persist for a time before clearing, but there are no guarantees. Place your hand over your right eye and tell me what you see."

Shailiha did as Faegan asked. She looked around the room to find that she could see shimmers of candlelight and irregular shapes mixed with the fog, but little else. After lowering her hand she explained her findings to the wizard.

"Do not be discouraged," he said. "As I said, the *Inkai* warned that this might be the case. In the meantime I suggest that you wear the eye patch and let your damaged eye rest."

"Before I do, I want the mirror," she said adamantly. "I must know . . ."

After thinking for a moment, Faegan nodded, then reluctantly gave her the mirror. Shailiha raised it before her injured face without hesitation. As the shock overcame her she took a quick breath.

At first she didn't recognize herself. Her left iris had been invaded by a milky-white substance and the skin around her eye was red and swollen. Then she looked at the left side of her face. Deep red pock marks pitted her cheek, neck, and jawline. Closing her eyes, she lowered her head.

"The damage to your skin will heal," Faegan said, "and the pain and stiffness in your joints and muscles will eventually subside. But I cannot say what added progress your left eye might make."

Finding that she had no words, Shailiha only nodded. When she had first realized that she was wearing an eye patch, she would have gladly done anything to be rid of it. But as Faegan gently put it back into its place and her vision was no longer occluded, she found wearing the simple black piece of felt and accompanying string to be strangely reassuring. Steeling her resolve, she looked Faegan squarely in the face. What was done was done. It was time for her to start giving orders rather than taking them.

"Help me out of this bed," she demanded.

Faegan shook his head. "No," he protested. "You need to rest."

Summoning what strength she had, Shailiha reached out to take hold of Faegan's worn black robe and pull him nearer. The wizard curiously raised one eyebrow, reminding her of Wigg. He could easily have used the craft to stop her but he didn't.

"I'm quite serious," she said. "Get me on my feet. If I am to rule Eutracia in Tristan's absence, I refuse to do so from my bed!"

After pondering her order for a moment, Faegan decided to obey. *Perhaps taking charge of the future is the best medicine for her,* he thought, *rather than lying there and wondering what it might do to her.* He smiled and gave her a nod.

"As you wish, Princess," he said.

Faegan raised one arm and summoned the craft. At once the bedsheets and comforter lifted away to drift to the floor. Then the craft levitated the princess into the air and onto her feet. As the spell dissipated, she gradually found her footing.

"Can you walk without help?" Faegan asked.

"I think so," she answered. Then her expression softened. "I'm sorry if I was harsh with you, but I must do this. Please leave me. I need to dress."

"As you wish," he said. "Do you have any other orders?"

Shailiha nodded. "I'm starving," she said. "I know that it's late, but I want Shawna to prepare a full breakfast for me, including lots of hot, extra-strong tea. I want Traax to personally deliver his battle report to me as soon as he awakens. And return my medallion to me. I can guess why you took it, but I'll have it back. When the *Inkai* contact me I will inform you at once."

Nodding, Faegan removed the enchanted medallion from his person and handed it to her. As she placed its chain around her neck, her expression fell. She gave the wizard a worried look.

"There's one more thing," she added quietly. "I realize that Morganna will be fast asleep, but have her brought to me. There is something that I must know."

Faegan understood, and his heart went out to her. "Of course," he replied.

Knowing that there was little more to be said, he swiveled his chair around and wheeled it across the princess's quarters. Calling the craft to open the door, he steered his chair into the hallway and the door closed quietly behind him.

Shailiha shuffled painfully across the room toward her wardrobe, gingerly trying to become accustomed to her aching body and impaired vision. She hurt everywhere, but she also supposed that the more she pushed herself, the quicker she would recover. After lighting more candles, she changed from her gown into a pair of close-fitting black breeches, a white silk blouse, and a sleeveless brown leather doublet. Putting on her knee boots was an immense challenge, but she finally managed.

After running her fingers through her long blond hair, she was breathing heavily and sweating lightly. She slowly crossed the floor to sit gratefully in one of the comfortable balcony chairs overlooking the palace grounds. The night air was sweet and cooling. After taking a few deep breaths she regained a modicum of composure.

And so I am partly blind, she thought. *But my body and mind remain intact, so therefore I can still rule. And rule I shall.*

As the night creatures sang and the stars twinkled in the sky, Shailiha explored her feelings. Her personal circumstances had changed, perhaps forever. This pain was new, but older, even deeper wounds that had come long before these new ones still scarred her heart. Since the death of her husband, Frederick, she had felt desperately alone, despite all the people and Minions who shared this great palace.

Morganna had helped to fill the void left by Frederick's passing, but since then there had been no love like that which Frederick had given her. For a time after his death she believed that her love for her child and the love that Morganna gave her in return would be enough to fulfill her. But she later realized that this vacuum would be unique and long lasting, regardless of how much she and her growing child loved one another. She needed a man's arms around her. She wanted a man's strong but careful touch, his scent, his passion. She wanted to be swept away— even if only for one night—so that she might fully experience womanhood once more. But there had been no such passion in her life for more than three years, and she deeply mourned its loss.

Because of the new injuries to her face and eye, added concerns unfolded in her heart—concerns about which she was at once sure and unsure. If her injuries did not heal, the likelihood of finding romantic love would be dampened still further. As much as that thought plagued her, another plagued her more. Morganna's presence had partly filled the hole in Shailiha's heart, but without her daughter's love and trust, that hole would only widen again, perhaps irrevocably. And so she had demanded to see her daughter straightaway. She had to know, before trying to carry on and rule the land that she and her brother so loved.

As she sat there with her thoughts, a soft knocking could be heard against her doors.

"Enter," Shailiha called out hoarsely.

The doors parted to reveal Shawna and Morganna standing there. Shawna was dressed in her usual work clothes, and the precocious three-year-old obediently held the gnome's calloused hand. Morganna was clothed in a simple red and white checked dress, white leggings, and shiny black shoes. Her long blond hair lay behind her neck, collected by a jeweled pin. As Morganna looked toward the balcony to find her mother, her face suddenly changed from delight to fear. Cringing slightly, she lifted Shawna's apron before her face, trying to find safety there.

Shailiha felt her heart break, but she continued to smile for Morganna's sake. Shawna gave Shailiha a concerned but knowing look, telling the princess that she had been fully informed of her situation. Then the gnome pursed her lips and nodded, tacitly signaling her deep sympathy.

Shailiha stretched out her arms. "It's all right, Morganna," she said. "Please come to me. I've missed you."

Morganna moved slightly away from the protection of Shawna's apron, but she refused to venture farther. The look on her face now spoke of both fear and confusion.

"Mamma . . . ?" she asked softly.

"Yes, it's me," Shailiha answered. "I'm a little bit sick, but I'll be better soon."

Morganna looked up at Shawna as if silently asking what she should do. After giving the princess a wink, Shawna scowled at Morganna and put her hands akimbo.

"Don't just stand here, child," she said. "Go to your mother. I must get back to the palace kitchens and cook up a great breakfast for you two. Now scat!"

Morganna swallowed hard, then started taking small, unsure steps toward the balcony. As she neared, she realized that the person in the chair really was her mother, and her expression changed from fear to concern. But as she reached Shailiha's chair, the princess was overjoyed to see her daughter suddenly reach up to be taken into her arms.

No amount of pain could stop Shailiha now. She scooped her daughter up and sat her in her lap. As Morganna's young eyes explored her mother's wounds and the mysterious new eye patch, at first she seemed frightened again. Then, to Shailiha's delight, she smiled.

"It's a game isn't it, Mamma?" she asked. "You've made a game just for the two of us."

Unsure of how to respond, the princess decided to agree. Holding her daughter closer, she said, "Yes, Morganna, it's a game. And when it's over I will look the way I did before." Holding Morganna closer yet, she rocked her in her arms. Then she looked across the room to see Shawna brush away a nagging tear.

"I'll take my leave now, Your Grace," she said. "The breakfast and all . . ."

As Shailiha pressed her lips against her daughter's forehead she gave Shawna a little nod. The gnome let herself out and the doors closed again.

Morganna pulled away a bit to again look into her mother's face. This time the child's fear was gone, and Shailiha finally felt her heart calm. *The worst has passed,* she realized. Morganna again reached up to touch her mother's ravaged cheek.

"I love you, Mamma," came the soft, longed-for words.

"I love you too," Shailiha whispered back.

For the first time since she was injured, the *Jin'Saiou*'s tears flowed freely, and this time she did nothing to hold them back.

CHAPTER XXXIX

MASHIRO'S WORDS STRUCK TRISTAN NEARLY SPEECH-less. He quickly looked at Tyranny and Wigg and saw that they were as amazed as he.

Surely Mashiro can't mean what he just said! Tristan thought. *The Tome and the two Scrolls of the Ancients are priceless artifacts of the craft! How could he possibly suggest that they be destroyed? And what could Mashiro mean by "dismantling the craft"?*

Still unable to believe, Tristan stared incredulously at each *Inkai* member. The resolute expressions on their faces said that they were firmly committed to Mashiro's bizarre announcement.

Tristan glared at Mashiro. "Are you mad?" he breathed. "The Tome and the Scrolls are paramount in their importance! Hundreds of thousands of lives on both sides of the craft have been sacrificed to possess them! How could you even *suggest* that they be destroyed? And what did you mean about *dismantling* the craft when you have spent aeons trying to save it?"

"There is much for you and your friends to learn, *Jin'Sai,*" Mashiro answered calmly. "This decision was not reached lightly, I assure you. But to save the craft we must first eliminate some of its more advanced disciplines. Even then, we can do so only after Rustannica has been defeated and the world reunited under your rule. For the moment, let us not discuss our far-ranging plans for the craft. Instead, allow us to tell you about Rustannica, Shashida, and how we came to become embroiled in this terrible struggle. I will start by explaining the Rustannican government and culture."

For the next hour Mashiro described the dangerous nation lying to the north. He explained the Rustannican government workings in detail, including the roles of the *Pon Q'tar,* the emperor and empress, the Priory of Virtue and the Femiculi, and the many tribunes who together constituted the voting body called the Suffragat. He then went on to describe the workings of the horrific Rustannican war machine with its legions, armada, and Blood Stalkers. Giving a detailed description of the Rustannican social order, he explained the differences among the krithians, hematites, phrygians, and skeens. The grotesque role of Rustannica's many coliseums was then outlined, as was her dwindling gold supply and resulting economic emergency. Finally he told them of Vespasian's new campaign to take the Shashidan gold mines.

When Mashiro finished, Wigg, Tristan, and Tyranny sat for a time in silent astonishment. After casting an incredulous look at his fellow Conclave members, Tristan looked back at Mashiro.

"I beg the Afterlife," he breathed. "It sounds monstrous. Are the Rustannicans truly that barbaric?"

Mashiro nodded. "Interestingly, they call *us* the barbarians," he replied. "Rustannica is a victim of her own excesses. Although many laws exist, morality does not figure prominently in their writing or enforcement. Instead, all the laws are skewed in favor of those possessing endowed, left-leaning blood. Unless one is a member of the krithian class or of the Suffragat, his or her life belongs to the state. But to fully understand Rustannica there is much more that you need to learn."

After taking another sip of umake, Mashiro placed his hands flat on the table. "Things in Rustannica are far from what they seem," he said. "Only the *Pon Q'tar* and one other member of the Rustannican government know the whole truth. Everyone else—including Vespasian and Persephone—wrongly believes that the Vagaries are empowered by an eternal flame. This imaginative lie serves the *Pon Q'tar*'s needs well. Ever since the *Pon Q'tar* clerics banded together and convinced other mystics of left-leaning blood to follow them and break away from Shashida to form their own nation, they have told the Rustannican people that the Vagaries and Vigors are empowered by two opposing, magical azure flames. To add credibility to their lie, the *Pon Q'tar* clerics spun another falsehood, claiming that in a courageous act of heroism they stole the Vagaries flame from us barbaric Vigors worshippers. It was then supposedly brought to Rustannica, where it could be forever nurtured and protected from Shashidan tampering in our never-ending quest to destroy the Vagaries."

Pausing for a moment, Mashiro took another sip of the heady umake. "To add weight to their lie, they gave the flame a physical presence, then built a magnificent Rotunda in which to house it and to provide living quarters for the Priory Sisters," he added. "It is the Sisters' task to 'watch over the flame and ensure its life so that the Vagaries shall never perish.' As you can imagine, the populace sees the Priory Sisters as immensely important to protecting the craft and their continued way of life. In truth, the flame that the sisters protect is a sham that even they believe. It is the role of the reigning Femiculi to reenergize the flame on each coming of the new moon. But the enchantment taught to her by the *Pon Q'tar* to perform this 'miracle of the craft' does nothing but ensure that the useless flame burns for another month. Except for helping to convince the populace of the *Pon Q'tar*'s great hoax, the flame serves no purpose whatsoever."

"Why did the *Pon Q'tar* weave such an elaborate lie?" Wigg asked. "Why not simply tell their citizens the truth?"

"Rustannica is rife with secrets and lies," Hoshi answered. "As you already know, we believe that one side of the craft cannot exist without the other. The *Pon Q'tar* created the myth of the flame to disguise various truths about the craft, such as the Orbs of the Vigors and Vagaries. Because the two orbs remain trapped on the world's other side, their existences can be easily refuted. Like the Sorceresses of the Coven, the *Pon Q'tar*'s use of the Vagaries has blinded them to the truth. They are aware of the theory that each side of the craft needs the other, but like Failee and her followers, they refuse to believe it. They hope that with Vespasian's coming they can use his immensely powerful blood to finally smash Shashida and destroy all the Vigors practitioners west of the Tolenkas. Because the Orb of the Vigors is safe from their reach, the Vigors would continue to exist—at least in theory. But with no one of right-leaning blood left on our side of the world to employ the Vigors, here that side of the craft would be as good as extinct. That's another reason why the *Pon Q'tar* and the Heretics have done all they could to help destroy Vigors practitioners and the Vigors Orb on your side of the world. With those deeds done, much of their mission would be finished.

But what they refuse to believe is that should their ultimate goals be achieved, all magic would cease to exist and the entire world would be plunged into a unique form of mayhem and darkness from which it would never emerge."

"There is another reason why the *Pon Q'tar* perpetuates the hoax of the eternal flame," Midori spoke up. "Because of Rustannica's monetary woes, an internal revolt is brewing. If the Rustannican citizens knew the whole truth about the craft and what would truly happen to the world if the Vigors were destroyed, they might rise up and demand not only a halt to the war, but that all magic practitioners again try to live in peace. Because of the great manpower needed to prosecute Vespasian's new campaign, there are likely not enough legions left at home to quell a powerful civil uprising. Aside from a *Jin'Sai* or *Jin'Saiou* finally reaching Shashida, that is the *Pon Q'tar*'s greatest fear—especially now that their economy is on the verge of collapse and the government has launched an all-out war to seize our gold. If our mines are taken, the Rustannican war machine can continue to wreak havoc against us for aeons to come."

Tristan sat back in his chair. He grasped everything he had just heard, but hosts of questions remained. He turned to look at Mashiro.

"If Vespasian's advance is stopped and Rustannica can one day be brought to her knees, why would you then wish to destroy the Tome and the Scrolls of the Ancients?" Tristan asked. "And why would you 'dismantle' the craft? If the Vagaries disciples can be neutralized without destroying the orb that empowers their side of the craft, why would you contemplate such a thing?"

"Indeed," Wigg added. "We mean no disrespect, but what you're proposing suggests destroying everything we have spent our lives trying to protect."

Renjiro folded his arms across his chest and gave Wigg and Tristan a compassionate look. "We understand your concern," he said. "Your limited successes in better understanding and using the craft have been admirable. And from your less educated viewpoints, our suggestions must surely seem antithetical. But you must hear us out. Over the aeons, even our use of the Vigors has become a source of great concern, to say nothing of the death and destruction the Vagaries practitioners have caused. If we are to succeed in saving the craft, we must first eliminate some of its higher applications and destroy forever the tools that have allowed those applications to flourish. The craft is in desperate need of salvation, for its evolution during the last few thousand years has denigrated Vigors and Vagaries practitioners alike. Although this downward slide was started by the *Pon Q'tar* as a way to destroy us, we were forced to adopt some of the same techniques in order to fight off their constant onslaughts. If both sides of magic and their practitioners are to eventually live in peace, the craft must become much more the way it once was."

"Are you referring to the plan that was outlined to me by the Envoys of Crysenium?" Tristan asked. "It was their wish that I return to Crysenium and my blood signature be altered to the vertical so that it shows no bias. Then I was to try to find a rebel organization called the League of Whispers and eventually convince the Rustannicans that a peaceful solution could be found. The Envoys hoped that such a display of trust would carry much weight and perhaps lead us onto the road toward peace."

"As did the rest of us," Mashiro answered. "Some of those same Envoys once sat at this table, and it was in this room that their plan was approved. But the situation has changed markedly in the short time between then and now. Because of Rustannica's rapidly spiraling financial troubles and the advent of Vespasian's new campaign, the Suffragat members would never entertain a peace proposal now, because this campaign has simply cost them too much of their already dwindling treasury funds. The die has been cast, and for Vespasian and the *Pon Q'tar* this is a campaign of last resort. They simply don't have the funds to sustain their country while spending decades conducting peace negotiations. They know that we could simply wait them out as they grow progressively poorer and further unable to control their restless populace. Vespasian and the *Pon Q'tar* would never stand for that. We believe that the only way to stop them now is by vanquishing them in the field. In fact, we have no other choice, because if they take and hold our gold supplies we will soon find our economic situations reversed. But that is not to say that every facet of the Envoys' peace plan was without merit."

"I still don't understand," Tyranny said. "If you can vanquish the Rustannicans, what need would there be to 'dismantle' the craft?"

"Despite the craft's mazelike complexities, your question is perhaps best answered with two simple words," Mashiro said.

Wigg raised an eyebrow. "And what might they be?" he asked.

Mashiro looked deeply into Wigg's eyes. "Free will," he said softly.

Tristan glanced at Wigg to find a look of complete surprise. Then the First Wizard's expression morphed into one of deep thought.

"Are you all right?" Tristan asked.

His thoughts racing, Wigg stared at Tristan with unseeing eyes, then blankly looked back at Mashiro.

"I beg the Afterlife," he breathed. "The Paragon, the forestallments, the Tome, and the Scrolls of the Ancients—they were all crutches! Everything is gradually spiraling out of control and taking craft practitioners from both sides into the abyss with it! The more advanced our craft use becomes, the more we hurt ourselves!"

Pausing for a moment, Wigg simply stared into space. "I'm right, am I not?" he breathed. "I beg the Afterlife—how could we have been so blind? We worked so hard . . . we always believed that what we were doing was so right . . ."

Tristan gave Wigg a concerned look. "What do you mean?" he asked.

"As I said, we're talking about free will," Mashiro answered in the wizard's stead. "The true purpose of uniting Shashida and Rustannica goes far deeper than just ending the War of Attrition. The unification's greater goal will be not only to return all blood signature leans to the vertical, but also to forever rid the world of forestallments. This will allow a return to free will, which, because of blood signature lean, neither side truly possesses. Despite what you might have been led to believe, blood signatures did not always show a perceptible lean one way or the other. As endowed human beings evolved, so did this trait that so strongly influences them to pursue one side of the craft or the other. The stronger the blood quality, the stronger the compulsion. If all blood signatures can be aligned to the vertical without exception, perhaps blood signature lean can be wiped out for good. And without forestallments, people will again spend lifetimes learning to use magic rather than simply having its many gifts so easily imbued into their blood, thereby ending the overuse of the craft. Because the craft's many gifts can be so readily imbued into endowed blood by forestallment, even here in Shashida many of our endowed persons have dedicated themselves to little more than lives of outright leisure. We have not yet succumbed to the depravity of the Rustannicans, but that is not to say it couldn't happen. Hard work and the satisfaction of the struggle needed to learn the craft the traditional way—and with it a better appreciation of its many gifts—are becoming a thing of the past. Something earned by sweat and toil is far more treasured than that which has been effortlessly given. A new, unified culture will be forced to begin again, and to live in peace for the good of the craft and all mankind despite our differences. Forestallments were first conceived by the *Pon Q'tar* to quickly empower their mystics with powerful, destructive gifts. They believed—and rightly so—that if they could do this fast enough, their mystics and soldiers could easily crush us. They nearly succeeded."

Amazed by what he had just heard, Tristan looked over at Renjiro. "This is what you meant earlier, isn't it," he asked, "when you said that if we are to succeed in saving the craft and ourselves, we must first banish some of its applications and forever destroy the tools that have allowed those applications to flourish? That also means destroying the Tome and the two Scrolls."

"Yes," Renjiro answered. "And all such documents and research on this side of the world as well. Here in Shashida, the Tome and two Scrolls do not carry the great importance that you place on them. To us, they are little more than children's craft primers, and they are not needed. The Vagaries Scroll was created by the *Pon Q'tar* and left behind on the world's eastern side so that future generations of Vagaries practitioners might find it and put its forestallment calculations to the same use as here. Failee found the Scroll, but it came into her grasp too late to help her win the Sorceresses' War. The next time the Scroll surfaced it was in Nicholas' hands. Then it came to be owned by Krassus, Wulfgar, Serena, and finally you and your Conclave. Although doing so went against our better judgment, we were forced to create a Vigors Scroll and leave it behind so that it might counterbalance the Vagaries Scroll. It also came into Nicholas' grasp but was stolen by the orphans called Marcus and Rebecca and was later given to you. The Tome and the Paragon were also created by us and left behind for the same reasons. Because we feared that the Tome might fall into the hands of Vagaries practitioners, we were forced to make its revelations purposely obscure."

Tristan looked over at Wigg and Tyranny. Tyranny still seemed stunned, but Wigg's expression had become resigned, accepting.

"You agree with this plan, don't you," Tristan said.

Wigg nodded soberly. "Now that I understand it, I do indeed," he answered. Lacing his long fingers together and placing his hands atop the table, Wigg looked at Mashiro.

"But I suspect that there is something more to your hopes and dreams than what you have told us," he said. "And as you told Tyranny, it might be best summed up in two words."

Mashiro smiled. *The wizard has grasped it,* he thought. "And what might they be?" he asked.

"Respectful tolerance," Wigg answered. "The concept that all Vigors and the Vagaries practitioners have done the things they did because they were compelled to do so by the nature of their blood. And that if this concept can be universally accepted and all blood signatures made the same, each side can forgive the other. Then the healing can truly begin."

"Well said," Kaemon spoke up from the other side of the table. "Now you understand that your many struggles east of the Tolenkas were only the beginning. The real war is here, and you have become a part of it."

Tristan suddenly felt a distant memory tug at his mind. It was a puzzling recollection whose meaning had long eluded him. At long last he had his answer.

"Krassus . . . ," he said softly.

"What of Krassus?" Wigg asked.

"It happened the day I awakened to find myself a slave on one of his demonslaver ships," Tristan answered. "Before condemning me to the galleys, Krassus ordered me tied to a chair and he beat me. I defied him, and I told him that like Nicholas, he represented nothing but evil. Until this moment, his answer mystified me."

"What did he tell you?" Wigg asked.

Tristan thought for a moment, trying to remember the Vagaries wizard's words.

"*Evil?*" Tristan quoted. "*He who has yet to be trained calls me evil? Don't you know that there are no such things as good or evil, Chosen One? There are only the Vigors and the Vagaries. Tell me, dear prince, do you really believe that Failee was 'evil'? Or was she simply doing what she was compelled to do? Given the undeniable call of her left-leaning signature, did she truly have a choice? Don't you see, you fool? It is the same with me. I'm not 'evil.' I don't even know the meaning of the word.*"

Tristan looked at Mashiro. "You speak of tolerance," he said. "Do you mean to say that all the Vagaries practitioners—no matter how vile— should be forgiven their terrible deeds because their blood compelled them to perform them?"

Mashiro sighed. "That is a question that has plagued us ever since the discovery of blood signature lean and the terrible realization that it easily induces us into vastly opposing actions and beliefs," he answered. "Shashidan philosophers have spent aeons trying to learn the answer to that question but to no avail. I cannot say whether the Vagaries practitioners should be forgiven any more than we should be, for what they believe are the many transgressions that we perpetrated on them. But what I do know is that it calls into question the conflicting natures of 'good' and 'evil.' Perhaps this is what Krassus was trying to tell you. Can one exist without the other? I don't know. But like the two sides of the craft, it seems that they at least need one another, if for no other reason than to justify their existence. Perhaps the true answer will only be found if everyone's blood signatures are altered to the vertical. With the full and lasting return of free will, if people freely choose to practice the Vagaries and to hurt and enslave others, perhaps only then might they legitimately be pronounced 'evil,' and rightly punished for their deeds. But until that day, all this is simply a matter of semantics. Before our dreams can come true, Vespasian must be stopped. If not, we and the Vigors that we so cherish might well perish from the earth. Should we fail, at the least Rustannica's ability to continue this monstrous war will be prolonged, perhaps interminably so. And because we believe that if one side of the craft perishes, then so too will the other, we fight from a unique perspective and for a far different goal than do the Rustannicans. Unlike them, we do not fight to destroy the opposite side of the craft, but to save both sides."

"How do you plan to stop Vespasian's advance?" Tyranny asked.

"Our forces are gathering to meet them as we speak," another female *Inkai* answered. "The only reason that we haven't engaged them yet is because we learned that a reigning *Jin'Sai* was finally crossing the Azure Sea. With you in our midst the entire nature of the battle plan must be changed. Now that you are here, our new plan can begin in earnest— provided, of course that you agree to help us defeat Vespasian. Contrary to what you might have guessed, so far we have purposely not provided his forces with much resistance."

"Why not?" Tristan asked.

"Because the place from which he must take our gold is unique and also the best place in which to trap his forces," she answered. "Vespasian surely knows this, but because he needs the gold, he has no choice."

Tristan looked across the table at the *Inkai* whom Mashiro had introduced as Haru of the House of Eagles. She seemed younger than the other elders, with dark hair that was streaked with gray. Her sky-blue robe bore white embroidered eagles. She was an attractive woman with piercing blue eyes.

Tristan gave Haru a curious look. "Why would your choice of a battle plan depend on my participation?" he asked. "I remain untrained in the ways of the craft. The powers of my Conclave mystics do not begin to rival yours, and my Minions are but a paltry few when compared with your reputedly immense forces. We will of course do all that we can to help. But how can such less powerful souls as we possibly make any difference in this struggle?"

Renjiro leaned forward and looked directly at Tristan. "You and Vespasian possess the highest quality endowed blood in the world," he answered. "His blood is the full equal of yours. Your crossing paths this way is earth-shattering in its importance to the craft and the world that it governs. Had you not been born when you were, Vespasian and his forces would surely defeat us. It is highly unlikely that a confluence of such amazingly powerful opposing bloodlines will ever occur again. You two have the potential to become the world's greatest leaders and warriors—you of the Vigors and he of the Vagaries. Thanks to Gracchus' teachings, Vespasian will soon reach his full potential. But you have not had such training, and it will be our task to ready you at last. What follows will surely be the final battle for dominance. Either we will win and both sides of the craft will flourish for the good of all mankind, or Vespasian and his forces will defeat us and the craft will cease to exist, plunging the world into never-ending darkness and chaos."

His gaze growing sterner, Renjiro locked his dark eyes onto Tristan's. "For you see, *Jin'Sai*," he said, "Vespasian has been carefully groomed and trained all his life by the *Pon Q'tar* to serve only one purpose—to lead them to final victory over Shashida. We suspect that his blood holds gifts of which even he is not aware—gifts that his *Pon Q'tar* masters will unleash at the right moment. Vespasian believes that he is their ruler, and in some ways that is true. But he is also their puppet and their ultimate tool of war. If you agree, we will train you in the same fashion, for only you can lead us to victory against the human abomination that the *Pon Q'tar* has produced. The result will be a battle between titans such as the world has never seen. In this way your fabled destiny will finally come to fruition."

Shocked yet again by Renjiro's words, for several moments Tristan sat in silence. Finally he found his voice.

"But Vespasian has had a lifetime to prepare for this struggle!" Tristan protested. "What you suggest seems impossible. How can you train me so fast?"

"By making you Vespasian's equal," Renjiro answered sternly.

"But *how* . . . ?" Tristan asked.

"We must to do the very things that we have so come to dread," Renjiro answered quietly. "Because of their supreme quality, only your blood and his are strong enough to survive what must be done to them to achieve ultimate power in the craft. Some among us consider our plan to be the ultimate abuse of the craft, but we have little choice if we are to survive." Pausing for a moment, Renjiro gazed again into Tristan's eyes.

"Just as the *Pon Q'tar* did with Vespasian, we intend to imbue your blood signature with forestallments that have long been banned because they might literally mean the end of the world."

CHAPTER XL

RISING FROM HER SEAT AT THE WAR TABLE, PERSEPH-
one walked to the command tent flap and gazed outside. The
day had grown late, but aside from the lengthening shadows, the view
had changed little since Vespasian and Lucius had departed to inspect
the battle zone. Gracchus had grown weary of waiting for Vespasian's
return and went to attend to other matters. Saying that she was tired,
Julia Idaeus had gone off to rest in her private tent chamber. Persephone was glad to have some quiet time alone.

As she looked down the long slope, she saw that it was still blanketed
with row after row of legionnaires marching to the front. This was the
empress's first foray into war, and although she took no part in the fighting, she believed herself to be an important part of this campaign. Vespasian wisely relied on the advice of all his counselors before making
important decisions. But Persephone had always been his greatest confi-
dante and most trusted friend, and in many ways he valued her opinion
above all others. Although her experience afield was limited, her schooling in military tactics and the history of war was every bit as comprehen-
sive as her husband's. One look at a war map was all she needed to sum
up a situation and give Vespasian a valid and well-conceived opinion.

But Vespasian valued Persephone's advice for more than just her
schooling, her intelligence, or her powerful command of the craft. Un-

like Vespasian's other advisors, she had no need to curry favor by agreeing with him when she might otherwise not, or by fawning loyalty so as to win a higher position in the government pecking order. Be her always frank advice welcome or unwelcome, Vespasian could rest assured that it came from her heart rather than from some ulterior personal need.

Walking back to the table, Persephone poured another cup of wine, then sat down and again consulted the many war maps lying there. So far the campaign was succeeding brilliantly. But like Vespasian and Lucius, she was concerned by their string of easy successes, and couldn't entirely dismiss the feeling that their legions were marching into a Shashidan trap. But also like her husband and their trusted First Tribune, she believed that it was too early in the campaign for the Shashidans to suspect their ultimate goal.

There were valid reasons for optimism. The Rustannican forces were still too far away for the *Inkai* to be sure of their enemy's ultimate objective, and Vespasian's invasion route into Shashida had been used several times before by other emperors whose purposes had been vastly different. From their current position, the Rustannican legions could turn in various directions, each one heading toward a worthwhile objective. It was hoped that only when the legions came far closer to the gold mines would the *Inkai* realize the daring nature of the Rustannicans' plan.

Moreover, taking the Shashidan mines had never been tried. Conquering Shashida's gold supplies had long been considered by both sides to be reckless to the point of military insanity. The Shashidans knew that their mines were nearly unassailable and that any attempt by the enemy to take them would result in huge, perhaps devastating Rustannican losses, even if the mines were taken. Vespasian's intelligence reports claimed that because of these beliefs, the Shashidans had grown complacent about protecting the mines and sometimes reduced the number of troops there to employ them elsewhere in the war.

Persephone was no fool, and she knew that Vespasian's ability to convince the Suffragat was due to more than his well-known powers of persuasion. Much of the Suffragat's agreement was because Rustannica's economic woes had dramatically worsened and this attack or something much like it simply had to occur. The Suffragat could only hope that like the Rustannican general populace, the Shashidan *Inkai* were ignorant of the desperate state of the Rustannican treasury. For if they knew the truth, the true motive behind this invasion would come to light too soon and perhaps spell an early defeat.

Because of the vast Borderlands separating the two nations, the Suffragat had long believed that the likelihood of Shashidan agents spying in Rustannica was small, lending strength to the hope that taking the mines was still a military secret. But even the Suffragat could not know for sure. Random blood signature examinations meant to ferret out Shashidan spies were regularly carried out by roving bands of centurions, but few such agents were ever found. And given the millions of people living in Rustannica, trying to randomly unmask enemy spies this way was haphazard at best. Even so, rumors of a Shashidan spy network called the League of Whispers persisted.

After putting down her wine cup, Persephone looked around the command tent. Although she was a lady through and through, she was no shrinking violet. She enjoyed the campaign's noise, activity, and sense of urgency. In a way she even enjoyed the simpler but still comfortable surroundings in which she now lived.

This war tent and those adjoining it were large and ornately decorated. Many more colorful tents like it stood nearby, each one topped with red banner bearing the imperial eagle embroidered in gold. One dozen of these tents housed the *Pon Q'tar*, another served as Lucius' personal quarters, yet another as Julia Idaeus' living area, and the fourth and largest held Vespasian and Persephone's private rooms. The area in which the empress sat was the communal command tent, its spacious focal point connected by canvas corridors to the other tents. In this way the Femiculi, the emperor and empress, the First Tribune, and the *Pon Q'tar* could reach the command tent without having to trespass through each other's private quarters. This series of interconnected tents was an ingenious arrangement that the Rustannican war machine had used in the field for centuries.

Like her and Vespasian's private areas, the central command tent was sumptuous and comfortable. Patterned rugs lay on the grass and tapestries hung on the tent walls. Supported by golden poles, the eight-part canvas ceiling rose to a high point in the center of the room. Upholstered chairs, sofas, and benches were placed about, and oil lamps hung at regular intervals from the golden roof beams. A long sideboard offered up food, wine, and other delicacies. Before a tray or pitcher could become empty or its contents stale, camp skeens immediately refreshed them. Watchful centurions always stood guard outside the command tent and the connecting tents.

Tired of studying the war maps, Persephone rose from her chair and walked across the room to gaze into a full-length mirror. Although the dress she wore was simpler than something she might have chosen at the imperial palace, she looked lovely. The light blue silk highlighted her eyes, and her gold jewelry sparkled in the soft, warm light cast by the many oil lamps. As a matter of practicality while afield, she had collected her long blond hair behind her neck with a sapphire clasp, allowing it to fall along the graceful arch of her back. She was a beautiful woman, and despite her lofty position she carried herself without pretension or arrogance.

Persephone was everything Vespasian could have asked for in a mate—save for the one flaw that had produced a crack in her heart and stubbornly refused to heal. She had gladly given him everything she had, everything she was, and everything she would ever be. In return he loved her with an ardor and fidelity unheard of during the reigns of past emperors, who brazenly took lovers despite their empresses.

Yet there was one last gift that she had yet to bestow, and she deeply mourned her failure to do so. Worse, it was the one thing that she wanted to give him most of all, and what she knew that he hungered most to receive. She had yet to give him an heir.

Persephone knew that she was a strong woman and a Vagaries sorceress without equal. Should Vespasian die, she believed that she could effectively rule in his stead. Even so, she felt unfulfilled. Despite her immense command of the craft and the fact that she was one of the most powerful people in Rustannica, her inability to do what most women took for granted often made her feel inferior and alone. Vespasian always comforted her during these times of self-doubt, telling her that it didn't matter and that there was still much time left in which to try. But when he said such things she could sense the pain lying behind his words. The *Pon Q'tar* had chosen her to be his bride, and neither of them had been given any choice in the matter. Because of that she often wondered whether Vespasian harbored any resentment about not being able to live his life as he chose or with whom he chose. Another woman would have probably given him a child, she knew.

But Persephone also knew that right now it didn't matter—nothing did, save for their loving each other and overseeing the final death blow to the Vigors. And so she would do her best to put her personal inadequacies aside until the campaign was through. If they were victorious, she and Vespasian could keep trying to have a child. And if not it wouldn't matter, for they would probably be dead.

Just then she saw Lucius stride into the command tent. She was surprised not to see Vespasian by his side. After looking around, the First Tribune hurried toward her and took her hands into his. His face bore a worried expression.

"Are you alone?" he whispered.

Persephone nodded. "Where is Vespasian?" she asked.

"I'm glad you're here, Empress," he said loudly, as if trying to make sure that he was heard outside the tent. Then his conspiratorial look returned.

"There is something I must show you!" he whispered. "Stay here, and no matter what happens, let me give the orders!"

As Persephone watched him hurry from the tent, she noticed that the two centurion guards were gone. Then Lucius' booming voice called out again.

"Bring it into the tent!" she heard him order. "The empress is waiting!"

To her surprise, three legionnaires carried a great rug into the tent. The rug was rolled up and lay across their strong shoulders. On Lucius' order they placed it on the ground.

"Shall we unroll your prize?" one of them asked the Tribune.

"No," Lucius answered. "I will do so myself. I had to kill three Shashidans to get it and it is to be a personal gift for the empress. Now begone!"

After giving the First Tribune crisp salutes, the legionnaires left the tent to go about their other duties.

Persephone scowled and placed her fists on her hips. "Why would you bring me a rug?" she asked. "Where is Vespasian? And what has become of the two guards who were outside the door?"

Before answering, Lucius pointed at the rolled-up tent flap. At once it came loose and fell earthward to close out the world.

"I sent the guards away!" he whispered. "You will soon see why!"

Lucius pointed at the rug and it began to unroll across the ground. As it reached its full length, Persephone was amazed to see Vespasian lying atop it. He was clearly in distress. His eyes were closed, he was bathed in sweat, and his body shook uncontrollably.

Persephone immediately realized that Vespasian was in the grip of another day terror. Before going to him, she grabbed Lucius by the shoulders. Calling on the craft, she augmented the strength in her arms and swiveled him around to face her. The look on her face was desperate.

"Does the *Pon Q'tar* know about this?" she demanded.

"No!" Lucius whispered quickly. "But it is likely that some legionnaires on their way to the front saw him like this, and we cannot assume that word of it won't reach Gracchus! Just before losing consciousness, Vespasian told me to hide him in the chariot and bring him straight to you. He said that no one else was to know. I did as I was told."

Lucius looked down at his friend of so many years. In all his life he had never seen Vespasian so helpless. The sight of the most powerful mystic in the world humbled and struck down so quickly by an unseen enemy had unnerved the stalwart tribune.

"What is wrong with him?" he asked Persephone. "He talked as though this has happened before."

"It has," she answered. "And now that you have seen it, there can be no going back for you. I'm sorry that you had to become involved in this, Lucius, but what's done is done. This was never our intent. I thank the Afterlife that you were there when it happened! You did well to bring him to me unnoticed."

Persephone sat down on the rug and took Vespasian into her arms. Lucius watched sadly as she rocked her husband back and forth like the child she never had.

"Shall I call for a healer?" Lucius asked.

"No!" Persephone answered. "I know of nothing that can be done for him. He must return to us on his own." Suddenly the look on her face became commanding.

"And now you too know the secret," she declared.

Looking down at her stricken husband, she wiped his brow and smoothed his damp blond curls. Despite her legendary skills in the craft, she was helpless to save the person she most loved in the world. That painful awareness caused her recent thoughts to resurface, and she realized that this was yet another way in which she had failed him. *I can't cure him, but I can protect him,* she decided. She looked back up at Lucius.

"What I am about to tell you must remain a secret," she said. "Only we three know about the emperor's affliction. If the *Pon Q'tar* or any other Suffragat members learn of it they might declare him unfit to lead this badly needed campaign. In the end, that defeat would crush Vespasian as surely as this affliction might. The Suffragat has the right to declare him unfit, but we must hide his secret. If word of this gets out I shall know that it came from you and I will kill you myself, do you understand?"

"Yes, Empress," Lucius answered respectfully. "I love him too. But is there nothing that we can do for him?"

"Pick him up," she ordered. "We must take him to our private quarters before anyone else comes in! Only there can I protect him and explain away his absence! Hurry now!"

Lucius bent down to take Vespasian into his arms. With the empress leading the way, the First Tribune carried Vespasian down one of the many connecting canvas corridors and into the safety of the emperor's personal quarters.

SCARCELY ABLE TO BELIEVE WHAT SHE HAD JUST HEARD, Julia Idaeus stood stock-still, praying that she hadn't been noticed. She stood only two meters away, just out of view down the long canvas corridor that connected her private quarters to the communal war tent. Finished with her rest, she had decided to rejoin Persephone to see whether she could coax the empress into telling her something that might be useful to the *Inkai*.

Never in her wildest dreams had she expected to hear such revelations as these. As she neared the war tent and heard the urgent conversation taking place there, she had immediately halted, then called a spell to cloak her endowed blood so that the empress and the First Tribune would not sense her presence.

After Persephone and Lucius spirited Vespasian away, she stood in the canvas corridor, thinking. They would likely not return for some time, she guessed.

Deciding to enter the war tent, with shaking hands she poured a cup of wine, then went to sit on one of the finely upholstered benches. She could not know how long she might have the luxury of being alone, and she would use every precious moment to think.

What she had just overheard was vastly important, and the *Inkai* must be informed at once. She had found but one safe occasion to commune with them since that day in the Hall of Antiquity, using that instance to supply them with vital details regarding Vespasian's advance. To her delight, she had been told that the *Jin'Sai* had finally reached Shashida.

But the news that she had just stumbled across might be even more valuable, she realized, and the *Inkai* must be told straightaway. All she needed was another safe opportunity to do so, but when and where?

Taking another sip of the excellent wine, she smiled to herself as she ended the spell cloaking her blood.

CHAPTER XLI

RENJIRO'S WORDS HIT TRISTAN LIKE A THUNDERBOLT.
"Just as the *Pon Q'tar* did with Vespasian, we intend to imbue
your blood signature with forestallments that have long been banned
because they might literally mean the end of the world. . . ."

Renjiro's mention of banned spells immediately reminded Tristan of
his first visit to Crysenium and what the envoy Miriam had told him
about the early days of the War of Attrition. She too had mentioned
spells that had been banned from use by both sides of the conflict. As
Tristan thought about it further, the pieces of Renjiro's mysterious announcement fell into place. The sudden awareness was terrifying.

The *Pon Q'tar* was about to take the struggle to the highest level. The
only thing holding them back had been their need for an endowed person of supremely powerful blood whom the Shashidans could not effectively counter. With the birth of Vespasian they finally had one. And
only Tristan's blood was the supposed equal of the emperor's.

Tristan looked into Renjiro's eyes. "It's true, then—I'm the only one
who can stop this," he said. "The *Pon Q'tar* will try to take your gold because no matter what else happens, they still need the gold to keep their
nation from falling apart. But afterward they will try to accomplish far
more. They wish to destroy Shashida completely—to wipe its civilization from the face of the earth with one stroke. Using the banned spells,

they mean to do with this one campaign what they have failed to achieve in aeons of relentless conventional war. You're right, Renjiro. With Vespasian's coming they finally have the ultimate weapon with which to realize their dreams."

A blank look on his face, Tristan sat back in his chair. "I beg the Afterlife," he breathed. "Despite its disastrous consequences, it's an inspired plan." Suddenly something else occurred to him and he shot a quick glance at Mashiro.

"Does Vespasian fully understand his role in all this?" he asked.

Mashiro sadly shook his head. "We can't be sure, but we have reason to doubt it," he answered. "Our best guess is that he still believes that the entire battle plan concerns only taking the mines. If we're right, the *Pon Q'tar* will tell him soon enough. We suspect that Vespasian's blood already possesses these awful gifts, but that he remains unaware of them."

"Why would the *Pon Q'tar* not inform him?" Tristan asked.

"Excuse me," Wigg interjected. "Would someone please explain what you're talking about?"

A short smile crossed Tristan's lips. "As you have been so fond of telling me over the years, you already have the needed information," he answered. "You simply don't understand how it all falls into place. I must say that it feels good to explain something to *you* for a change."

Wigg pursed his lips. "Then I suggest that you enlighten this simple old wizard and your Conclave privateer," he said. Sitting back in his chair, he crossed his arms over his chest.

"It all goes back to something Miriam told me in Crysenium before she and the other Envoys were killed," Tristan answered. Before continuing he shot a questioning glance at Mashiro. "Am I right?" he asked.

"I don't know," the *Inkai* elder answered. "After all, I wasn't there. Any time I know you speak in error I'll humbly correct you, *Jin'Sai*."

"Fair enough," Tristan answered.

"And so?" Wigg eagerly pressed.

Tristan looked back at the First Wizard. He took a deep breath, as if even he couldn't believe what he was about to say.

"I told the Conclave the things Miriam said to me about the early days of the War of Attrition," Tristan said. "Surely you remember them."

Wigg nodded. "Yes," he answered. "But it seems that you have taken those revelations a step further in meaning."

Tristan thought for a moment as he tried to recall Miriam's words.

"Aeons ago, everyone here lived in a fragile and tense coexistence," he said. "Then the Vagaries practitioners became fanatically devoted to the dark side of the craft. Eventually they split away and started the civil war. What followed was a miscalculation beyond description."

Wigg nodded. "Go on," he said.

"During the war's early years the Vagaries rebels used especially dark magic to influence the forces of nature," Tristan explained. "Spells were formulated that allowed them to employ natural phenomena as weapons of war. The destruction was unprecedented, and millions died. To survive, the Vigors practitioners had no choice but to do the same thing, even though it went against their principles." Suddenly realizing something else, Tristan again glanced over at Mashiro.

"These environmental spells are much like the forestallments, aren't they?" he asked. "They represent a direction in which you would have preferred not to take the craft, but you had to follow the *Pon Q'tar*'s lead to ensure the survival of the Vigors."

Mashiro nodded. "Well done," he said. "Please continue."

"Before the war started, what we now call Eutracia and Parthalon were part of this world," Tristan added. "The Tolenkas didn't exist, nor did the Sea of Whispers. The lands encompassing Eutracia and Parthalon were one and the same. Once loosed, the dark environmental magic produced devastating and unexpected side effects. The Tolenkas suddenly arose and the land mass separated, creating the Sea of Whispers. Since then these environmental and seismic arts have been abandoned by both sides because their far-reaching effects might kill their users as easily as the enemy. But the formulas were held in reserve by each side, in case the other should try such madness again."

Tristan looked at Mashiro. "The *Pon Q'tar* plans to resurrect these ancient arts, don't they?" he asked. "The only reason why they abandoned them at all was because they knew that you could retaliate in kind. But with Vespasian among them, they know that if they imbue these gifts into his blood, Shashida will be defeated once and for all. Nothing could stand against the lethal combination of his blood quality and those dark arts."

"Well done," Hoshi said. "But there remains much that you don't know. Long ago, a treaty was signed between Rustannica and Shashida that outlawed environmental spells by both sides. Until now the *Pon Q'tar* has kept its word. Every *Inkai* you see here took part in the negotiations, and at first we had hoped for an outright end to the war. We were rebuffed on that score, but the *Pon Q'tar* did agree to ban the nature spells because they realized that more than anything else, those particularly powerful craft devices could mean their defeat. Gracchus and I were the treaty's chief architects, and it was signed in the no-man's land that is the Borderlands. Every *Inkai* and *Pon Q'tar* member signed the document. Many of those people are still alive. The Borderlands Treaty has survived the test of time, but we fear that the *Pon Q'tar* is about to violate it."

"How long ago was the treaty signed?" Tyranny asked.

"One hundred and fifty-one centuries past," Hoshi answered. "Each side agreed to never use this terrible kind of magic again. But two unique occurrences have intersected in time to tempt the *Pon Q'tar* into rethinking their position. One is the depletion of the Rustannican treasury, and the other is the birth and coming to manhood of Vespasian Augustus I. Had either of these events occurred separately, the *Pon Q'tar* mightn't feel so emboldened yet also so deeply threatened at the same time. If the banned spells are used by Vespasian, he will summon unheard-of power. We have no wish to reply in kind, but if we are to survive, it seems we must fight back with a weapon of equal ferocity. Our use of such spells was stopped, but our research into their workings was not. Surely the *Pon Q'tar* has been doing similar, if not superior, study. In the entire world only the *Jin'Sai's* blood and Vespasian's are strong enough to accept these advanced but untried spells without dying. But the stakes might rise even higher than that. If Vespasian uses these gifts improperly, it could mean more than the destruction of Shashida. It could cause the vaporization of the entire planet."

Tristan sat quietly for a moment. "And you wish me to become a weapon like Vespasian, an ultimate destroyer of worlds," he said. "I thought that my mission was to be one of peace."

"That was our wish as well," Mashiro said, "and so we agreed to the Envoys' plan. But as we have said, that prospect is dead. We asked for none of this, *Jin'Sai*. Now it seems that if we are to find a lasting peace, there is but one way. As I said, while the *Pon Q'tar* fights to destroy the Vigors, we fight to save *both* sides of the craft. Not to resist Vespasian and the *Pon Q'tar* would mean the end of Shashida. With our civilization gone, the *Pon Q'tar* could turn their full efforts toward finding a way across the Tolenkas to your side of the world. One day they will eventually succeed, or perhaps Vespasian might use his banned spells to do it for them. No matter how it happens, your sister and her meager forces will never stop them. Their next step would be to destroy the Vigors Orb, just as Wulfgar twice tried to do and failed. But the *Pon Q'tar* will not fail. With the Vigors destroyed, the world will plunge into a craftless, endless chaos from which it will never recover. The many gifts of peace, order, and balance that the craft provides will be no more, and barbarism will forever reign. The *Pon Q'tar* embrace a frame of mind in which madness is their only muse."

Tristan quietly looked around the table. *The War of Attrition is indeed aeons old,* he realized. *And after all this time, things are about to change radically. Vespasian will be the catalyst of this seismic shift in the craft, and it falls to me to try to stop him.*

"There can be but one way that you are so well informed," Wigg suggested. After taking another sip of umake he set the cup back on the table, then placed his hands into opposite robe sleeves.

"You've placed a spy in their midst, haven't you?" he asked. "Given the quality of your information, this must be a person of some importance in Rustannica. And brave, too, considering the heinous things we have heard about the place. You have my compliments. Inserting a spy into the upper reaches of the Rustannican power elite was surely no easy feat. I suspect that doing so took a very long time, and that this asset is of immense value to you."

"You are correct," Haru replied. "Her name is Julia Idaeus. Not only is she the reigning Femiculi, she is also a member of the League of Whispers. The League is a secret society in Rustannica made up entirely of Shashidan mystics who feign loyalty to the empire and adopt Rustannican names. Unknown to the *Pon Q'tar,* two of the Priory's many Sisters are League members. After gaining the post of Femiculi, Julia was able to influence the *Pon Q'tar* into unknowingly accepting another League woman into the sisterhood. Her name is Agrippina Sertorius."

"How did the League come about?" Tyranny asked.

"During the early days of the war, the Borderlands did not exist, and it was far easier to enter Rustannica than now," Midori answered. "We asked for volunteers of right-leaning endowed blood to go and live in Rustannica with the understanding that they could never return home. Tens of thousands of loyal Shashidan men and women offered to join the newly forming League. The selection process was rigorous. So as to constantly disguise his or her blood, each volunteer had to be an expert mystic. In the end, more than two thousand were chosen." Renjiro took another sip of umake and looked around the table.

"After being trained in certain specialized gifts, they were secretly inserted into Rustannica by way of azure portals," he added. "To avoid being seen, they were sent to sparsely populated areas, then told to make their way to the cities and begin Rustannican lives. Because they had endowed blood and large sums of gold were transported with them, they soon became well-respected krithians. This part of the ruse was needed because only krithians can rise to positions of power in Rustannica. Most are acquainted with at least some of their fellow League members. If not, they can identify one another by way of whispered code phrases that have remained largely unchanged for aeons. Despite their wealth and status, their lives are difficult, and they live in constant fear of being found out. Each member carries a death forestallment in his or her blood that allows for instantaneous suicide without need of a physical weapon. We could not grant them time enchantments for fear of drawing undue attention their way. To avoid the adulteration of their right-leaning blood and to maintain the survival of the League, they can only marry other League members. Finding a mate is often difficult, but they manage. To help in that regard, many marriages are secretly arranged at childhood."

"Do you mean to say that the League members now living in Rustannica were all born there?" Tristan asked. "They must have been, because so much time has passed. It would also follow that your spies are many generations removed from the people you first sent there, and that those first League members are long dead, and that your current spies have never seen home."

"That's right," Mashiro answered. "When children of right-leaning blood are born to two League members, they are raised by them. On reaching a responsible age they are secretly taught our customs and beliefs as well as those of Rustannica. In this way it was hoped that some of them might reach stations of prominence in the Rustannican hierarchy. Because League children are born there, their Rustannican heritage is not questioned, and there is no limit to how high they might rise. Long ago one League member rose to the rank of Heretic, but he was unknowingly killed in battle by our troops."

"But now there is Julia Idaeus, the Priory Femiculi," Renjiro said. "Julia rose from humble beginnings and never took a husband or lover so that she might keep her virginity and apply for Priory membership. To our delight she was accepted, then worked hard and sacrificed much to become the reigning Femiculi. She is the first and only League member to become a voting member of the Suffragat, and her loyalty to Shashida is unshakable. Vespasian unwittingly made a great mistake when he ordered that Julia be a member of the committee responsible for devising the war plan. Julia is not only conversant with the entire scheme, but she also travels with the legions to perform the auspiciums. Because of her membership in the Suffragat, she must be informed of any changes to the battle plan. She communes with us when she can to supply us with vital information. She is also the lone Suffragat member to whom the citizens may come bearing their supplications. As such, she is well informed regarding the mood of the Rustannican citizenry. I daresay that she is more in touch with the common people than is Gracchus or Vespasian, which is yet another advantage to her position. We cannot overemphasize her importance to our cause."

"What are the 'auspiciums'?" Wigg asked.

"The auspiciums are yet another of the *Pon Q'tar*'s carefully crafted fabrications," a male voice said from across the table.

Tristan looked at the *Inkai* who had been introduced as Jomei of the House of Water Lilies. Like Mashiro, he wore a drooping white mustache, and battle scars crisscrossed his aged face like lines drawn on a wrinkled old war map. His long white hair was pulled behind his head and secured with the traditional gold ornament. Embroidered white lilies adorned his white silk robe. Like Faegan's eyes, Jomei's seemed to burrow straight into Tristan's.

"The auspicium is a ritual during which a host of white birds is released into the air by the reigning Femiculi," Jomei added. "For propaganda purposes, this is usually done in full view of the populace, and always in view of the Suffragat. It is supposedly a sign of impending good or bad fortune and is performed before an important event. The direction in which the birds fly supposedly indicates whether the venture will succeed. As you might guess, Gracchus uses the craft to influence the birds' direction of flight and thus help manipulate popular opinion."

"And Julia understands that the rituals of the azure flame and the auspiciums are clever frauds?" Tristan asked.

"Yes," Jomei answered, "but the *Pon Q'tar* doesn't realize that she knows. In many ways Julia's existence is a great contradiction. She spent her entire life trying to acquire and hold a position that she knows is meaningless, yet it is that same meaninglessness that allows her to serve the highest calling of her right-leaning blood."

"When will she next commune with you?" Wigg asked.

"When she has important information and can safely do so," Kaemon answered. "Because of her dangerous situation, the timing must always be hers. Her survival requires that she perform the most delicate of balancing acts—that is, deciding when her information is of enough value to risk performing a communion. It took aeons for a League of Whispers member to rise to such a lofty station as reigning Femiculi, and we can't afford to lose her."

"You mentioned that Vespasian might not know that his blood holds the banned forestallments," Tristan said to Mashiro. "What leads you to that theory?"

"Julia informs us that the emperor has been behaving strangely," Mashiro answered. "During a recent coliseum spectacle he was taken ill and had to leave. As far as we know, Vespasian has never been sick a day in his life. The banned gifts in his blood might be adversely affecting him. His recent episode is not proof of our theory, but Julia is watching him closely, and she will report any other aberrant behavior that she sees. The other reason is that he made no mention of the banned forestallments when he proposed this unprecedented campaign to the Suffragat. Had he known, he would likely have assured the Suffragat of his willingness to use every power at his disposal. Moreover, one of the *Pon Q'tar*—Gracchus, most likely—would surely have demanded it. This is not Vespasian's first command. He has led other strikes into Shashida, some of them quite successful. Admittedly, not one of them was the size or scope of this latest one. But if he had known about his gifts during previous campaigns, he would have surely used them."

"Are you saying that the *Pon Q'tar* might have imbued these forestallments into his blood without telling him?" Tyranny asked. "Why would they do that?"

"You must never underestimate the *Pon Q'tar*'s legendary paranoia," Hoshi answered. "Their marked tendencies toward suspicion and distrust—even of others who share their blood lean—were one of the prime causes of the War of Attrition. Although Vespasian is the ultimate product of their depravity, that doesn't mean that they trust him. Despite the emperor's supreme command of the Vagaries, the banned spells are so powerful and tempting that if he knew about them, even he might be unable to resist their use. Doing so without the supervision of the *Pon Q'tar* could be disastrous, even to them. Or perhaps Vespasian's blood or psyche wasn't mature enough until now to survive the forestallments' use and so the *Pon Q'tar* did not tell him. It stands to reason that the forestallments were granted to him while he was too young to remember, or while he was in a suppressed mental state induced by the *Pon Q'tar*, or both. With the maturation of his blood, these banned forestallments might be calling out to his mind, begging to be used. This could be the reason for his recent episode and why the empress seemed so eager to rush him away. Now that the Rustannican treasury is at the breaking point, had Vespasian not suggested this campaign, the *Pon Q'tar* would surely have proposed something very much like it. In a way, he played right into their hands. The *Pon Q'tar's* ultimate weapon is ready for use, and his name is Vespasian Augustus."

"If that's true, then why don't they influence Vespasian to use his gifts straightaway?" Wigg asked.

"For the *Pon Q'tar*, one need stands far above the rest," Kaemon answered. "If Vespasian uses the banned spells first, our gold supplies might be scattered to oblivion. Remember, the research in banned spells that the *Pon Q'tar* has presumably carried out since the Borderlands Treaty likely remains untested. If so, even they cannot fully know what the results might be. Despite their other goals, the *Pon Q'tar* needs our gold to maintain order at home. The gold simply must be secured and sent back to Rustannica before Shashida is decimated. Even the *Pon Q'tar* can't risk national bankruptcy."

"But there is a more compelling reason why we believe that Vespasian's blood carries these special gifts," Hoshi said. "For research purposes, we once asked for a Shashidan volunteer of highly endowed blood into whom we might impart our own environmental spells. We had no intent to unleash them, but a host was needed to continue our studies. The results were much like what Julia sees in Vespasian, but far worse because of the volunteer's less powerful blood."

"What happened to him?" Tristan asked.

Hoshi's face took on a sad look. "He succumbed to crippling mental terrors and died soon after," she answered softly. "But he lived long enough for us to recognize the same signs in Vespasian, should Julia report them."

"There remains another reason why we must believe that Vespasian carries these banned spells in his blood and that the *Pon Q'tar* will soon unleash him on us," Mashiro said quietly.

"And what is that?" Wigg asked.

"It's too dangerous not to," the worried elder answered softly.

For several moments no one spoke. Tristan looked out through the colonnaded far wall into the lush gardens to see that night was approaching. There was still much to learn, he realized. But one supreme mystery still haunted him. It was the same one that had burned in his soul since first discovering the Caves of the Paragon and learning that his and Shailiha's blood and destiny were special. He was the *Jin'Sai,* but even now he didn't fully understand what that meant, or who he really was.

"Miriam tried to tell me something just before she died," he said to Mashiro, "but she never finished the sentence. She said: 'Your parents weren't . . . ,' and then she passed. Can you tell me what she meant?"

"Perhaps," Mashiro answered. "But it would only be an old man's guess."

"Tell me," Tristan asked.

"Had she lived, Miriam would have probably said that your parents weren't *selected.*"

"Selected?" Tristan asked.

"It has to do with why your and Vespasian's blood is so special," Hoshi answered. "The appearance of your supreme blood quality was a very rare but also a natural occurrence. Vespasian's, however, was engineered by the Heretics and the *Pon Q'tar.*"

"What do you mean?" Wigg asked.

"Like the Consuls of the Redoubt who serve your Conclave, the Rustannican Heretics serve the *Pon Q'tar,*" Hoshi said. "Many are legionary officers, second in power only to the eighty tribunes. But others of them once followed another, darker purpose. For aeons it was their task to examine the blood signatures of all newborn endowed Rustannican infants. They searched for one specific female blood signature and one male signature. Many centuries ago they found the female, and they kidnapped her. When she reached her prime childbearing years, she was granted the time enchantment so that she would grow no older. She was imprisoned in luxurious surroundings in Ellistium and zealously guarded by the *Pon Q'tar* as they waited for the needed male signature holder to be found. Fifty Seasons of New Life ago, that male child finally came to light. Thirty years later he reached his sexual peak, then he and the woman were forced to mate under the watchful eyes of the *Pon Q'tar* until she conceived. The result was Vespasian Augustus I. He was taken from his parents and suckled by numerous veiled wet nurses so that no maternal or parental attachments would form in his psyche. From the day of his birth, his only 'parents' and mentors have been the *Pon Q'tar.*"

Tristan shook his head. "It's monstrous," he breathed. "Are you saying that he has no knowledge of his true past?"

"Precisely," Jomei answered. "But there is more to this twisted tale. Immediately after Vespasian was born, his mother and father were again locked away in separate prisons. We surmise that they remain alive. Vespasian is unaware of their existence. He and Persephone believe that Vespasian was an orphan, raised and trained by the *Pon Q'tar* out of the 'goodness' of their hearts."

"I can understand why the *Pon Q'tar* wants Vespasian to believe that his parents are dead," Tyranny mused. "It helps to ensure his loyalty. But why does the *Pon Q'tar* keep Vespasian's parents alive? Surely their continued existence represents a threat to the *Pon Q'tar*'s credibility should Vespasian somehow learn the truth. His rage over how they have been treated might be incalculable."

"Can't you guess?" Wigg asked the privateer.

"They want to be able to bring another child of Vespasian's blood into the world, should their first creation fail them," Tristan breathed. He shot a questioning look at Mashiro.

"That's it, isn't it?" he asked. "That's also what you meant when you said that to save both sides of the craft, Rustannica and the *Pon Q'tar* must first be totally defeated. If Vespasian is killed and the *Pon Q'tar* live, they can do the same monstrous thing again."

"Yes," Midori said. "The thirty or so years needed to bring another such abomination to manhood or womanhood is but a blink of an eye in the maze that is the craft. All that the *Pon Q'tar* wants from Vespasian is for him to use his potent blood to help take our gold and then summon the banned forestallments that will reduce Shashida to ashes. To them he is simply a tool of war—a means to an end and nothing more. Persephone was betrothed to him in an arranged marriage in hopes of keeping him from pursuing and impregnating other women. They even went so far as to cast spells over the empress, making it impossible for her to conceive. They add credibility to their supposed compassion for her plight by giving her useless potions said to enhance her fertility. She is told that the worthless concoctions might help, but in truth the *Pon Q'tar* doesn't want Vespasian to father children. Being a father would create a needless distraction from his ceaseless training in the craft and might produced an unwanted reluctance in him to risk his life for their cause. When he has served their purposes, they might well kill him. Some sort of terrible accident, no doubt, that can be explained away to a grieving populace. He remains too great a threat to their power for him to live into old age."

"Who are Vespasian's parents?" Tyranny asked. "Where did they come from?"

"The girl was found in a peasant village in the Rustannican highlands," Midori answered. "The boy came from a well-placed krithian family in Ellistium. To maintain secrecy the children's families were killed by elite legionary assassins, and the murders were blamed on thieves and cutthroats who were never 'caught.' "

"How can you know all this?" Tristan asked Mashiro. "Julia is too young to have told you these things."

"Do you remember my saying that one of the League members rose to the rank of Heretic but that he was killed in battle?" Mashiro answered.

Tristan nodded.

"That man found the boy child who would later become Vespasian's father," Mashiro answered. "He was also one of the few Heretics who were granted full knowledge and participation in the *Pon Q'tar's* plan. Part of his duties included guarding the imprisoned woman who became Vespasian's mother. As a reward he was granted the time enchantment, and he lived for centuries. Being forced to participate in that travesty for so long nearly drove him to madness, but he persisted and was able to commune with us often. By then Julia had risen to the station of Priory Sister, and she and the League 'Heretic' knew each other. It was she who told us of his death, a terrible blow to our cause. Vespasian's parents still lived at the time of our rebel Heretic's death. But we have no way of knowing whether that is still the case, for even Julia has not been made privy to that information. Even so, keeping them alive would seem to be in the *Pon Q'tar's* best interests, would it not?"

"In a strange way I'm almost sorry for Vespasian," Tristan said.

Mashiro sternly shook his head. "I understand how you feel," he said. "But you cannot afford to sympathize with his plight, *Jin'Sai*. If you meet him on the battlefield you must strike quickly and with everything you have. He is the ultimate product of the Vagaries, and he would as soon kill us as draw his next breath—you above all."

"And what about me and Shailiha?" Tristan asked. "You said that our blood signatures occurred naturally. What did you mean?"

Mashiro smiled. "Unlike Vespasian's parents, yours found one another on their own. Wigg and the other Directorate Wizards chose Nicholas I to be king, and Nicholas later took Morganna as his queen. Your parents' union was natural, as were your and your sister's twin births. Unknown to your father, mother, and the late Directorate, Nicholas and Morganna carried the supreme male and female blood signature halves needed to produce the *Jin'Sai* and the *Jin'Saiou*. Your parents were each of highly endowed blood, to be sure. But only when these two magnificently powerful and opposing gender blood signature halves join to form a new one does the resulting child's blood take on such transcendent strength. You and Shailiha became those two children. In the entire history of your world, only three other such random pairings occurred. This also means that your blood signature and Shailiha's are identical with that of every *Jin'Sai* and *Jin'Saiou* who preceded you."

"And the previous *Jin'Sai*s and *Jin'Saiou*s that the Scroll Master spoke of," Tristan said, "were they our forebears?"

"In a way, they were," Kaemon answered. "But as you can imagine, for the vast majority of recorded time these two supremely gifted blood signature halves drifted apart from one another as they resided in various people's blood and were handed down from generation to generation. You and your sister are the first and only *Jin'Sai* and *Jin'Saiou* born to royalty. Nicholas and Morganna were more than just your parents—they were also the human vessels that carried the transcendent blood signature halves for a short time. They made you and Shailiha who you are, and you are right to keep on loving them and holding your memories of them dear."

Tristan sat in respectful silence for a moment, remembering. Then another question occurred to him. "Save for its lean, is my blood signature identical to Vespasian's?" he asked.

Mashiro shook his head. "We do not know. Our rebel Heretic had no opportunity to see Vespasian's blood signature before he was killed, nor has Julia. Our scholars believe that they are probably different in appearance but equally powerful."

"But what is it that gives these two—or should I say four—uniquely powerful signature halves such amazing qualities?" Wigg asked. "Why does their joining create people of such transcendent blood?"

"Our scholars have long believed that it has something to do with the two orbs," Renjiro answered. "That the orbs perhaps somehow influenced their evolution—one pair for the Vigors, another for the Vagaries. Each pair produces vastly different tendencies, to be sure, but they are probably equally powerful. In truth even we do not know. If we survive to defeat Rustannica, perhaps that will be one of the mysteries we will solve together. Aside from that, who is to say why these unique blood signatures produce such talented and extraordinary mystics? Why do some of us become geniuses of science and mathematics, or great prodigies in music and art? Nature still has her ways, and I daresay we humble humans have yet to fully understand them."

Tristan again looked through the gaps in the colonnade to the gardens lying beyond. The sun had set in earnest, and the various night creatures had started singing. A cool wayward breeze flowed through the magnificently appointed gardens, its invisible tentacles sometimes reaching into the room to gently caress his face. They brought with them unfamiliar scents, sounds, and seemingly even greater mysteries.

Because of the many things he had learned this day, Tristan had at last found a sense of quiet peace in Shashida that he had known nowhere else. At last he knew who he really was, and how he and Shailiha had come to be, and why. Questions remained, but he understood enough to put his heart at rest—at least for now.

Then his eyes caught the lovely Hoshi's once more. He was about to speak to her when Mashiro garnered his attention. Leaning over the table slightly, the *Inkai* elder gave the three newcomers a serious look.

"It is late," he said. "I fully understand that you have more questions, but the three of you should retire. But before you leave us, there is something more that you need to know. You will probably find the news disturbing."

"What is it?" Wigg asked quietly.

"You three brave travelers and everyone still aboard your Black Ships will likely never see Eutracia again," Mashiro said. "Like us, you have become trapped on this side of the world. Because of this, you should consider making Shailiha the Queen of Eutracia. Tristan will likely never return home, and Eutracia must have a ruler."

Tristan looked over at Wigg and Tyranny to see resigned expressions. Wigg nodded; Tyranny took a deep breath and tried to give Tristan a reassuring smile.

All the expedition members who had come with Tristan had done so willingly and with the knowledge that if they reached Shashida, they might never return home. But now that possibility had become fact, and the stark reality was settling in.

Tristan was not concerned for himself. He would miss Eutracia, the other Conclave members, and most of all his sister. But with Celeste dead, and knowing that his destiny lay here, he was content to stay. Wigg had lost Abbey, so there was now less reason for him to return home even if he could. Tyranny was not romantically involved, as far as Tristan knew; her great love was for the Black Ships. With the *Ellistium* destroyed and the *Cavalon* damaged beyond use, the only serviceable Black Ships resided on this side of the world. Tristan couldn't know whether she might command the great vessels again, but for her sake he hoped that she would. The other Conclave mystics who had traveled here with him had left no mates behind, and Tristan had insisted that the Minion warriors who accompanied him be unattached.

But in the end none of that mattered, for the die was cast. Reaching Shashida meant starting new lives—lives that would surely be filled with wonder and amazement. But they would also be dangerous lives that would test the limits of their courage and faith in the Vigors. What Tristan, Wigg, and Tyranny didn't know was why they couldn't return home. Pursing his lips with thought, the *Jin'Sai* turned to look at Mashiro.

"We all knew that if we reached Shashida we might never see Eutracia again," Tristan said. "But before we retire, please tell us—why are we all trapped here? What keeps everyone from crossing the Tolenka Mountains? Why can't we sail the Black Ships back the way we came?"

"The story is a complicated one," Mashiro answered, "and even we do not fully understand it. Because the hour is late, I will be brief. When the *Pon Q'tar* first used the spells that were later banned by the Borderlands Treaty, their calculations were crude by today's standards and resulted in acts of the craft that were nearly uncontrollable. As you know, when the *Pon Q'tar* employed them, the Tolenka mountain range unexpectedly arose and the land mass separated to create the Sea of Whispers. We too had immense difficulties trying to control our versions of the spells. One such spell was designed to create the Azure Sea and the stone maze that would allow only persons of right-leaning blood to sail back and forth across it and to move easily from one side of the world to the other. When we realized that the spell was going awry, we created the Tome and the Vigors Scroll to leave behind for future generations of right-leaning blood to find and use. Some of us—like the Scroll Master and the Watchwoman of the Floating Gardens—volunteered to stay behind in hiding, in the hope that Vigors practitioners would find them and that they might help you to better understand the workings of the craft. But even they could not tell you about crossing the Azure Sea because it did not yet exist. Like the *Pon Q'tar's* best efforts, ours too went awry. After the Azure Sea and the stone maze that brought you here formed, the spell took on a life of its own. That is the major drawback to the banned spells—in some cases they seem to come alive to create their own sentience and purpose. To our amazement, it evolved further and of its own choosing. Since that fateful day, we have not been able to undo it."

"Amazing," Wigg said. "What was the result?"

"As you know, the spell allows travel from east to west across the Azure Sea, but only by those possessing right-leaning blood, lest the maze's course become different and continually repeat itself," Jomei answered. "Regardless of one's blood—be that blood unendowed or endowed of any type—should he or she try to sail the Azure Sea and head east, the maze walls rise, but afterward they join, crushing everything and everyone caught between them. You were lucky. Had you turned your ships around and headed back, everyone aboard them would have suffered that terrible fate. Despite our scholars' best efforts, no answer to repairing the spell has been found. And even if one was devised, using it would violate the Borderlands Treaty, because its calculations are environmental. Even so, if the Rustannican break the treaty, our survival will mean that we must do the same."

"But that is not to say that others of right-leaning blood can't come from east to west," Tristan said.

"True," Mashiro answered. "But before doing so, they should be warned that they can never return."

"Why can't the Tolenkas be crossed from this side?" Tyranny asked.

"We are stymied by the same limitations as those living in the east," Midori answered. "The mountains are simply too high for even us to cross. The air becomes so thin that every mystic group we sent up the mountainsides returned in failure. Despite much trying, we have found no spell to overcome this obstacle. The *Pon Q'tar*'s early spell that unexpectedly created the mountain range also developed a life of its own. To this day it morphs to protect its matrix against tampering."

"If that is true, then the craft has entered a dangerous and startling new phase," Wigg said. "Or should I say, new to us three."

"Indeed," Mashiro answered.

"Because we can't go back, you are right about the need for Shailiha to become queen," Tristan said to Mashiro. He looked over at Wigg. "Do you agree?" he asked.

Wigg nodded. "She is the rightful heir, and her time has come," he said.

"Before you retire, there is something that I must ask you, *Jin'Sai*," Mashiro said. "Can you decide soon whether you will help us to defeat Vespasian? As we said, to do this we must grant you the banned fore-stallments. Because of their great power, it is likely that even we cannot imbue your blood with these gifts without causing you great physical pain. If you choose not to help us, no shame will be attached to your decision. But if the answer is to be yes, we must alter our war plan, and time is precious. We also understand that all this news is overwhelming and that you will need time to decide. But know this: Our futures and the survival of the craft are inexorably tied to yours. Vespasian and the *Pon Q'tar* must be defeated, be it now or later. If you accept, we will do everything in our power to help you." Mashiro gave Tristan a short smile, and the gleam in his eyes seemed to brighten.

"After all, even the reigning *Jin'Sai* does not discover a new world every day," he added.

Tristan needed no time to decide. From the moment he took a seat at the meeting table, he had known that this strange land was where he would finally meet his destiny.

"I will answer now," he said quietly. "I cannot speak for those who accompanied me here, but for my part I will do all that I can to defeat Rustannica and her servants who wish to destroy us." Pausing for a moment, he looked over at Wigg and Tyranny.

"What say you?" he asked. "Are you with us?"

Despite the painful loss of Abbey, Wigg dredged up the semblance of a smile. "I have been alive for more than three centuries," he said. "I have loved and lost, and this night I find that is the case yet again. During all that time, I have striven to learn everything I could about the craft and to protect it from those who would see it destroyed. And now it seems that the real struggle is about to start." The wizard stared into Tristan's eyes. "I watched you and your sister come into this world not so long ago," he added softly. "From that moment forward, I have been and always will be yours."

"Thank you," Tristan answered. He turned to look at Tyranny. She in turn looked at Mashiro before answering.

"I have no endowed blood," she said. "I want to help, but how?"

Mashiro smiled. "Although you cannot summon the craft, you have unique seafaring talents," he answered. "I'm sure that something can be arranged to your liking."

"Then I'll join you," she said. "It's good for a simple privateer of un-endowed blood to know that she can contribute to the cause."

Tristan let go a short laugh. He then looked into every face around the table and raised his cup. Everyone followed suit.

"We're yours," he said. He raised his cup higher, as did the others.

"To new beginnings!" he offered.

"To new beginnings!" everyone answered.

After draining his cup, Tristan looked across the table to see Hoshi smiling at him. This time her smile was genuine and offered without reservation.

CHAPTER XLII

AS THE BOY AWAKENED, HE AGAIN FOUND HIMSELF LYING on a cold stone floor. Something hard lay between him and the stones, biting into his skin and causing him pain. Rubbing his eyes, he sat up. The familiar room was dark, but this time a burning candle in a golden holder stood atop the usual wooden stool. The candle seemed out of place, the boy realized, but it provided some welcome light.

Coming to his feet, he felt an unexpected heaviness clinging to his left hip. He looked down, and what he saw surprised him. A short sword in a tooled leather scabbard lay there. The scabbard was attached to a leather belt cinched around his waist. Reaching down, he grasped the sword hilt and slowly drew the weapon. As the blade came free, it produced a ringing sound.

Holding the sword before the faint candlelight, the boy regarded it carefully. It was at once a beautiful and a terrible thing, and its weight felt good in his hands. Lowering the sword a bit, he ran one finger across the blade to find that it was razor sharp.

Still wondering why he had been given such a magnificent weapon, he slid the sword into its scabbard, then walked to the shabby stool. Taking the candleholder into his hands, he climbed atop the stool to wait in silence for his master to arrive. Although the sword was a mystery, the boy believed that he would have the answer soon.

Unlike the times before, today he was unafraid. During his last training session with the still unidentified master, the boy had lost something but gained far more. His dreaded fear of the faceless man in the hooded robe was gone, replaced by a strange gift that the master called *K'Shari*. With the coming of that gift, rather than dread the imminent arrival of his teacher he hungered to learn the object of today's lesson. He was sure that the sword lying at his hip would be instrumental in his understanding, although he couldn't imagine how.

The door slowly opened and a shaft of light streamed into the room, hurting the boy's eyes. *This time I will not look away,* he resolved, *nor will I cover my face with my hands. I will stay strong and look into the light with courage.*

The robed figure walked into the room. Saying nothing, he placed his hands into opposite robe sleeves. The boy gazed unafraid into the dark recesses of the empty hood to again see nothing but blackness. This time the sight did not frighten him, and for a time neither student nor master spoke. Finally the hooded master took a step nearer.

"You didn't shield your eyes from the light this time," he said. "Did its sudden brightness not hurt them?"

"It did," the boy answered. "But I now know that keeping my eyes open was needed, despite the pain it brought."

"And why would that be?" the master asked.

"Because a warrior cannot fight what he cannot see," the boy answered. "I could not know who was entering the room. The pain caused by the light would surely be less than that of being killed by an unseen enemy."

"Well done," the master said. "It is time for your next lesson." Reaching out, he beckoned the boy to leave the stool and follow him.

The hallway was just as the boy remembered it. Endless and stark white, it held countless doors with golden handles. Saying nothing, the master turned left and started walking. The boy followed willingly, the heaviness of the sword at his side a reminder of its still unexplained presence.

After a long walk the master stopped before a door. He pointed a finger at the golden handle, and it levered downward. The boy and his master entered the room beyond, the door closing behind them with quiet finality. The scene before the boy was surprising. Like the hallway, the room was stark white. Two incongruous things stood before the boy, neither of which made sense to him.

On one side of the room stood a huge white bull. An iron ring was secured through its nostrils, and a chain led from that ring down to another one embedded into the floor. The bull was magnificent. Two wide black horns protruded from the top of his skull, each curving forward to nearly touch the other's point. His face was broad, his dark eyes wide apart, large, and lustrous. Strong muscles rippled beneath his skin, and as he stood there he turned to look at the boy. Everything about the animal conveyed power, courage, and strength.

On the other side of the room stood a large artist's easel. The simple wooden tripod was two meters high and one across. It held a stark white canvas, its four sides framed with simple wooden slats. An identical canvas stood propped against one wall. Save for the deep, rhythmic breathing of the great bull, the room was silent. Although the scene was bizarre, the boy did not ask about it, for he knew that the answer would come soon enough.

The master stepped forward to face the boy. The darkness of the hood seemed limitless, all-knowing.

"Slaughter the bull," the master ordered. "Do not question my order—simply follow it. Draw your gladius and kill the beast with a single stroke across its neck."

The boy did not hesitate. Reaching down to grasp the sword hilt, he pulled the weapon free with a quickness and economy of movement that he didn't know he possessed. As the blade appeared, it shone in the bright light of the room. The boy took three steps toward the white bull and raised his sword.

Without hesitation he brought the blade around in a perfect arc, slicing the bull's throat. At once the arterial spray from the gaping wound showered the boy's hands and face, but he remained undaunted. The boy again raised his sword, ready to strike again if need be.

The beast screamed in agony, then slumped to the floor on its massive cloven forelegs. As its blood poured onto the floor, the mammoth creature's hind legs also collapsed, and the bull crashed heavily onto its side. Moments passed as the exsanguination became complete and deep red blood flowed across the floor to approach the boy's boots. As if it were second nature, the boy started to wipe the sword blade against the simple robe he wore, but the master reached out to stop him.

"No," the master said. "Do not clean your weapon. Instead, dip it in the warm blood and collect more of it onto the blade."

Again the boy obeyed. Walking toward the dead bull, he bent down and ran the flat side of his sword as best he could through the growing blood pool. When he lifted the blade, the blood ran freely down the groove and onto his hands. The sight did not deter him.

"Come here," the master said. "Bring your sword and stand before the easel."

The boy did as he was told. The stark white canvas was devoid of markings. The master then walked nearer and reached out to touch the bloody sword. At once it shrank to the size of a dagger, its blade still covered with dripping blood.

"Hold the dagger not as you would a weapon, but as you would an artist's paintbrush," the master ordered.

The boy scowled, not from a wish to disobey but because he found his master's words bizarre. Even so, he adjusted the dagger in his grip, awkwardly holding it as best he could the way an artist might hold a brush. To his surprise, the blood no longer ran down the blade, but magically collected near the dagger's tip.

"Good," the master said. "Now look at me. Take in my robe, my hands, my faceless hood. Then use the dagger to paint my image on the canvas in blood. Do the best that you can. When you have finished I will comment on your effort."

Again the boy did as he was told, and to his amazement the blood flowed evenly from the dagger blade onto the canvas, just as paint would from a brush. He did the best he could, but when he was finished the result was unremarkable. Standing back from the canvas, he told the faceless one that he was done.

"A poor likeness of me, is it not?" the master asked. "Do not fret, my young charge. The results were as I expected. Can you tell me why you failed?"

The boy thought for a moment. "The tool was wrong for the task," he answered.

"True," the master answered. "But there is more to it. *Think.*"

Again the boy pondered the question. "I am the wrong person for the job," he answered. "I am a warrior, not an artist."

"Also partly correct," the master answered. "You are a warrior—that much is true. But because your blood carries the gift of *K'Shari,* you are also an artist—a *martial* artist."

The master reached out and again touched the bloody blade. At once the dagger morphed back into the original sword.

"Go to the blood pool and again dip your 'brush,' " he ordered. "Then return to me."

As the boy again dipped his sword into the blood, the master waved one arm. The crude, bloody painting sitting on the easel rose into the air and flew to the far side of the room to land on the floor. The second blank canvas then levitated to take the place of the first one. The boy returned with his bloody sword and stood before the fresh canvas.

"This time I want you to call on your gift of *K'Shari,*" the master said. "I know that the sword is cumbersome, but wield it as best you can. Use it like a great paintbrush and again try to fashion my portrait." Standing back a bit, the master clasped his hands before him and he waited.

The boy called on his new gift. As it came, he felt his blood tingle, telling him that its arrival was a matter of letting it rise to overtake his senses rather than trying to summon it from his blood. As it came, he surrendered to it willingly. Soon his sword blade glowed azure beneath the blood.

Again the boy painted his master's portrait, and this time the result was far different. As he used the sword, his movements became more abandoned, his strokes surer and more unthinking. Soon he was wielding the sword as it was intended, using great, swinging strokes and stabbing lunges as he cast the bloody "paint" onto the canvas. Exhausted, the boy finally stopped, then stood back from the easel and lowered the bloody sword. What he saw astonished even him.

The once blank canvas now held a perfect image of his master, fashioned from the blood of the bull. Every nuance of the faceless one had been captured, right down to the haunting feeling the boy always experienced when looking into the empty hood. Coming nearer, the master laid one hand on the boy's shoulder.

"Excellent," he said. "I could not have hoped for more. Can you tell me the object of today's lesson?"

All that the boy could say was to repeat his earlier answer about being the wrong person using the wrong tool. The master's hood shook to and fro, telling him he was wrong.

"There is far more to it than that," he said. "Because the answer is unusually elusive, this time I will tell you, rather than force you to search for it. As I said before, you are a martial artist, not a painter. Your task in this world is to take life, not to create beauty. When you summon your gift, wield your sword like a paintbrush, and your death-dealing will be as flawless in its own way as the portrait that you just created. Use your sword like a paintbrush, my young charge, and every stroke of your deadly art will be perfect. As it is now, your sword will again become bloodied, but no enemy will defeat you."

"I understand," the boy said quietly. Lifting the sword before his face, he looked at the drying blood that still lay on it. *How long will it be before my sword blade drips with human blood?* he wondered.

"And the bull?" he asked, turning to look into the dark hood. "Why did you have me slaughter the bull when red paint would have done as well?"

"Would it have?" the master asked. "I think not. I asked you to kill the bull so that your 'paint' would be more meaningful in the context of your lesson. Blood is the source from which all our endowed gifts flow—there is nothing else like it in the world. I wanted its warmth and texture to flow onto your hands so that you might understand how it will feel in battle, and what it means to kill. Slaughtering the bull served another purpose. Sacrificing the strongest and proudest animal in creation takes heart. It will be that same great sense of heart that will see you through your most challenging battles."

The boy nodded. "Thank you for the lesson."

"It is I who will one day be thanking you," the faceless one said.

No sooner had the master spoken than the boy heard a voice tugging at his mind. It was a woman's voice, he soon realized, coming from somewhere far away. His master was suddenly gone, as were the dead bull, the blood, and the two canvases. As he felt his consciousness slipping away, the voice grew louder and more insistent.

"Vespasian," the somehow familiar voice called out from everywhere, nowhere. "Vespasian . . . Vespasian . . ."

VESPASIAN AWOKE FROM HIS DAY TERROR WITH A GASP. AS he came around, he found himself lying on his bed in his private tent chambers. Persephone and Lucius sat by his side, worried expressions on their faces. He had been stripped of his dress armor and lay clothed only in a silk robe. Exhausted, pale, and bathed in sweat, he looked at them weakly. Then he remembered what had happened, and panic threatened to seize him anew.

Lucius and I, he thought. *On our way to the front . . . the chariot . . . the rows of tortured katsugai mosota . . . I fainted . . .*

When he again looked into Lucius' worried face, he knew. More than just he and Persephone now understood his terrible secret. He had unwittingly drawn his best friend and greatest tribune into his lie, and for that he would be eternally sorry. Not for himself, he realized, but for his dear friend who would also be forced to carry this heavy burden of secrecy and intrigue.

After trying to smile at Persephone, he again looked at Lucius. Lucius bent down and clasped his forearm to Vespasian's as one legionnaire to another.

"I'm here, my friend," he said. "Persephone told me all about it. Your secret is safe with me."

Vespasian was about to answer when Gracchus' booming voice was heard just outside the entrance to the emperor's chambers.

"I don't care whether the empress left orders not to be disturbed, you fools!" he shouted at the two centurions standing guard. "There's been a report that the emperor has been taken ill, and I demand to see him! Stand aside or there will be two more sudden deaths to add to the legions' casualty lists!"

Gracchus burst into the tent and immediately rushed to Vespasian's bed. Remembering her promise to Vespasian that his secret be kept from the *Pon Q'tar* at all costs, Persephone angrily leapt to her feet and confronted the cleric.

"How dare your enter our private quarters without permission!" she shouted. "I could have you shackled for this intrusion!"

Without responding, Gracchus stopped and looked over Persephone's shoulder at Vespasian. He then projected a commanding gaze toward the empress that rattled even her.

"Don't pretend with me, Persephone," he said sternly. "Besides, the chains have yet to be forged that could hold me, and we both know it." The lead cleric cast another quick glance at the stricken emperor.

"He has suffered an unconscious terror, hasn't he?" Gracchus demanded. "You may calm yourself, Empress, for they were expected. So, at long last they have come—and not a day too soon, I might add! Your husband isn't about to die, nor is he ill. Tell me—how many terrors has he suffered?"

Unsure what to say, Persephone looked at Vespasian. Realizing that

Gracchus somehow understood what was happening, Vespasian nodded his consent.

"This was the third," Persephone answered angrily. "What is happening to him? Explain yourself, cleric! I demand to hear what you know of this!"

Ignoring her pleas, Gracchus brushed past her and hurried to Vespasian's side. Sitting down beside Lucius, he reached out to take Vespasian's free hand. The emperor's skin felt cold and lifeless.

"What is wrong with me?" Vespasian whispered. "Am I going mad?"

Gracchus smiled and stroked Vespasian's brow. "No, my liege," he answered. "You are anything but mad. Your blood has finally matured to its fullest, and some wondrous gifts that you didn't know you owned are calling out to your mind, begging to be used. That's why the terrors have come—they are the signs that I have been waiting for. Trust me when I say that despite your fears, all is well. Tell me of your dream."

"I slaughtered a bull," Vespasian said weakly. "I used his blood to paint two portraits . . . I was but a young boy . . ."

"Ah, yes," Gracchus answered. "I remember."

Reaching out, Vespasian seized Gracchus' white and burgundy robe and pulled the cleric nearer. "How could you possibly remember *my* dream?" he shouted.

Calling the craft, Gracchus gently freed his robe from Vespasian's grasp. "Because I was there," he answered. "Your day terror was no dream, Vespasian. It was real—they all were."

Vespasian slumped back down on the bed. "Can you make them stop?" he begged. "I fear that they will tear my mind apart!"

Shaking his head, Gracchus smiled again. "Only you can make them stop," he answered.

"*How?*" Vespasian demanded. "I will do anything!"

"You can stop the terrors by using your untested gifts to help us win this war," the cleric answered. "The story is a complicated one, and at long last it is time for you to hear it. Please allow an old mystic to tell the tale."

As Gracchus started his story, Persephone approached, and Lucius eyed the cleric cautiously. As the shadows lengthened outside the tent and day turned into night, Vespasian, his empress, and the First Tribune found themselves engrossed in Gracchus' unfolding saga.

CHAPTER XLIII

 "YOU *BASTARD*!" VESPASIAN SCREAMED. "HOW *DARE* YOU gamble with my *life?*"

The emperor's face was red with rage and the cords in his neck tensed as though they were about to snap. Rising from his bed, Vespasian grabbed Gracchus' robe and pulled him so close that their faces nearly touched.

"I should kill you where you stand!" he screamed. "You, and all those other scheming harpies who make up the *Pon Q'tar*! You used *all* of us—me, Lucius, Persephone—the legions, the Priory—*everyone*! Is there no end to your treachery?"

Given the depth of Vespasian's rage, Gracchus knew that he would have but one chance to make his case. If he failed to convince the emperor here and now, Vespasian would likely kill him on the spot or send him home to suffer a violent death in the coliseum. At the least he would linger for all eternity in the Ellistium dungeons.

Just now he had few allies in this war tent. Vespasian was enraged, Persephone would do anything to protect her husband, and Lucius would like nothing better than to see the *Pon Q'tar* stripped of its power. Gracchus knew that he must convince all three that his secret reasons had been just or suffer Vespasian's wrath. Just as Gracchus had feared, his explanation of Vespasian's special gifts had sent the emperor into a heated frenzy. If Vespasian chose to kill him, even Gracchus' vaunted gifts in the craft couldn't save him from the Blood Royal's anger.

His rage taking over again, Vespasian summoned the craft, and he threw Gracchus the entire length of his private quarters. Gracchus landed hard, taking down an ornate table as he crashed to the ground. Lucius smiled broadly at the sight, and Persephone gave her husband a quick nod of support.

Gathering himself, Gracchus stiffly arose, then took a seat in an upholstered chair. He could not overpower Vespasian, so he would be forced to rely on his wits. The success or failure of his entire life's work would be decided in the next few moments.

"You haven't answered me, you piece of filth!" Vespasian snarled. "Give me one good reason why I shouldn't kill you here and now!"

"We clerics did what we must to ensure our eventual victory over Shashida, Your Highness," Gracchus answered calmly. "The entire *Pon Q'tar* was in agreement. When you were brought to us as a helpless orphan, we were astounded to learn that your blood signature held the long-sought-after Vagaries halves that would one day allow the ultimate supremacy to your blood. We had searched for such a child for aeons. In the name of Rustannica, we made the best use of your upbringing that we could. But there remains more to tell you. Should you wish to kill me after hearing me out, I cannot stop you. But if you want to live and to see Shashida vanquished once and for all, you will listen to what I have to say."

At once Lucius stood and drew his gladius. Striding toward the cleric, he placed the point of his sword beneath Gracchus' chin and forced it higher.

"You dare to bargain with the emperor's life?" he demanded.

"I only wish to save him," Gracchus answered. "Sheathe your sword, Tribune. If you kill me, he will surely die. There will be nothing that you, the empress, or anyone else will be able to do to stop it."

"Explain yourself!" Persephone demanded. "No more tricks, cleric!"

Although Gracchus had rehearsed his speech a thousand times in his mind, for his explanation to succeed, it must be heartfelt and believable. More importantly, Vespasian must be convinced that what had been done to him was in his own best interests. But Gracchus remained confident of his chances, for although what he was about to say was not the whole truth, it was the truth nonetheless. Moreover, the emperor would have little choice but to follow Gracchus' orders if he wished to avoid a gruesome and painful death. Taking a deep breath, Gracchus gave Vespasian a beseeching look.

"Your highness, the *Pon Q'tar* has long awaited the terrors that you have been experiencing," Gracchus said. "But not because we wished to see you harmed. In fact, your continued well-being is of prime importance to us. The terrors are your blood's way of calling out to your mind, begging you to make use of the banned spells. These spells are much evolved from those that caused the unexpected rise of the Tolenka Mountains so long ago. They are the strongest forestallments ever conceived by man. Only your blood and the blood of the reigning *Jin'Sai* can accommodate them without causing your deaths. By reaching out to your psyche, the spells are indicating that your blood is finally mature enough to employ them without harm to your person. We enchanted some memories of your darker youthful training sessions to remain hidden from your consciousness and to arise only when your blood finally came of age. This is *your* time, my emperor—the era of Vespasian Augustus I. There has been none like it in the history of the world, nor is there likely to be again."

Vespasian was still seething, but he had calmed enough to resist killing the cleric. With a wave of one hand he ordered Lucius to sheathe his gladius.

"You said that if I do not listen to you, I will die," Vespasian demanded. "Explain yourself."

"We granted you these spells so that one day you might summon unheard-of power and vanquish Shashida once and for all," Gracchus answered. "That time has finally come. If you do not heed my advice, the banned forestallments in your blood will keep causing the terrors to unfold in your mind. The banned forestallments and the memories of your training sessions were planted in your psyche by me and the other *Pon Q'tar* clerics while you were still young. It had to be this way lest you become too powerful and perhaps choose to refuse the forestallments because their use would violate the Borderlands Treaty. Even so, far darker sessions still linger in your subconscious. Many of them were put there before you lost your youthful fear of me, such as the one during which you watched the two dogs fight to the death. If they keep surfacing, they will drive you mad, the madness soon leading to your death. In the end, they will literally tear your mind apart."

"You toyed with my very *life*!" Vespasian shouted, his rage surfacing again. "You took a great chance, did you not? How could you be sure that you would recognize the signs before the terrors killed me?"

"It was a certainty that as the terrors increased in frequency and strength, you would be taken ill," Gracchus replied. "I must admit that you did an excellent job of keeping them a secret, for even we of the *Pon Q'tar* did not know. Even so, they would soon have become so terrible that you would have been forced to seek out our help. So you see, the end result would have been the same."

His thoughts racing, Vespasian started angrily pacing the tent. So much of his world had been irrevocably turned upside down that he scarcely knew what to believe. After a time he stopped pacing and looked Gracchus in the eyes.

"Is this all that I am to you?" he demanded. "Am I but some ultimate tool of the craft that you would use for your own purposes? Why didn't you tell me about this before now?"

Despite the emperor's anger, Gracchus realized that Vespasian was reaching out to him, begging to understand. *Now is the moment,* Gracchus thought. *I must console him and reclaim my role as his mentor and his friend. Only then will he do what we ask of him.*

Rising from his chair, Gracchus walked across the room and took Vespasian's hands into his.

"It was for your own good that we did not tell you," Gracchus answered. "Had you known, we believe that the temptation to use the banned spells would have been far too great for even your will to resist. Using them without our guidance could have killed you, and at the very least, might have resulted in harm to Rustannica. We need each other, Vespasian, and the time has come. You cannot resist or ignore the spells. If you wish to survive, you must activate one of them. Only then will you have attained all that the craft has to offer and cause the terrors to stop."

The anger in Vespasian's eyes flashed again. "What other lies have you told me?" he asked. "If I learn that you have deceived me further, your life won't be worth a single sesterce!"

"Nothing, my liege," Gracchus answered. "I swear it."

"How do I end the terrors?" Vespasian asked.

"Use one of the banned forestallments and the terrors will forever vanish," Gracchus answered. "Once one of them has been employed, your blood signature will sense it, and the spell that brings your long-repressed memories to the surface will be lifted."

"There is no other way to break the spell aside from using one of the banned forestallments?" Persephone asked.

"No," Gracchus answered. "Even we of the *Pon Q'tar* cannot otherwise undo it. It was conceived this way for a reason."

"Indeed," Vespasian answered skeptically. "It must be done your way, or I die."

"That is true," Gracchus answered. "But rather than being enraged by this news, I suggest that you look upon it as the final step in the long process that will bring you supreme mastery in the craft. When it is accomplished, you will thank me, I promise you. You will be known all through history as the Rustannican emperor who finally destroyed Shashida and the Vigors."

"How does he go about using one of these gifts?" Lucius demanded angrily. His tone said that as always, he still mistrusted the cleric's motives.

"Vespasian must use one of the banned gifts now—this very day—so that his terrors are forever put to rest," Gracchus answered. Smiling, he raised one hand and gripped the shoulder folds of his robe. "I suggest that he begin with the town to which we currently lay siege," he added.

"That means violating the Borderlands Treaty!" Vespasian protested. "We have honored that agreement for untold centuries!"

"That is also true," Gracchus replied. "But if you do not violate the treaty, you will die, and the Vagaries might be forever defeated here and now. The choice seems clear."

As Vespasian considered Gracchus' words, he suddenly remembered the katsugai mosota he had killed only hours before, and the dire warning that the Shashidan had given him. Vespasian and Lucius had dismissed it as a lie, but now the emperor wasn't so sure.

"There is something that you need to know," Vespasian told Gracchus. "At first I thought it was nothing more than the desperate ravings of a dying man. But now it seems to have greater importance."

"Tell me," Gracchus said.

"A captured katsugai told me that he had recently come from the south," Vespasian answered, "and that he was privy to secret information. He said that the *Jin'Sai* was trying to cross the Azure Sea. If that is true—"

"It *is* true," Gracchus interrupted. "The Viper Lord tried to kill Tristan at the edges of the Azure Sea, but he failed. We cannot know whether the *Jin'Sai* has reached Shashida, but we must assume that he has. It is all the more reason to take the initiative and be the first to use the banned spells! Think for a moment, Vespasian! There can be only one reason why the *Chikara Inkai* would welcome the *Jin'Sai* into their midst! They wish to imbue his blood with banned forestallments as well! Now there is surely no choice—we must violate the Borderlands Treaty first, before they can give the *Jin'Sai* such powers and order him to do the same! And if the *Jin'Sai* is indeed there, we will finally succeed in killing him! Right now we may still have the upper hand, but if we wait until he reaches Shashida, the moment will be lost forever! But before we completely destroy Shashida, the gold mines must be safely in our possession, for we must first ensure that we can maintain stability at home. Without greatly adding to our treasury, a revolt is an eventual certainty."

Vespasian tiredly walked to a chair and sat down. The issues that had been put before him were earthshaking. The longer he considered Gracchus' words, the more difficult his decision became.

He had to agree that the *Pon Q'tar*'s scheme would likely succeed. If his gifts were in fact as powerful as Gracchus claimed, using them would likely mean taking the gold mines, vanquishing Shashida once and for all, and forever ending Vigors use on this side of the world. The *Jin'Sai* would be dead, and the only remaining impediment to the world domination of the Vagaries would be the *Jin'Saiou*. Moreover, his terrors would end and his life would be spared.

Despite all these temptations, Vespasian hesitated. As Emperor of Rustannica, he had strictly abided by her laws and agreements—especially the Borderlands Treaty. Vespasian had not been one of those who so long ago devised and ratified that agreement, but like every emperor since then, he had respected it.

Vespasian was a devout Vagaries worshipper, but what Gracchus was asking him to do would clearly violate not only the treaty, but also his personal sense of honor. Millions would die by his hand, and the earth's devastation might be forever unredeemable. That was the very reason the Borderlands Treaty had been proposed by the Shashidans and later agreed to by both sides. His mind awash with concern, Vespasian looked worriedly at Gracchus.

"Can you guarantee that only Shashida will be destroyed?" Vespasian asked. "I know nothing of these spells. I must have your assurances that they can be controlled!"

"Like these spells, your blood is the most potent known to man,"

Gracchus answered. "We believe that they can be controlled, but only by you and the *Jin'Sai*. Despite their immense power, you will find summoning them to be a relatively simple matter. Controlling their use will be more difficult, but not impossible. I will teach you all that you need to know. If Shashida is to be crushed and the *Jin'Sai* killed, these spells must be used. Only they can provide the raw power needed to do so—to say nothing of saving your life."

"And what of my personal legacy?" Vespasian asked. "Can you guarantee that as well? I desire nothing more than to be known as the emperor who finally accomplishes these wondrous things. But the Borderlands Treaty is well known throughout Rustannica, and I have no wish to be the first emperor to violate it. If I do, history might not be as kind to me as you predict."

Gracchus smiled. "*We* rule Rustannica," he answered, "not the citizens. Our history has always been what we make of it. If we die trying to win this war, it won't matter. Should we win, just as we censor the meetings of the Suffragat, we can easily explain our victory to the Rustannican citizens in any way that we like. If you do not wish to be known as the emperor who first violated the treaty, we will say that the Shashidans were the aggressors. Always remember that history is written by the victors, not the vanquished."

Vespasian looked over at Persephone to see worry on her lovely face. Although at first she had been enraged, now more than anything she worried for her husband's life. If that meant violating the treaty, so be it. After taking a deep breath, she gave Vespasian a nod, indicating her agreement.

Persuading the First Tribune would be another matter. As Vespasian turned to look at him, a dark look overcame Lucius' face. He hated Gracchus, and he had never tried to hide it. Hearing that the lead cleric had duped them all for the sake of the craft had seemingly angered Lucius more than anyone. Even so, he recognized the need to go forward with Gracchus' plan, for it seemed that the opportunity was far too tempting to squander. And so he too would consent to Gracchus' wishes. But in payment for his agreement he would first demand his pound of flesh.

Raising one arm, he quickly pointed it at the lead cleric. At once Gracchus' throat started to constrict as though someone had slipped a rope around it and was strangling him. Although Gracchus was a powerful craft practitioner, so was Lucius. If Lucius could subdue Gracchus fast enough, the cleric would likely be unable to summon enough power to strike back. As Gracchus choked and struggled, Lucius levitated the cleric off his feet. Then he looked at Vespasian.

The emperor nodded. "Very well," he said. "Because of his treachery, you may have your fun. Just see that he doesn't die."

With Gracchus firmly in his power, Lucius walked over to stand before him. By this time there was nothing that Gracchus could do to break Lucius' hold over him. Placing his hands on his hips, Lucius looked up into Gracchus' eyes.

The cleric's face was growing red and his feet were wildly kicking as if trying to gain a purchase on thin air. Saying nothing, Lucius let him linger a bit longer. As precious seconds ticked by, drool started forming in the corners of the cleric's mouth, then ran down his chin and onto his white and burgundy robe.

"Should any harm befall the emperor because of your secret spells, or should I learn that you have withheld any part of the truth, I'll see to it that you and every other *Pon Q'tar* member dies," he said quietly. "You are not in Ellistium, Gracchus. Your fawning citizenry is not here to protect you. And unlike them, you do not command my worship. Instead, you are surrounded by hundreds of legions, each of which owes its allegiance first to Vespasian, then to the empress, and then to me. They would as soon see you die as I would. I suggest that you remember that."

Finally releasing his grip on Gracchus, Lucius let him crash to the floor.

Gracchus fell hard, causing Vespasian to wonder whether Lucius had miscalculated and killed him. Then the cleric gasped. Coughing wildly, he spat up more drool, then finally sat up. As he recovered, he looked at Lucius with hate-filled eyes.

One day you will pay dearly for this insult, First Tribune, he thought as he shakily came to his feet. *No one dares treat the lead cleric this way and lives. But that will not be today. Today my only goal is to initiate my ultimate war weapon, and so I shall.*

Weakened but undaunted, Gracchus ignored Lucius and looked into Vespasian's eyes. Everything had come down to this moment.

"May I have your answer, my liege?" he asked, his voice hoarse. "The time is now. Not only does the war effort need you, but your next terror could come at any time. If so, it might kill you."

Vespasian found much of the cleric's proposal unpleasant, but he realized that he had little choice. Besides, he reasoned, if for some reason the *Pon Q'tar* had wanted him dead, they had had ample chances to kill him before now. Striding toward Gracchus, the emperor looked sternly into his eyes.

"I will do what you ask of me," he said. "But hear me well, cleric. You and Lucius are both right. There are no citizens here to protect you, and only the victors write history—including yours. Should any harm befall me from these secret spells, I hereby grant Lucius and Persephone the right to avenge me in any way they see fit, including the total elimination of the *Pon Q'tar.* Do we understand each other?"

Gracchus fell to his knees and kissed the back of Vespasian's hand.

"Agreed, my liege," he answered. "You will soon command wonders of the craft that the rest of us can only dream of. To begin, you must order a full-scale retreat of our forces from the riverside village that they continue to sack."

Vespasian gave Gracchus a suspicious look. "Why?" he demanded.

Gracchus came to his feet. "Because they are no longer needed," he answered with a smile.

Vespasian turned toward Lucius. "Make it so," he ordered.

"But my liege!" Lucius protested. "We have lost many legionnaires in this latest struggle! Only now are we starting to gain control of the city! The gold mines lie just beyond! If we abandon our fight, what message does that send to our troops?"

"It sends the message that their emperor is still in command of these forces!" Vespasian shouted back. "I'm not asking for your permission, Lucius! Besides, I should think that you would be eager to put the cleric's words to the test! Should I be harmed, you and Persephone can take your revenge in any way that you like!"

"Even if we order a retreat by azure portals, it will take at least three hours," Lucius countered.

"Then I suggest that you start now," Vespasian answered.

Clearly upset, Lucius would nonetheless do as his emperor ordered. Gathering up his helmet, he strode angrily from the tent and into the night. At once he could be heard barking out orders that the other tribunes would find nearly impossible to believe. Pouring two cups of wine, Persephone gave one to Vespasian, and the three Rustannican rulers listened as Lucius' voice faded into the night.

As they waited, Gracchus further detailed Vespasian's many new gifts and how to use them. As the cleric talked on, Vespasian and Persephone could scarcely believe their ears.

FOUR HOURS LATER, VESPASIAN, GRACCHUS, PERSEPHONE, and Lucius stood atop the long, sloping hill that lay just north of the partly destroyed Shashidan city. The remaining *Pon Q'tar* members and Julia Idaeus were also in attendance. Only moments ago Vespasian had received word that by his orders, his forces had abandoned the struggle. At Gracchus' suggestion, those same legionnaires now surrounded the three rulers by the hundreds of thousands, waiting to see what would happen. *Let them witness your reasons for their unexpected retreat,* Gracchus had suggested to the emperor. *Not only will it justify your decision, but it will assert your ultimate mastery of the craft for all time.*

A great and terrible thing was about to occur, the stunned legionnaires had heard. The coming wonder would mean a quick victory here, allowing them to finally push forth toward the Shashidan gold mines. The rumor went on that the emperor himself was about to single-handedly finish destroying this enemy city. Eager to see what might happen, the legionnaires stood in strict ranks as they waited for their beloved emperor to act.

The night was clear and calm as the many thousands waited atop the hill. Magenta light beaming down from the three red moons provided more than enough illumination for everyone to see the suffering of the beleaguered city nestled in the valley below. Dawn would break in less than two hours, and a soft breeze caressed the waiting Rustannicans. The grass was shiny with dew and the hillside was peaceful, its tranquillity in stark contrast to the desperate scene at the bottom of the valley.

The Shashidan city was called Kagoya. Parts of it were still ablaze, but there were fewer such areas than earlier. With the retreat of Vespasian's legions, the Shashidan civilians and the katsugai mosota who had been rushed from Ryoto to help defend Kagoya had worked tirelessly to quell the flames and to tend the wounded. Even so, the city remained engulfed in an insane uproar.

Katsugai and civilians rushed about, trying to quell the flames and bring order to the chaos. Dead bodies and body parts from both sides of the conflict lay everywhere, the blood from their gaping wounds running red in the streets. Children cried, buildings still caved in here and there, and many wounded souls wandered the city aimlessly.

Earlier this night the dwindling Shashidans had watched as hundreds more Rustannican azure portals suddenly formed. *Surely this will mean the end,* they thought. But rather than see more enemy troops pour forth from the spinning vortices, the katsugai commanders couldn't believe their good luck as legionnaires by the thousands abandoned the fight to enter the portals and be gone. Hours later, not one living enemy soldier could be found in the city. *We are saved,* everyone thought. *We will live on to fight another day.* And so, although their desperate struggles to quell the fires and to save the wounded continued, at least they now sensed a modicum of hope.

The fools, Vespasian thought as he sat atop one of his white stallions and he looked down on the scene. *Little can they comprehend the forces that I am about to unleash.*

Gracchus' instructions to Vespasian regarding his new gifts and the various powers that they would unleash had been awesome in their mazelike complexities, stunning Vespasian and Persephone nearly into speechlessness. The cleric went on to say that because of the supremely gifted nature of Vespasian's blood, the emperor would be able to call them forth with relative ease. The difficult part, Gracchus had warned, would be to control their ferocity once they had been unleashed.

Through his amazing revelations, Gracchus had at least partly redeemed himself in his emperor's eyes. Even so, before using his new gifts, Vespasian had insisted that Julia Idaeus perform an auspicium to foretell whether his imminent use of the craft would bring good results or bad. As Julia expected, Gracchus embraced the idea warmly. Vespasian nodded to Julia, telling her to begin.

As the Femiculi walked toward her white birds, she again suffered the bizarre combination of emotions that always roiled up inside her whenever she was forced to participate in this sham of the craft. So as to protect her identity, she must conduct the ritual flawlessly, all the while appearing to believe in its power to help guide the empire. Yet she couldn't help but worry for Shashida, the land in which she now stood and truly revered. It was not unusual for the Femiculi to perform auspiciums on the battlefield—she had done so many times. But this one would surely be even more awful in its portent, for like the *Pon Q'tar* members, she too had finally been informed of Vespasian's special gifts. The mere thought of being a part of any ritual that might grant good tidings to such a terrible scheme brought fear and disgust to her heart.

She knew full well that the *Chikara Inkai* would want her to perform her part of the auspicium normally. They would forbid her to try to affect Gracchus' tampering with the birds' direction of flight, should Gracchus do so to ensure the favorable outcome that the lead cleric needed. Such interference would surely tell Gracchus that someone was plotting against him, perhaps causing his sharp brown eyes to turn toward her. Above all else, her secret identity as a League of Whispers member and her august position of Priory Femiculi must be preserved.

Even so, she felt that her refusal to expose Gracchus for the charlatan that he was somehow made her a traitor to Shashida. Knowing that she must do nothing to prevent Gracchus from subverting the ritual, she prepared to perform the auspicium.

The ten white sacred birds sat tethered to a golden rail. After coming to stand before the cooing birds, Julia pointed a finger in their direction. At once the tethers binding the birds' feet to the rail vanished. This time, rather than wing their way home to the Rotunda after their direction of flight had been made clear, the birds would obediently return to the golden rail. Just as she had done many times before, Julia bowed her head.

"O sacred flame of the Vagaries, grant us the wisdom to perform this auspicium and to be guided by its decree," she recited. "Allow your divine magic to drive the sacred birds skyward and show your humble craft servants which path is best. In our emperor's name we ask for your guidance. In your name we offer our thanks and our continued servitude."

With that, Julia raised her arms higher. Amid a quick flurry of white wings, the birds took to the sky.

As always, for several tense moments the birds circled overhead, giving no inkling as to their decree. Then they gathered to fly due north for a short distance before returning to their perch. As the birds landed one by one, from behind the protection of her veil Julia desperately blinked back her tears.

Northward, she thought, her heart breaking. *The auspiciums are good and Vespasian will surely act. With Gracchus in attendance, was there ever any doubt?*

Julia looked over to see that the lead cleric and the other *Pon Q'tar* members were beaming with delight. She couldn't know whether Gracchus had secretly altered the birds' direction of flight, nor did it matter. All that mattered now was that Vespasian would use his new powers for the first time, and the entire dynamic of the War of Attrition was about to change forever.

"The time has come, my liege," Gracchus said to Vespasian. "Unleash one of your gifts and finish off Kagoya once and for all. Then we will take the gold fields. Soon we will walk the streets of Ryoto as our own."

"Do you have a suggestion as to which gift should be summoned?" Vespasian asked.

"I do," Gracchus answered simply. The lead cleric turned to look down upon the stricken city. "Much of Kagoya still stands," he said. "I suggest that the same force of nature that began its destruction be allowed to finish the task."

Vespasian nodded. After giving Persephone a somber look, he again turned his attention toward the beleaguered city. Following Gracchus' training, he closed his eyes and raised his arms skyward.

At once Vespasian saw the many elaborate banned forestallment calculations whirling in his mind. Their computations were elegant, allpowerful. Selecting the one he wanted, he caused the others to vanish. As the chosen spell came to life for the first time, Vespasian opened his eyes.

Soon the eager Rustannicans could not believe their eyes. The clouds in the heavens were literally obeying Vespasian's commands and combining into a single huge veil in the sky. As the clouds coalesced, thunder arose, its rumblings terrible, nearly deafening. The rising wind began to howl, and with it came bright lightning that streaked majestically across the sky. Everyone watched in awe as the lone cloud drifted directly over Kagoya, its immense size easily reaching from one end of the city to the other. Soon the cloud slowed, the city beneath it entirely unaware that it was about to be wiped from the face of the earth.

Closing his eyes again, Vespasian summoned the second half of the needed spell. At once the massive cloud began changing from milky white to a bright, raging red. Soon the red form in the sky glowed even brighter. Heat radiated from it, the torridness rising so quickly that it could be felt even by the Rustannican multitudes lining the hill. With another great crack of lightning the raging form split apart, showering down its contents. As Julia watched them fall onto Kagoya, her heart broke in two.

Vespasian's terrible creation was raining liquid fire.

The orange-red fire fell not as flames, but as great molten gobs, like volcanic lava loosed from the sky. It did not start at one end of Kagoya and work its way toward the other, for that might have allowed the terrified Shashidans a chance to flee. Instead, the awful stuff fell upon the city as a whole, sparing no part of it.

As the gathered Rustannicans watched, Vespasian's awesome creation immediately ignited every remaining building and flowed down each street, engulfing everyone and everything in its path. Soon it joined forces with the fires that were already raging in the city, turning Kagoya into a gigantic torrent of flame. When the craft's terrible work was done, the fire vanished, leaving only dense smoke and the smell of burning flesh rising into the air. Nothing moved within the dead, blackened city. It seemed to everyone on the hillside that not only had Kagoya been destroyed, its very soul had been vaporized.

His task done, Vespasian lowered his arms. So exhausted that he could barely remain atop his stallion, he closed his eyes, drew a deep breath and gripped his saddle pommel. When he finally opened his eyes, the sight before him was awesome, unexpected.

Every living soul atop the hill and for as far as he could see into the night was on his or her knees before him, head bowed. Even the *Pon Q'tar* had never witnessed such an amazing use of the craft and they too had taken postures of supplication before the wondrous demigod they had created.

Vespasian ordered everyone to rise. Thunderous victory cheers soon rose into the night, and the throngs of legionnaires banged their gladii against their shields in honor of the great emperor and craft wielder whom it was their privilege to serve. Victory wine flowed among the joyful troops.

Wending his way through the crowd, Benedik Pryam came to stand beside Gracchus. Looking down at the smoldering ruins of Kagoya, he smiled and handed the lead cleric a cup of wine.

"So it seems that you have finally realized your masterpiece of the craft after all," he whispered. "I must admit that some of the more skeptical *Pon Q'tar* members were starting to have their doubts. It is fortunate for all of us that Vespasian's impending terrors reached out to his mind no later than they did. Otherwise we might have begun a campaign that we couldn't finish."

"I am as delighted as you," Gracchus answered as he continued to grin and wave theatrically at the triumphant emperor. "Although we take a major step toward ultimate victory this night, do not think for one moment that the battle is won. If the *Jin'Sai* has reached Shashida, our real fight may have only started. Either way, the War of Attrition is forever escalated."

As Benedik watched the beloved emperor being joyfully pulled from his saddle and into the waiting arms of the legionnaires who so loved him, he smiled again.

"Tell me, Gracchus," he whispered. "Now that you have created this wonder of the craft, did you leave the proper spells in place as we agreed? Can you in fact still control Vespasian? The *Pon Q'tar* has fears along those lines as well."

"Of course," Gracchus answered. "After all, when one creates such a monster as this, one must be sure that it is kept in a very strong cage."

"And that cage remains in place?" Benedik asked.

"Yes," Gracchus answered. "As we planned, his terrors were not in fact vanquished after the use of his first banned forestallment. Instead, they still lurk in his subconscious. But unlike before, they will no longer spring up of their own choosing. Should our creation become rebellious, I will order the terrors to revisit him. Only then will I tell him how and why."

Turning to Benedik, Gracchus smiled.

"So you see, my friend, all is as it should be," the lead cleric said. "Soon the Shashidan gold will be traveling home to Ellistium and we will be dining in the fabled gardens of the Kyuden Shimin."

Smiling broadly, the two clerics linked arms and drank heartily of the rich victory wine.

CHAPTER XLIV

"JUST HOURS AGO, JULIA IDAEUS AGAIN SECRETLY COM-muned with us," Mashiro said sadly. "She was lucky to do so without detection, for it is a dangerous thing to accomplish while traveling with Vespasian's armies. I'm sorry to report that her news is grave." Before continuing, Mashiro paused and he looked down at his hands.

"Kagoya has been totally destroyed," he announced. "It was not a large city, but it was a culturally important one. Worse, it was the last bastion between Vespasian and our gold mines. Julia watched the carnage as every Kagoyan civilian and every katsugai mosota posted to its defense was killed. Vespasian used one of his banned gifts to rain liquid fire down onto the city. After more than one hundred and fifty centuries, the Rustannicans have finally violated the Borderlands Treaty. What we have long feared has come to pass, and this war's deadly ferocity has been forever heightened."

Tristan looked at Mashiro as the *Chikara Inkai* elder sadly wiped away tears. Although he and his fellow pilgrims were new to Shashida, they felt the pain as sharply as if a Eutracian city had been destroyed. For several long moments the *Inkai* meeting chamber went silent.

It was the morning of the Eutracians' second full day in Shashida. Tristan, Wigg, Jessamay, and Tyranny had been asked to participate in a hastily called meeting of the *Chikara Inkai.* Tristan had dined with them the previous night, giving them a chance to brief him. All the Eutracians, the Black Ships, and the Minions of Day and Night had arrived safely, Wigg had said. As Tristan might have guessed, the Minion warriors elected to live aboard the ships rather than take up residence in the elegant Kyuden Shimin, or "People's Palace." Everyone else had been housed in the palace's visitors' wing.

Mashiro had ordered that cradles be quickly built to hold the vessels. They were much like those that the Minions had constructed in Eutracia, Wigg said, but they also showed the stylistic elegance that was common to Shashida. The great ships and their cradles were stationed on the manicured inner grounds of the Kyuden Shimin.

Tristan had retired early last night and he awoke refreshed. After bathing, he walked to his wardrobe. Hoshi had seen to it that his Eutracian vest, breeches, and knee boots had been cleaned and returned. Tristan had never seen his Eutracian clothes so well laundered, and he was sorely tempted to wear them. The breeches were spotless, and the leather vest and boots had been cleaned and shined to a high gloss.

He finally selected a dark blue Shashidan robe. He took up a pair of sandals and socks from the dozens that sat side by side on the spotless wardrobe floor. He then strapped his dreggan and throwing knives into place behind his right shoulder.

He was about to depart his chambers when Wigg, Tyranny, and Jessamay appeared to tell him that the *Chikara Inkai* urgently requested their presence. Like Tristan, they were dressed in Shashidan garb. Leaving Tristan's rooms, they hurried to the meeting chamber. That had been only moments ago, and as he again gazed into Mashiro's ancient eyes, he knew that the next few hours would shape Shashida's future for centuries to come.

"So your assumptions were right," Wigg said to Mashiro. "Banned forestallments have in fact been lurking in Vespasian's blood."

Mashiro nodded. "Yes," he answered. "And at long last he has chosen to use them. We cannot say why this has not occurred before now, because Julia is not privy to that information. But one thing remains crystal clear. Vespasian's next goal will be to secure our gold deposits. If he takes and holds the area, he might then lay waste to the lower reaches of Shashida and then finally to the nation as a whole."

"There is something about Rustannica's violation of the Borderlands Treaty that confuses me," Wigg said. "Each time the Borderlands are summoned by the *Pon Q'tar,* their environment is made toxic, so as to kill anyone trapped there. It would seem that the only way to do that would be to use one or more of the banned forestallments. And if that's true, then the *Pon Q'tar* has already violated the Borderlands Treaty untold times."

"Given your limited understanding of the treaty, that would be true," Kaemon said. "When the treaty was ratified, it included a provision saying that because the Borderlands are Rustannican territory, the *Pon Q'tar* is free to use the banned spells there—but only there. We objected, of course, but the Rustannicans remained firm. In the end we were forced to grant the concession or there would have been no treaty at all."

"If Vespasian's gifts are as powerful as you suspect, how does the *Pon Q'tar* hope to control him?" Tristan asked.

"They don't need to *control* him," Hoshi answered. "They only need to *unleash* him."

"But Shashida is vast," Tristan said. "It seems impossible that even Vespasian's gifts could destroy the entire nation."

"We tend to agree," Midori replied from across the table, "but we cannot be sure. If he alone can crush one major objective after another, his legions will be free to leave his side and then attack lesser targets at will. Julia reported that Vespasian destroyed all of Kagoya in less than one hour! Because of this, he might decide that only a few of his legions need accompany him from here on. He could then delegate command of the others to Lucius Marius, his First Tribune and closest friend. Lucius' task would be to overwhelm the smaller targets traditionally while Vespasian uses his new gifts to destroy the larger ones. In this way, the Rustannican war machine could cover great expanses of Shashida quickly and spread our forces thin."

After thinking for a moment, Tristan looked at Mashiro. "Do the Rustannicans know that I am here?" he asked.

Mashiro sighed. "Julia tells us that they worry about your arrival, but that they cannot confirm it. Because you escaped Khristos at the edge of the Azure Sea, they of course know that you were trying to come here. They are not fools and they will take your possible arrival into their planning. Only one thing remains certain, *Jin'Sai.* If Shashida is to be saved, we must grant you our versions of the banned forestallments soon—today, if you will permit it. During yesterday's emergency session, our governing body ratified our request to do so, and to allow you to then confront Vespasian. Once the spells have been imbued into your blood, you and our armies will be rushed by azure portals to meet him head-on. We humbly ask your forgiveness for throwing you into the fray so abruptly, but the hour is late and there is no other choice. Because of Vespasian's far superior training in the craft, it is doubtful that you can defeat him outright. But if you can counter his ability to employ the banned forestallments with your own, he might halt his advance and order his legions home. We Shashidans would view Vespasian's retreat as a victory."

"But I know nothing about your military and your tactics," Tristan countered, "not to mention my complete lack of familiarity with Vespasian's forces. How can I be expected to lead Shashida against an enemy about whom I know so little?"

"By *not* leading her," Renjiro answered. "Forgive me, *Jin'Sai,* but although you have commanded your Minions to victory many times, things are vastly different here. You are right—you cannot be expected to lead forces about which you know little or nothing. Therefore, Hoshi and I will lead them. You will be with us, providing the one weapon that we cannot. When suddenly confronted by your gifts, Vespasian might put a stop this madness and return home. As we speak, hundreds of Shashidan cohorts are being sent by azure portal to a staging area south of where our gold deposits lay. The other *Chikara Inkai* members will remain here. We will inform them of events by way of mental communion."

Tristan nodded. "I will do so gladly," he answered. "But I have some requests of you."

"What are they?" Hoshi asked.

"I want to take my Minions into battle with me and I want complete control over them," he said. "I know that you find them crude when compared to your katsugai mosota and perhaps they are. But my Minions are gifted and ruthless killers, and their advantage of flight will be useful. Vespasian might not be expecting that."

To Tristan's surprise, Hoshi smiled. "Truth be told, we were about to suggest that very thing," she replied. "What is your other request?"

"I want my Black Ships to participate in the fight and Tyranny to command them," Tristan said. "Your portals can easily accommodate them. I, my Minions, and my fellow Conclave members will ride the Black Ships to the battle site. Once there, I will gladly follow your orders."

Mashiro nodded, and Tristan turned to look at Wigg, Jessamay, and Tyranny. "What say you all?" he asked. "Will you come with us?"

Despite the recent loss of Abbey, Wigg managed a short smile. "I can answer for everyone," he replied. "You were born to take part in this struggle. It will be an honor to serve by your side."

After nodding at Wigg, Tristan looked back at Mashiro. "Then it's settled," he said. "When will I be granted the banned forestallments?"

"Within hours," Mashiro answered. "But first there is another concern that deserves our attention. I'm sure it has not escaped your mind."

Tristan nodded again. "Shailiha," he said softly. "I'm mad to know her condition and to help her defeat the Viper Lord."

"To those ends, we have a gift for you," Kaemon said. "Since the moment you arrived in Shashida, our best craft researchers have been diligently working to perfect some needed spells. We believe that you will find them interesting."

"What spells are these?" Wigg asked.

"You will see soon enough," Mashiro answered. The *Inkai* elder turned to look at Tristan.

"Activate your medallion," Mashiro told him.

"IS THERE STILL NO NEWS OF KHRISTOS?" SHAILIHA ASKED.

"No, Your Highness," Traax answered. "Night Witch patrols continue to scan Eutracia's rivers from the air, but there has been no sign of him or his servants. Mashiro suspects that as long as the enemy remains submerged, Failee's original spell will provide them with sustenance. If that is true, they have no need to surface until they wish to attack. They lurked beneath the water for three centuries before emerging to take the First Mistress's revenge. Staying submerged for mere days at a time must be a comparatively simple feat."

The hour was late and Shailiha was tired. Even so, she demanded that her Conclave members meet again to discuss the ongoing situation. This would be the last briefing of the day, and for that she was glad.

Khristos' ability to raze Tammerland and to set fire to one of the Black Ships and nearly steal the other had enraged every Conclave member. The loss of the *Illendium* had been disastrous, and many days would pass before the *Cavalon* would again be airworthy. With her two Black Ships unavailable and yet more Minions dead, Shailiha's ability to fight Khristos had been severely compromised.

Moreover, her physical condition still plagued her. Her facial skin was healing, but her body ached badly from the effects of the viper venom, causing her to move like a woman twice her age. The vision in her left eye had improved slightly, but not enough to persuade her that it would ever return to normal. *It will take time*, Mashiro had told Faegan, and she clung to that belief. Of necessity she still wore the black eye patch, and by now everyone in the palace had grown accustomed to its presence. *At least there is that,* she thought.

Faegan, Traax, Aeolus, and Adrian sat with her at the mahogany table in the Conclave meeting room, deep in the Redoubt. It was not the first time that the remaining members had gathered since their friends had left for Shashida. Even so, the empty chairs still lent the room a desolate feel, and the chair that had once been Abbey's seemed the most forlorn of all.

Sighing, Faegan placed his forearms on the highly polished table. "We can do little but wait, Princess," he said. "We should continue to send out Night Witch patrols, but because our enemies can hide in the rivers, the likelihood of finding them before they again emerge is not great."

Sadly, Shailiha was forced to agree. In Tristan's absence she ruled Eutracia, but her inability to act was frustrating. She knew that if Tristan were still there, he would be equally stymied, and the advice being offered to him would be identical. Unlike her twin brother, the princess more carefully considered her options before acting. But because those options were so few, she was finding it increasingly difficult to stifle the same kind of impetuousness that characterized the *Jin'Sai*.

Just then Faegan gave her a strange look, and she realized that he was staring not at her face, but at the gold medallion hanging around her neck. She looked down to see that it was glowing. *Tristan!* she thought. *He's reaching out to me from Shashida.*

Rather than turn over the medallion, Shailiha hesitated. Tristan and the other Conclave members had yet to see her since she was injured. As at the moment when Morganna first saw her injured face, she worried about how they would react—especially her brother. The last thing she wanted from them was their pity. As the medallion continued to glow, she looked into Faegan's eyes.

The crippled wizard reached out to pat her hand.

"He's your brother," he said. "He worries for you, as they all do. It is best that you put this behind you."

Shailiha nodded, then turned over the medallion so that everyone around the table might see into it. Her first viewing of the *Inkai* meeting room and the many people there took her breath away.

 WHEN TRISTAN SAW HIS SISTER, HE FELT HIS HEART BREAK. He knew that she had been injured, but seeing her that way greatly disturbed him just the same. He knew that there was no use in speaking to her, so he tried to give his best smile of support.

"Has contact been established?" Mashiro asked.

"Yes," Tristan answered.

"Please remove the medallion and place it on the meeting table," the *Inkai* elder said.

Tristan gave Mashiro a questioning look. "It was my understanding that the medallion must be worn by one of endowed blood to do its work," he said.

Mashiro smiled. "That is no longer altogether true," he said.

Tristan removed the medallion and placed it face up on the table. At once Mashiro caused the medallion to levitate about two feet above the table. Then the gold disc and its chain started to spin. Faster and faster they went until they became only a blur, then disappeared altogether.

In their place appeared another representation of what Tristan had seen in the medallion, but this time the scene was far larger. The images of the people sitting at the Redoubt table had become life-sized. Amazed, Tristan turned to gape at Mashiro.

"How did you do this?" he breathed.

"We altered the spells that Miriam cast over your medallions before she died," he answered. "It took our craft researchers some doing, I can assure you."

Tristan looked back at the scene floating before his eyes. The new image was about two yards broad by one yard high. It was so clear and sharp that Tristan felt he was there in the Redoubt and could actually reach out and touch his sister's ravaged face. As he looked closer, he saw that the far wider scope of the new image allowed him to see everyone in the Redoubt chamber at once. Every Conclave member's face wore an equally amazed expression. Because the new image floated above the *Inkai* meeting table, everyone could see it easily.

"Has their view of us been similarly changed?" Tristan asked.

"Yes," Mashiro answered. "This was made possible because Shailiha's medallion is an exact duplicate of yours, created by the craft while she was imprisoned by the Coven of Sorceresses. Because of its origins, an enchanted connection has always existed between them. Miriam simply brought it to life, then we enhanced it. Now when either of you calls the needed spell, your medallions will create enlarged views, and they will not have to leave your bodies to do so."

Still amazed, Tristan looked over at Mashiro. "I wish to communicate with her," he said, "but I will need paper and ink to do so. May I be given some?"

Mashiro shook his head. "You won't need them," he said.

Wigg's eyes narrowed and he leaned over the tabletop. "Do you mean to say—"

"That's exactly what I mean," Mashiro answered.

Before Wigg could reply, Mashiro closed his eyes and called the craft. At once the image floating over the table glowed brighter, then blurred for several moments. When the scene came back into focus, Tristan heard an eerily familiar sound that did not originate from the *Inkai* meeting chamber. He soon realized that it was the crackling of the burning logs in the Redoubt fireplace, far on the other side of the world. Mouth agape, he sat back in his chair.

"I beg the Afterlife!" he breathed. "I can hear them!"

Mashiro nodded. "That's right, *Jin'Sai,*" he said, "and they can hear us. Please accept these augmentations to your and your sister's medallions as humble gifts from the *Chikara Inkai.*"

When she unexpectedly heard her brother's voice, Shailiha reacted with a start. Faegan, Aeolus, Traax, and Adrian seemed similarly stunned.

"Tristan . . . ?" Shailiha said.

"I'm here," he answered. "The *Chikara Inkai* has augmented our medallions so that we may now also hear each other. I find the effect as amazing as you do."

Pausing for a moment, Tristan looked sadly into his sister's eyes. "Are you all right?" he asked quietly.

At first Shailiha didn't answer. After pausing for a moment she bravely lifted her eye patch for all to see, then she put it back in place. A quick rush of air left Tristan's lungs, but he did his best to stifle his shock.

"My vision is a bit better," Shailiha answered. "On behalf of all of us, I wish to offer our condolences on the death of Abbey. We all miss her."

Shailiha then cast her handicapped gaze about the *Inkai* chamber and looked at each of the members in turn. "Which of you is Mashiro?" she asked.

Mashiro stood and bowed. "My apologies, Princess," he said. "I should have made the needed introductions sooner. Please allow me to correct my mistake."

Mashiro asked the *Inkai* members to stand one by one. As they did, he introduced them to the Conclave members watching from so far away. When he finished, Shailiha did the same for her followers. Because of the sharpness of the scene and the amazing clarity of the Conclave members' voices, it was almost as if everyone were seated at one great table.

For the next hour the two groups exchanged information on their respective situations. Shailiha informed the *Inkai* that there had been no sightings of the Viper Lord or his followers but that Night Witch patrols continued to search them out. She then explained that the *Cavalon* was under repair, but it would be many days before she would again be airworthy. Traax then provided the *Jin'Sai* with an updated casualty report.

When Traax finished, Mashiro informed the Eutracian Conclave of everything that he had told Tristan and his fellow travelers during their earlier meetings. He then went on to explain Vespasian's recent violation of the Borderlands Treaty and the *Inkai*'s plan to imbue Tristan's blood with their versions of the banned forestallments. He also described in detail the *Inkai*'s wish that one day everyone's blood signature might be altered to the vertical and that a new, unified nation might be born that was devoid of forestallments and dedicated to the ideal of free will. The Conclave members sat in stunned silence, absorbing every word. When Mashiro finished, many quiet moments passed as those in Eutracia considered the astounding news.

His expression stern, Faegan leaned across the Conclave meeting table and looked straight into Wigg's eyes.

"Tell me, First Wizard," he asked. "Assuming that the lands west of the Tolenkas can ever again be united, do you agree that all blood signatures should be altered to the vertical and that the Tome and the two Scrolls of the Ancients should be destroyed?"

"I do," Wigg answered. "The Shashidans are right to feel this way. But before such awesome changes can happen, Rustannica must be defeated for good. Only then can the *Inkai* turn their attention to the betterment of the craft for the sake of all mankind."

Faegan sat in silence for some time as he considered Wigg's words. "Despite how radical the concept seems, I must say that I agree," he answered. "I envy your being there, old friend. I can only imagine the wonders that you have seen and those that still await you. Abbey would have been proud."

Wigg's face darkened for a moment. "Thank you," he said simply.

"Now then," Mashiro said. "I must ask the Conclave whether Failee's grimoire is available."

"It is," Aeolus answered. He rose from his chair to walk across the Redoubt meeting chamber to where the red leather-bound book sat atop a pedestal. Bringing it back, he placed it on the table.

"Why do you wish to see the late First Mistress's grimoire?" he asked. "Surely there can be nothing in it that supersedes your knowledge of the craft."

"Although that is probably true, you must never forget how brilliant Failee was, or how limitless were the depths of her distrust," Mashiro answered. "Like the *Pon Q'tar,* she always constructed a way of destroying her own creations should the need arise."

"I don't understand," Faegan protested. "Aside from the Vigors, what would she have wished to destroy?"

"Not what, but *whom,*" Renjiro answered.

Faegan's face suddenly came alight with understanding. "You're talking about Khristos, aren't you?" he asked. "If for some reason he ever turned on her, he and his Blood Vipers would have presented a deadly threat to her rule—especially while she was still struggling to win the Sorceresses' War."

"Correct," Midori said. "We suggest that you scour her grimoire for any references to Khristos. If the First Mistress devised a secret way to destroy him, her grimoire is where she probably hid it."

"We have already done so," Shailiha said. "Aside from a few entries describing her overall plan for Khristos, nothing more is said about him."

"Nothing that you can see," Mashiro said to Shailiha. "It's what you *can't* see that interests us."

"What are you talking about?" the princess asked.

Mashiro turned to look at Wigg. "Correct me if I'm wrong, First Wizard," he said. "Isn't it true that during the Sorceresses' War, the Coven used spells to camouflage secret documents?"

"We always suspected as much," Wigg answered. "If they did, they took the knowledge to their graves. Despite the combined efforts of the late Directorate of Wizards, we were never able to unravel the secret. I have long suspected that hidden writings lay in her grimoire, but there is no way to know for sure."

"Until now, perhaps," Mashiro said. He turned back toward the hovering image and looked at Faegan. "Wigg tells us that he left some of the subtle matter behind in Eutracia. Do you still have it?"

"Yes," Faegan answered.

"Would you be kind enough to have it brought to your meeting chamber?" he asked. "You will have need of it."

Faegan nodded and asked Traax to fetch it from its resting place in the Redoubt Archives. Soon Traax returned with a small glass flask filled with subtle matter, not unlike the one that Wigg had brought to Shashida. Taking the flask from Traax, Faegan placed it on the table alongside the grimoire.

"Now, then," Mashiro said to Faegan. "Using your gift of Consummate Recollection, please open the grimoire to the section that makes mention of Khristos."

Faegan closed his eyes and called the craft. Soon the grimoire opened of its own accord, and its pages began turning madly. After a few moments they stopped.

"It is done," Faegan said.

"Good," Mashiro said. "Now if you would be so kind as to sprinkle a small bit of the subtle matter onto the pages."

Faegan did so, but nothing happened. He said as much to Mashiro.

"Do not be dismayed," Mashiro said. "Subtle matter has many uses, but few of them can be achieved without an accompanying spell. If you would, please repeat the Shashidan incantation that I am about to recite. You will find it complex, so I suggest that you first call on your Consummate Recollection to ensure that you repeat my words perfectly. Otherwise you might find the results distressing, to say the least. But if you recite it correctly and our suspicions about Failee are true, the results might be intriguing."

"Very well," Faegan answered. "I am ready."

Mashiro enunciated a long incantation in his native Shashidan. As Tristan listened, he found the language far more beautiful and elegant than his native dialect. Throughout Mashiro's incantation, Tristan recognized but one word: "Khristos."

When Mashiro finished, Faegan closed his eyes. Calling on his special gift, he carefully repeated the incantation word for word. As he finished, all eyes turned toward Failee's grimoire.

For a moment, nothing happened. Then the grimoire started to glow with the same white light that had emanated from the Tome and the two Scrolls of the Ancients when the subtle matter decoded them in the Archives. Letters, numbers, and craft symbols lifted from the pages to hover above the Conclave meeting table. Then the grimoire pages started flurrying by again, and yet more marks went flying off the pages. Soon the pages stopped turning, and Failee's writings ceased lifting from the pages.

Everyone watched as the thousands of glowing characters swirled about to form lines. The lines then formed a text many paragraphs long incorporating two involved spell formulas. As Faegan read the glowing text, his mouth fell open.

"I beg the Afterlife!" he exclaimed. "You were right."

Both chambers went silent as everyone read the glowing text. It soon became clear that it was a craft treatise that had been written by Failee and described in detail how to deal with Khristos and his servants should they ever become a threat to her. Filled with awe, Tristan let go a deep breath and sat back in his chair.

"Well done, Faegan, and worthy of an *Inkai*," Mashiro said to the crippled wizard. "This should greatly aid you in your struggle."

"Indeed," Shailiha answered. "I thank you."

Remembering the other reason he had wanted to contact his sister, Tristan again looked at her. The time had come, and there could be no denying it.

"Now that you have the needed information from Failee's grimoire, there is one thing left to say," Tristan told her. "It is important, and you must heed my advice well."

"What is it?" Shailiha asked.

"It is unlikely that I will ever return to Eutracia," he said. "Because of that, it is time for you to become Queen. I fully realize that this is a burden that you never thought you'd have to shoulder, but in the name of our late parents, you must. Our country needs a formal ruler."

Before the princess could answer, Aeolus reached out and took one of her hands into his.

"The *Jin'Sai* is right," he said. "We must accept the fact that although we can communicate with one another, the Conclave of the Vigors is probably forever divided, and our struggles have become separate and distinct. You are the reigning *Jin'Saiou* and rightful heir to the throne. It is only right that you take power."

Taking a deep breath, Shailiha looked at her brother. Although she could see and hear him as if he were sitting by her side, she missed him badly. She missed his impetuousness, his strength, his laughter, even his moodiness. But she also knew that he might never actually be with her again, and because of that, he was right. It was time for her to shoulder her responsibility.

"I accept," she said to everyone. "And I thank you for your trust in me. But I think it only right that I not succeed to the throne until our struggle with the Viper Lord is finished. We must focus all of our attention on the calamity at hand. This is no time to prepare for a coronation."

Wigg smiled broadly at her. "Spoken like a true queen," he said. "Your parents would be proud."

Mashiro reached out and touched Tristan on one arm. "With all due respect, *Jin'Sai,* we must end this viewing," he proposed. "Both the Conclave and the *Inkai* have urgent matters to attend to, and time is of the essence."

Although Tristan did not want to see his sister go, he knew that the *Inkai* elder was right. Looking back into Shailiha's eyes, he told her so.

"I agree, brother," she said. "Please stay safe, and may your coming battle see a victory for the Vigors."

"And yours," Tristan said.

With that, Mashiro dismantled the spell, and the image vanished.

After taking the medallion into his hand, Tristan held it thoughtfully for several moments before again placing its chain around his neck.

"Now, then," Mashiro said soberly. "It is time."

Tristan and the others knew full well what Mashiro meant. The *Inkai* elder would now imbue Tristan's blood with Shashida's versions of the banned forestallments and the language fluency forestallments. Each time before, the process had been excruciating and this time would likely be worse. Even so, there was no other choice, no going back.

"I understand," Tristan said. "Where shall it be done?"

"The venue is immaterial," Mashiro answered. "This meeting chamber is as good a place as any. The process will take some time and you must remain strong. If you survive the ordeal, you and Vespasian will be the two most powerful mystics in the world. You will not be as well trained in the craft as he, but your gifts of manipulating nature will be equally strong. Aside from Vespasian's ability to rain fire as described by Julia, we cannot know the natures of his other banned gifts, or how many he possesses. But the *Pon Q'tar* will not know that of yours, either. Are you still sure that you wish to do this thing?"

"Yes," Tristan answered simply. "It has to be."

"Very well," Mashiro replied. "Because of the exquisite pain that you will suffer, Hoshi will place a warp about you to keep you from thrashing. We apologize for such crudeness, but it is needed to keep you from harming yourself."

Mashiro nodded at Hoshi. She in turn looked at Tristan with sad eyes.

"Forgive me," she said quietly.

At once Tristan felt himself engulfed in a warp the likes of which he had never experienced. Although it was not painful, his immobilization was perfect, unrelenting. The only movements allowed him were his quickening breath and the blinking of his eyes. Nervous perspiration started on his brow in anticipation of the horror to come.

Out of respect, Mashiro cast a sad look at Wigg, the man who had for so long been Tristan's best friend and mentor. Although he too was saddened by what was about to happen, the First Wizard knew that there was no other choice if Shashida and the Vigors were to survive Vespasian's onslaught. Closing his eyes, he gave Mashiro a reluctant nod.

At once a terrible fire poured through Tristan's bloodstream. He desperately needed to move, to scream, to cry out and beg that it stop. But he couldn't. He could only endure it. On and on the pain went, coursing through his system like a raging river. Sweat poured into his eyes, his heart raced, his soul shrieked in torment. As the process continued unabated, some were forced to turn their heads, while others brushed away tears that only kept returning.

In the end, the torturous process would take five full hours.

CHAPTER XLV

TWO DAYS AFTER DESTROYING THE CITY OF KAGOYA, Vespasian triumphantly stood in the Shashidan valley through which ran the mighty Alarik River. It was midday, the weather clear and bright. As he looked out across the amazing scene, the emperor couldn't have been more pleased.

His destruction of Kagoya had been total. Despite the lengthy warnings that he had received from Gracchus, even he had been astonished by his new gifts. As Gracchus said, choosing a particular forestallment and then summoning its power had been simple things. Controlling it as it went about its awful work and then causing it to vanish on command had been far more difficult, however. With experience, your ability to control your new gifts will only grow, Gracchus had told him. Like some highly addictive drug, Vespasian's new gifts beckoned tantalizingly, and he hungered to taste them again. With his day terrors finally gone and the banned forestallments waiting to be summoned, he had never felt so alive.

On seeing their emperor destroy Kagoya, his legionnaires had acquired an even greater reverence for him. They now considered Vespasian a demigod, his awesome command of the craft unlimited in its scope and fury. The final victory over Kagoya had fully redeemed the scheming lead cleric in the emperor's eyes, and everyone believed that the total dominance of the Vagaries would not be long in coming.

Aside from his supply lines that stretched ever northward, Vespasian's entire war machine had been moved to this valley by way of hundreds of azure portals. The Shashidan resistance had been stronger here, and many legionnaires had died.

Even so, the campaign had progressed too easily, Vespasian thought. His massive war machine's string of successes continued to worry him and his advisors. It was almost as if the Shashidans *wanted* them to succeed, but the Rustannicans were at a complete loss as to why this might be the case. What was done was done, Vespasian realized, and there would be no turning back until their mission was complete. To stop the campaign now that the gold deposits had been taken would be absurd, even though the newly empowered warlord and every advisor in his service feared that a Shashidan trap was in the making. They had come for the gold, and they would stay in this place and take it.

Trying to cast off his concerns, Vespasian turned to admire the lush, beautiful valley and the majestic river that flowed through it. This area was one of the most awe-inspiring that he had ever seen, not to mention the richest. In the Rustannican dialect it was called Vallesis Majestatis, or the Valley of Majesty. The Shashidans called it Tani Kinkiro, the Valley of Gold. Vespasian found both names apt.

Running due north and south for more than one hundred leagues, at the valley's heart laid the mighty Alarik River, fed by its seemingly endless branches. Legend said that hundreds of centuries were needed for the river to carve its way south through the imposing granite peaks and to divide them into two separate mountain ranges. On leaving the valley the river flowed south toward the broad, flat plains that would later give rise to Ryoto, the capital of Shashida.

The opposing mountainsides rose leagues into the air, their tops so high that they lay perpetually covered with snow and ice. The craggy slopes had long ago become laden with pine trees, their green needles casting a clean scent into the air. Lush pastures and knolls lay on either side of the Alarik, their gentle swells extending from the riverbanks to where the mountainsides began rising toward the sky. Fish filled the Alarik and its many branches, and wildlife of every kind flourished amid the serene protection granted by the opposing mountain ranges.

To everyone's surprise, the phrase "Shashidan gold mines" had been a misnomer. On reaching the Vallesis Majestatis, Vespasian and his forces were stunned to find that there were in fact no "mines" at all. Instead, the gold lay all about for the taking, the earth humbly offering up her treasures without demanding a great struggle of any kind.

Gold nuggets—the smallest among them easily the size of man's hand—could be seen lying atop the Alarik River bed, their bright yellow color waving temptingly up through the rushing water. More gold could be found in countless veins that reached up the mountainsides, their vast wealth easily dislodged with the craft to tumble down the hillsides and land literally at the legionnaires' feet. The pickings were easy, and seemed too good to be true. No matter from what source the gold came, more was found beneath it.

As best the Rustannicans could tell, these amazing deposits abounded for the entire length of the valley. Vespasian could easily understand why guarding this place was so difficult for the Shashidans. Because the valley was so huge, protecting it would require the presence of so many katsugai mosota that few would be left to fight the war. And because the gold fields lay so deep in Shashidan territory, an attack on them was highly unexpected. Even so, there had been many katsugai mosota here. Killing them had come at a cost, but not so great as to stop Vespasian's legions from ruling the day.

After dispatching the enemy, Vespasian's legions set to work harvesting the golden bounty that so temptingly presented itself. As an incentive to speed the task, he issued a decree that every legionnaire who survived and returned home at the end of the campaign would share in the plunder.

Hundreds of thousands of men toiled at picking up the gold, their sweating, bent backs stretching away toward each end of the valley as far as the eye could see. War tents by the thousands stood along the riverbank, forming an impromptu city made of canvas. The southerly flowing Alarik ran particularly fast through the valley, making Vespasian's planned use of his barges to ferry the gold upstream largely unworkable. Even so, many tons of gold had already been sent home to Ellistium by way of the azure portals, and more was leaving Shashida by the minute.

Despite this place's obvious temptations, a great danger lay here, and Vespasian knew it. The very idea of his army being enclosed in a valley was a military nightmare. If the Shashidans closed off both ends of the Vallesis Majestatis, his forces' only avenue of escape would be the azure portals, which in turn would mean abandoning the gold fields. Unless his trapped legions escaped by portal, the barbaric katsugai mosota would come charging down the valley from both ends, trapping Vespasian's legions in the middle. In hopes of preventing an attack inside the valley, he had sent three legions to guard each valley entrance. As his worries taunted him, Vespasian was soon reminded of a famous military tenet. *No man fights so hard as he who defends his homeland,* he remembered. If and when the katsugai arrived in force, they would fight very hard indeed.

Vespasian turned to see Lucius and Persephone approaching. The First Tribune held a wax diptych in one hand. Smiling broadly, he removed his helmet and placed it under one arm. Persephone came to her husband's side and looped one arm though his.

"It goes amazingly well, my liege," Lucius said, handing the diptych to Vespasian.

"Is this the latest count?" the emperor asked.

Lucius nodded. "Even so, it grows by the moment! The gold deposits are staggering in their abundance! It seems that no matter how much we take, more always lies beneath, ripe for the picking!"

Vespasian opened the diptych and he ran his eyes down the single page. As expected, the report was in Gracchus' handwriting. Even the emperor was stunned by what it said.

The amount of gold already sent home to Ellistium was greater than the largest amount that had ever existed in her treasury. At this rate, in mere days the empire's coffers would hold a nearly incomprehensible amount. Vespasian smiled as he realized that the Rustannican imperial mint would be stamping new coins for decades or longer, and that each coin would bear his likeness.

Despite the encouraging tally, as Vespasian looked around the valley again his expression saddened. Unable to understand why, Persephone gave her husband a questioning look.

"What troubles you, my love?" she asked. "In only a few more days we will have sent more gold home than we could ever have imagined! Who knew that it would be so easily harvested? Your campaign is a towering success!"

"Perhaps," he answered. "Even so, our problems have not ended." Vespasian shook his head.

"It's this *place,* Persephone," he said quietly. "We must tarry here because the gold lies here. But as a military stronghold, this valley is a nightmare. We must soon decide how long to stay and loot the fields, because every moment that passes brings us that much closer to engaging the Shashidans. If they somehow close off both ends of the valley—"

"A necessary gamble, my liege," Lucius said. "We have legions posted at both the northern and southern valley entrances. At the first sign of the Shashidans, our forces will engage them, and they will personally inform us by way of one of the azure portals. You may put your entire trust in them. They have never failed us."

"I know, I know," Vespasian answered, rubbing his brow. His heart was filled with a strange blend of euphoria and impending doom, and the conflicting emotions showed on his face. "It's not a matter of whether the Shashidans come, but when. They'll divide their forces, then try to seal off both ends of the valley, I'm sure of it."

"How can you be so certain?" Persephone asked.

"Because that's what I would do," Vespasian answered grimly. "A schoolchild could grasp its effectiveness! But there's more to my worries. Being imprisoned between these imposing peaks makes me wonder whether our campaign plan should be changed."

"To what end?" Lucius asked.

"Persephone said it best," Vespasian answered. "Because we can simply pluck the gold from nature as one might harvest fruit from a tree, our work proceeds exceedingly fast. Soon we will have sent more gold home to Ellistium than we ever dreamed possible. Perhaps we should then abandon this valley and move on, for it is too far away from home for us to hold as conquered territory. I long for the maneuvering room that only being away from these imposing peaks can afford. Here in this valley we toil like rats in a trap."

"There is little else that we can do for now," Lucius said. "I suggest that we review the process for sending the gold home. More than anything else, it will remind us why we ventured into this barbaric land."

Letting go a short smile, Vespasian nodded. "Very well," he said to Lucius. "Lead on."

The trio sauntered along the Alarik toward one of the many staging areas where the gold was being weighed and the sums tallied before being shipped home. Many such stations lay up and down the length of the valley. Despite the hundreds of thousands of eager legionnaires working away, Vespasian knew that even if his forces toiled here for months, they couldn't harvest a fraction of the massive Shashidan deposits. Although their take would be vast, in a strange way that knowledge also disheartened him.

In the end, what will we have accomplished? he wondered as he walked. No matter how much gold his legions took from this place, the amount would be finite. He could imagine the imperial coffers back in Ellistium full to overflowing as never before. But for how long would the plunder last?

Unless he struck Shashida a fatal blow here and now, not even the *Pon Q'tar* could predict how long the War of Attrition might continue. Given the great wealth of this valley, Shashida might be able to finance her war needs endlessly. Soldiers and weapons of war were replaceable, up to a point. But because Rustannica's indigenous gold deposits were nearing depletion, Rustannica could again become a victim of her own successes, and even the stolen gold reserves would one day be used up.

Taking Ryoto was the key, he knew. If he could kill the members of the *Chikara Inkai* and the *Kokkai Kokumen*, the total defeat of Shashida would soon follow. But how much gold should be harvested before he ordered this valley abandoned? And when he did, in what direction should he send his legions—homeward to safety, or onward toward Ryoto and an uncertain future?

At first his goal had been only to send as much gold as possible to Ellistium, then retreat homeward to fight this war another day and with vastly renewed strength. But no Rustannican force in history had advanced this close to Ryoto. Taking the Shashidan capital was so tempting that he knew he must strategize only with his head, not his heart. Then Vespasian smiled wryly as he remembered that being on campaign was always a far different and far uglier thing than was proposing it to the Suffragat in the luxurious surroundings of the Aedifficium.

Were his legions' recent successes due to luck, he wondered, or were the Shashidans cleverly drawing him in? Now that his new gifts had been realized and Ryoto lay before him, should he continue this fight to its finish? That was what Gracchus wanted. And what of the *Jin'Sai?* he wondered. If Tristan reached Shashida, he was surely in Ryoto, plotting with the *Chikara Inkai.* As Gracchus said, there would be no better time for Vespasian to kill the *Jin'Sai* than now, hopefully before the Vigors mystics could imbue Tristan's blood with spells that might match his own . . .

"Here we are," Lucius announced, returning Vespasian to the issue at hand. "What say you, my liege? It goes well, don't you think?"

The scene before them was amazing in its scope and efficiency. No other force on earth could accomplish so much so fast, Vespasian realized as he watched his legionnaires and mystics go about their unique labors.

Like the many other staging areas dotting the valley, this one was supervised by a tribune. Vespasian knew Antonius Tertia well, as they had served together on many campaigns. As the Lead Tribune of the Thirty-third Legion, Antonius had acquired a fearsome battle reputation, and like Lucius he was a legendary womanizer. Tall and broad, he wore a great red beard. Like the other legionnaires toiling under the hot Shashidan sun, he had stripped down to his waist, and his bare skin shone with the sweat of his labors. As the trio approached he did not look up, involved as he was in recording the latest tallies in a beeswax diptych.

Vespasian smiled. "Are you so greedy to collect Shashidan gold that you have no words for an old friend?" he chided the tribune.

Looking up from his book, Antonius smiled back and gave the three visitors a perfect salute.

"Indeed not, my liege!" he said robustly. "Your visit is an honor!"

After paying his respects to the empress and Lucius, Antonius gestured toward the amazing sight. "Impressive, is it not?" he asked. "All of this gold, ours for the taking!"

As the legionnaires harvested the gold by hand from the riverbeds and mountainsides, it was loaded onto horse-drawn carts. The six-horse teams then drew the gold toward larger wagons. The larger wagons measured ten meters long by five meters wide and were built of stout Rustannican oak with iron-braced floors. When filled to the brim, each cart carried about ten tons of pure gold. Then each cart was pulled by a team of six great beasts into the azure portal located at each staging area, where it was sent by way of the craft to Ellistium. There the cart was unloaded, and it and its beasts were returned to the valley by tribune mystics under the command of Flavius Maximus, Vespasian's choice as Imperator Tempitatus.

Suddenly Vespasian heard a great noise and turned to look. *The Bedevilers seem unusually ill-tempered today,* he thought. Smiling, he watched the great beasts that stood harnessed to the larger carts, impatiently waiting as the carts were filled.

Bedevilers were massive creatures that had been conjured by the *Pon Q'tar* to serve a variety of wartime purposes. Standing ten meters tall, each creature stood upon four huge cloven hooves. Their powerful legs allowed them to run swiftly if need be and to move great loads. They possessed dark, shaggy bodies that were stout and powerful, and they had thick, bull-like necks. Their wide heads were also bovine in nature, with long black horns and dark eyes set far apart. Another long, sharp horn meant for stabbing enemy troops and throwing them into the air extended from either side of the beasts' pink snouts.

Bulls were revered in Rustannica for their strength, loyalty, and fertility, and sacrificing one to the Vagaries was considered a sacred rite. It was for those same qualities that the *Pon Q'tar* chose bulls as the template for these creatures that served the mighty legions so well. Each Bedeviler carried a roofed wooden platform strapped to its wide back. Each platform could accommodate ten legionnaires or mystic tribunes at one time. Huge leather bridles adorned the Bedevilers' heads, the reins leading back to the legionnaire controlling the great beast from the protection of the roofed platform.

Vespasian smiled as he watched the nearest team of Bedevilers snort and paw at the ground while they waited for their cart to be loaded. They could be impatient, ill-tempered beasts and quite difficult to control. Each Bedeviler had one mystic master who oversaw its training and use, and several lesser legionnaires who saw to its care and feeding. Aside from being the perfect beasts of burden, Bedevilers also provided excellent platforms from which legionnaires could hurl azure bolts or use the craft to shoot perfectly aimed arrows.

Their tough hides nearly impervious to any weapon other than one born of the craft, the beasts had been known to charge through Shashidan forces with abandon, causing havoc and crushing katsugai mosota by the scores in their wakes, thereby earning their names. If needed, they could be relied on to mow down trees as they cleared pathways for Vespasian's foot soldiers. They were highly valuable tools of war and perfectly suited to the task of hauling the captured Shashidan gold toward the waiting portals. As he stood watching them, for the thousandth time Vespasian found himself glad that they were not servants of the Shashidan cohorts.

Again opening the diptych, Vespasian took another glance at the gold tally inscribed at the bottom of the single beeswax page. His legions had been at the task for but one day and half of the next, but the tonnage was already huge, most of it safely in Ellistium's coffers and loyally guarded by Flavius Maximus and his home legions. Balancing his nation's pecuniary needs against the greater objective, Vespasian made a fateful decision. He handed the diptych back to Lucius.

"I will permit the legionnaires to harvest gold for the rest of today and all of tomorrow," Vespasian told Lucius. "When dawn rises the day after next, I want this entire army ready to move. Whatever gold has been sent home by then will simply have to suffice."

"As you order, my liege," Lucius answered. He gave his friend and emperor a wry smile. "May the First Tribune inquire as to our new destination?"

Vespasian thought somberly for a moment before answering.

"Order the *Pon Q'tar* to prepare portal calculations that will transport our army onto the flat plains south of here, near where the Alarik again divides," Vespasian answered. "From there we advance on Ryoto. The attack will be risky, but there might never again come such an excellent chance to kill all the Shashidan leaders and the *Jin'Sai* at the same time."

As Vespasian's eyes again scanned the snowy peaks that so worried him, his expression darkened further.

"My heart tells me that Tristan is plotting with the *Inkai*," he said softly. "Since the days that we were born, our meeting was meant to be. Let us finally make it so."

CHAPTER XLVI

PULLING HER STRONG WINGS THROUGH THE EVENING air, Sigrid soared eastward high above Eutracia. The night was clear, allowing her an excellent view of the ground below. Perhaps more than any other Minion, she was the one most eager to begin this fight. More important, she considered it her personal mission to ensure that Valda and the twenty-eight other members of the Night Witch patrol she once commanded had not died in vain. *Our revenge will be sweet,* she thought as her dark eyes scanned the Sippora River slipping by beneath her.

Despite her broken arm, soon after she reported back from the slaughter in Tanglewood she had begged Traax for command of another Night Witch group. Traax had agreed heartily, adding that although her group had perished, no one considered her personally responsible for the defeat. In fact, her service and bravery had been exemplary, he said. It was because of these qualities that she had been given the honor of leading this vastly important war party through the night. Although her fellow Minions saw her as a hero, Sigrid did not share that opinion. For her, this new command was a rare opportunity to redeem her honor, and she would sooner die than waste it.

Looking rearward, she saw her twenty-nine new Night Witches steadfastly following her. Rather than accept command of an established group, Sigrid had requested only Minion females whose special-ized Night Witch training was still incomplete, so that she might mold them to her liking. After Traax granted her request, Sigrid hand-picked the twenty-nine who would become hers. Despite her injured arm, Sigrid had been training these women since the Tanglewood slaughter, and they were ready to serve. Sigrid had learned much from that fight, and in some ways her new group was superior to the one she lost. Their new war cry "Remember Tanglewood!" was heard each time her group took to the skies and went on patrol.

Show yourself, Khristos, she thought as the cool evening air rushed past her face. *This time you will not find my warriors to be such easy prey.*

Half the entire Minion force followed her lead, six of them carrying a litter bearing Shailiha, Faegan, and Traax. Determined never to make the same mistake again, Shailiha ordered that Aeolus, Duvessa, Sister Adrian, all the consuls and acolytes, and the other half of the Minion force remain behind to guard the palace and the Redoubt. They would be sorely missed in the coming fight, but every Conclave member had agreed with the princess's decision.

Gambling that Khristos and his vipers were heading toward the coast, the war party had left the palace two hours ago to fly east, follow-ing the course of the Sippora River. In truth the Conclave could not know the enemy's position. But if Khristos and his forces wished to remain unseen, they had no choice but to remain submerged in the Sippora.

That left the Viper Lord only three options. He could remain in the river, he could head upstream and deeper into Eutracia, or he could head downstream toward the sea. Staying in place seemed unlikely, for Khristos surely knew that the section of river where the recent fighting had taken place would be swarming with Minion warriors desperate to kill him and his followers. The enemy might proceed upriver, but Traax had wisely ordered several thousand of his troops to swoop low over the river and continuously dredge its bottom with weighted nets. Khristos could easily use the craft to destroy the nets, the Conclave realized, but if he did, they would know it, and Shailiha's war party could be called home to deal with him there.

Heading toward the sea was Khristos' likely choice, the Conclave de-cided. Perhaps of greatest concern was that the Sea of Whispers would provide a huge place in which Khristos and his Blood Vipers could hide. No longer limited to Eutracia's rivers, they could travel up and

down the length of the Eutracian coastline at will, then surface anywhere of their choosing and travel overland. They could also again slink
up the length of the Sippora River, or choose the Vitenka River lying to
the south from which to reenter Eutracia.

The theory that Khristos was heading for the sea was but one of several possibilities, but by necessity it must be the first place that the
Conclave searched. Once the Viper Lord and his followers were loosed
into those waters, all the advantages would be theirs. Searching the sea
itself would be pointless, for if Khristos had already managed to reach
it he could be lurking anywhere in its depths. And so the Conclave's
search would start at the coast of the Cavalon Delta and backtrack westward along the Sippora's winding length. It was hoped that Khristos
and his vipers would be found somewhere between the delta and where
the Minions dredged the Sippora in Tammerland.

Sitting in the speeding litter alongside Faegan and Traax, Shailiha
looked eastward with worry. Unlike the many other times when she had
faced danger, tonight she felt hesitant. Despite the wondrous help given
to the Conclave by the *Chikara Inkai,* the marked absence of so many
Conclave members was causing her to feel uneasy, as if an important
part of her human arsenal were missing. Abbey's death had heightened
this feeling, as did her brother's absence. If was as if little by little the
membership of the Conclave was being stripped away and she would
one day be left all alone to face Eutracia's foes.

A great portion of her misgivings could be attributed to her infirmi-
ties, she knew. Because her body still ached, she had reason to doubt
her swordsmanship. Her hampered vision had improved little, and it
handicapped her not only physically but psychologically as well. Of
necessity she continued to wear the black eye patch, and its presence
still caused her to feel freakish and conspicuous. Even so, she staunchly
resolved to keep her personal insecurities hidden and to command her
forces with decisiveness. Suddenly reminded of her late mother, she
closed her eyes.

A queen cannot always let her feelings be known, she thought, *even if she is
only a queen in waiting. At least this eye patch has taught me that much.*

Sensing her discomfort, Faegan reached out to touch her hand. "A
kisa for your thoughts," he said.

She gave him a slight smile. "There's no need to pay me for my
thoughts," she answered. "You've always been able to sense my moods
and you know it. It has something to do with being a wizard, I imagine."

Faegan smiled. As the litter jounced through the air he cradled the precious vial of subtle matter lying in his lap.

"Each of us has a part to play," he answered. "And we can do so only according to our gifts. Your gifts are great, Shailiha. Never forget that. Despite all of the things that seem to overwhelm you just now, when the time comes, you'll do well. I'm sure of it."

Shailiha's good eye looked at the vial in Faegan's lap. "Is that all of it?" she asked.

"I'm afraid so," Faegan answered. "The length of the Sippora between the delta and Tammerland is vast. Despite the *Inkai*'s advice, I hope that there will be no need to use it all. Unless a safe way is found to travel back and forth between Shashida, we on this side of the world might never see its like again."

"Do you agree with the *Inkai*'s plans for the craft?" Shailiha asked. "Banning the use of forestallments and destroying the Tome, both Scrolls, and their indexes seem to be drastic measures. I must admit that such radical theories would never have occurred to me."

"Nor to me, had they not first been explained to us by the *Inkai*," Faegan answered. "Although seeing things from our perspective is probably impossible because you are so young, you must always try to remember what has gone before," he added. "Because the Tome has been in our possession for hundreds of years and because it taught us how to use the craft, we always viewed it as a treasure to be protected at all costs. But the *Inkai* see it as nothing more than some obsolete old text, and rightly so. The same is true of the Scrolls and their indexes. So you see, it is all a matter of perspective. Like Wigg and Tristan, we have come to believe that the *Inkai* are right. Once Rustannica and Shashida are united, only radical changes to the craft and to everyone's blood signatures will enable both sides to live together in peace. If these things are not done, the continued pull of the Vigors and the Vagaries on the human condition will doom history to repeat itself. A radical notion, you say? You are right, my dear, but it is far more than that! To us old mystics, it seems downright treasonous! But that's the strange thing about a truly honorable peace, Shailiha. For it to last and to be effective, each side—even the victors—must make sacrifices. That's the mistake that the late Directorate made with the Coven of Sorceresses, and no one need tell *you* about how that came back to haunt us! If Tristan and the *Inkai* can one day defeat Rustannica, the craft and the world it governs will likely change forever."

Taking his gaze from hers, Faegan looked out toward the eastern horizon.

"I hope we will all live to see that day," he added quietly.

"As do I, old friend," replied the princess.

Just then a Night Witch flew up alongside the litter and shouted something to Traax. Traax nodded, then ordered her to return to the formation. He was by Shailiha's side in seconds.

"Sigrid informs us that the coast is near, *Jin'Saiou*," he said. "What are your orders?"

Shailiha looked eastward to where the sea met the shore. The Cavalon Delta lay there, the Sippora separating into three streams across its marshy land before it flowed into the sea. Khristos could be hiding in one or more of those branches, or in none of them, she realized.

"We will perform this search one stream at a time," she ordered. "If he is not found, we will search the next one and finally the third, if need be. Only when we know that all three branches are free of him will we turn westward and search the river proper. Order Sigrid to lead us toward the shoreline where the southernmost branch meets the sea. We will start our search there."

Traax stood and snapped his boot heels together. "Very good, Highness," he answered. Looking toward his warriors, he immediately began barking out orders. At once the entire war party started its descent and turned southeast.

Within moments they had arrived. As the flight of warriors swooped low over the estuary, Shailiha turned to Faegan and nodded.

At once the crippled wizard lifted the precious vial from his lap and poured some of the precious subtle matter onto the surface of the stream. As it landed atop the water, he recited the incantation supplied to him by the *Inkai*.

When he finished, Shailiha gave him a worried look. "Can this actually work?" she asked. "It seems impossible . . ."

"I understand," Faegan answered, his eyes glued intently on the water. "Even so, because this part of the process has been taught to us by the *Inkai*, I do not doubt its efficacy. Once Khristos has been found, it's the next part of the plan that gives me pause."

"Why?" she asked.

"Because we will then be relying on Failee's mastery of the craft, rather that the expertise of the Shashidans," he answered, still searching the water for signs of life. "The First Mistress was brilliant, but the se-

cret spell that she devised to deal with Khristos and then hid in her grimoire remains untested—it must be so, or the Viper Lord and his servants would already be dead. Thus, we cannot be sure that it will work.
An unproven spell is a dangerous thing, Princess. For each way that it
can go right, there are always one hundred ways for it to go wrong. We
agree that it worked at one time, because as you know, Succiu once used
it centuries ago to torture someone who would later become a member
of the Conclave. But that person had been human, and our enemies are
not. If the spell does not perform exactly as outlined in Failee's grimoire, we might accomplish no more than to unleash an even greater
monster of some kind. I suspect that even Failee was unsure how her
original spell might have affected Khristos and the viper embryos when
she first condemned them to that river in Hartwick Wood. If they were
somehow further changed without her knowing, all of this might be a
grave mistake."

Faegan shook his head as he suddenly grasped a bizarre irony.

"For the first time in my more than three centuries of existence, I am
forced to hope that one of the First Mistress's spells works perfectly," he
said ruefully. "May the Afterlife forgive me for this use of the Vagaries."

Shailiha looked back down at the southernmost stream and saw that
the telltale phenomena described by the *Inkai* were not appearing.

"We have failed here," she said. "We must search the next branch."

After Shailiha shouted out new orders to Traax, the Minion commander relayed them to Sigrid and the war party turned north. Soon they
were at the shoreline where the middle stream met the sea. Again the
Jin'Saiou nodded to Faegan, and the wizard started the painstaking process anew. After more subtle matter had been dropped onto the water,
Faegan again recited the incantation. Tense moments passed as the war
party hovered, every eye trained on the dark, rippling water below.

Suddenly Shailiha saw the glow of the craft appear. The process was
mesmerizing. Little by little, azure dots of light were gathering atop
the surface of the tributary. Before she knew it there were thousands of
them, each one signifying the exact place where a Blood Viper lurked in
the water below.

Then her blood ran cold as she realized that the multitudes of haunting azure dots were slowly moving toward the restless ocean. In mere
moments the first of them would enter the Sea of Whispers and perhaps
escape forever. Desperate to start the second part of the process, she
turned toward Faegan.

"We've found them!" she shouted. "But we have little time! You must call Failee's spell before they reach the sea!"

Everyone in the war party knew how vitally important it was that Faegan perform the next part of the attack flawlessly, lest the monsters and their terrible leader escape them forever. Summoning all of his power, Faegan began reciting Failee's centuries-old incantation:

> 'Tis your blood that is sought;
> 'Tis heat to be wrought;
> No god or man can end my toil;
> No savior may cause this enchantment to spoil;
> I command your blood essence to writhe and churn;
> You shall feel your very soul to burn.

Her heart in her throat, Shailiha stared breathlessly at the water.

CHAPTER XLVII

STANDING ON THE FOREDECK OF THE *TAMMERLAND,* Tristan could scarcely believe his eyes. The scene unfolding all around him was overwhelming, proving once and for all that the War of Attrition was indeed conducted on a scale that he and his fellow Eutracians could once have scarcely dreamed of. Yet here they were, about to become a part of it. Simply contemplating the coming fight caused his newly gifted blood to pulse stronger.

Two days had passed since the *Inkai* granted him their versions of the banned forestallments. Just as the elders had feared, the ordeal had almost destroyed him. Twice during the agonizing process he nearly died, his heart beating so wildly that it almost ruptured as Wigg, Tyranny, Jessamay, and the *Inkai* watched and worried.

Only Mashiro's craft skills kept Tristan from perishing as the spells first assaulted his blood, then finally became part of it. The process complete, he had lain senseless in his private quarters for four more hours before regaining consciousness.

Tristan had awoken weakened and confused. Wigg, Jessamay, Tyranny, and Hoshi were all there waiting to welcome him back to the world. He spent the remainder of that day and night resting. On the following morning he felt much like his old self again and he had demanded a hearty breakfast.

With Wigg and Jessamay looking on, Tristan spent the following day with Mashiro as the *Inkai* elder explained his new gifts and instructed him in how to summon and dismiss them. Tristan's new abilities sounded so awesome that he and the other Eutracians could scarcely believe what they were hearing. Along with his instruction to Tristan, Mashiro added a grave warning: Because you are still unaccustomed to your powers, they are not to be summoned until they are needed on the battlefield, he cautioned the *Jin'Sai*. And only on Hoshi's orders, he added.

Later that day, the *Inkai* granted him, Wigg, Jessamay, Astrid, and Phoebe the much-needed language forestallments that allowed them to speak both Shashidan and Rustannican. The Eutracian mystics were astounded at how suddenly their new gifts took hold, causing them to involuntarily slip from one of the three languages now at their command into another one almost without knowing. Smiling at their ineptitude, Mashiro told them that with practice, their control over the languages would soon improve.

The next morning, Tristan stood squarely on the deck of the *Tammerland* watching the Shashidan forces gather for the coming fight. He understood all too well that he was an irrevocably changed man. Never again would he return to the lesser being that he had once been, nor could he envision wishing to so do. It was his destiny to take part in this fight.

Tristan had never felt so powerful, so alive. He knew instinctively that even his gift of *K'Shari* paled when compared to the new powers flowing through his veins. He felt like a towering giant among men, as if his will alone could shape the world and its events to his liking. Moreover, it was all he could do to keep from using his gifts here and now. They beckoned to him, begging to be used. But as much as these new feelings enthralled him, they also worried him.

He wisely confided in Wigg and Mashiro his desire to loose his gifts prematurely. As Wigg listened, he became very concerned. Mashiro did his best to reassure them by saying that the *Inkai* believed this was to be expected. Given the nature of the *Jin'Sai's* blood and the immense power it now held, how could one imagine otherwise? he asked.

He went on to say that the *Inkai* also believed that Tristan's mind would overcome these temptations, just as they guessed Vespasian's had done. Although Tristan's blood had been granted these unprecedented gifts, it had not been fundamentally changed. Tristan's great need to be errant was not dangerous, Mashiro added, provided the *Jin'Sai* controlled his new gifts to the best of his abilities and employed them only in the service of the Vigors. By granting him the banned forestallments, the *Inkai* had placed more trust in him than in any other human being that had ever existed in the history of Shashida. *Listen to Hoshi and use your new gifts wisely,* Mashiro said, *lest the world suffer at your hand rather than be helped by it.*

With the arrival of Tristan's new gifts, everyone seemed to regard him with awe and apprehension. The Shashidans bowed deeper toward him, and when they spoke their tones conveyed even greater humility and reverence. Even his fellow Eutracians seemed unsure how to behave in his presence. Such behavior toward him seemed only to heighten his newfound sense of separateness.

Hearing boot heels strike the deck, Tristan turned to see Wigg approaching. Like Tristan, the First Wizard had chosen to go to war wearing his customary Eutracian clothes. Although he and Tristan had become accustomed to Shashidan garb, today their old clothes felt more appropriate. Tristan's worn leather vest, black breeches, and knee boots seemed like old friends, as did his dreggan and his throwing knives. Like Tristan's clothes, Wigg's boots and worn gray robe had been spotlessly cleaned. For a long time the two friends simply stared in awe at the gathering Shashidan forces.

"Have you ever seen the like?" Tristan asked, using the Shashidan dialect.

Remaining silent for a time, Wigg placed his hands into opposite robe sleeves.

"There simply are no words," he finally answered in kind.

As the Shashidan war forces gathered around the two Black Ships, Wigg empowered the *Tammerland* while Jessamay piloted the *Ephyra,* the Eutracian vessels hovering side by side at an attitude of about one hundred meters. Tyranny, Scars, and Ox were also aboard the *Tammerland,* while Phoebe and Astrid were stationed on the *Ephyra.* The Black Ships' decks were swarming with Tristan's Minions, each warrior spoiling for a fight. Even the stalwart Minions had been rendered speechless as they too watched the massive Shashidan army gather in the sky around them.

The Black Ships' journey from Ryoto to these distant flatlands had been accomplished by way of azure portals. Several Shashidan divisions, or *bunkatsu,* had gone through first to make sure that the staging area south of the lower Tani Kinkiro entrance was clear of the enemy. Each division held ten thousand male and female katsugai mosota. Only after the staging area was deemed free of the enemy were Tristan's two Black Ships and the remainder of the Shashidan army allowed to follow. As Tristan watched the Shashidan forces continue to pour forth from the whirling airborne portals, their growing ranks seemed endless.

Once gathered, the Shashidan forces would be staggering in their power. Each cohort, or *kensai,* held ten divisions, for a total of one hundred thousand fighters. Like the Rustannican legions, each kensai was commanded by an expert mystic or *mahotsukai.* The Shashidan army held thirty kensai, meaning that it easily numbered three million katsugai. Julia Idaeus had informed them that the Rustannican legions numbered at least that many soldiers, perhaps more. As Tristan looked around he realized that when finally assembled, the Shashidan forces would stretch across the sky as far as the eye could see. Six million warriors would soon clash in one of the mightiest struggles ever witnessed on earth.

The Shashidan attack would be partly an airborne assault and a partly a ground assault, Mashiro had told the Eutracians. The goal was to strike with speed and surprise while Vespasian's troops were still busy plundering the gold. Half of the Shashidan forces were already on their way north by azure portal to a point above the far entrance to the Tani Kinkiro. When both staging areas were ready, two opposing Shashidan attacks would crush Vespasian's legions guarding the valley entrances and then proceed toward each other down the valley's length, killing as they went. Vespasian's legions situated in the valley would be forced to hold their positions if they wished to keep on harvesting gold. But the trapped Rustannican forces would surely fight back with everything they had, and the struggle would be savage in its ferocity.

The *Inkai* guessed that Vespasian would realize it was better to keep what gold he had taken and retreat to fight another day, rather than remain in the valley and fight it out. The loss of the gold would be unfortunate, Mashiro said, for it would enable Vespasian to continue fighting this war for decades to come or longer. Even so, during the brief time available to them, the Rustannicans could not have pilfered enough gold to make any appreciable difference to the Shashidan coffers.

Taking back the valley was the main goal, the *Inkai* decided. But should Vespasian foolishly decide to fight to the end, the katsugai would gladly oblige him. So as to speed the lightning Shashidan attack, no slow-moving supply lines would be established unless the battle became a protracted one. Like the Rustannicans, the Shashidans had conjured beasts at their disposal. But because transporting and handling the various Vigors beasts was a laborious process, it was decided that they would not be employed despite the presence of Rustannican Blood Stalkers and Bedevilers. The katsugai mosota understood that they alone would bear the full weight of the attack, and they accepted the responsibility with relish.

As Tristan and Wigg watched, ever more Shashidan airborne war barges exited the azure portals, each one crammed full of katsugai mosota. Soon the great airships would blot out the sky. When Tristan had first seen the Black Ships, he was staggered by their size. He couldn't imagine that any vessel of the sea or of the air might eclipse them in sheer magnitude. But he had been wrong.

Unlike the frigatelike Black Ships, the Shashidan vessels were true barges. Also known as *tataki fune,* their primary mission was to bring as many katsugai to the fight as possible while protecting them at the same time. Azure portals were infinitely faster at transporting soldiers and materiel, but their inherent drawback was the immediate vulnerability of those rushing from its depths as they emerged onto the battlefield. Although far slower, the flying barges afforded greater protection to the troops while deploying them where the real fighting raged.

Each tataki fune was square in shape, measuring four hundred meters on every side. Their hulls were flat, and each one could accommodate a full Shashidan division of ten thousand katsugai. Made of wood and protected against harm by *Inkai* enchantments, they carried no sails but were empowered by expert katsugai craft practitioners, four to each barge. Their wooden sides were straight and flat, with portholes through which the katsugai mosota and barge pilots could look out. Each tataki fune was painted a vibrant color matching the armor color of the katsugai division that it carried. To give them a fearsome appearance, intricately carved heads representing various Shashidan mythological beasts projected from their bows, and corresponding tails were fixed to their sterns. They were truly amazing craft constructs, and their magnificence only added to Tristan's growing sense of awe.

And commanding it all—her authority over all the Shashidan forces absolute—was the woman called Hoshi of the House of Lotus Blossoms.

Tristan had not seen Hoshi that day, but he knew that she was there somewhere, busily preparing the Shashidan forces for their attack. He knew so little about her, he realized.

How old was she really, he wondered, and how had she come to be the supreme commander of all the Shashidan forces? Was she in fact ancient and protected by time enchantments, as were the other members of the *Chikara Inkai*? Her youthful appearance was incongruous among the *Inkai* elders, yet her vision and counsel were equally respected. Tristan assumed that only the *Inkai* superseded her military authority, but he could not be sure. One thing was certain, however: She was a true warrior. Moreover, she brooked no misbehavior from her katsugai, and her orders were sometimes expertly enforced by the use of her sword. *As well they should be,* he thought grimly.

Just then Tyranny, Scars, and Ox approached. Saying nothing, Tyranny produced her gold case and lit a cigarillo. Like Wigg and Tristan, today she wore her Eutracian clothes. Tristan smiled as he was reminded how piratical she could appear.

Tousling her dark hair in disbelief, she took another deep lungful of smoke as she watched the huge tataki fune taking up their massive formations in the sky.

"I see it, but I still can't grasp it," she breathed.

"I know," Tristan answered, remembering to speak only Eutracian in her presence.

"Ox always believed Black Ships big," the huge Minion said. "They be nothing next to Shashidan vessels."

Tristan was about to respond when one of the Shashidan war barges floated dangerously near the *Tammerland.* It was packed to overflowing with eager katsugai. As the barge pulled alongside, its katsugai bowed to Tristan reverently, but foremost in his mind was the worry that the two vessels might collide. He was about to order Wigg to shear the *Tammerland* away when he saw an armored katsugai mystic officer levitate from the barge to land on the Black Ship's foredeck.

The fighter stood there for a moment, looking at him from behind an elaborate war mask. This was Tristan's first glimpse of a fully armored katsugai close up, and the effect was chilling.

Armor covered the katsugai's head and body, leaving virtually no place vulnerable to attack. It was constructed of lightweight metal plates bound together by leather cords, each plate overlapping the next. The plates had been lacquered a shiny black to make them waterproof and to identify the cohort and the air barge to which he belonged. Chain mail connected the plates at strategic joints, allowing for freedom of movement. The various pieces included a breastplate and backplate, greaves, gauntlets, footwear, and an elaborate helmet. Broad shoulder pads of bright red woven metal draped down over the upper arms. The gloves were of black chain mail.

The helmet was particularly fascinating. Also made of black lacquered metal, it was rounded on the top, with a wide brim to keep the sun out of the fighter's eyes. A broad, low-slung metal shield attached to the back of the helmet protected the katsugai's neck from rearward blows. The helmet was held in place by a thick black leather cord tied under the katsugai's chin in a large bow.

Of all its amazing features, the helmet's face mask was the most intimidating. It too was made of shiny black lacquered metal, and the image engraved upon it was fearsome. The eye slits were slanted and wicked-looking, the facial expression warlike, the open mouth and sneering lips twisted into a seething grimace. More chain mail protected the katsugai's throat, and the traditional long and short swords were secured at the fighter's left hip. Taken as a whole, the effect was daunting. To an uninitiated enemy, the mere sight of this armored warrior might well cause him to throw down his weapons.

Tristan was about to speak when the katsugai extended one gloved hand and grasped the chin of his mask. The mask swiveled upward ingeniously and disappeared into the space between the crown of the katsugai's head and the top of his helmet. Removing the helmet, with a shake of her head Hoshi tossed her long black hair free. She gave Tristan a solemn bow which he politely returned, once he recovered from his astonishment.

"We are ready, *Jin'Sai*," she said simply. "It is time for you to come with me."

Tristan nodded. It would feel strange to leave his friends just before the battle, but it had to be this way, for he was not leading this fight. Hoshi was in command and he had pledged to obey her. He turned to look at Wigg.

"I leave command of the Minions and the Black Ships to you," he said. "Aid the struggle to the best of your abilities. I will be on Hoshi's barge, also doing what I can."

A somber look on his face, Tristan stepped forward and embraced Wigg.

"Goodbye for now, old friend," he said quietly. "In Abbey's name, kill as many Rustannicans as you can."

Nodding, Wigg blinked away a tear. "Take care, *Jin'Sai*," he answered. "Above all, remember Mashiro's warnings and use your new gifts wisely."

After again looking into Wigg's misty eyes, Tristan turned and walked to Hoshi's side. Hoshi put her helmet back in place, then pulled down her war mask and raised one hand in Tristan's direction. They levitated up and away from the *Tammerland*'s bow deck to land on Hoshi's war barge.

Moments later, the order was given, and the mighty Shashidan armada turned to sail into history.

CHAPTER XLVIII

FROM HER PLACE IN THE HOVERING LITTER, SHAILIHA looked breathlessly down at the Sippora River's middle stream. *Failee's spell is working!* she realized.

Faegan's recitation of the incantation found in Failee's grimoire was initiating a Blood Pox on Khristos and his vipers. It was succeeding exactly as it would have done for the First Mistress, had she lived and found it necessary to destroy her terrible creations. The first part of the plan had been to find Khristos by following the *Inkai*'s instructions in the use of the subtle matter. Now that the second part of the attack plan had taken effect, every pair of eyes in the hovering war party watched with rapt fascination as Failee's ancient, long-forgotten spell went about its grisly work. The spell was designed to raise the blood temperature of Khristos and his followers until they died. They would suffer horrible, torturous deaths, the punishments more than appropriate for the crimes that the Viper Lord and his gang of monsters had committed against humanity.

There was a welcome kind of rough justice about unleashing Failee's Blood Pox against her own creations, Shailiha thought as she watched the waters of the Sippora writhe and churn. Not only would the Viper Lord and his followers be tormented, but there would be an added sense

of retribution in the name of a departed Conclave member. For this was
the very spell that Succiu, Second Mistress of the Coven, had used to
trap and to torture Geldon, the hunchbacked dwarf that she first discovered in the Parthalonian Ghetto of the Shunned. Later she would employ him as her personal slave, forcing him to scour Parthalon for
suitable victims on whom she would practice her bizarre predilections.
The Blood Pox had left Geldon impotent and sterile—two afflictions
that Succiu refused to cure. Geldon had been loyal and brave, and he
had been instrumental in helping the Conclave to win some of its most
important battles over the Vagaries. But an assassin in the service of the
Vagaries had killed him, and to this day his fellow Conclave members
missed him deeply.

Taking her eyes from the churning water, Shailiha looked to the
nighttime sky and toward the seemingly limitless number of stars suspended from its ebony canopy. Since the day she had learned of Geldon's
death, she liked to believe that one of those stars represented his soul,
that soul that had been so much greater than the stunted body that contained it. *May you now rest peacefully, my friend,* she thought.

Looking back down at the roiling, steaming water, Shailiha suddenly
felt the need to attain another form of justice. This need was personal,
and it quickly overpowered her. Her face a mask of grim determination,
she turned to Faegan.

"Stop applying the spell," she ordered.

Faegan was stunned by her words.

"But it's working, Princess!" he protested. "You mustn't order me
to stop now! Given more time, their blood will literally boil, killing
them all! Why in the name of the Afterlife would you order me to
stop?"

Incensed, Shailiha glared into Faegan's eyes. "If you stop the spell,
are Khristos and his followers likely to emerge?" she demanded.

Faegan looked at her quizzically. "I would suspect so," he answered,
still bewildered by the *Jin'Saiou*'s demand. "They will likely attribute
their suffering to the boiling water, not knowing that it is in fact their
own rising blood temperatures that are causing the water to heat."

"And will Khristos still be able to call the craft?" she demanded.

"I do not know," Faegan answered. "But because the Blood Pox
raised his blood temperature to such a high level, his powers have probably been at least somewhat lessened. That might have been the goal of

Failee's spell all along. His Blood Vipers will probably be similarly affected."

"Good," Shailiha answered. "Now stop employing the spell! That is a direct order!"

Still confused, Faegan simply stared back at her. If he was to do this thing, he was determined to understand her reasons.

"But *why*?" he again protested, this time fairly screeching at her.

Raising one hand, Shailiha pointed to her black eye patch. "*This* is why!" she shouted. "And I do this for Abbey as well! I want that abomination of the craft to know that it was I who killed him! Now are you going to obey my orders before it's too late?"

"Very well," Faegan answered. "But after the spell is gone, what are your plans?"

"The plan is simple," Shailiha answered. "When they emerge, I will take the Minions down and kill them all. You may participate if you like. But this is going to happen with or without you approval."

Her face grim, the *Jin'Saiou* looked back down at the roiling water.

"I fully understand that dead is dead, no matter how it is arrived at," she added quietly. "But how these abominations meet their end has meaning for me. The Blood Pox seems too easy. I want them butchered in the same way that they butchered so many of us. I forbid you to use your powers against the Viper Lord's person unless he kills me."

Finally consenting, Faegan ended the spell. Soon the water stopped churning and the rising steam vanished. Tense moments passed as the hovering war party waited and watched. As the first of the many reptilian heads broke the surface of the river, Shailiha turned toward Traax.

"Order your warriors and Night Witches to attack," she said. "Take every head, but leave Khristos to me."

"I live to serve!" Traax answered. He quickly shouted out a series of orders to the Minions and they started peeling off from their formations to dive toward the ground.

"Now get me down there," Shailiha ordered Traax.

Traax quickly lifted the *Jin'Saiou* into his arms and turned to fly from the litter. Before he launched into the air, he looked down to find an empty landing spot. What he saw caused his muscles to clench.

"Look there!" he shouted.

Shailiha quickly swiveled her head and looked down.

Khristos stood on the riverbank, his face and body covered with boils and his skin scalded red by the water. As his thousands of Blood Vipers slithered up the banks, Shailiha saw that they were similarly plagued. Khristos looked up and saw the litter, and his reptilian eyes locked onto Shailiha's. Raising one boil-infested hand, he beckoned her down with a sneer.

Without hesitation, Traax snapped open his wings and took flight.

CHAPTER XLIX

AS TRISTAN STOOD BESIDE HOSHI IN THE BOW OF HER black war barge, ten thousand heavily armed katsugai stood waiting in strict lines behind them, filling the vessel to the gunwales. Having been ordered to stay behind, Tristan's Eutracian comrades and his beloved Black Ships were nowhere to be seen. But he couldn't risk worrying about them now, he realized. History was about to be made, and once it began, there could be no going back for either side.

Hoshi had strategically dispersed the war barges that hadn't already been sent to wait near the upper entrance of the valley. Some remained near the lower valley staging area with Tristan's Black Ships, while the rest had been divided into two opposing flight groups. Closely hugging the outer slopes of the valley mountain ranges, they quickly flew north and stationed themselves one league apart from each other in two hovering lines lying along each side of the valley. Then the great lines of barges levitated at once up the mountainsides, coming to a stop just below the peaks and out of sight of the Rustannicans raiding the gold below.

Hoshi and Tristan's barge also hovered very near the snowy summit. So far, it seemed that the Rustannicans had not detected the Shashidans' presence. Off in the distance, the *Jin'Sai* could make out a war barge dutifully floating at the same altitude on either side of his own. Knowing that they were there was reassuring.

The weather was brutally cold here, causing Tristan to wish that he had chosen to wear a shikifuku rather than his Eutracian vest and breeches. Hoshi had offered him traditional katsugai armor, but because he was unaccustomed to it, he respectfully declined. Snow had started to fall on the lurking barges, adding a surreal quality to the nerve-racking wait. Soon the mountain winds arose, causing Hoshi's black war barge to sway with the familiar creak of a great ship under way.

The Shashidan battle plan sounded effective, but Tristan believed that it would be difficult to execute, considering the thousands of barges that were to take part. When the assigned time arrived, the attack was to begin en masse. Because the barges lined the valley on both sides, it was hoped that the sudden onslaught would be overwhelming, causing the Rustannicans to react with confusion.

As the katsugai being released from the war barges stationed at the lower and upper entrances pushed their way into the valley and toward each other, those barges hovering on either side of the mountains would fly up and over the peaks, then soar down into the valley and also spill forth their fighters. Tristan still believed that the hugely scaled plan would be immensely difficult to coordinate, and he tactfully told Hoshi as much. But after Hoshi explained the devices that had been specially designed to help unify the attack, he quickly changed his mind.

A stout wooden pedestal stood in the bow of their barge. Atop it sat a unique hourglass, enchanted by the *Inkai.* Its upper globe was filled with black sand that fell into a matching lower globe. Both globes glowed with the azure hue of the craft. Each of the thousands of barges was thus equipped, Hoshi explained. On leaving the staging area, she had enacted the spell that would cause the sand in every one of the thousands of upper globes to begin falling at once. At the same time, the enchantment placed into the many upper globes would ensure that all the grains of sand fell at precisely the same rate. When the sands fully emptied into the lower globes, all the barges would attack simultaneously.

Tristan looked at the hourglass to see that the grains of sand had nearly all fallen. The attack would start soon, he realized. Pulling him to one side, Hoshi raised her war mask. Her gaze was searching, concerned.

"It is doubtful that we will become separated, because the *Inkai* have ordered you and me to stay on this barge at all costs," she said. "It seems that the elders consider us valuable commodities," she added with a little laugh.

She then removed a bright red scarf from beneath her armor and tied it around her upper arm. "Should we lose each other, this will help you to find me again," she said.

Pausing for a moment, she again looked toward the enchanted hourglass. "The moment grows near," she said. "It is time for you to learn your part in all this."

As Hoshi outlined Tristan's orders, he listened intently. When she finished, something unexpected happened. Hearing a rustling of armor, Tristan turned and looked toward the stern of the tataki fune.

All ten thousand katsugai mosota were on bended knees, heads bowed. There seemed to be a sea of them on this barge alone. He turned to again look at Hoshi.

"They do not bow to me, *Jin'Sai*," she said. "They bow to you. As I speak, the same act of reverence is happening on every Shashidan barge, but these katsugai here with you and me will stay with us as our personal bodyguards. It is your time now. Let us start this battle."

Overwhelmed by the unexpected displays of devotion both seen and unseen, Tristan bowed in return. The thousands of katsugai mosota came quickly to their feet.

Hoshi lowered her mask, then turned to watch the last sand grains fall into the lower globe. She quickly shouted a series of orders to her barge's pilot mystic.

At once the barge soared up the craggy mountainside, its ascent so steep that for a time Tristan saw nothing but snow-filled sky. On reaching the crest, the barge suddenly righted for the briefest of moments, then pivoted downward to begin the sharp descent into the valley.

The battle to reclaim the Tani Kinkiro had begun.

CHAPTER L

TO SHAILIHA'S SURPRISE, KHRISTOS TOOK NO IMMEDI-
ate action against her and Traax as they descended into the fray.
Minions were landing by the thousands to begin fighting the Blood
Vipers, and the erupting chaos was growing by the second. Faegan and
Adrian wasted no time in launching azure bolt after azure bolt down
onto the viper hordes still emerging from the tributary. As Traax and
Shailiha landed to face Khristos, the sounds of explosions, screaming,
and death-dealing rose into the night air.

Knowing full well that Shailiha would not be denied her revenge,
Traax decided that she must be protected from the vipers as she confronted the Viper Lord. Shouting out a quick series of orders, he commanded a group of warriors to form a thick protective ring around the
place where Shailiha and Khristos stood facing each other. Reluctantly
joining the ring, Traax grew increasingly worried as he watched the
drama unfold.

Even now Khristos took no direct action against Shailiha, choosing
instead to stand his ground and give the princess a leering smile. His
smile broadened further when he noticed her eye patch. Widening her
stance, Shailiha raised her sword.

"So," Khristos said, "I see that you did not escape the fighting in
Tammerland unscathed after all! You and your wizards likely do not

know it, but there is no known cure for viper venom. By the way, I'm informed by my lead vipers that your herbmistress bitch named Abbey died like the squealing pig that she was. Partial adepts aren't like you and me, are they? They're really little more than pretenders to the craft."

Finally choosing to move, Khristos raised his silver staff. "But worry not about your injured eye, Princess," he said. "You are about to die, and your darkness will become eternal. The same will soon be true of your Minions and mystics. I come to this happy conclusion because I can readily see that my forces outnumber yours. Either we killed far more warriors then we first believed, or you left a sizable force behind to guard the palace. Even now my vipers slaughter your warriors."

As Shailiha stood her ground, Khristos smiled again. "Ah, that's it, isn't it?" he asked. "Determined to never make the same mistake again, you made an even greater one by not bringing your entire force to search us out. Once you and the winged freaks you brought here are dead, taking the palace and ransacking the Redoubt should be easy."

Pausing for a moment, Khristos casually spun his staff as he started circling Shailiha. Just as Tristan had taught her, she pivoted in place as he moved, saving her energy while Khristos expended his.

"Your method of finding us was very clever indeed," Khristos said. "We nearly escaped forever into the Sea of Whispers. But heating the tributary in order to kill us was not so effective, I fear. Did you not realize that we could simply emerge in order to save ourselves? While it's true that we are scalded, we are still quite able to defeat you. It seems that your vaunted Vigors mystics have finally miscalculated after all."

Shailiha remained quiet as she glared into his eyes. No longer sleek and smooth, his olive skin was covered with red, angry boils. The vertical pupils embedded in his almond-shaped yellow irises still seemed vibrant, and they missed nothing. His black robe lay in even greater tatters and scarcely clung to his body. As she watched, his bright red tongue slithered in and out of his mouth, testing the night air.

"We did not heat the river water," Shailiha said at last. "You and your vipers did that. I allowed you to emerge so that I might kill you personally."

Khristos threw back his head and let go a wicked laugh. "The *Pon Q'tar* told me that you were not trained in the ways of the craft," he answered. "Even so, I never dreamed you were so stupid! I am a powerful wizard, you fool! Do you believe that I can be tricked so easily?"

"It's quite true," Shailiha answered. "The spell that we used was of

Failee's making. She hid it in her grimoire for safekeeping, should she need to kill you and your horrible servants. It wasn't the water surrounding you that first became heated." Smiling slightly, she widened her stance a bit more, putting Khristos on notice.

"You are the victim of a Blood Pox," she added quietly.

At the mention of Failee's name, Khristos looked stupefied, as if he had been struck across the face.

"You're lying!" he shouted. "The First Mistress would never have done me harm! We loved each other!"

"No, Khristos," Shailiha answered. "*You* might have loved *her*, but I doubt that she ever really loved you. From the time she went mad and left Wigg, she loved only the Vagaries."

Her expression becoming darker as her memories of the First Mistress surfaced, Shailiha glared hatefully at Failee's reptilian creation.

"I should know," she said menacingly. "For a time, I too was under that bitch's aegis."

"I still say you're lying!" Khristos raged. "And you are about to pay for those lies with your life! I'll enjoy watching my vipers eat your liver! It is a prize to which they have aspired for a long time!" Taking a step closer, he pointed the tip of his silver staff directly at Shailiha's chest.

To everyone's amazement, Shailiha lowered her sword and stepped toward the Viper Lord. Holding her arms wide, she brazenly offered herself up for the killing.

"Then do it, if you're so sure!" she hissed. "Kill me now and prove the First Mistress's love for you! Kill me, you twisted freak!"

Shailiha's taunting finally put Khristos' hatred into action. Summoning all his power, he called the craft.

Shailiha tensed as she watched the craft's power slowly build in the tip of Khristos' staff. With a wicked smile, he let it loose.

The azure beam that streaked toward Shailiha was narrowly focused, yet far slower than any she had seen before. Whirling to one side and trying to ignore her pain, she avoided it.

Screaming with frustration, Khristos began to grasp the terrible truth. Again pointing his staff at the *Jin'Saiou*, he did his best to call the craft. This time the results were even less powerful, and the azure bolt that erupted from the staff's point fizzled in midair and crashed to the ground between them, knocking clumps of dirt and grass into the air.

Shailiha took a deep breath, then raised her sword again. "It's over for you, Khristos," she said. Although they were lessening, from time to time she could still hear the sounds of her warriors struggling with the vicious vipers.

"Kneel before me and I promise to grant you a quick death," she offered. "I suggest that you do it. It's a far more compassionate way to die than being impaled on a stake and disemboweled."

Seething with anger, his powers all but gone, Khristos glared viciously at her.

"Never," he whispered.

Screaming wildly, he raised his staff like a sword and charged straight at her.

Whirling on her heels, Shailiha sidestepped Khristos' staff as it came flashing down, then brought her blade around swiftly. Her sword cleanly severed Khristos' head from his shoulders and it fell to the ground, its reptilian eyes still wide open. The lifeless corpse crashed down beside it.

The *Jin'Saiou* took several precious moments to look around. The azure bolts had stopped raining down, and it seemed that Khristos' Blood Vipers had been all but vanquished by her Minion warriors. Given the monsters' depleted condition, she had gambled that they could be defeated by a lesser force, and she had won. Wanting to be sure, she called out for Traax.

The Minion commander was by her side in seconds. He appeared exhausted, and his dreggan blade was covered in blood. Hissing and screaming still pierced the cold night.

"What is our situation?" she demanded.

"Viper stragglers are being killed as I speak," he answered. "Given the enemies' weakness from the Blood Pox spell, our losses were light."

Shailiha nodded as she sheathed her sword. "See to it that every viper head is taken," she said. "Not one of those creatures is ever to walk the earth again."

"I live to serve!" Traax answered, then quickly turned away to carry out his orders.

Shailiha watched the Minion litter descend and land nearby. As Faegan and Adrian disembarked, Shailiha approached them tiredly. The look on Faegan's face told her that he was relieved but perturbed. Scowling, he folded his arms across his chest.

"You took a great chance, did you not?" he asked. "After all, I said that I couldn't be sure about Khristos' waning powers." Then the wizard looked at the beheaded corpse and he let go a quick smile. "But don't think we're not glad to see him dead," he added.

"I trust your judgment," Shailiha answered simply. "I always have."

She looked up at the nighttime sky. "It will start soon now, won't it?" she asked.

Faegan nodded. "No matter how many times I witness it, I remain amazed."

"As do I," the princess replied.

No sooner had she spoken than lightning streaked across the sky, accompanied by thunder so loud she thought her eardrums might burst. On and on the display continued as Khristos' many forestallments left his blood to go and find their way back into the Well of Forestallments. The wind howled, the trees shook, and the gentle waves that had once hidden Khristos and his Blood Vipers turned into swiftly moving whitecaps. And then, as quickly as it had begun, it was over. Shailiha placed one hand on Faegan's shoulder.

"Let's go home," she said.

Saying nothing, Faegan grasped her hand and nodded.

CHAPTER LI

AS TRISTAN AND HOSHI'S BARGE PLUMMETED DOWN-
ward, at first the *Jin'Sai* could see nothing but snow as it rushed
toward him. Soon the snowfall became so dense that it became difficult
to see Hoshi, even though she stood at his side.

For a few terrifying moments Tristan wondered how the katsugai officer piloting the barge could possibly see through the blizzard, then he
remembered that the warrior was a Shashidan mystic. The wind was
bitter cold, and had Tristan not been so intent on wanting the barge to
clear the blizzard, he would have realized that his body was trembling
and his teeth chattering.

Although he couldn't see them, Tristan knew that thousands more
tataki fune were flying down the mountain slopes from every direction.
Thousands more would be unloading their katsugai divisions at the north
and south valley entrances to claw their way through Vespasian's legions.

Just then the barge burst from the squall to reveal the lush valley
that the Shashidans called the Tani Kinkiro. The valley was so spectac-
ularly beautiful that Tristan forgot his fear. The rolling pastures were
lush and green, the river running through the valley's center majestic
and swift. Even from such a great altitude Tristan could see gold veins
glinting in the mountainsides and nuggets twinkling in the riverbed.
Then he got his first glimpse of the Rustannican legions, and he gasped.

Rustannican soldiers blanketed the valley floor. Even now they were hurriedly gathering up all the gold they could steal. Vespasian's war tents stretched for leagues toward each end of the valley. Great herds of exotic beasts could be seen hauling the purloined gold toward hundreds of whirling azure vortices. Tristan couldn't begin to imagine how much plunder Vespasian had sent to Ellistium.

Nor could he guess why the legions had yet to notice the thousands of katsugai-laden barges that were streaking down the mountainsides, until he grasped how silent was their approach and how intently the Rustannicans toiled at their labors. But that would soon change, he knew, and he would be the catalyst of that change.

On Hoshi's command, their pilot leveled the barge, then caused it to stop and hover about two hundred meters above the valley floor. None of the other barges was stopping, but Tristan expected this. His first salvo of the craft was to come straightaway. The goal was for Tristan to cause as much devastation to the Rustannicans as possible from above, before Vespasian guessed what was happening and responded in kind. When Tristan unleashed the first of his new powers, the Rustannicans would immediately realize that they were embroiled in a battle of unprecedented ferocity.

Hoshi turned to look at the *Jin'Sai* and pointed toward a group of canvas tents about four hundred meters away, their tops adorned with bright red battle flags.

"There!" she shouted. "That is Vespasian's compound! Strike there, *Jin'Sai,* and with all your power!"

Although Tristan knew that he must do this thing, he couldn't escape the feeling that he was committing murder. How many unsuspecting people would die during his first attack alone? he wondered. Then another concern gripped him.

"What if Julia Idaeus is killed?" he shouted.

"That is a risk we must take!" Hoshi shouted back. "She knows the time of the attack and she promised to be near one of the hundreds of Rustannican portals when it starts! You must attack, *Jin'Sai!* The time is now, before they see us!"

Tristan closed his eyes, raised his arms, and called the craft. Just as Mashiro had foretold, the craft obeyed him effortlessly, and he felt its power rise in his veins. Soon hundreds of elegant spell calculations came roaring into his mind's eye. Singling out the one that Hoshi and the *Inkai* wished him to employ, he caused the others to vanish. Concentrating fully on the lone spell, Tristan opened his eyes and loosed the first of his wondrous gifts.

Twin beams shot from his hands, their brilliance nearly blinding. Some Rustannican legionnaires immediately noticed the bolts streaking across the heavens, and they started shouting urgent warnings to their officers. But it was already too late. Concentrating harder, Tristan called forth the second part of the spell.

Subtle matter exists everywhere, Mashiro had taught him. *Like the energy of the craft, it can be gathered. But while the uses of azure beams are limited, subtle matter's applications are many. Use it in the name of the Vigors, Jin'Sai, for only you can do so. Reclaim the Tani Kinkiro and send Vespasian's invading legions fleeing back to Rustannica.*

Despite Mashiro's careful instruction, when Tristan looked to the sky he could scarcely believe what he saw. Near where his beams streamed, dozens of great meteors were forming from subtle matter collected by his spell. Bright azure in color and burning and revolving with the immense power of the craft, each meteor was easily one hundred meters across. As they grew in size and their surging power begged to be unleashed, Tristan quickly pointed one arm downward, sending the first of them plummeting straight toward Vespasian's command post.

The monstrous ball landed with a great crash, destroying everything within its sphere. Tents, legionnaires, horses, gold, great mounds of earth, all went flying hundreds of meters into the air and were vaporized. When the smoke cleared, nothing remained where the meteor landed save for a great smoldering crater.

With Tristan's first attack the entire valley came alive. Hundreds of thousands of legionnaires stopped working and quickly formed military ranks. Bugles were urgently blown and war drums beaten. This instinctive assembly of Vespasian's legions was just what the *Inkai* had hoped for. As soon as the forming legions presented more compact targets, Tristan caused another meteor to come barreling down out of the sky.

The second one landed directly in their midst. Tens of thousands of legionnaires were killed on the spot, the body parts of those not instantaneously vaporized flying through the air like so many dried leaves on a stiff wind. Like the time before, when the smoke cleared there was nothing to show for the many brave soldiers who had once assembled there, save for another great crater and a quickly growing odor of burning flesh.

Tristan was about to send another meteor crashing down when Hoshi grabbed his arm, stopping him. "Wait!" she ordered. Then she pointed toward the valley floor. "Look!"

As Tristan gazed down into the valley he quickly grasped why Hoshi had ordered him to desist. Had he sent another meteor plummeting down, it would have killed as many attacking katsugai as Rustannican legionnaires. From now on his targets would be fewer because the battlefield was changing by the second, breathtaking in its vast scale and terrible in its quickening ferocity.

The thousands of Shashidan war barges had landed on the valley floor to discharge their katsugai. Screaming madly, the Shashidan warriors flooded against the still-forming Rustannican legions in mighty clashes of muscle, armor, and steel. Mystic officers on each side of the struggle soon began using the craft against each other, and the resulting carnage was stupefying.

Aside from hand-to-hand combat, azure bolts crisscrossed the battle scene, killing hundreds at a time. Explosion after explosion rocked the valley, sending dark smoke hundreds of meters into the air. Endowed archers from either side launched so many shafts that sometimes the sky went nearly black with them, each one invariably finding an enemy soldier by way of the craft.

And with the death of so many craft mystics, there soon arrived the stunning atmospheric phenomena always associated with passing of their blood and the forestallments that that blood carried. Lightning ripped across the sky and the wind howled violently, threatening to overturn Tristan and Hoshi's barge. Tristan had seen these phenomena before, but never with such fury as this.

Wondering when his fellow Eutracians might join the fight, Tristan looked toward the southern end of the valley. To his surprise, the *Tammerland* and the *Ephyra* had arrived and were soaring northward, low over the valley floor. The ships must have flown over the legions guarding the southern pass, Tristan reasoned.

Even from this distance he could see his mystics' azure bolts streaming down from the ships and tearing into the swarming legions, and he could imagine Tyranny prowling the topside of the *Tammerland,* anxiously shouting out orders. Then he watched the ships suddenly come to a stop and hover over the green pastures south of his and Hoshi's position. As ever more azure bolts streamed down from the Black Ships' decks, Tristan saw his Minion phalanxes take flight to attack the nearest legionnaires. He smiled grimly as he realized that Vespasian's troops were about to confront a new and more ruthless foe than they had ever seen before.

As the battle raged and lightning continued to tear across the heavens, Hoshi saw something that made her breath catch in her lungs. Not far from where her and Tristan's barge hung in the sky, a host of legionnaires were running furiously toward the Bedeviler pens. Thousands of the enchanted beasts were being held there, waiting their turns to haul the stolen gold. Screaming and pawing the ground, the monsters clearly wanted to be unleashed against the flood of attacking katsugai. Hoshi knew all too well that the pens were craft constructs, their glowing azure bars impervious to even the massive Bedevilers. Only the legionnaire mystics could release the beasts, and it would happen in moments.

Hoshi again pointed downward. "There!" she shouted. "That is where you must strike next! Kill the Vagaries monsters before they can be freed!"

Without hesitation Tristan raised one hand and called down another azure meteor. With a thunderous crash it landed squarely in the center of the Bedeviler holding area. The beasts and the frantic legionnaires trying to free them simply disappeared in an eruption of earth and smoke, never to be seen again.

At Hoshi's renewed insistence, Tristan again refrained from using his gifts. With their hearts in their throats, they anxiously waited and watched.

"DO NOT ARGUE WITH ME!" VESPASIAN SCREAMED AT Persephone. "The battle is lost! You must go while you still can!"

As the fighting raged all around them, Vespasian gripped his wife's arms and glared into her eyes, trying to make her understand. Lucius stood faithfully beside him, he too refusing to go until his emperor did the same.

Vespasian's legions were fighting back valiantly, and for a time he believed that they might be able to vanquish the attacking Shashidans. Even when he learned that his forces had been surrounded and that the north and south valley entrances had been breached, he clung to the hope that his legions might somehow hold out. But when he saw the first azure meteor rush down from the heavens, he knew that it could have been summoned by only one living being other than he. After quickly conferring with Lucius and Gracchus, Vespasian decided to abandon the Vallesis Majestatis and retreat homeward.

Although taking Ryoto and killing the *Inkai* would remain dreams for another day, Vespasian had stolen enough Shashidan gold to finance the War of Attrition for centuries, perhaps longer. From the start of the campaign, the legionnaires had had standing orders that should their leaders need to flee, they would defend the portals at all costs while sending as many soldiers home to Ellistium as they could. Only when the situation was completely hopeless would they close the portals, so as to keep the hated katsugai from surging through them and invading Ellistium. Many legionnaires would die while defending the portals. Many more would die once the portals were withdrawn, their fates sealed to the seething katsugai. But to save the emperor and to ensure the safety of Ellistium, there was no other way.

Julia Idaeus and the *Pon Q'tar* had already entered one of the azure portals, and by now they would have safely reached Ellistium. In a supreme effort of the craft, Gracchus and the other *Pon Q'tar* members had managed to force the entire Oraculum Tempitatium into the portal ahead of them. It had been only the will of the fates that the Rustannican hierarchy had all been away from their tents supervising the transfer of yet more stolen gold when the first of Tristan's meteors devastated the Rustannican war compound.

Vespasian was desperate to learn Tristan's position and respond in kind, but in the confusion not one of his legionnaires could say from where the *Jin'Sai* was unleashing his powers. Immediately after the Rustannican rulers made their decision to flee, the gold transfers were stopped and they entered the portals. But when Vespasian told Persephone to go without him, she staunchly refused.

"What are you going to do?" Persephone screamed at Vespasian. Just then the second of Tristan's meteors had slammed into Vespasian's assembled legions, killing tens of thousands more.

Despite the carnage all around him, Vespasian was determined to face the *Jin'Sai*. He had no death wish, but the *Jin'Sai* was here in this valley slaughtering his troops with abandon. Another chance to kill him such as this one might never come again. After Vespasian had seen to it that his advisors and Persephone had been safely sent home, he was determined to do what no one else could. He would remain behind for as long as possible and attack the *Jin'Sai* in kind. Knowing that he had little time, he turned to look at Lucius.

"You are my most trusted friend!" he shouted. "Trust me one more time and do as I order you! Take my wife and go!"

Lucius looked into Vespasian's eyes with a mixture of respect and fear for his old friend. After shaking his head angrily, he finally relented.

"Very well!" he shouted. "Do what you must, but you cannot allow yourself to fall into Shashidan hands!"

Vespasian heartily slapped his forearm against Lucius' and grasped it not as an emperor to a tribune, but as one legionnaire to another.

"Thank you," he said simply.

He then turned to look at his wife. "My love, forgive me," he said.

The swift blow that Vespasian delivered to Persephone's chin was enough to render her unconscious, but not so powerful as to do her permanent harm. As she crumpled, Vespasian caught her in his arms. He could have used the craft to subdue her, he realized, but she would surely have fought him in kind, wasting valuable time. After kissing her on the cheek, he handed her over to Lucius.

"Go!" he commanded.

Knowing that he had no other choice, with Persephone in his arms Lucius turned and ran as fast as he could toward one of the hugely swirling portals. After turning to give his emperor a final look, he stepped into the portal, and he and Persephone were gone.

Vespasian immediately ran to where his chariot stood waiting. Snatching the reins from his horse handler, he slapped them across the stallions' rumps and headed straight for the worst of the fighting. If he was to find the *Jin'Sai* he must reach his legion scouts, for only they might know from where Tristan was launching his powers.

Charging his careening chariot into the heart of the carnage, Vespasian offered a silent prayer to the Vagaries flame on behalf of Lucius and Persephone.

AS TRISTAN WATCHED THE GROTESQUE BATTLE RAGE ON, he remained stunned by the wanton loss of life. The death-dealing was extreme and without mercy. Hundreds of thousands were dying on either side, and the green valley floor was becoming littered with corpses, dead horses and Bedevilers, and smashed wagons and chariots. Although the vast gold deposits had been the reason for all this carnage, they had no meaning now. Nothing did, save for staying alive.

More than once it seemed that the Shashidans were about to rule the day, only to have the Rustannican legions regroup and attack again with renewed fury. Even so, Tristan came to realize that the advantage belonged to the katsugai. By and large, Hoshi's plan had worked, and the legions were surrounded, their valiant soldiers corralled near the valley's center.

Just then Tristan saw a shadow loom over the valley floor, not far from where their barge hovered. Looking up at the sky, he saw a huge, very dark cloud forming in the sky. It hovered higher than their barge and lay about one hundred meters west of them. It would not have seemed unusual had it not been so much larger and darker than the others. He mentioned the strange-looking cloud to Hoshi. As she lifted her war mask to take a better look, the blood suddenly drained from her face.

Knowing that there was no time to warn her barge pilot, Hoshi immediately called the craft and wrested control from him. At once she caused the barge to lunge forward and heel over hard on her starboard side.

But even Hoshi's quick actions hadn't been enough to avoid disaster altogether. As the first of Vespasian's conjured lightning bolts loosed from the dark cloud that he had created, it streaked toward the tataki fune and struck a thunderous glancing blow to its starboard stern quarter.

The corner of the barge exploded into matchsticks and its bow tilted skyward as the craft careened through the air. Hundreds of katsugai were instantaneously burned to cinders by the lightning bolt and hundreds more tumbled through the partly destroyed wall to fall end over end toward certain death. Holding on to the front wall of the barge for dear life, Tristan and Hoshi struggled to remain standing while Hoshi fought to regain control of the pitching craft.

Finally she righted the barge. After desperately searching the valley floor, she turned back toward Tristan.

"Only Vespasian could have done that!" she shouted. "The emperor lives! Worse, he has found our position, but we do not know his!"

Before Tristan could answer, more terrible lightning ripped free of the ominous black cloud. Hoshi again did her best to maneuver the barge out of its path, this time barely succeeding. Tristan watched in awe as the lightning narrowly missed the leading edge of the barge. It passed so near that everyone aboard felt its heat and heard it crackle with energy as it plummeted earthward.

Using the craft to augment her sight, Hoshi searched desperately for Vespasian's well-known gilded chariot and white stallions. She knew that she had little time to search him out before another lightning bolt struck. Suddenly she spied the chariot and the tall blond figure commanding it.

"There!" she shouted to Tristan. "Near where the river bends, there are three azure portals lying side by side! Do you see? Vespasian is there!"

Tristan found the bend in the river, and he could just make out the three azure portals. But because he could not call the craft in ways that Hoshi might, he did not see Vespasian.

"I see the portals!" Tristan shouted.

"Send one of your meteors there!" Hoshi shouted. "If you do it quickly, even he will not be able to escape it in time!"

Just as Tristan was about to act, to his horror he saw another dark shadow forming across the valley floor. Much as the first one had done, it too started to move.

Vespasian has called forth another cloud! Tristan realized. If the emperor simultaneously launched two lightning bolts from different directions, even Hoshi's gifts wouldn't be able to save them and they would be obliterated. Raising his hands, Tristan quickly launched another azure meteor. But even as he saw the meteor start plummeting earthward, he realized that another of Vespasian's lightning bolts had been loosed.

Hoshi swung the barge over hard again, but this time the blow was far more direct. Striking the barge amidships, the lightning bolt blasted much of the craft to bits. Blown head over heels, Tristan, Hoshi, and thousands of katsugai tumbled toward the ground.

Because his use of the craft had been affected by the exploding barge, Tristan's meteor plummeted crazily toward the valley floor. Careening madly, it headed in Vespasian's general direction, then veered north before it hit the ground. Tens of thousands of legionnaires and katsugai were vaporized instantly. The resulting concussion reached Vespasian, throwing him from his chariot.

As Tristan fell earthward he caught a quick glimpse of Hoshi to see that she had used the craft to stop her descent, but she had apparently been unable to do the same for him. Over and over he went, his lungs gasping for air and his limbs flailing wildly. Hoshi acted again, this time sending down an azure bolt to try to catch him. But she missed widely, the bolt streaking by him.

Suddenly Tristan felt a jolt so great that he thought his back might break. The wind was quickly knocked out of him and he felt his left shoulder dislocate. As he slipped from consciousness, he turned to see Ox's eyes looking into his.

That's why there were two lightning bolts coming at us at once, he realized. *The second shadow didn't come from another of Vespasian's clouds . . . it came from the* Tammerland.

Finally losing consciousness, the *Jin'Sai* dangled limply in Ox's arms as the faithful Minion warrior reversed direction and soared upward.

LYING PRONE ON THE GROUND, VESPASIAN GASPED AS HE tried to gather his senses. His chariot was wrecked and his stallions had run away. Screaming fighters still hacked viciously at one another all around him, and azure bolts from both sides wildly crisscrossed the battlefield. Coming to his feet, Vespasian called the craft to stem his growing nausea, then tried to assess the situation.

Screaming katsugai were attacking his forces on all sides. While he had been trying to kill the *Jin'Sai,* the Shashidans had closed their circle even more, forcing the legions into a compact group near the valley's center. Although Vespasian found himself at the center of that group, the end would come soon, he realized.

He turned to see three azure vortices nearby. One gallant tribune had taken charge of them, deciding that the time had come to save as many legionnaires as he could by ordering them home to Ellistium. As legionnaires swarmed into the vortices, the situation was becoming hopeless, chaotic. Soon Vespasian was engulfed by soldiers begging him to issue new orders.

Ignoring them, he turned and ran toward the three vortices. As the raging katsugai continued to press his forces from all sides, Vespasian was forced to make a fateful decision.

He turned to look at the senior tribune who had taken charge of the three portals. Although admitting defeat was abhorrent to the legions, the tribune was following his orders to the letter. Still dazed and wobbly, Vespasian staggered toward him and gripped the man's forearm with his own.

"You know your orders!" Vespasian shouted as yet another azure bolt tore through the air just above their heads. "Save as many as you can, then close the portals forever, and see to it that the same is done with all the others!"

Standing tall, the tribune gave his emperor a perfect salute.

"It shall be done!" he shouted. "I speak for all of us left behind when I say that it has been a pleasure to serve with you!"

At first Vespasian could find no words. "If you wish to surrender to the katsugai, I will attach no shame to it!" he finally shouted back. "They do not kill their prisoners! I will return to this land and free those of you who live, I swear it!"

"You must go now, my liege!" the tribune shouted. "The time grows short!"

Despite the insane fighting closing in on them, for several moments the two men looked each other in the eye with the unique brand of understanding that only years of service in the legions could provide. Vespasian did not know this man, nor would he ever get the chance to do so. Even so, he would never forget this stalwart soldier who sacrificed his own life for that of his emperor.

Vespasian ran into the depths of the whirling portal and vanished.

CHAPTER LII

VESPASIAN SMILED AS HE LOOKED ACROSS THE ARENA. The day would again be hot, and the two blood-red canopies had been stretched toward one another to provide shade for the multitudes that had come to take part in their emperor's victory celebration. So as to keep the growing crowd amused, he had ordered an initial slate of killings. Blood, wrecked chariots, and dead skeens littered much of the arena floor.

Because so much Shashidan gold had been brought home to Ellistium, no expense would be spared on this celebration day. Attendance would be free, thousands of wild animals and Shashidan skeens would be slaughtered, and the food and wine would be without charge. Every seat was filled, and Vespasian had issued an unprecedented decree that the public might also stand in the aisles.

A fortnight had passed since the Battle of the Vallesis Majestatis. Many legionnaires had been killed, but many katsugai had died as well. To the tribunes' credit, a surprising number of Vespasian's soldiers had escaped through the azure portals before the vortices had been closed. Vespasian's dream of taking Ryoto and killing the *Inkai* had not been realized, but his most urgent need had been fulfilled beyond his wildest dreams.

Even now, the gold count was still being tallied, to say nothing of how busy the Imperial Mint was stamping out new coins. Soon Rustannica's treasury would be filled to overflowing—creative ways would be needed to deal with all the money. Most important of all, the war against Shashida could be prolonged for centuries if need be.

Vespasian turned to look at his wife. Persephone had long since forgiven the way in which he had forced her to escape the battle scene. Dressed in a long red gown, she wore new jewelry of her own design that had been crafted from the stolen gold.

Lucius Marius sat beside her. Because this celebration was to be unique, he had asked Vespasian if his latest female conquest might be allowed to accompany him to the emperor's box. His mood generous since returning home, Vespasian had approved. The woman was a lovely creature with long dark hair, and she hailed from an Ellistium krithian family of some note. The way Lucius coddled her caused Vespasian to wonder whether the legendary First Tribune had perhaps met his match.

The usual box reserved for the tribunes was full, as was the section meant for the women of the Priory of Virtue. All twelve members of the *Pon Q'tar* had survived the battle, and they were in attendance as well. Tray after tray of sumptuous food was served by Shashidan skeens, and wine flowed without end. As he waited for the celebration to begin, Vespasian pointed toward his goblet and caused it to float into his grasp. The rich red wine had been made from the best Rustannican highland grapes, its finish sweet and strong.

On arriving home, Vespasian's first order of business had been to call a meeting of the Suffragat, whereupon Lucius had given the war report and detailed their losses. Many legionnaires and tribunes had perished, and not one of the Bedevilers had returned. By necessity, vast amounts of supplies, food, and support troops had been left behind in Shashida.

Even so, these losses paled when compared with the amount of stolen gold that had been taken. Because the treasury had been so amply refilled, replacing the war materiel would be a simple matter. Given time, the *Pon Q'tar* could easily conjure even larger herds of Bedevilers and other creatures. Even the loss of so many troops did not greatly concern the Suffragat, for now the empire could afford to offer large financial bonuses to entice enlistees. New blood had been needed in the legions for a long time, and at last they would have it.

Vespasian and his counselors knew that the campaign losses should not be publicized; therefore they would be made up a little at a time so as not to arouse suspicion. The Suffragat's usual report to the citizenry had been censored even more heavily than usual, and it contained only the details of a great Rustannican victory and the taking of much gold. Because the treasury was so full, Vespasian also announced that taxes would be lowered, especially on the trading of slaves. The mood in the country was joyful, and any hint of rebellion had vanished.

Even so, as Vespasian waited for the celebratory portion of the day to begin, concerns still plagued him. On returning home, the Oracle had informed Gracchus of Shailiha's victory over Khristos, and he had told the Suffragat. When compared to the threat that Shashida continually presented, the world's other side remained a relatively minor concern. Even so, the reigning *Jin'Saiou* would have to be dealt with in some way.

Most worrisome of all, the *Jin'Sai* had reached Shashida and he too now commanded forestallments banned by the Borderlands Treaty. Vespasian had destroyed the Shashidan barge from which the *Jin'Sai* had thundered down azure meteors, but as Vespasian's chariot had overturned he had not been able to determine whether Tristan had been killed. Sitting back in his marble throne, Vespasian pursed his lips, thinking.

In a strange way it didn't matter whether he knew the *Jin'Sai*'s fate, he realized. If Tristan died during the battle of the Vallesis Majestatis, so be it. If not, Vespasian would soon know, for only he and the *Jin'Sai* commanded such awesome gifts of the craft, and they would surely meet again.

Just then, legionary buglers and drummers entered the arena through the Gates of Life and the crowd stood and cheered. On a signal from Vespasian, the one-eyed Games Master quickly swiveled a new sign that had recently been crafted from stolen Shashidan gold.

On seeing the order, hand-picked centurions stationed on the arena floor quickly exited through the Gates of Life. When they returned, at first the amazed spectators gasped, then they cheered as never before when they saw what the centurions carried. From the woven baskets lying in their arms, the centurions began throwing newly minted sesterces—complete with Vespasian's likeness—into the surging crowds.

Smiling, Gracchus Junius sat back in his chair and took another sip of wine. Seated by his side, Benedik Pryam leaned closer.

"You were right," Benedik said quietly.

"I usually am," Gracchus answered. "But even I do not know to which of my recent accomplishments you refer."

"I speak of our young charge, of course," Benedik answered, tilting his head in Vespasian's direction. "He truly knows what Ellistium is. It's the mob, pure and simple. His decrees to lower taxes and to throw money into the crowd are master strokes. They are sure to love him as never before."

Rubbing his chin, Benedik scowled. "Even so, it seems that in some ways we are right back where we started."

Gracchus laughed. "If that is what you believe, then you are as blind as you are foolish," he replied. "Aside from the total destruction of Shashida, we have gained all that we could have hoped for. Our treasury is bursting, and the mood of the populace has again swung in our favor. Rustannica's ability to finance her war against the Vigors has never been so robust. Our emperor has accepted his immense gifts and he has proven that he is willing to use them. Even better, he believes that his terrors have been forever banished."

As he again turned his attention to the arena, Gracchus plopped a grape into his mouth.

"So you see, my dear Benedik, aside from the arrival of the *Jin'Sai* on this side of the world, all is as it should be," he added. "And given time, even he will be dealt with."

Hearing the buglers again blow their horns, everyone in the royal box looked toward the arena floor. On Vespasian's order, Shashidan skeens were entering the arena. They wore only meager loincloths and were shackled hand and foot. Each slave carried something across his or her back, their bodies bent low under the crushing weight. As they were whipped, they staggered across the arena floor as best they could.

When the crowd realized the nature of the slaves' burdens, they cheered and stamped so loudly that they could be heard in the farthest reaches of Ellistium. They were witnessing the ultimate humiliation, and its savage cleverness endeared their young emperor to them even more.

Across each slave's back, tied together with stout rope, lay several bars of their own gold, recently stolen from the Vallesis Majestatis. Sitting back in his ivory chair, Gracchus smiled.

From behind the protection of her gauzy veil, Julia Idaeus wiped away a tear.

ABOUT THE AUTHOR

ROBERT NEWCOMB is the author of The Destinies of Blood and Stone: *Savage Messiah* and *A March into Darkness,* as well as The Chronicles of Blood and Stone: *The Fifth Sorceress, The Gates of Dawn,* and *The Scrolls of the Ancients.* He lives in Florida with his wife, a neuro-psychologist and novelist. Visit the author's website at www.robertnewcomb.com.

ABOUT THE TYPE

This book was set in Garamond No. 3, a variation of the classic Garamond typeface originally designed by the Parisian type cutter Claude Garamond (1480–1561). Claude Garamond's distinguished romans and italics first appeared in *Opera Ciceronis* in 1543–44. The Garamond types are clear, open, and elegant.